D0586704

READER'S DIGEST
CONDENSED BOOKS

With the exception of actual
personages identified as such, the
characters and incidents in the
fictional selections in this volume
are entirely the product of the
authors' imaginations and have no
relation to any person or event in
real life.

www.readersdigest.co.uk

The Reader's Digest Association
Limited 11 Westferry Circus
Canary Wharf London E14 4HE

For information as to ownership of
copyright in the material of this
book, and acknowledgments, see last
page.

Printed in France
ISBN 0 276 42550 2

READER'S DIGEST CONDENSED BOOKS

*Selected and edited
by Reader's Digest*

CONDENSED BOOKS DIVISION

THE READER'S DIGEST ASSOCIATION LIMITED, LONDON

CONTENTS

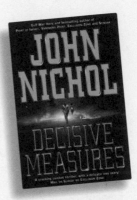

PUBLISHED BY HODDER & STOUGHTON

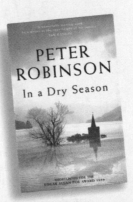

PUBLISHED BY MACMILLAN

24 HOURS

Greg Iles

Joe Hickey has got kidnapping down to a fine art. Twenty-four hours, that's all he needs, plus the foolproof communication system he's set up with his cousin. But as he plans his next target—the young daughter of top-flight anaesthetist Dr Will Jennings, Hickey makes one serious mistake: he underestimates the Jennings family's determination to fight back. Emotion-packed, high-voltage drama.

PUBLISHED BY HODDER & STOUGHTON

NORA, NORA

Anne Rivers Siddons

Adolescent Peyton McKenzie doesn't want to share her widowed father with anyone—let alone the red-haired, bohemian cousin who breezes into their lives one day. But Nora's free spirit and life-affirming wisdom become an inspiration to the frustrated teenager growing up in the Deep South. A coming-of-age story, deliciously rich in character.

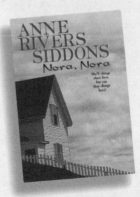

PUBLISHED BY LITTLE, BROWN

JOHN
NICHOL

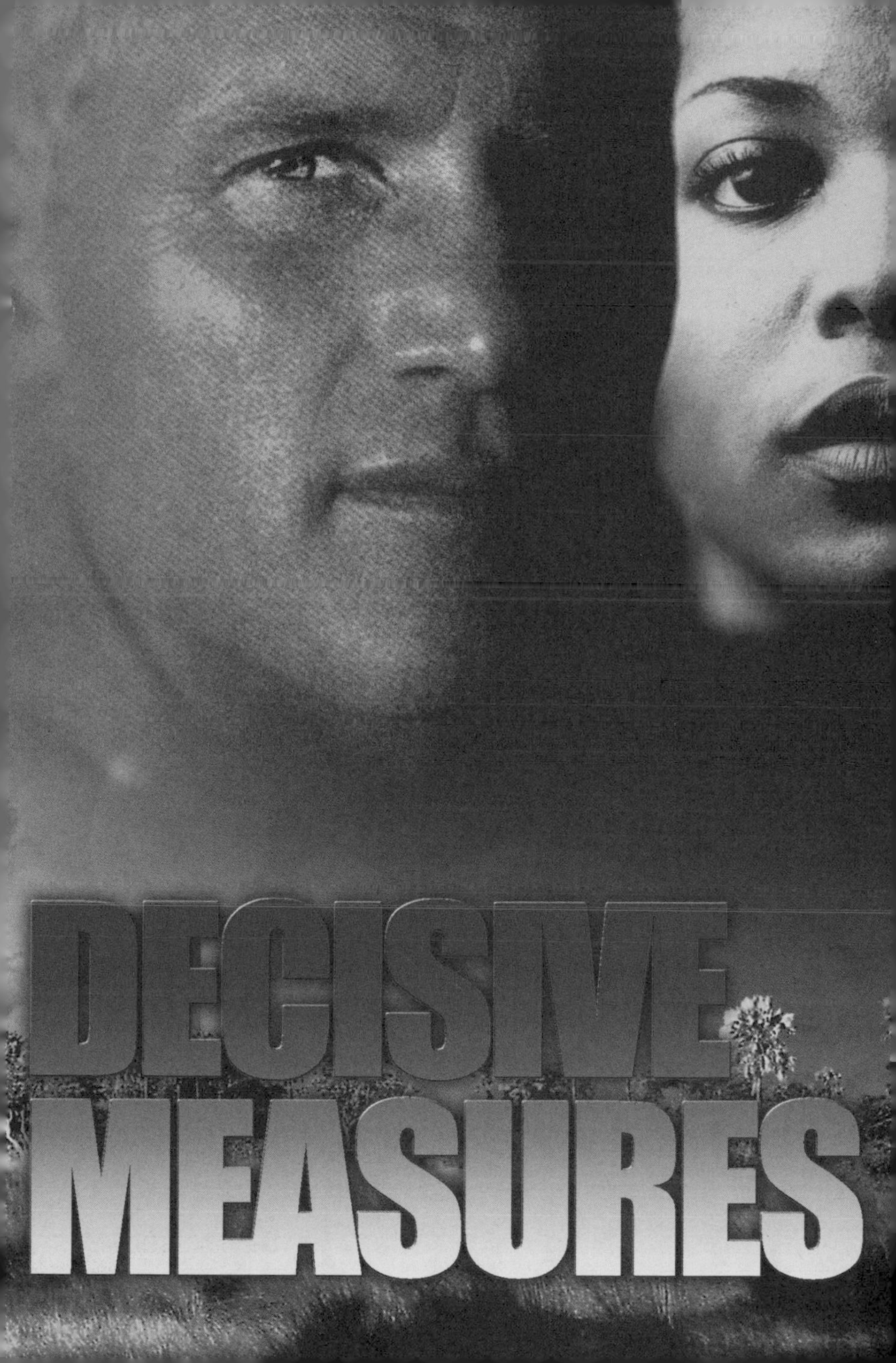
DECISIVE
MEASURES

Helicopter pilot Jack Griffiths arrives in war-torn Sierra Leone to take up a job transporting supplies and personnel to a Western-owned diamond mine. A respite, he hopes, from his recent, horrific experience of military combat.

But, in the torrid heat of Africa Jack finds himself involved, yet again, in fierce fighting. And among those he has to protect is Layla, a beautiful local doctor to whom he is powerfully drawn.

# PROLOGUE

The sunset was already reddening the sky and casting long shadows across the hills when the radio crackled into life again. 'Echo Fourteen. Hostiles reported 179502. Investigate.'

I suppressed a groan and acknowledged the order. We had been flying for over eight hours, sortie after sortie over a land already scarred by fighting, arriving always too late, to find another village in ruins, another pillar of black smoke reaching up into the sky.

I banked the heli around and headed northeast over the dusty Macedonian hills. I dropped to low level as we approached the Kosovan border, and began twisting and turning, hugging the contours of the land. We soared to clear a last mountain ridge and then dropped into the target valley.

Ahead was a familiar scene: a hamlet, a cluster of houses sheltering in the lee of the hills, surrounded by a belt of woodland. I could see columns of smoke and the flicker of flames piercing the jagged outlines of ruined houses. Of the inhabitants there was no sign.

I put the heli into a broad turn around the hamlet, my eyes raking the open ground and the edges of the woodland. Out of the corner of my eye, I glimpsed a group of rectilinear outlines in the shadows among the trees—trucks or maybe even tanks using the wood for cover. My flesh crept, but I maintained the same course until we had passed out of sight beyond the end of the wood. I radioed base. 'Possible hostiles sighted. Over.'

Then I jabbed the intercom. 'Keep alert, guys. There are at least six vehicles among the trees. I'm making another pass along the edge of the wood. Echo Thirteen, follow me through.'

I heard a thud behind me as the gunner slid open the door of the cab and swung his gun to cover the target. I swooped in low and fast past the edge of the wood, using my peripheral vision to search for the outlines among the trees. Once more there was no sign of people and no firing, only the tantalising, half-hidden shapes.

I had now made out eight distinct forms under the trees and a long, tapering black cylinder angled upwards at 45 degrees. It could have been the barrel of a tank gun; it could equally have been a fallen tree. I passed beyond the end of the wood and banked in a tight turn, as my wingman followed me through. The intercom crackled as he completed his pass. 'Definite hostiles,' he said. 'Let's go for it.'

I hesitated. 'Negative. Am not sure. Going in again.'

As we dropped back towards the wood, I lowered our speed. A flash of the dying sunlight reflected from my copilot's helmet as he turned to look at me. 'Jesus, Jack,' he said. 'How much of an invitation are you going to give them?'

'We've got to be sure.'

'We'll be sure enough when we're dead.'

As we reached the midpoint of the wood, I flared the heli, putting it into the hover. The force of the downwash threw the branches aside for a moment and I at last saw movement—figures sprinting towards the vehicles. I sped up and away from the wood.

I reached for the radio. 'Figures and vehicles sighted.'

The answer came back before I had posed the question. 'Clear engage.'

I kept circling. My wingman's voice came over the intercom. 'What are we waiting for?'

My copilot's gaze was still fixed on me. 'Well?' he said.

Abruptly I made the decision. 'Engage.'

I headed out in a wide loop and then dropped to minimum level, accelerating back towards the long shadow of the wood. The trees rose like a dark wall ahead of us. I held the heli level for a few more seconds as I stared into the cross hairs. They intersected on the largest shape inside the trees and I pulled the trigger once, twice.

There was a *whoosh* as the rockets streaked from the pod. I sent the heli soaring up into the sky. A moment later, there was a massive explosion and a bubble of oily flame and black smoke belched upwards through the trees. The gun thundered as the door gunner raked the edge of the wood. There was no answering fire.

I saw my wingman complete his attack run as I banked for another pass. I dropped in low, the turbines screaming, my finger once more tightening on the trigger. A microsecond before I fired, a figure burst from the wood, a human torch burning from head to toe. The long black skirt flapping around the woman's legs was a sheet of flame.

I jabbed the intercom button. 'Abort. Abort.' I peered down. The woman was still wreathed in flame, her arms raised, her hands spread wide in supplication. She threw her head back. I saw her mouth opening in a silent scream. Then she slumped to the ground, a shapeless, burning mound of rags.

I turned for base, the ground blurring before my eyes as tears trickled down my face.

 # CHAPTER 1

A wall of heat and humidity hit us as the door of the aircraft swung open. Sweat beaded my forehead at once as I watched two Africans in threadbare overalls push a rusting flight of steps to the plane.

Tom leaned past me and stared out at the airfield. From his expression he was less than impressed. Over forty years old, and a career RAF man, he was finding it hard to adjust to life on the outside. 'That must be the welcoming committee,' he said, as a cloud of flies formed around us.

'Welcome to the real world, Tom. Better get used to it. There's no more soft postings and squadron dinners for us, and no more people to hold our hands and tidy up after us. We're on our own now.'

He scowled and the ever-present frown lines deepened on his forehead. 'What a dump. Remind me what we're doing here, Jack.'

'We're doing the only job we know, making a few quid for ourselves and upholding Her Majesty's vital interests at the same time.'

He gave a sour smile. 'Vital interests spelt D-I-A-M-O-N-D-S. If they're that vital, why doesn't Her Majesty send some of her own boys to look after them? No, don't tell me, let me guess: because some things are better done at arm's length.'

I met his gaze. 'Listen, it's a job of work. We agreed to the terms when we signed the contract. It's a bit late now for regrets.'

We hurried down the steps and walked across the potholed concrete towards the terminal building. It was stained and crumbling and its windows were filthy and starred with bullet holes.

Tom's thinning, sandy hair was darkened and plastered to his head by sweat. I could feel my shirt sticking to my back.

Although the shedlike arrivals hall was out of the sun, it felt little cooler. Two soldiers in grease-stained uniforms got up as we approached. They pored over our passports, then dropped them onto the table in front of them. We waited in silence, searching their impassive faces for some clue to the next move.

A group of African men, women and children, most in torn clothes and ragged T-shirts, stood on the far side of the steel gates beyond the arrivals hall, staring at us without apparent interest. There was a commotion and the group parted to allow two men through. They opened the gates and came striding towards us.

The leader was a powerful figure, his skin tanned to mahogany from long exposure to the sun and his hair flecked with grey. A broad grin showed beneath his walrus moustache. Ignoring the soldiers, he walked over and slapped us on the back. 'Glad you made it, boys. Grizz Riley. You can't imagine how pleased I am to see you here. I was beginning to think we'd never get another heli crew.'

As he spoke, his companion, a paunchy African with a gold tooth and a shiny suit, began talking to the soldiers in confidential tones. I recognised the type, a local fixer paid to smooth our way past police, customs and other local piranhas.

I heard the words 'Decisive Measures', and the rustle of leone bills—the local currency. Pocketing the bribe, the two soldiers, now all smiles, handed us back our passports and waved us through.

Grizz led us outside to a battered pick-up. A bullet-headed, square-jawed soldier in faded fatigues stood guard over it. His blond hair was cropped so short that his scalp showed through it, and a network of scar lines gleamed white against the tanned skin. He remained unsmiling, scrutinising each of us in turn.

'Another new kid on the block,' Grizz said.

'Jack Griffiths,' I said, holding out my hand. 'Pleased to meet you.'

The soldier scowled, but shook my hand. 'I'm Rudi,' he said in a thick Afrikaans accent.

Rudi and the fixer got in the front while we climbed into the back with Grizz. A few heads turned to watch us drive off.

It was an uncomfortable ride. The airport road was potholed and badly scarred by tank tracks. The rusting, burnt-out wreck of one tank had been bulldozed off the road and then left to rot.

We reached the main road that led up the peninsula towards Freetown. Its surface was marginally better and we accelerated towards the capital. The sun was now directly overhead and I was glad of the patches of dappled shade as the road weaved through fringes of rain forest. At intervals there were clusters of mud-and-thatch huts, and an occasional concrete building. Signs advertised bars, shops and cafés, but all appeared to be closed, and many were smoke-blackened and pockmarked by gunfire.

We climbed a forested ridge and saw Freetown sprawling below us, a mosaic of bare earth, grey concrete, palm thatch and multi-coloured tin roofing, all overlaid with a layer of red dust.

Beyond the capital, palm-fringed, white-sand beaches, stretching south along the peninsula as far as I could see, looked deserted. This was clearly no place for tourists. Commanding the ridge line were rows of colonial houses raised above the earth on stilts and shaded by breadfruit and cotton trees. Grizz followed my gaze. 'It was named Hill Station by the British,' he said.

Like their former occupants, the houses had once been white, but they were now faded to a dull khaki brown, stained by rivulets of damp. All of them were surrounded by high brick walls or tin fences topped with shards of broken glass and coils of razor wire.

Mango and breadfruit trees grew in the lush grounds of the Presidential Palace on Signal Hill, but the white walls, unrepaired from years of coups and countercoups, were pitted by shellfire. Lower on the steep hillside the slopes festered with an ugly, sprawling shantytown that ran down to the creek at the bottom of the hill. The shacks were built of packing cases and scrap wood, and roofed with rusting corrugated metal or palm fronds.

Ahead of us, a few overloaded, battered pick-ups drove down the hill into the city, laden with firewood and farm goods to sell. As we rounded a bend on the steep descent, we came to a juddering halt. A pick-up and a beaten-up old Mercedes taxi had collided. Both drivers were out of their vehicles, remonstrating with each other.

As they argued, a human tide began pouring out of the shanty-town on the hillside just below the road. Ignoring the drivers' protests and tearful pleas, the mob began looting the vehicles, stripping them of everything they could carry. The Mercedes driver tried to save his car radio, but he was punched to the ground.

Drivers coming up the hill stopped, sized up the situation and either reversed or pulled three-point turns and disappeared in clouds of dust. A moment later a police car appeared round the corner. It braked to a halt and sounded its siren. The looters barely glanced up from their work of stripping the cars. No policemen emerged from the car and after a moment it, too, reversed down the hill.

Grizz glanced at me. 'Welcome to Sierra Leone,' he said. He reached for his rifle, stood up and fired a burst into the air. Then he lowered the barrel, pointing it at the looters. There was a moment's silence, then they fled in panic and we drove on into the city.

At the Kissy roundabout we turned west through the Lebanese district and drove down East Street past the mosque and the prison. The decaying façades of once-imposing colonial buildings lined the broad streets at the centre of Freetown, but City Hall was a crumbling wreck, surrounded by rows of shabby two-storey buildings. Tattered washing hung from lines suspended across the street, and most of the houses had a fire pit in the yard in place of a kitchen.

We pulled up in Garrison Street by a row of battered shops with buckled and scorched steel shutters. Most were run by Lebanese traders, but few had any goods to offer; only a handful of tins and flyblown packages on otherwise empty shelves.

The general store at the end of the street was slightly better equipped, though the goods seemed more appropriate to a frontier town than a capital city. There were mosquito nets, candles, axes, bush knives and the shovels and sieves used by gold panners.

Grizz busied himself collecting supplies, which Rudi took out and loaded onto the pick-up, while the store owner ran around scribbling notes on a pad. We left the fixer to argue about the price, and Grizz led us round the corner to a hotel. It resembled a Soviet apartment block and had perversely been built back to front. The balconies faced inland and the bathrooms looked out over the sea.

Grizz left us at the check-in desk.

'When do we start work?' I said.

He smiled. 'Decisive Measures are generous employers. You get one night's acclimatisation and R 'n' R. Then we go upcountry to the Bohara mine first thing in the morning. I'll leave you guys to sort your kit. I'll be back at six to give you a briefing and then show you what passes for a good time in these parts.' He sauntered out.

My room was everything I expected: the lights didn't work, nor did the rusting fan at the centre of the bedroom ceiling. There was a rustle of cockroaches from the bathroom and a stench that made me reluctant to investigate further.

A kerosene lamp stood by the bed, which was draped with a mosquito net. I turned back the covers, lay down and closed my eyes.

I woke soaked with sweat, my heart pounding, the thunder of gunfire still resounding in my ears. Only the noise of the cicadas broke the silence of my room. As I lowered my head back to the pillow, cursing the nightmare that had frightened me awake, I heard the banging of fists on the door and Grizz's voice shouting, 'Come on, you lazy bastard. I've nearly worn my knuckles off on this door.'

I croaked a reply.

'Twenty minutes, in the lobby,' he said.

When I heard his footsteps recede down the corridor, I dragged myself out of bed and walked into the bathroom.

I turned on the shower and stood under the dribble of brackish water for a few minutes, then towelled myself dry. I pulled on jeans and a clean long-sleeved shirt, then headed down the stairs, not wishing to try my luck with the lift.

I found Grizz, Rudi and Tom in the lobby, staring out through the plate-glass window at the skyline. There had been a slow build-up of cloud throughout the afternoon, climbing the wall of the mountains and piling higher and higher into the sky, building the thunderheads that would bring the evening rain. The sun had almost set and lightning was sparking over the mountains.

As the sky darkened, the lights all over Freetown went out. Tom started and looked round in alarm. 'Just another power failure,' Grizz said. For a moment the city was in darkness, then scores of generators fired up in a metallic chorus, counterpointing the croaking of the frogs in the swamps.

We walked to a small meeting room off the lobby. Marks of smoke damage and the crudely repaired outline of an impact from a heavy round or rocket were clearly visible where the wall met the ceiling.

We settled into chairs as Grizz closed the door. He strode to the front of the room. 'Rudi, you can sleep through the first bit if you want, unless helicopter-spotting is one of your hobbies.'

He turned to Tom and me. 'Have you guys flown together before?'

'You mean apart from the training course on the Huey?' I said. 'Not for a while. Tom trained me though, nearly ten years ago.'

'It won't be a problem,' Tom said. 'We both know our own jobs.'

Grizz nodded. 'OK, as I'm sure you've been told, you'll be flying a

Huey XI. The helicopter is vital to the resupply and support of the garrison at the Bohara mine. You'll be based here in Freetown, but your job is to keep Bohara supplied with everything from mining equipment and ammunition to food and medical supplies. The Huey is twenty years old, but it's been upgraded many times and I can vouch for its condition. It has a door-mounted mini-gun, a nose gun and forward-firing rockets, and chaff and flare dispensers. It's also been fitted out for flight with night-vision goggles.'

'What about the rebels?' Tom said. 'What have they got?'

Rudi stirred and began to show some interest.

'They're backed by Liberia,' Grizz said, 'and a lot of their weapons come through that regime. They have plenty of AK rifles, a few rocket-propelled grenades and a couple of heavy machine guns. They also captured a ZFU antiaircraft gun from the government some years ago, but we're uncertain whether they have the know-how to fire it effectively. The Liberians do have Hind helicopters, however, and there are rumours that one has been allocated to the rebels. You'll have read about Sierra Leone in the papers, but in some ways the reality here surpasses anything you've heard. The government is theoretically in control of the country, but in practice its writ barely runs as far as the outskirts of Freetown.'

He gave a bleak smile. 'Lives have no value here. Only one thing counts: diamonds. The government owns the mines but is powerless to protect them without the help of private military companies like Decisive Measures, and, like everybody else, the companies take their reward in gemstones. Don't get the idea that we operate on a lavish budget though, we operate on a shoestring.'

'What are the rebels fighting for?' I said.

Grizz shrugged. 'Just diamonds. They want to defeat the government, but only so they can take control of the diamond-producing areas. The rebels are bloody and brutal fighters but they're not particularly well equipped; the Liberian regime that backs them creams off most of the diamond wealth that the rebels steal or smuggle out.

'The regular army is supposed to be on our side but, despite the diamonds, this is the poorest country in the world and the soldiers certainly aren't growing too fat for their uniforms. When they're paid at all it's sporadic, and they're going hungry: they're supposed to get one bag of rice a month plus clothing and a gun, but the senior officers keep back as much rice as they can to sell on the black market.

'In short, we can rely on no one but ourselves here. If it all goes to ratshit, the British government and the UN won't want to know. There will be no SAS rescue parties flying in to save our arses. We either look after ourselves or we go under.'

He paused. 'That's the bad news; the good news is that for the moment we're in a lull in the fighting. The rebel offensive in the northeast has stalled because of the rainy season. With the dry season almost upon us we must expect an upsurge in activity. For the moment, though, Decisive Measures are simply tasked with keeping the Bohara diamond mine running smoothly. Your job is to get the supplies and the personnel out there to enable it to do so. That's it. Any questions? Then let's go and have a beer.'

WE WENT OUT into the hot, humid night. It was low tide and the sickly, fetid smell of mud and mangroves filled the air.

Women sat at the side of the street, their goods—dried fish, rice, cassava roots, chillies and potato leaf—spread in front of them on palm leaves laid in the dust. Their hungry, pot-bellied children played around them as they waited.

Here and there a solitary street light flickered into life as the power was restored, but most were broken, their wiring stolen and sold for scrap, or cannibalised for other uses.

We passed several burnt-out and derelict houses. Those that remained intact had iron-barred windows, stout locks and razor-wire fences. The walls were still clapboard, however.

Grizz led us along the road fringing the beach. It was lined with restaurants. From the nameboards over the doors, most of them, like the shops, were run by Lebanese. Many were deserted, but at one the owner still presided over his bamboo-fronted bar, perched on a rusting stool, his paunch spilling out of his torn, stained T-shirt. The bar was full of expatriate mineworkers, traders, soldiers and government officials, and a scattering of dull-eyed whores.

The menu was limited: groundnut soup and rice. I ordered food and beer for all four of us.

Grizz took a swig of his beer, lit a cheroot and glanced at Tom. 'So what brings you here, Tom? Apart from the money, of course. Bottom line, that's what we're all here for, isn't it?'

Tom sipped his drink. 'Money and boredom, I suppose,' he said. 'I've been pensioned off by the RAF, but it's a bit early in my life to be getting out the pipe and slippers, so I thought I'd give this a go.'

'Any family?'

'No. Well, I've two children, but they're grown up now. One lives in Australia and the other's in New York.'

'And your wife's back in England?'

As Tom stared down into his beer, the overhead light deepened the furrows in his forehead and he looked even older than his forty-five years. 'She left me a few months ago.'

Grizz studied him for a moment. 'So your break-up would have been another reason for a change of scene?'

Tom didn't reply. After a moment, Grizz switched his attention to me. 'What about you, Jack? You're too young to have been pensioned off. What's the story? Rub some air marshal up the wrong way?'

'Something like that.'

Grizz waited for me to continue. As the silence lengthened, he smiled. 'Fair enough. It's none of my business, anyway, as long as you do your job here.' He shot a glance at Rudi. 'And you're certainly not the only one working for Decisive Measures who's got a bit of a history behind him.' He paused. 'So . . . got any wives or children?'

'Not last time I looked,' I said. 'What about you?'

'Plenty of each—three wives, four children. All in the past tense now, though.'

'Even the children?'

'Oh, I send them a card on their birthdays and things, but it only upsets them if I go to see them. It's better all round if I stay away.' He tried to force a smile, but his eyes belied it.

'And you, Rudi?' I said.

'Fifteen years in the South African Defence Force fighting bush wars against the ANC. I quit the day Mandela was sworn in.'

'Any family?'

He shook his head and ended the interrogation by walking over to the bar. By the time he returned with more beer, Tom, Grizz and I had moved the conversation on to less personal ground.

Rudi stayed aloof from the chat, downing a succession of beers and replying in monosyllables to any remarks directed at him, but his watchful eyes showed that he missed little of what was said. Finally, as if we had passed some secret test, he banged another four beers down on the table and gave a broad smile. He took a long pull on his drink, then put his feet up on the table and rocked his chair back.

'This could be God's country, Jack—perfect beaches, diamonds, any woman you want for the price of a pack of cigarettes, and just enough trouble from the rebels to keep us in work. You couldn't have a better posting.' His speech was a little slurred, and though he smiled he had the air of a man who could change moods in a second.

As Rudi was warming to his theme, a taxi pulled up outside. A few moments later two tall, striking women entered the bar. One had long black hair cascading around her powerful shoulders, a mouth lipsticked in vivid red and skin so dark it seemed blue-black in the dim light. The other was model-thin with close-cropped dark brown hair, coffee-coloured skin and eyes of piercing blue. I could not take my eyes off her.

'Jesus,' Rudi said. 'Some good-looking whores at last.'

He had just reached the two women when Grizz returned from the bar with another round. He took in the scene and winked at us. 'This should be entertaining.'

Rudi's bulky figure loomed over the two women as he propositioned them, waving a ten-dollar bill. The black woman ignored him, turning her back and talking to the barman. The other heard Rudi out in silence, eyeballing him without blinking. Then she took the bill, tore it in quarters and dropped it on the floor.

'Even if I was a whore,' I heard her say, 'it would take more than you could earn in a lifetime to persuade me to sleep with an ox like you. But I'm not a whore, I'm a paramedic. Part of my job is to patch up dumb mercenaries when they get shot. I look forward to making your acquaintance again under those circumstances.'

Rudi stared at her, the veins knotting in his forehead. I was afraid he might strike her, but he shambled back across the room.

He swore in Afrikaans. 'That bitch needs teaching a lesson.'

Grizz raised an eyebrow. 'That bitch is a bloody good medic. Now have a drink and take your beating like a man. There's plenty of whores will take your money without hitting on women who won't.'

Rudi reverted to sullen silence.

'So who is she?' I asked Grizz.

'She's called Layla. She works for Medicaid International, but she's seconded to us part of the time. She deals with medical problems at the mining compound and holds clinics in the villages.' Grizz smiled. 'And don't waste your time; we've all tried.'

I saw her move to the bar. 'I'll get the next ones,' I said.

I walked over and stood next to her as I ordered the beers, then glanced at her. 'Hi, I'm Jack,' I said. 'I fly helicopters. I gather we'll be working together now and again.'

She looked me up and down. 'I'm Layla.' Her accent was English but with a faint lilt. 'I don't think so. I work with mercenaries as little as possible. My job's to save lives.'

'So's mine.'

'Sure,' she said. 'Just like your friends over there.' She walked back to her table, leaving me staring after her.

I went back to the others. Rudi was still mechanically downing one beer after another and his mood was turning increasingly ugly.

Grizz glanced at him and then at us. 'Maybe we could round the evening off with a couple of beers back at the hotel,' he said.

Rudi shook his head, his eyes still fixed on Layla and her friend. 'Not me. I'll see you later.'

Grizz shrugged. 'You guys with me? I'll just hit the can and we'll be out of here.'

On his way back from the stinking lean-to that acted as the communal toilet, I saw him stop and speak to Layla. She turned and looked at Rudi, then frowned and nodded.

Grizz walked back over to us. 'Let's go.'

Tom and I followed him outside. The taxi that had brought Layla and her friend was still waiting, parked a few yards away. Grizz signalled to it and we climbed in.

'Wait a moment, please,' Grizz said.

Tom looked puzzled. 'What for? Rudi said he was staying put.'

He smiled. 'I think you'll enjoy this company more than Rudi's.'

As we waited, the rain began to fall. In seconds it was battering down, blanking out the view and turning the brown water coursing down the road to foam.

Layla and her friend appeared in the doorway of the bar. They hesitated at the sight of the rain, then glanced behind them and ran for the taxi. By the time they had reached it they were soaked to the skin, their hair plastered to their scalps.

Layla jumped in next to me, her wet clothes clinging to her, showing every contour of her body. As her friend also squeezed onto the crowded back seat, Layla was pressed against me. My nostrils were full of the musky aroma of her perfume, and I could feel the soft swelling of her breast against my arm. The heat of her body seemed to burn all the way down my side.

The taxi moved off along the road, inching through the flood. I glanced behind us. The huge figure of Rudi was visible for a second, framed in the doorway of the bar, staring after us, then the curtains of rain blocked him from view.

We were halfway back to the hotel when the storm ended as abruptly as it had begun. The floods began to ebb away and a watery moon appeared as the clouds parted. Even this late, traders came out of the buildings and doorways where they had been sheltering and began setting up again, lighting candles and storm lanterns to illuminate their wares.

The hotel bar was deserted but still open. 'Fancy a last drink?' I said, unsuccessfully trying to hide my disappointment when Layla exchanged a glance with her friend, then shook her head.

'Nothing personal. We've all got an early start in the morning.'

'Have we?'

'You guys are the helicopter pilots, aren't you?'

'Yes, but—'

'Then don't stay up all night drinking. I'm flying up to Bohara with you in the morning to run a clinic at the mine.' For the first time all evening, she gave me a smile. I could still smell a faint trace of her perfume in the air long after she had disappeared up the stairs.

 **CHAPTER 2**

We set off early the next morning. Layla rode up front with Grizz. Tom and I were once more perched in the back, with Rudi.

The glass had been knocked out of the small window in the rear of the cab, allowing us to talk to Grizz and Layla, though we had to shout to be heard above the roar of the engine.

When we reached the Kissy roundabout, Grizz continued straight on. 'This isn't the way to the airport,' I shouted.

'I know. That's because the helicopter isn't kept there.'

We passed through the belt of dismal shantytowns surrounding the capital, the smoke from cooking fires mingling with the stink of refuse and decay, ragged people moving among the shacks. 'Every rebel offensive sends a few more thousand fleeing to Freetown,' Layla said. 'They all end up in the shantytowns.'

The road ran out into open country along fringes of dense jungle and swamp, and the tarmac gave way to red earth and crushed rock as the road climbed steadily towards the mountains. Looking back I could pick out the huge cotton tree in the centre of Freetown.

We drove on, the surface of the road potholed and fissured by rainwater and floods. Ahead I saw savannah grassland. It looked fertile, studded with breadfruit, papaw, guava, mango and locust trees, but the villages were few and sparsely populated.

The road curved to the left and, as we reached the bend, Grizz hit the brakes hard. A tangle of branches had been thrown across the road. Beyond it stood a row of armed men.

I reached down to the rifle beneath my feet. Rudi already had his across his lap, and I heard a click as he eased off the safety catch. There was no way of telling whether the men were soldiers or rebels, since all wore the same battered uniforms, topped with whatever lurid T-shirts or other clothes they had managed to loot. They stood in silence, fingering their weapons and gazing at us with hostility.

'I think they're government men,' Grizz said out of the corner of his mouth. 'Not that it makes much difference. They're hungry and they haven't been paid. That's enough to make anyone bad tempered. Give them some smokes.'

I reached for one of the packs of American cigarettes stashed in the back and held it out over the side of the pick-up as Grizz drove slowly to the makeshift barrier. The leader of the soldiers stepped forward and took the cigarettes. He remained unsmiling, but after a few moments he nodded and signalled his men to move the barrier.

As we moved off, Rudi kept his rifle trained on the group of men, swinging himself slowly round as we nosed through the narrow gap in the barrier, until he was facing back over the tailgate.

We left the road for a rutted dirt track leading away through the bush. It doglegged right and left, and as we swung round the second bend I saw a stretch of rusty wire fencing and a pair of open double gates. The legend on the peeling signboards was just about legible: SIERRA LEONE DEFENCE FORCES, CAMP 17.

Beyond the fence was an expanse of beaten earth and concrete. The barrack huts ahead were so ruinous it seemed inconceivable that the base could still be in use, but a squat soldier appeared from the guardhouse and pointed a Kalashnikov in our direction. His scowl changed to a smile as he recognised Grizz, and he saluted.

Grizz returned the salute and I tossed the soldier a pack of cigarettes as we bounced and jolted our way across the base. We rounded a barrack block and came to a halt by an old Huey parked on the concrete. Even through the camouflage net covering it, I could see it was riddled with holes.

'We're not flying that,' I said. 'Are we? It looks like a wreck.'

Grizz smiled. 'It is. The one you're flying is inside the hangar.' He pointed towards an arch of corrugated-tin sheeting walled with mud bricks. A soldier dozing by the doors leapt to attention and was rewarded with another pack of cigarettes.

Grizz kicked at the rotting wooden doors to loosen them, then we dragged them open. 'Same model,' he said, 'just better nick.'

Rudi turned the pick-up round and backed it up close to the doors. He ran out the winch cable and connected it to the helicopter and we began half dragging and half pushing it out of the building. It was covered in a thin layer of red dust and its body panels were a jigsaw of repaired and reclaimed pieces, suggesting it had had a hard and bullet-riddled life, but the rotor hubs were greased and, when I opened the engine covers, the turbines looked well maintained.

'It looks better than the other one,' I said. 'Where's the engineer?'

Grizz smiled. 'You're looking at him.'

'I thought you were the door gunner,' I said.

'That too. Versatility is the first rule of these kind of ops.'

'So why keep it here? What's wrong with the airport in Freetown?'

'If we left it there, it would be flogged by the first government minister who was short of a few quid. This way it's under our control.'

'Hardly,' I said. 'It's still guarded by government soldiers.'

He smiled. 'But the government doesn't pay them. We do. If the President says one thing and I say another, they'll do what I say.'

Rudi jumped down from the pick-up and disappeared into the gloom of the hangar. He returned rolling a drum of aviation fuel and began topping up the tanks as Tom, Grizz and I began a detailed check of the heli. Layla settled herself to wait in the shade, but a queue of soldiers formed next to her. All complained of aches and pains and pestered her for medicine. They wore a baffling variety of uniforms, collaged together with multicoloured T-shirts and sandals cut from old tyres. Their weapons were a similar mixture, but the guns did at least look well maintained.

It took us an hour to check the heli. The oil pressure on one of the engines was low and, as Grizz tinkered with it, I strolled over and sat next to Layla, who had just sent her last patient away.

'You had quite a queue there,' I said.

'It's the same wherever I go.'

'So what do you do?'

She met my gaze. 'Treat the sick ones as far as I'm able, and give the others a placebo—you'd be amazed how well it works.'

'What brought you to Sierra Leone?' I said.

'I'm a medic.'

'I know, but why here?'

'Why not? They need all the help they can get. Sierra Leone should be one of the richest countries in the world; it has platinum, gold, iron ore and diamonds. But it's the poorest country on earth. The national wealth's all held by foreign corporations or in Swiss bank accounts. By the time the mining companies'—she glanced at me—'and their mercenaries, the President, the army officers, government officials and rebels have had their share, there's precious little left. Know what they call the mining district? The Wild West. Officially, two million carats of diamonds are being exported every year, but even on the most conservative estimates, for every one legally exported, another two are smuggled across the border. There are no diamonds in Liberia and yet there are more diamond merchants in Monrovia than there are in Amsterdam.

'Of course, some of the theft is institutional. The government has no foreign currency reserves, so Decisive Measures are paid in mineral rights. They now get sixty per cent of the diamonds. Once they'd done that deal, they lost whatever interest they had in fighting the rebels. All they want to do is protect their diamond concessions.'

'And Medicaid International?'

'Are willing to get involved in places where no one else will. We can't change things but we can at least help to ease the misery of people who have nowhere else to turn.' She frowned. 'That's me. What persuaded you to join the mercenaries?'

'They don't like to be called that, but—'

'But that's what they are, hired killers.'

'So are all soldiers.'

'And pilots.'

'And pilots.' I paused, seeing yet again in my mind the burning woman with her arms outstretched. I hurried on, trying to banish the image from my mind. 'Yes, sure. We're all trained to fight and kill; it's the last resort, but that's our job and sometimes we have to do it. In peacetime we're hated for it and in wartime people love us for it. But we're doing our government's bidding.'

'Mercenaries aren't.'

'Some aren't. Companies like Decisive Measures are. They're here to defend the diamond mines, but by doing that they're also keeping the rebels at bay. They're like the armed forces, but at one remove, doing the jobs the UK doesn't want to be seen doing for itself.'

She looked across at Rudi, who was cleaning and oiling his rifle. 'Like killing Africans.'

'That's not why I'm here. I'm here because I don't want to see . . .' My voice trailed away. 'Decisive Measures would say we're here to protect Western interests.' I changed tack. 'Listen, I'm a trained military pilot. I've left the RAF; what else can I do?'

'Why did you leave?'

I ducked the question. 'It's a job, it's money, but please don't call me a hired killer. I'm just flying people around, dropping guys on patrols, ferrying in supplies; it's like driving a bus or a truck.'

She pointed to the rocket pod under the body of the Huey. 'And where you come from buses are fitted with those, are they?'

'If you feel so strongly about this,' I said, 'why do you work with Decisive Measures yourself?'

'We have no helicopters and very few vehicles. So I treat Decisive Measures' mercenaries and the expats at the Bohara mine, because it also enables me to treat the African workers there and run clinics at some of the villages.' She stared at me. 'But that doesn't mean I condone what Decisive Measures do.'

Grizz wandered over, wiping the oil from his hands with a piece of rag. 'Don't let Layla pile too much guilt on you, Jack. Mercenaries have been a part of Sierra Leone for centuries. Chiefs, merchants and traders all hired professional warriors; nothing's changed.' He paused. 'Now if you and Comrade Layla have finished your dialectical discussion, I've got a helicopter I'd like you to fly.'

Tom and I began the preflight checks. I scrambled into the cockpit. The dusty, scratched Perspex canopy was etched with the fine lines of stress patterns, casting a blurred halo around every object seen through it. I settled myself into the tiny, bone-hard seat and looked around. Tom and I had only a three-week familiarisation course on the Huey behind us, but already it felt as familiar to me as the driving seat of a family car.

I connected the helmet and radio and we ran through the first round of cockpit checks. Then I gave the wind-up signal to Tom and pressed the starter. The turbines coughed like a man clearing his lungs with the first cigarette of the day, and puffs of blue-black smoke drifted away behind us. Then they fired, roaring into life.

I shifted the lever into flight idle and the rotors began to turn, ponderously at first then accelerating to a blur. The noise increased to a thunder and a cloud of dust rose, obscuring the compound.

We made the last round of preflight checks, a rapid-fire exchange of question and response—fuel, hydraulic pressures, oil temperature, turbine outlet temperature, torque gauge and oil pressure.

Checks complete, I flicked the intercom switch. 'All ready?'

The answers came back at once. 'I'm ready,' Tom said.

'Ready in the back,' Grizz said.

I raised the collective and we lifted clear of the ground. The Huey was an old model, the workhorse of the US forces in Vietnam, but it was solid, well engineered and reliable.

I glanced across at Tom. 'Happy?'

'As happy as I can be seven hours' flying time from the King's Head.'

We made the short hop to Freetown airport and loaded the heli with supplies from Decisive Measures' storage bunkers. Then we took off again, tracking the road we had taken that morning. We passed the base and flew east over a plain of red earth and elephant grass studded with brown huts as round and fat as mushrooms.

Clumps of tall trees cast dark pools of shadow onto the baking earth and a broad river wound its way down from the distant mountains. Its banks were lined with trees, but beyond their shade the surface of the water sparkled like silver in the glare of the sun.

Layla leaned through from the cab, resting an arm on the back of my seat. 'What do you think?'

'Looks great, doesn't it?' I said.

'From here, maybe,' Tom said. 'Get down there with just the tsetse flies, mosquitoes and rebels for company and see how great it is.'

Layla stared at him. 'Perhaps you should reserve judgment until you've actually seen the place and met the people.'

'I don't need to. I already know what it's going to be like.'

'It must be nice to be so certain about everything.'

'Don't worry about him,' I said. 'He's got a mind like a steel trap—it's permanently closed.'

She stayed where she was, standing silent, watching me flying the Huey. 'It looks unbelievably complicated,' she said.

I glanced over my shoulder and smiled at her. 'It's not really. When we're airborne there are only four controls that matter—the rudders, the throttle, the collective and the cyclic.' I pointed towards the floor of the cockpit. 'The rudders are controlled by those foot pedals.

'On my left'—I waggled the control slightly—'is the collective. It increases and decreases the pitch angle of the rotors—pull it up and the heli rises, lower it and the heli goes down. The throttle grips are on the end of the collective—you twist power on and off.

'The cyclic is this long, thin stick that comes out of the cockpit floor between my legs. Whichever way you tilt the cyclic—forward, backward, left or right—the disc of the rotors, and therefore the heli itself, will tilt in the same direction.

'That's really all there is to it . . . except that none of the controls can be operated in isolation—not if you want to stay airborne. Movements of the cyclic and the collective have to be synchronised.'

We flew east for another hour, as the terrain grew steadily higher and rougher below us. Finally we climbed towards the last steep ridge separating us from the Bohara Valley. As we cleared the ridge line, I gasped at the desolation below us.

Whole forests had been felled, the ground cleared and levelled and then stripped to the bedrock. A river had been diverted and a huge dam built, flooding a vast area with water that was a sickly shade of orange. Manmade mountains of crushed rock, the tailings from the mine workings, rose hundreds of feet, bare of any vegetation. As far as my eyes could see, nothing grew in the entire lower valley.

A few antlike figures scurried around the monstrous machines gouging at the ground. Enormous draglines ripped at the diamond-bearing gravels, biting out tens of tons of rock at a time. Massive dumper trucks moved in an unending procession down to a smoke-belching mill, where they dumped gravel onto conveyor belts as wide as roads that disappeared into the gaping maw of the plant.

More conveyor belts moved the debris away, building fresh spoil heaps that seemed to grow as I watched them, and a torrent of discoloured water flowed constantly from an opening at the base of the mill. In the far distance beyond the mine I could see an ugly sprawling town, an island of a few concrete buildings rising from an ocean of mud huts and tarpaper shacks.

A much smaller shantytown surrounded the perimeter fences of the mining compound. The outer fence was a surreal combination of US cavalry fort and Belfast army base—a wooden palisade of sharpened stakes topped by a tangle of barbed wire. Inside the palisade was an altogether more modern fortification: a chain-link perimeter fence topped with coils of razor wire.

Right at the heart of the compound inside the fences was a helipad of beaten red earth.

CHAPTER 3

I circled the compound, determining the best approach to the landing site, clear of the worst obstacles and heading into the wind.

I came in and pushed the nose of the heli upwards, flaring towards the landing. The downwash threw up such a dense cloud of red dust that I had to use the artificial horizon indicator to hold the craft level. Turbulence from the ground threw the helicopter around as we descended the last few feet. I levelled the nose but still made a heavy landing, thumping down onto the springs.

I shut down the engines, stripped off my flying helmet and wiped the sweat from my forehead as the wind from the slowing rotors blew away the last traces of the dust cloud. Then I climbed stiffly down from the cockpit to join the others.

A tall, dark-haired man was waiting to greet us. He was in civilian clothes, but he wore them like a uniform; everything from his immaculately parted and combed hair to his unrolled sleeves and sharp-creased trousers marked him out as an ex-army officer.

'Welcome to Bohara,' he said. 'I'm Colonel Henry Pleydell, CEO of Decisive Measures, but don't worry'—he did his best to put a twinkle in his eye—'this is just a flying visit. We're here to protect the integrity of this site and ensure the smooth running of one of the world's largest diamond mines.' He gestured to the town just visible in the distance. 'That was a cluster of half a dozen huts when diamonds were discovered here. It's now a town of seventy-five thousand people, the biggest in the country after Freetown.

'Most of the processes are automated. There are few hand operations because of the opportunities for pilfering they would allow. There are thousands of illegal miners.' His lips pursed in distaste. 'They work at night in the hope of avoiding our security and they make a bloody nuisance of themselves. Areas levelled for mechanical mining one day are often scarred with hand-dug pits by the next morning.' He studied them for a moment. 'Well, I hope you enjoy your stay here.'

As he turned to consult one of the mining engineers, I took a look at his kingdom. All round the inside of the outer palisade were palm-roofed sheds that looked like Second World War Japanese prison huts.

Layla followed my gaze. 'The native workers live in them,' she said. 'The mine operates twenty-four hours a day, seven days a week and the miners work twelve hours on, twelve hours off. The day shift sleep in the beds the night shift have just vacated. Some of their wives and dependants live in the shanties just outside the wire . . .'

She broke off as Pleydell began shaking hands all round, then he climbed into a heavily armoured Land-Rover. Six mercenaries took up gun positions on it before it was driven out of the gates.

'So it's back to the golf course for the colonel then,' Grizz said.

I continued my scrutiny of the compound. Eight shipping containers had been stacked together in a double-tiered block in the centre. Door and window openings had been cut into them and steel grilles had been welded over the windows. The whole construction was surrounded by an earth mound, capped with a sandbag wall. It was obviously the last redoubt.

A row of single-storey breeze-block houses surrounded it, the accommodation for the expatriate workers. Awnings round the sides gave the houses a little shade. There were sun loungers, swing seats and barbecues on the stoops, and inside each house, no doubt, were TVs, freezers, and fridges full of cold beer.

Layla peeled off to begin her clinic, a row of Africans waiting patiently next to the fire pit where the cooking was done. The rest of us walked over to the stacked containers and filed through a gap in the sandbag walls. Grizz showed us around. The mining company used the upper tier for offices. The front half of the lower tier served as a combined mess hall, satellite TV lounge, briefing room and relaxation area for the mercenaries, and an end section was used as a dormitory. Rudi had already bagged a spare bunk and made himself comfortable. Tom and I chose a couple as far from him as possible.

Most of the other soldiers were watching videos, an arsenal of weapons propped against the walls. We were introduced to them: white officers and NCOs, commanding black troops. Few of the latter were in evidence and I wondered if their quarters were with the black workers beyond the wire. From their accents, the majority of the white soldiers were Rudi's fellow countrymen, but there were five Englishmen, two of whom claimed to be ex-SAS.

'I'm from Hereford—enough said,' one growled as he crushed my hand in an iron handshake. 'Call me Raz, everybody else does.' He was at least a couple of years younger than me, with keen blue eyes and a square, pugnacious chin.

'That's my mate Reuben,' he said, pointing out another young mercenary with a round, moon face and a facial tic that made him blink his eyes in a constant rapid motion. It gave him an air of permanent surprise. He raised an arm in greeting, blinked, smiled, blinked again and turned his attention back to the television.

'The thick-looking one is Hendrik,' Raz said, gesturing towards a bull of a man picking his teeth with the point of a knife, who gave us a curt nod at the mention of his name. 'Don't let his table manners put you off. He's not a bad guy—for a South African.'

The three of them were the only ones who bothered to shift their eyes away from the television screen. So we left them to their videos and moved back to the dining area. Grizz reached into a battered old fridge and passed Tom and me a beer.

I dropped my voice. 'Are those two real Hereford or bullshitters?'

'Bullshitters. One of the guys is an ex-Para. The rest are infantrymen or South African veterans of the bush wars against the ANC.'

There was a sudden burst of fire outside. It provoked a flurry of activity. Soldiers grabbed their helmets and weapons and sprinted for the door. Grizz strode across the room and ran outside.

There was no further shooting and Grizz and the others soon returned. 'No big deal,' he said. 'A couple of rebels taking a few pot shots. A patrol's gone out, but they'll have legged it by now.'

Remembering that Layla had been outside right through the shooting, I hurried out into the bright sunlight. The queue waiting for treatment had dwindled to a handful of people. I stepped back into the shade by the door and watched Layla as she worked.

Some of the African workers had brought their wives and children into the compound to be treated, and even the smallest child, a little boy, showed no fear as Layla examined him. With one hand she stroked his forehead as she tested his distended stomach wall with the other. She gave the parents a reassuring smile, but I saw her bleak look as they turned away with the medicine she had given them.

She started as I stepped out of the shadows next to her. 'Sorry,' I said. 'Didn't mean to startle you. Was that a placebo?'

She nodded. 'But it won't do any good in that case.'

'Is there anything you can do for him?'

'Not really . . .'

'We could fly him to Freetown.'

She looked up in surprise. 'You obviously haven't read the Decisive Measures manual—no inessential passengers allowed.'

'Sod the manual. If it's a matter of life and death, let's do it and worry about it afterwards.'

'Thanks.' I felt the cool touch of her fingers on my arm. 'But it's not that simple. Even in Freetown there are neither the drugs nor the expertise to cure him, and he'll be far from his parents and his village if—when—the worst happens. It's better that he stays here.'

By the time she had seen her last patient, night was falling.

'I've never got used to how quickly the sun sets in the tropics,' I said. 'I really miss those long summer evenings back home.'

'Me too.' She fell silent, staring up at the darkening sky.

'Where is home for you?'

'Don't laugh, I'm an Essex girl; not the best place to grow up for someone of my—' She hesitated. 'Of my background.'

'What do you mean?'

'What do you think I mean?' She shot me a suspicious look. 'My mother was a nurse. She met my dad when he was in hospital after an accident. He'd been an engineer in Guyana; the only job he could get in England was on the assembly line at Dagenham. Maybe things are different there now, but it seemed to me that I was always too black for some and too white for others.' She fell silent and gave a slow shake of her head. 'I don't know why I'm even telling you this. You're no different—just another white mercenary that fancies his chances with me.'

'That's not true.'

'Isn't it?'

I looked around. It was now full dark. A solitary soldier was patrolling the perimeter wire, his boots scuffing in the dust. There seemed to be no one else around. The normal noise of the African bush—the chatter of monkeys, the croaking of frogs and the whine and buzz of a billion insects—was absent. In this valley of desolation, almost nothing moved except men and machines.

The night had a strange beauty of its own, however. The stars dusting the sky overhead were mirrored by a myriad pinpricks of light, moving slowly through the mine workings like glow-worms in the darkness of some vast cave.

'What are they?' I said.

'The illicit miners. They work at night by candle- or lantern-light. They dig out the gravel and carry it in baskets on their heads to the nearest stream. They sieve and jig it, then turn it upside-down and handpick any diamonds.' She paused. 'If they have time before the guard patrols chase them away or shoot them.'

'There must be at least a thousand of them.'

'Why be surprised? There's no other work to be had. The mines have destroyed or flooded most of the farmland, and wrecked the fisheries too.' She searched my face for a moment. 'If you want to see the real Sierra Leone, come with me tomorrow. I'm doing a clinic in Boroyende, a village a few miles north. Some of what you'll see is far from pleasant but it can be inspiring. It'll give you an insight into what the country could be like if the war ever ends and the mines start to be run for the benefit of Sierra Leone, not Britain and America.'

'All right,' I said. 'I'd like that.'

She gave me a dazzling smile. 'Good. Now I'm pretty tired and we have an early start in the morning. I'm going to get some sleep.'

She walked across the compound to one of the breeze-block houses. As she closed the door and walked through the house I saw her shadow outlined against the blinds. I stood watching for some time before I went back into the container building.

Grizz gave me an old-fashioned look when I asked him if I could go with Layla. 'I've told you, you're wasting your time with her.'

I remained impassive. 'So may I go?'

'Yeah, I suppose so. I could do with the time up here to lick these useless bastards into shape. But don't get captured by the rebels. They're not that far from Boroyende. Take a rifle as well as your pistol, and ammunition. And be back in time to get us back to Freetown before dark.'

As I walked to my bunk, Grizz's mocking voice came floating after me. 'Oh and Jack? Want Tom to come with you for company?'

'If he wants to,' I said.

'No chance,' Tom said. 'I'll let you do the tourist bit. I'm quite happy here, thank you very much.'

I smiled to myself as I stretched out on my bunk.

I closed my eyes and lay there replaying in my mind the shape of Layla's body outlined against the blind, trying to hold off sleep as long as I could, knowing that the familiar nightmare would once more be lying in wait.

I GOT UP as soon as the first grey light of dawn showed in the sky, but by the time I'd showered and grabbed some breakfast, Layla was already waiting for me.

'We drive part of the way and then walk the rest,' she said. She climbed into the driving seat of one of the mine's pick-ups.

'The mining companies do have some uses, then,' I said.

She gave me a sharp look. 'It's part of the deal with Medicaid.'

We drove out of the gates of the inner and outer compounds through the shantytown outside and up a steep track skirting the spoil heaps from the mine and climbing towards the ridge. The narrow summit plateau bridged two vastly different worlds. Behind was bare rock, polluted water, the din of heavy machinery and ugly shantytowns shrouded in a pall of dust and smoke. Ahead was a lush valley, a patchwork of villages and small fields, surrounded by broad swaths of dense forest. Only as we began to descend the hillside did I see the scars of war on the land—smashed buildings and abandoned fields slowly reverting to forest.

We drove on towards the distant mountains. The vegetation grew sparser and more patchy and the few tribespeople looked desperately poor and thin. Some men were dressed in rags, others wore no clothes at all. All carried pangas—bush knives

'They subsist on slash-and-burn agriculture,' Layla said. 'In the last few years, the fighting has forced many of them to flee before they've even been able to harvest their crops.' She shrugged. 'Some say it's deliberate; the rebels and the government forces drive them out, then share the crops between themselves.'

Some villages had disappeared altogether, their sites only detectable from the overgrown orange and mango trees and the circles of burnt, blackened earth where huts had been torched.

Layla pulled up at one set of ruins and parked the pick-up.

I picked up my rifle and a rucksack heavy with ammunition, and followed Layla through the ghost village and out along a path leading into the forest. It was green and cool at first, after the heat of the sun, but before long our clothing was soaked with sweat.

We walked for an hour. Eventually the path widened and small, cultivated fields began to appear, niches carved out of the enclosing wall of the forest. We passed women with head-loads of firewood, and men carrying hoes and pangas. All gazed warily at my rifle, but broke into broad welcoming smiles as they recognised Layla. Many of them embraced her and the women held up babies for her inspection, their faces glowing with pride. Layla was soon surrounded and she stopped to carry out her first impromptu treatment at the side of the track.

I walked the last few yards to the village alone. It appeared to be deserted. The path ended in a clearing of beaten earth. A breadfruit tree stood in the centre, casting a pool of shade. Around the edge of the clearing were a dozen mud huts, roofed with palm thatch.

I glanced inside the first hut; it was empty. The earth floor was swept clean, the cooking pots and bowls were stacked on a shelf nailed between two of the stout bush poles supporting the roof, and the sleeping mats were neatly rolled.

The next hut must have belonged to the village carpenter. There were tools with the dull glint of age and the patina of constant use, and a handful of nails burnished where they had been hammered to straighten them. There were also scraps of wire, rope and string and a broken saw blade refitted with an improvised handle. The furniture included a beautifully carved and jointed rocking chair that any English craftsman would have been proud to have made.

I stepped back outside and a moment later Layla joined me. 'That was quite a welcome you got back there,' I said.

'I was based in Boroyende for three years when I first came out here and I've been doing clinics in the village ever since—eight years all told. I've nursed them through a few illnesses, delivered their children, come to their weddings.' A shadow passed over her face. 'And the funerals of those I could do nothing for. They're good people.'

She walked to the centre of the clearing and called out. Slowly the frightened people began to reappear from the forest. A grizzled, white-haired old man led the way. He embraced Layla and talked animatedly to her in the local language.

She replied, then gestured to me. What she said must have been reassuring, for the old man gave a broad smile and shook my hand.

'This is Njama,' she said to me. 'He understands a little English.'

I introduced myself and made the ritual congratulations on the village and the crops. He smiled, bowing his head in acknowledgment, then clapped his hands and signalled for food to be brought. They had little enough but it was shared without a second thought.

As people moved around the village, I noticed that several of them had only one arm. 'What happened to them?' I said.

'The rebels,' Layla said. 'Anyone suspected of supporting the wrong side at the election had an arm severed in punishment. You get the idea: cut off the arm that voted for the government. Thousands of people were mutilated. You see them everywhere. Worse things are done every day here.' She looked past me and called out to a boy who was loitering at the edge of the clearing. He hesitated, then made his way over to us. He seemed no more than nine years old, but, when his gaze met mine, the sad, world-weary eyes of a far older man looked back at me.

'Kaba is from a different tribe,' Layla said. 'But Njama's people have taken him in. He has no family of his own.' She stroked his hair as she spoke. 'His tribe are traditional hunters. At first, they fought to defend their villages against the army and the rebels alike, but then they were recruited by the government as mercenaries or forcibly conscripted by the rebels.

'When the rebels attack a village, they usually kill the adults and take the children. The boys are formed into "Small Boys Units", brutalised, drugged and sent into battle. They're highly valued as soldiers because they're fearless. They go into battle believing that bullets cannot hurt them.'

'And has their belief in their own invulnerability survived the evidence of their friends dying around them?'

'They are told that if one of them dies it is because he has broken one of the rules. They are not allowed to have sex with a woman before they fight. Kaba was too young anyway. He speaks good English. Let him tell you his story.' She gave the boy a gentle smile and held his hand as he began to speak.

'I was a captain in one of the Small Boys Units,' he said. 'Our job was to cut off people's hands, to kill and burn houses. I was promoted because I did it well. The rebels gave us tablets with our food. They gave us power; they made us brave.'

'They feed them a mixture of amphetamines, marijuana, alcohol and gunpowder,' Layla said.

'It made our hearts strong,' Kaba said. 'We were not afraid of anything. Sometimes we drank the blood of those we had killed. The men ate the hearts and livers, as well. We were told it gave us power.'

I shuddered. 'What happened to your parents?'

'They are dead.' He hesitated, twisting his hands together. 'I killed them. The rebels told me, "Kill your mother and father, and your brothers and sisters, or we will kill you." '

He pulled his hand from Layla's and walked back across the clearing.

The food had arrived, so we sat down to eat. Kaba's story had left me with little appetite, but out of politeness I took a little of the dried, smoked fish and rice.

'As you can see, it's a limited but adequate and healthy diet,' Layla said, 'provided they can harvest their rice. They also eat fruit, potato leaf, cassava and okra, and catch fish in traps.'

A jug of palm oil was passed round and poured over the food. 'It makes it more palatable,' Layla said. 'They use palm oil for everything. They cook with it and preserve food in it; fish in oil keeps for months. It's also mixed with ashes and used as soap.'

Njama began to speak to me, pausing to allow Layla to translate. 'We have lived here for many generations, our land is good, but we have lost too many people. We dare not stray far from the village. We have to clear and cultivate where we can, when we can.'

As soon as we had finished eating, a queue of patients formed for Layla to examine. As she worked, Njama took my arm and led me away across the village towards his hut. He ushered me inside.

His sons, four beetle-browed men ranging in age from twenty to thirty, I guessed, followed us in. It was a few minutes before I realised that three of the four had had their right hands severed at the wrist.

The sons stared at me but did not speak as their father proudly showed me around. The internal walls were bare mud. The men's weapons—pangas, spears and an old hunting rifle—hung from pegs and nails driven into the walls. A line of shell casings held water, rice, dried fish and palm oil, and metal from the doors and body panels of wrecked vehicles had been beaten into plates and bowls.

Njama raised his eyes to the ceiling, his face glowing with pride. I followed his gaze and found myself staring at a fly-specked electric light bulb dangling from the thatched roof.

Njama pulled a switch. The light bulb lit with a feeble glow, casting a fitful light into the recesses of the hut.

I shook my head in disbelief. 'How?'

He laughed, then led me out and around the side of the hut. We walked down to the river, where the rusting wheel of a truck had been set up on an axle attached to the river bank. Rough metal paddle blades, cut from the truck's bodywork, had been fixed at intervals around the rim. They spun in the current, powering a dynamo.

I smiled. 'You remind me of my father. When I was a small boy, he was always out in his shed in our garden, trying to find uses for bits of metal and wire or the motor from an old vacuum cleaner.'

I reached in my pocket and took out my Swiss Army penknife. I showed him the different tools and blades, then folded it up and pressed it into his hand. His sons clustered around him, exclaiming at each new blade or tool that he produced from the handle, like a conjuror pulling rabbits from a hat.

When I made as if to leave, Njama detained me for a moment. He stared hard into my eyes. 'You will not take Layla away from us?'

I shrugged, embarrassed. 'I hardly know her. We work together, that's all.'

He smiled. 'But I have seen the way you look at her . . . I think you will bring her happiness.' He spread his hands, encompassing the whole village. 'And if you do, you will have many friends here.'

I was silent most of the way back from the village, mulling over what I had seen and heard. Layla glanced at me frequently as we walked along the forest path and drove back to Bohara.

'It's both better and worse than I imagined,' I said at last. 'They have nothing and yet they have everything they need. But when you hear Njama or Kaba talk . . .' I paused, seeing Kaba's young-old face in my mind as he recounted those unspeakable horrors in his expressionless voice. 'I wish there was something I could do for them.'

'There is. But you have to be willing to work for someone like Medicaid for the benefit of the villagers, not the mercenaries and the mining corporations. I'm not sure you'd be able to do that.'

It was more of a question than a statement. I didn't reply.

 # CHAPTER 4

We collected Grizz and Tom from Bohara and flew back to Camp 17 that afternoon. The flight was uneventful, and as I swung in towards the base I was thinking about a cold beer when there was a sudden silence. The whine of the turbines had disappeared. In its place there was just the rush of wind and the slowing noise of the rotors. Then there was the scream of a siren.

I shouted a warning. 'Engine failure! Prepare for autorotative landing. Get back in the cab, Layla. Hold on for your life!'

A helicopter in free fall drops at around 1,700 feet per minute. Already under 200 feet, I had less than six seconds to react to the power failure, identify a clear area and land in it. Instinctively I rammed the collective full down to neutralise the pitch angle of the rotors. If they remained at flying angle the blades would slow and stop immediately. Rigid, they would then fold up like a bird folding its wings, with similar results. But once I'd made sure they were flat, the uprushing air would continue to turn the rotors and provide enough uplift to cushion the impact. That was the theory, at least.

There was a clear, roughly level patch of land just inside the perimeter of the base. I aimed straight at it, and fifty feet from the ground I hauled back on the cyclic to flare the heli and bleed off the forward air speed down to zero. I kept the nose in the flare as we plummeted groundwards, then at the last minute I levelled it.

We crashed down with a sickening thud. My teeth crunched together and my neck was whipped back into the headrest. The heli bottomed on its springs and gave an almost human groan as it bounced up again. We came to a rest, canted at a slight angle.

The rotors wound down and stopped and there was a sudden silence. I was already tearing at my straps and twisting to look back into the cab. The cockpit was cushioned by powerful shock absorbers, but the cab had almost no protection. People in the back often suffered crushed vertebrae after an autorotative landing.

'Layla.' I struggled through the narrow gap between the seats and into the cab. She was still strapped in, her eyes closed, her face deathly pale. 'Layla!'

Her eyes flickered open. 'I'm all right. I was just scared to death, that's all.' She started to unbuckle her harness.

'Don't move until you're sure your back's all right.'

She made some cautious exploratory movements of her neck and shoulders, then eased herself away from her seat. 'I'm OK.'

'Thank God for that.' I began to help her towards the door.

'Well, don't worry about me, will you?' Grizz said.

'Sorry, Grizz. Are you all right?'

'As a matter of fact I am, yes, but thanks for asking anyway.'

Tom began to giggle and within seconds we were all creased up with laughter. The release of tension made it seem the greatest joke we'd ever heard.

We clambered down from the heli and began looking it over.

'Nothing broken as far as I can see,' I said, 'but I'd rather not take it up again until we know why the engines cut out like that.'

'I'm with you on that,' Grizz said. 'I'll get the guys here to haul it back to the hangar, then I'll strip it down and put it back together.'

'What about us?'

'I'll need one of you to give me a hand. The other one can take Layla back to Freetown and come back out here tomorrow.'

I turned to look at Tom.

He stared at me for a moment. 'All right, you win. I'll stay here.'

I tried hard not to look too pleased.

Grizz handed me a rifle and some spare clips. 'It never hurts to be prepared. And take this radio so we can stay in touch.'

'All right. But I don't want you bothering me all the time when I'm trying to relax.'

He gave an enigmatic smile.

'What?'

'Nothing. Just have a nice night, that's all.'

Layla studied him, arms folded, head on one side. Then she looked around the dusty, fly-blown base and laughed. 'I tell you what, Grizz. We'll be hard-pressed to have a worse night than you.'

WE REACHED FREETOWN in the late afternoon. The sky was pale, almost white, and the low sun was a faint ghost of itself, obscured by dust. The months of rain had at last given way to the dry harmattan wind, laden with fine sand carried from the Sahara. As we drove down the hill to the city centre, it hung like fog in the air.

Before I got out of the pick-up, I wrapped a piece of rag round my face like a mask, but almost at once I could feel the dust in my nose and taste it in my mouth. The air was full of creaking sounds as the wooden buildings dried in the wind.

When I reached my hotel room, I found that the dust had seeped in round the edge of the windows and suffused my books and clothes. It had even passed through the mosquito net and settled like talc on my bedding.

After a quick shower I met Layla for dinner. The hotel menu had a choice of smoked fish, rice and okra—or an unidentified stew.

We chose fish and, more in hope than expectation, I ordered a bottle of wine. I took a dubious sip, then another. 'It's delicious,' I said, 'full-bodied and Lebanese—just like the hotel owner.'

She smiled, and the stress lines etched into her face disappeared.

'That's better,' I said. 'Leave your problems outside and relax.'

'I get the feeling that's not something you're very good at doing.'

I bowed my head. 'Guilty,' I said.

She studied me. 'So why are you here? I'll grant you this, you don't seem like the other mercenaries. They're pushing forty. Yet what are you? Twenty-eight? Twenty-nine?'

I nodded. 'Right first time.'

'You could have had another ten years in the RAF? So why leave? And why come here?'

'I guess I needed a change.' It sounded lame even to me.

She waited in silence for me to continue.

'I—I just wanted a steady job, I suppose. No excitement—'

'And no responsibilities?'

'That too.'

She gave a wry smile. 'Sierra Leone isn't exactly noted for its quietness, and when things go wrong here, even those on the sidelines find themselves involved whether they like it or not.'

I poured us each another glass of wine. 'So what about you?' I said. 'Why are you here?'

'I got into trouble at my last posting. I expressed my opinions a bit too forcefully to a politician. It took some hasty diplomacy to prevent the entire medical team being expelled. I was lucky not to be sacked, but this was the worst posting they could think of.' She smiled. 'Funnily enough, despite all the deprivation and violence, I love it here. I feel as if I belong.'

The hotel owner cleared away our plates and brought tiny cups of thick, black Lebanese coffee with powdered milk and gritty sugar. We sat talking late into the evening, long after the other diners had left. As we said good night outside my room, I leaned forward to kiss her.

She let my lips brush against hers, but when I tried to prolong the embrace, she pushed me away. 'Let's just keep it friendly, Jack,' she said. 'I'd need to know an awful lot more about you before I'd even consider being the next notch on your bedpost.'

'I know that,' I said. 'I didn't—' But she was already walking down the corridor.

When I got into bed, I lay staring into the darkness for a long time but, like almost every night since Kosovo, the familiar nightmare was waiting for me when I at last fell asleep. This time there was a difference, however: a hand began beckoning from the flames and a man's voice shouted over and over, 'Come in. Come in.'

I awoke. The voice continued. 'Jack, come in. Jack, come in.'

I lay there trying to make sense of it, as cold sweat trickled down my forehead. Then I sat upright, clambered out of bed and began to rummage through the pitch-dark room for the radio Grizz had given me. I found it at last, buried under my discarded clothes.

'This is Jack. What's happening, Grizz?'

'There's shit flying at Bohara. A big rebel assault. The guys have taken casualties. Get Layla, and get out here to the base. We must take the heli and go as soon as we can.'

'But the heli's not fit to fly until it's been fixed.'

'We've sorted it,' he said. 'Now get out here pronto.'

I dragged my clothes on then ran and pounded on Layla's door.

A sleepy voice answered and she came to the door wrapped in a towel. Even half asleep she looked heart-stoppingly beautiful.

'Grizz has been on the radio,' I said. 'There's trouble at Bohara. We've got to get going at once.'

She stared at me for a moment. 'What sort of trouble?'

'The rebels.'

She turned back into the room. Through the half-open door, I saw the sheen of starlight on her skin as she dropped the towel and pulled on a T-shirt and jeans. A moment later she was hurrying out of the door, holding her medical bags.

We ran downstairs and out into the darkness.

I revved the engine of the pick-up and we drove off through the deserted streets. Layla sat silent in the passenger seat staring out through the windscreen, her lip caught between her teeth.

'Are you all right?' I said.

'What? Yes, sorry, I was just thinking about Njama's people, wondering if they're safe.'

We left the city and began the climb through open country towards the mountains. As we approached the bend where we'd encountered the roadblock, I slipped the radio and my pistol under the seat. The rifle that Grizz had given me was still sitting in the hotel room. I cursed, but it was too late to go back for it now.

I was only half expecting the barrier to be manned, but as we rounded the corner, I brought the pick-up to a juddering halt. A dozen heavily armed men stood guard on the barrier. They levelled their rifles at us as soon as we came into view.

'This doesn't look too clever,' I said.

'Give them some cigarettes and we should be all right,' Layla said.

I wound down the window and held out the carton as we stopped in front of the barrier. The soldiers looked tired and edgy. One of them—the leader, I guessed, going by the mirrored sunglasses he wore like a badge of office—walked to the door of the pick-up, took the cigarettes from me, then jerked his head. 'Get out of the car.'

We got out and the soldier searched us in turn. I saw Layla flinch as he handled her breasts while pretending to search for concealed weapons. Then he stepped back and signalled to two of the others to search the vehicle.

They handed him Layla's medical bag, then one of them found the radio and pistol under the seat.

The leader turned the pistol over in his hands. 'What is this?' he said angrily. 'Who are you? What are you doing here?'

'As you can see from our medical bag, we're doctors with Medicaid International,' I said before Layla could speak. 'We're on our way to treat a very ill patient. Please let us pass.'

'Since when do doctors carry guns?'

I spread my hands. 'These are dangerous times. I carry it only for protection from robbers and bandits.'

He studied me for a moment. 'Where is this patient of yours?'

'At the army camp at the top of the hill.'

He stiffened. 'He is a soldier, then.'

'No,' I said. 'She is a civilian. The soldiers took her to the camp because she was so ill.'

'What is wrong with her?'

Layla jumped in before I could reply. 'She is with child. She has been in labour for almost two days. If we do not get to her soon, both she and her baby will die.' She held his gaze. 'Please. Imagine if this was your wife and your baby. One day it might be.'

He hesitated, then gave a curt nod. With some show of reluctance, his men began moving the barricade.

'My pistol and my radio?' I said.

He shook his head. 'Radios are the tools of spies, not doctors.'

I thought about arguing, then let it go. 'And my pistol?'

He slipped it into his pocket. 'You will have no need of this. I and my men control this road. We permit no thieves or bandits.' His smile challenged me to argue with him if I dared.

We got back into the pick-up. I drove away up the hill.

As we passed out of sight of them I heard machine-gun fire coming not from behind us but from somewhere in the darkness ahead.

I braked to a halt, switched off the lights, then put the pick-up in gear and began creeping forward again, steering only by the faint glow of the moonlight reflected from the surface of the road.

When we crested the brow of the hill, I saw a reddish glow away to our left. It pulsed and flickered, sending sparks spiralling upwards.

'The base,' Layla said. 'What do we do?'

I pulled the pick-up off the road into a small clearing at the edge of the forest. 'We go forward on foot and see what's going on.'

We climbed out and inched our way forward through the trees, stumbling over dead branches. I was soaked with sweat, as much from tension as the exertion in the heat of the night. Pumped up on adrenaline, I was hyperalert, straining my eyes to see into the darkness ahead, imagining rebel soldiers hiding behind every bush.

We crawled the last few yards through the undergrowth at the edge of the base. I raised my head a little and parted the branches in front of me, then flattened myself at once.

Not more than thirty yards away was a rebel position. Their commander was directing fire, shouting orders into the radios he held in either hand. Other groups of rebels were scattered around the perimeter and the heavy machine gun we had heard from the hill was set up a hundred yards to his right.

Inside the base, the huts nearest to us were ablaze, but through the smoke I could glimpse the hangar where the heli was. It looked intact and was still protected by a cordon of defenders.

Even so, the position seemed hopeless. There were no more than a couple of dozen soldiers at Grizz's disposal and at least ten times that number of rebels.

'We have to get into the base,' I said. 'If I can get the Huey airborne we've a chance of driving these bastards off.'

'We can't,' Layla said. 'They've got it completely surrounded.'

'We've got to do something. If we just sit here, Grizz, Tom and everybody else will be slaughtered. We've got to create a diversion somehow. Come on.'

'Where are we going?'

'Back to the pick-up.'

 **CHAPTER 5**

With the crash of gunfire reverberating in our ears, we retraced our steps through the forest.

Before I drove away, I ripped my shirtsleeve off, then unscrewed the cap from the fuel tank and dowsed the cloth in petrol. I left half of it protruding from the neck of the tank, then drove slowly, without lights, down the track to the base.

The thunder of gunfire grew louder and, as we rounded a bend, I saw the glare of burning buildings and the muzzle flashes of scores of weapons. I stopped the pick-up in the darkness beneath a clump of trees overhanging the track.

The rebel commander's position was directly ahead of me down the track, just beyond a parked truck. I turned my head and let my gaze travel slowly along the perimeter of the base, picking out the other groups of rebels.

I touched Layla's arm and pointed to a section of the fence almost midway between two groups of rebels. A tree grew close to the wire and the ground dipped down towards the fence, giving a little cover. 'That's the best place,' I said. I stripped off my flying jacket. 'Take that and sprint down to the fence. Wait under cover of the tree until the balloon goes up, then throw the jacket onto the barbed wire and climb over it.'

'And where will you be?'

'Right on your heels all the way.'

'It's too dangerous, Jack. Even if the rebels don't shoot us, when Grizz's men see us climbing over the wire, they're not going to wait for us to identify ourselves, they're just going to shoot us.'

'That's the chance we have to take. If we don't get into the base and get that heli airborne, they'll all be killed.'

I leaned across the seat and kissed her. She stared at me, then took my flying jacket and slipped out of the pick-up.

I watched her run down the slope to the tree, then I reversed along the track a hundred yards. I got out of the pick-up, found a good-sized rock and slipped it into the vehicle's footwell, then walked back to the tailgate. I struck a light, ignited the cloth trailing from the neck of the petrol tank and sprinted for the cab. I accelerated through first and second gears, then lined up the pick-up on its target, rolled the rock onto the accelerator, jamming it to the boards, and dived out of the side. The impact as I hit the ground drove the air from my lungs.

Still accelerating, the pick-up bucketed along the track and hit the rear corner of the truck. There was a beat of silence then a blast as the petrol tank exploded and fire erupted into the air. Before the glare had faded, I was running bent double down the slope.

I saw Layla throw the jacket onto the barbed wire and begin to climb. I reached the bottom as she struggled over, and heard her stifle a cry of pain as a barb spiked her hand. Then she was dropping to the ground on the other side.

I was almost at the top when I heard a shout from inside the base and a burst of gunfire was directed at me. A moment later I was also spotted by the rebels. Caught in the lethal crossfire from both sides, I threw myself forward. I felt the barbs ripping and tearing at me, then I was falling to the ground.

I landed heavily on my side, but staggered to my feet and was off, stumbling after Layla, running for cover as bullets cracked and whined around me. We flung ourselves into a hollow and lay still as bullets chewed at the earth above our heads.

I waited for a lull in the firing then, still in cover, I shouted, 'Grizz!' I raised my arms. There was an isolated shot, then silence. I straightened a little, and advanced a couple of feet out of cover. Four black soldiers had their guns levelled at my guts. I could see their puzzlement at my white skin.

Beyond them I saw Grizz with his back to me, crouching behind an earth mound and directing fire towards the far side of the compound. I heard Layla start to follow me. 'Not yet,' I said. 'Wait there.'

She ignored me and came alongside me, her arms also raised. I shouted again at the top of my voice. '*Grizz!*'

I saw him turn, stare at us, then shout at the soldiers. They kept us covered as we moved slowly forward. A moment later Grizz came sprinting towards us. He pushed past the soldiers, dragged us down behind the earth mound and grabbed us both in a bear hug. 'Thank God,' he said. 'I'd written you off. Can you get airborne and give us some help here?'

'Just watch me. Get your boys to give us some cover while we get the heli out. It will fly, won't it?'

'Let's hope so. We fixed it, but we've had no time to test it.'

'Guns?'

'Fully loaded. No time for the rocket pod, though.'

'Right.' I turned and ran at a crouch towards the hangar. Grizz followed. 'Where's Tom?' I called over my shoulder.

'You'll have to manage without him. He's been hit in the leg.'

We dragged the hangar doors open. I put on the night-vision goggles and then fired up the engines while the heli was still inside the building. The defenders laid down a barrage of fire until Grizz gave them the signal, then a dozen of them dropped their weapons and ran to push the Huey out of the hangar into the open.

When the nose of the heli appeared the rebels redoubled their fire, raining down everything they had to try to stop the Huey getting airborne. Even though an embankment partly shielded it from the rebel fire, rounds were cracking and rattling on the heli's metal skin. I tried to force myself to concentrate on the controls in my hands.

As soon as the tips of the rotor arms cleared the hangar door, I gunned the engines. The rotors turned, blurred and accelerated into an unbroken disc overhead.

Grizz threw himself into the cab as the Huey lifted on its springs and then we were airborne. I banked hard away from the main concentration of rebels, climbing rapidly to 200 feet, then I swung round and came in low and fast at my first target, the rebel command position.

I heard the chatter of the mini-gun as Grizz opened up from the door of the cab, laying down a barrage of fire, but I held off with the nose gun until the cross hairs intersected on the left-hand man in the rebel group. Then I squeezed the trigger, easing the right rudder down to walk the line of fire right across the cluster of rebel troops. The nose guns thundered and I heard the heavy rattle of ejected cartridges and smelt smoke and the tang of cordite.

I was already banking to bring the next group of rebels into my sights: the men manning the heavy machine gun. I squeezed the trigger again, swinging the heli around to move the line of fire through the target. The ground below me shook and erupted. Clods of earth were flung high into the air and dust mingled with smoke.

A few rebels returned fire, but it was ragged stuff. They began running in all directions. I saw the commander jump into the truck and begin urging the driver back, but its way was blocked by the burnt-out pick-up. I lined up the guns and riddled the truck from bumper to bumper. It disappeared in a cloud of smoke and flame.

I pursued a group of fleeing rebels until I had emptied the guns, then banked around, back to the base.

We landed and I climbed down from the cockpit. Slowly the defenders began to emerge from behind the barricades.

Grizz slapped me on the back, 'Great shooting, ace.' His men fanned out across the base, pausing to examine each fallen rebel. There was a drum roll of single shots as the injured were finished off with a bullet in the head. I turned away.

Grizz caught my eye. 'That's the nature of war for all sides here,' he said. 'The Geneva Convention didn't make it this far. There's not enough medicine, food or anything else to supply your own side, let alone prisoners of war. So . . .' He put his forefinger against his temple and mimed pulling a trigger.

Layla emerged from a bunker looking drawn and deathly pale. We looked at each other. Grizz's face was a mass of cuts and bruises. I didn't paint too pretty a picture either.

'Where's Tom?' I said, suppressing a guilty twinge that I had only just thought about him.

Grizz gestured towards a low building alongside the hangar. 'He's in the hut there. Like I said, he's wounded, but he's OK, I think. He caught a bullet in the thigh, a flesh wound, but he made a lot of fuss about it—you know what pilots are like—so we dosed him up with morphine.' He switched his gaze to Layla. 'Now the heat's off, you can look him and the rest of the casualties over.'

He led us over to the hut. Inside, the casualties lay on the floor or were propped against the wall. Tom was slumped just by the door. He stared up at us and smiled and waved in recognition, but his speech was a blurred, morphine-fuelled stream of incoherence.

The water canteen he had been carrying on his hip had been shattered but it had saved his leg and maybe his life. There were messy wounds where shards of metal had been forced into his thigh, but the bones were not broken.

Some of the other casualties had horrific wounds, but Layla moved among them, fast but purposeful, showing no trace of panic as she assessed them. 'This one will wait. This one now.'

'What's our next move?' I said to Grizz, who had been talking on the satcoms while Layla was working.

'We must get the heli to the airport, load up as much ammo as we can carry and get back out to Bohara fast. It's still under attack.'

We loaded Tom and the worst of the wounded into the back of the Huey. Grizz once more manned the door gun.

'You can sit in the front,' I said to Layla. 'The copilot won't be needing the seat and you're as safe there as anywhere.'

I called the tower at the airport, making sure they were aware that the incoming helicopter was friendly. 'This is Decisive Measures helicopter Grizzly One, flying from Sierra Leone Defences Force Camp Seventeen, seeking clearance to land.'

'Come on in, Grizzly One,' a laconic voice replied. 'You've got the place to yourself.'

We lifted off. I kept the Huey climbing to 5,000 feet, then banked towards Freetown. As we approached the airport I could see a transport aircraft with Nigerian markings unloading near the runway.

We landed and I helped Grizz and Layla unload the casualties.

The most seriously injured were taken away in a rattletrap ambulance emblazoned with the Medicaid International logo; the less seriously wounded, Tom included, were seated on the ground.

Tom still looked spaced out. 'Will he be fit to fly?' I said.

Layla frowned. 'His leg is no problem; it's only a flesh wound. But he needs a few hours to get the morphine out of his system. Four hours absolute minimum, OK?'

I nodded then turned away to help Grizz.

We unlocked one of the bunkers and began loading boxes of ammunition, grenades and RPG rounds into the cab of the heli, stacking them roof high and lashing them to the sides with webbing.

'What about Layla?' I said, as we worked.

'What about her? She comes with us.'

'It's too dangerous,' I said.

'It's too bloody dangerous everywhere these days. Besides, she's needed; they've taken casualties.'

WE WAITED FOR DUSK and the cover of darkness before taking off. Soon, it was a moonless night. The mountains rising to the north of us were blacker even than the night sky and the distant river winding beneath the canopy of the forest gleamed like dull pewter.

The airfield was blacked out and the only light was the faint glow of the instruments, but the darkness would give us some protection from rebel ground fire, and with night-vision goggles I could have flown the Huey down a coal mine at midnight.

Tom limped over to the Huey and climbed into the cockpit. I glanced behind into the cab. Grizz was stationed by the open door, squatting behind the mini-gun. Layla was precariously perched among the ammunition boxes. If we encountered ground fire and rounds went through the cab . . . I shook that thought off.

Just before I started the engines I shot a sideways glance at Tom. 'Are you really all right to take over control if you have to?' I said.

'No problem. Get on with it.' The waspish note in his voice gave me more reassurance than his words.

I fired the engines, grabbed the rotor brake and pushed the lever forward into flight idle. The drooping rotors creaked into life. The *whock-whock-whock* as they began to turn accelerated into a blur of noise and motion.

I pulled the night-vision goggles down over my eyes and switched them on. There was a faint electronic whine and the dark landscape turned green before my eyes, sparkling into life. The course of the river shone like a ribbon of light and the starlight flickered from the rotors like sparks of green fire.

I pressed the intercom. 'Here we go. Hold on, it's going to be a bumpy ride.'

I raised the collective and the Huey rose into the air. I held it at 100 feet as I got clearance from the tower and radioed ahead to Bohara. 'We're on our way. ETA twenty fifteen hours. Over.'

The reply was masked by static. 'The sooner the better.' I could hear the sounds of gunfire punctuating his words.

I put the Huey into a gradual descent. The changing air pressure in my ears told me we were descending without even having to look at the gauges or out through the canopy.

I waited until the altimeter hit fifty feet, then levelled. Still accelerating, we thundered eastwards into the night, rising and falling in response to my green-tinged vision of the unfolding terrain. I pushed us up to clear a ridge, then down again in a gut loosening plummet to a valley floor, and rising once more to the next ridge. As I moved the controls, I gave a running commentary to Grizz and Layla in the back to help them brace themselves for the next lurch as the Huey swooped and soared, twisted and turned.

There had been no ground fire so far. I tried to imagine the unseen groups of rebel soldiers in the darkness ahead. They would have little warning of our approach, only a distant rumble of engines, swelling rapidly to a deafening clamour. There would be a storm of wind from the rotors and an unlit shape, black as a bat, flashing overhead. By the time they brought their weapons to bear, it would be too late.

We had been climbing steadily for some time to clear the last major ridge separating us from Bohara. As we neared the summit, the first starfires of shots pierced the darkness below us. I felt sweat start to my brow and gripped the controls even tighter. We cleared the ridge and lurched downwards in a sickening fall. I thumbed the radio. 'Bohara, this is Grizzly One. We are on approach now, taking incoming fire.'

I switched my gaze forward, looking for the signal from the unlit base. Then in the distance I saw a single square of beads of light begin to glow in the enveloping velvet blackness.

The ground fire was increasing in intensity now and I pushed down towards the rocky moonscape created by the mines.

As we approached Bohara, a blizzard of rounds filled the air and arcs of tracer seared upwards. Heavy-calibre tracer could cut through the heli's armoured skin like paper. I tried to ignore the stabbing streaks of red and orange light reaching up towards us. It seemed impossible that anything could fly through that inferno and not be carved into pieces. I jerked the heli left and right and sent it rising and falling, trying to unsettle the rebels' aim.

I looked ahead. A line of fierce red tracer slashed through the sky ahead of us. If we held our course, flying straight into a curtain of fire, we would be shot down.

I pulled an abrupt turn, swinging through 360 degrees in barely more than the Huey's own length. I heard a cry of surprise from Grizz in the back and a rattle as an ammunition box broke loose from its ties.

I held my breath, then saw the tracer exploding harmlessly behind us. It snapped off for a few moments, then reappeared, again slicing though the sky to overtake us. I pulled the same manoeuvre. Once more the tracer whipped past us and disappeared in our wake.

The compound lights had been extinguished after that one brief showing but one of the mercenaries was guiding me in using a torch with tape across the glass to leave only a thin, faint lozenge of light glowing in the darkness. I pulled back the cyclic, banking to land.

'Ground speed fifty, altitude one hundred feet,' Tom said.

I stamped alternately on the rudder pedals, twitching the tail from side to side in the hope of throwing off the aim of the rebel gunners, but, as I prepared to land, the torrents of ground fire increased still further. A moment later a string of flares ignited. As they drifted slowly down, they lit up the compound and the heli.

'We can't land,' Tom said. 'Just ditch the ammo and let's get out of here.'

I began to argue but I knew he was right. I pushed the intercom. 'We're going for a rolling drop. Get ready and I'll count you in.'

The seconds crawled by as we cleared the fence line and reached the drop zone. 'Three . . . two . . . one . . . Drop!'

Grizz and Layla started pushing and kicking out the cases of ammunition as I kept the Huey creeping forward over the floor of the compound. We were dropping the cases from thirty feet and I saw one split open as it hit the ground, spilling rounds onto the dirt, but Grizz was already shouting, 'Load clear. Go! Go! Go!'

I rammed up the collective and, free of the heavy load, we bucked into the air. I nosed the Huey over hard as soon as we were clear of radio antennae and satellite dishes on the accommodation block. I kept us climbing fast, moving out of range, disappearing back into the blackness of the night.

I grabbed the intercom. 'Everyone OK back there?'

'A few more holes in the cab,' Grizz said, 'but none in us.'

We flew back to the airport, but returned to Bohara twice more during the night, each time dumping more ammunition into the compound and then disappearing as rounds buzzed around the cockpit like angry hornets. On the second trip we managed to get Layla safely to the ground so that she could treat the wounded.

Dawn was breaking as we flew back to Freetown Airport again. We reached the airfield and I saw a giant Hercules transport drawn up near the Decisive Measures compound.

As soon as we'd landed, we began checking over the Huey. There were a few more perforations in its metal skin and some nicks in the edges of the rotors, but no significant damage. We turned away from the Huey in time to see a field gun being unloaded from the Herc.

'That's ours,' Grizz said. 'Let's grab some breakfast and then get that gun up to Bohara.'

'We're a sitting target already without a two-ton pendulum hanging underneath us,' Tom said. 'Do they really need it?'

'Those weren't fireworks the rebels were throwing, Tom,' I said. 'Of course they need it.'

I studied him for a moment. I'd been trained by him at Finnington when I was beginning my air force career in helis, but that was all I knew of him. When I discovered we'd be flying together again, I had asked the air-force rumour mill for information about him.

It appeared that Tom was a moderate pilot with an unexceptional career. There were no black marks on his record, but there was a whisper about him. The guy had served for twenty years in the air force—a period including the Falklands War, the Gulf War and Kosovo—and yet somehow he had never been in combat. My informants tapped their noses and hinted at a lack of bottle.

On the back of thirty hours with virtually no sleep, we had now been flying for over twelve hours nonstop. Close to exhaustion, I was flying as if on automatic pilot, but there was no question of refusing to fly the mission, least of all when the guys at Bohara were taking incoming fire. I sensed a difference in Tom's attitude, however, and his state of mind was already beginning to worry me.

'That's the job, Tom,' I went on. 'They need it, we deliver it.'

'Even if it gets us killed?'

'That's why they pay us the money.'

Grizz looked up. 'Listen, Tom, you've got a hard job, but it's nowhere near as tough as the one the guys at Bohara are doing.' He gave Tom a look that contained little sympathy, and walked away.

Tom watched him go, then turned to face me. He held my gaze, his voice quavering with barely suppressed emotion. 'I didn't come here to die, Jack. I came to get my life back on track and give myself a breathing space, not get shot to pieces over some stinking jungle.' He paused and softened his tone. 'You're younger than me. Things look more clear-cut to you: there's right and wrong and not much else in between. And you fly—like all the young guys—as if the shoot-downs only happen to other people.' He gripped my arm tightly. 'Well, they don't, Jack. They happen to people just like you and me. My luck's run out. I've been hit already. The next one'll kill me.'

As gently as I could, I disengaged his hand from my arm. 'You copped a flesh wound in your leg, Tom, that's all. If your luck had run out it would have killed you.' I paused, trying to find words to rally him. 'We're both knackered and by the book we've flown too many hours already, but we're going to get the job done. In a few hours' time we'll be sitting with our feet up and a cold beer in our hands, laughing about this conversation. Now let's get some food and water and then get airborne.'

He turned away. I watched him limp towards a street vendor who had set up shop on the edge of the airfield selling bean soup, smoked fish and rice. The price had gone up fivefold since the news of the rebel attacks had broken and he would take payment only in dollars, but there was little choice: it was that or K-rations.

While we ate, Grizz shouted and cajoled his private army into preparing the field gun. It was an ancient 25-pounder.

'I didn't know you were an antiques collector, Grizz,' I said.

He grinned. 'We use what we can get, smart arse. It's British Army surplus, but it still works all right and it'll land a round on a target just as well as a modern artillery piece—maybe even better.'

As we talked, the others sweated to loop two thick wire cables beneath the gun and stack the boxes of shells into the heli. When all was ready, we refuelled the Huey and I fired up the engines to pick up the 25-pounder. I flew forward and a guy crouching near the gun reached up and swung four cables over the hook as I held the heli in the hover. Then I heard Grizz shout, 'Got it. Let's go.'

The rotors struggled to haul the load off the ground. But finally, engines groaning, we began to climb. The controls felt sluggish under the added load and the drag of the gun. I adjusted the controls with small, almost imperceptible movements, knowing the danger of beginning a pendulum swing in the load that would increase until it threw the heli out of flying trim.

The flight to Bohara seemed to take for ever. The weight of the 25-pounder dangling below the Huey made every manoeuvre ponderous, and I knew that when we came under heavy fire it would be impossible to fly the normal patterns of evasion. Any attempt to climb or descend too steeply would simply send us crashing to earth.

The one trick I could employ was to approach from an unexpected direction. It was one of the first things we were taught in combat training: never use the same approach path twice or the enemy will set up guns under it and cut you to pieces the next time you fly in.

Instead of the direct approach to Bohara from the west, I therefore circled south and east of the compound, coming in from the opposite direction to the one the rebels would be expecting.

The drop-off was still fraught with danger, however. With the field gun trailing below us we could not even approach at low level. Instead, I came in high and then dropped towards the compound in a dive that, because of the destabilising weight of the 25-pounder, was neither as tight nor as rapid as I would have wished.

The rebel gunners opened up with everything they had. I could see scores of muzzle flashes and moments later rounds began to clip the fuselage. More bullets struck sparks from the field gun below us and then ricocheted away.

Grizz and Tom talked me down as a hail of rounds rattled from the armoured underside of the Huey. One whined away from the metal frame of the Perspex canopy. The next one pierced it, punching twin holes in either side of the cockpit a few inches from our heads and showering us with fragments of Perspex that rattled against my visor. Tom's voice cracked as he tried to give me instructions, but Grizz remained imperturbable, his words interspersed with bursts from the mini-gun. The rebels' brightly coloured T-shirts made them highly visible targets.

'Left thirty feet,' Grizz said. 'Hold it there and descend.' At last, he gave the command. 'That's it. Hold it there. Release!'

'Release,' Tom said, the relief evident in his voice. The heli lurched upwards as he hit the button and the dead weight dropped away.

We had hovered for no more than a minute, but in that time we were riddled with fire. More rounds struck the rotors and ripped through the cab walls. As we returned fire, spent casings from the mini-guns cascaded down onto the tin roofs in the compound.

Grizz already had the cases of shells for the field gun poised at the edge of the deck. I nosed the heli forward another twenty yards, clear of the 25-pounder, and he began kicking them out. More and more rounds struck the fuselage of the Huey. It seemed impossible that none had yet pierced a vital area. At last I heard Grizz's voice on the intercom. 'Last one clear. Go! Go! Go!'

I piled on the power. Free at last of the massive load, the Huey shot upwards into the sanctuary of the skies.

 # CHAPTER 6

We returned safely to the airfield at Freetown, but my thoughts of rest proved optimistic. We were back in action at once. As well as the field gun, fresh reinforcements had arrived in the Herc. There was a group of black South African troops and their white NCOs, and a ragged looking bunch of white mercenaries—German, Russian, French and South African—all with the hard-eyed look of men who had killed before and would do so again.

'Decisive Measures seem to be getting a lot less choosy about where their recruits come from,' I said.

Grizz shrugged. 'Needs must. Let's get moving.'

By now, the run to Bohara had become almost routine, a high-level approach, followed by a breakneck, low-level dash over the last few miles, dodging the ground fire. Each run added a few more holes to the Huey, but I'd begun to feel almost invulnerable. I was at one with the machine, sure of its responses as I pushed it to the limits, the rotors skimming the treetops. We flared and landed or went into the hover over the compound only for the few seconds it took to drop the load we were carrying before we were airborne again in a fog of dust.

This time we landed, keeping the rotors turning fast as the mercenaries dumped out their weapons and kit and jumped down. As they did so the landing zone erupted with hostile fire. I heard the crack and tick of rounds piercing the helicopter's steel skin and ripping through the Perspex canopy above my head.

The seconds crawled by as the soldiers dragged their equipment out. 'Come on,' Tom shouted. 'Come on, let's go.'

'We're waiting for Layla,' Grizz said.

She had been treating some wounded at the compound, but was now returning to Freetown. I saw her come sprinting from the fortified container building, ducking and weaving as she ran across the compound and dived into the cab.

It seemed an age before Grizz called, 'She's in. Go. Go. Go.'

Before he had finished speaking, I was climbing and banking away from the rebel fire, swinging away as dust and smoke obscured the battlefield behind us.

Among the lines of ineffectual small-arms fire, I suddenly saw a series of huge, vivid red starbursts ripping upwards, outlined for a fraction of a second against the backdrop of bare rock and forest and then soaring up across the blue sky towards us. For a moment I refused to believe the evidence of my eyes.

'That's antiaircraft fire,' Tom said. 'That ZFU they told—' His voice trailed away.

Sweat poured from my brow as I jerked and twisted the Huey around in a frantic pattern of evasion. The unseen gunner tracked us, and the fireballs drifted closer. I pulled a maximum break and the red fires blasted the empty sky where we had been heading only a few seconds before.

I pulled another gut-wrenching turn, then froze. Red fire burned a line through the sky towards us like an oxyacetylene torch cutting metal. It disappeared in the blinding glare of the sun, then reappeared as a red flash directly ahead of us.

Time seemed to stop, then there was a blast and a crash, and a blurring frenzy of light, noise and heat. The red flares were on the inside of the cab, punching up through the armoured floor and out through the roof. The line burned its way across the floor, up through Tom's seat and out through the back of the cab.

There was the stench of burning, and a snowstorm of metal, plastic, rubber and fabric flew around me. Tom twitched a little, and then settled into his seat as if dropping off to sleep, but from the corner of my eye, I saw a rich, red stain spread over his flying suit.

For a second every screen was blank. Then there was a blizzard of flashing lights and a rising cadence of shrieking alarms. The Huey gave a savage lurch and went into an accelerating spin. Tracer rounds, red earth, dark green vegetation and blue sky blurred into a continuous multicoloured stream flashing past the cockpit.

Agonisingly slowly, each movement a huge effort, I pulled the levers, throttling back, cutting the power and the torque in an effort to hold it level. The landscape came back into focus.

I nursed the failing helicopter towards a gash in the trees where some forest giant had collapsed. It was strictly too narrow for the rotors but we had zero options. I lined up the heli, setting the tail rotor directly along the length of the gap.

I took a deep breath. Modern craft were lighter, constructed from materials unknown when the Huey was built, but the sheer solidity of the old helicopter had some advantages. The main rotors were almost fifty feet from tip to tip and the ballast weights at the ends gave the heavy blades such inertia that they could slice through brush and small branches without damage.

I began to inch us down. The body of the heli dropped below the treetops. As it sank lower there was a noise like gunfire and a snow-storm of wood fragments flew through the air.

The noise and the blizzard of splinters increased as we dropped. The rotors made harder work of cutting their way through the thicker lower branches and we were still sixty feet above ground when they hit an immovable object—the spike of a broken branch as thick as my thigh. The blurring rotors froze in front of my eyes and then shattered, sending silver shards knifing through the air.

The Perspex cracked, and a fragment of rotor blade smashed through it like a machete. Its leading edge sliced through my harness and into my chest. The Huey hit the ground with a crash that drowned out the warning siren, and I blacked out.

WHEN I OPENED my eyes, fragments of leaf were fluttering down onto the crumpled cockpit and a fog of orange-brown dust hung around it. My head was pounding and there was a stabbing pain in my chest. I could hear the hiss of fluid dropping on hot metal and the clicking of the engine as it began to cool. There was no sound from the surrounding jungle; every bird and animal had been put to flight by the crash of the helicopter.

I shook off my flying glove and touched my chest. My hand came away dark and sticky with blood. Then I looked to my right. Tom lay motionless in the copilot's seat. His flying suit from chest to ankles was a sodden mass of blood, his face as grey as if it had been cast from clay. I shuddered and looked away.

I called to Layla and Grizz. There was silence. Panic rose inside me. I called again, twisting my head to look behind me, then winced as the knife-sharp fragment of rotor blade sliced deeper into my flesh. It had been stopped by the breastbone. Had it penetrated a couple of inches further, I would have been dead.

I heard Grizz mutter something and then Layla's hesitant reply. I almost cried with relief. 'Don't try and move for a moment. I'll get myself free and then help you.'

I undid my harness, then pulled myself as far back into my seat as I could. The broken rotor blade had a barbed edge and the skin on my chest caught and pulled. I stifled a cry of pain as it tore free, leaving a small gobbet of flesh impaled on the hook like fishing bait.

As I squeezed through the gap into the cab I heard the crack of gunfire. Grizz was already out of his seat, wrenching the mini-gun from its mounting.

'Get Layla out and make a break for it,' he said. 'I'll give you cover.' He handed me a grenade. 'Blow the tanks with this when you're ready to go. The diversion'll give us all a better chance.'

'Where do we wait for you?'

'You don't. We'll RV back at Bohara.'

'But Grizz—'

'Don't argue. Get going.' He loosed off a burst into the forest, then jumped out and sprinted for cover on the far side of the clearing.

I turned to Layla. 'OK?'

She nodded. 'What about Tom?' She read the answer in my face.

I grabbed a rifle and as many clips as I could stuff into the pockets of my combat vest. Then I slid open the door on the far side of the cab, waited for a burst of gunfire from Grizz, and waved her away towards the undergrowth at the edge of the clearing. She ran fast, low to the ground, dodging and weaving. As she dropped into cover behind a rotting tree trunk, I swung out of the door. I stuck the grenade into the neck of the fuel tank, pulled the pin and sprinted away from the Huey, throwing myself into cover alongside Layla.

The grenade exploded, followed at once by an even more massive blast as the fuel tank detonated. A pillar of flame shot into the air and debris whistled over our heads. As the echo of the blast faded, I was on my feet, grabbing Layla's arm. 'Come on.'

We turned and ran into the forest. The firing began again almost at once, but no shots followed us as we crashed through the under-growth. We ran on until the gunfire was only the faintest of echoes, then slowed to a walk. It was hard to navigate through the dense forest, but I tried to keep us on a northwesterly bearing.

'What do we do?' she said.

'I don't want to make directly for Bohara. If the rebels are pursu-ing us, that's the direction they'll assume we're taking. We'll aim to pass north of the compound and then approach from the east—though there's a high chance of getting lost in this maze.'

We moved on. The trees soon began to thin, with patches of cleared land hacked and burned out of the forest. Some were planted with crops, showing that a village was not far away.

We reached the edge of the forest and looked out over a broad valley. A river wound through it and I could see a village set in a sea of elephant grass, a cluster of huts made of crude wattle-and-daub walls and palm-thatched roofs supported on bush-pole rafters.

We moved through the chest-high grass and crept up a low ridge to peer down at the village. It seemed a picture of tranquillity. Women sat in the doorways of their huts as children played around them. A few scrawny hens scratched at the dust. The younger women were returning from the river bank carrying head-loads of water and clean washing.

We lay watching for some time. 'What do you think?' I said.

'I know these people,' Layla said. 'I think we're safe here.'

As I began to get to my feet, I heard a faint noise behind me and then a blow exploded against my temple. I staggered and collapsed to my knees. When I raised my head, shaking it to clear my blurred vision, I found myself facing a group of at least twenty men. I closed my eyes, cursing myself for my stupidity. Our headlong flight through the forest must have left a trail a blind man could have fol-lowed. We should have kept moving through the grasslands, rather than pausing here, allowing the rebels to overtake us.

Their hair was tangled into rough dreadlocks plaited with scraps of ribbon, thread and shards of broken mirror. Their eyes were bloodshot and their pupils like pinpricks. Most were little more than boys, but there was no mistaking the murderous look in their eyes.

Their leader, a bloated, brutish-looking veteran at least eighteen years old, stood watching as we were searched. My combat vest was ripped from my back and handed to him, together with my rifle and ammunition clips. He emptied my wallet, tucking my money into his pocket. My survival equipment was picked over, then distributed among his men. When he found the GPS navigating device, however, he put it on the ground and drove the butt of his rifle down on it.

We were pushed down the hillside towards the village and there were shouts of alarm as we were spotted by the villagers. People began to run, only to find more rebels advancing into the village on all sides. The men and boys who had been out working in the fields were dragged in a few minutes later and the whole population was herded together on the trampled earth at the heart of the village.

The rebel leader pushed Layla and me into a corner by one of the huts. Two rebel soldiers stood guard over us.

I touched Layla's hand. 'I'm sorry I got you into this.'

'You didn't. I got myself into it. If you make it out of here, Jack, go and see my parents for me, will you?' A tear trickled down her cheek. 'Tell them what happened and say that, though I wished it hadn't ended this way, I still didn't regret having come here.'

'You can tell them yourself, the next time you're home.'

She gave an impatient shake of her head.

'All right,' I said. 'I promise I will.'

She held my gaze a moment longer.

We fell silent and sat huddled together, frightened and alone as the rebels looted the village. Food and jugs of palm wine were brought out of the huts and passed from hand to hand, and they were soon drunk. They began to interrogate the villagers, but after a few minutes, they gave up even a show of interest in the answers. They began chanting and singing, stamping their feet, moving ever closer, crowding the villagers together. Pangas began to rise and fall, the sun glinting from the blades. Layla stifled a scream and buried her face in my shoulder as a bloodied man collapsed to the ground. Then the rebel leader severed his victim's head with three strokes of his panga. He impaled the head on a stick and thrust it towards us, jeering at the terror he saw written on our faces.

The slaughter went on until the village was full of dead. The smell of blood hung over it, sweet and sickly.

The boys were forced to become recruits. Each was made to identify his parents and then ordered to kill them. If he refused, he was killed himself. But after this had happened three or four times the boys began killing their parents as soon as they were ordered to.

Tears running down our cheeks, we watched the surviving boys and young men, most too stunned even to cry, being marched away. Now only the girls and young women remained in the village. The leader stayed with the two rebels guarding us. The rest of them dragged the girls away, ripping off their clothes and holding them down as each soldier took his turn. It was like a soundtrack from hell, with cries, groans and screams coming from all sides.

The leader watched for a moment, a smile on his face, then turned towards us. His gaze switched from me to Layla as he licked his lips, his tongue darting out like a snake tasting the air.

He signalled to the other two to take my arms. As I strained against the two holding me, I felt sharp steel prick my throat and forced myself to remain still.

The leader moved round behind Layla, placing one hand on her hip. Clutching a panga in his other hand, he began to propel her towards one of the huts, thrusting his hips against her buttocks to push her forward.

As he reached the entrance he paused and called out to the two men guarding me. They gave a burst of harsh laughter. One of them propped the RPG he was carrying against the wall of the hut and held a blade against my neck. The other stood in front of me. His T-shirt was stained with blood, dirt and sweat and when he spoke he showed a mouthful of black and rotting teeth. He stretched out a hand and stroked my cheek, then said something to the other rebel. They both laughed again.

He took a knife from the sheath on his belt and pressed the point against my chin, forcing my head up. I felt a stab of pain and blood trickled down my neck. The knife point worked lower, tracing a line down my throat and chest. He cut off the buttons of my shirt one by one and then slid the knife down the waistband of my trousers.

Suddenly there was a terrible screaming from the hut where the rebel leader had taken Layla, so high-pitched it sounded as if no human voice could have made such a sound. Even my captors were momentarily nonplussed.

I gave up the last shreds of hope. Layla was dead. I would be next. Better to die fighting than humiliated and murdered. I tensed myself, poised to attack. I might at least get one of them before the other cut me to pieces.

Then I heard a footfall and a thin, sibilant sound, 'Sssst! Sssst!'

I looked up. The face of the rebel guarding me had become a red mask of blood. The sound came again, 'Sssst!'

There was a squeal like a slaughtered hog and the bulk of the other man crashed down on my back. Writhing to be free of his dead weight, I forced myself away from him and swung around. Then I saw his staring eyes and the gaping gash in his neck. Blood still spilled from it, but he was already dead.

I looked up. Layla stood there, her skirt ripped and stained. Blood dripped from the blade of the panga she held in her hand. She met my gaze, her eyes blank and hard, but as she looked down again at the bodies, her face crumpled and the panga dropped from her grip.

I hauled myself to my feet. 'We've got to get out of here,' I said, my voice cracking. 'Now.'

The rebel commander staggered into view, blood drenching his thighs, screaming and shouting. I looked round. The soldiers' weapons were still propped against the wall of the hut. I reached for a rifle, eased off the safety catch and took aim.

The shot hit him low and slightly left, ripping through the side of his abdomen. The force of the impact spun him round and his body jerked as I fired again and again. At last he dropped and lay still.

I dropped the rifle and stared at my hands. To pilots, war could sometimes seem an arcade game. Now I was mired in the bloody, terrifying, ground-level reality of the most brutal and vicious warfare that the mind of man could devise.

'Jack!' Layla's fingers were digging into my arm.

I looked up. A group of rebels was sprinting towards us, yelling and screaming. I reached for the rifle, then checked and picked up the RPG instead. I fumbled with it, pressed it into my shoulder, sighted and pulled the trigger. Nothing happened. I jerked it down, groped for the safety catch and then pulled it up again.

The lead rebel was no more than twenty yards away. As I sighted along the barrel I saw his face change as he spotted the RPG. Then I pulled the trigger. There was a roar and a blast. The rocket punched a hole through his guts and detonated against a rock a yard away from him. The shrapnel cut down all the other rebels within range, but the noise brought the rest of them swarming back into the centre of the village like hornets.

Smoke filled my lungs and I coughed. The wall of the hut was on fire, ignited by the back blast of the RPG. Half-blinded by smoke, I grabbed the panga, the rifle and a belt of ammunition, and pushed Layla away. We stumbled towards the forest, hearing the shouts of the rebels in our ears. The first shots whined around us.

As we reached the trees I turned to loose off a burst from the rifle. One rebel toppled but the others did not even falter in their pursuit. I turned again and we ran for our lives along the track, deeper and deeper into the forest.

We ran until I thought my lungs would burst, then I checked at a faint break in the wall of vegetation. We dived through it, then twisted round, spreading the foliage back across the gap. We flattened ourselves, worming our way down into the leaf litter of the forest floor, and lay still.

The wild beating of my heart drowned any sound of pursuit at first, but then I heard the slap of bare feet running towards us. The rebels loped into view, indifferent to their own safety, running steadily, confident of overhauling us. Through the screen of foliage I saw the face of the lead man, scanning the jungle for marks that might show where we had gone.

I dropped my head and lay still as they moved closer, though my flesh crept. The footsteps slowed. I held myself motionless, though every instinct screamed at me to run before it was too late.

The seconds dragged by. Then I heard the footsteps move on again down the track. I waited until the sounds had faded and my heart had stopped its pounding, and was about to raise my head when I caught a faint noise. I froze. The sound grew louder, a soft scuffing in the dust of the forest track.

The noise stopped. I saw a bare foot no more than a yard away. The hairs on my neck rose. Knowing that any movement, however slight, would give us away, I forced myself to remain motionless, gritting my teeth and offering silent prayers that the rebel would miss us and move on. There was nothing separating us from death but a single scrubby bush and a thin covering of leaf litter. I could feel a faint trembling in my arm, but could do nothing to stop it.

I heard the soft rustle of cloth and saw the foot move as he turned towards the other side of the track, but after a moment he turned back. An arm came into my view as he reached down and fingered a broken plant stem.

A voice broke the silence and I almost jumped out of my skin. He had spoken in the local language, and, though I did not understand the words, his tone told me the game must be up. He had seen us and was telling us to come out.

I was tensing my muscles to ease myself up slowly enough to avoid alarming him and provoking a shot, when he was answered by another man behind him on the track.

There was a long silence, then an abrupt word of command and I heard again the faint scuffing noise and saw two pairs of feet moving away along the track.

I remained absolutely motionless, my heart still hammering in my chest until the calls of birds told me we were safe, for the moment at least. I rose slowly, peered along the empty track, then took Layla's arm and led her deeper into the jungle.

CHAPTER 7

We kept walking for another hour before I felt it was safe enough to pause. We stopped at the bank of a forest stream and Layla sank to the ground at once. Her face was bruised and cut and her hair was matted with blood. I took off my tattered shirt, rinsed the sweat and dirt from it and then gently cleaned her face. As I reached over to dab at a cut over her eye, I put a hand on her arm to steady myself. She recoiled and pulled away from me at once.

'Are you all right?' I said.

She didn't reply. Her eyes remained fixed on mine, but she seemed to be staring straight through me.

'Did he—' I checked and changed the question. 'How did you get away from him?'

Her voice was harsh and flat. 'I don't want to talk about it and if we get out of this alive, I never want anyone else to know what happened back there in that village.'

I saw her eyes fill with tears and tried to cradle her head against my shoulder, but she pushed me away, fury in her face. She stood up and walked off, turning her back to me, but I saw her body racked with sobs. I waited in silence until she had grown quiet again.

'Do you want to wash yourself?' I said. 'I'll keep watch.'

She shivered, as if waking from a nightmare, then turned her tear-stained face towards me. 'I'd like that, thanks.'

I moved away a few more yards and stood with my back to her as she stripped off and bathed herself in the stream water.

When she had finished, we changed places. I took off my clothes, crouched on the bank and began washing myself. I scooped up handfuls of sand from the bed of the stream and scoured myself with it. I felt I could have washed myself for a week and still not got clean.

'What do we do?' Layla said, after I'd pulled my clothes back on.

'I don't know. I thought we might make Bohara, but with no map and no GPS, I think our only hope is to make for Freetown.'

'But we can't cross the country on foot. And how will we navigate?'

'The river was north of us, wasn't it? All we can do is use the sun to navigate and make our way north until we find the river.'

'And then?'

'Try to steal a boat, I suppose.'

I moved a few paces upstream and then took a rough bearing from the sunlight filtering through the forest canopy.

The twists and turns we had to make around the impenetrable stands of trees and dense undergrowth made our progress slow, and it was easy to get disorientated. The direction of the sun was often obscured by the tree cover.

The foliage frequently reduced visibility to no more than five yards, but my other senses seemed heightened in compensation. I paused every few steps to listen for the sound of movement or the distress cries of birds, and I sniffed the faint breeze for any human trace.

At length I heard a faint sound. It grew into the steady ripple of moving water. I caught a glint through the undergrowth and, parting the leaves, looked out on a broad, slow-moving river.

We tracked the river westwards. Shortly before sunset I saw a dark shape on the far bank. As we drew closer, the shape resolved itself into the mud walls and rough thatch of a ferryman's hut.

A battered craft was tied up at the water's edge on the far side and a wire cable ran from bank to bank, sagging into the river in the middle. It was secured at the base of thick posts driven into the soil on either bank. The cable passed through steel eyes at each end of the boat; the ferryman could punt across the river, guided by the cable.

We lay down to wait for full darkness.

Half an hour after the faint glow of a candle or lantern in the building had been extinguished, I left Layla in our hiding place and crawled forward through the vegetation. I got to my feet next to the post securing the cable and gave the rusting wire an experimental pull. The boat remained motionless, but the protesting squeal of rusty metal penetrated the night.

I dropped to the ground. A second later the hut door opened and I saw the outline of a rebel soldier, the barrel of his gun black against the sky. He made a desultory search around the hut, but he found nothing and moments later I heard the bang of the door.

I waited ten minutes, then knotted the carrying loop of my rifle, clenched the strap in my teeth and lowered myself into the water. I began to haul myself along the cable, hand over hand, my head tilted back to help keep the rifle free of the water.

Dark shapes sent my heart racing as they swirled past me. They were only branches but, to my frightened eyes in the gloom of the night, each looked like a water snake or an alligator.

My arms were aching with the effort and I began to shiver with cold. I forced myself on again, but had hardly moved when a log, carried on the current, crashed into my shoulder. I gasped with shock.

Just as I felt I could go no further and my numbed fingers were beginning to lose their grip on the cable, my right hand bumped against something hard. The shallow, metal, flat-bottomed ferryboat was no more than ten feet long and less than half that in width. I worked my way alongside it and crawled out onto the bank. I lay gasping on the mud, waiting for my strength to return.

I stared towards the hut, straining my ears for any sound, then began to work on the rotting post that held the steel cable. I heaved at it with all my strength, but it barely moved.

I saw the pale disc of Layla's face watching me from the far bank. I had to release the boat. It was our only hope. I knew what I had to do—for her as well as for me.

I crouched down behind the ferryboat no more than five yards from the hut and set the rifle on automatic. I aimed six inches above the ground and then raked the hut from left to right and right to left. I heard a scream. Then, a rebel trailing one leg behind him lurched through the door of the hut, shooting without aiming as he stumbled towards the boat where I lay hidden. I fired another burst. The impacts hurled him back against the wall of the hut and he slumped to the ground and lay still. I put another burst into the hut to be sure, then I stepped out of cover and moved to the doorway.

In the faint glow of the embers from their dying fire, I could see another body lying inside the hut. This was no soldier. The ferryman had been unarmed and unprotected, wearing only shorts and a faded T-shirt. The shots I had fired had hit him in the head, chest and thigh as he lay asleep. The burning taste of bile was in my throat as a wave of shame swept over me.

I searched the hut, aware that every second was now vital. The noise of the gunfire would have been heard for miles up and down the river, and even now a rebel patrol might be moving to investigate.

I had hoped to find an axe or a shovel but there was only a panga. I took it outside.

I ran to the dead soldier, intending to use his rifle as a crowbar, but as I picked it up I saw a grenade hanging from his belt. I hacked at the post with the panga until I had carved out a rough hollow beneath the cable. Then I forced the grenade into it, pulled the pin and sprinted for the cover of the boat. There was a flash and a blast and I heard shrapnel rattle against the metal hull.

I ran back to the post. Most of the cable had been shredded but a few strands still held. I picked up the panga and hacked at them.

There was a crack as the last strand snapped. The ferryboat began to drift away from the bank. I ran down the slippery mud bank and half jumped, half dived for the boat, just managing to catch the gunwale as it swirled away on the current. I dragged myself up and over the side and fell onto the bottom boards. Still attached to the cable on the far bank, the boat swung in a pendulum curve out across the water, past the midpoint of the river and in towards the far bank. Then the cable tautened and the boat held station, some twenty yards from the water's edge.

I called to Layla but she was already racing along the bank towards me. As she began wading out towards the boat, I heard a scraping sound and then a twang as the cable pulled free of the guidehole in the stern. The end snaked past me. It was checked for a moment by the guidehole on the bow of the boat, then it pulled clear and fell away with a splash.

Layla lunged for the gunwale as the boat gathered speed, and I grabbed her arm and dragged her bodily into the boat. We lay flat, gasping with exertion, as our craft moved away downstream.

We were soon well downriver of the ferryman's hut, carried head-long by the rip of the current. Within seconds the fear of striking a rock in the darkness pushed me upright. There was no rudder, only a long punt pole lying in the bottom of the boat. I trailed it over the stern and used it as a makeshift rudder. Eventually, when we encountered a long stretch of rapids, I tried to steer for the bank, but the strength of the current was too great and we were carried sideways towards the rocks. The noise of the rapids reverberated around us as we entered a steep ravine, its walls smoothed and scoured by the force of rainy season floods. I could barely steer.

I shipped the punt pole, and Layla and I clung to the sides of the boat with both hands as it barrelled through the water, cannoning off the flanks of the rocks in its path. Finally our luck ran out. The boat was driven headlong onto a massive rock in the centre of the channel. I felt a bone-jarring shock and was thrown out.

As it was swept away into the darkness, I heard Layla scream, then I was fighting for my life, floundering and only just keeping my head above water. The rapids hurled me onwards. I was bumped and battered so hard from rock to rock that I could hardly draw breath. My fingers clawed for grip on the smooth, slimy rocks but each time I was dragged away again. I could see nothing in the darkness and hear nothing but the thunder of the water echoing from the bare rock walls of the gorge. It was as much as I could manage to gulp in a fresh mouthful of air before the next surge of water swept over my face and whirled me away again downstream.

The thunder of the rapids seemed to fade, then the waters again closed over my head and blackness enveloped me.

I regained consciousness, choking and retching. I could feel water still lapping round my legs but there was gritty sand against my cheek. Then strong hands pressed down on my chest and a fresh spasm of coughing shook me as more water poured from my mouth.

I opened my eyes. Layla sat astride me. When she saw me looking at her, she hugged me and kissed my face. 'Thank God. I thought I'd lost you.'

I raised my head a little. The boat was drawn up on the narrow beach a few feet away. Upstream to my right, I could make out the rapids spilling out of the entrance to the canyon. The river flowed fast and silent past the beach where I lay. I pushed myself up to a sitting position and took a few deep breaths. 'Let's get out of here.'

In the grey light of approaching dawn, we clambered back into the boat and Layla pushed off with the pole. We slipped downstream, fast at first, but as we drifted farther from the rapids, the river began to meander on a leisurely course across the marshlands that separated us from the coast.

We drifted with the current, peering into the water, trying to discern the telltale eddies troubling the surface as the river passed over shallows and swirled around sandbars and sunken rocks. Three times we had to beach the boat and half drag, half carry it over the shallows to the next navigable stretch.

The river bank was now barely a foot above the surface of the water. We passed islands from which palm trees grew. Herons stalked through the shallows, stabbing at the black mud with their beaks.

The river divided and then split again and, as the sky lightened, we found ourselves drifting through a series of progressively narrower and more sluggish waterways, with the mangroves growing so close around us that they scraped the sides of the boat.

Finally we came to a mud flat and a slight break in the wall of mangroves. As I stared at the mud in the dawn light, I saw a series of footprints leading away from the water. Whatever the dangers it might herald, it at least promised a way out of the swamps. We dragged the boat out of the water and began to follow the trail. Stumbling over submerged roots, we worked our way at snail's pace through the thickets, trying to steer a course between the main channel of the river and the first signs of habitation—the settlements fringing the shore.

As we plodded on, exhausted and weak from hunger, the path became better defined. Palm logs were laid as bridges over the creeks and small rivers, and among the mangroves were patches of paddyfields studded with vivid green rice shoots.

At last the mangroves began to thin and the track started to open out ahead of us. After the gloom of the swamp, I had to shield my eyes from the morning light.

The tide was low and the river channel was flanked by broad expanses of glistening mud. Boats were drawn up on the opposite bank. The near bank was empty. A steep hillside half a mile ahead hid Freetown from us, but I could see smoke rising from its shantytown.

'If we can get past here we should be safe,' I said.

'Always assuming the rebels haven't attacked the capital while we've been making our way back here,' Layla said.

'Let's assume the worst but hope for the best,' I said.

We struck out along the bank. It was slow going, skirting treacherous stretches of mud that sucked at our legs like quicksand, and picking our way over rotting logs and past shacks and shanties that were perched just above the high-water mark.

Suddenly a figure appeared no more than thirty yards in front of us. We dropped to the ground and froze. A woman walked out to the edge of the river, her footprints black against the wet mud. She filled a cooking pot with water and then returned the way she had come.

We moved on again, our progress slower and slower as more people appeared at the river's edge to wash or fetch water. As we passed the mouth of a filthy street lined with mean shacks, a dog barked at us and then slunk away between two huts.

My heart was in my mouth. If the alarm was raised we would quickly be surrounded by hundreds of people. I had seen some of the inhabitants of the shantytown at work on the way in from the airport the day I had arrived in Sierra Leone. They might hand us over to the rebels, or they might rob and murder us themselves.

I was torn between the need to avoid rousing the people and a wave of panic that made me want to run headlong for the mouth of the river and the relative safety of the beaches that lay beyond.

As we rounded a bend we came face to face with a woman carrying a bucket of water on her head. She froze for a moment, her jaw dropping with astonishment at seeing us there. Then she dropped the bucket and turned and ran.

Layla laid a restraining hand on my arm. 'There's nothing we can do,' she said. 'Let's just keep moving.'

Past the last, ragged fringes of the shantytown the mud began to give way to yellow sand, speckled with grey grass stalks. I heard the roar of breakers and we hurried on, along a beach alive with small crabs. The fronds of the ragged palms fringing the sands rustled overhead like dry brown paper.

 **CHAPTER 8**

We worked our way along the deserted beach until we were almost directly behind our hotel. Then we crawled forward through the dune grass and peered out at the building and the city beyond.

My head was pounding. I ran my tongue over my dry, cracked lips. We needed water. I felt an overpowering urge to run straight to the hotel, but I fought it down. We had been out of touch for days. Had a rebel offensive been launched against the capital, we could be heading straight into a deathtrap.

We lay in hiding, watching and waiting. The streets were almost deserted—a worrying sign that something was wrong—and yet there was a disarming air of normality about the few people and vehicles we did see moving about. It was the arrival of a delivery van at the rear of the hotel that led to my next movements. The scent of warm bread wafting to us on the breeze set the saliva flowing in my mouth and my stomach rumbled in anticipation.

'Come on,' I said, getting to my feet. 'It's OK, I'm sure of it.' We walked down the slope from the dunes, crossed the concrete access road and entered the building.

There was a handful of people in the lobby. None carried weapons and I felt the tension ebbing from me,. The hotel guests lapsed into a stunned silence as we walked in. I caught a glimpse of our reflections in a mirror and could see why. Two mud-stained, wild-eyed, near skeletons stared back.

The Lebanese owner peered at me from behind the reception desk, trying to identify the mud-covered stranger in front of him. 'We need water,' I said. 'And food. And then a shower and a bed.'

He continued to stare at me, uncertainty written on his face.

I tried again. 'We were staying here a few days ago. I'm Jack Griffiths. I'm with Decisive Measures.'

His face now wreathed in smiles, he clapped his hands to summon his staff. 'Mr Griffiths, of course. I will have your room prepared at once. Perhaps you would prefer to shower before you eat.'

I shook my head. 'Water and bread now.'

He barked an order at a slouching waiter, then ushered us to the dining room. I felt my knees buckle and had to slump in a chair before I fell. The waiter brought a jug of water and I gulped some down, then fell on the basket of naan bread he proffered.

Layla laid a warning hand on my arm. 'Take it easy,' she said. 'Eat and drink a little, then wait before you swallow some more. Give your body time.' She sipped at her water as she spoke, then took a small mouthful of bread.

We sat there for half an hour, hardly speaking a word, just eating, drinking and smiling at each other. At length, I pushed back my chair and got unsteadily to my feet. 'I've got to have a shower but I think I'm too hyper to sleep.'

She nodded. 'Me too. Let's get away from these people, though.'

As we walked through the lobby, I stopped at the desk and picked up the phone, planning to call the Decisive Measures HQ in the hope of getting word on the situation at Bohara. The line was dead. The owner spread his hands. 'Out of order, I'm afraid. The phones seem to be out all over the capital.'

I tried to read his expression. 'Is everything quiet here?'

He gave a flustered smile. 'It's very quiet. Not many guests.'

'That's not what I meant. I was talking about the rebels.'

'There is fighting in the mountains, but they will not dare attack

Freetown.' He glanced around the lobby, measuring the effect of his words on the hotel guests, then leaned over the counter and lowered his voice. 'There are rumours, though. People are leaving the city.'

'What rumours? Which people?'

'The President is unpopular. The army has not been paid. The President's son flew to Guinea yesterday.' He tapped his nose. 'They say the aircraft that took him has returned to await its next passenger.'

'We'll get a better idea later,' I said to Layla as we walked to the stairs. 'If the phones are still knackered I'll go to the High Commission and contact Decisive Measures from there.'

'And I'll go to Medicaid International,' she said. 'I should have reported in already, they'll be worried about me.'

'To hell with it,' I said. 'Let's catch up on the world later on. We've earned a bit of rest after what we've been through.'

When we reached the first floor, we stood in silence on the landing, looking at each other. I ached to take her to my room, crush her to me and bury myself in her body, then sleep with our arms wrapped around each other, cut off from whatever awaited us. But still I hesitated, unsure of her response. 'Would— Do you—' I began at last.

She stood on tiptoe, took my face in her cool hands and kissed me, but when she felt me responding, she stepped back. 'I'm sorry,' she said. 'I can't, not yet. It's too soon. But I don't want to be on my own. Can we just . . . ?'

For answer, I put my arm around her waist, supporting her as we shambled away down the corridor to my room.

The rifle I had left behind a week before was still propped in a corner down the side of a wardrobe. I sat down on the edge of the bed. 'You shower first.'

She emerged twenty minutes later, her hair damp and her body wrapped in a threadbare towel, barely long enough to cover her. I saw the marks of lacerations and dark, purpling bruises on her thighs and felt anger burning in me. As she looked towards me I averted my gaze, as if I'd been caught spying on her.

I stood under the trickling shower, soaping my hair and body until the dirt had been washed away. I checked myself in the bathroom mirror and was shocked at my condition. There were black, sunken hollows under my eyes, I had lost several pounds in weight and my skin was a mass of abrasions, bruises and insect bites.

I pulled on some clean clothes and walked through to the bedroom. Layla was lying on the bed covered by the sheet. She held out her arms to me. 'Come and hold me while we talk.'

I lay next to her, feeling the unaccustomed softness of the bed beneath me, and very aware of the warmth of her body against mine.

'There's something I have to ask you,' Layla began. 'The last time we were in this hotel, you spent most of the evening avoiding telling me why you were in Sierra Leone. After all we've been through, do you feel ready to tell me yet why an otherwise apparently sane and decent human being would want to become a mercenary here?'

'All right.' I hesitated. I didn't want to lie to her but I was afraid of what she might think if I told her the truth. 'There was an operation in Kosovo,' I said at last. 'It went badly wrong.'

'Tell me about it. Only if you want to, of course, it's none of my business, but . . .' Her voice trailed away.

I held her gaze. 'No, I want to tell you. It was when the Serbs were really tearing the country apart. We were flying nonstop missions looking for targets—tanks, artillery, anything that presented itself. Then base picked up intelligence on some suspected hostiles. My wingman and I were sent to investigate. We made a few passes over the area and I glimpsed some vehicles hidden in the woods. I made another pass, then another, trying to decide. I was also hoping to draw some fire that would have confirmed them as hostile.

'My wingman said they were definitely hostile, but I still wasn't sure. I went round again, put the heli into the hover near the wood and then I saw people sprinting for the vehicles. I hesitated a little longer, then I made up my mind. We attacked. We flew in at low level and I fired my rocket pods at the vehicles. I was circling for another attack when I saw a figure running out of the trees. It was a woman wearing a long black skirt. She was on fire. She raised her arms above her head as if she were pleading with me. Then she fell to the ground.' Tears were now streaming down my face. 'She'd managed to escape from the Serbs. A group of her people were hiding in the woods with their farm trucks and tractors and carts. If the Serbs had found them, the men would have been killed and the women raped. But they'd survived. The Serbs had gone. Then I killed them.'

Layla didn't reply, but she reached up and stroked my face as I got myself under some sort of control.

'I'm sorry,' I said. 'I've never told anyone about that before.'

We lay in silence for some time. 'I used to dream that one day I would be famous,' Layla said. She smiled. 'But the older I get, the more I realise that life is about really small things. If we can do a little bit more good than harm while we're passing through, that's probably about as good as it gets for most people.'

'In that case, my personal ledger is way out of balance,' I said.

She gripped my arm, her fingers digging into my flesh, trying to impress upon me the importance of what she was saying. 'Then that's all the more reason to start balancing the books now. You can't change the past, but you can change the future. You don't want to be looking back in old age and still seeing that woman in Kosovo.'

She fell silent, studying my face, and when she spoke again her voice was little more than a whisper. 'I killed a child once. It was when I was training as a doctor. I was a houseman, a junior doctor. I was dog-tired at the end of a very long shift, but of course that's no excuse. Somehow—I don't know how, I knew what the right dose should be—I gave the baby three times the normal dose of a drug. Her heart stopped. I killed her.'

'But you've saved hundreds of others since.'

'I killed that one. When I close my eyes I can still see her little crumpled figure in the cot and her parents turning to look at me and asking, "Why? What happened?" And do you know what? I didn't even have the guts to admit what I had done.' She fell silent again, staring past me. 'So, we've both had to learn to live with mistakes,' she said eventually. 'I can understand why you left the air force, but that still doesn't explain why you came to Sierra Leone.'

'I didn't ever want to be in a position where I could get it so terribly, horribly wrong again. But flying helicopters is what I do. There's no civilian work; there are thirty pilots for every job that's going. I thought this would be a safe option; not many people want this kind of posting, but it suited me.'

She gave me a gentle smile. 'If the reasons you joined the air force were good ones, what happened in Kosovo shouldn't negate them. It was a tragic accident, but you can't just run away from it.' She paused. 'I ducked my responsibilities to the family of that dead girl and I'll never forgive myself for that, but I didn't give up medicine because of it. I know that nothing I can ever do will end the heartbreak her parents must feel. All I can do is try to help other sick children and make sure I never make such a terrible mistake again.' She held my gaze as she spoke. 'You've got to do the same kind of thing, Jack. You can't just sit on the sidelines, least of all in Sierra Leone. If you're here at all, you're either part of the problem or part of the solution.' She fell silent. 'I'm sorry. I'm a fine one to lecture you, aren't I? I spend my life butting my head against every obstacle that presents itself.'

'We make a good team then,' I said. 'We cancel out some of each other's weaknesses.'

She gave me a long, thoughtful look. 'That's one way of looking at it. But what if we cancel out each other's strengths instead?'

'If we did, we wouldn't be having this conversation now. We'd be lying dead back there in that jungle somewhere.'

The light was fading now. She kissed me, then sat up. 'I'm going back to my room,' she said. 'I need to sleep now.'

'Sleep here,' I said.

She shook her head. 'I need to be alone for a while to think things through.' She held on to my hand for a moment, then stood up.

I watched her all the way to her door and as it closed behind her, I whispered, 'I love you,' to the empty corridor.

Despite my exhaustion, it was a long time before I fell asleep. When I did, I was soon in the grip of the familiar nightmare: the thunder of guns, the burning figure, and the crushing feelings of helplessness and guilt. Then, finally, I was awake, with the sound of explosions and gunfire in my ears. This was no dream.

I went to the window and peered out. Dawn had not yet broken, but I could see the flash of explosions and the lurid glare of flames.

I picked up the rifle. As I felt my way along the darkened corridor towards Layla's room, I heard a door open and saw her silhouetted in the flash of another explosion in the heart of the city. I called her name and we clung to each other.

'I was just coming to find you,' she said, her voice shaking with fear. 'What do we do?'

'Try to find out what's going on.'

'Are we safe in the hotel?'

'I guess so, as safe as anywhere. If we go charging out into the night, we're just putting ourselves in greater danger. We'll stay here until we know what's happening.'

We groped our way to the stairs and went down to the lobby. There was no one to be seen. The hotel staff and, more worryingly, the security guards paid to protect the building had obviously reached their own conclusions about the shooting. All had fled.

The owner was not in evidence, but his office was unlocked. I tried to dial the British High Commission, but the lines were still dead. There was a transistor radio on the desk, but when I turned it on I heard only the hiss of static from the local channels. It was another ominous sign.

I tuned the radio to the BBC World Service instead. We had to endure forty minutes of magazine programmes before the next news bulletin. We were the lead item: 'Reports are coming in of an attempted coup in Sierra Leone. Sections of the armed forces have mutinied and made simultaneous attacks on the airport, the radio station and Government House in the capital, Freetown. There are unconfirmed reports of killing and looting in the capital . . .'

I returned to the local channel. A scratched recording of martial music was playing, but a few minutes later it was replaced by a rebel spokesman. He announced that the government and 'key installations' were already in rebel hands and proclaimed an immediate curfew, breaches of which would be punished by death. He warned 'foreign troops not to get involved with the internal affairs of the now republic of Sierra Leone'.

I forced a smile. 'I guess that means me and the rest of the boys.'

'What do we do now?'

'We need to know a bit more about what's going on. Meanwhile we stay put. We'd be safest from the firing somewhere near the heart of the building, but I guess we'll be better off up where we can see what's happening. If the rebels decide to storm the hotel, we need enough warning to be able to make a break for it. I don't fancy our chances'—I held her gaze—'especially yours—if they find us here.'

We went back to the lobby. The handful of other residents had congregated there. They had dressed in haste and now stood debating what to do. Some were for making a dash for the airport at once; others preferred to wait for daylight.

The hotel owner had appeared and was fussing around the group, imploring them not to panic, to wait to see what daylight brought. It was hard to tell if his concern for them was personal or financial.

We left them and went down to the kitchens for some food and water, then up to the first floor. The door to the corner suite was locked, but I kicked it open. The suite had windows looking south along the beach road where some of the expatriate houses were, and east, down the hill to the city centre. We drew the curtains, leaving only a chink through which we could see out, then we sat back to watch and wait, huddled together, her head resting on my arm.

Explosions continued to light up the night and there were regular, sustained bursts of small-arms fire.

Just before dawn, two vehicles crammed with people stormed out of the hotel car park and away down the hill. The group advocating a break for the airport had obviously won the day.

We tracked the taillights of the cars until they disappeared from sight. Shortly afterwards there was a prolonged burst of gunfire from the direction they had taken. Our eyes met, but neither of us spoke, though I felt Layla shaking as she cried soundlessly.

The first light of dawn revealed a pall of grey smoke hanging over the city. Peering out through binoculars from our hiding place, I saw rebel soldiers advancing along the road. Most wore sunglasses, T-shirts and stolen clothes piled layer upon layer over their threadbare fatigues. Like the rebels we'd encountered before, they had mirror fragments and bits of multicoloured plastic woven into their hair.

As they moved through the streets, they searched each building by shooting wildly into it. Then the looting began. The streets lower down the hill were soon strewn with debris and smashed glass.

'Where are the government troops?' I asked.

'Don't hold your breath. They defected to the rebels en masse in the last uprising. They're on whichever side they think will win.'

From the windows facing the beach road, I could see the homes of expatriates being stripped. The Lebanese traders were the most vulnerable targets. Those who had not taken the precaution of buying the protection of the rebel leaders—and perhaps even some who had—were robbed of everything. Most people had already fled or gone into hiding. The terrible screams we could hear echoing through the deserted streets told of the fate many others were suffering.

At noon, the rebels began to advance towards the hotel.

'Come on,' I said. 'If we stay, we're finished. Let's get out of here.'

'To where?'

I shrugged. 'The High Commission.'

She gave me a doubtful look. 'I think our best destination is the Medicaid International compound. I'll be needed there anyway. There'll be a lot of wounded. And whatever else the rebels are destroying, I'm sure they won't attack there.'

'I wish I shared your confidence,' I said. 'The High Commission has well-armed guards to protect it. The rebels are likely to leave it alone because they won't want to provoke a direct intervention by British troops. It's a much safer bet.'

'For you maybe, but I have to reach Medicaid International. I'm a medic, Jack, I'm needed there.'

We ran down to the lobby. Only the owner remained, sobbing and wringing his hands. He ran to us and seized my arm. 'What will I do?' he said. 'Please bring help, bring soldiers before it is too late.'

I gently disengaged his hand. 'You should get out now,' I said. 'If you stay, you'll be in great danger.'

'If I leave my hotel, it will be destroyed.'

'Perhaps, but if you stay, they will loot it anyway. Don't let them kill you too. You must leave now.'

He turned away and disappeared into his office. A moment later, I heard the sound of the key being turned.

We went downstairs to the deserted kitchens, took some more water and a little food, and then slipped out of the back door of the hotel and ran off down the access road to the beach.

We sprinted along the sands, using the dunes flanking the beach to screen us from any pursuers. We ran for half a mile, then threw ourselves down, gasping for breath.

'We can't stop yet,' I said, as soon as I could speak. I grabbed a handful of dead palm fronds. 'Come on. Down to the sea.'

When we reached the water's edge, I led Layla through the shallows for another few hundred yards. Then, lungs bursting, I stopped again. I turned to make sure the beach was still empty behind us, then gave Layla the rifle and sent her on ahead into the dunes. I followed, walking backwards, erasing our tracks with the palm fronds.

Layla found a hiding place among the dunes from where we could keep watch. I swept away the last marks we had made and then lay down beside her. I could feel her heart pounding, but when she turned to speak to me her voice was level. 'What now?'

'We wait for nightfall and then move out.'

CHAPTER 9

We lay there throughout the day, eking out our precious water supply and using the palm fronds to give us a little shelter from the sun. The faraway sounds of shots, screams and explosions continued, but the only visible movement was the flapping of the circling vultures.

Then, in late afternoon, a utility truck crammed with soldiers cruised slowly out of the approach road and down the beach. I sank back deeper into hiding, as they slowed and stopped at the tracks leading down to the sea. Four rebels jumped down and began pacing the beach, staring down towards the sea and back towards the dunes. I inched the rifle forward and eased off the safety catch.

I felt Layla tense as one of the rebels appeared to stare directly at us. 'Keep still,' I said. 'I'm sure they can't see us. Don't move and give us away.' I squeezed her hand and felt an answering pressure.

They began to drive on slowly down the beach. I saw their heads swivel from side to side as they scanned the edge of the dunes. I froze, hardly daring to breathe as they drew level with us. From high in the dunes I could still see faint marks where I had brushed away our tracks. I could only pray they were invisible from beach level.

The truck slowed and then moved on out of sight, but we remained motionless, listening to the engine note. It faded then swelled again, as they turned and began to make their way back.

The truck came into sight, moving even more slowly, and stopped again at the line of tracks. We heard the murmur of voices rising as an argument began, then there was a crash of gears and it drove off again, speeding away up the beach towards the city.

Even when nightfall came we remained where we were, for in the darkness we still heard the occasional burst of firing and the sounds of shouts and brutish laughter, carried to us on the breeze.

Towards midnight Layla said, 'Come on. We can't stay here for ever.'

We moved off through the dunes, slowly working our way along the fringes of the beach. We needed water. My plan was to get some from the hotel if it seemed safe to do so, and then strike across the city to the Medicaid International compound. If we found that untouched, I would leave Layla there and make my way on alone to the High Commission, to obtain some means of communicating with Decisive Measures HQ.

We inched our way along the edge of the approach road from the beach and lay in the shadows behind the hotel for some minutes. There were no lights on and no sign of movement. After watching for ten minutes, I took a last careful look around, then reached across and squeezed Layla's hand. 'OK,' I said. 'Let's go for it.'

We broke cover and sprinted for the back of the hotel, flattening ourselves against the wall at the corner of the building. We edged along it, ducking under the windows, until we reached the rear door. It hung slightly ajar, banging softly in the breeze.

I slid the safety catch off my rifle and eased the door further open with my toe, then paused and listened. There was no sound but the faint drip of water from somewhere inside.

We moved into the dark deserted basement. Everything had been looted. The kitchens were stripped and even the sink and cooker had been ripped from the wall and carried off. All that was left were broken pipes and smashed tiles.

We slaked our thirst and refilled our empty water bottles from a dripping pipe and then crept up the stairs to the ground floor. It was deserted, but everything of value had again been torn out in an orgy of destruction. As we moved through the lobby, our boots crunching on broken glass, I heard a faint noise from the owner's office.

I motioned Layla to silence and crept round the broken brick plinth on which the reception counter had stood. I listened at the door, eased it open a chink and then burst into the room.

A bruised, bloodied figure sat in the far corner, half-burrowed into a pile of broken furniture and fallen plaster. He was rocking slowly to and fro, keening to himself.

It was the hotel owner. He looked up at me for a moment then scrambled to his feet. 'My English friends, thank God, you have come back.'

His speech was slurred, and as his mouth gaped open, I saw by the moonlight the stumps of broken teeth.

'Are there soldiers with you?' His smile faded as I shook my head.

'Are the rebels still here?' I said.

He shuddered and shook his head. 'All gone. Everything gone.'

'Other people?'

Again he shook his head. 'I don't know. I don't know.'

'Do you have food?'

'Nothing. Nothing.'

I left him there. We hurried through the rest of the ground floor searching for food, but the rebels had stripped the place bare. We paused just inside the broken doors of the hotel, peering out into the dark. At last I stepped out again into the heat of the night.

The streets were almost deserted and the handful of people we did see were as nervous and frightened as we were, scuttling away into hiding as soon as they saw us approaching. We kept to the side streets as much as possible and moved a few yards at a time, pausing to scan the way ahead from each doorway or alley.

There was devastation on all sides and mingling with the stink of smoke was the sickly stench of blood. Several times we had to step over corpses, but we saw no other living thing save the rats sharing the fruits of the rebels' victory.

The double doors of the World Food Programme's warehouse stood wide open and the building had been completely emptied of rice. Layla's workplace lay a few yards further down the street. Here again the gates of the compound were unmanned and gaping open. We crept across the yard and entered the darkened building.

We searched it from one end to the other. There were no signs of struggle, no bloodstains, and few bullet holes, but there was no trace of the doctors and nurses who had worked here either and the store rooms had been stripped of every last drug and dressing.

Layla's shoulders sagged. 'What's happened to them?' she said.

I cradled her to my chest. 'They'll be all right,' I said. 'Even if they didn't get away in time, the rebels know the value of them both as medics and as hostages. They'll be well treated.'

She exhaled heavily, still staring around her. 'So what now?'

'The High Commission. Let's hope that hasn't been looted too.'

We had been walking for about twenty minutes when we reached the junction of a broad street and a narrow alley running up the hill in roughly the direction we wanted to follow. We inched our way along the alley, paused at the corner listening and looking, then sprinted across a broad street and dived into another alleyway. As we did so, I heard a shout and the sound of running feet.

We sprinted up the alley. There was another shout followed by the crack of a rifle. I heard the howl and whine of the bullet as it smashed against the wall and ricocheted away.

The words of a combat-survival briefing I had been given as a rookie pilot came into my mind: 'Bullets ride walls. If you're trapped in a street and you have no cover, you're safer in the middle than pressed flat against the walls.'

The theory was fine, the practice less attractive. More shots rang out and more rounds whistled past us. I dived into a doorway, heaving at the door and trying to ignore the running feet and the hail of bullets whining around us. The wood creaked, groaned and at last gave way and we tumbled into a single deserted room.

The running footsteps stopped. There was a moment's silence, then a grenade exploded outside the sagging door. The blast threw us against the wall. I heard a thunderous concussion and a flash of heat seared me. There was the sour taste of chemicals in my mouth.

We dragged ourselves up. The stout door now hung from one

hinge, part-blocking the doorway. It had absorbed much of the shrapnel that would otherwise have shredded us. We were both scratched and cut but otherwise unhurt.

Through the ringing in my ears, I heard the sound of running feet again. There was no way out but the way we had come.

I looked up. Thick beams supported the shallow, pitched roof above us. Blackened and ancient, they sagged in the middle and sprouted fungus where they joined the walls. I could only pray that they would bear our additional weight.

The running feet were closer now, almost at the doorway. I threw myself upwards and my fingers grabbed and caught on a beam. I hauled myself onto it, squeezing between the beam and the roof, the muscles of my arms screaming with the effort, then reached down and pulled Layla up and alongside me.

I put my mouth close to her ear. 'Lie on your side along the beam and don't move.' She gave a small nod and did as I said.

We lay lengthways, head to head, our hands clasped. A moment later, the remnants of the door were kicked aside and there was the thunder of automatic weapons.

The shooting stopped. The walls were riddled with bullet holes. There was a pause, then two figures darkened the doorway.

They began firing upwards. Rounds blasted through the roof on either side of us. More rounds smacked into the beam beneath me. I felt it twitch with the impacts and splinters of wood filled the air.

The shooting seemed to go on for ever. I shook with fright, wanting to scream out my terror, beg, plead, anything to make it stop. There was a sudden pause. I heard voices. Then the dark shadows disappeared from the doorway. I fought the urge to peer down.

The next moment there was the thunder of another grenade below us. I heard a rumble as part of the rear wall collapsed. The beam we were lying on twisted and we fell together, crashing down among a torrent of falling masonry and timber. I hit the ground with a thump that drove the breath from my lungs and lay there, helpless, as fragments of stone and tile crashed down around and on top of me.

I heard rough laughter. A few moments later there was the faraway sound of footsteps retreating up the alley.

As the ringing in my ears slowly subsided, I managed to raise my head a little, forced my right arm up through the dead weight of rubble, then clawed at the mound covering me. It took several minutes of gruelling work to prise myself free. My eyes and mouth were gritty with dust and I had suffered cuts and bruises, but I was alive.

I looked around, panicking as I realised that Layla lay buried under the rubble. Then I spotted a foot protruding from the mound. I tore at the rubble until I found the beam, which now lay across her chest.

I dragged and scraped at the stones and dirt covering her head and found myself looking into Layla's eyes. They were red-rimmed and lined with dirt, and her face was covered in blood from a score of cuts. She was shaking with fright.

'Are you badly hurt?' I said.

'I—I don't think so. Just very fr . . . ' Her voice faltered and died.

'Can you move your legs? Your body? Your chest?'

Each time there was hesitation, then the faintest of nods. I felt for the underside of the beam and moved my hand along it. There was a fraction of an inch between her body and the beam, no more.

I glanced around. The building had almost completely collapsed. We were out in the open air, lit by the stars and the setting moon.

I turned back to Layla. 'I can't lift the beam off you, it's too heavy. I'm going to try to pull you out from under it.'

The lower end of the beam was wedged fast against the ground, buried in a mound of stones. The upper end was precariously poised, resting on a mound of loose material. I packed it as well as I could, forcing rocks and broken timbers under it. When I was satisfied that it wouldn't shift, I started to clear the rubble away from one side of Layla's body.

Her frightened face looked up at me. I leaned over and kissed her forehead. 'It's all right, you can do it.'

I pulled gently on her upper arm as she wriggled and strained to free herself. Each movement set off tiny avalanches of dust and stone fragments, causing me to look anxiously at the beam above her. She worked her legs and hips free, but her upper body was still directly under the beam. 'I can't get any further,' she said.

I took hold of her ankles. 'I'm going to try to pull you out.' Her face, beneath the streaks of dirt, looked deathly pale in the faint moonlight. I took hold and began to pull, steadily increasing the pressure on her legs. She moved a little towards me, then stuck. I saw her bite her lip as she tried to stop herself crying out with pain. I let go of her legs. 'It's no good. You're well and truly stuck. I'm going to have to try to lever the beam up a fraction.'

She was silent, but at last I heard her murmur, 'All right.'

I clambered back over the rubble towards what had been the front of the house. One side of the doorway still stood; the rest had collapsed. I leaned out and peered up and down the alley. There was no one in sight and not a sound to be heard.

I took hold of the thick post that had formed one upright of the door frame and began to heave on it, working it to and fro. Dust and mortar dropped away from it and each time I was able to rock it a little further. Finally the fixings gave way. I pulled the timber free, and carried it back to the rubble heap where Layla was buried.

I forced it in under the beam as close to Layla's head as I dared. 'When you feel it lift,' I said, 'scramble for your life . . . Ready?'

I took the strain and then heaved down on one end of the timber, it creaked ominously and for a moment nothing happened. I redoubled my effort. The blood was pounding at my temples and the veins stood out on my arms. There was a creak and a rustle of dust and stone and the beam rose an inch. *'Now, now!'*

Her legs kicked and her head disappeared from my sight under the beam as she wormed her way downwards. The timber creaked once more then split with a crack like a pistol shot. The beam crashed down, the mound of rubble collapsing beneath it. I dropped the useless end of the timber and dragged my eyes towards the other side of the beam. The top of Layla's head was a bare inch from the beam. She rolled over and dragged herself to her feet.

'Thank God,' I said. I crushed her to me and kissed her face, clinging to her, as our tears made tracks in the dust on our cheeks.

She returned my kiss then eased my arms from around her and began gingerly feeling her ribs.

'Anything broken?'

'I don't think so.'

The sky was still dark, but the eastern horizon was tinged with the faintest trace of red. 'We have to move,' I said. 'It'll be daybreak soon and if we're caught on the streets . . .'

Hugging the wall, we moved away through the deserted alley.

We paused before each crossroads then hurried on, moving up the hillside using whatever cover we could find.

As we neared the intersection with the main road to the east, we lay flat and crawled our way forward, then paused by the edge of the road, hidden by the rubble from a collapsed shop front. I could hear the crack and whine of small arms and the thunder of heavy weapons from the direction of the airport.

Layla's expression was bleak. I squeezed her arm. 'It gives us some hope. It shows the rebels are still being resisted.' As I spoke, I glimpsed two shapes outlined against the sky over the airport and heard the distant howl of jet engines. 'The rebels don't have any ground-attack planes,' I said. 'The Nigerians might be on the way in.'

Peering through the tangle of broken timbers on top of the mound of rubble, I could see a steady stream of people moving slowly along the road. They were unarmed civilians, and there seemed no sense or purpose in their movement. If they were fleeing from the fighting, they were fleeing in both directions, for as many were heading towards the hills as were trudging towards the centre of the city. Old men, women and children plodded past us. There were no teenage boys or girls or young men or women to be seen, however. I could guess what their fate had been.

As the last of the refugees disappeared from sight, we crossed the road. With the sky lightening by the minute, we had to press on, hoping there would be no rebel patrols or roadblocks.

We worked our way up the hillside, starting at every faint sound. I almost wept with relief when at last I saw the harsh white light over the gates of the High Commission.

We still had a hundred yards of open ground to cross. I took a careful look around us and then we sprinted across the road, the sound of our footfalls seeming to thunder in the semidarkness as we ran.

The High Commission was a concrete blockhouse, protected by steel-barred gates and an eight-foot wall topped with razor wire.

The gates were locked and the door of the guardhouse beyond was closed. I saw a dark figure outlined behind the bulletproof windows and could hear faint music from inside. I called in a low voice. There was no response. I took another look around and then shook the gates. The metallic rattle seemed deafening to me, but still the man did not look up.

I heard the noise of an engine lower down the hillside behind us. I scrabbled frantically in the dirt and at last my fingers closed round a clod of earth. I picked it up and hurled it through the gates at the window. There was a dull thud and the guard stared at us, shaking his head with disapproval. He opened the door, his rifle loose in his right hand. 'What do you want?'

My heart sank. What we needed right now was a trained British soldier, not some local recruit.

'We're British citizens. We need to speak to the High Commissioner.'

He shook his head. 'My orders are to admit no one.'

I heard the noise of the engine growing louder behind us. 'Then get your boss here now,' I said.

'He's asleep.'

'This is life or death. Wake him up.'

'If I do that, I'll be in trouble,' he said.

The noise of the engine grew still louder. There was no time for further discussion. I swung the rifle up to cover him. 'If you don't, you'll be dead. Now drop your rifle and walk towards the gates.'

He put the rifle down and began to move slowly towards the gates, a sheen of sweat on his brow. The glow of headlights lit up the sky behind us and the engine note grew to a roar.

'Faster,' I said. 'Now open the gates.'

He opened his mouth to argue, but I pushed the rifle forward and the barrel dug into his ribs. He stepped to the side of the gates and pushed a button. There was the whine of an electric motor and a rumble as the massive steel gates began to slide slowly apart.

As soon as the gap was wide enough, we squeezed through. 'Now shut them.'

He pressed the button again. As the gates began to close again, the vehicle I had heard cleared the top of the hill behind us.

It skidded to a halt. There were shouts and then a ragged volley of shots as we dived for the cover of the guardhouse. Rounds pinged off the steel gates and one smacked into the bulletproof glass of the window. After another volley of shots I heard the pick-up drive on.

I jabbed the barrel of my rifle into the guard again. 'Now get your superior,' I said.

We followed him into the guardhouse. He picked up the phone and dialled a number, his eyes fixed on the muzzle of my rifle. I heard a distorted voice giving a sleepy reply, and the guard gabbled an explanation. 'I'm being held at the gate by armed gunmen,' he said.

'British armed gunmen,' I shouted.

A moment later a siren began to sound. The seconds ticked by with no sign of movement from the building. Then suddenly the door of the High Commission swung open. As it did so, I saw a flurry of movement to either side of the building, and armed soldiers sprinted out and dived for cover.

I had no wish to be shot by British soldiers so I kept myself clearly visible through the armoured windows of the guardhouse as I held the rifle away from my body and dropped it to the ground. Then I raised my hands over my head and Layla did the same.

A voice barked at us from the darkness. 'Step forward, five paces. Now down! Down!'

I spread-eagled myself in the dirt and heard Layla drop alongside me. There was the sound of running feet, and my arms were grabbed and jerked up behind my back. I winced as the flexicuffs bit into my wrists. Then I was hauled to my feet.

'Who are you?'

'Jack Griffiths. Helicopter pilot with Decisive Measures.'

'Who's she?'

Layla replied for herself. 'Layla Edwards, a paramedic with Medicaid International.'

'We were shot down upcountry a few days ago,' I said. 'We made it back to Freetown just in time to be caught up in the coup.'

'It's not been your lucky week, has it? Where's your ID?' Already the voice was friendlier.

I jerked my head towards my pocket. One of the soldiers took our documents and passed them to his boss. He checked them.

'OK,' he said. 'Bring them inside.' We were hustled in through the main door of the building. 'And you can lose the cuffs,' he said. As they were removed, I rubbed the feeling back into my wrists.

We were shown into a room. A moment later an attaché strode in. I took his outstretched hand. 'Glad you made it,' he said. 'We were worried about you.'

I outlined our experiences. When I fell silent, he wrinkled his nose. 'Now, from the state of you, I'd say you need a shower, fresh clothes, something to eat and a stiff drink. Get yourselves cleaned up and then I'll have someone show you to the dining room. You'll find someone else there who will be even more pleased to see you.' He had walked out before I could ask him who he was talking about.

I spent a long time in the shower, soaping the filth and sweat from my body. I was covered in cuts, bruises and mosquito bites, some already turning septic, but it could have been a lot worse. When I was ready I dressed in clean clothes—not my own, but approximately the right size—and followed a soldier to the dining room.

As I entered, Grizz leapt up from a table and clasped me in a bear hug, nearly crushing my ribs. 'I didn't expect to see you again,' he said. 'You're either a military genius or the luckiest bastard alive.'

'You must be a bit of a lucky sod yourself,' I said.

He shrugged. 'Those rebels are brave but they're not soldiers. I just kept firing and moving. Their leader called them off in the end. I probably had the same idea as you—head for Freetown, not Bohara. Luckily, when I hit the road I was able to'—he paused and smiled—'to borrow a pick-up from a group of rebels I came across. They didn't look like they had any further use for it by then. I was parked up here waiting for orders from HQ when the coup started.'

He broke off as Layla came in, and hugged her. 'Great to see you,' he said. 'Now, you two eat and I'll talk. Here's the situation.' He gave a grim smile. 'As you've probably already noticed, the city's disintegrated—no police, no army, no one in control. The Nigerians are holding the airport and have apparently started a push out towards the city, but I'm not too optimistic about their enthusiasm for a fight if the rebels make a stand.'

'Do you think they will?'

'Hard to know. Their usual practice is to loot everything they can carry and then take off for the hills. The Nigerians won't pursue them there. The rebels might let them have Freetown for now; what they really want are the diamond mines.

'Anyway, we've been given three objectives: to help secure the existing government in power if possible, to evacuate European workers if necessary—but only if necessary—and to hold the diamond mines at all costs.' He gave a sour smile. 'Not necessarily in that order. Our first job is to get as much ammunition as we can carry up to Bohara. The garrison's still holding off the attacks at the moment, but once the rebels have finished looting the capital, the odds are they'll begin an all-out assault on the mines. We need to be there to help fight them off, or get our guys out before they're wiped out.'

I glanced towards Layla. 'What about the Medicaid people?'

Grizz shrugged. 'No sign of them and no ransom demands yet.'

Layla said nothing, but I saw her expression as she turned away.

'Try not to worry,' I said to her. 'Like I told you, they won't be harmed. They're too valuable to the rebels.'

'Anyway,' Grizz said, 'the boys at Bohara are in shit street. They're low on supplies and ammunition and hard-pressed by the rebels. Now we've got you back, though, we're in with a shout, apart from one big problem. Her Majesty's Government are running scared about being seen to support our activities. Which means that despite our friendly welcome here, the supply of helis or heavy weapons is not going to be permitted. They won't even look the other way this time while we bring them in from elsewhere.'

'So what can we do?' I said. 'The heli's in pieces in the jungle.'

He shook his head. 'There is one more.'

I stared at him for a moment, then I shook my head. 'Oh no. You're not thinking of that wreck at Camp Seventeen, are you?'

He nodded. 'Exactly.'

'We'd never get it off the ground.'

'We'll have a bloody good try. What else can we do? The rebels are pounding Bohara. We need to give our guys some fire support.'

I looked around. Layla was sitting at the other end of the table, sipping a cup of coffee as if it were the most beautiful thing she had ever tasted. I lowered my voice. 'What about Layla?' I said.

'She comes with us, of course. There are wounded at Bohara.'

'No!' I almost shouted it.

'You were happy enough to have her along before,' Grizz said.

'That was different.'

'I think I'm entitled to a voice in this,' Layla said. She had walked the length of the table and now stood directly behind me. 'I'm going back to Bohara with you.'

'It's too risky, Layla, too dangerous,' I said.

She smiled. 'More dangerous than what we've been through already?'

'But we had to do that; you don't have to do this.'

'I'm a medic, Jack. Of course I have to.'

'But you can't—' I began.

Her eyes flashed. 'Don't presume to tell me what I can and can't do. I'm doing my work, just as you're doing yours. I'm going to Bohara with you. End of story.'

I was ready to go on with the argument, but her expression showed me I'd be wasting my time. 'Anyway,' I said, turning back to Grizz, 'how do we get to Camp Seventeen without a vehicle?'

'We've got the one I borrowed.'

'And what do we do for weapons?'

He winked and tapped his nose. 'The High Commissioner is not unsympathetic. Officially he can't do anything, of course, but I've called in a couple of favours from the garrison here.'

'But what about spare parts for the heli?'

'What we have, we'll use. What we don't, we'll improvise.'

'So when do we leave?'

'As soon as we're ready,' he said. 'I'll just get the latest sit-rep here and call HQ for an update, then we're on our way.'

He returned to the room a few minutes later. 'The Nigerians' push out along the airport road ended after a couple of miles,' he said. 'They pulled back at the first sign of resistance. No surprises there. HQ reckons they'll just hold the airport and await developments.'

He led the way to the compound at the back of the High Commission. A battered utility truck was parked there. Two general-purpose machine guns had been lashed onto it, on either side of the roll bar. 'OK,' he said. 'Layla will drive. You and I'll take charge of the guns. Have you fired one before?'

I shook my head.

'With luck, the threat should be enough anyway. But if we meet any roadblocks and the usual cigarettes and bribes don't do the trick, use very short bursts. It'll save ammunition and it'll stop you from shooting up the treetops instead of the rebels.'

I helped him to load fuel, water and rations, and we shoved a few cartons of cigarettes under the dashboard. Then we climbed in the back and Layla gunned the engine.

 **CHAPTER 10**

We bucketed out of the gate in a cloud of dust and I hung on to the roll bar for support as we bounced down the road. It was early in the morning and most of the rebel soldiers were no doubt sleeping off the previous night's looting and drinking.

We tore through the outskirts of the city with Layla at the wheel, swerving expertly around piles of rubble, abandoned vehicles and the remains of barricades. As we turned onto the road towards the mountains, however, we hit a roadblock guarded by eight soldiers.

Grizz swung the barrel of his GPMG to cover them. I followed suit, keeping a particularly wary eye on a man with an RPG. 'Government soldiers or rebels?' I asked.

'Who knows?' Grizz said. 'They look more like government men, but it doesn't necessarily make any difference anyway.' With the fore-finger of his right hand curled round the trigger of his weapon, he raised the other hand, palm outwards in a gesture of friendship.

Layla pulled out a carton of cigarettes and held it out of the window. One of the soldiers took it from her. They shared the cigarettes out, but still made no move to raise the barrier.

'Where are you going to?' their leader said.

'Just to the hills to try to buy food.'

'Not to Bohara?'

'See for yourself, we have nothing here, just water and a little fuel.'

The soldiers debated among themselves, staring at the GPMGs. Finally the leader shrugged. 'Twenty dollars and you can pass.'

'We have only leones,' Grizz lied.

The leader motioned one of his soldiers forward and Grizz handed him a bundle of crumpled notes. The leader counted them, then jerked his head to his men, who began dismantling the barricade.

We ground on up the hill, turned off the main road and followed the winding track through the forest. We were on maximum alert as we approached the base, but the familiar listless soldiers still sprawled in the dust by the fire-blackened buildings inside the fence. They jumped to their feet and shouldered their weapons when they heard our approach, but at the sight of Grizz and yet another carton of cigarettes they dragged the gates open.

We drove into the compound and across to the rusting helicopter. Layla and I stripped the dust-laden camouflage net from it as Grizz disappeared into the Nissen hut and began dragging out spare parts, tools and a pile of what looked like scrap metal.

I looked the heli over and shook my head. 'We'll never fix this.'

Grizz brandished a roll of metallic tape. 'There's nothing that can't be fixed with speed tape.'

I began checking the heli externally, while Grizz worked on the engine. Then I began bolting lengths of aluminium section across the worst of the holes in the cab walls.

It was four hours before Grizz was satisfied with the engines. We paused for a brew and a bite to eat, then I ran through the cockpit checks while Grizz removed the GPMGs from the pick-up, fixed brackets improvised from scrap metal to the door frame of the heli and bound the guns to them with swaths of speed tape.

Next he beckoned to me and I followed him into the Nissen hut. Together we dragged a rocket pod from the hut and levered it into position on the underside of the nose of the cockpit. I tried to blank off the memory of what had happened the last time I had fired a rocket pod in action, but the thought kept returning to me.

When it was securely attached, Grizz connected a firing cable to the trigger on the stem of the collective, holding it in place with speed tape.

I helped Grizz to load the rocket pods and we took on maximum fuel and maximum ammunition for the mini-guns. When we had finished, the helicopter looked as if it had been assembled from scrap metal and Meccano, and bound together with speed tape.

I did the preflight checks and then pressed the starter. The turbine stuttered and whined like an old banger on a frosty morning. Then the engine coughed and died as a cloud of black smoke belched out. I exchanged a glance with Grizz, then tried again. Once more it faltered, spluttered and then caught. I tried the other engine and the whine of the turbines swelled to a roar as it also caught and fired. Grizz gave a thumbs-up and ran for the cab. The heli seemed in surprisingly good mechanical nick. I let the engines idle for five minutes as I checked the gauges, watching for any warning signs.

I glanced across at Layla in the copilot's seat. Her expression was relaxed, but the whiteness of her knuckles and the way she caught her lip between her teeth showed how nervous she was.

I reached across to squeeze her arm with my gloved hand, then I pushed the lever into flight idle. I raised the collective and eased the cyclic forward as we rose from the ground, and I paddled the rudder pedals, banking us to the east.

The Huey's response to the controls was sluggish, but that was hardly surprising. Even through my helmet I was deafened by the noise as the slipstream howled through the bullet holes in the body, setting metal vibrating against metal in a cacophony of noise.

There was only sporadic ground fire as we flew over the outskirts of the capital. Looking down, I could see smoke still rising from scores of fires. Ragged lines of vehicles were moving in both directions, empty trucks and pick-ups heading into the city, and heavily laden ones making for the mountains to the east.

The airport road was scarred with the marks of recent fighting, the road surface blackened, burned and part-blocked by the wrecks of vehicles. Bodies still lay sprawled in the dirt around them.

The two Hawk jets I had seen flying sorties the previous night were drawn up on the hard standing at the far side of the airfield, near a couple of Nigerian military transport planes that were unloading supplies. Groups of soldiers were dug in around the perimeter and a large force of men was milling about near the arrivals hall.

I kept the heli high until the last possible moment, then made a steep descent over the heart of the airfield to touch down safely.

We climbed down from the Huey and followed Grizz over to the

main airport building. A group of Nigerian officers had comman-
deered the airport administration offices for their own use.

Grizz introduced himself to the senior officer, a bulky figure in
combat fatigues and the inevitable mirrored sunglasses.

'What's the situation here, Major?' Grizz asked.

'We have secured the airfield,' he said. 'And when we are ready, we
shall advance on Freetown and drive the rebels back into the hills.'

We walked over to the small barbed-wire compound that Decisive
Measures maintained at the airport. Some of the Sierra Leonean
soldiers detailed to guard it were still there, but they seemed cowed
by the presence of the Nigerians.

There was no sign that there had been any fighting in the immediate area, but there had been a serious attempt to force the locks on
the heavy steel doors of the store bunkers. In one case it had been
successful. The doors hung off their hinges and the interior of the
bunker had been stripped bare.

'The rebels?' I said.

Grizz shook his head. 'They never breached the airport perimeter.
More likely our saviours here.'

He walked over and spoke to the Nigerians. All shook their heads
or shrugged their shoulders.

Grizz led the Sierra Leonean soldiers off to one side and began
talking to them. I couldn't hear what they said, but their body language showed their uneasiness. They kept their faces averted from
Grizz's probing stare and raised their eyes only to dart nervous
glances at the Nigerians.

Grizz pointed a finger towards the city. 'You want to keep working
for us? Or do you want to take your chances out there?'

A couple of the men hesitated, then muttered something in reply.
He walked back to us. 'Come on.'

We made our way back to the administration building. The
Nigerian officer made no attempt to conceal his impatience as Grizz
stated his grievance. 'One of our store bunkers has been looted of
grenades, rifles and ammunition.'

'Of what concern is this to me?'

'Your men are the culprits.'

'You dare to accuse my men of this? Where is your proof?'

'The word of the soldiers we pay to guard it.' He paused. 'If we
don't get them back, those weapons will be sold to the rebels who
have been robbing, raping and killing in Freetown, while your men

sit here doing nothing. Are you here to protect the people or are you waiting for the rebels to leave so that you and your men can take their turn at whatever is left?'

The Nigerian strode from behind his desk and stood toe to toe with Grizz. 'We are Africans.' He jabbed his stubby thumb into his chest. 'I am African. These are my people, they have my protection. We Africans know who the real oppressors are. Get out before I have you arrested.'

'Go ahead. See how much shit hits the fan after that. With the amount we pay in bribes to Nigerian generals, I don't think we'll have any difficulty in finding one willing to bust you back down to private.' He paused. 'We want those weapons back, Major, and if any of those other bunkers are tampered with again, we'll be asking our generals for a favour.'

'Do Decisive Measures really have some Nigerian generals on the payroll?' I asked as we walked back across the airfield.

Grizz laughed. 'I don't know, but you'd have to be a brave major to call the bluff, wouldn't you?' He opened one of the other bunkers and we loaded more ammunition for the garrison at Bohara. Then I fired up the engines and took off, staying above the safe haven of the airport as I maintained a tight spiral climb to height.

I levelled at 2,000 feet and set the nose of the Huey directly towards Bohara. The landscape had been transformed into a scene of devastation. Villages had become blackened ruins, their fields stripped bare of crops. Everywhere there were fleeing figures, scattering in panic at the sight of the helicopter. Whether they were rebels, government troops or simply refugees it was impossible to know.

We dropped into the Bohara Valley. Grizz and I began a three-way conversation with the radio operator at the mine compound. Grizz was also talking to Rudi on the net.

'We need to get the expats out,' the operator said. 'The mines have been shut down for the last week anyway and we're taking a storm of incoming fire. We can't guarantee their safety any longer.'

'Have them ready to ship out,' I said.

Grizz chipped in. 'Hostiles are reported advancing twelve miles. Let's see if we can quieten those bastards down first before we start worrying about the expats.'

We passed over the compound and swung away onto the bearing Grizz indicated. We swooped over a ridge line and down towards the target valley. As if my Kosovo nightmare had again become reality, I saw a burning hamlet ahead of me, the ruined buildings standing stark among the flames and smoke. Beyond it was dense woodland and forest.

As I skimmed along the tree line, the downwash lashing at the branches revealed shapes moving in the shadows of the trees. There were no muzzle flashes, no tick of rounds against the Huey's skin. I could see figures running between the trees but I had no way of telling if they were refugees from the burning village or rebel soldiers.

Not again, please God, not again, I thought. I made another, slower pass. Still there was no fire from the woods.

I flicked the intercom switch. 'What do you get, Grizz?'

'Figures. Hostiles.'

'They could be villagers.'

'Negative. I can see men with weapons.'

'They might be sticks or spears,' I said. 'Hold your fire, I'll make another pass.' I did, and then another, putting the heli into a hover directly in front of the half-hidden figures, inviting them to shoot.

I heard the clank of the ammunition links for the door gun.

'Hold your fire.'

'What?' Grizz said. 'Jesus, Jack. What are you trying to do?'

I ignored him, my thoughts echoing in my brain: *Why don't they shoot? Why don't they shoot?*

I glanced at Layla. Her face showed her fear, but her voice was firm and level. 'This isn't Kosovo, Jack,' she said. 'Trust your judgment. Do what you have to do.'

I strained to look beyond the camouflage of the foliage. I saw a few angular shapes and what might have been the glint of metal. Then the sunlight glancing from the metal fuselage of the heli was picked up and reflected by a score of tiny mirrors, gleaming like Christmas lights in the darkness of the forest.

That decided me. I had seen enough rebels with mirror fragments woven into their hair or dangling from their clothing, part of the juju they believed would ward off evil and keep them alive.

I swung the heli away from the forest then banked in a sweeping turn. 'Are you ready in the back?' I said.

The answer from Grizz was immediate. 'Just give me the word.'

'On my shot.' My finger began to close on the trigger. A microsecond before I fired, a figure came sprinting from the tree line—a woman blundering directly into the cross hairs of my sights.

The vision of the burning woman from Kosovo flooded my mind.

'Abort! Abort! Abort!' I pulled my hand from the trigger as if it had been burned, and banked us up and left, away from the wood.

'Jack? What's going on? Jack?'

I couldn't answer him for a moment. My hands were trembling so much I could barely grip the controls and my body shook with shivers. I offered a silent prayer of thanks that I'd been saved from repeating the terrible crime I'd committed in Kosovo.

I glanced back over my shoulder and saw the woman still running. Then she stopped, jerking from side to side as if some giant invisible hand was shaking her. She toppled forward and lay still.

Then there was a red flash from the edge of the wood and I heard Grizz's warning shout. 'Missile launch! Evade! Evade! Evade!' I was already throwing the Huey into a savage right-hand break as the RPG round blasted up at me trailing a plume of dirty grey smoke. I watched it with a curious detachment as it knifed past us, so close it appeared to pass through the whirling disc of the rotors. Then it was gone, diminishing to a black speck in the sky, before it exploded in a ball of orange flame.

I glanced down. At once I glimpsed the stooping figure of a rebel soldier, a squat black tube extending from his shoulder. I swung the heli back to face the forest.

The rebel soldier had reloaded and was raising the launcher back to his shoulder. He froze as he saw the Huey blasting in towards him. I nudged the nose of the heli right a shade, and as the cross hairs intersected, I squeezed the firing trigger. There was a *whoosh* as the rocket blasted from the pod. The soldier disappeared in a burst of crimson flame and clods of earth were blasted into the air.

I heard the clatter of the GPMG as Grizz began raking the tree line. He gave a warning shout. 'Muzzle flashes four o'clock.' I swung the heli right to bring my weapons to bear and squeezed the trigger of the rocket pod again. Driven by a cold rage, I attacked over and over, indifferent to danger, as I laid the ghosts of my past. I was wreaking vengeance as much for what I had done in Kosovo as for the terror the rebels had inflicted here.

I launched all the rockets from the pod and kept firing the nose gun long after every sign of movement from the rebels had ceased, then I turned away, back towards Bohara.

Suddenly there was a flash and a blast strong enough to throw the Huey sideways. Shrapnel ripped into the side of the cab.

'What the—' I froze. In the corner of my eye I glimpsed a black shape just above the forest canopy, as sinister and ugly as a taran-tula, but far more deadly.

It was a Hind helicopter gunship. The markings on its flanks had been painted out, but there was little doubt where it had come from. The Liberians had obviously decided to gamble on an intervention to tip the fight for the diamond mines in favour of their protégés.

There was another flash and a streak of smoke and flame. 'Flares! Flares! Flares!' I yelled.

Layla's hand hovered over the buttons, then pressed one.

'Not chaff, flares! The next button!'

She pressed the correct button and the fierce light of miniature stars burned at the periphery of my vision as a burst of flares ignited in our slipstream.

I put us into a dive even as I spun the heli round to mask the heat of the engines from the missile streaking towards us.

The Huey screamed downwards. I held the dive until my vision was filled with the sight of onrushing trees, then almost broke the Huey's back as I pulled the steepest climbing turn I could manage. I could feel the blood draining from my brain as the G force bit, but I held the turn until the colour began to wash from my vision. It was the grey-out—the prelude to unconsciousness.

I eased back on the controls and, as my full vision returned, I whipped my head round searching for the Hind. 'Where is it?'

'In your five,' Grizz said, hanging out of the door of the cab to keep the enemy in sight. 'Go left. Go left.'

I stamped down on the rudder again, forcing the Huey into another juddering turn. The Hind flashed across my sights. I'd have given a year's wages for just one of the rockets I'd blasted into the forest only a few minutes before, but the pod was empty.

As the cross hairs intersected on the Hind I squeezed the trigger of the nose guns and rounds spat out, punching a rising line though the Hind's fuselage. Then the firing stopped abruptly. I squeezed the trig-ger again, holding the turn to keep the enemy heli in my sights, but the guns were useless—empty or jammed.

I could barely control a mounting wave of panic. I had no rockets and now no guns—no armaments of any sort to take into a duel with one of the deadliest gunships ever built. And the Hind was already turning to bring its own weapons to bear once more.

I tried to manoeuvre to bring Grizz's guns to bear, but though he loosed off a couple of bursts, sighting through the doorway of the cab barely gave him enough time before the Hind was out of his line of sight again.

The Hind flashed towards me. I faked a left turn, then kicked hard right and dived, passing under the Hind, its blind spot. We were so close that its downwash shook the Huey like a terrier on a rat and my own rotors scythed the air within feet of its metal belly.

In that instant, I saw one glimmer of hope. I accelerated and set the nose due west as if bugging out from the fight and running for home. The Hind immediately turned in pursuit and the gap that had begun to open narrowed again. He was now in perfect position to plant a heat-seeking missile straight into the exhaust of the Huey's straining engines . . .

I dumped the collective and booted the right rudder, sending the Huey into the most savage break yet. There was a strangled cry from Layla alongside me as the force of the turn threw her against the side of the cockpit and I heard a thud and a curse behind me as Grizz lost his footing and fell against the wall of the cab.

The Huey's momentum carried it through the turn and as the nose dipped and we started to drop, a flash of fire trailing smoke blasted past the cockpit mere feet from my face.

It detonated with a blinding flash behind us, but I had no time to spare it a thought. We were now nose to nose, a mile apart and closing fast. If neither of us evaded, we would impact in seconds.

The Hind opened up again with a burst from its nose gun and then jinked left. I matched the move exactly. We were still nose to nose. He went right and left again, then climbed, and each time I matched him, focusing only on the helmeted figure I could just glimpse through the tinted Perspex bubble of the Hind's canopy. We were now no more than 200 yards apart. I sensed as much as saw him start to climb and once more matched his move.

'Jack! What are you doing?' Layla screamed. 'You'll kill us all!'

A fraction of a second later I saw the Hind's nose dip. I twitched the cyclic upwards as its ugly black shape filled my vision. The disturbed air threw the Huey around, but I held the controls with rigid arms as I saw the nose of the Hind slide towards us. I could see the pilot's expression freeze as I jerked the cyclic forward and the Huey began to drop towards the blur of razor-edged motion—the rotors of the Hind. There was no margin for error. A couple of feet too low and we would all die together.

Then there was the crack and whine of metal on metal from

behind and below me. The back of our skids had caught the tips of the Hind's main rotors.

I was powerless to do anything but wait. If I had misjudged our angle of dive, I would have set us on an irreversible path to destruction. There was a deafening crash and my helmet smacked against the edge of the canopy as the Huey was thrown sideways. The floor of the cockpit beneath my feet was buckled by the impact.

I heard Grizz curse and yell as he was thrown around. The force of the impact had spun us round so that the Hind again filled my vision. Its main rotors were still turning at blinding speed, but the tail had disappeared, smashed away like rotten wood. With no tail rotor to control the torque, the giant body of the Hind was already beginning to spin out of control. Whipping around its own axis, it drilled downwards towards the ground and then disappeared in a massive orange and yellow flash.

I pushed up my visor to wipe the sweat from my eyes. 'Jesus,' I said. 'That's the first and last dogfight I ever want to go into with no ammunition. If they've got another Hind, we're finished.' I heard Grizz's rumbling laugh over the intercom. 'I think you just wrecked at least fifty per cent of the Liberian air force. I don't think there's much danger of them risking the other half as well.'

Layla, too, joined in the laughter, but her face was deathly pale.

 **CHAPTER 11**

I set the heli climbing to clear the ridge, sighting on a notch in the skyline where a landslip had cut away a section like a small quarry. Beneath it the slopes were barren and strewn with scree. 'A great place to hide,' I said as we flashed over it. 'You could lie up there for weeks and never be found.'

We cleared the ridge and flashed down towards Bohara. The ground fire from the rebels began at once and rounds clipped the rotor blades, tracing a brief fiery trail of sparks in the sky.

I pressed down lower and kept the heli weaving from side to side as I radioed the compound, 'Grizzly One, coming in.'

Almost at once the garrison put out a barrage of fire at the rebels. As I dropped fast and low towards the helipad, I could make out people gathered in knots around the perimeter wire, and a jostling mass pressing against the gates of the inner compound. The rebels had driven villagers and mineworkers alike towards Bohara. They were pinned between the advancing rebels and the mercenary garrison. I could see them shouting, pleading and waving fistfuls of leone bills. It felt like the fall of Saigon.

We landed. As the engines wound down, I looked at Layla. 'Your patients are waiting,' I said. 'You haven't got long, though.'

As I spoke, I cast an uneasy glance out of the cockpit. The arrival of the helicopter seemed to have driven the people into a frenzy. They were clawing at the razor wire, indifferent to the cuts on their hands as they tried to haul themselves up and over.

One boy succeeded. He sprawled in the dust and then pulled himself to his feet only to be clubbed to the ground again by a mercenary. I recognised Rudi's powerful figure standing over the prone figure. As the boy raised his face from the dust, Layla stared through the cockpit, then began tearing at her harness.

She jumped down from the cockpit and sprinted towards the fence, ignoring the crackle of small-arms fire. I hurried after her. She was crouching over the boy. I helped her carry him towards the two-storey container building at the centre of the compound.

We laid him down at the side of the doorway and, screened by the wall of sandbags, Layla first tested his skull for fractures and then began to bandage his torn hands. Only when he opened his eyes and spoke did I realise that the boy was Kaba.

Layla was trying to calm him, but he kept gabbling out the same refrain, 'You must come to Boroyende. Njama is wounded.'

'What happened?' I said.

He turned his bleak gaze on me. 'The rebels came. They knew you had been to the village; they'd seen your truck. They said we were spying for you.' He stared me out. 'They found the knife you gave him. They said it was payment for spying. They tried to kill everyone. A few of us managed to get away and hide.'

A sick feeling grew in my stomach. 'But Njama? He is alive?'

He nodded. 'He was in the fields, otherwise they would have killed him too. But he is sick, wounded. He needs medicine.' He turned back to Layla. 'He needs you. You must come.'

Layla took my arm and led me off to one side. 'We have to go there,' she said. 'What's happened is our fault, our responsibility.'

'I can't,' I said. 'I have to take the expat workers out of here.'

'And then?'

'Whatever my orders are next.'

'And the black mineworkers?'

'You know the answer to that, I'm afraid. They're on their own.'

'In other words, you're going to leave them to die.'

I couldn't hold her gaze.

'And Boroyende?'

Again, I couldn't meet her eyes as I answered. 'The same.'

'So, you look after the expats and the diamonds and leave the people themselves to die.'

'It's not that black and white.'

'You're wrong, Jack. Black and white is exactly what it is.'

She stared at me for a moment. There was a look in her eyes I could not read.

'What is it?' I said.

She looked away. 'Nothing,' she said. 'I made a mistake, that's all.'

She turned her back on me before I could reply.

Grizz had been conferring with Rudi and now came racing back to the Huey. 'Let's get things moving, fast.'

A group of white expatriates, each clutching a single case, stood waiting for the signal to load. Fear and anger vied for control of their faces as they stared at the mob outside the compound, held back only by the threat of the mercenaries' guns.

I walked over to Layla, who was huddled in a corner talking to the boy. I touched her shoulder but almost flinched at the look she gave me. 'We have to get ready,' I said.

She shook her head. 'You mean you do. I'm staying here.'

'You can't do that. It's crazy.'

She gave me a level stare. 'You're coming back for the mercenaries, aren't you? Or are they to be left to die too?'

'Of course I'm coming back.'

She shrugged. 'Then I'll return with them.'

Grizz came charging over. 'Jack, for God's sake get out there before that heli's overrun.' I hesitated, still holding Layla's gaze, then I turned and ran for the Huey.

The expatriates ran for it too as I fired up the engines. A crowd of black workers began trying to force the gates of the compound. The massive figures of Hendrik and Reuben were at the heart of a group of mercenaries firing over their heads and into the dust at their feet, trying to hold them back. At a command from Rudi, Reuben turned and jogged to the helicopter. He swung himself up into the cab.

'Grizz? What's going on?' I said into the intercom. 'The Huey's already seriously overloaded. You're the door gunner. We don't need him as well.'

'I'm also the boss,' Grizz said. 'We've two GPMGs. I can't fire both of them and we need every gun hand we can load onto this crate.'

'If we're too overloaded, we won't get airborne.'

'Just try it, will you?'

I hesitated, sick at heart, staring back towards the entrance to the container building, where Layla's slim figure was still hunched in the shadows next to the boy.

'What are you waiting for? Let's get out of here,' Grizz said.

The turbine whined its way up the octaves. I raised the collective to bring the Huey to a hover, but it barely lifted on its springs. I pushed the collective right up to the stops but the heli remained rooted to the ground, shuddering with the vibrations of the engines as they strained at maximum power.

'I'll have to try a running takeoff,' I said.

I used the cyclic to set the heli lumbering slowly across the compound. It ground its way slowly forward, the skid plates scraping and rattling at the earth. If I could squeeze enough momentum out of it to lift the rotors into clean, undisturbed air, free of the turbulence of the ground effect, in theory we would achieve translational lift—the rotors would bite and send us soaring upwards.

That was the aim. At the moment, we were still bumping along the ground, carving furrows in the red dirt of the compound with the skids. Just short of the perimeter fence I paddled the right rudder—turning with the torque increased the available power to the main rotors—and came around.

We accelerated again across the compound. The heli rocked as the skids rumbled over the rutted ground.

We were moving too fast to make another ground turn and the fence was now looming. I hauled on the collective. For a moment the heli remained earthbound, but then I felt a sudden jerk as the rotors bit into clean air, free of the turbulence of the downwash.

As the perimeter wire seemed to rush towards us, we crept a few feet above the earth. I swung the heli around just in time to miss the fence and nosed it back across the compound, barely airborne and still trapped by the fence surrounding us.

We crawled back across the compound, not gaining an inch of

altitude. I brought the Huey to a hover a few feet above the floor of the compound. The vibrations increased and after a moment the by now familiar screech of the low RPM warning began to sound.

The battle between power and weight was being lost, and inch by inch the Huey was slowly sinking back towards the ground. I had to find a way to reduce the power demand for a moment or I'd lose control of the ship altogether.

I eased the collective down a fraction, letting the Huey drift downwards. My reward was to hear the turbines pick up. The warning siren died away, and as soon as the heli stabilised I eased the collective up again and the Huey rose back into the air.

Once more, however, even though I pulled in maximum power, as soon as the Huey began to rise out of the ground effect, it started to settle back down again. I repeated the manoeuvre and, perhaps helped by the loss of fuel weight as I kept the engines bellowing, this time I managed to squeeze a few more revs and at last got the Huey level with the top of the compound fence. I kept parallel to it, building the revs as much as I could. Then I took a deep breath and banked hard right, praying that the power boost I could nick from allowing the Huey to swing with the torque would be enough to lift us clear of the fence.

The coils of razor wire along the top disappeared beneath us. I was just beginning to exhale when there was a savage jerk. The nose dipped and I fought the controls to stabilise the heli, holding it in a hover as the engines screamed under the load.

Grizz's voice came over the intercom. 'We're caught. One of the wheels has snagged the razor wire.'

I glanced behind into the cab. He was hanging out of the door. 'I'll have to free it. Get me roped up.'

He wriggled back in and Reuben tied a rope around his chest, padding it with his shirt. Grizz picked up a pair of metal shears from the toolkit and Reuben lowered him out of the door. He hung suspended for a moment out of reach of the wire and the skids. Then Reuben began to swing him like a pendulum.

Slowly at first, Grizz swung away in a wider and wider arc. I heard him grunt as he grabbed and missed the shaft of the skids, then he grabbed again and held.

His voice came again over the intercom. 'Back five.'

I eased the heli back. I saw a strand of wire curl up into my vision as he cut through it and heard his laboured breathing.

A gust of wind hit the heli, pushing it a few feet. 'Hold it,' I said into the intercom, working the controls to bring us back. Just then I heard the snap of the razor wire parting, followed by a scream. The heli lurched and one end of the severed wire lashed the side of the cockpit like a whip. It left a bloody trail across the Perspex.

Reuben's voice cut in on the intercom. 'We've got to land again. Grizz is down there.'

I swung the heli around, craning my neck to look down. A figure lay sprawled in the dirt, one leg twisted underneath him. The flying razor wire had sliced through the rope and sent Grizz plunging to the earth, but the fall was not what had killed him. The wire had also cut clean through his neck, severing his head.

Reuben's voice came again. 'We have to land.'

'We can't,' I said. 'We're overloaded already and the fence is down. If we land there those guys will rush us. Besides, there's nothing we can do for Grizz. He's dead. We'll have to leave him here.'

'You don't leave a comrade behind, even if he is dead.'

'This time we'll have to. I thought the world of Grizz too, but if we land to pick up his body, we'll never get airborne.' I raised the collective again and pushed the cyclic forward, ending the argument.

The ship groaned and shook as it climbed slowly away from the compound. I flew in a daze, only dimly aware of the landscape passing below me and the feel of the controls in my hands.

At last, in the distance ahead, I saw the surf haze hanging over the coast. Then the grey rutted concrete of the airport runway came into view. As we made our approach, a few bursts of ground fire greeted us, but it was sporadic and barely threatening.

I eased down the collective, flared and landed.

I killed the engines and slumped in my seat, feeling the sweat soaking through my flying suit. The expats tumbled from the heli, laughing and joking as they hurried across the concrete towards the terminal. I went the other way, to the edge of the airfield where I bought some food and a drink from a stall.

I sat down in the shade of a fuel bunker as a fuel bowser trundled across the hard standing towards the Huey. Then I heard the scrunch of feet on the dusty concrete and a shadow fell across me. I looked up.

'Don't get up,' said a clipped, English voice. 'Henry Pleydell. We met at Bohara when you first came out here.'

I nodded. 'I remember you, Colonel.'

'You've done a great job for us, Jack,' he said. 'Grizz has told us.'

103

'Grizz is dead.'

He pursed his lips, and a bead of sweat trickled down his forehead and splashed onto the front of his neatly pressed shirt. 'I'm very sorry to hear that,' he said. He nodded to himself, then went on, his manner once more brisk and businesslike. 'We have reports that Liberian troops are massing on the frontier. Some may even have crossed it. The mining company is no longer prepared to meet the cost of countering a full-blown invasion. So we're pulling out, Jack, and leaving the Nigerians to fight it out.'

'Until the next time,' I said.

'Oh, I'm sure we'll be back when the situation permits. But in the meantime we need you to fly just a couple more missions, to bring out the rest of the garrison and a package.'

'What sort of package?'

He rolled his eyes. 'It *is* a diamond mine, old boy.' He paused. 'Get airborne as soon as you can. There'll be a healthy bonus in it for you when they're safely delivered.'

'The diamonds or the men?'

A fleeting look of irritation passed across his face. 'Both, of course. You don't think we'd leave them to die, do you?'

'I need a door gunner and a copilot' I said.

'Door gunner is no problem. Take Reuben. But I'm afraid you'll have to keep flying solo. We've moved heaven and earth to try to find one in these last few days. We even offered double rates, but there were still no takers. People believe all sorts of rumours.'

'Quite,' I said. 'So what ordnance have you got here? Are there rockets for the pod?'

He shook his head. 'Just rounds for the guns, I'm afraid.' He glanced at his watch. 'Well, good luck then.'

As he walked away, Reuben began to load boxes of explosives into the heli.

'Demolition charges?' I said.

Reuben didn't even turn his head. 'You fly the helicopter,' he said. 'We'll take care of the rest.'

IT WAS DUSK before we took off and I made the customary transition to night-vision goggles for the flight. For once there was little gunfire to greet us as I flew in towards Bohara. It was as if, secure in their impending victory, the rebels had pulled back to recuperate before the final assault.

Rudi supervised the unloading of the demolition charges. They were at once fitted into backpacks and Raz, Reuben and Hendrik, their faces obscured with cam cream, slipped out of the gate and disappeared into the darkness, moving towards the mine workings.

Rudi spat in the dust. 'Waste of good plant,' he said. 'The Kaffirs couldn't use it anyway.'

I turned and walked away from him into the container building. I searched both tiers from one end to the other, then walked right around the compound. There was no sign of Layla.

I began stopping everyone I passed. 'Where's Layla?' I asked. 'Where's Layla?' All shook their heads or shrugged. I reached the main gate. 'Where's Layla?' I said to the guard.

'She went out an hour before dusk,' he said. 'She insisted she had some medicines for a patient in the workers' compound and wouldn't take no for an answer.'

'Was there a boy with her, an African kid?'

'Yeah.'

I knew at once where she had gone.

I returned to the building sick at heart. Rudi was sitting at a table. 'Layla's missing,' I said.

He shrugged. 'So?'

'I have to find her.'

He laughed. 'When you've done the job you're paid for then you can go walkabout in the bush, crybaby. Right now, we've enough to do without worrying about some coloured bitch who's gone native.'

I looked away, waiting until I had controlled my anger. 'How soon do we leave?'

'The first group will go as soon as the demolition teams are back.'

'And the rest?'

'We'll hold the fort until you come back for us.'

We sat in silence for an hour until the demolition teams returned. Rudi selected eight men and sent them out to the heli. With all their kit, it was once more going to be dangerously overloaded.

'There's one more passenger,' Rudi said.

As I began to protest, I saw two men running from the container building, carrying a burden between them.

Grizz's corpse had been flexicuffed at the wrists and ankles to make it easier for them to carry. They ran stooping with it to the heli and tossed it inside without ceremony. Hendrik returned a final time with the severed head wrapped in a piece of sacking. He threw it onto the floor of the cab and I saw one of the mercenaries push it under the seat with the toe of his boot.

Only Rudi, Raz, Reuben and Hendrik now remained to hold the compound. 'Make sure you're back to lift us before dawn,' Rudi said.

I held out my hand. 'The diamonds.'

'Oh no. The diamonds stay here. If we let you fly out of here with them, what guarantee do we have that you'll come back for us?'

'I don't give a shit about the diamonds,' I said. 'All I want to do is get everybody out alive.'

'I'm touched by your concern, but perhaps Decisive Measures might have other priorities. This way we have an insurance policy.'

I fired up the helicopter and took off into the night. Somewhere in the blackness below me was Layla, if she was still alive.

As soon as we landed back at the airport, Colonel Pleydell and the Decisive Measures quartermaster strode out to meet us. The colonel was immediately surrounded by the mercenaries, airing the traditional soldiers' grievances about pay. While they argued, I shouted for a body bag. The quartermaster sauntered to a bunker and came back with a black rubber bag. I spread it out on the ground. 'Help me carry him out of the cab,' I said.

We lifted Grizz's body and laid it down on the rubber. 'We need to cut the flexicuffs off him,' I said.

'It doesn't matter to him.'

'It does to me. Just do it.'

He shrugged and cut off the flexicuffs with a knife.

I climbed back into the cab and pulled out the head from under the seat. I unwrapped it from the sacking, but could not bring myself to look at the face as I tried to arrange it in the body bag to give it some semblance of dignity.

'Make sure anyone who handles that shows some respect,' I said.

The quartermaster nodded. We lifted the bag onto the back of his Jeep and he drove across the airfield towards a waiting charter jet.

The colonel brushed the angry mercenaries aside and pushed his way through to me. 'You have the diamonds?'

'They're coming on the next trip.'

His thin, bloodless lips tightened. 'Those were not your orders.'

'I know that. Rudi and his mates back there weren't too eager about the original arrangement.'

He made a visible effort to control his anger. 'How soon can you be airborne again?'

'As soon as I'm refuelled.'

He turned away and started barking orders at the ground crew. They responded with sullen indifference and it was a good forty minutes before the fuel bowser had been brought out to fill up the tanks.

There was an understandable lack of enthusiasm among the mercenaries for one of them to act as a door gunner for the final mission to Bohara. The colonel tried bluster, cajolery and bribery in turn.

The plan that had been forming in my mind crystallised while I listened to the arguments. 'Don't sweat it, Colonel,' I said. 'I've managed without a copilot for the last few missions. I'm sure I can fly this one without a door gunner.' I settled the matter by turning away and pulling on my helmet as I hurried towards the cab.

I checked in with the tower, then I was airborne in a cloud of dust, banking southeast, back towards Bohara. Assuming I made it there, what happened after would depend entirely on Rudi, but I was pretty confident that I had his measure.

I switched on the night-vision goggles at 2,000 feet, allowing time for my eyes to become accustomed to the green-tinged, negative vision of the world below me before I began the descent.

I maintained radio silence until I was only a few miles from Bohara, then jabbed the radio button. 'Bohara, this is Grizzly One. Time for the last bus home. Give me a little light there, will you?'

Rudi's guttural Afrikaaner tones came at once through the static. 'Stand by. We'll light you in. There'll be a little diversion too.'

I saw the specks of green light flare in the distance as they began the prearranged signal: two long flashes, one short, three long.

As I slowed, preparing to land, the darkness beyond the base was lit by a series of blinding flashes as the demolition charges on the mine equipment erupted in succession.

A moment later the first ground fire cracked around me. I jinked and dodged, keeping the Huey moving around. The compound loomed ahead of me and I landed close to the container building.

Heavy weapon rounds were crashing down around the compound and the incoming fire redoubled as the remnants of the garrison— Raz, Reuben and Hendrik—sprinted for the cab.

Rudi was the last to leave the building. He sprinted low to the ground, clutching his rifle in his right hand and a chained steel case the size of a small cash box in his left. He dived through the door of the cab, yelling 'Go! Go! Go!'

I rammed up the collective and the Huey was airborne again.

Torrents of tracer fire ripped through the night around us.

We were a bare 300 feet above the compound when the container building detonated. Flames climbed halfway towards the Huey.

The lack of return fire from the base must have told the rebels the last of the garrison had gone, and the ground fire ceased all at once, as if it had been switched off. I imagined them running through the darkness, tearing down the gates to loot whatever was left.

'Next stop R 'n' R,' Rudi said.

'Come up front a minute,' I said. 'I want to talk to you.'

'What about?'

'I'll tell you when you're up front.'

He pushed his way through the gap between the seats and slumped into the copilot's seat.

'Put the helmet on,' I said.

He gave me a suspicious look, but picked it up from the floor of the cockpit and pulled it onto his head.

'It keeps it private,' I said. 'Just between us. I've got a proposal.'

'And what do you propose?'

'A deal,' I said. 'I need your help to reach Layla.'

'You don't even know where she is.'

'I do know that. She's at Boroyende. I want you to help me find her and bring her and everyone else there to safety.'

He laughed. 'What have you got that could interest me?'

'Nothing much. Only ten million pounds' worth of diamonds. Colonel Pleydell is waiting to collect them at Freetown Airport. But we're here, while he's hundreds of miles away. So stuff him,' I said. 'You guys can split them between you. I'll ditch the heli and say we got shot down, the rebels got the diamonds and as far as I know they got you, too. You'll be posted missing in action. Just one of those diamonds'll buy you a new identity and a one-way ticket to a new life anywhere in the world.'

'Aren't you overlooking one thing? I have the diamonds, not you.'

'Sure you do, but at the moment we're at two thousand feet and heading for Freetown. When we land there, Decisive Measures and their friends will share the spoils and you will be left with a few thousand dollars in back pay and bonuses . . .'

I shot a quick glance at him and could see the predatory glint of his eyes in the darkness. I smiled to myself; I had him. 'All you've got to do is persuade the other guys to come with us,' I said.

'You're overlooking something,' Rudi said. 'What's to stop us taking off with the diamonds anyway, and leaving Layla and her Kaffir friends to rot?'

'Nothing, except if I set you down here, it'll take you three weeks to walk out . . . if you make it. But do as I ask and I'll drop you anywhere you want. We've got the range to go to Guinea, the Ivory Coast, even Senegal. We've plenty of fuel, I made sure of that.'

He sat in silence for some time, thinking it over. 'OK. You've got yourself a deal. But we'll keep it between ourselves for now. As far as the other guys go, this is part of the mission. OK?'

'OK,' I said. 'As long as you're sure you can persuade them.'

'I don't have to,' he said. 'They're soldiers, they take orders, and I outrank all of them.'

I gave an anxious look towards the eastern horizon. The first hints of dawn were already beginning to appear in the sky.

I switched my gaze back to the steep rocky ridge ahead of us, scouring it for the notch in the skyline that I was seeking—the landslip I had spotted some days before. Then I saw it a few miles ahead.

The instant that the ridge line cleared beneath me, I flared the heli and set it down in the notch in the hillside. Screened on either side and hidden from below by the lip of the landslip, it was invisible except from the air.

I shut down. Rudi was already climbing through to the cab. 'One more patrol, guys,' he said. There was a chorus of groans and argument, then Rudi's guttural voice rose, cutting through the dissent. 'I don't like it any more than you do, but those are the orders. We just get in and out; we get the job done, then we go home. And there's a bonus in it,' he said. 'Ten thousand dollars a head if we bring the coloured nurse out alive. She has some powerful friends.'

As they began to clamber down from the cab, I jumped down myself. Reuben and Hendrik helped me drag a camouflage net from the cab and drape it over the heli. I took particular care to obscure the Perspex canopy, covering it with branches and showering it with handfuls of dust to prevent it shining like a searchlight when the sun's rays struck it.

I glanced around. Rudi was standing off to one side, the case of diamonds still clutched in his left hand. 'Let's get moving,' he said. 'We need to be off this mountain before the sun gets much higher.'

I walked over to him and lowered my voice. 'Just one more thing first,' I said. 'We leave those diamonds here.'

He gave a brief humourless laugh, stuffed the case into the bottom pocket of his combat trousers, fastened the chain round his ankle and snapped the lock shut. He held the key in his closed fist for a moment, then turned and hurled it outwards, over the lip of the landslip. It glittered as it caught the light, then dropped from sight, tumbling down somewhere into the scree below us.

I shrugged and turned away. We formed a column and moved out, bathed in the strengthening light of dawn. Rudi and Raz led the way with Hendrik and Reuben bringing up the rear. I had the novice's position in the centre of the column, the safest place if we were ambushed and the one from where I could also put the others in the least danger through my inexperience.

Rudi paused for several minutes at the lip of the landslip, scanning the scree-strewn hillside below us, then led us out of the shade into the warmth of the rising sun. We moved along the slope for half a mile until we reached a dry stream bed. Then, half hidden by the cover of the jumble of rocks in the stream bed, we began to descend towards the distant line of the forest at the foot of the slopes.

The gradient eased as we descended. We passed the first stunted bushes and trees on the scree slopes, and we moved more slowly and cautiously as we neared the tree line. We paused on the edge of the forest to give our eyes time to adjust to the dim light under the tree canopy. Then we began to advance through the trees.

Birds and the occasional monkey moved through the roof of the forest high above us and butterflies fluttered through the pools of light where a fallen tree had pierced the canopy and allowed the sun to break through. Insects whined around my ears, feeding hungrily on any exposed flesh. We advanced slowly in total silence, communicating by hand signals. We paused every few yards to watch and listen, and check the GPS.

Boroyende lay no more than fifteen miles ahead of us, yet it would take us at least the rest of the day to reach it.

I could scarcely believe my recklessness in placing my trust in Rudi, but I could see no way that I could have made it through the forest and back without the help of his mercenaries. For all their brutality, these men were trained and experienced jungle fighters.

The fact that Rudi had lied to the others also concerned me. If he was planning some double-cross, he would certainly not want any witnesses to it.

As the slope grew more gradual, the ground became wetter and wetter. We crossed sluggish streams and waded through the first shallow ponds. Then, over the forest floor ahead of us, I saw the beginnings of a swamp. There was no way round it, for it spread for miles across the valley. We just had to go through it.

 **CHAPTER 12**

We were still two miles short of Boroyende as night began to fall. We huddled together, thigh deep in swamp water, as we discussed in whispers our next move.

'It's only two miles,' I said. 'Can't we just keep going?'

Rudi turned a scornful look on me. 'Have you ever tried to move through jungle at night? It's as black as your hat. All you would do is alert every rebel for miles around by the noise you made blundering through the undergrowth and scaring the wildlife.' He shook his head. 'We find some dry ground and bivouac there till morning.'

I knew he was right, but the thought of spending another night so near and yet so far away from Layla tore at my heart.

We stopped at a low hillock rising above the surface of the swamp. Rudi and the others had hammocks, brew kits and survival rations in their backpacks. I had almost nothing.

As dark fell we ate some rehydrated rations and drank a mug of tea, then Rudi ordered Raz and Reuben to keep guard as he and Hendrik settled into their hammocks slung between the trees. I curled up on the ground.

The swamp was alive with the noise of frogs and insects, and mosquitoes fogged the air around me. I barely slept and it was a relief to see the light filtering through the forest canopy as dawn broke.

We ate a frugal breakfast, brewed up some tea, and then moved out again on the trek over the last two miles to the village. After a mile we met rising ground and emerged at last from the dank waters of the swamp into the leaf litter of the forest floor.

The trees began to thin almost at once. As we reached the cultivated land, garden plots slashed and burned from the forest, we advanced slowly and stopped at the tree line. The village appeared utterly deserted, not even a scrawny chicken rooting in the dust.

The mercenaries worked their way through the village, covering each other as they cleared each hut. I followed them, the sense of foreboding growing inside me with each step. I peered into the village carpenter's hut. The neat rows of carefully polished tools had disappeared and the beautiful rocking chair lay in bits.

I moved on to Njama's hut. There were stains of dried blood in the dust just inside the doorway. The interior of the hut had been wrecked and the storage jars and plates had disappeared.

I looked up at the ceiling. The light bulb still hung there, but the glass had been shattered, leaving only a dangling bent and broken filament. It was a similar tale of destruction in every hut in the village; there was no sign of the occupants.

As I came out of the last hut, I saw Rudi and the other mercenaries standing just beyond the edge of the village, staring down into something at their feet. A feeling of dread overwhelmed me.

A crude pit had been dug in the ground where a mound now rose from it, covered in something black that seemed to move and shimmer as I looked at it. As I reached the edge of the pit, Rudi stretched out his rifle and prodded the mound. The black shimmering curtain rose into the air, a cloud of flies lifting to reveal the corpses beneath.

I found myself staring into the dead face of one of Njama's sons. Before I knew what I was doing, I had climbed down into the pit and begun to tear at the bodies, pushing them and dragging them aside, barely aware of the terrible stench of decaying flesh.

Three of Njama's four sons were dead. I dragged their bodies aside in turn and searched through the rest, finding old men and women, children and even babies buried there.

I crawled out of the pit, walked away from the others and stood alone, staring into the forest. I shook my head. 'There's no sign of Layla or Njama or Kaba here.'

'That doesn't mean they're alive. The rebels could have killed them somewhere else, or taken them away with them.' Rudi paused, studying my face. 'They'd certainly have wanted to have their fun with Layla before they killed her.' He was almost laughing at me.

My fists clenched, but this wasn't the moment to fight him. 'They could still be alive. We have to search for them.'

'How? Where? Even if they are alive, they could be anywhere.'

'They won't have strayed far from the village. We could light a signal fire, or fire a shot.'

'Don't be stupid. The only people that would bring running would be the rebels. Now I've kept my part of the bargain, it's time for you to keep yours.'

I thought of Layla lost in the forest around us. I threw back my head and cried out her name. I heard the scrape of steel on steel.

Rudi's rifle was pointing towards me and the safety catch was off. 'You do that again,' he said, 'and I'll leave you in the pit. Now'—he wrinkled his nose as he stepped closer to me—'get down to the river and wash or the rebels will be able to track us from the stench of dead meat and the trail of flies following us.'

I walked down to the river bank, sluiced the stench of death from me with river water and turned to walk back towards the village.

As I did so, I glimpsed a face peering at me from the undergrowth. I froze. Then the leaves parted and Kaba walked into the open. His hair was matted and his ribs showed through his skin but his face broke into a grin at the sight of me. 'You have come for us,' he said.

'Layla?' I hardly dared ask the question.

'She is safe.'

Relief washed over me. 'How many others?'

'Twelve.' The population of the village had been at least eighty.

'Where are they?' I said.

'In hiding a little way from here. I will take you to them.'

'Wait,' I said. 'We must bring the soldiers with us.'

I led him back into the village. His expression darkened when he saw Rudi. 'Why is he here?'

'He's here to help you—to help us all.'

'They're still alive,' I said to Rudi. 'They're near by. We must go and get them.'

His expression was unreadable. He studied me for a long time in silence. Then he shrugged his shoulders. 'Let's get on with it.'

The boy led the way down to the river, stepped into the current and began to wade upstream through the chest-deep water. We followed, holding our rifles above our heads. The river narrowed as it curved away out of sight. Both banks were smothered in vegetation, and branches and lianas hung down over the water, forming a tunnel through which we moved. It was as dark as dusk under the dense vegetation, but ahead I could see the glow of daylight.

We were approaching a sweeping bend in the river. Silt and sand had formed a small beach ending in a sheer rock face. The beach was only a dozen yards wide and at either end it was screened by a curtain of tree branches and lianas.

I glanced upstream and down. The curve of the river hid the beach from sight; the only way to come upon it was to wade the river as we had done or to fight our way through the jungle down to the bank opposite.

Kaba called softly from the shallows, then moved up onto the beach. I saw the foliage stir at the far end and an old woman stepped into the open. She gave an uncertain look from the boy to the semicircle of mercenaries flanking him, then she saw my face. She smiled, turned and said something to the people still hidden behind her.

Then Layla stepped into view. A moment later she was in my arms. I pulled her close and kissed her. She stiffened for a second, then leaned into me, holding my face in her hands, staring into my eyes. 'I'd given you up,' she said. 'I'm sorry that I doubted you.'

'You were right to doubt me,' I said.

She glanced over my shoulder at Rudi and the others. 'But why are they here? Don't tell me they've suddenly discovered a conscience.'

'It's strictly business for them. I bribed Rudi: diamonds for lives.' When I released her and looked up, I saw that the other survivors from the village had also emerged from hiding. There were two small children, a girl, a couple of teenage boys, and a number of older women. Njama was the last to emerge, leaning heavily on the shoulders of two of the women. There were dressings over wounds in his stomach, chest and arm, and his face bore the ravages of pain and grief, but he managed a flicker of a smile as he saw me.

I turned back to Layla. 'Is he fit to travel?'

'Not really, but if he stays here he'll die.'

Rudi took my arm and pulled me to one side. 'If we try to take the old man, we put all our lives at risk.'

'Just the same, he comes with us. I'm not leaving him to die.'

He stared at me in silence, then turned away. 'Come on.'

I lifted Njama onto my shoulders, waded out into the river and followed Rudi and the others back downstream. When we reached the village, I lowered Njama to the ground. Kaba and I helped him as he hobbled up the track and into the village.

Rudi led the way straight through and disappeared into the forest on the far side. As we made to follow him, Njama stopped us. He took a last look at what had once been his village. His eyes filled with tears as he turned his back and walked with us into the forest.

The four mercenaries spaced themselves through our ragged column with Rudi at the head and Hendrik bringing up the rear. We were very vulnerable to attack, however, strung out over forty yards in forest where the visibility was no more than five or six.

We made painfully slow progress at first, working our way through the dense vegetation, but after a while we found an animal track made by pigs or brush deer.

At my insistence, we stopped for a few minutes every hour. As soon as we did so, Njama sank to the ground and closed his eyes, his face grey. Each time, Layla examined him and checked his dressings; the wound in his stomach was beginning to weep again.

She met my gaze. 'He needs to rest.'

'We can't stop yet; we've too far to go.'

She bit her lip. 'All right, but not much further, then he must rest.'

The old man's frail voice cut through our discussion. 'I will make it,' he said. 'I will not let you down.'

We began to wade through the murky water of the swamp. I was soon exhausted from the effort of half carrying, half dragging Njama along, and I could hear his rasping breath at each step.

We collapsed to the ground when we reached the low mound rising above the surface of the swamp, where we'd slept the previous night. Layla examined Njama again. 'He can't go any further without proper rest,' she said.

I looked upwards. The light filtering through the forest canopy was bright; the sun must still have been quite high in the afternoon sky. I hesitated, then nodded. 'That's it,' I said to Rudi. 'We'll have to stop here. Njama can't go any further until he's rested.'

Rudi glowered at me as the other mercenaries clustered around him. 'What is this?' Reuben said. 'A patrol or a picnic in the woods?'

Raz took up the grievance. 'What are we doing here?'

'We're following orders,' Rudi said. 'We have a job to do.'

'Nursemaiding Kaffirs?' Hendrik said. 'Since when has Decisive Measures been interested in that?'

They looked on the point of mutiny. 'Maybe we should level with them,' I said.

Rudi met my gaze with a ferocious scowl and pulled me to one side, out of earshot. 'Need-to-know basis,' he said. 'They don't.' The others gave us sullen stares and I could hear them muttering to each other as we settled down to rest and prepare for the night. Rudi posted Raz and Reuben as guards, keeping them apart, I thought, so that they would have no further chance to share their grievances.

We had little food between us, and though Raz and Reuben shared some of their rations, albeit with ill grace, Rudi and Hendrik kept all theirs for themselves. I cut brushwood and made a crude bed for the old man, raised a few inches above the sodden earth. He lay down, closed his eyes and was asleep at once.

Layla sat by him, her face etched with concern. As night began to fall, we curled up together on the ground.

Layla studied me in the twilight. 'Why did you come back?'

'I finally realised that what you told me was true. You can't escape responsibility by sitting on the sidelines or looking the other way. You've got to take sides and get involved; otherwise you're no better than the rest of them.'

We fell into an exhausted sleep, our arms round each other, but we were awake again before first light. As the light strengthened, we began moving on through the water. Kaba and I supported Njama, carrying him through the deepest parts of the swamp.

A few hours later, we stopped to drink a mug of swamp water, strained through a gauze dressing, and eat a few grains of rice and a piece of dried fruit. When we set off again, Rudi changed the marching order, putting the two younger mercenaries, Raz and Reuben, at the front of the column and bringing up the rear himself with the more experienced Hendrik.

In the gloom under the dense vegetation we could see no more than five yards ahead or behind us. We had been wading in single file through the swamp for almost two hours, when there was a burst of gunfire from the forest behind us. We hurried forward.

Raz and Reuben had stopped dead at the head of the column. They dropped into firing positions at either side of the animal track we were following.

Raz jerked his head at me. 'Take them on ahead,' he said. 'We'll follow when we've cleared the danger.'

Layla took over my role of supporting the old man as I moved to the head of the column. As I had seen Rudi and the others do, I paused every few yards to watch and listen, and kept checking the GPS, trying to keep us on a direct bearing to the helicopter. I lost all track of time as I inched forward through the swamp, my nerves jangling at each noise—the plop of a frog splashing into the water, the faint rasp of a snake's belly as it slithered away through the undergrowth or the cries of birds in the canopy high above us.

At last I could see the land beginning to rise ahead of us. We had reached the end of the swamp. One by one we emerged out of the water onto dry ground.

There was brighter light ahead and we reached a natural clearing where a giant tree had collapsed, tearing a hole in the forest canopy. I hesitated, peering towards the shadows on the far side of the clearing. A track ran through the middle at right angles to our course. I stayed hidden in the undergrowth, looking and listening.

Nothing moved and I heard no sound. After a couple of minutes, I waved the column forward, trying to cover them with the rifle as they crossed the clearing and disappeared back into the forest. Layla, Njama and Kaba had just begun to cross when I saw movement from up the track to my left. I shouted to them, 'Take cover! Fast!'

They dived into cover. I looked back to my left. A woman was walking slowly towards me. I stepped out into the centre of the track and held up my hand, palm out, to show her she had nothing to fear from us. Her face remained nervous, frightened.

That was nothing unusual; these were desperate times, when every stranger was to be feared, but something made me look again. As I peered at her, I saw the black mouth of a rifle poking out from under her arm, and in the dust behind her I saw a double shadow—the woman herself and another figure crouching behind her. I swung up my rifle and shouted at the woman, 'Get out! Get out of the way!'

She gave me a terrified look, whimpering with fright, but she didn't move. I saw the black mouth of the rifle swinging towards me and threw myself back into the cover of the undergrowth. There was the crack of a rifle and a bullet smashed through the vegetation a couple of feet from my head. I rolled sideways and then belly-crawled a few more feet. As I did so I heard another single shot, and then a burst of gunfire shredded the undergrowth where I had been hiding. I slid my rifle forward and raised my head a few inches to peer out through the fronds of a fern towards the clearing.

The woman lay sprawled in the track, apparently dead, a pool of blood slowly widening around her. She had outlived her usefulness to the rebel soldier. He was now moving towards where I had disappeared into the undergrowth. He walked erect, not even bothering to stoop, certain of his own invulnerability.

I took aim, then squeezed the trigger. The rifle was set on semiautomatic. The first couple of rounds ripped through his chest, hurling him backwards. The rest of the burst sprayed high and wide, but he was already dead, slumped over the body of the woman he had killed.

I waved the rest of the column through, urging them on, then I dropped back to the rear. We had gone no more than fifty yards when I heard the sound of pursuit.

I wormed my way into the undergrowth, my rifle pointing back along the track we had made. I heard the sound of people moving fast, crashing through the undergrowth after us. Easing off the safety catch, I squinted along the barrel, drawing a bead where the track disappeared from sight, aiming about three feet above the ground. A figure burst into the open. My finger was already tightening on the trigger when I recognised the burly figure in camouflage fatigues. Rudi had only Raz and Reuben with him.

I called 'Rudi!' and, not wanting to be shot by reflex, I waited until I saw recognition in his eyes before I stood up.

'I saw your handiwork back there on the track,' he said. 'Not bad. We might make a soldier of you yet.' He paused. 'But I didn't think you English gentlemen killed women.'

'I didn't,' I said. 'The gunman killed her.'

He smiled. 'I believe you, English. I believe you.'

'What happened to you?' I said. 'What was the shooting?'

'Rebels. A small group. They won't be troubling us again, but they may have been the advance guard of a larger group.'

'There are only three of you. What happened to Hendrik?'

'Hendrik is dead. The rebels shot him.'

Something in the way he said it made the hairs on the back of my neck stand on end. He pushed past me and began to walk off up the track we were following.

Raz was white-faced and I could see a muscle tugging insistently in Reuben's cheek, counterpointing the rapid blinking of his eyes.

'I'm sorry about your mate,' I said. 'Were either of you with him when it happened?'

Raz shook his head and turned away to follow Rudi. I stood staring at the ground, a growing chill in the pit of my stomach.

 **CHAPTER 13**

We overtook the struggling column within fifty yards and pushed on together, finally beginning the long, slow ascent towards the mountain.

I moved up alongside Rudi as he scanned the open hillside beyond the last of the trees. There was nothing moving on the whole expanse of hillside but, hampered by Njama's wounds, I knew that we would be exposed in the open for at least two hours before we could reach the landslip where the helicopter was hidden.

Rudi took a last look around, then turned to me. 'You go on with the others. We'll loop the track and make sure we're not being followed. If they catch us in the open out there, they'll cut us to pieces.'

I had the feeling that his words concealed more than they revealed.

He stood for a moment and touched his pistol, his ration pack and the grenades attached to his webbing, as if he were carrying out a mental checklist. Then he turned and hurried away. He hissed an order to the other two and they followed him back into the forest.

The rest of us moved out of the trees and we laboured up the hillside, slipping and stumbling over the loose rock and scree.

Njama's head lolled on his shoulders and his mouth hung open. He was exhausted. I handed Layla the rifle and hoisted the old man onto my back. As I stumbled slowly upwards, my head pounded from dehydration. We were still creeping up the dry stream bed and had another fifty yards or so to go to reach the contour line that would take us round to the mouth of the landslip. Then there was an explosion from the forest behind us, followed by a burst of gunfire. I urged the others on and redoubled my own efforts.

I climbed until I thought my lungs would burst, then set Njama down for a moment and turned to look back down the hillside.

Rudi was just beginning to climb the stream bed behind us. He was alone and climbing fast, never once turning to look behind him.

He overtook us just as we reached the landslip. 'Where are the others?' I said.

'We were followed. They threw a grenade. They killed Raz and Reuben. I shot those rebels, but there'll be others. We have to get out of here fast.'

I stared at him.

'What's up with you?' he said. 'Let's go. Let's go.'

I kept staring at him. There was a gap on his webbing where a grenade had been hanging when he'd gone back into the forest.

'I only heard one grenade and one gun firing, Rudi,' I said.

He looked down, following my gaze. When he raised his eyes again, there was a cold murderous look in his eye and I now found myself staring down the barrel of his rifle.

He studied me for a moment, chewing his lip as he pondered his options. Then he shrugged. 'Less people to share the diamonds with, Jack. That's all you need to worry about. Just fly this heli over the frontier, ditch it in the jungle near a city and we walk out with a few million in diamonds each.'

I shook my head. 'No way.'

'You don't have a choice, Kaffir-lover,' he said.

I glanced towards the others and he laughed at me. 'You think that coloured whore or those Kaffirs will help you? If it means saving their own necks, they'll stand there and watch you die.'

Just the same, he moved slightly, trying to keep them in his sight as he confronted me. Njama's son just stood there blank-faced, but I saw Kaba slink away from Rudi towards the rocks. I didn't blame him. I'd have run for it too, if I could.

'Kill me and you're trapped,' I said. 'You can't fly the helicopter.'

'I don't need it. You think in twenty years' Kaffir-killing I haven't learned how to survive in the bush?'

'Then you'd better go ahead and shoot me,' I said. 'Because I'm not going anywhere without these people.'

His jaw worked and I saw his knuckles whiten as he tightened his grip on the trigger. The crack of a rifle shot reverberated from the rock walls around me. A bullet smashed into my shoulder, hurling me to the ground. I tried to push myself upright, then collapsed again as my shattered shoulder gave way beneath me. I stared stupidly at the blood soaking my right sleeve.

I looked up. Rudi's mouth hung open in a silent scream of pain and rage. His head was tilted to one side, and his right arm hung at a strange angle. A dark stain was spreading over his fatigues. I saw his fingers spread and his hand fall limp at his side. The rifle dropped to the ground, its butt streaked with blood.

Rudi turned to face his assailant, but as he did so Kaba struck again, reaching up on tiptoe like a kid stretching for a sweet jar, except that in his hand he held a bloodstained panga. Rudi let out a bellow and aimed a punch at the boy's head with his one good arm, but Kaba ducked underneath it and swung the panga again at the back of Rudi's knees. His hamstrings snapped like guitar strings and he collapsed to the ground.

Rudi and I stared at each other, both sprawled in the dirt, as Kaba advanced and stood over Rudi, his face devoid of expression.

'Kaba! No!' I shouted, but it was too late. The panga was already rising again. He held it two-handed, high over his head for a moment, then brought it whistling down with all his force across Rudi's neck, hacking his head from his body.

Kaba stood motionless, his face impassive as he stared at the dead man. No one moved until Layla got to her feet, walked over to the boy and laid a hand on his arm. He started, but made no resistance as she gently eased the panga from his fingers, and turned him away from the dead body, cradling his head against her chest.

One of the old women led him away as Layla ran to my side. I stifled a yell of pain as her fingers probed the wound. 'It's badly broken,' she said. 'I'll tie off the bleeders and then I'll have to set it and strap it up. I'll give you some morphine. It's going to hurt.'

'No morphine,' I said. 'I've got to fly the heli.'

'With a broken shoulder? You can't.'

'I have to. And you'll have to help me.'

'But I can't fly a helicopter.'

'You can if I tell you how to. If we don't get out of here we'll die, Layla. Either the rebels will kill us, or we'll starve to death. Now patch up my shoulder so I don't bleed to death on the way back and then let's get out of here. But, Layla,' I held her gaze. 'No morphine. I need to be alert or we're all dead.'

'You can't imagine how painful this is going to be.'

'Just do it,' I said.

She gave me a twisted piece of cloth to bite on and then began to clean the wound, picking out fragments of bone and tying off the severed veins. I kept my eyes averted most of the time, but it hurt like hell and I felt waves of hot nausea sweeping over me.

She paused for a moment and our eyes met. She kissed my forehead. 'Hold on,' she said. 'This is the really painful bit. I have to move your arm to set the bone, then I'll strap it across your chest.'

She called to Kaba and one of the women. They knelt either side of me and held me down as Layla straddled my chest and took hold of my arm. Electric stabs of agonising pain shot through me. I heard the dry scrape of bone on bone. The pain built and built until I thought my head would explode. Then I blacked out.

When I came round, Layla was still crouching over me, watching my face. The worry lines etched into her forehead faded as my eyes flickered open and she gave a gentle smile. 'Are you all right?'

My shoulder throbbed with a dull ache. I glanced down. My right arm was strapped across my chest. 'I think so. Help me up.'

She and Kaba supported me as I struggled to my feet. The effort sent more hot waves of pain coursing through me and I had to steady myself against Layla and close my eyes until it subsided.

'It's too soon,' she said.

I shook my head. 'Help me get this net off the helicopter.'

We hauled at the camouflage net and I sent Kaba up to wipe the thick layer of dust off the canopy.

Layla and Kaba then helped Njama to climb into the cab and laid him on the floor. The other villagers clustered around him.

I led Kaba over to Rudi's body. 'We need that case he's carrying,' I said. 'Can you break the chain with the panga?'

He studied it for a moment, then nodded. 'I can get it for you.' He raised the panga above his head and brought it down. There were no sparks and no sound of metal on metal, just a noise that was now all too familiar to me—a dull, wet thud like an axe chopping sodden wood. I looked down. Rudi's left foot had been severed at the ankle. Kaba reached down and pulled the bloodied chain over the stump and offered me the case.

'Just put it in the cockpit of the helicopter,' I said. I turned to Layla. 'Let's get airborne. I can still do most of the work, but you'll have to operate the cyclic for me.'

She stared at me. 'This is madness. I can't help you fly this. We'll crash and be killed. We can walk out instead.'

I shook my head. 'We'd be dead long before we reached the frontier. How long would I or Njama last? Or the old women? Or you? Even Kaba would struggle to make it. It's the only way, Layla.

'I told you all this once before, remember? I can still operate the rudders, the throttle and the collective, all you've got to worry about is the cyclic. The controls are duplicated for the pilot and the copilot. All you have to do is move your cyclic when I tell you. The movements required are very small, absolutely minimal. If I see you do anything wrong, or feel, by the other controls, that you've over-cooked it, I'll get you to correct it. We may fly like a drunk on a rollercoaster, but we will keep airborne. Trust me?'

She studied my face, then gave a slow, reluctant nod.

I smiled with a bravado I was far from feeling. 'Then let's do it, before either of us realises what fools we're being.'

Layla slid the cab door closed, then helped me up into the cockpit. I couldn't get my flight harness over my injured arm, so I remained unstrapped. She put on her own harness, then sat back in the seat as far as possible and closed her eyes.

I settled my feet on the rudder pedals and gripped the collective with my left hand. The pain in my shoulder had subsided a little, but it was still bad enough to make the sweat stand out on my brow, and any movement sent a fresh stab of pain searing through my body.

'Right,' I said. 'Get the feel of the cyclic before we do anything else.'

She opened her eyes and took hold of it in a tentative grip, her forearm resting across her thigh.

'You have to hold the cyclic more firmly than that,' I said. 'When we fire up the engines it'll start to shake around.'

She took a firmer grip on it.

'That's better,' I said. 'Now practise moving it around. Go left . . . right . . . forward . . . back . . . That's fine, except that you're moving it too far. Try again, but no more than a quarter-inch in any direction. Better to have to nudge it further than ram it over and then drag it back again.' I paused. 'Right, helmets on.'

She helped me fasten the strap under my chin, then fixed her own. I turned a little in my seat to look back into the crowded cab and it caused an agonising stab of pain to shoot down my arm. I gasped.

Layla shot me an anxious look. 'All right?'

I nodded. 'Let's get this thing airborne.' Reaching awkwardly across my body with my left hand, I stretched up and pushed the levers into ground idle. I waited until the fresh jolt of pain in my shoulder had subsided a little, then pressed the starter. There was an electric whine over our heads and the left engine began to turn over.

I stared at the RPM gauge, waiting for it to reach double figures, then pushed the fuel switch. The engine roared and I repeated the process for the right engine. When both were running, I checked the gauges and warning panels, then pushed the control into flight idle. I raised the collective gently until the heli lifted on its springs, poised to take flight. I looked at Layla. 'Don't worry. You'll do fine. Just don't panic and keep listening to what I'm telling you. Even if we seem to be out of control, we can pull it all back together as long as neither of us panics.'

I could see her hand shaking with the mechanical vibrations through the cyclic, and her knuckles whitened as she grasped it still more tightly.

'Now, our first problem is to get out of this landslip without touching the sides. If we can do that, the rest should be a doddle. All we'll have to worry about then is landing at Freetown. So, in a moment I'm going to raise the collective, and as I do so I want you to ease the cyclic forward a touch. Don't move it to either side, just forward. There's a fractional time-lag before the heli responds, so don't think it isn't working and give it some more, or we'll be heading down again rather quickly.'

I turned my head to call into the back. Even that slight movement caused another wave of pain. 'All right back there? Hold tight to the sides, we're taking off in a second and it's bound to be a rough flight.' I heard the frail voice of Njama translating what I had said.

'Right, this is it,' I said, and raised the collective. 'Cyclic forward a touch.' As the heli began to lift, sluggish under its heavy burden, Layla moved the control forward. She hesitated and then nudged it forward again. 'That's too much,' I said. 'Wait for the response.'

She corrected it, but the Huey clattered down again and bounced back into the air. Unrestrained by any harness, I was thrown up with it, and then crashed down again onto the seat, jerking the controls around in my hands. I bit my lip as a fresh burst of pain hit me.

The Huey was airborne again, but beginning to drift left. 'Ease it right a fraction,' I said.

'It's not responding.' Again she moved the cyclic further.

'Give it time,' I snapped. 'Move it left.' I saw the rock wall looming beyond her. 'Left now!'

She responded, but overcorrected and we began to drift towards the left-hand rock face. 'Forward,' I said, raising the collective again. The engine note and the beat of the rotors picked up, but we were now both dipping towards the rocky floor of the landslip and drifting dangerously close to its wall. 'Now back and right again. Right!'

We lurched away from the rocks and shot up into the air. I raised the collective to stop us from stalling, but Layla was already making a semi-instinctive correction, pushing the cyclic forward again. We hurtled down, caught the lip of the landslip with a thud that sent us bouncing back high into the air. The disc of the rotors scythed through the air by the right-hand rock wall, shredding the parched shrubs clinging to its face.

'Left, left!' I shouted. 'Forward!'

I raised the collective again and we lurched out of the mouth of the landslip. I heard Layla's indrawn breath as she saw the land falling away below us. 'It's all right,' I said. 'You're doing great.'

I risked a glance at her. Through the Perspex of her visor I could see her hair matted with sweat against her forehead. 'Now we need to pick up some speed,' I said, 'and climb to clear the ridge. Just hold it steady and give it a little forward nudge.'

This time I waited a fraction of a second before raising the collective, realising—not before time—that it was easier for me to adjust to her movement of the cyclic than the other way round.

As I moved the controls, even above the thunder of the rotors, I heard the crack of gunfire. I looked down. 'Shit!' I said. 'Rebels.' The mountainside below us was black with soldiers. Bullets chipped fragments from the rocks around the mouth of the landslip and a moment later there was a whoosh, a crash and a starburst of smoke and flame as a round from an RPG streaked inches past the Huey.

'Climb!' I shouted. 'Back and left on the cyclic. Back and left!'

I yanked the collective upwards, twisting the throttle viciously as I stamped on the rudder pedal, swinging us round to face the cliff. There were cries and groans from the cab as the villagers were thrown around by the manoeuvre.

Rounds continued to clang against the armoured underside of the heli. If the soldier with the RPG got his next shot on target, it would pierce the armour as if it were paper and blast us out of the sky.

We had to put the ridge line between us and the rebel gunner before he could get off another shot, but an even more immediate danger was now threatening us. Taking me at my word, Layla had made the most minimal movement of the cyclic. It was not enough. The rock face just below the ridge loomed in front of the cockpit, filling my vision. 'Back on the cyclic! Back! Back! Give it more!'

Slowly, ponderously, the Huey responded and the nose began to come up. Weighed down by the people in the cab, the engines were screaming as they strained to deliver the power I was demanding through the controls.

Although we were climbing slowly, the ridge line was rushing to meet us. Blue sky showed in the top half of the canopy, but the rest of my vision was filled with black, unforgiving rock. 'We're not going to make it,' I yelled, trying to brace myself for the impact.

There was a crash and a sickening lurch as the skids hit the rock just below the summit. More cries came from the back and I almost passed out with pain. As the heli tipped forward, and even before I had time to speak, Layla had begun to correct, forcing the cyclic back to counter the dip of the nose.

There was another crash and a terrible scraping, gouging sound as the skids bit into the solid rock. The turbines climbed the octaves, shrieking at the strain imposed on them, then the Huey spun to the right and its momentum threw it clear.

At once we were climbing almost vertically, still with the sound of bullets smacking against the metal skin of the heli. The screaming engines faltered at stalling point. 'Forward, now!' I said.

The engines picked up again and we began to level, but rounds were still puncturing the fuselage. 'Forward again. More.'

The sounds of gunfire faded and stopped as we plummeted down the far side of the ridge, out of sight of our pursuers. I fought for control of the Huey and, as soon as we levelled, I piled on the power again, putting as much distance as possible between us and the ridge line before any rebel soldiers reached it.

I glanced at Layla. 'You were fantastic,' I said, as soon as I had got my breath back. 'A natural pilot. Now let's get out of here.'

 **CHAPTER 14**

We flew on into the west. Layla tried hard to hold the Huey in straight and level flight, but we still kept drifting from side to side as she corrected, recorrected and overcorrected the cyclic.

'It's got a mind of its own,' she said.

I could hear the tremor of fear in her voice. 'You're doing great.'

After a few more minutes she was able to hold it within a five degree arc of the direction I wanted us to be facing. We made slow progress, like a ship tacking into the wind, but with every minute we were cutting the distance separating us from Freetown.

I got Layla to push the radio button and spoke to the tower at the airport. 'Mayday. Mayday. Mayday. This is Grizzly One. Pilot wounded, helicopter overloaded, request immediate clearance to land. I repeat, immediate clearance. Over.'

A voice cut through the hiss of static. 'Grizzly One, this is Freetown tower. We have operational military traffic flying from here in support of a ground offensive. Request you divert to Conakry.'

'Negative, tower. I have insufficient fuel and we're close to falling out of the sky and so overloaded we can't even hover. We're coming in from the east, repeat east, and we'll need a clear runway to set down. ETA five minutes. Over and out.'

The radio squawked again at once, but I ignored it. 'Here comes the tricky bit,' I said to Layla.

Almost as soon as the words were out of my mouth, I saw streaks of red and orange tracer stabbing up into the sky. 'We've got to keep moving,' I said. 'And not offer a predictable target.'

'You mean keep flying it the way I have been?' she said. It was a brave attempt at a joke, but her voice cracked as she made it.

We were at 2,000 feet, a questionable range for an assault rifle, but well within range of anything heavier. The tracer bursts kept coming, lines of fire bright enough to show even against the afternoon sun. They began to get our range and the wavering lines cut through the sky towards us.

'Push it right and forward.' As I spoke, I hit the right rudder pedal and dumped the collective. The force of the diving turn pinned me against the side of the cockpit. I couldn't stifle a yell of pain. 'Sorry,' I said. 'But I'm all right, really. Now take it left and pull back.'

I waited until I saw her hand start to move, then raised the collective. Each manoeuvre was greeted by a chorus of screams and cries from the back, for few of the villagers had any handholds and they toppled and slid from side to side as we threw the heli around.

As we continued the evasion, Layla moved the cyclic to send us lurching upwards and downwards, and drifting from side to side in a way that even I could not predict. 'If they hit us it'll be sheer fluke,' I said. 'No gunner in the world could track this pattern.'

If it was hubris, it got the punishment it deserved. A few seconds later, the orange fires of bursting flak flared up across our track. I stamped on the rudder and shouted an order to Layla, but even as she moved the cyclic I heard the tinny rattle of shrapnel against the fuselage and then a crack from the tail boom.

I felt the tail of the heli begin to swing left. The tail rotor countered the torque from the main rotor. If it was damaged, the torque would force the body of the heli around. If it had been destroyed altogether, the heli would gyrate around its own axis until it hit the ground or tore itself apart.

I stamped on the right rudder, trying to counter the swing of the fuselage. There was a heart-stopping pause before I felt it begin to slow. We began to make forward progress again, but if I relaxed the pressure on the rudder it immediately began to spin.

My calf muscles were beginning to ache from the effort of holding down the rudder pedal, and I found it hard to concentrate on what Layla was doing with the cyclic. Our flight became ever more erratic, the Huey staggering across the sky like a drunk.

There was another burst of flak, another rattle as shrapnel knifed into the fuselage and then the clamour of a warning siren.

We had to contend with the smoky, choking stench of burning oil as the pressure gauge on the right engine registered a drop. Almost at once I heard it choking and banging. The altimeter began to unwind in jerks, dropping a few feet, levelling as the engine caught and fired smoothly again, then dropping once more as it spluttered and almost died.

I stared straight ahead, ignoring the flak, willing the heli on towards the airport, now clearly visible ahead.

I called the tower once more. 'Mayday. Mayday. Mayday. Tower, this is Grizzly One. Now losing oil, engine failure imminent. Please clear the airfield and prepare for crash landing. Over.'

The flak faded away behind the heli and I saw below us the front line of the fighting. Nigerian armour was rolling along the airport road towards Freetown.

Now safe from ground fire, I was torn between the need to keep enough altitude to reach the airport and the knowledge that if the engines failed at this height no autorotative landing on earth would save us.

The heli steadied, rose a little and then dipped again. We lurched from side to side as Layla tried to correct with the cyclic. Fresh waves of hot pain jabbed through me as I was thrown around in my seat.

The airfield perimeter was now less than a mile ahead, but the oil-pressure gauge had ceased to register, the engine was banging and clanking, belching filthy black smoke, and the smell of burning and hot metal was almost overpowering.

The effort of forcing down the rudder pedal was making my leg shake and tremble. I let the pressure slip for a fraction of a second and the heli at once slewed sideways. I gritted my teeth and stamped down again, counting silently to myself as I tried to hold it down and faintness and nausea once more threatened to overwhelm me.

I heard Layla's voice from a long way off. 'Hold on, Jack, we're almost there. Hold on.'

We were fifty yards from the perimeter fence when the right engine exploded into flame. The heli gave a sickening lurch. 'Cyclic left. Left!' I shouted as we slid sideways and downwards.

Layla jerked it too far and we began to slip the other way. The perimeter fence loomed ahead of us. The drop had at least allowed a microsecond for the revs to build in the remaining engine. I squeezed another couple of feet of altitude from the feeble increase in power.

Smoke began to fill the cockpit and the heat from the burning engine overhead was fearsome. If we didn't get it down in the next few seconds we might be blown apart in midair.

We had reached the fence. The heli jerked and almost stalled as it snagged the wire, then began to topple sideways. Spontaneously, I released the rudder pedal and kicked down hard on the opposite rudder. Driven by the torque, the tail boom whipped round. The force catapulted us clear of the fence, but the heli smashed down on its right-hand side, shattering the flailing rotors like toothpicks.

I howled in agony as I was thrown across the cockpit and landed full on my fractured shoulder, on top of Layla. As the wave of pain ebbed away, I shouted 'Out! Out! Out! Jump for your lives!'

Black smoke swirled around us, and even through the visor of my helmet I felt the searing heat of the blazing engine. The steel case containing the diamonds had been crushed by the impact. Its twisted lid lay ajar and half a dozen diamonds glittered in the dust of the cockpit floor. I began scrabbling for them.

'Stuff the diamonds,' Layla said. 'Leave them.'

'You get out, I'm right behind you,' I said. 'Run. Get away from the heli.'

As she dropped from sight down the side of the cockpit, the heli burst into flames. With the fire spreading and dense smoke filling the body of the Huey, the bruised and battered villagers scrambled for the cab door. They began to tumble out of it, falling the few feet to the concrete and crawling away from the heli.

Coughing and choking, I fumbled with the steel case, then pushed at the cockpit door. It was stuck fast. Above the roar of the flames licking around the fuselage, I could hear Layla screaming for me to get out. I lay on my back, barely able to breathe for the stinking clouds of smoke enveloping me, and kicked out with my feet. There was a crack and an inrush of air as the door sagged open.

Still clutching the steel case in my good hand, I launched myself outwards and fell heavily to the ground. I lay there winded, my clothes smouldering, until Layla helped me to my feet.

'Did everyone get out?' I said.

She nodded. She helped me up and supported me, an arm round my waist, as I hobbled away from the stricken Huey. The villagers were strung out ahead of me in a ragged line across the concrete.

I heard the clamour of a fire truck, but before it could reach the heli, there was a bang like a sonic boom. We were blown forward, hurled into the dirt as the blast wave flashed over us and burning fragments rained down around us. I looked back. The Huey was a smoking ruin, a tangle of black, twisted metal. Layla helped me up and we moved on again to the dirt and parched grass at the edge of the airfield. Then I sank down, resting my head on my good arm.

Layla took my pulse and pulled off my helmet and laid a hand on my brow. Then she peeled back the dressing to examine my shoulder wound. 'It looks all right,' she said. 'Do you feel OK?'

'Never better.' I began to laugh at the stupidity of my remark, but it ended in a choking fit. 'My shoulder hurts like hell, of course, but thank God we all made it safely. You did a great job to get us here.'

'Are you sure you feel all right? Your speech is slurred again.'

'I'm fine. Just dog-tired.'

I put my hand to my mouth, then pressed it against my shoulder, wincing as if another spasm of pain had hit me.

She reapplied the dressing. Over her shoulder, I saw Colonel Pleydell marching over the concrete towards us, flanked by a posse from Decisive Measures.

I let my head sink onto my chest and half closed my eyes, waiting until I saw the colonel's immaculately polished toecaps come to a halt in front of me before I raised my head again. 'Sorry about the Huey, Colonel,' I said. 'Hope it's insured.'

He stared at me for a moment. 'You left for Bohara three days ago. Where the hell have you been?'

'Engine trouble, Colonel. We were damn lucky I managed to patch it up enough to get back here at all.'

He gave me a dubious look, then waved his hand towards Njama and the others. 'Who the hell are all these people?'

'Human beings. Refugees.'

'Where are the others?'

'Rudi and the guys? They took off into the bush. Said they preferred to take their chances with the rebels than risk the flight back with me. Since I was coming back empty I took the opportunity of bringing these people with me.'

It took him a full minute before the implications of Rudi's disappearance hit him. 'Where are the diamonds?'

I handed him the steel case. He stared suspiciously at the battered lid, then knelt down, opened it and tipped out the diamonds to make a gleaming mound in the dust. He began counting them. When he straightened up again, his face was contorted with anger. 'There should have been seventy-four diamonds in this case. Six are missing.'

'Well, I haven't got any. Maybe they're still in the cockpit. You're welcome to go and search for them. Or talk to Rudi and those guys about it. They just handed me the case; I didn't ask how many were in it.' I paused as if the thought had just struck me. 'Maybe that's why they were so happy to risk it in the bush.'

He stared at me. 'Search him.'

His heavies manhandled me to my feet. I yelled in pain as one took my right arm.

'What are you doing?' Layla said. 'He has a serious wound and a fractured shoulder, and he's lost a lot of blood. Leave him alone and get him an ambulance.'

Pleydell swivelled to look at her. 'Who are you, pray?'

'I'm a paramedic with Medicaid International.'

He sneered at her. 'When I want advice from representatives of communist front organisations, I'll ask for it. This man is suspected of the theft of a number of diamonds and whether you like it or not, he will be searched.'

'It's OK, Layla,' I said. 'I'll be all right.'

The heavies looked to Pleydell for guidance. 'Get on with it,' he said. 'Search him.' Half-apologetically, one of them began to pat me down. 'Not like that,' Pleydell said. 'We're looking for diamonds not a pistol, for Christ's sake. Strip-search him.'

They stripped off my boots and trousers and searched every seam. Then they undid my shirt and body-searched me. They even began pulling back the bandages and peering at my wound, but I let out such a yell that they stopped at once. The sweat on my ashen face should have been enough to convince them that I was not faking.

'That's enough,' Layla said.

Pleydell gave me a long stare. Then a faint smile crossed his face. 'His mouth,' he said. 'Search his mouth.'

His men stared uncertainly from him to Layla.

Cursing, he pushed them aside. I obliged him by opening my mouth. He peered into it, and felt between my teeth and my cheeks with his finger. 'Lift your tongue,' he said.

'What?'

'Lift your tongue.'

I made a show of hesitation, then did as he asked.

He felt around under my tongue then stepped back, wiping his fingers on his trousers.

Pleydell still directed his baleful stare at me. 'Don't think for a moment this is over. I'll have more to say to you when we get back to England. The charter's waiting. I want you aboard inside ten minutes.'

'You don't understand, Colonel,' I said. I looked from him to Layla. Beyond her Njama and the other villagers sat silent and watchful. Layla stared back at me, holding my gaze with a look that told me all I needed to know.

I turned back to face Pleydell. 'I like it here. So as far as I'm concerned, you can stick your orders and your diamonds. I'm going nowhere, I'm staying here.'

Pleydell's mouth worked. 'To hell with you then. You're in breach of contract, and your wages are forfeit. See how long you last without money in this stink-hole of a country.'

He turned and marched away, followed by his men. As our ragged band made slow, shambling progress around the perimeter towards the airport buildings, I saw the Tristar's doors close. The engines fired and it taxied to the end of the runway. A couple of minutes later it took off towards the setting sun.

As the rumble of its engines faded, I turned to Layla. 'Could you change my dressing? Those diamonds are bloody uncomfortable.'

She stared at me for a moment and then began to laugh. She carefully peeled back the dressing and a few moments later she dropped six perfect, if bloodstained, diamonds into my hand.

I turned them over, watching the light shimmering through them, then passed them to Njama. 'These belong to you,' I said. 'You'll need them. Once the rebels are beaten, we've got a lot of rebuilding to do.'

JOHN NICHOL

John Nichol first hit the headlines while serving in the RAF during the Gulf War of 1991. He and his fellow officer, Flight Lieutenant John Peters, were shot down, captured by the Iraqis, tortured and paraded on television. The story captured the popular imagination and the men's book about their experiences, *Tornado Down*, was a best seller. Since then, Nichol has pursued a successful and varied career as a broadcaster and writer.

Decisive Measures is a book that has been in his mind for some time. 'Sierra Leone was in the military news for quite a while before it came into the public eye,' he points out. 'I had been chatting to friends who had been on earlier missions to the country, but when I started to research the area, back in the summer of 1999, it was just too unstable to go and visit.'

Instead, Nichol spoke to many people who had spent time in Sierra Leone, both military and civilian, and read up on the country in newspaper reports and books. 'One book that provided a lot of the inspiration was Ian Fleming's *Diamonds Are Forever*, which is partially set in Sierra Leone and has a lot of information in it. You've got to ask yourself, if Sierra Leone exported bananas instead of diamonds, would there still be British intervention? I rather doubt it.'

The hero of the book, like Nichol himself, is an airman, in this case a helicopter pilot, but although the author is keen to describe the flying accurately, that is not what the novel is about. 'The most important thing to me,' he says, 'is not how to be a helicopter pilot, but the people themselves, the men and women, and how they react to combat and the stressful situations that confront them.'

IN A DRY SEASON

Peter Robinson

When the village of
Hobb's End in Yorkshire
was submerged beneath a
reservoir in the 1950s,
evidence of a terrible
death was concealed.

Forty years on, when the
heat of summer exposes
the bones of a young
woman in the dry valley
bed, the secrets of the
past re-emerge.
DCI Banks, called in to
investigate, finds himself
piecing together clues to
a wartime drama of
sexual rivalry and
thwarted passion.

Prologue

It was the Summer of Love, 1967, and I had just buried my husband when I first went back to see the reservoir that had flooded my childhood village.

I made the journey only a few months after Ronald and I had returned from one of our frequent long spells abroad. Spells that had suited me well for many years. Ronald, too, had suited me well. He was a decent man and a good husband, quite willing to accept that our marriage was one of convenience. I believe he saw me as an asset in his diplomatic career, though it was certainly neither my dazzling beauty nor my sparkling wit that had snared him. I was, however, presentable and intelligent, in addition to being an exceptionally good dancer.

Whatever the reason, I became adept at playing the minor diplomat's wife. It seemed a small price to pay. In a way, I was Ronald's passport to career success and promotion, and—though I never told him this— he was my passport to flight and escape. I had married him because I knew we would spend our lives far away from England, and I wanted to be as far away from England as possible. Now, after more than ten years abroad, it didn't matter very much. I would be quite happy to live out my days in the Belsize Park flat. Ronald, always a shrewd investor, had left me a tidy sum of money. Enough, at least, to live on for some years and to buy myself a new Triumph sports car. A red one. With a radio.

Singing along with 'All You Need Is Love', I headed back to Hobb's

End for the first time in over twenty years. For some reason I enjoyed the raw, naive and whimsical new music the young people were listening to, even though I was in my early forties. It made me long to be young again: young without the complications of my own youth; young without the war; young without the heartbreak.

I don't think I saw another car after I left the main road outside Skipton. It was one of those perfect summer days when the air smells sweet with the perfume of grass and flowers. I fancied I could even smell the warm exhalations of the dry-stone walls. Berries shone like polished garnets on the rowan trees and sheep bleated their plaintive calls from the far dalesides. The colours were all so vibrant—the green greener than ever, the blue of the sky piercingly bright.

Not far beyond Grassington I lost my way. I stopped and asked two men repairing a dry-stone wall. It was a long time since I had heard the characteristic broad speech of the Dales and at first it sounded foreign to me. Finally I understood, thanked them and left.

The old lane stopped at the edge of the woods, so I had to get out and walk the rest of the way along a crooked dirt path. Clouds of gnats whined above my head, wrens flitted through the undergrowth and bluetits hopped from branch to branch.

At last I broke out of the woods and stood at the edge of the reservoir. My heart started to pound, and for a moment I thought I was going to faint. But it passed.

When I had lived there, Hobb's End had been a village in a valley. Now I gazed upon a lake surrounded by forest.

The water's surface, utterly still, reflected the trees and the occasional shadow of a gull or a swallow flying over. To my right, I could see the small dam where the old river narrowed as it flowed into Harksmere. I sat on the bank and stared over the scene.

I was sitting where the old railway branch line used to run, a single track that ran to and from Harrogate, our only real access to the larger world beyond Hobb's End during the war. Many a time had I waited on the platform with rising excitement to hear the distant chugging and whistling of the old steam engine.

As I sat there remembering, time went by. I had started out late from London. Soon, darkness infused the woods around me. A whisper of a breeze sprang up. Then a full moon rose, scattering its bone-white light, in which I fancied I could see clear through the water to the village that used to be there.

I saw a vision of the village as it had been when I lived there, smoke curling from chimneys over the slate and flagstone roofs, the dark mill at the west end, the squat church tower, the High Street curving beside the narrow river, people going about their daily business. In my vision, I could even see our little shop, where I met her for the first time that blustery spring day in 1941.

Chapter One

Adam Kelly loved to play in the derelict houses, loved the musty smell of the old rooms, the way they creaked and groaned as he moved. He loved to leap the gaps between the broken stairs, and hop from rafter to rafter, kicking up plaster dust.

This afternoon, Adam had a whole village to play in.

He stood at the rim of the shallow valley, staring at the ruins below. This was the day he had been waiting for. The future of the universe depended on Adam today; the village was a test, one of the things he had to conquer before advancing to the Seventh Level.

The only other people in sight stood at the far end, near the old flax mill: a man in jeans and a red T-shirt and a woman dressed all in white. They were pretending to be tourists, pointing their video camera here and there, but Adam suspected they might be after the same thing he was. He had played the game often enough on his computer to know that things were never what they seemed.

He half slid and half ran down the dirt slope, skidding to a halt when he reached the red, baked earth at the bottom. The sun beat down and made him sweat at the back of his neck. His glasses kept slipping down his nose. The Talisman was here somewhere, and it was Adam's job to find it. But where to begin? He didn't even know what it looked like, only that there must be clues somewhere.

He crossed the old stone bridge and walked into one of the half-demolished cottages. It smelt like a bad toilet.

Sunlight slanted in through the space where the roof had been. In places, the heavy stone flags that formed the floor had shifted and cracked, and thick gobbets of mud oozed up between them.

There was nothing in this house. Time to move on.

Outside, Adam noticed an outbuilding near the bridge, about seven feet high, with a slanting flagstone roof still intact, the kind of place that had perhaps once been used to store coal or keep food cold. Whatever it had been, The Destructors had left it largely alone. Here, at least, was a structure he could mount to get a clear view.

On one side a number of stones stuck out like steps. Carefully, Adam rested his weight on the first one. It was slippy, but it held fast. He started to climb, and soon he was at the top.

He pulled himself onto the roof. It was easy enough to walk on. But when he got to the middle the thick stone slabs gave way beneath him. With a scream, he plunged down into the darkness.

He landed on his back on a cushion of mud; his left wrist cracked against a fallen flagstone and his right arm, stretched out to break his fall, sank up to the elbow.

As he lay there, winded, looking up at the square of blue sky above him, he saw two of the remaining roof slabs tilt and fall towards him, each one about three feet square and six inches thick, enough to smash him to a pulp if it hit him. But he couldn't move.

They seemed to drift down in slow motion. He felt no panic, no fear, just acceptance. He knew there was nothing he could do to avoid whatever fate had in store for him. This must be the Seventh Level, he thought as he held his breath, waiting for the impact.

One slab fell to his left and embedded itself in the mud; the other fell to his right and cracked in two against one of the floor flags.

So he had been spared. He felt light-headed. There was nothing seriously damaged, he thought, as he started to move his limbs slowly. His left wrist hurt a lot, but it didn't feel broken. His right arm was still thrust deep in the mud. He tried to wiggle his fingers under the mud and they brushed against something hard.

It felt like a cluster of smooth, hard spindles, or a bundle of short rods. Curious, he pushed his arm in deeper and grasped the object tightly; then he tugged. The mud made sucking, slurping sounds as, inch by inch, he dragged his arm free. Finally, he was able to see the object he was holding.

It was the skeleton of a hand.

BANKS STEPPED BACK to survey his handiwork, whistling along with the habanera from *Carmen*, which was playing loudly on the stereo. Not bad for an amateur, he thought, dropping the paintbrush in a bowl of turpentine, and a definite improvement over the mildewed wallpaper he had stripped from the walls of his new home yesterday.

He particularly liked the colour. The man at the DIY centre said it was calming, and Banks needed all the calming he could get. The shade of blue reminded him of the Greek island of Santorini, which he and his estranged wife Sandra had visited. He hadn't bargained on that memory, but he thought he could live with it.

Pleased with himself, Banks pulled a packet of cigarettes from his top pocket. Only three gone since morning. Good. He was trying to restrict himself to ten a day or less. He walked into the kitchen and put on the kettle for a cup of tea. The telephone rang.

Banks turned off the stereo and picked up the receiver.

'Dad?'

'Brian, is that you? I've been trying to get in touch with you. Where are you?'

'I'm staying at Andrew's flat.'

'Where?'

'Wimbledon. Look, Dad . . .'

'Isn't it about time your exam results were out?'

'Yeah, well, that's why I was calling you . . .'

'Go on,' Banks prompted. 'You *did* pass, didn't you?'

'Course I did. It's just that I didn't do as well as I expected.'

'What did you get?'

Brian almost whispered. 'A third.'

'A *third*? That's a bit of a disappointment, isn't it?'

'Yeah, well, it's more than you ever got.'

Banks took a deep breath. 'It doesn't matter a damn what I did or didn't get. It's you we're talking about. Your future. You'll never get a job with a third-class degree. Do you want to be another statistic? Another unemployed yobbo?'

'Thanks a lot, Dad. Nice to know you believe in me. Anyway, as a matter of fact, I'm not on the dole. We're going to try and make a go of it. Me and the band.'

'You're *what*?'

'Andrew knows this bloke who's got a studio, like, and he's said we can go down and make a demo of some of my songs. People like us. We've got gigs coming out of our ears. We're making plenty of money.'

'Money's not everything. What about the future? What are you going to do when you've peaked at twenty-five and you don't have a penny in the bank? Have you talked to your mother about this?'

'Well, I sort of thought, maybe . . . you could do that.'

Him talk to Sandra? They couldn't even discuss the weather these days without an argument.

The kettle started whistling.

'I think you'd better ring her yourself,' he said.

'Thanks a lot, Dad,' Brian said, his voice hard-edged with bitterness. 'I thought you'd understand. I thought you *liked* music. Go see to your kettle.'

'Brian—'

But Brian hung up. Hard. Banks stormed into the kitchen and turned off the kettle. He didn't even feel like a cup of tea any more.

Before he had a chance to think any further, the phone rang again. This time it was Chief Constable Jeremiah 'Jimmy' Riddle. Must be my lucky day, Banks thought. The new call also meant that Banks couldn't dial 1471 to get Brian's Wimbledon phone number, which he had neglected to ask for. He cursed and reached for his cigarettes again. At this rate he'd never stop. Bugger it. He lit up.

'Skiving off again, are you, Banks?'

'Holiday,' said Banks. 'It's official. You can check.'

'Doesn't matter. I've got a job for you to do. Now.'

Banks wondered what kind of job Jimmy Riddle would call him off his holidays for. Ever since Riddle had had to reinstate him reluctantly after dishing out a hasty suspension the previous year, Banks had been in career Siberia, his life a treadmill of reports. Not one active investigation in nine months. Surely the situation wasn't going to change this easily? There had to be more to it; Riddle never made a move without a hidden agenda.

'We've just got a report in from Harkside,' Riddle went on. 'A young lad found some bones at the bottom of Thornfield Reservoir. It dried up over the summer. Used to be a village there, I gather. Anyway, there's nothing but a section station in Harkside, and all they've got is a lowly detective sergeant. I want you down there as senior investigating officer.'

'Old bones? Can't it wait?'

'Probably. But I'd rather you get started right away.'

'What about Harrogate or Ripon?'

'Too busy. Don't be so ungrateful, Banks. Here's the perfect opportunity for you to drag your career out of the slump it's fallen into. You'll find the local DS already at the scene. Cabbot's the name.'

Banks stopped to think. What the hell was going on here? A detective chief inspector would not, under normal circumstances, be dispatched to the remote borders of the county simply to examine a pile of old bones. Riddle was clearly not doing him any favours; he must have got tired of confining Banks to the station and had thought up some new and interesting way to torture him. He obviously believed the case would be boring and unpleasant, and that it would lead to certain failure and embarrassment.

'And, Banks. Don't forget your wellies.'

Banks could have sworn he heard Riddle snigger.

He dug out a map of the Yorkshire Dales. Thornfield was the westernmost in a chain of three linked reservoirs built along the River Rowan, which ran more or less east from its source high in the Pennines until it turned south and joined the River Wharfe near Otley. Banks traced a route on the map. Getting there would probably take an hour or more.

After a quick shower, Banks picked up his car keys and wallet, then walked out into the afternoon sunshine. Before setting off, he stood for a moment, resting his hands on the warm stone wall, and looked down at the bare rocks where the Gratly waterfalls should be. A quote from a T S Eliot poem came to his mind: 'Thoughts of a dry brain in a dry season.' Very apt. It had been a long drought; everything was dry that summer, including Banks's thoughts.

He wished his conversation with Brian hadn't ended the way it had. Well, he thought, getting into the Cavalier, Brian was old enough to make his own decisions. If he wanted to chuck everything in for a shot at fame and fortune, that was up to him, wasn't it?

At least Banks had a real job to do. Jimmy Riddle had made a mistake this time. No doubt he believed he had given Banks a filthy, dead-end job; but he had overlooked the one overriding characteristic Banks possessed, even at his lowest ebb: *curiosity*. Feeling, for a moment, like a grounded pilot suddenly given permission to fly again, Banks drove off.

THE BOOK SIGNING STARTED at half past six, but Vivian Elmsley had told her publicist, Wendi, that she liked to arrive early, get familiar with the place and have a chat with the staff.

There was already a crowd at a quarter past. All of a sudden, after twenty novels in as many years, Vivian Elmsley was a *success*. Her Detective Inspector Niven series had made it to the small screen; the first three episodes had been shown, to great critical acclaim, and Vivian had become about as familiar a face to the general public as a writer ever is. She had been interviewed by Melvyn Bragg on *The South Bank Show* and had featured prominently in *Woman's Own* magazine. After all, becoming an 'overnight success' in one's seventies was quite newsworthy.

At 6.30 on the dot, Adrian, the event organiser, introduced her, and to a smattering of applause Vivian picked up her copy of the latest Inspector Niven story and began to read. About five minutes was enough, she reckoned. Anything less made her look as if she couldn't wait to get away; anything more risked losing the audience's attention.

After the reading, people formed an orderly queue, and Vivian signed their books, pausing to chat briefly with everyone, asking if they wanted any specific sort of dedication and making sure she spelt their names right.

Vivian looked down at her hand as she signed. Talon-like, almost skeletal, dotted with liver spots. Hands were the first to go, she thought. The rest of her was remarkably well preserved. She had remained tall and lean. She hadn't shrunk or run to fat like so many elderly women. Steel-grey hair, pulled back tightly and fastened at the back, created a widow's peak over her strong, thin face; her deep blue eyes were almost oriental in their slant, her nose was slightly hooked and her lips thin. Not a face that smiled often, people thought. And they were right, even though it had not always been so.

'You used to live up north, didn't you?'

Vivian looked up, startled. The man appeared to be about sixty, thin to the point of emaciation, with a long, gaunt, pale face and lank fair hair. He was wearing faded jeans and a gaudy, short-sleeved shirt. He held the book out for her to sign.

Vivian nodded. 'A long time ago.' Then she looked at the book. 'Who would you like me to sign this to?'

'What was the name of the place where you lived?'

'It was a long time ago.'

'Did you go by the same name then?'

'Look, I—'

'Excuse me, sir.' It was Adrian, politely asking the man to move along. He did as he was asked, and left.

Adrian brought Vivian a glass of wine and she carried on signing.

When it was all over, Adrian and the staff suggested dinner, but Vivian was tired. All she wanted to do was go home to a long hot bath and a gin and tonic.

'I'll drive you home,' said Wendi.

Vivian laid her hand on Wendi's forearm. 'No, my dear,' she said. 'I'll be perfectly all right. I'm not over the hill yet.'

Wendi blushed. She had probably been told that Vivian was prickly. Someone always warned the publicists.

'I'm sorry. I didn't mean to suggest anything like that. It's my job.'

'A pretty young girl like you must have far better things to do than drive an old lady home.'

Wendi smiled and looked at her watch. 'Well, perhaps if I phone my boyfriend we could get some last-minute theatre tickets. But only if you're sure.'

'Quite sure, my dear. Good night.'

As she walked to the tube, Vivian thought again about the strange man in the bookshop. She didn't like to dwell on the past but he had pushed her into a reminiscent mood, as had the recent newspaper photographs of the dried-up Thornfield Reservoir.

The ruins of Hobb's End were exposed to the light of day for the first time in over forty years, and the memories of her life there had come crowding back. Vivian shuddered as she walked down the steps to the underground.

BANKS PAUSED FOR BREATH after his walk through the woods. From where he stood on the edge of Thornfield Reservoir, the entire elongated bowl of ruins lay open below him, about a quarter of a mile wide and half a mile long. On the opposite embankment, the difference in soil colours showed where the water line had been. Beyond the high bank, Rowan Woods straggled away to the north.

The most dramatic part of the scene lay directly below: the sunken village itself, bracketed by a ruined mill on a hillock to the west, and by a tiny packhorse bridge to the east. There was no road surface, but the course of the old High Street by the river was easy enough to make out. It eventually forked at the bridge, one branch turning towards Rowan Woods, and the other continuing over the bridge, then out of the village along the embankment to Harkside.

Below him, a group of people stood by the other side of the bridge, one in uniform. It was a warm evening, and he was sweating by the time he got to the bottom of the narrow path. The valley bottom wasn't as muddy as it looked. Most of the exposed reddish-brown earth had been caked and cracked by the heat.

As he crossed the packhorse bridge, a woman walked towards him. 'Excuse me, sir,' she said. 'This is a crime scene. I'm afraid you can't come any further.'

Banks smiled. He knew he didn't look like a DCI. He wore a blue denim shirt open at the neck, with no tie, light tan trousers and black Wellington boots. 'Why isn't it taped off, then?' he asked.

The woman frowned. She was in her late twenties or early thirties, long-legged, tall and slim. She was wearing blue jeans and a herringbone jacket that followed the contours of her waist. Her chestnut hair fell in waves to her shoulders and she had a smooth, tanned complexion. She wasn't conventionally good-looking, but her looks showed character and intelligence. And the red wellies set it all off nicely.

Banks smiled. 'Do I have to throw you off the bridge before I can cross, like Robin Hood did to Little John?'

'I think you'll find it was the other way round, but you could try it,' she said. Then, after they had scrutinised one another for a few seconds, she squinted, and said, 'You'll be DCI Banks, then?'

'DS Cabbot, I presume?'

'Yes, sir.' She smiled. It was no more than a twitch of her mouth and a brief flash of light behind her eyes, but it left an impression.

'And these people?' Banks pointed to the man and woman talking to the uniformed policeman. The man was aiming a video camera at the outbuilding.

'They were scouting the location for a TV programme when they saw the boy fall. They ran to help him. Seems they also had their camera handy. I suppose it'll make a nice little item on the evening news.' She scratched the side of her nose. 'We'd run out of crime-scene tape at the section station, sir.'

'There's nothing we can do about the TV people now,' Banks said. 'You'd better explain to me what happened. All I know is that a boy discovered some old bones here.'

DS Cabbot nodded. 'Adam Kelly. He's thirteen. I sent him home. He seemed a bit shaken up, and he'd bruised his wrist and elbow. Nothing serious. He was walking on the roof and it gave way under him. Lucky he didn't break his back.' She pointed at the outbuilding. 'The rafters must have rotted. Anyway, the mud broke his fall, his arm got stuck in it, and he pulled up a skeleton of a hand.'

'Human?'

'Don't know, sir. I mean, it *looks* human to me, but we'll need an expert to be certain. I've read that it's easy to mistake bear paws for human hands.'

'*Bear paws?* When was the last time you saw a bear around these parts?'

'Why, just last week, sir.'

Banks paused a moment, saw the glint in her eye and smiled. There was something about this woman that intrigued him. Most junior police officers, when questioned about their actions by a senior, generally either let a little of the 'Did I do the right thing, sir?' creep into their tone, or they became defensive. But DS Cabbot simply stated things as they had occurred, completely self-assured without being at all arrogant or insubordinate.

'Right,' he said, 'let's go and have a look.'

DS Cabbot led the way. Banks followed her to the outbuilding.

It was about six or seven feet square. Banks stood in the doorway and looked at the depression in the mud where the boy had landed, then at the two heavy slabs of stone on either side. DS Cabbot was right; Adam Kelly had been very lucky indeed.

His gaze alighted on the skeletal hand curled round the edge of a broken stone slab. The bones were dark and clotted with mud, but it looked like a human hand.

'We'd better get some experts in,' he said. 'Then we'll need a forensic anthropologist. In the meantime, I haven't had my tea yet. Is there somewhere nearby we might be able to get a bite?'

'The Black Swan in Harkside's your best bet.'

'Have you eaten?'

'No, but—'

'You can come with me, then, fill me in over a meal.'

VIVIAN ELMSLEY FELT bone-weary when she got home from the signing. She put her briefcase down in the hall and walked through to the living room. Most people would have been surprised at the modern chrome-and-glass decor, but she far preferred it to the antiques and knick-knacks that so often cluttered up old people's houses.

She poured a stiff gin and tonic and made her way to her favourite armchair. Supported by chrome tubes, upholstered in black leather, it leaned back at just the right angle to make reading, drinking or watching television sinfully comfortable.

Vivian glanced at the clock. Almost nine. She would watch the news first. After that, she would have her bath and read.

The news was the usual rubbish. Politics, for the most part, a botched assassination attempt in the Middle East. Then, towards the end, came one of those little human-interest bites.

This one made Vivian sit up and take notice.

The camera panned a cluster of familiar ruins as the voice-over

147

explained that the drought had brought the lost Dales village of Hobb's End to light for the first time since it had been flooded in 1953. The camera angle changed, and she could see a group of people standing by the bridge.

'Today,' the voice-over went on, 'a young boy exploring the scene discovered something he hadn't bargained for.'

It was a mystery worthy of Miss Marple, the narrator went on, part of a skeleton was discovered, not in a cupboard, folks, but under the muddy floor of an old outbuilding. How could it have got there? The police were refusing to comment at this early stage.

Vivian let her body sag in the chair, and took a deep breath. Then she reached for her gin and tonic. The programme was well into the weather forecast by the time she had recovered from the shock.

When she felt a little calmer, she went into the study and dug through her filing cabinet for the manuscript she had written in the early 1970s, a few years after her last visit to Thornfield Reservoir. She carried it back through to the living room. It had never been intended for publication. In many ways, it had been a practice piece, one she had written when she became interested in writing after her husband's death. She had written it when she thought the old adage 'Write about what you know' meant 'Write about your own life'. Now she still wrote about what she knew—guilt, grief, pain, madness—only she put it into the lives of her characters.

As she started to read, she realised she wasn't sure exactly what it was. A memoir? A novella? She had tried to stick to the facts, had even consulted her old diaries for accuracy. But because she had written it at a time in her life when she had been unclear about the blurred line between autobiography and fiction, she couldn't be sure which was which. Would she see it any more clearly now? There was only one way to find out.

DS CABBOT LED the way to Harkside in her metallic purple Astra, and Banks followed her along the winding streets lined with limestone and gritstone cottages.

They parked beside the village green, where a few scattered trees provided shade for the benches. Old people sat in the late-summer dusk as the shadows grew long, watching the world go by. The essentials were arrayed around the green: a bank, newsagent's, butcher's, grocer's, a fifteenth-century church and three pubs.

'Do you live here?' Banks asked.

'For my sins, yes, sir.'

They walked over to the Black Swan, a whitewash-and-timber façade with gables and a sagging slate roof. Inside, a few tourists and ramblers lingered over after-dinner drinks at rickety wooden tables. Banks walked to the bar with DS Cabbot, who asked the barmaid if they could still get food.

'Depends what you want, love,' she said, and pointed to a list on the blackboard.

Banks decided on a beef and Stilton pie with chips. DS Cabbot ordered a salad sandwich, no chips.

'Diet?' Banks asked.

'No, sir. I don't eat meat. And the chips are cooked in animal fat. There's not a lot of choice.'

'I see. Drink?'

'Like a fish.' She laughed. 'Actually, I'll have a pint of Swan's Down Bitter. I'd recommend it very highly.'

Banks took her advice and was glad that he did. He had never met a vegetarian beer aficionado before.

They took their pints over to a table by the open window and Banks fished out his cigarettes. 'Do you mind?' he asked.

She shook her head. 'I usually manage to control my cravings.'

'Reformed?'

'A year.'

Banks lit up. 'I'm thinking of stopping soon myself.'

'Best of luck.' DS Cabbot took a sip of beer and smacked her lips. 'Ah, that's good. Do you mind if I ask you something?'

'No.'

She leaned forward and touched the hair at his right temple. 'What's that? The blue bit. I didn't think DCIs went in for dye jobs.'

Banks felt himself blush. He touched the spot she had indicated. 'It must be paint. I thought I'd washed it all off.'

She smiled. 'Never mind. Looks quite nice, actually.'

Banks tried to concentrate on the job at hand. 'I called my sergeant on the way here,' he said. 'He'll organise a team to dig out the bones tomorrow morning. A bloke called John Webb will be in charge. He's studied archaeology so he ought to know what he's doing. You can phone around the universities in the morning, see if you can come up with a friendly forensic anthropologist. In the meantime, tell me all about Thornfield Reservoir.'

DS Cabbot leaned back in her chair and crossed her legs at the ankles. She had swapped her red wellies for a pair of white sandals, and her jeans rode up to reveal tapered bare ankles. Banks wondered again what she could possibly have done to end up in such a god-forsaken outpost as Harkside.

'Thornfield Reservoir was created in the early fifties,' she began. 'The village had already been empty a few years by then. Since the end of the war, I think. It was called Hobb's End.'

Their meals arrived. Banks stubbed out his cigarette. 'Why was it empty? What drove people away?'

'Nothing drove them away. It just died. Places do. The flax mill was the village's *raison d'être* in the nineteenth century. The mill owner, Lord Clifford, also owned the land and the cottages. Very feudal.'

'You seem to be an expert.'

'I read up on the area when I came here. Anyway, the flax mill started to lose business—too much competition—and old Lord Clifford died. After the Second World War people moved away to the cities or to the other dales. Finally, the new Lord Clifford sold the land to Leeds Corporation Waterworks. They rehoused the remaining tenants, and over the next few years they created the reservoir.'

'So our body, if indeed there is one, and if it's human, has to have been down there since before the early fifties?'

'Unless someone put it there this summer.'

'I'm no expert, but from what I've seen it looks older than that.'

'Whoever buried it there could have moved it from somewhere else.'

'I suppose it's possible.'

'Whatever happened, there's no way a body could have got under those stone slabs on the outbuilding floor without a little human intervention, don't you think, sir?'

IT WAS A BLUSTERY AFTERNOON in April 1941, when she appeared in our shop for the first time. Even in her land girl uniform: the green V-neck pullover, biscuit-coloured blouse, green tie and brown corduroy knee breeches, she looked like a film star.

She wasn't very tall, perhaps about five foot two or three, and the drab uniform couldn't hide the kind of figure I've heard men whistle at in the street. She had a pale, heart-shaped face, perfectly proportioned nose and mouth, and the biggest, deepest, bluest eyes I had ever seen. Her blonde hair cascaded from her brown felt hat. I was immediately put in mind of Hardy's novel, *A Pair of Blue Eyes*. Like Elfride Swancourt's, this land girl's eyes were 'a misty and shady blue, that

had no beginning or surface . . . looked *into* rather than *at'*.

'I don't suppose you've got five Woodbines, have you?' she asked.

I shook my head. 'Sorry, we don't have any cigarettes at all.' It was one of the toughest times we'd had in the war thus far: the Luftwaffe was bombing our cities to ruins, the U-boats were sinking Atlantic convoys and the meat ration had been dropped to one and tenpence a week, but here she was, bold as brass, a stranger asking for cigarettes! I was lying, of course. We did have cigarettes, but what small supply we had we kept for our regular customers.

She broke into a bright smile. 'I didn't think you would have,' she said, 'but it was worth asking. Oh well, can't be helped.'

'Are you the new land girl at Top Hill Farm?' I asked, curious now.

She smiled again. 'Word gets around quickly, doesn't it? That's me. Gloria Stringer.' Then she held her hand out. Her hand was soft and slightly moist, like a summer leaf after rain. Mine felt coarse and heavy wrapped around such a delicate thing. 'Gwen Shackleton,' I muttered. 'Pleased to meet you.'

Gloria looked around. 'Not a lot to do here, is there?'

I smiled. 'Not a lot.' I knew what she meant, but it still struck me as an odd thing to say. I got up at six o'clock every morning to run the shop, and on top of that spent one night a week fire-watching. I also helped with the local Women's Voluntary Service.

I had heard how hard a land girl's job was, of course, but to judge by her appearance, you would swear that Gloria Stringer had never done a day's hard physical labour in her life. But in this, as in most of my first impressions about Gloria, I was quite wrong. She could spend the day hay-making, threshing, milking, snagging turnips, yet always appear fresh and alive, with energy to spare.

On first impressions, she struck me as being vain, common, shallow and selfish. Not to mention beautiful, of course.

Then Michael Stanhope walked in.

Michael Stanhope was something of a village character. A fairly successful artist, somewhere, I'd guess, in his early fifties, he was wearing a rumpled white linen suit, a shabby lavender shirt and a crooked yellow bow tie. He also wore his ubiquitous broad-brimmed hat and carried a cane with a snake-head handle. As usual, he looked quite dissipated. He had at least three days' stubble on his face, and emanated a sort of general fug of stale smoke and alcohol.

A lot of people didn't like Michael Stanhope because he wasn't afraid to say what he thought and he spoke out against the war. I quite liked him, in a way, though I didn't agree with his views. Half the time he only said what he did to annoy people.

'Good morning, my cherub,' he said, as always, though I felt far from cherubic. 'I trust you have my usual?'

'Er, sorry, Mr Stanhope,' I stammered. 'We're all out.'

'All out? Come, come now, girl, that can't be. I'll bet if you looked in the usual place,' he said, leaning forward and rapping on the counter with his cane, 'you would find them.'

I knew when I was beaten. Mortified, I reached under the counter and brought out two packets of Piccadilly.

'That'll be one and eight, please,' I said.

'Outrageous,' Mr Stanhope complained as he dug out the coins, 'the way this government is taxing us to death to make war.'

When I glanced at Gloria guiltily, she smiled at me and shrugged.

Mr Stanhope must have caught the gesture.

'Ah, I *see*,' he said, turning his gaze fully towards Gloria and admiring her figure quite openly. 'Do I take it that you were enquiring after cigarettes yourself, my dear?'

Gloria nodded. 'As a matter of fact, I was.'

'Well,' said Mr Stanhope, 'I'll tell you what, perhaps we can come to some sort of arrangement. I have but one stipulation.'

'Oh,' said Gloria, narrowing her eyes. 'And what might that be?'

'That you smoke in the street every now and then.'

Gloria started to laugh. 'That won't be a problem, I assure you.'

And he handed her one of the packets.

I was flabbergasted. Cigarettes weren't cheap or easy to get.

Instead of protesting that she couldn't possibly accept them, as I would have done, Gloria simply said, 'Why, thank you very much, Mr . . .?'

He beamed at her. 'Stanhope. Michael Stanhope. It's my pleasure, my dear. It's a rare treat indeed to meet a woman as comely as thyself around these parts.' Then he moved a step closer and scrutinised her, quite rudely, I thought, rather like a farmer looking over a horse he was about to buy.

Gloria stood her ground.

'You know, you really must visit my studio, my dear. See my etchings, as it were.' And with that, Mr Stanhope was gone.

In the silence that followed, Gloria and I stared at one another for a moment, then we both burst out giggling. I told her I was sorry for deceiving her, but she waved the apology aside. 'You have your regulars to attend to,' she said.

'I must apologise for Mr Stanhope, too,' I said. 'I'm afraid he can be quite rude.'

'Nonsense,' she said. 'I rather liked him. And he did give me these.'

She opened the packet and offered me a cigarette. I shook my head. She put one in her mouth and lit it with a small silver lighter. 'I can see these will have to last me a while.'

'I can put some aside for you in future,' I said.

'Would you? Oh, yes, please! That would be wonderful. Now if I might just have a look at that copy of *Picture Goer* over there, the one with Vivien Leigh on the cover—'

But before I could get the magazine for her, Matthew dashed in.

Gloria turned at the sound of the bell, eyebrows raised in curiosity. When he saw her, my brother stopped in his tracks and fell into her eyes so deeply you could hear the splash.

THE FIRST THING Banks did when he got back to the cottage that night was check the answering machine. Nothing. Damn it. He wanted to put things right after his miserable cockup on the phone earlier that day, but he still had no access to Brian's number in Wimbledon. Sandra might know, of course, but the last thing he wanted to do was talk to her.

Banks poured himself a whisky, lit the last cigarette of the day and took his drink outside. The cottage stood on a narrow, unpaved lane about fifty yards west of Gratly. Before the drought it had been an ideal spot for ramblers to stop and admire the falls, but at night there was never anyone there. Banks liked to stand out there in the evening. It helped him to think, get things sorted.

Tonight, sharp starlight pricked the satin sky, along with the lights of a distant farmhouse; a gibbous moon hung over the valley, and the square church tower stood solid against the night.

Banks thought again about the odd way he'd come to live in this isolated limestone cottage. Over his last few months alone in the Eastvale semi, he had drifted so far from himself that he hadn't even cleaned or tidied the place. He spent most of his evenings out in pubs and his nights falling asleep half-drunk on the sofa, takeaway cartons piling up in an ever-widening circle around him. In April he seemed to reach his lowest ebb. There was a new man in Sandra's life, a photojournalist called Sean. As a result, Banks was full of anger and self-pity. When Sandra decided that their separation was to be permanent, they sold the semi.

After the sale, Banks began to seek isolation. When he first saw the cottage from the outside, he didn't think much of it. The view of the dale was terrific, but it was a squat, ugly little place that needed a lot of work. A typical Dales mix of limestone, grit and flag, it had originally been a farm labourer's cottage. Inside, the place smelt of camphor and mould, and all the furniture and decor seemed dark and dingy. Downstairs was a living room with a stone fireplace at one end; upstairs, only two small bedrooms. But when he walked into the kitchen he experienced a feeling of well-being and peace. He *knew* he had to have the cottage.

The cottage became his long-term project—his therapy, and his refuge. Working on the cottage was like working on himself. Both needed renovating, and both had a long way to go. Somehow he had lost his way over the past year, and he wanted to find a new one. So far, he had fitted some pine cupboards in the kitchen, installed a shower unit, and painted the living room. It hadn't kept the depression away completely, but made it more manageable.

Banks stubbed out his cigarette and went back inside. As he got ready for bed, he thought of the skeletal hand, possibly human; of DS Cabbot, definitely human; and of Hobb's End, that lost, ruined village suddenly risen from the depths with its secrets.

Chapter Two

Banks watched from the edge of the woods the next morning as the Scene of Crime Officers slowly lifted the skeleton from its muddy grave under the expert direction of John Webb.

First, they had to take down the wall next to which the bones were buried, then they made a trench round the area and dug down until the bones were exposed, about three feet below the surface. Next they slipped a thin sheet of metal into the earth under the bones, and finally they got it in place, ready to lift out.

The bones came up on the metal sheet, still packed in earth, and four SOCO pallbearers carried it up the slope, where they laid it out on the grass at Banks's feet. It was just eleven and DS Cabbot still hadn't shown up. Banks had already talked to Adam Kelly, who hadn't been able to add anything to his previous statement. He was still shaken, but Banks sensed a resilience in him. The little adventure had done him no lasting harm, and he would enjoy celebrity status among his school pals for a while.

Banks stared at the filthy, twisted shape at his feet. The bones had taken on the muddy brown colour of the earth they had laid in for so long. The skull looked full of it—mud in the mouth, the nose, the eye sockets—and some of the long bones looked like rusted metal pipes.

The SOCOs had already photographed the skeleton during every stage of its excavation and now went back down and started their detailed search of the area, digging deeper and further afield. John Webb also searched through the dirt for any objects that had been buried at the same time.

Banks leaned against a tree trunk and watched Webb work. He was tired; most of the night he had tossed and turned, and the morning heat made him drowsy. Giving in to the feeling for a moment, he closed his eyes and rested his head on the tree. He was at the edge of sleep when he heard a rustling behind him, then a voice.

'Morning, sir. Rough night?'

'Something like that,' said Banks, moving away from the tree.

'Sorry I've been so long,' said DS Cabbot. 'A lot of university profs are still away on holiday. Anyway, I've tracked down a Dr Ioan Williams, University of Leeds, a physical anthropologist with experience in forensic work. He said if we could get the remains to the university lab, he'd manage a preliminary look by early evening.'

'Good,' said Banks. 'The sooner we know what we're dealing with here, the better.'

If the skeleton had been lying there for a hundred years or more, the investigation wouldn't really be worth pursuing. On the other hand, *if* it turned out to be a murder victim, buried there during or since the war, there was a chance that the killer was still alive.

'Want me to supervise the move?' Webb asked.

Banks nodded. 'If you would, John.'

Webb looked at his watch. 'With any luck, we can have it in the lab by one o'clock.'

'I need to know a lot more about the village,' Banks said to DS Cabbot. He pointed towards the ruins of the cottage near the bridge. 'The outbuilding clearly belonged to that cottage, so I'd like to know who lived there and who the neighbours were. It seems to me that we've got three possibilities. Someone used the empty village as a dumping spot to bury a body during the time it was in disuse—'

'Between May 1946 and August 1953. I checked.'

'Right. Or the body was buried while the village was still occupied, before May 1946, and the victim was buried not far from home. Or it was put there this summer. It's too soon for speculation, but we do need to know who lived in that cottage before the village emptied out, and if anyone from the village was reported missing.'

'Yes, sir.'

'Where are the parish records now?'

'I don't know. I imagine they were moved to St Jude's in Harkside.'

'They might be worth a look if you draw a blank elsewhere. There's the local newspaper, too. And, DS Cabbot?'

'Sir?'

'Look, I can't keep calling you DS Cabbot. What's your first name?' She smiled. 'Annie, sir. Annie Cabbot.'

'Right, Annie Cabbot, do you happen to know how many doctors or dentists there were in Hobb's End?'

'I shouldn't imagine there were many. Most people probably went to Harkside.'

'Try to find out, anyway. It's a long shot, but if we can find any dental records matching the remains, we'll be in luck.'

'I'll look into it, sir. And what should I do next year?'

Banks smiled. 'I'm sure you can conscript one of your PCs to help. Do you happen to know if anyone who lived in Hobb's End is still alive, maybe living in Harkside now?'

'I'll ask Inspector Harmond. He grew up around these parts.'

'Good. I'll leave you to it and see these bones off to Leeds with John. Meet me at the lab at six o'clock. In the meantime,' he said, 'here's my mobile number. Ring me if you come up with anything.'

'Right you are, sir.'

BANKS WAS AN ODD FISH, Annie thought as she drove back to Harkside. She'd heard a few rumours. She knew, for example, that Chief Constable Riddle hated him, that Banks was under a cloud, though she didn't know why. Someone had even hinted at fisticuffs between the two. Whatever the reason, his career was on hold.

Annie had also heard that Banks's wife had left him not too long ago. Not only that, but there were stories going around that he had a woman in Leeds. She had heard him described as a loner and a skiver. He was a brilliant detective gone to seed, they said, over the hill and burnt out since his wife left.

On first impressions, Annie liked him. She certainly found him attractive, and he didn't look much older than mid-thirties, despite the scattering of grey at the temples of his closely cropped black hair. He seemed tired, but she could sense that the fire still smouldered somewhere behind his sharp blue eyes. On the other hand, perhaps the fire she sensed was simply embers, just about to cave in on themselves. Well, if Annie had learned one thing over the past couple of years, it was not to jump to conclusions about anyone.

She parked beside the section station and walked inside. Only four of them worked directly out of the station: Inspector Harmond, Annie and PCs Cameron and Gould. They seemed a pretty decent bunch of men, as men go. She certainly felt no threat from any of them. PC Cameron was married with two kids, to whom he was clearly devoted. Gould seemed to be one of those rare types who have no sexual dimension whatsoever, content to live at home with his mum and add stamps to his album. Inspector Harmond was, well, avuncular.

The office area of Harkside police station was open-plan—apart from Inspector Harmond's office, partitioned off at the far end. Annie's desk took up a corner, part of which included a side window. It wasn't much of a view, only the cobbled alley, a gate and the back wall of the Three Feathers, but at least she was close to a source of light and air. These little things mattered so much, Annie had discovered. She had had her shot at the big time, the fast track, with all its excitement, but it had ended badly for her. Now she was slowly rediscovering what mattered in life.

Harkside was generally a law-abiding sort of community, so there wasn't a lot for a detective sergeant to do. There was plenty of paperwork to keep her occupied, but it was hardly a high-overtime posting, and there were slack periods. That also suited her fine.

She headed first to the coffee machine and filled her mug, then she knocked on Inspector Harmond's door.

Harmond looked up from his desk. 'Annie. What is it, lass?'

'Got a minute?'

'Aye. Sit down.'

In his early fifties, Harmond seemed content to be a rural inspector for the rest of his working life. He had a pleasant, open face. The features were a bit coarse, and a few black hairs grew out of the end of his misshapen potato nose, but it was the kind of face you could trust.

'It's this skeleton thing,' she said, sitting. 'DCI Banks wanted to know if anyone who used to live in Hobb's End lives here now.'

Harmond scratched his temple. 'You remember Mrs Kettering, the one whose budgie escaped?'

'How could I forget?' It had been one of Annie's first cases in Harkside.

Inspector Harmond smiled. 'I know she used to live in Hobb's End. Remember where she is now?'

'Up on the Edge, isn't it?'

The Edge was what the locals called the fifty-foot embankment that ran along the south side of Harksmere Reservoir. Only one row of cottages overlooked the water, separated from the rest of Harkside village by about half a mile of open countryside.

'Anyone else?'

'Not that I can think of. Not offhand, at any rate. Leave it with me, I'll ask around. You'll keep me informed?'

'I will.'

'And, Annie?' Harmond scratched the side of his nose. 'This DCI Banks. I've heard a bit about him. Better watch yourself, lass.'

BEFORE I TELL YOU what happened next, let me tell you a little about myself and my village. My name, as you already know, is Gwen Shackleton, which is short for Gwynneth. My father died before the war began, and by 1940 my mother was an invalid, suffering from rheumatoid arthritis. Sometimes she was able to help out in the shop, but the brunt of the work fell to me.

Matthew helped me as much as he could, but university kept him busy most of the week and the Home Guard took up his weekends. He was twenty-one, but despite the call-up the Ministry was encouraging him to finish his engineering degree at Leeds University. They believed that his training would come in useful in the forces.

Our little newsagent's-cum-general store was about halfway along the High Street, and we lived above it. We didn't sell perishable goods, just things like newspapers, sweets, cigarettes, tea and tinned goods—depending, of course, on what was available.

Though most of the able-bodied men had joined up, the village had never seemed busier. The old flax mill was operating at full strength and most of the married women worked there. The military wanted flax for parachute harnesses and other things.

There was also a big RAF base about a mile away, and the High Street was often busy with Jeeps and lorries. The airmen sometimes came to the village pub—the Shoulder of Mutton—except when they went to Harkside, where there was much more to do.

These things aside, though, I think that at first the war impinged upon us very little. Even with rationing, our diets didn't change as much as those of city folks, for we had been used to eating plenty of vegetables, and in the country there were always eggs, butter and milk.

Perhaps the hardest thing to get used to was the blackout. We had to tape up our windows to prevent damage from broken glass, and we also had to hang up the heavy blackout curtains. On moonlit nights, especially if there was a full moon, the effect could be spectacular: the hills were dusted with silver powder, and the stars glittered like cut diamonds on black velvet. But on cloudy or moonless nights, people bumped into trees and even cycled into the river. You could use a torch if you wrapped the light with several layers of tissue paper, but batteries were scarce. All car and bicycle lights had to be masked, too. There were a lot of car accidents, until petrol became too scarce and nobody drove any more except on business.

The day before Gloria Stringer arrived, the war hit closer to home: Matthew got his call-up papers, and was due to report for his medical in Leeds in two weeks.

DS CABBOT WAS JUST PARKING her Astra when Banks arrived at Dr Williams's lab just off the main campus. He watched her get out and stepped up beside her.'

She turned. 'Ah, sir.'

Banks smiled and nodded towards the building. 'Let's go inside.'

He followed her up the steps. This evening she was wearing a mid-length black skirt and matching jacket over a white blouse. She was also carrying a black leather briefcase. Much more businesslike. Banks caught a brief whiff of jasmine as he walked behind her.

He pressed the intercom and got them buzzed in.

Dr Ioan Williams waited for them on the first-floor landing. He was a tall, rangy fellow with long, greasy blond hair and wire-rimmed glasses that magnified his grey eyes. Much younger than Banks had expected, Dr Williams wasn't wearing a white lab coat but was dressed casually in jeans and a T-shirt advertising Guinness. His handshake was firm, and judging by the way he lingered over DS Cabbot, his mind was not 100 per cent focused on science.

'Come in,' he said, leading the way down the corridor and opening the lab door.

In the centre of the room the skeleton lay on a long table. The bones looked different now that Williams's assistants had been to work on them. Much of the crusting remained, but the skull, ribs and long bones were easier to examine. They were still a dirty yellow-brown, but at least the whole resembled something more like a human being.

'There are a number of odds and ends my lads found,' Williams said. 'They're over there on the bench.'

Banks looked at the collection of filthy objects on the lab bench along one wall. It was hard to make out what they were: A ring? Shreds of old clothing?

'Can you get them cleaned up and sent over?' he asked.

'No problem. Now let's get down to work.'

Annie took out her notebook.

'First of all,' Williams began, 'let me confirm, just for the record, that we *are* dealing with human remains, most likely Caucasian.'

'What about DNA analysis?' Banks asked.

Williams grunted. 'People seem to think DNA analysis is some sort of miracle answer. It's not. Right now, I can tell you a hell of a lot more than any DNA could. May I continue?'

'Please do. But get a DNA analysis done, anyway. It might be useful for determining identity.'

Williams nodded. 'Very well.' He turned back to the skeleton. 'The height of the subject was easy enough to determine: a hundred and fifty-five centimetres.'

'What's that in feet and inches?' Banks asked.

'Five foot two.' Dr Williams looked over and smiled at DS Cabbot. 'But I can't be sure about the eyes of blue.'

Annie gave him a chilly smile. Banks noticed her roll her eyes when Williams had turned away.

'Also, you are dealing with the remains of a young woman. In general,' Williams explained, 'a male skeleton is larger, the bone surfaces rougher. The male skull is thicker.'

'Well, what do you know,' Annie muttered.

Williams laughed. 'Anyway, in this case, the pelvis is intact, and that's the easiest way for the trained eye to tell. The female pelvis is wider and lower than the male's, to facilitate childbearing.' Williams ran his hand over the skeleton's pelvic bone. 'This pubic curve is definitely female, and here, the sciatic notch is also unmistakably female. Much wider than a male's.' He looked at DS Cabbot again, but Annie kept her head down.

Williams picked up a small magnifying glass from the lab bench and handed it to Banks. 'And look at this.' Williams pointed to where the two pelvic bones joined at the front of the body. Holding the glass Banks could just about make out a small groove.

'That's a parturition scar,' Williams said. 'It's caused by the stresses that attached ligaments put on the bone.'

'So she'd given birth to at least one child?'

'Well,' Williams went on, 'there's only a single pit on either side of the pubis, which would strongly suggest that she only gave birth once in her life.'

'How old was she when she died?'

'I'd have to do more comprehensive tests to be certain of that.'

'What do you have to go on at the moment?'

'Well, there's epiphysial union, for a start. Here, at the very ends of the long bones in both the arms and the legs, the epiphyses have all firmly united with the shafts, which doesn't usually happen until the age of twenty or twenty-one. But look here.' He pointed towards the collarbone. 'The epiphysis at the sternal end of the clavicle, which doesn't unite until the late twenties, has *not* united yet. So I'd say about twenty-two to twenty-eight.'

'Any idea how long she's been down there?'

Williams folded his arms. 'Well, there are certain indications that we're dealing with recent, as opposed to archaeological remains. What do you notice most about the bones?'

'The colour,' said Banks.

'Right. And what does that tell you?'

Banks wasn't too sure about the usefulness of the Socratic method at a time like this, but he had found that it is usually a good idea to humour scientists. 'That they're stained or decayed.'

'Good. Good. Actually, the discoloration is an indication that they have taken on some of the colour of the surrounding earth. Then there's this.' He pointed to several places on the skeleton. 'The bone surface is crumbling, or flaking. Now if you take all this into account, then I'd estimate it's been down there for a few decades. As we already know, it's unlikely she was buried after 1953. I'd go back about ten years from there.'

'Nineteen forty-three?'

'Hold on. This is a very rough guess. The rate of skeletal decay is wildly unpredictable. Obviously, an odontologist will be able to tell you a bit more, narrow things down, perhaps. There are a number of tests I can carry out. But I'll need more information about soil, mineral content, bacterial content, temperature fluctuations and various other factors. I'll visit the site first thing in the morning and take some samples.' He looked at Annie. 'Perhaps DS Cabbot here would be willing to escort me there?'

'Sorry,' said Annie. 'Far too busy.'

His eyes lingered on her. 'Pity.'

'Visiting the site's no problem,' Banks said. 'I'll arrange for a car and make sure the SOCOs are expecting you. Can you tell us anything at all about cause of death?'

'I think I can help you a little with that, though it's not really my area of expertise, and you should definitely get your Home Office pathologist to confirm this.'

'Of course.'

'See those markings on the bones there?' Dr Williams pointed to triangular notches on several of the ribs and the pelvic area.

Once Banks saw them he knew he'd seen them before. 'Stab wounds,' he muttered.

'Exactly. See those little curls of bone there, like wood shavings? They're still attached to the bone, and that only happens with living bone. There's no sign of healing. If she'd remained alive after these injuries, the bones would have healed to some extent, starting about ten days after the injury. Add to that the fact that the position of these wounds indicates the blade would certainly have pierced vital organs, and I'd conclude that she was stabbed viciously, more than once, almost certainly causing death.'

Banks looked at Annie Cabbot.

'Murder, then,' she said.

THE FOLLOWING MORNING Mrs Ruby Kettering was squatting in the garden spraying her dahlias. She looked up as Annie opened the gate and introduced herself.

'I know who you are,' the old lady said, placing her hands on her thighs and pushing herself to her feet. 'I remember you. You're that nice policewoman who found Joey, my budgie.'

Mrs Kettering was wearing a red baseball cap, a loose yellow smock and baggy white shorts down to her knees.

'What can I do for you?' she said, wiping the streaks of sweat and soil from her brow with her forearm.

'It's about Hobb's End. I understand you used to live there.'

Mrs Kettering nodded. 'Seven years Reg and me lived there. From 1933 to 1940. It was our first home together, just after we got married. Listen, dear, would you like a cold drink? Lemonade, perhaps?'

'Thank you.'

'We can sit over there,' Mrs Kettering said. She pointed to a flagstone patio where two deck chairs sat, half in the sun.

'That'll be just fine,' Annie said, walking over.

Mrs Kettering disappeared inside the house. Annie settled herself into one of the deck chairs, stretched out her legs and luxuriated.

'Here we are, dear,' said Mrs Kettering, coming back out with a tray. She offered a tall glass to Annie, then took the other for herself, set the tray aside and sat down.

'Hobb's End,' Mrs Kettering said. 'That takes me back. What do you want to know?'

'As much as you can tell me,' Annie said. And then she told Mrs Kettering about the skeleton.

'Yes, I saw something about that on the news. A young woman, about five foot two, with a baby?' Mrs Kettering repeated, brow knotted in concentration. 'Well, there was the McSorley lass, but she'd have been well over thirty by the time we left. No, dear, I can't honestly say anyone comes to mind. The far cottage, you say, the one by the fairy bridge?'

'Fairy bridge?'

'That's what we used to call it. Because it was so small, only fairies could cross over it.'

'I see. That's right.'

Mrs Kettering pulled a face. 'Sorry, love, it's a blank. I certainly don't remember any young woman living there.'

'Never mind,' said Annie. 'What can you tell me about the village itself? What sort of people lived there?'

'All sorts, really. Shopkeepers, milkmen, publicans, farm labourers, dry-stone wallers, van drivers, salesmen of one sort or another. We even had our very own famous artist. Michael Stanhope. Well, he's not very fashionable these days. Come with me a minute.'

She struggled out of her deck chair and Annie followed her into the house. Mrs Kettering pointed to a large watercolour that hung over the dark wood mantelpiece. 'That's one of his,' she said. 'He gave it to me as a going-away present. Don't ask me why, but he took a bit of a shine to me. Maybe because I wasn't a bad-looking lass at the time.'

Annie had a passion for art. She stared at Stanhope's painting. 'Is that Hobb's End before the war?'

'Just after war broke out, actually. It was painted from the fairy bridge, looking towards the mill.'

Annie stood back and examined the work carefully. The first thing she noticed was Stanhope's peculiar use of colour. The season was autumn, and he seemed to take the hues and tones hidden deep in stone, fields, hillsides and water and force them out into the open, creating a pattern of purples, blues, browns and greens. It was uncanny, almost surreal in its effect. Next, she noticed the subtly distorted perspective. The mill was there, perched on the rise in the top left corner, and though it *should* dominate the scene, somehow it didn't. The church managed more prominence through its dark and subtly menacing square tower.

The rest of the composition appeared simple and realistic enough: a busy village high-street scene whose people reminded her of Bruegel's. The villagers were shopping, gossiping, pushing prams. A man straddled a roof repairing a chimney; a tall girl stood arranging newspapers in a rack outside the newsagent's shop; a butcher's boy was cycling down the High Street. Normal life. But there was something sinister about it. If you looked long enough, you could almost believe that the man on the roof was about to drop a flagstone on some passer-by, and that the butcher's boy was wielding a cleaver ready to chop off someone's head.

The only characters who looked attractive were the children playing in the shallows of the river, splashing one another, paddling. Some of them looked angelic; all of them looked innocent. There was something religious, ecstatic, in the children's aspects, and the water brought to mind baptism. It was a powerful work.

In the bottom right-hand corner, just above the artist's signature, stood the outbuilding where the skeleton had been found, next to a small cottage. A wooden sign announced the name: BRIDGE COTTAGE.

'What do you think?' Mrs Kettering asked.

'Have you noticed the way everyone looks? As if—'

'As if they were all either hypocrites or sadists? Yes, I have. That's Stanhope's vision. I must say I didn't see Hobb's End like that at all. Would you like to go back out to the garden?'

Annie followed Mrs Kettering outside and sat down again.

'What became of Stanhope?'

'I think he stayed in the village until the bitter end, and then I heard he moved to a small studio in London. But I don't think he managed to find a foothold in the big city art world.'

Annie sat quietly for a moment, taking it all in. 'Bridge Cottage,' she said. 'It looked neglected in the painting.'

'I noticed that, too,' said Mrs Kettering, 'and it made me remember something. I think an old lady lived there. Bit of a recluse, so I can't tell you anything about her. I just remembered, looking at the painting, that some of the children thought she was a witch. I'm sorry I can't be of much help.'

Annie stood up. 'You *have* been helpful. Believe me. Thank you.'

WHEN MATTHEW MET GLORIA that first time, I could feel their immediate attraction like that eerie electric sensation you get before a storm. It scared me; I don't know why.

From that first April meeting, events progressed quickly between them. That very afternoon, Matthew showed her round the village. A few days later they went to the pictures in Harkside and then to the May Day dance there. I was helping out behind the refreshments counter, and I could see the way they danced so close together, the way they looked at one another.

I wasn't at all surprised when Matthew announced that he had invited Gloria to tea one Sunday. Mother was in one of her states, so the preparation all fell to me.

I was listening to *The Brains Trust* after putting the rabbit stew on to simmer, when Gloria popped her head round the door, Matthew right behind her. Mother was still titivating herself in her bedroom.

Gloria's golden hair, parted on the left, tumbled in long wreaths of sausage curls over her shoulders. She was wearing a blue blouse with padded shoulders and puffed sleeves tucked into a simple black skirt with silver buttons down the side. On her lips was just a trace of lipstick. I felt dowdy in my plain old pinafore dress.

'Look what Gloria's brought for us,' Matthew said, holding out a pint of milk and half a dozen eggs. I thanked her.

'Hello, Gwen,' Gloria said. 'I should have known you'd be a *Brains Trust* fan. Tell me, who's your favourite? Joad or Campbell?'

'Joad. He's the most intelligent, the best-read, the most eloquent.'

'Hmm. Probably,' said Gloria, sitting down on the sofa. Matthew sat next to her looking like the proud new owner of . . . well, of something. 'I like Campbell,' she said. 'He's more entertaining.'

'I wouldn't have thought you listened to something like that,' I said, regretting my rudeness almost as soon as the words were out.

Gloria just shrugged. 'I've heard it once or twice.' Then her eyes lit up in that way they had. 'But you're right. If I had a wireless, I'd listen to nothing but music all day long.'

'You don't have a wireless?' Surely everyone had a wireless.

'Mr Kilnsey won't have one in the house. He's rather a strict sort of Methodist, you know. Thinks they're the devil's loudspeaker.'

'Oh, good heavens,' said Matthew, shaking his head.

Gloria nudged him. 'It's true! He really talks like that. Anyway, I don't mind. All I do is work and sleep there.'

'I must go and see to the food,' I said. I put the kettle on to make us all some tea, then I peeled a few potatoes and prepared the carrots and parsnips. We had some onions from the garden and some rhubarb for a pie. If I say so myself, it was a good meal.

The kettle boiled. I made tea and carried it through. With rationing, you had to be sparing, and the tea was a lot weaker than we were used to. With sugar rationed at only a pound a fortnight, and most of that in the rhubarb pie, the three of us had all stopped taking it. I didn't know about Gloria, so I offered her some.

'I gave it up,' she said. 'Actually, I've got a far better use for my sugar ration.' She shook her curls. 'If you mix it with warm water, you can use it as a setting lotion.'

'It must make your head feel terribly sticky,' I said.

She laughed. 'Well, sometimes it's hard to get my hat off, I can tell you. But that can be quite a blessing in the wind.'

At that moment, Mother made her grand entrance. She walked slowly because of her arthritis and her stick tapped against the bare floorboards. She was wearing one of her old flower-patterned frocks, a small, frail-looking figure, a little stooped, with a round, ruddy, pleasant face. It was a kind face, and she was a kind woman.

'What a lovely blouse, my dear,' Mother said after the introductions. 'Did you make it yourself?'

'Yes,' said Gloria. 'I managed to scrounge a bit of parachute silk, then I dyed it. I can make one for you, if you like. I've got a bit more put away up at the farm.'

'Good heavens, my dear, you don't want to waste your time making fancy clothes for an old crippled woman like me. No, what I've got will do to see me out.'

The Brains Trust ended and a special about Jerome Kern came on. Gloria liked that better; she had heard all the songs in her beloved

Hollywood musicals. Mother and Gloria got talking about how they both loved Fred Astaire and Ginger Rogers in *Swing Time*.

We turned the wireless off while we ate. 'So, my dear,' said Mother when the stew was served, 'tell us all about yourself.'

'There's not much to tell, really,' Gloria said.

'Oh, come, come. Where are you from?'

'London.'

'Oh, you poor girl. What about your parents?'

'They were both killed in the bombing.'

'Oh dear, I'm so sorry. When was this?'

'Last year. September. I'm all alone now.'

'Nonsense, my dear,' said Mother. 'You've got us.'

I almost choked on my rabbit. 'It's not as if we're adopting her or anything, Mother,' I managed.

'Don't be so rude, Gwen. People have to pull together.'

'Anyway,' Matthew said, 'Gloria's away from all that now, aren't you, darling?'

She looked at him with those big beautiful eyes of hers, adoration just dripping out of them like treacle. 'Yes,' she said. 'I am. And I'm never going back.'

'Is there no one left?'

'No one. I was out visiting a friend a few streets away when the air raid came. I thought my family would go to the underground like we always did in air raids, but they didn't make it in time. My grandparents lived next door, and they were killed, too.'

We were all silent for a few moments, digesting the matter-of-fact horror of what Gloria had just told us.

'What made you decide on a godforsaken place like Hobb's End?' Mother asked.

'That's where they sent me, the Land Army. I was just glad to get away to the countryside.'

After the rhubarb pie, Matthew and Gloria lit cigarettes. Then Matthew cleared his throat and said, 'Mother, I invited Gloria here tonight because, well, we have something to tell you.'

My heart started to thump against my rib cage.

'We want to get married.'

I gaped at Matthew: tall, dashing, handsome, that charming lock of dark brown hair always slipping over his eye, the dimples at each side of his mouth when he smiled, the clear eyes and strong chin. And then I looked at Gloria, saw her radiance.

At that moment, I hated her.

'Ah,' said Mother. 'You do, do you?'

'Very much,' said Gloria, taking Matthew's hand. 'I know we haven't known one another for long, but it's wartime and—'

Mother interrupted her. 'Have you thought, though, that Matthew might be going far away soon?'

'We've thought about that, Mother,' he said. 'Even though I passed the medical, I'll still have my military training to do after the degree, and there's a good chance I'll be able to come home every weekend until after Christmas.'

'Matt will be at Leeds University until July,' Gloria said, 'then he'll go wherever they send him for training. I know it's not perfect. We'd love nothing more than to be together *all* the time, but we know that's not realistic.'

I couldn't believe it; she called him *Matt*. How could she? He had always been Matthew to Mother and me.

'A lot of couples are waiting to marry,' Mother said. 'Until times are less uncertain.'

'But a lot of people are getting married, too,' Matthew argued, 'making the best of the time they have. If anything happens to me in the forces, I'll die a far happier man for having been married to Gloria. Even if it was only for a day.'

Mother glanced at me. 'What do you think about all this, Gwen?'

I swallowed. 'Me? Well, I suppose if it's what they really want to do, then there's nothing we can say to stop them.'

'Good old Gwen,' said Matthew. 'I knew I could depend on you.'

'Where will you live?' Mother demanded. 'It's not that we wouldn't have you, but there's not enough room here, you know.'

'We're going to live in Bridge Cottage,' said Matthew.

Mother frowned. 'What? That run-down hovel by the fairy bridge?'

'Yes. I've talked to Lord Clifford's agent, and he says that the evacuees there are moving out next week. I know it'll need a lot of fixing up, but I'm good with my hands. And it's only five shillings a week.'

'What about children? Have you thought about that, too?'

That sad look came over Gloria's face the way it did sometimes, a dark cloud blocking the sun. 'We haven't planned to have children,' she said. 'Not yet, anyway.' Then she smiled again. 'After the war, though, we'll see. Things will be different then.'

Mother was silent for a moment, then she said, 'You've thought of everything, haven't you?'

Matthew beamed. 'Everything, Mother. Please say you'll give us your blessing. Please!'

Mother looked at Gloria again. 'And you have no living relatives, my dear?'

'None. But you *did* say I've got you, didn't you?'

Mother smiled. 'I did, didn't I? Go on, then, you have my blessing.'

SOME MORNINGS, Vivian Elmsley liked to walk up Rosslyn Hill to Hampstead High Street, take a table outside one of the cafés and linger over her morning coffee to think about the book she was working on; she would sit and scribble a few ideas as she sipped.

Today, though, the book was far from her mind. She opened her newspaper. The item she was looking for appeared on an inside page.

North Yorkshire Police indicated yesterday that the skeletal remains found under Thornfield Reservoir, on the site of a village called Hobb's End, were those of a female murder victim. Detective Chief Inspector Alan Banks said that the body is that of a woman in her twenties. All indications are that she was stabbed to death. Preliminary information indicates that they are dealing with a twentieth-century crime. Anyone with information is asked to get in touch with the North Yorkshire Police.

So they knew that much already. Her hand trembling slightly, Vivian put the newspaper down.

It was funny, she thought, how over the years she had managed to distance herself from the past: the years with Ronald; her early struggles as a writer after his death; the slow rise to success; the television series. Before Ronald, she had thought her life completely blighted by fate. Instead, it had been far more fulfilling than she could ever have dreamed. But there is always a price to pay, and that was the deep, gnawing guilt that, while it fuelled her imaginative flights of fancy, brought on black moods and sleepless nights.

Vivian glanced back at her newspaper, folded open at the Hobb's End item, and sighed.

Well, it shouldn't take the police long now, should it? And then what would become of her hard-earned peace?

BANKS STARTED with Brian's university administration office, and ten minutes later, after a few white lies, he had managed to convince the assistant to break her 'strict code of privacy'. On the pad in front of him was Andrew Jones's telephone number in Wimbledon. When he dialled the number, no one picked the phone up, and there was no answering machine.

As soon as he put it down, the phone rang. It was John Webb.

'I've just picked up the stuff we dug up with the Hobb's End skeleton,' he said. 'Dr Williams's lads have given it a good clean.'

'What did you find? Not much, I imagine.'

'Actually, you'd be amazed at the things that *do* survive. I found a few buttons and some metal clips that might have come from a brassiere or a suspender belt. I also found some small leather shoes.'

'So you're saying she was buried in her clothes?'

'Looks like it.'

'Anything else?'

'Yes, some other material, black and heavy. Definitely not clothing. Some sort of curtains, perhaps?'

'Did you find a wedding ring?' he asked.

'I think so. That's what it looks like all right.'

'Any sign of the murder weapon? Most likely some sort of knife. Handbag or a purse? Anything with identification.'

'Sorry, no. Just what I've told you.'

'OK, thanks a lot, John.'

'No problem. I'll have it sent over to you later today.'

Though the health fascists had finally succeeded in banning smoking from every police station in the country, Banks lit a cigarette. He had his own office. With the door closed and the window open, who would know? Banks started to drift into pleasurable fantasies involving Annie Cabbot and her red wellies.

Dream on, he told himself. The truth was that Annie Cabbot wouldn't have him, and he wouldn't try it anyway. He was too old to go out on dates and worry about whether a good-night kiss would be welcome. He wouldn't know where to begin.

He had had only one sexual encounter since Sandra left, and that had been a disaster. In his cups at a farewell party in the Queen's Arms, Banks had picked up a woman called Karen something-or-other. Karen was tipsy and definitely frisky. Without much preamble, they went back to his place where, later, Banks awoke around four in the morning with a pounding headache, a naked woman wrapped around him and a burning desire to be alone. He never saw her again.

The telephone dragged him out of his depressing memory. It was Geoff Turner, the forensic odontologist.

'Geoff. Any news?'

'Nothing dramatic. Too soon for that. But I was keen to make a start. What I wanted to do first of all was confirm Dr Williams's estimate of her age. He's right. The third molars are up—wisdom teeth—but the apexes haven't quite closed yet, nor have the medial sides of the incisal sutures. The third molars don't usually come up until your early twenties. The apexes are usually closed by the age of twenty-five and medials by thirty. Which makes her mid-twenties.'

'Thanks, Geoff. Any idea how long she's been down there?'

'What few fillings there are seem to indicate fairly recent dental work, not later than the fifties, if that's any help. We're not talking top-quality dental work here. There are several missing teeth—pretty clean extractions—and signs of neglect, which may indicate we're dealing with someone who couldn't afford the best treatment. Another possibility is wartime.'

'Really? Why do you say that?'

'Think about it. Most of the good young dentists and doctors were in the forces, and there were only old dodderers left. Poor equipment. Repairs were hard to get done.'

'Right. I didn't think of that. Thanks. I owe you, Geoff.'

'Best of luck, Alan. Talk to you later.'

Banks put down the receiver and thought about what he had just heard. If the victim had been between twenty-two and twenty-eight when she was killed, she would probably have been between seventy and eighty had she lived. So her killer might still be alive, then, and so might a witness, or at least someone who *remembered* her.

Chapter Three

As weddings go, Matthew and Gloria's was a relatively small affair. A few family members came from as far away as Eastvale and Richmond, but Gloria had no family, of course, so the rest of the guests were made up of people from the village. Gloria had insisted on inviting Michael Stanhope, as they had become quite close friends. At least he had made the effort to shave, comb his hair and wear a decent if rather frayed suit.

I must say Gloria looked radiantly beautiful. With her angelic face and earthly figure, she had a natural advantage to start with. She had found her wedding dress on sale at Foster's in Harkside for two pounds ten shillings. It was a simple white affair, both elegant and tasteful. She had made her own veil out of lace.

Wouldn't you know it, clothes rationing came into force the Sunday before the wedding. Luckily, we had all got used to mending and making do by that stage of the war. Cynthia Garmen and I were bridesmaids and we wore matching taffeta dresses made out of some old curtains.

It was June 7, 1941, and a lovely day, with clouds like trails of spilt milk in the sky. The Reverend Graham conducted the service at St Barts and the reception was held in the church hall. Our first American food had just arrived in the shop, so we had Spam for sandwiches, and tinned sausage meat for sausage rolls. We managed to get a keg of watery beer from the Shoulder of Mutton and there was some sweet sherry we had been keeping in our cupboard.

Matthew's friend, Richard Bright, played trumpet with the Victor Pearson Dance Band, so we got at least half the band to come and play for their supper. Gloria and Matthew led off the dancing, of course, and a lump came to my throat as I watched them.

Michael Stanhope remarked on how beautiful he thought Gloria looked and what a lucky man Matthew was. Betty Warden sat with her nose in the air most of the night, disapproving of everything and everyone, but when she danced with William Goodall she seemed like a different person. Alice Hill was cheerful and talkative as ever, and I rather think she developed a fancy for Eric Poole that night. They certainly danced closely together often enough.

Gloria came up to me at one point. 'This is the happiest day of my life, Gwen,' she said. 'Do you know, just six months ago I thought I would never laugh or dance again. But thanks to you, your mother and, of course, dear Matt . . . Thank you, Gwen, thank you so much.' Then she clasped me to her bosom, giving me a little peck on the cheek. 'I haven't seen you dancing,' she said.

I shook my head. 'I don't. I mean, I can't.'

'I'll teach you,' she said. 'Not right now of course . . .'

She excused herself, and went to talk to Mother, smiling on everyone she passed with those Hardy-heroine eyes of hers.

Matthew and Gloria went to Bridge Cottage for their first night together as man and wife. Whether this was their first *time* together, I have no idea. It may be hard to believe now, but I knew very little of such things back then, being only sixteen at the time. The next day they were going to Scarborough for a three-day honeymoon. After that, it was back to university for Matthew and back to Top Hill Farm for Gloria, though she would live at Bridge Cottage.

I finally excused myself through tiredness and set off home alone. It had been a long, hard day. Back home, I made sure the blackout curtains were drawn tightly, then I went to bed.

It was only when I was on the very edge of sleep and heard the thrumming and droning of the bombers taking off from Rowan Woods RAF Base that I realised that there had been no wedding bells. All the church bells had been silent since 1940 and were only supposed to ring if there was an invasion. I thought that was very sad, and I cried myself to sleep that night.

ANNIE CABBOT PAUSED with the dusty file in her hands when she heard footsteps on the stairs. She was surprised when she saw DCI Banks.

'Inspector Harmond told me you were down here,' Banks said.

Annie gestured around at the musty-smelling, ill-lit basement room. 'Welcome to Central Records,' she said. 'You can see how often we dip into our history around here.'

Banks smiled and walked over to join her. 'Anything yet?'

'Quite a lot. I've been on the phone most of the day, and I was just checking some missing-persons files.'

'And?'

'It's a bit of a confusing period for that sort of thing. Just after the war, so many people coming and going. Anyway, most of the ones who went missing seemed to turn up eventually, either dead or alive, or in the colonies. There are a couple of young women who fit the general description still unaccounted for. I'll follow up on them.'

'Fancy a pint? The Black Swan?'

Annie smiled. 'You took the words right out of my mouth.' What a relief, she thought. She had been in the stifling basement for the best part of the afternoon.

Comfortably ensconced on a padded bench just a few minutes later, pint already half finished, Annie smacked her lips.

'I checked the voters' register first,' she said, 'but the clerk in the council office told me it was frozen at the start of the war. The last person listed for Bridge Cottage is a Miss Violet Croft. I had a bit more luck with the Land Registry. Violet Croft rented the cottage between the 14th of September, 1919, and the 3rd of July, 1940, so she must be the old lady Ruby Kettering remembered. The cottage remained empty until June 1941, when a Mr and Mrs Shackleton took up residence there. It might have been requisitioned for the billeting of evacuees or military personnel in the interim period, but there was no record of that.'

'What happened to Miss Violet Croft?'

Annie flipped over a page in her notebook. 'I dropped by St Jude's next. They've got all the old parish registry records and magazines from St Bart's stored there. Violet Croft, spinster of the parish, died in July 1940 of pneumonia. She was seventy-seven.'

'That lets her out. What about the Shackletons?'

'They were married at St Bart's on the 7th of June, 1941. The husband's name was Matthew Stephen Shackleton, the wife's maiden name Gloria Kathleen Stringer. The witnesses were Gwynneth Shackleton and Cynthia Garmen.'

'Were they Hobb's End residents?'

'Matthew Shackleton was. His parents lived at 38 High Street. They ran the newsagent's shop. The bride's listed as being from London, parents deceased.'

'Big place,' Banks muttered. 'How old was she?'

'Nineteen. Born on the 17th of September, 1921.'

'Interesting. That would put her within Dr Williams's age range by the end of the war. Any mention of children?'

'No. I looked through the registry of baptisms, but there's nothing there. Was he certain about that, do you think?'

'He seemed to be. You saw the pitting for yourself. Do you know what? I'm beginning to get a vision of St Catherine's House looming large in your future.'

Annie groaned. Checking birth, marriage and death certificates was one of the most boring jobs a detective could get. The only positive aspect was that you got to go to London.

'Any luck with the education authorities?' Banks asked.

'No. They said they lost the Hobb's End records, or misplaced them. Same with the doctors and the dentist. I think we can say goodbye to that line of inquiry.'

'Pity. What does your instinct tell you, Annie?'

Annie was surprised. No senior officer had ever asked for her *feelings* before. Banks was certainly different. 'Well, sir,' she said, 'for a start, I don't think it's a killing by a stranger. It *looks* domestic. Like that bloke who killed his wife and sailed off to Canada.'

'Dr Crippen? He buried his wife under the cellar.'

'Cellar. Outbuilding. Same difference.'

'All right, I take your point. Conclusion?'

'Victim: Gloria Shackleton. Killer: husband, or someone else who knew her.'

'Motive?'

'God knows. Jealousy, sex, money?'

'*Blackout curtains*.' Banks slapped his palm on the table.

'Come again, sir?'

'Blackout curtains. John Webb said they found some heavy black material with the body. It makes sense now. The body was wrapped in blackout curtains, Annie. And Geoff Turner mentioned possible wartime dental work. I think we're dealing with a wartime crime.'

'Brilliant, Holmes.'

'Elementary. Anyway, Gloria Shackleton fits the bill as victim. Before we go any further, let's find out all we can about her. She hasn't shown up as missing?'

'Not in any records I've seen.'

'Right.' Banks looked at his watch. 'How about something to eat? I'm getting hungry. Are there any decent restaurants in Harkside?'

Annie paused for a moment, then gave in to a little surge of devil-may-care excitement and said, 'Well, sir, there's always my place.'

AFTER THE HONEYMOON, Gloria continued to report for work at the farm, and at weekends she was at Bridge Cottage, looking fresh and beautiful, ready for Matthew's arrival. Matthew passed his engineering degree, and started his military training at Catterick, which wasn't too far away. Most days I was busy with the shop.

We managed to get to the pictures in Harkside together a few times. Gloria just loved films.

Sometimes we accepted a lift with some of the RAF boys from Rowan Woods, and we even became quite friendly with a couple of Canadian airmen attached to the RAF: Mark, from Toronto, and Stephen, from Winnipeg. Mark was the handsomest one, and I could tell he liked Gloria by the way he looked at her. Gloria seemed amused by it all. Sometimes we let them take us to the pictures and they were both very well behaved.

For Gloria's twentieth birthday, in September, I took her to Brunton's Café on Long Hill, where we gorged ourselves on grilled sausage with mashed potatoes and braised butter beans, followed by jam roll and custard. Matthew couldn't be with us because it was a weekday. After tea, we went to the Lyceum to see *Ziegfeld Girl*, starring Jimmy Stewart and Lana Turner. It was so memorable that the next day I couldn't remember a single melody. It was Gloria's choice, of course. Unfortunately, our tastes couldn't have been more different. Gloria liked empty-headed Hollywood musicals and romantic comedies with beautiful stars and handsome leading men, whereas I preferred something with a bit of meat on its bones.

Sometimes Alice, Cynthia and Betty came to the pictures with us, even Michael Stanhope on occasion. While he often delighted us with his wicked critical commentary on the way home, he disappointed me in leaning more towards Gloria's sort of film.

Matthew and Gloria tried to furnish Bridge Cottage as best they could. You had to scrounge for the simplest of things, like curtain rods and coat hooks. They went to auctions some weekends, bought a wardrobe here, a dresser there, and bit by bit managed to make a home out of Bridge Cottage. Gloria's pride and joy was the radiogram they bought from the Coopers after their son, John, was killed when HMS *Prince of Wales* was sunk just before Christmas. His mum and dad couldn't bear to keep it after he died.

Gloria honoured her promise to give me dancing lessons and I spent an hour or so over at Bridge Cottage each weekend while Matthew read the newspaper after dinner. I learned the waltz, the quickstep and the foxtrot. I actually tried out my skills at a Bonfire Night dance in the Harkside Mechanics Institute. I did very well at dancing, and that worked wonders for my confidence.

By Christmas, Matthew had almost finished his training, and there was talk of a posting, but he said there wasn't much hope of a shopkeeper's son getting a commission.

It was also that Christmas when I got my first real inkling of Gloria's problems with men.

ANNIE'S PLACE turned out to be a squat, narrow terraced cottage at the centre of a labyrinth. Banks left his car parked by the green and they walked through so many twisting narrow streets and ginnels that he was lost within seconds.

'Why do I keep thinking I should have left a piece of thread attached to the Black Swan?' he said as he followed her.

Annie cast a glance over her shoulder and smiled. 'Like Theseus, you mean? I hope you don't think I'm the Minotaur?'

Banks's mythology was a bit rusty, but he remembered an ancient vase he had seen on a school trip to the British Museum. It depicted Ariadne outside the Labyrinth holding one end of the thread and Theseus at its centre killing the Minotaur.

Annie opened a high wooden gate in a stone wall, led him through a small flagged yard and in the back door.

'Where do you park?' Banks asked.

Annie laughed. 'A long way away. Look, it's tiny, there's not much of a view and very little light. But it's mine. Well, it will be when I've paid off the mortgage.'

Annie led him through to the living room. It was small but cosy, and she had decorated much of it in whites, lemons and creams because of the lack of outside light. As a result, the room seemed airy and cheerful. There was just enough space for a small white three-piece suite, a TV, mini-stereo and a small bookcase under the window. Several miniature watercolours hung on the walls. Local scenes, mostly. There was also one oil portrait of a young woman with flowing Pre-Raphaelite hair and laughing eyes.

'Look, I feel really grubby after being down in that basement. I'm going up for a quick shower first, then I'll start dinner. Make yourself at home. There's beer in the fridge.' Then she left the room. Banks heard stairs creak as she walked upstairs.

This woman was an enigma, he thought. She had a DCI, her boss, as a guest in her house, yet nothing in her behaviour indicated a deferential relationship. He heard the shower start.

First, he did what he always did when left alone in a new room; he nosed around. Curiosity was part of his nature. He crouched down and checked the CD titles in the cabinet under the stereo. It was an odd collection: Gregorian chants, Don Cherry's *Eternal Now* and several 'ambient' pieces by Brian Eno. There was also an extensive blues collection. Next to these stood a few pop and folk titles. The books mainly centred around Eastern philosophy.

Then Banks wandered into the kitchen, opened the fridge and took out a bottle of Black Sheep beer. He found an opener and a pint glass in one of the cupboards. Carefully, he poured out the beer, then he took a sip and went back into the living room. He took *Eternal Now* from its case and put it in the CD player. He had heard of Don Cherry, a jazz trumpeter, but didn't actually know his work.

Before the first track had finished, Annie breezed into the room exuding freshly scrubbed warmth.

'I never took you for a Don Cherry fan,' she said, a wicked grin on her face.

'Life is full of surprises. I like it.'

'I'll start dinner now.' She disappeared into the kitchen. 'You can keep me company,' she called out over her shoulder.

Banks carried his beer through. He sat down at the kitchen table. Annie was bending over, pulling vegetables out of the fridge.

'Pasta OK?' she asked, half turning her head.

'Great. It's a long time since I've had any home cooking. Mostly these days it's been either pub grub or something quick and easy from Marks and Sparks.'

'Ah, the lonely eater's friends.'

Annie filled a large pan with water, added a little oil, then set it on the gas ring. She washed and chopped mushrooms, shallots, garlic and courgettes. There was a certain economic grace to her movements; she seemed to possess a natural, centred quality that put Banks at ease. Soon the oil was hot in the frying pan and she was dropping the vegetables in. When they were done, she added tinned tomatoes and herbs. About the time Banks finished his beer, Annie announced that dinner was ready and delivered two steaming plates to the table. Banks grated Parmesan onto the pasta and tucked in. He complimented Annie.

'See,' she said. 'It's not all salads and tofu. You learn to be more inventive in the kitchen when you're a vegetarian. Wine?'

'Please.'

Annie brought over a bottle of Bulgarian Merlot, poured herself a glass and one for Banks. 'You know, I'd really like to find out more about this Hobb's End artist, Michael Stanhope. He *was* living in Hobb's End during the war. Maybe he knew the Shackleton woman. There may be other paintings. They might tell us something.'

'They might,' Banks agreed. 'Though I'm not sure how far art could be trusted as evidence.'

Annie smiled. 'Not technically, perhaps. But artists often distort reality to reveal the truth about it. The artist's reality is as valid as any other. Perhaps more so because an artist struggles to see more deeply, to illuminate. Stanhope obviously perceived something odd about Hobb's End, something that went beyond the superficial ideas of village life. He saw something *evil* there.'

'Isn't that a bit far-fetched? Maybe it was just because there was a war coming?'

'I'm not trying to make out he was a visionary. Just that he really *looked* and maybe he saw something other people could not see that might be useful to us.'

Banks sipped some wine. 'You seem to know a lot about the subject.'

'My father's an artist.'

'Is he well known?'

'Not really. In some circles, perhaps.' She smiled crookedly. 'Ray will never go down in history as one of the greats.'

'What about your mother?'

Annie was silent for a few moments. 'She died,' she said at last. 'When I was six. I don't really remember her very well.'

'That's sad. I'm sorry.'

'More wine?'

'Please. That oil portrait in the living room, is it your mother?'

Annie nodded.

'Your father painted it?'

'Yes.'

'She was a beautiful woman. You look a lot like her.'

It was almost dark outside now. Annie hadn't put on any lights, so Banks couldn't see her expression.

'Where did you grow up?' he asked.

'St Ives.'

'Nice place. I've been there on holiday a couple of times.'

'I don't get down as often as I should. In the sixties it became something of an artists' colony. Over the years my father's done all kinds of odd jobs to support his art. Now he paints local landscapes and sells them to tourists. He's quite successful at it.'

'He brought you up alone?'

Annie pushed her hair back. 'Well, not really. We lived in a sort of artists' colony on an old farm just outside town, so there were always lots of other people around. My extended family, you might call them. Ray's been living with Jasmine for nearly twenty years now.'

'It sounds like a strange set-up.'

'Only to someone who hasn't experienced it. Some of the locals thought we were having orgies every night, doing drugs, the usual stuff. Actually, though there always seemed to be some pot around, they couldn't have been further from the truth. On the whole it was a pretty good environment to grow up in.'

'What made you join the police?'

'The village bobby took my virginity.'

'*Seriously.*'

Annie laughed. 'It's true. He did. His name was Rob. He came up to see us once, looking for someone who'd passed through. He was good-looking. I was seventeen. He noticed me. It seemed a suitable act of rebellion. I'd had enough of that lifestyle by then. Too much talk and not enough done. And Rob seemed solid, dependable, more sure of himself and what he believed in.'

'Was he?'

'Yes. We went out until I went to Exeter University. Then he turned up there a year or so later as a DC. He introduced me to some of his friends and we sort of started going out again. I suppose they found me a bit weird. I was into yoga and meditation. I didn't really fit in anywhere. I don't know why, but being a detective sounded exciting. *Different*. It was a bit impulsive, I'll admit.'

Banks wanted to ask her why she was in a dead-end place like Harkside, but he sensed that this wasn't the moment. 'What happened to Rob?'

'He got killed during an armed drugs bust three years later. His gun jammed.'

'I'm sorry.'

Annie fanned her hand in front of her face. 'Ooh, I'm hot. Listen to me go on. I haven't talked to anyone like this in ages.'

'I wouldn't mind a cigarette. Would you like to stand outside with me? Cool down a bit, if it's possible?'

'OK.'

They went out into the back yard. It was a warm night, though there were signs of a breeze. Annie stood beside him. He lit up, inhaled and blew out a plume of dark smoke.

'I'm like you in a lot of ways,' she said.

'What do you mean?'

'Well, how much have you told me about your past? You're a loner, like me. I don't just mean now, because you're . . .'

'Because my wife left me?'

'Right. I mean I think you've got a lonely, isolated nature. It colours the way you see the world, the detachment you feel. I think I'm the same.'

It was what Sandra had said when they had their final argument. There was something in him that always stood apart, that she couldn't reach and he wouldn't offer. It wasn't just the job and its demands, but something deeper. He had been on the outside, an observer, even as a child. As Annie said, it was a part of his nature, and he didn't think he could change it if he tried.

'Maybe you're right,' he said.

Banks dropped his cigarette and trod on the red ember. Suddenly a chill gust of wind rustled the distant trees and passed through the yard. Annie shivered. Banks put his arm around her and moved her gently towards him. She let her head rest on his shoulder.

'Oh dear,' she said. 'I don't know if this is a good idea.'

'If it's the rank thing that's bothering you—'

'No. No. I don't give a damn about that. It's just that . . . I've had some bad experiences with men. I mean . . . Oh, shit, why is this so difficult?' Banks kept silent. Annie sighed deeply. 'I've been celibate,' she said. 'By choice. For nearly two years now.'

'I don't want to pressure you,' Banks said.

'Don't worry. I wouldn't let you. I make my own choices.'

'I'll never find my way out of this labyrinth alone.'

'I'd lead you,' Annie said, facing him and smiling. 'If I really wanted you to go.' She rested her hand on his chest. His heart beat loudly. 'There are a lot of reasons for not taking this any further, you know,' she went on. 'I've heard you're a bad lot. A womaniser.'

'Not true.'

They looked at one another for a few moments. Annie bit her lip, shivered again and said, 'Oh, hell.'

Banks leaned forward and kissed her. Her lips yielded and her body moulded itself to his.

MATTHEW AND GLORIA had decided to have a party on Christmas Eve. The guests started to arrive at Bridge Cottage at about seven o'clock, including airmen from the base, some with their girlfriends. Alice's Eric was away in North Africa by then, but Betty's William hadn't passed his medical, so they would only let him in the Home Guard. Michael Stanhope came dressed in his usual artistic 'costume', but he did bring two bottles of gin and some wine, which made him most welcome indeed. Mark and Stephen had also contributed a bottle of Canadian Club whisky.

Matthew and Gloria had decorated the tiny front room as best they could, with balloons, concertina streamers and fairy lights over the mantelpiece. There was a Victor Sylvester concert on the radio that night, and soon people were dancing close together in the cramped space. Cynthia and Johnny Marsden hogged the sofa and kissed one another. Gloria drank too much Canadian Club and then switched to gin. She wasn't loud or falling down or anything, but there was a sort of glaze to her eyes and a slight wobble in her step.

I got distracted by an RAF radio operator who first dragged me under the mistletoe and gave me a kiss that tasted of tinned sardines, then proceeded to explain radiolocation to me. I should have told him I was a German spy.

I realised I hadn't seen Gloria for a while and wondered if she was sick or something. I needed to go to the toilet anyway, so I disengaged myself from the radiolocation lecture. It was cold and dark outside, so I put my coat over my shoulders, picked up a torch with its tissue-filtered light and headed out into the back yard.

Bridge Cottage had two outbuildings; one was the toilet and the other was used for storage. As I made my way down the flagstones to the toilet, suddenly I heard sounds nearby. I paused, then I heard a grunt and a muffled voice calling out. The sounds were coming from behind the toilet. Puzzled, I tiptoed over and pointed my torch.

What I saw made my skin tingle. Gloria was pinned to the wall by Mark, the Canadian airman. Her dress was bunched around her waist, and the white flesh of her bare thighs above the stocking-tops stood out in the darkness. Mark was crushed forwards into her, one hand over her mouth, the other fumbling at his waist.

Gloria was calling out in a muffled voice, 'No, please, no!' over and over again, trying to struggle against him. When he saw my light, he swore at me and took off round the front of the house.

Gloria leaned back against the wall, gasping and sobbing. Then she straightened her dress, leaned forward and was sick.

I didn't know what to do. I wasn't even sure what I had witnessed—except that there was something very wrong about it. All I knew was that Gloria looked hurt, upset and in pain. So I did what came naturally; I opened my arms and she fell into them.

THERE WAS ENOUGH LIGHT through the thin curtains for Banks to see Annie breathing softly beside him. She lay on her side, curled away from him, hands clasped in front. Gently, Banks touched her. Annie stirred a little but still she didn't wake.

He rolled onto his back and closed his eyes. His only fear last night had been that he would feel the same way he had when he slept with Karen. He should have known better. He should have known this would be different. Afterwards, Annie had rested in the crook of his arm and he knew then that he wouldn't wake with a burning desire to be alone.

Just for a moment he wondered if this was a trap Riddle had set for him. Were there hidden cameras in the bedroom? Were the two of them plotting Banks's final downfall? Then, as quick as it came, the paranoia was gone. Jimmy Riddle clearly didn't know DS Cabbot, otherwise he wouldn't have sent Banks within twenty miles of her.

Annie stirred and Banks ran his hand slowly all the way from her hip to her shoulder.

'Mmm . . .' she murmured. 'Good morning.'

'Good morning.'

Banks hooked his arm over her side and rested his palm on her stomach, easing her closer. He kissed the soft flesh between her shoulder and neck, then slid his hand up to cup her small breast. Annie sighed and Banks turned her gently towards him.

'THE OTHER NIGHT,' said Gloria the next time I saw her alone. 'At the Christmas party. I want to thank you. If you hadn't come along, I don't know what would have happened. I just don't want you to think it was something it wasn't.'

'I don't know what I think it was,' I said. I felt embarrassed, her talking to me like this.

'He followed me out there,' she said. 'I didn't mean to, but I suppose I might have given him some encouragement. He called me a tease, said I'd been leading him on all night. Things just got a bit out of hand, that's all.'

'What do you mean?'

'Oh, I don't know. Men. It seems like they just can't stop themselves. They're so strong. And sometimes it's easier just to give in.'

'Is that what you were doing? Giving in?'

'No. I was struggling, but Mark had his hand over my mouth. I love Matt, Gwen, I didn't want to cause a fuss, get Matt upset. Can we just forget about it?' Gloria pleaded.

I nodded. 'That's probably for the best.'

She gave me a hug. 'Good. And we're still friends, Gwen?'

'Of course.'

AFTER BANKS HAD GONE, Annie did her usual twenty minutes of meditation, followed by a few yoga exercises and a shower. As she dried herself, she realised how good she felt.

She hoped Banks wasn't the kind who felt a moral obligation to fall in love just because he slept with a woman. She wanted to see more of him, yes; she wanted to sleep with him again, yes; but beyond that, she didn't know what she wanted. Still, maybe it would be nice if he did fall a little bit in love with her. Just a little bit.

For the moment, another beautiful summer's day beckoned, and it was a great luxury not to have to make any more serious choice other than whether to do her washing or go shopping in Harrogate.

Before going anywhere, though, she picked up the phone and dialled a number she knew by heart.

It rang six times before a man's voice answered.

'Ray?'

'Annie? How are you doing, my love? We're having a bit of a party.'

Annie could hear laughter and music in the background. 'But it's only ten o'clock in the morning,' she said.

'Is it? Oh, well, you know how it goes. *Carpe diem* and all that.'

'Dad, when are you going to grow up? Haven't you realised yet that we're in the nineties, not the sixties? One day the police will come and bust the lot of you.'

'Police? They're not interested in a couple of teeny-weeny joints, are they? Anyway, how is my little WPC Plod? Getting any, lately?'

'*Dad!*' Annie felt herself blushing.

'All right. Sorry. Just showing a bit of fatherly concern, that's all. Anyway, wonderful as it is to talk to you, it's not like you to phone before discount time. Anything I can help you with? Like me to beat up a couple of suspects for you?'

'As a matter of fact,' Annie said, 'there is something you might be able to help me with. The artist, Michael Stanhope.'

'Stanhope . . . Sounds familiar. Wait a minute . . . Yes, I remember. Let me see. He didn't live up to his early promise. Died some time in the sixties, I think. Why?'

'I saw a painting of his in connection with a case I'm working on.'

'What was it? The painting.'

Annie described it to him. 'Yes, that'd be Stanhope. He had a reputation for Bruegelesque village scenes. Touch of Lowry thrown in for good measure. That was his problem, you know: too derivative and never developed a style of his own.'

'Do you know where I can find out more about him? Is there a book?'

'I don't think so. He wasn't that important. Most of his stuff will be in private collections, maybe spread around the galleries, too. Why don't you try Leeds? They're bound to have a few Stanhopes, what with him being local and all.'

'Good idea,' Annie said. 'I'll do that.'

AND FRIENDS WE REMAINED. **We saw the New Year in together, linked arms and sang 'Auld Lang Syne'. Hong Kong had fallen to the Japanese on Christmas Day and the fighting in North Africa and in Russia went on as bitterly as ever.**

Though I often thought about what I had witnessed, I had no way of knowing how culpable Gloria had been. So I did the best I could to put the whole episode out of my mind.

On January 15, 1942, Sergeant Matthew Shackleton shipped out. He didn't know where he was headed, but we all assumed he would be going to North Africa to fight with the 8th Army.

Imagine our surprise when Gloria got a letter from Matthew in Ceylon, then another from Calcutta, India. I could have kicked myself for not guessing earlier. They didn't need bridges and roads in the desert, of course, but they needed them in the jungles of the Far East.

ANNIE PARKED north of Leeds city centre and walked down New Briggate to The Headrow. The place was busy, pavements jammed with shoppers. Annie put on her sunglasses and set off through the crowds towards Cookridge Street. A little research had revealed that Leeds City Art Gallery had several works by Michael Stanhope.

Once inside, she picked up a guidebook at the reception area. The Stanhopes were on the second floor. Four of them. She started up the broad stone staircase.

When she found the Stanhopes, she was at first disappointed. Two of them were rather dull landscapes, not of Hobb's End, but other Dales scenes. The third showed a distant view of Hobb's End, the bright vermilions and purples of sunset splashed across the sky. A fine effect, but it told Annie nothing she didn't know.

The fourth painting, though, was a revelation.

Titled *Reclining Nude*, according to the catalogue, the painting reminded Annie of Goya's *The Naked Maja*. The woman reclined on a bed in much the same pose, propped on a pillow, hands behind her head, looking directly at the painter with a highly charged erotic challenge in her expression. Also, like the *Maja*'s, her round breasts were widely spaced and her legs bent a little, awkwardly placed as her lower half twisted slightly towards the viewer. There were differences, though. Stanhope's model had golden-blonde hair rather than black, her large eyes were a striking blue, her lips fuller and redder.

But there was more to Stanhope's vision. If you looked very closely, you could see images of tanks, aeroplanes, armies on the march, explosions and swastikas in the background. Eroticism and weapons of mass destruction. Make of it what you would.

Annie glanced at the note on the wall beside the painting, then she stepped back with a gasp.

There it was, plain as day, below *Reclining Nude*. A subtitle: *Gloria, Autumn 1944*.

ON MONDAY MORNING, Banks looked again at the postcard reproduction of *Reclining Nude: Gloria, Autumn 1944* that lay on his desk. It was an uncanny and disconcerting experience to see an artist's impression of the flesh that had probably once clothed the filth-covered bones they had found last week.

Thrilled by her discovery, Annie had phoned him late on Saturday afternoon. They met for dinner at Cockett's Hotel, in Hawes, with every intention of going their separate ways later, both having agreed that they shouldn't rush things. After the second bottle of wine, though, instead of leaving, they took a room and woke to Sunday-morning church bells. After a leisurely breakfast, they left, agreeing to restrict their trysts to weekends.

As he looked at Gloria's pose—beautiful, erotic, sensual, playful, but also challenging, mocking, as if she shared some sort of secret with the artist—he felt that on this case he was needed as much as he'd ever been. All the petty duties and details of a policeman's job aside, Banks's obsession was with bringing down as many bullies as possible. When the victims were dead, of course, he couldn't defend them, but he could damn well find out what had happened to them and bring the bullies to justice. He was convinced that Gloria Shackleton was the victim they had found buried at Hobb's End, and he wanted to know what had happened to her.

A call from Dr Glendenning, the Home Office pathologist, cut into his thoughts.

'Ah, Banks,' he said. 'I'm glad I caught you in. You're very lucky I happened to be in Leeds, you know. Otherwise you could have whistled for your post-mortem. There are plenty of fresh cadavers craving my expert attention.'

'I'm sure there are. My apologies. What have you got?'

'Nothing much to add to what Dr Williams told you, I'm afraid. She was stabbed viciously, fifteen or sixteen times, as far as I can tell. It's not possible to say what killed her, though judging from the angles and positions of the knife wounds, the blade would almost certainly have pierced several vital organs.'

'Did you find evidence of any other injury?'

'Patience, laddie. That's what I'm getting to, if you'll slow down and give me the chance. I found possible, and I stress *possible*, signs of manual strangulation.'

'Strangulation?'

'That's what I said. And stop echoing me. If I needed a bloody parrot I'd buy one. I'm going by the hyoid bones in the throat. Now, these are very fragile bones, almost always broken during manual strangulation, but the damage could have occurred over time, due to other causes. The weight of all that earth and water, for example. I must say, though, the skeleton was in remarkable condition considering where it's been for so long.'

'Would that make it more probable than possible?'

Glendenning sighed theatrically. 'All right, shall we say it's certainly not impossible, and even quite *likely*, that the poor woman was strangled.'

'Before she was stabbed.'

'It would seem very unlikely to me that her killer felt any need to strangle her *after* he had done this. I'd say the strangulation came first and then, for whatever reason, the stabbing. That kind of thing is statistically more common, too.'

'So why the stabbing? To make sure she was dead?'

'I doubt it. Whoever did it got carried away with killing. Either that or he knew exactly what he was doing and he enjoyed himself.'

'Right,' said Banks, scrawling away on the pad he'd pulled in front of him. 'Thanks very much, Doc.'

ALL THROUGH FEBRUARY 1942, day after day, I followed the news reports. I read about the estimated 60,000 British taken prisoner in Singapore, and the fighting near the Sittang River, from where Matthew wrote Gloria another letter, telling her not to worry. Then, on March 8, we heard about the fall of Rangoon.

Our morale at home was pretty low. One week you couldn't get fish for love or money; the next it was poultry. The civilian petrol ration was cut out completely in March. In April, the Germans gave up all pretence of bombing military and industrial targets and started bombing cities of architectural beauty, such as York, which was getting very close to home.

I wrote to Matthew every day, which was probably more often than Gloria did. She was never much of a letter writer. Matthew didn't write back that often, but when he did he would always assure us he was well. Mostly, he complained about the monsoons and the humid jungle heat. For a long time we didn't even know if he had been in battle. Once, though, he wrote: 'Long stretches of boredom relieved only by the occasional brief skirmish.'

That September, *Pride and Prejudice,* with Laurence Olivier and Greer Garson, finally came to the Lyceum. Gloria had just had a tooth extracted by old Granville, the dentist, after suffering toothache for several days. As usual, Granville did more damage than good, and poor Gloria had been bleeding for over a day. She was just beginning to feel a little better and I managed to persuade her to come to the pictures with me. It made a nice change from all the comedies and musicals she had been dragging me to see lately.

It was a beautiful autumn evening tinged with smoky green and golden light. As we walked across the fields that night, I could see the purple heather darkening on the distant moor-tops to the west and could smell clean, hay-scented air.

Despite the war, I felt deeply content at that moment. Yet as we came down towards the fairy bridge in the gathering darkness, I felt a chilling shudder of apprehension, as if a goose had stepped over my grave, as Mother would say.

As the weeks passed, I tried to dismiss the feeling, but it had a way of creeping back. There was plenty to rejoice about, I told myself: Matthew continued to write regularly; the Red Army seemed to be making gains at Stalingrad; and the tide had turned in North Africa.

But after the victory at El Alamein that November, when the church bells rang for the first time in years, all I could do was cry because Matthew had had no bells at his wedding.

'FIRST OFF,' Annie told Banks over the phone later that day, 'I can find no official record of Gloria Shackleton at all after the wedding notice in 1941. There's no missing-persons report in our files and no death notice anywhere.'

'OK. Go on.'

'Well, I was able to dig up a bit more about her life at Hobb's End, mostly from the parish magazine. In the May 1941 issue, she's welcomed to the parish as a member of the Women's Land Army, assigned to work at Top Hill Farm, owned by a Mr Frederick Kilnsey and his wife, Edith. They had one son called Joseph, who was called up. That's why they got Gloria. Joseph didn't come back. Killed at El Alamein. By then, Gloria was living at Bridge Cottage. Unfortunately, the parish magazine stopped publication early in 1942. Paper shortage.'

'Pity. Go on.'

'That's about it, really. Matthew Shackleton's younger sister Gwynneth—who witnessed the marriage—was still around in March 1942. Wrote a piece on growing your own onions, in fact.'

'How fascinating. What about Matthew?'

'The last time he was mentioned he was shipping overseas. Didn't say where. Secret, I suppose.'

'Any idea where any of these people moved to when they cleared out of Hobb's End?'

'No. But I rang Ruby Kettering. She's remembered that she knows two people who lived in Hobb's End during the war. There's Betty Goodall, who lives in Edinburgh, and Alice Poole in Scarborough.'

'OK. Which do you fancy: Edinburgh or Scarborough?'

'Doesn't matter to me.'

'I'll toss for it. Heads or tails?'

'How can I trust you over the telephone?'

'Trust me. Heads or tails?'

'This is crazy. Heads.'

Banks came back on. 'It was heads. Your choice.'

'I'll take Scarborough.'

'OK. If I get an early enough start I can be up to Edinburgh and back by early evening. I'd like to get something on tonight's news, first. I want to put Gloria's name out, see if anything comes back.'

'So JIMMY RIDDLE thinks he's dropped you in it with this one, then?' said DS Hatchley after swallowing his first bite of toasted tea cake.

'To put it succinctly, yes,' said Banks.

They were sitting in the Golden Grill, just across the street from Eastvale Divisional HQ. Outside, Market Street was packed with tourists, cameras round their necks. Like sheep up on the unfenced moorland roads, they strayed all over the narrow street.

Once they had given their orders to the bustling waitress, Banks told Hatchley about the skeleton. By the time he had finished, their order had arrived.

Banks knew his sergeant had a reputation as an idle sod and a thug. His appearance didn't help. Hatchley was big, slow-moving and bulky, and he usually looked as if he had just been dragged through a hedge backwards. But it had always been Banks's experience that once Hatchley got his teeth into something, he was a stubborn and dogged copper.

'Anyway, what I'd like you to do is take PC Bridges and go down to London, to St Catherine's House, tomorrow. Here's a list of information I'd like.' Banks passed over a sheet of paper.

Hatchley glanced at it. 'Can't I take WPC Sexton instead?'

Banks grinned. 'And you a married man? I'm ashamed of you, Jim. Before you go, could you put out a nationwide request for information on similar crimes in the same time period? It's an old crime, but there's a chance someone might have something similar on the books.'

'You think this was part of a series?'

'I don't know, Jim, but what Dr Glendenning told me about the MO made me think I shouldn't overlook that possibility.'

The door opened and WPC Sexton walked over to them. DS Hatchley nudged Banks and pointed. 'Here she is. The belle of Eastvale Divisional.'

'Piss off, Sarge,' she said, then turned to Banks. 'Sir, we just got an urgent message from a DS Cabbot in Harkside. She wants you to get down there as soon as you can. She said a lad named Adam Kelly has something he wants to tell you.'

THE TELEGRAM, in its unmistakable orange cover, came to the shop, for some reason. I remember the date; it was Palm Sunday, April 18, 1943. Gloria was working that day so, heart thumping, I had to run up to Top Hill Farm.

I found Gloria collecting eggs in the chicken shack.

'What are you doing here, Gwen?' she said.

Panting, I handed over the telegram to her. She read it, her face turned ashen and she sagged back against the wall. The chickens squawked and the sheet of paper fluttered to the dirt floor. 'Oh, no,' she said. 'No.' Then her whole body started to tremble. I wanted to go to her, but somehow I knew that I must let the first pangs of grief shake her and rip through her alone.

MRS KELLY ANSWERED the door and asked them in. Banks could sense the tension immediately. The aftermath of a scolding.

'He won't say owt,' Mrs Kelly said. She was a plain, harried-looking woman in her early thirties, old before her time. 'I challenged him on it when he came home from school and he ran up to his room. He won't come down.'

'Challenged him on what, Mrs Kelly?' Banks asked.

'What he stole from that . . . that there skeleton. I left it where I found it when I were cleaning his room. Anyone would think I haven't brought him up right. It's not easy when you're on your own.'

'Calm down, Mrs Kelly,' Annie said, stepping forward. 'Nobody's blaming you for anything. Or Adam. We just want to get to the bottom of it, that's all.'

'May I go up and talk to him?' Banks asked.

'Suit yourself. You'll get nowt out of him. Left at the top of the stairs.'

Banks glanced at Annie, who tried to settle Mrs Kelly in an armchair, then he made his way up. He knocked first on Adam's door and, getting no response, opened it and stuck his head round. 'Adam?' he said. 'It's Mr Banks. Remember me?'

Adam lay on his side on the single bed. He turned slowly, and said, 'I didn't mean nothing, honest I didn't. I don't want to go to jail.'

'Nobody's going to take you to jail, Adam. Why don't you just calm down and tell me what happened. Can I come in?'

Adam sat up on the bed. His eyes were red with crying. 'Suppose so,' he said.

Banks sat on the edge of the bed. Posters of muscular sword-and-sorcery heroes hung on the walls. A small computer sat on a desk.

'Why don't you tell me about it?' he asked.

'I thought it were magic,' Adam said. 'The Talisman. That's why I went there. Hobb's End. It's a magic place. It were destroyed in a battle between good and evil, but there's still magic buried there.'

'You found something that day, when you fell, didn't you?'

Adam nodded.

'Will you show it to me?'

The boy reached under his pillow and pulled out a small round object. He hesitated, then passed it to Banks. It was a metal button, by the look of it. Corroded, but clearly a button of some sort.

'Where did you find this, Adam?'

'It fell into my hand, honest.'

Banks turned away to hide his smile. 'All right,' he said. 'What were you doing when it fell into your hand?'

'Pulling the hand out.'

'It was in the skeleton's hand?'

'Must've been, mustn't it?'

'Why didn't you tell us about it sooner?'

'I thought it were the Talisman. It's not easy to get. You have to pass through the veil to the Seventh Level.'

Banks hadn't a clue what the boy was talking about. Not that it mattered. 'You did well,' he said. 'But you should have passed this on to me the first time I came to see you. It's not a talisman, it's just an old button.'

Adam seemed disappointed. 'Is it important?'

'I don't know yet. It might be.'

'Who was it? Do you know? The skeleton?'

'A young woman.' He held out the button on his palm. 'This might help us find out who killed her.' Banks stood up. 'You can come down now. Nobody's going to do you any harm.'

'But my mum—'

'She was just upset, that's all. Come on downstairs.'

Adam's mother was in the kitchen making tea, and Annie was leaning against the counter talking to her.

'Oh, so you've decided to join us, have you, you little devil?' said Mrs Kelly.

'Sorry, Mum.'

She ruffled his hair. 'Just don't do owt like that again.'

VIVIAN ELMSLEY SAT DOWN with her gin and tonic to watch the news that evening. The drinks were becoming more frequent, she had noticed, since her memories had started disturbing her.

Tonight, the news shook her to the core.

Towards the end of the broadcast, the scene shifted to Hobb's End, where crime-scene searchers were still digging up the ruins.

'Today,' the reporter began, 'in a further bizarre twist to a story we have been covering in the north of England, police investigating some skeletal remains are almost certain they have established the identity of the victim. Detective Chief Inspector Alan Banks, who is heading the investigation, talked with our northern office.'

The camera settled on a dark-haired man with intense blue eyes.

'Can you tell us how this discovery was made?' the reporter asked.

'Yes.' Banks looked straight into the camera as he spoke. 'When we discovered the identity of the people living in the cottage during the Second World War,' he began, 'we found that one of them, a woman called Gloria Shackleton, hasn't shown up on any postwar records. Of course, there could be a number of reasons for this, but one thing we are forced to consider is that she hasn't shown up because she was dead.'

'How long have the woman's remains been buried?'

'It's hard to be accurate, but we're estimating between the early to mid-forties.'

'That's a long time ago. Is there any way the public can help?'

'Yes, there is.' The next moment, the screen was filled with the head and shoulders of a woman. Surely it couldn't be? But there was no mistaking who it was: *Gloria*.

Vivian gasped and clutched her chest.

It looked like part of a painting. Gloria must have been lying down as she posed. Michael Stanhope? It looked like his style.

In the background, Banks's voice went on, 'If anyone recognises this woman, who we think lived in London between 1921 and 1941 and in Hobb's End after that, would they please get in touch with the North Yorkshire Police.' He gave out a phone number.

All Vivian could see was Gloria's face: Stanhope's vision of Gloria's face, with that cunning blend of naiveté and wantonness, that come-hither smile and its promise of secret delights. Then she thought, with a tremor of fear: if they had already discovered Gloria, how long would it take them to discover *her*?

Chapter Four

'It only said he's *missing*,' Gloria insisted over two months later at the height of the summer of 1943. We were standing by one of Mr Kilnsey's dry-stone walls and looking out over the gold-green hills. She thrust the most recent Ministry letter towards me. 'See: "Missing during severe fighting east of the Irrawaddy River in Burma."'

What had kept us going the most since we heard the news of Matthew's disappearance was our attempt to get as much information as we possibly could about what had happened to him. First we had written letters, then we had even telephoned the Ministry. But the most we could get out of the man on the phone was that the area in which Matthew had disappeared was in the hands of the Japanese. Matthew was not among confirmed casualties. He might have been killed, taken prisoner. It was impossible to get anything further out of him. Gloria had been brooding over what to do next.

'I think we should go down to Whitehall,' she said. 'Get some answers.'

For the rest of that month I tried to talk her out of the London trip, but she was adamant. Even Michael Stanhope said it would be a waste of time: government bureaucrats would tell us nothing.

I had never been to London, and the prospect scared me stiff.

It was finally arranged for September. Gloria decided it would be best if we went and returned by night train. That way she would only have to rearrange her one and a half days off for midweek. Cynthia Garmen said she would look after Mother and the shop. Mother gave Gloria some of her clothes coupons to use if we had time to visit the big shops. Though she accepted them gratefully, for once clothes were the last thing on Gloria's mind.

IT WAS ABOUT TEN O'CLOCK when the road crested the hill and Banks could see Edinburgh spread out in all its hazy glory: the stepped rows of tenements; the dark Gothic spire of the Scott Monument, the hump of Arthur's Seat; the castle on its crag.

Betty Goodall, lived just off Dalkeith Road, not far from the city centre. She had given him precise directions, and after only a couple of wrong turns he found the narrow street of tall tenements.

Mrs Goodall answered Banks's ring promptly and led him into a high-ceilinged living room that smelt of lavender. She was a short, stout woman and her recently permed hair was almost white. Its waves looked frozen, Margaret Thatcher style.

She bade him sit in a sturdy damask armchair, its arms and back covered by white lace antimacassars.

'Well, then, you're here. Tea?'

'Please.'

She disappeared into the kitchen. Banks surveyed the room. It was a nondescript sort of place: clean and tidy, but not much character. A few framed photographs stood on the sideboard, but none of them showed Hobb's End.

Mrs Goodall walked back into the room slowly, carrying a china tea set on a silver tray. She set it down on a doily on the low table in front of the sofa, then sat down.

'We'll just let it mash a few minutes. Now,' she said, hands clasped on her lap, 'let us begin. You mentioned Hobb's End on the telephone. What do you wish to know?'

'Do you remember Gloria Shackleton?' Banks asked. 'She lived in Bridge Cottage during the war.'

Mrs Goodall looked as if she had just swallowed a mouthful of vinegar. 'Of course,' she said. 'Dreadful girl.'

'Oh? In what way?'

'Not to put too fine a point on it, Chief Inspector, the girl was a brazen hussy. I knew it the first moment I set eyes on her in church. She was still called Gloria Stringer then.'

'Was she religious?'

'No true Christian woman would go about flaunting herself the way she did.'

'Why did she go to church, then?'

'Because the Shackletons went, of course. She had her feet firmly under their kitchen table.'

'She was from London originally, wasn't she? Did she ever say anything about her background?'

'Not to me, though I vaguely remember someone told me her parents were killed in the Blitz.'

Mrs Goodall sat up, back erect, and poured the tea. The cups were tiny, fragile bone-china things with a handle he couldn't possibly get a finger through.

'Of course,' she went on, 'one hoped that over time she would make attempts to fit in, to alter her manner according to the standards of village society, but she made no attempt at all.'

'Did you know her well?'

'Chief Inspector, does she sound like the kind of person whose company I would cultivate?'

'Did you have any dealings with Gloria at all?'

Mrs Goodall nodded. 'Indeed I did. It fell to me to advise her that her behaviour was unacceptable, as was the way she looked.'

'Looked?'

'Yes. The sort of clothes she wore, the way she sashayed about, the way she wore her hair. It was not ladylike.'

'You say it *fell* to you? On what authority? Was there strong general feeling against her?'

'In my capacity as a member of the Church of England.'

'I see. How did Gloria react when you rebuked her?'

Mrs Goodall flushed at the memory. 'I pointed out that it might do her much good, morally and socially, were she to become active in the Women's Institute and the Missionary Society. She called me an interfering busybody and indicated that there was only one missionary position she was interested in, and it was *not* the Church's. And she used language I would not expect from the mouth of the lowest mill girl.'

'She married Matthew Shackleton, didn't she?'

Mrs Goodall sucked in her breath with an audible hiss. 'Yes. Matthew was an exceptional boy. I expected far better of him than that. He went missing in action, poor Matthew, some time in 1943. Captured by the Japanese.' She gave a shudder. 'I presume he died.'

'You lost touch?'

She fiddled with her wedding ring. 'Yes. My husband, William, was posted to Scotland early in 1944. I accompanied him and we didn't have anything more to do with Hobb's End.'

'Do you know if Gloria had affairs?'

Mrs Goodall sniffed. 'Almost certainly.'

'Who with?'

She paused, then uttered just one word. 'Soldiers.'

'What soldiers?'

'This was wartime, Chief Inspector. There were soldiers everywhere. Not all of them British, either.' For the first time in their conversation, Mrs Goodall let a small smile slip. 'Oversexed,' she said, 'overpaid and over here.'

'Americans?'

'Yes. The RAF handed Rowan Woods over to the American air force. They often used to come and drink in the village pubs, or attend our dances at the church hall. And I needn't tell you about the opportunities for immorality and indiscretion that a wide area of wooded land like Rowan Woods had to offer, need I?'

Banks wondered if she would take a positive answer as an indication of personal experience. He decided not to risk it. 'Did Gloria have anyone in particular?' he asked.

'I have no first-hand knowledge. I kept my distance from them. According to Cynthia Garmen, she had more than one. Not that Cynthia was one to talk. She married one of them, didn't she? Went off to live in Pennsylvania.'

'So there was no one serious for Gloria?'

'Oh, I've no doubt her liaisons were every bit as serious as such a woman was capable of. A *married* woman.'

'But you said she thought her husband was dead.'

'Missing, *presumed* dead. It's not quite the same.' Mrs Goodall remained silent for a few moments, then said, 'May I ask why you are asking me about the Shackleton girl after all these years?'

'Don't you watch the news? Read newspapers?'

'I prefer historical biography.'

Banks told her about the discovery of the body they believed to be Gloria's. Mrs Goodall paled. 'I don't like to speak ill of the dead,' she muttered. 'You should have told me sooner.'

'Would that have changed what you said?'

'Probably not. I have always considered telling the truth to be an important virtue. I can tell you, though, that Gloria Shackleton was alive and well when we left Hobb's End in May 1944.'

'Thank you,' said Banks. 'That helps us narrow things down a bit. Do you know if she had any enemies?'

'Nobody who would do what you have just described. Many people, like myself, disapproved of her. But that's quite a different thing. Given Gloria's wayward nature, don't you think you should be looking at this as a *crime passionnel*?'

'Perhaps.' Banks shifted in his chair. 'What about Michael Stanhope?' he asked.

She raised her eyebrows. 'There's another one. Debauched, perverted. Birds of a feather, him and Gloria Shackleton.'

'I wonder if you knew anything about a nude painting of Gloria?'

'I can hardly say it surprises me, but no. It was *not* public knowledge in Hobb's End while I was there.'

'Do you think she might have had an affair with Stanhope?'

'I can't say. I wouldn't rule it out. They did spend a lot of time together.'

'Did Gloria and Matthew have any children? There were certain indications in the post-mortem.'

'Not that I ever knew of. It's hard to hide such things in a small village. Of course, she could have had a child after we left in 1944.'

'It's possible. Or perhaps she gave birth *before* she arrived in Hobb's End.'

'But . . . but that means . . . Surely that would indicate she was already married?'

'Just one more sin to add to her list,' said Banks. 'But it wasn't necessarily so. I imagine even back then, in the good old days, the odd child was born on the wrong side of the blanket.'

Mrs Goodall's lips tightened. 'I don't appreciate your sarcasm, Chief Inspector, or your coarseness.'

'I'm sorry, Mrs Goodall. I don't mean to be sarcastic, really, but I'm trying to get to the bottom of a particularly nasty murder here. I believe the victim deserves my best efforts.'

'Of course. I stand corrected. Gloria Shackleton could not possibly have deserved what you say happened to her.'

'Did you know Matthew's sister, Gwynneth?'

'Gwen? Oh, yes. Gwen was always rather the quiet one, head buried in a book.'

'Do you know what became of her? Is she still alive?'

'I'm afraid we lost touch when William and I went to Scotland.'

'Were she and Gloria close?'

'Well, they were always off to dances together in Harkside, or to the pictures. But they were as different as chalk and cheese. There was some talk about Gloria leading Gwen astray. Gwen was a few years younger, an impressionable girl.'

'What did she look like?'

'Gwen? She was rather a plain girl, apart from her eyes. Remarkable eyes, almost oriental the way they slanted. And she was tall. Tall and awkward. A gangly sort of girl.'

'What about Matthew?'

'A dashing, handsome fellow. Very mature.' Again, she allowed a little smile to flit across her hard-set features. 'If I hadn't met my William, well . . . who knows?'

Banks stood up. 'You've been a great help.'

'If there's anything else I can help you with, please don't hesitate to telephone.'

GLORIA AND I TOOK the night train from Leeds, where the platform was crowded with young soldiers. We felt ourselves jostled along like corks in a fast-flowing river and finally managed to get ourselves more or less pushed onto seats in a cramped compartment.

Everyone was crushed too closely together for sleep to be possible. I couldn't even read. The blinds were drawn tight and the compartment was lit by one ghostly blue pinpoint of light.

We talked for a while with two young soldiers. Then people started to fall silent. For me it was a matter of gritting my teeth and enduring the long journey, the unexplained delays, the jerking stops and starts. Gloria dozed off after a while and her head slid slowly sideways until she was resting her cheek on my shoulder.

It was in the last hour or so that I caught my first sight of street after street of bombed-out London terraces. Rosebay willowherb and Oxford ragwort grew from the rubble, pushing between the cracks in the bombed masonry and brickwork. Some houses were split open like a cross-section. You could see wallpaper, framed paintings and photographs on the walls, a bed half-hanging over the jagged remains of the floor. I'm not sure that I had any real grasp of the full extent of the war's devastation until then.

It was after ten o'clock in the morning when we arrived at King's Cross and I was starving. Gloria wanted to head straight for Whitehall, but I persuaded her to stop and we found a Lyons, where we managed to get a rasher of bacon and an egg.

After breakfast, we walked back into the street. The whole place had a shabby, worn and slightly defeated air about it. I saw my first wounded soldiers, sad-looking men with bandaged heads, missing limbs, eye patches, some on crutches or with their arms in slings. Everybody looked pinched and pale, after years of rationing, bombing and uncertainty.

Gloria was in her element. We took a bus and got off on a broad street flanked with tall buildings where our search began. I felt like a small child dragged along by its mother as Gloria took me from building to building. Finally, Gloria found a minor clerk who did seem to know a little more about the war in the Far East than anyone else would admit to. And he appeared to take a shine to Gloria.

He was a tidy little man in a pinstripe suit, with grey hair parted at the centre and a neat, trim moustache. He glanced at his watch, before suggesting he might spare us ten minutes if we cared to accompany him to the teahouse on the corner.

We bought tea at the counter, and Gloria started to pump the poor fellow for information.

'What are the chances that Matthew might still be alive?'

The man, who told us his name was Arthur Winchester, hemmed and hawed a bit, then measured his words carefully. 'I'm afraid I can't really answer that question,' he said. 'As I told you, I have no knowledge of individual cases, merely a little general knowledge of the situation in the East.'

'All right,' Gloria went on, undaunted, 'tell me about what happened at Irrawaddy?'

Arthur Winchester paused and sipped some some tea. 'Burma,' he said, 'as you probably know, stands between India and China, and it would be of inestimable value if our forces could reopen the Burma Road and clear the way to China, which could then be used as a direct base for operations against Japan. This is general knowledge.'

'Not to me it isn't.' Gloria lit a Craven A. 'Go on,' she prompted, blowing out a long plume of smoke.

'To put things simply, since Burma fell, we have been trying to get it back. One of the offensives was the Chindit Operation, launched in February. They began east of the Irrawaddy, a river in central Burma. While they were there, the Japanese launched a major offensive on the Arakan Front and the British had to withdraw. The Chindits, the Allied fighters who operated behind Japanese lines, were trapped, cut off, and began to filter back in some disarray.' He looked at Gloria. 'This, no doubt, is why no one has been able to give you any specific information about your husband.'

'But we're still trying to get Burma back?'

'Oh, yes. It's of great strategic importance.'

'So there's still a chance that someone might find Matthew? When the British win back Burma?'

'I wouldn't get your hopes up, my dear. A long time might pass before that happens.'

'How do you know all this?' Gloria asked.

Arthur Winchester inclined his head modestly. 'I don't know very much, I'm afraid. But before the war I was a history teacher. The Far East has always interested me.'

'So you don't really have anything to tell us?' Gloria said.

'Well, any excuse to take tea with a pretty lady will do for me, if you don't mind my saying so.'

Gloria got to her feet in a fury. Arthur Winchester grabbed hold of her sleeve meekly. 'I say, my dear, I'm sorry. Poor taste. I really didn't mean to offend you. A compliment, that's all.'

Gloria sat down again, slowly, a hard, suspicious look in her eyes, and said, 'Can you tell us anything at all, Mr Winchester?'

'All I can tell you, my dear,' he went on gravely, 'is that during the retreat, many of the wounded had to be left behind enemy lines. They were left with a little money and a weapon.'

Gloria had turned pale. I found myself twisting the fabric of my dress in my fist over my lap until my knuckles turned white.

'And what if that is what happened to Matthew?'

Arthur Winchester paused. 'Well,' he said, 'the Japanese don't like taking wounded prisoners. It would depend how badly wounded he was, of course—whether he could work.'

'So they might have simply murdered him?'

'I'm saying it's possible. Or . . . He looked away. 'As I said, the wounded were left behind with a weapon.'

It took a second or two for what he was getting at to sink in. 'You mean Matthew might have committed suicide?' I said.

'If capture was inevitable, and if he was badly hurt, then I'd say, yes, it's a possibility.' His tone brightened a little. 'But this is all pure conjecture, you understand. Maybe he was simply captured and he's in the relative safety of a prison camp. The main problem is that our lines of communication are very poor. Even the Red Cross has great difficulties getting its parcels delivered and getting information. The Japanese are notoriously difficult to deal with.'

'So he may be a prisoner of war and nobody has bothered to let anyone know? Is that what you're telling us?'

'That is a distinct possibility. Yes. But . . .' He paused. 'Well,' he said. 'I don't want to upset you, but I'd say it's best to hope he's dead. It's best that way.' He paused again. 'Look. It's wartime. Things are very different. You have to let go of the past. Your husband is probably dead. Or, if he isn't, he might as well be. Nothing will ever be the same when it's done. All over the city people are living as if there's no tomorrow. How long are you staying in London?'

Gloria looked at him suspiciously. 'Until tonight. Why?'

'I know a place. Very discreet. Perhaps I could—'

Gloria got to her feet so fast she bumped the table and the remains of her tea spilt onto Arthur Winchester's lap. But he didn't stop around to mop it up. Instead, he bolted for the door saying, 'Good Lord, is that the time? I must dash.'

Gloria glared after him for a moment, then touched up her curls and sat down again.

We dawdled over our tea. Gloria smoked another cigarette and gazed out through the steamed-up window. 'What did he mean, "It's best that way"?'

'I don't know,' I said. 'I suppose he meant to say that the Japanese don't treat their prisoners as well as we do. It sounded to me as if he was saying that Matthew would be better off dead.'

ANNIE PARKED IN ONE of the hilly streets at the back of Scarborough Castle, and went looking for Alice Poole's cottage. The sky was bright blue, with only a few wisps of white cloud borne on the sea breeze.

She found the cottage easily enough. It was in a high, quiet part of town, away from the pubs and shopping centres crowded with holidaymakers. From the garden she could see a wedge of the North Sea far below, steely grey-blue today, dotted with small boats.

The woman who answered the door was tall, with thin, wispy hair. She was wearing a long, loose purple dress with gold embroidery round the neck and dangling gold earrings of linked hoops. A pair of black horn-rimmed glasses hung on a chain round her neck.

'Come in, love.' She led the way into a bright, cluttered room. 'Can I offer you coffee?' she asked, having settled Annie in an armchair. 'I usually have elevenses around this time.'

Annie smiled. 'Thanks, Mrs Poole.'

'Alice. Call me Alice. And why don't you have a look through this.'

She handed Annie a thick leatherbound photograph album and headed for the kitchen. Most of the deckle-edged black and white photographs were family groups, but several were village scenes. There were also a couple of pictures of the church and mill.

Alice Poole came back holding a mug of coffee in each hand and a KitKat between her teeth. 'A little indulgence of mine,' she said when she had freed her hands. 'Would you like one?'

'No,' said Annie. 'No, that's fine.' She accepted her coffee.

'You've come about poor Gloria, then?'

'You've heard?'

'Oh, yes. Your boss was on telly last night. How horrible. Have you got any suspects yet?'

'Not really,' said Annie. 'It's very difficult, what with it all being so long ago.'

'You don't say. I was seventy-five last birthday. Look, this is Gloria.' Alice turned to a photograph of four girls standing in front of a Jeep and pointed to a petite blonde with long curls, a narrow waist and a provocative smile. Underneath was written 'July 1944'. 'This one's Gwen, her sister-in-law.' Gwen was the tallest. She wasn't smiling and had half turned away, as if shy about her looks. 'And this one here is Cynthia Garmen. That one's me.' Alice had been a svelte blonde, by the look of her. Also in the photograph, standing in the Jeep, were four young men in uniform.

'Who are they?' Annie asked.

'Americans. That one's Charlie, and that's Brad. We saw quite a lot of them. I don't remember the names of the other two.'

'I'd like to make a copy of that photo, if you don't mind.'

'Not at all.' Alice detached the photograph from its corners. 'Please take care of it, though.'

'I promise.' Annie slipped it in her briefcase. 'You knew Gloria well?' she went on.

'Quite well. She married Matthew Shackleton, as you probably know, and while he was away at war, Gloria and Gwen, Matthew's sister, became inseparable. But quite often the gang of us would do something together.'

'What was she like?'

'Gloria?' Alice unwrapped her KitKat and took a bite. 'Well, I'd say she was a good sort. Cheerful. Fun to be with. Kind. Generous. She'd give you the shirt off her back.'

'Did she tell you anything about her past?'

'All she said was that she lost her family in the Blitz. It must have been very painful for her, so I just thought, if she doesn't want to talk about it, then that's all right with me. She did sometimes seem very distracted. She had deep, quiet, sad moods that would just come on her out of nowhere. But not often.'

'Did she have any enemies?'

'Quite a few people disapproved of her. She went in the pubs by herself, and she smoked in the street. I know that's nothing now, love, but back then . . . Well, to some people it meant you were nigh on a prostitute.' She shook her head slowly. 'And Gloria was far too cheeky and flighty for some people. Betty Goodall, in particular, could never take to her. Betty always was a bit too High Church, if you ask me.'

'Do you know whether Gloria actually *did* anything to merit such disapproval, or was it simply her personality?'

'Oh dear. You want me to tell tales out of school?'

Annie laughed. 'Not if you don't want to. But it *is* a long time ago, and it might help us find her killer.'

'Oh, I know, love. I know.' Alice waved her hand. 'Just let me get my cigarettes.' She got up and brought her handbag over, fiddled for a packet of Dunhill and lit one with a slim gold lighter. 'Now then, dearie, where was I?'

'I wanted to know if Gloria had affairs, slept around.'

'Certainly no more than a lot of others did then. She was a bit of a flirt, but that doesn't mean anything, does it? I may have been naive, but I think there was more smoke than fire. Most of the time.'

'What did you think of Matthew?'

'Oh, he was nice enough, handsome and charming, and one had to feel sorry for what happened to him later.'

'What happened?'

'Killed by the Japanese. Over in Burma.'

'How did Gloria take his death?'

'She was heartbroken. Devastated. I was worried about her. Gwen said she'd be OK in a while, but then Gwen didn't look too good herself, either. Very close, they were, her and Matthew. Anyway, when Gloria started to go out again a few months later, she was more devil-may-care, you know, the way some people get when they feel they've nothing left to lose.' She took a drag on her cigarette.

'When did Gloria form her relationship with Michael Stanhope, the artist?'

'Oh, he'd always been around. He was at their wedding. Gloria used to drink with him in the Shoulder of Mutton. They were both outsiders, freethinkers. On some level, they understood one another.'

'Did you know Stanhope?'

'Just to say hello to. He was an eccentric. Always wearing that floppy hat of his. And the cane. Very affected. There was no mistaking that he was an *Artist*. But I think he was harmless enough. Anyway, he wouldn't have had anything to do with Gloria. He was a homosexual, dearie. Queer as a three-pound note, as we used to say.'

'I see. Was Gloria involved with anyone in particular after her husband's death?' Annie asked.

'She had a bit of a fling with a Yank called Billy Joe something or other. She got a bit of a reputation for hanging around with American airmen, disappearing into the woods late at night, that sort of thing.' Alice winked.

'Do you think there was anything in it?'

'I'd be surprised if there wasn't. I think she was lonely. We met a lot of them, Betty, Cynthia, Gloria, Gwen and me. We'd go to dances, mostly at the base or in Harkside. Most of the local lads were at war, except those unfit for service or in reserved occupations and they just hung out in the Shoulder of Mutton and complained. The Americans were different. They talked differently, spoke about places we'd only seen at the pictures. They were exotic. Exciting. They also had all sorts of things we hadn't been able to get—nylons, cigarettes and that stuff. We were friendly with PX, the chap who ran their stores, and he used to get us all sorts of stuff. Gloria in particular. She was definitely his favourite. She was like a beautiful, exotic butterfly; she attracted every man who met her.'

'This PX, what was his real name?'

'Sorry, love, I don't know if I ever knew. We just called him PX.'

'Was there anyone else in particular?'

'After Billy Joe, she developed a real soft spot for Brad. She didn't want anything serious but Brad was head over heels.'

'Do you remember his second name?'

'Sorry, love.'

'How long did they go out together?'

'There you've got me. They were still seeing each other when I left at Christmas 1944. My Eric got wounded. Nothing serious, but it got him an early discharge. The doctor recommended a bit of sea air, so we came here, fell in love with the place and ended up staying.'

'Did Gloria ever mention anything about having a baby?'

Alice looked puzzled. 'No, not to me. I'm not even sure she liked children. Wait a minute, though . . . Once, after Matthew had gone, when I was crossing the fairy bridge I noticed a bloke turn up with a little lad in tow. They went in to see Gloria. I heard voices raised.'

'Who was he, do you know?'

'Sorry, dearie, I've no idea.'

'Did you ever ask Gloria about him?'

'Yes. She went all quiet on me. She did that sometimes. All she would say was that it was relations from down south. You don't think . . .?'

'I don't know,' said Annie. 'Did they ever come back?'

'Not that I ever heard of.'

'And what happened to Gwen and Gloria after you'd left?'

'I don't know. I never saw or heard of Gloria again. I sent her a postcard, must have been March or April of 1945, telling her we were going to stay in Scarborough. She never replied. You lose touch with a lot of people over the course of your life, I've found. It was the same with Gwen. But we did have some good times together.'

'Well, Alice,' Annie said, 'I think that's all for now. You've been very helpful.'

'It's so nice of you to say so, dearie. I must admit, I've enjoyed having a good chinwag. It's been years since I thought about all that stuff.'

ON HIS WAY BACK from Edinburgh, Banks called in at the station. He found about twenty telephone messages in response to Monday evening's television news appearance. He spent an hour or so returning calls, but most people simply wanted to relive wartime memories, and all he found out was that someone thought the Shackletons had moved to Leeds after V-E day.

There was also a message from John Webb, who said he had cleaned up the button. It was made of brass, probably, and had a raised pattern on the front, possibly reminiscent of wings. Clearly, he added, given the time period under consideration, the armed forces came to mind, perhaps the RAF.

When Banks had finished at the station, he phoned Annie and asked if she would mind coming up to Gratly. He would take her out to the Dog and Gun in Helmthorpe for dinner and hope to God there was something vegetarian on the menu. Then he went home and took a long shower. Next he tried phoning Brian again. Still no luck. He'd have to try again the next day.

When Annie arrived, she first showed him the photograph of Gloria and her friends. Then, after a lightning tour of his house, they walked to Helmthorpe in the hazy evening light, sharing the information each had learned that day.

It was early September now, and the nights were drawing in fast. When they got to the High Street, the sun was already low in the west, a red ball glowing like an ember through the gathering haze. Sounds of laughter and music came from the open pub doors.

They managed to find a table in the beer garden out at the back. Between the trees, the dying sunlight streaked the river shallows blood-orange and crimson. Annie sat down while Banks went to buy a couple of pints and order food. Luckily, Annie said she wasn't very hungry and a cheese-and-pickle sandwich would do her fine.

'Cheers,' Banks said when he came back. 'So who have we got now, then?' he asked. 'Now we've discovered that Matthew was killed before Gloria was?'

Annie leaned back and stretched out her long legs. 'What about the boyfriend?' she suggested. 'The American.'

'Brad? As her killer? Why?'

'Why not? I get the impression that Gloria exerted an enormous power over men. Alice thought he was more keen on Gloria than she was on him. Maybe she tried to shake him loose and he wouldn't go.'

'We definitely need to find out more about the Americans in

Hobb's End,' said Banks. 'The American Embassy might be able to point you in the right direction.'

'I notice the subtle pronoun usage there: "you".'

Banks laughed. 'Rank has its privileges. I'll be trying to get more information on Matthew Shackleton. Besides, you're so good at it.'

Annie pulled a face and flicked some beer at him.

Their food arrived, and they both ate in silence for a while.

'What about Michael Stanhope?' Banks suggested.

'What possible motive could he have had? They were friends.'

'Inordinate desire? If he was powerfully attracted to Gloria, if she wouldn't have anything to do with him sexually, then painting her in the nude might have inflamed him beyond all reason.'

Annie raised her eyebrows. 'You'd be surprised how dispassionate an artist can be. The impression I get is that a lot of villagers projected negative feelings onto Gloria. I think she was basically a decent woman, but her good looks and her free and easy attitude gave her no end of problems, especially with men. Eventually someone went over the top.'

'You sound as if you know what you're talking about.'

Annie turned away and stared at the dark river. It had only been a teasing, offhand remark, but Banks felt as if he had trespassed on some private reserve, set her hackles up. They still had to be careful with one another, he realised.

After a pause, Annie went on, 'Besides, Alice also said he was gay.'

'She couldn't know that for certain. He could have been bisexual. Anyway, there's one obvious flaw with the Stanhope theory. If anything happened between them, it would be more likely to have happened at his studio. That's where she was naked in front of him. If he killed her, I don't think he would have risked carrying the body all the way back to Bridge Cottage. He would have found somewhere closer to dispose of her. Another drink?'

'Better not,' Annie said. 'One's my limit when I'm driving.'

Banks paused a moment, his voice lost somewhere deep in his chest. 'You don't *have* to drive home,' he said finally.

Annie smiled and put her hand on his arm. Her touch set his pulse going faster. 'No, but I think I should, with it being a week night and all. Besides, we agreed, didn't we?'

'Can't blame a bloke for trying. Mind if I have one?'

She laughed. 'Course not.'

Banks went inside. He hadn't expected Annie to rise to his offer, but he was disappointed. Surely there was room for a little spontaneity now and then? He wondered if he would ever be able to figure out this relationship business.

He bought himself another pint and went back outside. Annie wasn't much more than a silhouette now—and a beautiful one to his eyes, with her graceful neck and strong profile—staring at the river in that peculiarly relaxed and centred way she had.

He sat down and broke the spell. 'What about this mysterious stranger and the child who turned up? Gloria's family was killed in the Blitz, but she told Alice that the man and boy who visited her were relations.'

'I know. It does seem odd, doesn't it?'

'If she ran off and left a husband or boyfriend stuck with her kid, that might be someone else with reason to be angry with her. He could have tracked her down later and killed her.'

'Yes, but maybe whoever it was didn't feel *stuck* with the kid. Maybe he loved the boy,' Annie said. 'I'd also like to know what happened to the sister-in-law, Gwynneth.'

'Maybe she's dead. Do you see her as a suspect?'

Annie frowned. 'Something could have happened between them.'

'There are a lot of things we don't know about what happened.'

'You realise we might never know who killed her, don't you?'

Banks finished his drink and nodded. 'If that's what it comes down to, we make out a final report based on all the evidence we've collected and point at the most likely solution.'

'How do you think you'll feel about that?'

'What do you mean?'

'It's become important to you, hasn't it? I'm not saying I don't care. I do. But for you it's something else. You have a sort of compulsion.'

Banks lit a cigarette. 'Somebody has to give a damn.'

'That sounds melodramatic.'

Banks tried to frame his nebulous thoughts. 'I know what Gloria Shackleton looked like. I've got some idea of her character, who her friends were, the things she liked to do.' He tapped the side of his head. 'She's real enough for me in there, where it counts. Somebody took all that away from her. Somebody strangled her, then stabbed her fifteen or sixteen times, and buried her in an outbuilding.'

'Murders happen all the time. What's so different about this one?'

Banks shook his head. 'I don't know. Partly, it's the war. Somehow the idea of this murder being committed while all that carnage was going on makes it seem even more of a travesty, and as far as we can tell, nobody reported Gloria missing. It looks as if nobody cared. Somebody has to. I seem to be good at it, overburdened with compassion, a natural.' Banks smiled. 'Am I making sense?'

Annie brushed his sleeve with her fingers. 'I care, too,' she said. 'Maybe not in the same way, but I do.'

Banks looked into her eyes. He could tell she meant what she was saying. He nodded. 'I know you do. Home?'

They walked out into the street, much quieter now night had fallen. Luckily, there was a moon, for there was no other illumination on the narrow, flagged footpath that curved round the steep banks of Gratly Beck up the daleside to the village itself.

Through the narrow stile at the other end, the pavement was broader, and Annie slipped her arm through his. They crossed the stone bridge, walked along the lane and stood at his front door.

'Coffee?' Banks asked.

Annie smiled. 'No, but I'll have a cold drink.'

He left her in the front room rummaging through his compact-disc collection while he went to the fridge.

He took out a carton of orange juice and poured them each a glass. An old Etta James CD started playing in the living room. Funky and fiery. He hadn't played it in years.

'You've got a hell of a CD collection,' Annie said. 'It's a wonder you can ever decide what to play.'

'It *is* a problem sometimes. Depends on the mood.'

Soon Etta was belting out 'Jump Into My Fire'.

'Sure you won't have a nightcap?' Banks asked when Annie had finished her orange juice.

'No. I told you, I've got to drive back.'

'It's a pity,' said Banks. 'I was hoping you'd change your mind.'

'Come to Mama' was playing now, and the music's rhythmic, slow-moving sensuality was getting to him. He had to keep telling himself that Annie was a detective sergeant, someone he was working with on a case, and he shouldn't even be thinking like this. But the problem was that Annie Cabbot didn't seem like any detective sergeant he had ever come across before.

'Well,' said Annie, smiling. 'I didn't say I had to go just yet, did I?' Then she stood up and pulled her T-shirt slowly over her head. With her head tilted to one side, she smiled, held out her hand and said, 'Come to Mama.'

THERE ARE GIANT redwood trees in California, they say, that can grow another layer round the dead and blackened wood if they ever burn in a forest fire. Matthew's disappearance burned out my core like that and while, over time, I did grow another skin over it, there was part of me inside that was always black and dead. There still is.

Of course, life went on. It always does. Gloria threw herself into her work at the farm. In time, we laughed and smiled again.

In October, *Gone With the Wind* finally came to Harkside, and Gloria and Mr Stanhope practically dragged me to see it. As it turned out, I enjoyed the film, and Gloria, needless to say, was potty about Clark Gable.

In September we had heard that the Rowan Woods Aerodrome had been closed and the RAF had gone somewhere else. One of the ground crew told me that the runways at Rowan Woods had to be converted to be able to handle four-engined bombers. A crew of labourers, mostly Irish, came in. Over the next couple of months, they brought in tons of cement, gravel and Tarmac to bring the runways up to standard. Shortly before Christmas, Rowan Woods became the new home to the United States 8th Air Force's 448th Bomber Group.

The Yanks had arrived.

THOUGH WORRY and fear had gnawed away at her since the TV broadcast, Vivian Elmsley tried to live a normal life: wandering up to Hampstead in the morning; sitting in her study for the day, whether she wrote anything worth keeping or not; talking to her agent and publisher; answering correspondence. All the while waiting for that knock on the door, wondering what she would say.

When it came, though, the shock was in a form she hadn't in the least expected.

That Tuesday night, the phone rang just as she was dropping off. When she picked up the receiver, all she heard was silence.

'Who is it?' she asked.

More silence.

She was just about to hang up when a voice she didn't recognise whispered, 'Gwen? Gwen Shackleton?'

'My name's Vivian Elmsley. There must be some mistake.'

'There's no mistake. I know who you are. Do you know who I am?'

'I don't know what you're talking about.'

'You will. Soon.'

Then the caller hung up.

Chapter Five

Christmas 1943. It was a gloomy, chill and moonless night when the 448th held their first dance at Rowan Woods. Gloria, Cynthia, Alice and I walked there together through the woods. We wore court shoes and carried our dance shoes because they were far too precious and flimsy to walk in.

Alice did a little dance. 'Ooh, just think of it, all those Yanks with money to throw away. They get paid much more than our boys, you know.'

'Don't you try to tell yourself they won't want *something* in return, Alice Poole,' said Gloria. 'And don't you forget your poor Eric away fighting for his country.'

We were all a bit quiet after that. I couldn't help thinking of Matthew. A fox or a badger suddenly flashed across the path and broke the silence. We were still excited, and we giggled like silly schoolgirls the rest of the way.

We had taken special care with our appearance—even me, who was generally not overly concerned about such superficial matters. We all had on our best dresses. Gloria, of course, looked gorgeous in her black velvet V-neck dress with the puffed sleeves and wide, padded shoulders. I was in a utility dress I had bought in London.

Cynthia was going for the Dorothy Lamour look—a black pageboy hairdo and a lot of make-up. Alice was in her Marlene Dietrich period: plucked eyebrows pencilled in a high arch, wavy blonde hair parted in the centre, hanging down to her shoulders. She was wearing a burgundy dress with long, tight sleeves and buttons all down the front. It came in at the waist to show how thin she was.

The dance was held in the mess. We could hear the music before we even got there. It was Glen Miller's 'Take the "A" Train'. We stood outside the door, checking our appearance in our compact mirrors. Then we put on our dance shoes and made our grand entrance.

Already the place was crowded with airmen and local girls, mostly from Harkside. The dance floor was busy and a knot of people stood laughing and drinking by the bar. Others sat at the rickety tables smoking and chatting.

'Take your coats, ladies?'

'Why, thank you,' said Gloria.

It was Gloria who had turned the heads, of course.

We handed our coats to the young airman, who was tall, slim and dark in complexion. He spoke with a lazy drawl. He had brown eyes, short black hair and the whitest teeth I had ever seen.

'Over here.' He led us to the far wall, beside the bar, where everyone's coats hung. 'They'll be safe here. And now, ma'am,' he said, turning straight away to Gloria, 'if I may have the pleasure of the first dance?'

Gloria inclined her head slightly, passed her handbag to me, and went off. It didn't take long before someone snapped up Cynthia, too, and I was holding three handbags. But a rather handsome young navigator called Bernard, from Hackensack, New Jersey, asked me to dance before his friend asked Alice. I passed the three handbags to her and left her standing there gawping.

After 'Kalamazoo', 'Stardust' and 'April in Paris', we gathered at the bar and the tall airman bought us all bourbon. His name was Billy Joe Farrell. He hailed from Tennessee and worked on the ground crew. He introduced us to his friend, Edgar Konig, who everyone called PX because on American bases PX meant the quartermaster's stores, which he ran. PX was a gangly young Iowan with a baby face and his fair hair shaved almost to his skull. He was tall, with Nordic cheekbones, pouting lips and the longest eyelashes over his cornflower-blue eyes. He was also very shy. He was the sort of person who never really gets noticed, and I think the reason he was so generous to us all was simply that it made him feel needed.

When I look back on that evening now, it seemed a whirl of dancing, talking and drinking, and it finished before it really began.

As the four of us walked tipsily back through the woods, arms linked with our gallant escorts, we sang 'Shenandoah' and after good-night kisses agreed to meet them in Harkside the next week.

IT WAS THE FIRST TIME Banks had been to the Queen's Arms for lunch in some months. Cyril, the landlord, welcomed him back like a long-lost friend. He bought a pint and ordered a Yorkshire pudding filled with roast beef and onion gravy.

He had brought with him a folder DS Hatchley had just dropped on his desk: information gleaned from the central registry of births, marriages and deaths. Already that morning he had phoned army records and asked about Matthew Shackleton's service history. They said they would call him back.

Hatchley's notes confirmed that Gloria was born on September

17, 1921. The official record listed Mile End as her place of birth.

Next, Hatchley had pulled death certificates for Gloria's parents, dated September 15, 1940, listing the same Mile End address and 'injuries sustained during bombing' as the cause of death.

Hatchley had been unable to find a death certificate for Gloria Kathleen Shackleton, but he did find one for Matthew, and the information on it caused Banks almost to choke on his beer.

Matthew Shackleton died on March 15, 1950, by his own hand. Cause of death was given as a 'self-inflicted gunshot wound'. At the time, he was thirty-one years of age, of no occupation, living at an address in Bramley, Leeds. The informant of his death was listed as Gwynneth Vivian Shackleton, of the same address.

He thought for a moment. Matthew Shackleton was supposed to have died in Burma, but obviously he hadn't. The three survivors of the old Hobb's End days that Banks and Annie had talked to had not mentioned Matthew Shackleton's returning, so he must have come back after they had left.

Which made him a definite suspect in his wife's murder.

And why had he killed himself five years later?

Banks carried on reading. A marriage certificate existed for Gwynneth Vivian Shackleton and Ronald Maurice Bingham. They were married on August 21, 1954. Ronald died of liver cancer at home on July 18, 1967. There was no death certificate for Gwynneth.

Hatchley had also discovered a child born to Gloria Kathleen Stringer at her parents' home address in Mile End, London, on November 5, 1937, shortly after her sixteenth birthday. The boy was christened Francis Paul Henderson, taking his father's surname. George Henderson was listed as 'dock worker'. There was no trace of a marriage certificate.

So Gloria had given birth over three years before she first appeared in Hobb's End. Had she turned over the boy's care to George Henderson? Was this the man who had turned up with the boy at Bridge Cottage during the war?

Banks tucked into the huge stuffed Yorkshire pudding.

According to Hatchley's final search, George Henderson had died of a heart attack just five months ago. There was no death or marriage certificate for his son Francis. Why hadn't Gwynneth Shackleton and Francis Henderson come forward? One possibility was that neither of them knew what was going on, which was too much of a coincidence for Banks to swallow. Maybe they had something to hide. But everything that had happened in Hobb's End had occurred before Francis turned eight, so he was hardly a suspect. Nonetheless, his DNA could help determine whether the skeleton really was Gloria Shackleton's.

Banks sighed, put the files back in his briefcase and walked across Market Street. He found a message waiting at the front desk from army personnel, informing him that Matthew Shackleton had been listed as 'Missing presumed dead' in 1943, and that was all they had on him. Curiouser and curiouser. Back in his office, Banks picked up the phone and called Detective Inspector Ken Blackstone at Millgarth station, in Leeds.

'Alan,' said Blackstone. 'Long time no see.'

There was a coolness and distance in his voice. They hadn't been in touch often over the past year or so, and Banks realised he had probably alienated Ken along with just about everyone else who had tried to be his friend during the dark days. 'You know how it is,' he said.

'Sure. What can I do for you? Don't tell me this is just a social call.'

'Not exactly.'

'I thought not.' Blackstone's tone softened a little. 'Any new developments between you and Sandra?'

'Nothing. Except I've heard she's seeing someone.'

'I'm sorry, Alan.'

'These things happen.'

'Tell me about it. I've been there. Want to get rat-arsed and talk about it some time?'

Banks laughed. 'It'll be a pleasure. By the way, have you ever heard anything on the grapevine about a DS called Annie Cabbott?'

'Can't say as I have. But then I've not exactly been around the grapevine much recently . . . So, then, what can I do for you?'

'Well, I'm looking for the details of a suicide. Leeds. Bramley. Gunshot wound. Name's Matthew Shackleton. Died on the 15th of March, 1950.'

'It could take a while.'

'You mean you're talking minutes instead of seconds?'

Blackstone laughed. 'Hours, more like. I'll get DC Collins to make some phone calls. I'll call you back later.'

'Thanks, Ken,' he said. 'Appreciate it.'

'You'd better. And, Alan . . . Don't be a stranger.'

'I know, I know. Curry and piss-up and talk about girls. Soon as you get the info.'

BILLY JOE AND GLORIA soon became a couple. Billy Joe was seen going alone to Bridge Cottage, and that got the village tongues wagging. Especially when PX was seen going there the next day. He, too, seemed to have taken a shy sort of shine to Gloria, happy to get for her whatever her heart desired. I suggested Gloria tell them to use the back door, where they couldn't be seen, but she just laughed.

Gloria told me she wanted sex and Billy Joe was good at it. I still didn't understand what *it* was all about.

Gloria also needed her Luckies, nylons, lipstick, rouge and whisky. And PX, of course, would get her all these things at the flutter of an eyelash. Whether she ever granted him any favours in exchange, I can't say for certain, but I doubt it. I couldn't imagine PX actually being *with* a woman in that way. He seemed too shy.

Billy Joe was essentially an aeroplane mechanic, but he could fix anything on wheels. When our Morris van gave up the ghost, Billy Joe came down with PX and a couple of others, fixed it in a jiffy, then the whole gang of us collected Gloria and went to the Shoulder of Mutton for a drink. A curious incident occurred that night.

They were the only Americans in the pub and we were the only women. In addition to getting us plenty of suspicious glances, this also drew a few loud and pointed comments.

'Think about it, Bert,' said one local as we bought our drinks. 'Our lads are over there fighting the Nazis, and them damn Yanks are over here sniffing around our women like tomcats on heat.'

We ignored them and took a table in a quiet corner.

The next time we were ready for drinks, Billy Joe went to the bar. He was drinking pints of watery beer, and I had told him to hold on to his glass because there was a shortage. As he was on his way back, one of the local strapping farm lads who hadn't been called up—something to do with an allergy—called out after him: 'Hey, Yank. Tha's ta'en me glass.'

Billy Joe tried to ignore him, but the man, Seth his name was, lumbered over from the bar and stood right behind Billy Joe. The place went quiet.

'I said that's *my* glass tha's got tha beer in, Yank.'

Billy Joe put the tray down on the table and shrugged. 'Same one ah've had all evening, sir,' he said in that lazy Southern drawl.

'"Same one ah've had all evening, sir."' Seth tried to mock him, but it didn't come out right. 'Well it's mine.'

Billy Joe picked up his glass of beer, turned to face Seth slowly and shook his head. 'Ah don't think so, sir.'

'Well, I bloody do. Gimme it back, Yank.'

Billy Joe nodded in that slow way of his, then he poured the beer all over Seth's feet and held out the glass to him. 'You can take the glass,' he said. 'But the beer was mine. Ah paid for it. And, by the way, sir, ah am not a Yankee.'

Even Seth's friends had started to laugh by now. It was that sort of fulcrum moment, when so much hangs in the balance.

Seth made the wrong move. He stepped back and raised his fist. Billy Joe's speed amazed me. Before anyone knew what had happened, there was the sound of breaking glass and Seth was screaming, hands over his face, blood gushing out between his fingers.

'Ah am not a Yankee, sir,' Billy Joe repeated, then turned his back and sat down. The mood had soured, nobody wanted anything more to drink, and we all left shortly afterwards.

VIVIAN ELMSLEY GOT UP at about one o'clock, turned on the bedside light and took a sleeping pill. She didn't like the way they made her feel woolly-minded the next morning, but lying tossing and turning all night was exhausting.

Slowly, the chemical insinuated its way into her system. She felt sluggish, her blood heavy as lead. She hovered on the threshold between sleep and waking, where thoughts take on the aspect of dreams.

She pictured Gloria's tilted head as she had appeared on the TV screen in the detail from Stanhope's painting, then Gloria covered in blood that oozed from cuts deep into the gristle of her flesh.

Vivian tried to stop it but she felt as if she were being held down by an anchor hooked deep into the horror. She struggled to wake and, as she did, the telephone rang. She shot up, gasping for air as if she had been drowning.

Without thinking, she picked up the receiver. A lifeline.

The monotone voice said, 'Gwen. Gwen Shackleton.'

'Go away,' she mumbled, her tongue thick and furred.

The voice laughed. 'Soon, Gwen,' the man said. 'Soon.'

BANKS AND ANNIE drove out to the estate from Millgarth police headquarters. Banks parked near Bramley Town End, and he and Annie strolled towards the street where Gwen and Matthew Shackleton had lived. Both were dressed casually; neither looked like a police officer. Sometimes, feelings against all forms of authority ran high on these estates.

'How are we going to approach this?' Annie asked.

'We'll play it by ear.'

It was another hot day; people sat out on their doorsteps or had dragged striped deck chairs onto postage-stamp lawns, where the grass was parched pale brown. Banks couldn't help but be aware of the suspicious eyes following their progress.

The address turned out to be on one of the narrower side streets. Most of the doors had scratched and weathered paintwork, and the whole street looked run-down. All the windows of the old Shackleton house were open and loud music blasted from inside.

Banks knocked on the door. A dog growled inside the house. Finally, the door jerked open and a young skinhead in a red T-shirt and torn jeans stuck his head out, holding a barking Rottweiler by its studded collar. Banks stepped back a couple of paces.

'Who the fuck are you? What do you want?' the skinhead asked. He couldn't have been older than eighteen or nineteen.

'Your mum and dad in?' Banks asked.

He laughed. 'I should think so. They never go anywhere. Trouble is, you'll have a bloody long journey. They live in Nottingham.'

'So *you* live here?'

'Course I fucking do.' The dog was still straining at its collar, drool dripping from its jowls, but it had turned quieter now.

'I'd like some information,' said Banks. 'Can we come in?'

'You must be joking, mate. One step over this threshold and Gazza here'll have you singing soprano in the church choir.'

Banks could believe it. 'Fine,' he said. 'Then maybe you can tell us what we want to know out here? It's the house I'm interested in.'

'Who is it, Kev?' came a woman's voice from inside.

Kev turned round and yelled back, 'Mind yer own business, yer stupid bitch!'

Banks sensed Annie stiffen beside him. He touched her forearm gently.

'How long have you lived here?' Banks asked.

'Two years. What's it to you?'

'I'm interested in something that happened here fifty years ago. Do you know who lived here before you?'

'Haven't a clue, mate. But you can ask the wrinklies over the road. They've been here since the ice age.' He pointed to the middle terraced house directly opposite.

'Thanks,' he said. Annie followed him across the street.

After Banks and Annie had held their warrant cards up to the letterbox for inspection, the deadlock and chain came off and a hunched man, probably somewhere in his early seventies, opened the door. He had a hollow chest, deep-set eyes, a thin, lined face and sparse black-and-grey hair larded back with lashings of Brylcreem.

He led them into the house. The windows were all shut tight and the living room had the atmosphere of a hot and stuffy funeral parlour; it smelt of cigarette smoke.

'What's it all about, then?' The old man flopped down on a sagging brown corduroy settee.

'The past,' said Banks.

A woman walked through from the kitchen. About the same age as the man, she seemed a little better preserved. She certainly had a bit more flesh on her bones.

The old man reached for his cigarettes and lighter and he coughed when he lit up. What the future holds in store for us smokers if we don't stop, Banks thought glumly.

'Police, Elsie,' the man said. 'They say it's about the past.'

'Aye, well, there's plenty of that about for everyone,' she said. 'Like a cuppa?'

'Please,' said Banks. Annie nodded.

'Sit yerselves down then. I'm Mrs Patterson, by the way. You can call me Elsie. And this is my Stanley.'

Stanley leaned forward and offered his hand. 'Call me Stan,' he said, with a wink. Elsie went to make the tea.

'How long have you lived here?' Banks asked.

'For ever. Or so it seems,' Stan said. 'It weren't really such a bad place when we first moved in.'

Elsie soon came back with the tea.

'Stan was telling me you've lived here a long time,' Banks said to her.

'Since we got married,' she said. 'This was our first home together.' She poured the tea into white mugs and sat beside her husband.

'And our last, way things turned out,' Stan said.

'Well, whose fault were that? You knew I wanted to move to that new Raynville Estate when they built it, didn't you?'

'Aye,' said Stan. 'And where is it now? They've had to knock the bloody place down now, things got so bad.'

'What year was it?' Banks butted in. 'When you came?'

'In 1949,' Elsie said. 'October 1949. I remember because I were three months gone with Derek at the time.'

'Do you remember anything about your neighbours across the street?' Annie asked.

Elsie spoke first. 'Weren't that those, you know, those . . . what's-their-names, Stanley? A bit stuck up. There were some trouble. That tall skinny young fellow, never said a word to anyone. Shot himself. What were his name?'

'Matthew Shackleton.'

'That's right. We had police all over the place.'

'Did you know the Shackletons?' Banks asked.

'Not really,' Elsie said. 'I tried to be friendly, you know, like you do. The time or two I did talk to her, she didn't say owt about where they came from, except to mention that things had been different back in the village, like. Well, la-di-da, I thought.'

Well, Banks thought, from Hobb's End to this Leeds council estate would have been quite a frightening journey into purgatory for Gwen and Matthew, unless they were in a purgatory of their own making already.

'How many of them lived there?'

'Just the two,' Elsie said. 'I remember her saying her mother used to live with them, but she died a year or so before.'

'Aye,' Stan chipped in. 'I remember them now. Just the two of them. Him and his wife. Tall, gangly lass, herself.'

'Nay,' said Elsie, 'she were never his wife. They didn't act like man and wife.'

'Don't be so bloody daft, woman,' Stan said. Then he looked at Banks. 'She were his wife. Take it from me.'

'What was her name?' Banks asked.

'Blodwyn,' said Stan. 'Summat Welsh, anyroad.'

'No, it weren't. Gwynneth, that were it.'

'What did she look like?'

'Ordinary, really, apart from them beautiful eyes of hers,' said Elsie. 'Like Stanley said, she were a bit taller than your average lass. She had a hard-done-by look about her. Tired, like.'

'Must've been from looking after her husband. He were an invalid. Battle fatigue. War wound.'

'What happened after the suicide?' Banks asked.

'She went away,' Elsie said.

'Do you know where?'

'No. She never even said goodbye. One day she were there, the next she were gone. I'll tell you what, though.' A wicked smile twisted her features. 'I know who that Gwynneth Shackleton is. That's not her name now, of course. Done right well for herself, she has. I've seen her on telly, seen her picture in *Woman's Own*.'

'Yer barmy, woman,' Stan piped up.

'I'm telling you, Stanley: it's her. Those eyes. The height. The voice. I don't forget things like that.'

Banks was trying hard to remain patient. 'Mrs Patterson. Elsie,' he said finally. 'Could you tell me *who* you think Gwen Shackleton is?'

'That woman writes those detective books. Always on telly. With that good-looking what's-'is-name playing the inspector.'

'She's thinking of that Vivian Elmsley woman,' sighed Stan.

'You don't agree?' Annie asked.

'Nay, I don't know, lass. I'm not good at faces, not the way our Elsie is. There *is* a resemblance, but . . .' He shook his head. 'It's so long ago.'

'Was Gwen in the house at the time of the suicide?' Banks asked.

Elsie paused. 'That's what they asked us back then,' she said. 'I don't know. I *thought* I saw her get back from the shops *before* I heard the bang.' She frowned. 'But I could have been wrong.'

'Did you tell the police this?'

'Yes. But nowt came out of it.'

Now Banks definitely wanted to have a look at the Matthew Shackleton file.

'Well, we might as well be off,' he said to Annie, then turned to Stan and Elsie. 'Thanks very much. You've been a great help.'

'Tell me summat,' said Stan. 'This Gwen, were she his wife?'

'His sister. We think.'

Elsie nudged her husband hard in the ribs. He started coughing. 'See, Stanley. I told yer so, yer great lummox.'

Banks and Annie walked gratefully out into the fresh air.

'What do you think about this Vivian Elmsley business?' Annie asked.

'I'm surprised that neither Betty nor Alice mentioned it.'

'Maybe they didn't know? Alice seems to have very poor eyesight, and Betty Goodall pays little attention to current affairs.'

'True,' said Banks. 'It's definitely worth looking into.'

'So,' said Annie back in the car. 'What next?'

'The local nick. I want to see Matthew Shackleton's file. Then back to Millgarth.'

'Have we time for a drink and a bite to eat later?'

'Sorry. I've got a date.'

She thumped him playfully. 'Seriously?'

'Seriously. With a detective inspector. A *male* detective inspector called Ken Blackstone.'

Banks explained his tenuous friendship with Ken and how he was in the mood for building bridges He realised that he had been neglecting his friends for too long.

'I see,' Annie said. 'A boys' night out, then?' If she was disappointed, she didn't show it.

BILLY JOE WAS CONFINED to base for a few weeks. They said his punishment would have been far more severe had not all the witnesses attested that he didn't start the fight. Gloria never said as much, but I think the incident put her off Billy Joe. Violence upset her.

It was while Billy Joc was confined to base that we first met Brad and Charlie.

We were walking out of the Lyceum. It was a miserable February night in 1944, not snowing, but freezing cold. We had been to see Bette Davis and Paul Henreid in *Now, Voyager*, and we were both humming the theme song as we put our coats back on in the foyer.

A young man in a fleece-lined leather jacket walked over, put two cigarettes in his mouth, lit them, then handed one to Gloria, as they had done in the film. We doubled over laughing.

'Brad,' said the young man. 'Brad Szikorski. And this is my pal Charlie Markleson.'

Gloria did a little mock curtsy. 'Charmed to meet you, I'm sure.'

'We're with the 448th, over at Rowan Woods. I don't mean to be forward,' said Brad, 'but would you ladies care to honour us by joining us for a drink?'

We exchanged glances. I could tell Gloria wanted to go. Brad was tall and handsome, with a twinkle in his eye and a little Clark Gable moustache. I looked at Charlie, who was probably destined to be my companion for the evening. He had intelligent eyes and a rather pale, thin face. His nose was too big, and it had a bump in the middle, but then mine was nothing to write home about, either. He also seemed reserved and serious. All in all, he'd do.

We walked to the Black Swan. Brad went to the bar and came back bearing a tray of drinks. We toasted one another and drank.

'What do you do?' Gloria asked.

'I'm a pilot,' said Brad, 'and Charlie here's my navigator.'

'A pilot! How exciting. Where are you from?'

'California.'

Gloria clapped her hands together. 'Hollywood!'

'Well, not exactly. A little place called Pasadena.'

'But you must know Hollywood?'

Brad smiled, revealing straight white teeth. 'As a matter of fact, yeah, I do,' he said. 'I did a little stunt flying there in the movies before I came over here.'

'You mean you've actually been in pictures?'

'Well, yeah, I guess so.' He named a couple of titles we hadn't heard of. 'That's what I want to do when all this is over,' he went on. 'Get in the movie business, have a shot at being a stunt man.'

As Gloria and Brad chatted away excitedly about films and Hollywood, Charlie and I started our own hesitant conversation.

He asked me what I did, nodding his head every now and then as I told him. Then he told me that he had completed his English degree just before the war, and wanted to go to Harvard to study law. The more we talked, the more we found we had in common—Jane Austen and Thomas Hardy, for example, and the poetry of T. S. Eliot. And Robert Frost and Edward Thomas. He hadn't heard of many of our younger poets, so I offered to lend him some issues of Penguin New Writing.

'Have you got a husband?' I overheard Brad ask Gloria. 'I mean, I don't mean to . . . You know . . .'

'It's all right. I did have. But he's dead. Killed in Burma. At least I hope to God he was.'

I turned from Charlie. There was still a lingering hope, at least in my mind, and I thought that was a terrible thing to say. I told her so.

She turned on me, eyes flashing. 'You must know what they're saying about the way the Japanese treat their prisoners?'

I had to admit that I had read one or two rather grim stories alleging that torture and decapitation were favourite pastimes in the Japanese POW camps. If the stories were true, then I should probably agree with Gloria and hope Matthew was dead.

'I've got friends fighting in the Pacific,' said Charlie. 'I hear it's pretty rough out there.'

'Well, he's dead, anyway,' said Gloria. 'Look, this is too depressing. Can we have another round of drinkies, please?'

Brad and Charlie drove us home in their Jeep. Charlie seemed a little embarrassed when Brad and Gloria started kissing passionately by the

fairy bridge, but he managed to pluck up the courage to put his arm round me. We kissed dutifully and arranged to meet again soon. Brad told Charlie to drive on, that he'd walk back to the base alone later, and he followed Gloria into Bridge Cottage.

THE INDIAN RESTAURANT Ken Blackstone had chosen was a hole-in-the-wall on Burley Road. Sitar music droned from speakers high on the walls, and the aromas of cumin and coriander filled the air.

'Did you find what you were looking for in those incident reports?' Blackstone asked as they shared poppadoms, samosas and pakoras.

'I wasn't after anything in particular,' Banks said. 'Elsie Patterson was unsure as to whether she saw Gwen Shackleton enter the house before or after she heard the shot. And she was the only witness. Nobody else saw Gwen or Matthew that day.'

'What did Gwen Shackleton say in her statement?'

'She just said she found Matthew dead in the armchair when she got home from shopping.'

'Was there any real doubt? Was she ever a suspect?'

'I didn't get that impression. Matthew Shackleton had had a history of mental illness since the war. He was also an alcoholic. According to the report, he had tried to kill himself once before, head in the gas oven that time. A neighbour smelt gas and saved him.'

'It was just a matter of time?'

'Seems that way. Though I suppose there's always the possibility that he was helped on his way, that he had become an intolerable burden to his sister. Remember, Gwen had been taking care of both her mother *and* her brother. It's not much of a life for a young woman, is it? But we'd never prove it.'

'Not unless Gwen Shackleton confessed.'

Their main courses arrived: rogan josh and king prawns, with aloo gobi, pilau rice, lime chutney and chapattis.

'What about forensics?' Blackstone asked.

'Single shot in the mouth. No evidence of a struggle. Empty whisky bottle by the chair. The angle of the wound was also consistent with the suicide theory.'

'Note?'

'Yes. The genuine article, according to forensics.'

'So what's bothering you?'

Banks ate some curry and washed it down with lager before answering. 'Nothing, really. I'm not very interested in whether Gwen

Shackleton helped her brother commit suicide or not. But I *would* like to know if he murdered Gloria Shackleton.'

'Perhaps he couldn't live with the guilt?'

'It's the most likely explanation. The only person who can tell us is Gwen Shackleton.'

'What happened to her? Is she still alive?'

'That's another interesting thing. Elsie Patterson swears she's Vivian Elmsley.'

Blackstone whistled. 'The writer?'

'That's the one. We'll have to talk to her. She certainly hasn't been in touch with us. But it's hard to imagine that many people don't know the story.'

'Which may mean that, if it is her, she has a reason for not wanting to be found?'

'Exactly. A guilty secret.'

Blackstone ordered a couple more pints of lager. Then he asked, 'This DS, Annie Cabbot. Good-looking woman?'

'I suppose so.'

'You involved with her?'

Banks paused. Why lie? Ken was a mate. He nodded briefly.

'Is it serious?'

'For crying out loud, Ken, I've only known her a week.'

Blackstone held his hand up. 'OK, OK. Just be careful, that's all. You're still vulnerable. When someone goes through what you're going through, he either ends up angry for a long time or he misses what he had. Or both. If he's angry at women he probably just shags them and leaves them. But if he misses the relationship, then he looks for another one to replace it, and his judgment isn't necessarily in the best of nick. If he's both, then he gets into another relationship and screws it up royally all round and wonders why everyone ends up in tears.'

Banks stood up. 'Well, thanks for the amateur psychology, Ken, but if I'd wanted Claire fucking Rayner—'

Blackstone grabbed on to Banks's sleeve. 'Alan. Sit down. Please. I'm not suggesting you do anything except be aware of the pitfalls. That's all the wisdom I have to offer.' He smiled. 'You've always struck me as a bit of a romantic underneath it all.'

Banks hesitated, still half ready to leave and half ready to punch Blackstone. 'What do you mean?'

'The kind of detective who cares just a bit too much about every victim. The kind of bloke who falls a little bit in love with every woman he sleeps with.'

Banks reached for a cigarette. He felt uncomfortable, as if he were in the dentist's chair and Blackstone were probing a particularly sensitive nerve.

'Alan,' Blackstone went on, 'ten months ago you thought you had a stable marriage. Then, all of a sudden, you find you've got nothing of the kind. The emotional fallout from that sort of upset doesn't go away overnight, mate, I can tell you. Enjoy yourself. Just don't make it more than it is. You're not ready to deal with that yet. Don't confuse sex and love.' He slapped the table. 'Shit, now I *am* starting to sound like Claire Rayner. Ignore me.'

Banks finished his pint. 'Look, I take your point, Ken, but to be honest, it's the first time I've felt comfortable with a woman since Sandra left—the first time I've really felt free enough to jump into something and say damn the consequences.'

Blackstone laughed and shook his head slowly. 'Sounds like you've got it bad.' He looked at his watch. 'What say we hit the flesh-pots of Leeds and get irredeemably pissed?'

Banks smiled. 'Most sensible thing you've said all night.'

WINTER FINALLY GAVE WAY to a slow spring, with its snowdrops in Rowan Woods, then the bluebells, crocuses and daffodils. Brad and Charlie became our regular 'beaux' and we saw far less of Billy Joe, who became very sulky. I was worried that Billy Joe would start a fight, given his violent streak, but he soon found another girl and started talking to us again when we met at dances and in pubs. He pestered Gloria on occasion to go back with him, but she was able to keep him at bay, even when she'd been drinking. PX, of course, remained absolutely essential, so we still cultivated him.

I won't say that my affair with Charlie was a grand passion, but we became less awkward with the physical side of things, and he did become the first man I ever slept with. He was gentle, patient and sensitive, and I came to look forward to those times we spent in bed together at Bridge Cottage, courtesy of Gloria. Our relationship remained more of an intellectual one; we passed books back and forth with abandon. Charlie wasn't dull and dry, though; he loved to dance and was a great Humphrey Bogart fan. He took me to see *Casablanca* and *The Maltese Falcon*.

When Michael Stanhope had an exhibition in Leeds, Charlie and I made a weekend of it and went to stay at the Metropole Hotel. Charlie, who knew a lot more about painting than I did, praised the exhibition to the skies. Even Gloria went to see Mr Stanhope at his studio that summer and autumn more often than she had before.

I tried not to dwell on the dangers inherent in Charlie's job and, for his part, he never seemed to want to talk about them. The war receded into the distance during those hours we spent together reading or making love.

In May, when it was warmer, we would often sit on the banks of Harksmere and read Coleridge and Wordsworth out loud to one another. We had picnics of Spam and potted-shrimp sandwiches.

Mother liked Charlie, I could tell, though she didn't say much. She never did. Matthew's disappearance had taken most of the wind out of her sails.

After the excitement of the Normandy landing, slowly things began to improve. The blackout was replaced by the 'dim-out' in September. If by autumn, then, we were feeling flush with the possibility of victory, we had little idea of the grim winter to come.

BY TEN O'CLOCK that night Annie was feeling so restless that even a large glass of wine didn't help settle her down.

She felt disappointed that Banks would rather go drinking with someone else than be with her. True, it was she who had suggested they limit their time together to weekends, but it was also she who had broken the rule the other night. Why couldn't he do the same?

But at least she hadn't wasted *her* time that evening. The long trail that had started on Wednesday, over the telephone, was beginning to bear fruit.

At first, she had come to the conclusion that it was easier finding a fully dressed woman in the *Sunday Sport* than getting information out of the American Embassy. She was shunted from one minion to another for the best part of an hour. By the end of the day, she managed to discover that the personnel at Rowan Woods in late 1943 would have been members of the United States 8th Air Force, and one of the more helpful employees suggested that she try contacting the National Personnel Records Center in St Louis, Missouri. She checked the time difference and after a little more shunting around was put through to a woman called Mattie, who just 'adored' her accent. Mattie told her she would see what she could do. When Annie mentioned the initials 'PX', Mattie laughed and said that was the man who looked after the store. She also warned Annie that some of their records had been burnt in a fire a few years ago, but if she still had Rowan Woods, she'd fax it. Annie thanked her profusely and felt absurdly pleased with herself.

But it didn't last.

Sometimes when she felt irritable and restless like this, she would go for a drive, and that was exactly what she did now. Without making a conscious decision, she took the road west out of Harkside, and when she reached the turnoff for Thornfield Reservoir, she turned right.

By then she had realised that Banks wasn't the problem; *she* was. She was pissed off at herself for letting him get to her. She was behaving like some sort of silly love-struck schoolgirl. Vulnerable. Hurt. Let's face it, Annie, she told herself, life has been pretty simple for some time now. No real highs; no real lows. She had been protecting her emotions from the harsh world 'out there'. Sometimes when you open yourself up to that life again, it can be painful. Your emotions are tender and raw, more than usually sensitive to little hurts and humiliations. So that was what was happening.

She pulled into the car park and got out. Silence. A misshapen harvest moon hung low in the western sky.

She took the narrow footpath towards Hobb's End. Hardly any moonlight penetrated the tree cover, but here and there she caught a slat or two of reddish-silver light between branches. She could smell the loamy, earthy smell of trees and shrubs.

Annie reached the slope and paused, looking down on the ruins of Hobb's End. Then she skipped down the slope and walked towards the fairy bridge. From there, she looked along the river and saw the blood-red moonlight reflected in the few little puddles of water that remained on its muddy bed. She walked on past the outbuilding where Gloria's skeleton had been found, and the ruins of Bridge Cottage next to it, and headed down what was once the High Street.

As she went, Annie tried to visualise the scene from Michael Stanhope's painting: children laughing and splashing in the river shallows; knots of local women gossiping outside a shop; the tall young woman arranging newspapers in a rack. *Gwynneth Shackleton*. That was who it was. Why hadn't she realised it before?

She looked at the ruins to her right and saw where once there was a detached cottage with a little garden, a row of terraced houses opening directly onto the pavement. Here was the Shackletons' newsagent's shop, here the butcher's, and a little further down stood the Shoulder of Mutton. So real did it all seem that she began to fancy she could even hear long-silent voices.

As she stood at the western end of the village and breathed in the air deeply, she realised how much she wanted to know what had happened here, every bit as much as Banks did. She identified with Gloria. This was a woman who had struggled and dared to be a little different in a time that didn't tolerate such behaviour. She had lost her parents, then had come to a remote place and fallen in love.

Suddenly, Annie noticed a movement and saw a figure scuttle across the fairy bridge. Her blood froze.

Finding her voice, she called out. No answer came. The figure disappeared into the woods. Annie set off in pursuit.

Just when she had got back up the slope, and was heading for the woods, she heard a car start ahead of her. There were two small car parks, separated by a high hedge, and whoever this was must have been parked in the other one, or Annie would have seen the car earlier. She put on an extra burst of speed but could only get to the road in time to see the taillights disappearing.

Chapter Six

'He asked me to marry him,' Gloria repeated.

'I still don't believe you,' I said.

It was early in the new year, 1945, and I had dropped by Bridge Cottage to see how Gloria was coping: she had had a terrible cold over Christmas—had even missed Alice Poole's farewell party. Though she was pale she seemed to be on the mend.

'Well, you can ask him yourself. It's true. You should have seen my nose when he asked me. It was red-raw.'

I laughed. It was good to laugh at something. Christmas that year had been a miserable affair because the advance that had seemed to be going so well earlier had bogged down in the Ardennes.

'What did you say?' I asked.

'I told him I'd think about it, but he'd have to wait until we could find out for certain about Matt.'

'Do you love him?'

'In a way. Not . . . Oh, I mean I don't really think I could ever love anyone like I loved Matt, but Brad and I get on well enough. And he's good to me. When the war's over, he wants to take me back to Hollywood with him.'

'It'll be a new lease of life, I suppose.'

'Yes.'

'And I'll have someone I can visit out there.'

'You will.'

'But? I still sense a "but".'

'Oh, I don't know, Gwen. You know I can't even consider getting married again until the war's over, for a start. But I will think about it. What about Charlie? Has he asked you yet?'

I blushed. 'No,' I said.

'Books, that's all you two ever talk about.'

'It's not.'

She smiled. 'I'm teasing, Gwen. I'm glad you're happy. Honest, I am. There's no hurry, I suppose. But you could do a lot worse. A lawyer! He'll be rich, just you wait and see. You can go to America, too. We can see each other all the time.'

'Gloria, Boston is miles away from Los Angeles.'

'Is it? Well, at least we'll be in the same country.'

And so we chatted on about what the future might offer us. Gloria soon recovered her health, and February brought the prospect of victory closer. I actually began to believe that we were entering the last spring of the war.

Everything changed one grey afternoon in March, when a tall, gaunt stranger walked down the High Street towards me, struggling against the wind.

BANKS REALLY MUST have had a night on the tiles, Annie thought. It was after nine, and he wasn't in his office yet. Was he still in Leeds? Had he and his friend picked up some women?

She fought back the acid-burn of jealousy that curdled in her stomach. Jealousy and suspicion had ruined relationships for her before. Just before Rob got killed she had suspected he was seeing someone else and had consequently treated him badly. She thought she had learned detachment, but perhaps she had only put her insecurity in mothballs. It was a frightening thought.

The fax machine hummed into action. Annie hurried over. It was a personnel breakdown of the 448th Bomber Group based at Rowan

Woods between December 19, 1943 and May 17, 1945, when they had left. There were a lot of names.

As she glanced over the list, Annie thought again about the Hobb's End incident last night. It had rattled her more than she realised at first, and she had had a difficult time getting to sleep. W*hy* should someone hide from her, and then why take off when she gave chase? There was nothing left at the site; the SOCOs had been over it thoroughly. Perhaps someone might *think* there was something there, though. Whoever it was hadn't been old enough to have murdered Gloria Shackleton over fifty years ago: people in their seventies or eighties don't usually move that fast.

So it remained a mystery. She wanted to talk to Banks about it, but he'd been off getting pissed with his mates. She hoped he had a hangover the size of China.

BANKS GOT BACK to Gratly safe and sane via the slow back roads. He didn't want Annie to see him until he had managed a change of clothes. The ones he was wearing stank of smoke and stale beer.

His head ached, despite the paracetamol he had downed at Ken's flat that morning. When he had woken up and looked around Ken's living room, he had groaned at the detritus of a wild and foolish night: an empty bottle of Glenmorangie on the coffee table, alongside an empty bottle of claret and an overflowing ashtray. Even a fifteen-year-old would have had more sense than to mix lager, wine and whisky that way. All the hangover clichés ran through his mind: *You're getting too old for this sort of thing* and *I'll never touch another drop as long as I live*.

After a shave, a shower and a change of clothes, Banks drove to his office. He hardly had time to turn on his computer when his door opened and in strode Chief Constable Jeremiah 'Jimmy' Riddle himself, making one of his rare forays to Eastvale. Banks muttered a silent curse. Just what he needed.

'Banks, you look bloody awful,' said Riddle. 'What have you been doing, man? Drinking yourself silly?'

'Touch of flu, sir. What can I do for you, sir?'

'Flu, my arse. I hope you're on top of things?'

'Definitely, sir.'

'Good. I want you to bring me up to date on that skeleton case. I've got to go to London today to tape an interview for *Panorama*. They're putting together a special segment on the investigation of old cases, how DNA makes a difference, that sort of thing.' He brushed some imaginary fluff from the front of his uniform. 'And you'd better make it quick. My train leaves in an hour and a half.'

Well, be thankful for small mercies, Banks told himself. He told him what he and Annie had discovered so far.

Riddle ran his hand over his shiny bald scalp and said, 'It's not much to go on, is it? Memory of a couple of old biddies?'

'We're not likely to get much better,' said Banks. 'Too much time's gone by. Anyway, we're still waiting for results of DNA tests from Dr Williams and our forensic odontologist. These things take time.'

'And cost money. Don't think I'm not keeping my eye on the bottom line on this one, Banks.'

'You mentioned DNA, sir,' Banks said. 'You might mention that it would be a great help if Gloria Shackleton's son could get in touch with us. That way we could verify the identity of the remains once and for all.'

Riddle stood up. 'If I've got time, Banks. If I've got time. By the way,' he said. 'DS Cabbot. How's she working out?'

She. So he did know. 'Fine,' said Banks. 'She's a good detective. Wasted in a place like Harkside.'

A malicious smile flitted across Riddle's face. 'Ah, yes. Pity, really. I understand there was some trouble in her previous posting.'

'Trouble, sir?'

'You should know all about that, Banks. Insubordination, failure to respect senior ranks.'

'I respect the rank, sir,' said Banks. 'But not always the person who fills it.'

Riddle stiffened. 'Well, I hope you're enjoying yourself—for your sake, Banks—because this is about as good as it's going to get.'

With that he walked out and slammed the door.

On his way to the coffee machine, Banks asked DS Hatchley to find out what he could about Francis Henderson, Gloria's illegitimate child. It was a loose end that nagged him.

Back at his desk there was a message from a Major Gargrave, in military personnel. Banks phoned him back.

'It's about that query you made the other day,' said Major Gargrave. 'Matthew Shackleton. It's all a bit embarrassing really.'

'He came back, didn't he? We found a death certificate dated 1950. I was going to ask you about it.'

'Yes, well, when my assistant was returning the file, he found some papers wedged down between two folders. It was a filing error.'

'When did he return?' Banks asked.

'March 1945. Place called Hobb's End. Does that make any sense?'

'Yes,' said Banks. 'Go on.'

'Sergeant Shackleton simply discharged himself from a London hospital and went home. The hospital said he'd been liberated from a Japanese POW camp and shipped home in pretty bad shape. No identification.'

'And that's all?'

'Yes. It would seem so. Very odd.'

'OK,' said Banks, 'thanks very much for calling, Major.'

After he hung up, Banks opened the window and let the sunshine in. He thought of lighting a cigarette but his throat and lungs still felt raw. There was something that didn't make sense in what the major had just told him, but he couldn't quite work out what. Too many dead brain cells in the way.

Banks steeled himself and picked up the phone. Annie answered on the third ring.

'You're back, then.' Her tone was icy.

'Yes.'

'Have a good time?'

'Pretty good, thanks. I'd rather forget this morning, though.'

'You probably deserve it.'

'Probably.'

'I've got the info on the Rowan Woods personnel.'

'Wonderful.'

'It's a long list, though. It'll take a bit of whittling down. There was more than one person working in the PX, for a start.'

'Is there anything else?'

Annie told him about what happened at Hobb's End.

'It was probably just a kid.'

'It didn't look like a kid. And it drove away.'

'There's not much we can do about it now, though, is there?'

'I just thought I'd let you know. For the record.'

'We'd better track down Vivian Elmsley,' Banks said.

'I've already done that.'

'Now I'm *really* impressed.'

'So you should be. While you've been recovering from your self-inflicted damage, I've been on the phone.'

Banks sensed that her tone was softening a little. 'And?'

'Well, in her case it was easy. She's in the London telephone directory. I've got her address. What do you want to do about it?'

'We should talk to her as soon as possible. If she really is the one we're looking for, she's holding something back. There was another thing nagging at me and I've just realised what it was.' Banks explained to her about the call from Major Gargrave. 'Why would Matthew have a gun? If he was a released POW, he'd hardly have his service revolver. I should imagine the Japanese confiscated the weapons from the people they captured, wouldn't you?'

'Unless his liberators gave him one?'

'I suppose that's just possible. Especially if they were Americans. Americans feel naked without guns. But I think it's unlikely. And why would he still have it when he went back to Hobb's End?'

'If he did have a gun, though, why didn't he use that on Gloria instead of strangling her and stabbing her?'

'*If* it was Matthew who killed her.'

'Have you considered Gwen as a serious suspect?' Annie asked.

'Certainly. According to everything we've heard, she was very close to her brother. If Gloria was running around with other men, Gwen might have fought back on his behalf. At the very least she should be able to tell us more about Matthew's relationship with Gloria after he came back. Fancy a trip to London tomorrow? There's a train leaves York at around a quarter to nine. Can you manage that?'

'No problem.'

After Annie hung up, Banks tried dialling Brian's Wimbledon number again. Still nothing. He hoped he might be able to see Brian tomorrow, have a talk, get things sorted. He didn't want Brian to keep on thinking he was disappointed in him.

He went back to his desk. For about the third time since the case began, he spread out the objects found with Gloria Shackleton's body. Detective Superintendent Gristhorpe might be able to tell him a bit about the button, he thought. Gristhorpe was a bit of an expert on military history, especially the Second World War.

Banks grabbed his jacket and was just about to leave the office when his phone rang.

'Hello, Alan.' A woman's voice.

'Yes?'

'It's Jenny. Jenny Fuller.'

He hadn't seen Jenny Fuller in almost a year, not since she'd decided to take a leave of absence from York University to teach in California.

'Jenny. It's been a long time. Where are you?'

'Home. Just got back yesterday.'

'A bit early, aren't you?'

'It's a long story.'

'I'm glad you called. I need some professional advice.'

'I might be able to manage that. The reason I'm phoning is, I'm in town and I wondered if you've got time for lunch?'

Banks had intended to drive out to Lyndgarth to see Gristhorpe, who was taking his annual holiday at home, but that could wait until later. 'Queen's Arms, half twelve?'

'Wonderful. I'll see you there.'

Banks smiled as he put down the receiver. His colleagues had expected him to sleep with Jenny Fuller after Sandra left. Perhaps he would have if she had been around. But timing is everything. Jenny was spending most of her time in California these days, and there was a man involved.

Now he and Jenny were having lunch in about an hour's time. Just enough time, in fact, to nip over to Waterstone's for a couple of Vivian Elmsley's novels. Her writing might give him some insight into her character.

FOR SOME REASON I was standing out in the street to check the window display when I glanced to my left and saw him coming across the fairy bridge. He was wearing a baggy brown suit and carrying no luggage. He was tall but stooped, as if suffering some affliction of the spine, and he walked with a stick. He moved slowly, as if he knew where he was going, but felt no hurry to get there. His frame was thin to the point of emaciation. As he came closer, I realised that he wasn't as old as I had first thought, though his lank, lifeless hair was tinged with grey.

The wind tugged at my clothes and chilled me to the marrow, but something about him compelled me to stand and watch, as if in a trance. When he got within a few feet, I saw his eyes. Deep, hollow, haunted eyes, turned completely inwards.

I don't know when the truth dawned on me; it could have been seconds; it could have been minutes. But I started to shake like a leaf. I ran to him and threw my arms round him but his body felt stiff and unyielding. Tears were pouring down my cheeks.

'Matthew!' I cried. 'Oh my God. Matthew!'

BANKS WALKED INTO the Queen's Arms a couple of minutes before twelve thirty, carrying two of Vivian Elmsley's paperback mysteries. He bought a pint and sat down at a table.

One was a suspense novel called *Guilty Secrets*—an interesting title from Banks's point of view—which bore review quotes to the effect that it was an 'amazing' and 'disturbing' achievement by one of our best mystery writers. The other was called *The Shadow of Death* and featured her series character, Detective Inspector Niven. The novel was praised for its 'compassionate realism in the portrayal of ordinary people' and its 'believable depictions of policemen's lives and police procedures'. Banks smiled. He'd see about that.

He was on page ten when Jenny dashed in, out of breath, tousled red hair flaming around her face. When she saw him she waved, hurried over and bent to give him a quick peck on the cheek. 'Sorry I'm late. My God, you look awful.'

Banks smiled and raised his glass. 'Hair of the dog.'

Jenny picked up the paperback he had set down on the table. 'I didn't think this sort of thing was up your alley.'

'Work.'

'Aha.' She raised her eyebrows.

Her figure looked as good as ever in tight black jeans and a loose jade silk top, Banks thought.

'So,' he said, when she had settled herself down. 'Can I get you a drink?'

'Campari and soda, please.'

'Food?'

'I've been craving scampi and chips for about a month now.'

'Scampi and chips it is.' Banks made his way to the bar, got them each a drink and ordered the food. He settled for plaice and chips.

He carried the drinks back and found Jenny poring over *The Shadow of Death*. Banks told her briefly about the case so far. By the time he had finished, their food arrived.

'Is it as good as you remembered?' he asked after she had taken a couple of bites.

'Nothing ever is,' Jenny said. He noticed a new sadness and weariness in her eyes. 'It's good, though.'

'What happened over there?'

'What do you mean?' She glanced at him, then looked away quickly. Too quickly. He saw fear in her eyes.

He thought of the first time he had met her in Gristhorpe's office, how he had been struck by her sharp intelligence and her quick sense of humour, as well as her flaming red hair, full lips and green eyes with their attractive laughter lines. His first impression had been that she was a knockout. He felt exactly the same today.

'Come on, Jenny,' he said. 'This sudden return wasn't on the agenda.'

She sighed, looked away, tried to form some words, sighed again. She seemed a lot more twitchy than he remembered, always moving her hands. 'It's all washed up, Alan. The job. Randy. My life.' She cocked her head. 'I never did have much luck with men, did I?'

Banks remembered one or two of Jenny's disasters.

'Just tell me what you want to, at your own pace,' said Banks.

She smiled and patted his arm. 'Thanks. You're sweet.' She snatched a cigarette from his packet and lit up.

'You don't smoke,' Banks said.

'I do now.' Jenny blew out a long plume. 'I've just about had it up to here with those nicotine-nazis out there. And to think California was a real hotbed of protest in the sixties. It's run by fascists now. As I'm sure you've gathered already,' she went on, 'Randy, my paramour, my reason for staying out there, is no longer a part of my life.'

'What happened?'

'Graduate students. Or, to put it more bluntly, blonde twenty-something bimbos with their brains between their legs.'

'I'm sorry, Jenny.'

She waved her hand. 'I should have seen it coming. Anyone else would have. Anyway, soon as I found out about what he was up to, there wasn't much to keep me there.'

'What are you going to do?'

'I'll be going back to my old lecturing job at York. Start next month. If that doesn't work out, I'll go into private practice. I'm quite the expert on deviants and criminal psychology. I've even been on training courses with the FBI profilers.'

'I want to ask your advice on something.'

'Go ahead. I'm finished blubbering and moaning. And I didn't even ask about you. How are *you* doing?'

'I'm doing fine, thanks.'

'Seeing anyone?'

Banks paused a moment. 'Sort of.'

'Serious?'

'What kind of a question is that?'

'So it *is* serious. What was it you wanted to ask me?'

'It's about Matthew Shackleton. Gwen's brother. Apparently he spent a few years in one of the Japanese prison camps. By all accounts, he was pretty disturbed when he came home. Ended up committing suicide. Thing is, all I can come up with in terms of psychiatric diagnoses are such vague terms as "combat fatigue". I was wondering what sort of diagnosis you'd come up with today.'

'That's a good one, Alan. You want me, a *psychologist*, to come up with a *psychiatric* diagnosis of a dead man's mental problems? This had better be between you and me.'

Banks grinned. 'Don't worry, you won't be called upon to testify in court.'

'Well,' Jenny said, 'I'm only guessing, but he was probably suffering from some kind of post-traumatic stress disorder.'

'This condition would have been caused by his experiences in the war and the camp, right?'

'Right. Basically, PTSDs are caused by some event or series of events well beyond the normal range of human experience—things like rape, kidnapping, military combat, earthquakes, fires, car crashes, torture, death camps.'

'I get the picture. What are the symptoms?'

'Recurrent nightmares about the event are common. Flashbacks and hallucinations. Anything that reminds the person of the event is painful, too; also things that were part of it. If a man was kept in a small cage for a long period, for example, then he would be likely to experience suffocating claustrophobia in a lift, for example. Strong feelings of detachment, estrangement and separation come with it. People who suffer from PTSDs often find it difficult to feel or accept love, they become alienated from their families and loved ones. Add to that insomnia, difficulty in concentrating, hypervigilance, panic disorders. Suicide is also not uncommon.'

'Might he be likely to become violent?'

'That's a difficult one. Anyone can become violent given the right stimulus. He would certainly be prone to irritability and outbursts of anger, but I'm not sure they'd necessarily lead to murder.'

'I was thinking he might have killed his wife because he found out she'd been having an affair.'

'I suppose it's possible,' Jenny said.

'But you don't think so?'

'Let me just say I hold reservations. The outbursts of anger in PTSD are usually fairly irrational. By linking them to his wife's behaviour, you're making it all far more logical. Cause and effect. And if he did feel detached and was unable to love, then where does the jealousy come in?'

'So could he or couldn't he?'

'Oh, no, you're not trapping me like that. Of course he *could* have committed murder. People do all the time, often for no reason.'

'Whoever did it probably strangled the woman, then stabbed her about fifteen or sixteen times.'

'Such rage. I don't know, Alan. From what I know of PTSD, I'd say that most of his pain and anger would have been directed inwards, not out at the world. Also, it's often too easy to pick on the mentally disturbed person as the most likely murderer. Most mentally ill people wouldn't harm a fly. Pathetic, perhaps, sometimes scary, but rarely dangerous.'

'Thanks. You've given me a lot to think about.'

They both sat in silence, nursing their drinks. Banks thought about Matthew Shackleton's suffering and his possible alienation from normal human affairs. If you couldn't feel love for someone, why would you feel hate? When Banks first found out about Sandra and Sean, he had hated them both because he still loved Sandra. If he hadn't cared, he wouldn't have felt so passionate.

'I fell apart, you know,' Jenny said suddenly.

'You did what?'

'I had a breakdown. After all that with Randy. I suddenly found myself completely cut off from everyone I'd grown up with, alone in a foreign country. It's one of the scariest feelings I've ever had. I fell to pieces. I even went to see a shrink.'

'Do any good?'

'Some. One of the things I realised was that I wanted to go home. That wasn't part of being ill. I *missed* this place too much. I actually missed winter. It gets you down, all that sun, day in, day out, only the occasional flood, fire or earthquake for variety. Anyway, as soon as I realised what I really wanted to do, I chucked my tranquillisers down the toilet and took the next flight home. Well, almost the next flight. I had a little act of girlish revenge to carry out first.'

'What did you do?'

Jenny flashed him a wicked grin. 'I planted one of those little voice-activated tape recorders in his office and taped one of his trysts. Then I sent the tape to the dean.'

'What happened?'

'I don't know. I left before the shit hit the fan. I should imagine he got suspended. Maybe fired.' She tossed back the rest of her drink and looked at her watch. 'Look, I'm sorry, I'll have to go. It's great seeing you again.'

She picked up her bag and paused. Then she looked Banks in the eye, and touched his hand softly. 'Why don't you give me a ring? We could . . . you know, have dinner or something together?'

Banks swallowed. 'I will. That would be great.'

She patted his hand, blew him a kiss and then she was gone in a whirl of red, jade and black, leaving a faint trace of Miss Dior behind. Banks looked down at his hand. It still tingled where she had touched him. Now that he had found the courage to start a relationship with Annie, Jenny was a complication he didn't need.

AFTER I HAD RUN and fetched Gloria from the farm, I was finally able to piece together what had happened. Matthew himself wouldn't say a word. He looked at us as if he remembered knowing us once, as if some deep homing instinct had brought him here, but our fussing didn't make much sense to him.

I went down to the telephone and began the long round of calls. The Ministry was about as much help as usual, the Red Cross a little more forthcoming, but it was ultimately a doctor in one of the big London hospitals who told me the most.

Matthew had been found at a Japanese POW camp near Luzon, in the Philippines. All his identification was missing, and all anyone could tell about him, from the scraps of his uniform, was that he was British. He hadn't spoken to any of the other prisoners and none of them had been captured at the same time as he had. Consequently, nobody knew where he had come from.

When I asked the doctor why Matthew wouldn't speak and why he also refused, when offered pen and paper, to write anything down, he paused, then said, slowly, 'I'm sorry to say, but one of the things we found was that his tongue had been cut out.'

I could think of nothing to say. I stood there, head spinning.

'Miss Shackleton? Miss Shackleton? Are you there?'

'I'm sorry . . . Please go on.'

'I'm the one who should be sorry. It must have sounded so abrupt and callous to you. I apologise.'

'That's all right, Doctor . . . So Matthew is incapable of talking?'

'Yes.'

'But he could write if he wanted?'

'There's no reason why not. All I can assume is that he simply chooses not to communicate. He's probably suffering from some form of combat fatigue.'

'Should we send him back to the hospital?'

'I can't see much point in doing that,' said the doctor. 'Physically, there's nothing more we can do for him. There's some deformity of the spine, probably due to being forced into a cramped environment, like a box or a cage, for long periods of time. A pronounced limp in the left leg, caused by an improperly set fracture. He was also shot in the arm and the abdomen. The wounds are healed now.'

I swallowed. 'And mentally?'

'As I said, we don't really know why he's refusing to communicate. It's a good sign that he came home, though.'

'Is there any treatment? Will he get better?'

'It's impossible to say. There are treatments. Narcosynthesis is the most common. It's a drug-induced re-enactment of the traumatic episodes, used to assist the ego to accept what happened. The problem is, of course, that Matthew can't express himself vocally, and that could mean a severe limitation to the value of narcosynthesis. If you give me your address, I'll put you in touch with a doctor who knows about these things. In the meantime, just take good care of him. I don't think I need to tell you that he has suffered appallingly.'

'No. Thank you, Doctor.' I gave him my address and went back upstairs, where Matthew was sitting staring towards the window. Mother and Gloria seemed at their wits' end.

'I don't think he even knows me.' Gloria said, voice quivering.

I told her what the doctor had said. 'He came back here, didn't he?' I said, to comfort her. 'Home. Don't worry, he'll be fine now he's back with the people who love him.'

Gloria nodded, but she didn't seem convinced. I wasn't either.

As HE EXPECTED, Banks found Detective Superintendent Gristhorpe out back working on his dry-stone wall. Walling was a hobby the superintendent had taken up years ago. He found it relaxing.

Gristhorpe was wearing a baggy pair of brown corduroy trousers held up by frayed red braces, and a checked shirt. He was holding a triangular lump of limestone in his hand. When Banks approached, he turned. His pockmarked face was redder than usual after the exertion and his unruly mop of hair lay plastered to his skull.

'Alan,' he said. It wasn't a greeting, just a statement.

'Sir.'

'They say a good waller doesn't put a stone aside once he's picked it up,' Gristhorpe said, then looked at the rock in his hand. 'I wish I could figure out where to put this bugger.' He paused, then he tossed the stone back on the pile. 'You'll have a glass of something?'

'Anything cold.'

'Coke, then. I've got some in the fridge. We'll sit out here.' Gristhorpe pointed to two fold-up chairs in the shade by the back wall of the old farmhouse. Banks sat down.

Gristhorpe went inside and returned with two glasses of Coke, and sat down.

'I hear Jimmy Riddle's given you a real case to work on.'

'Sort of. I'm sure he thinks of it as more of a dead end.'

Gristhorpe raised his bushy eyebrows. 'Is it?'

'I don't think so.' Banks told Gristhorpe what he had discovered so far and handed him the button. 'It's impossible to say,' he went on, 'but it *might* have been in the victim's hand. She could have ripped it from her attacker's uniform.'

Gristhorpe examined the button. 'It looks like an American army air force button,' he said. 'It's so corroded it's hard to tell, but that design looks like the American eagle. The button could have come from the collar. Usually it was worn on the right side. Officers wore them left or right with the branch of service below.'

'If she was being strangled,' said Banks, 'then it's quite likely she reached out to try to grab at her attacker's collar.'

Gristhorpe handed back the button. 'It sounds like a reasonable theory to me.'

'There's another thing that puzzles me. Matthew Shackleton committed suicide in 1950. Shot himself. I'm wondering where he got the gun. He was in no state to go out and buy one on the black market.'

'What kind of gun was it?'

'A Colt .45 automatic.'

'Really? That was the gun the American military issued their servicemen. It raises interesting possibilities, doesn't it? American button in the wife's hand. American gun in the husband's mouth.'

Banks nodded. Though what the possibilities were, he hadn't a clue. The two events were separated by five years or more.

'Alan, I might have a bit of good news for you, if you can promise to keep it to yourself.'

'Good news. That makes a change.'

'Between you, me and the stone wall, Jimmy Riddle might not be around much longer. A little bird tells me that the crooked finger of politics beckons. As you know, he can't enter into that as a copper.'

'Politics?'

'Aye. His local Conservative MP is practically gaga. High-echelon rumour has it that Riddle has already had several interviews with the selection committee and they're pleased with him.'

Banks began to feel a sort of warm glow deep inside. Maybe his dry season really was coming to an end.

CHARLIE WAS KILLED on March 19 during a big raid over Berlin. Their Flying Fortress got badly shot up by a Messerschmitt. Brad managed to fly the aeroplane back across the Channel and land in an airfield in Sussex. He escaped with cuts and bruises.

When he got back from Sussex, he came over to the shop with a bottle of bourbon and told me the news in person. I could tell he was devastated by what had happened.

Gloria had told Brad she couldn't see him again, that it would only upset her and would do them no good. Brad was angry and upset about her rejection, but there was nothing he could do except come to me and pour his heart out.

We sat in the small room above the shop after Mother had gone to bed and drank bourbon. Neither of us said very much; there was nothing, really, *to* say. Coming right after Matthew's return, this news was almost impossible for me to bear.

Not far down the High Street, Gloria was devoting her time to caring for a man who couldn't speak and wouldn't communicate, with no end in sight. That was what our lives had been reduced to by the war: the essence of misery and hopelessness. I laid my head on Brad's shoulder and cried.

ON THURSDAY EVENING Banks tried Brian's number yet again.

On the fifth ring, someone answered.

'Brian?'

'Andy. Who's calling?'

'His father.'

Pause. 'Just a sec.'

A few moments later, Brian came on the phone. 'Dad?'

'Where've you been? I've been trying to get in touch with you.'

'We were doing some gigs in South Wales. Look, Dad, I told you, we've got gigs coming out of our ears. You weren't interested.'

Banks paused. He didn't want to blow it this time, but he was damned if he was going to grovel to his own son. 'You have to give it a little time to sink in. We were all expecting you to come out with a good degree and start working at a good firm somewhere. It's a shock, that's all. Music's a great hobby but a risky living. Anyway, the main reason I'm calling is that I'll be down in your neck of the woods tomorrow, so I wondered if we could get together. Let me buy you a pint.'

'I don't know, Dad. We're really busy right now.'

'Half an hour?'

Another pause followed. 'Look,' Brian said, 'tomorrow and Saturday we're playing at a pub in Bethnal Green. If you want to come and listen, we can have that pint during the break.'

Banks got the name of the pub and said he'd do his best.

'It's all right,' said Brian. 'I'll understand if something crops up and you can't make it. Wouldn't be the first time. One of the joys of being a copper's son.'

'I'll be there,' said Banks. 'Goodbye.'

It was almost dark. Banks took his whisky and went outside to sit on the wall. A few remaining streaks of crimson and purple shot the sky to the west and the waning moon shone over the valley. The promise of a storm had dissipated and the air was clear and dry again.

Well, Banks thought, at least he had talked to Brian and would get to see him soon.

He heard his phone ring. Quickly, he went back inside.

'Sorry to disturb you at this time of night, sir,' said DS Hatchley, 'but I know you're off to London in the morning.'

'What is it?' Banks looked at his watch. Half past nine. 'It's not like you to be working so late, Jim.'

'I'm not. I mean, I wasn't. I was just over at the Queen's Arms, so I thought I'd pop in the station, like, and see if I'd got any answers to my inquiries.'

'And?'

'Francis Henderson. I've got an address. Dulwich.' Hatchley read the address. 'What's interesting, why it came back so quick, is he's got form.'

Banks's ears pricked up. 'Go on.'

'According to Criminal Intelligence, Francis Henderson started working for one of the East End gangs in the sixties. Not the Krays exactly, but that sort of thing. Mostly he dug up information for them, found people they were after. He developed a drug habit and started dealing to support it in the seventies. They say he's been retired and clean for years now, at least as far as they know.'

'Thanks a lot, Jim. Get yourself home now.'

'Don't worry, I will.'

'And give another push on that nationwide tomorrow if you can find time.'

'Will do. *Bon voyage.*'

Chapter Seven

Annie was waiting at York Station looking very businesslike in a navy mid-length skirt and silver-buttoned blazer over a white blouse. She had tied her hair back. For once, though, Banks didn't feel underdressed. He wore a lightweight cotton summer suit together with a red and grey tie.

'Good Lord,' she said, smiling, 'I feel like we're sneaking away for a dirty weekend.'

Banks laughed. 'If you play your cards right . . .'

The London train pulled out of the station and Banks and Annie chatted for a while, lulled by the rattling and rocking rhythm. Banks ascertained that whatever had been bothering Annie on the phone the day before was no longer a problem. He had been forgiven.

She started reading the *Guardian* and Banks went back to *Guilty Secrets*. In bed the previous evening, he had given up on *The Shadow of Death* when DI Niven arrested his first suspect, saying, 'You have the right to remain silent. If you don't have a lawyer, one will be provided for you.' So much for the realistic depiction of police procedures. Feeling that the author deserved a second chance, he started *Guilty Secrets* and had trouble putting it down. Despite the thinness of the plot, *Guilty Secrets* turned out to be a fascinating exploration of conscience and character. Banks finished the book just before Peterborough. Annie had closed her eyes by then and was either napping or meditating. He gazed out of the window.

King's Cross was the usual madness. Banks and Annie negotiated their way through the crowds and tunnels to the Northern Line and managed to cram into the first Edgware-bound train.

A few minutes later, they came out of Belsize Park tube station, walked up Rosslyn Hill and turned into the side street where Vivian Elmsley lived.

A woman's voice answered over the intercom.

Banks stated his rank and his business. There was a long pause then a resigned voice said, 'You'd better come up.' The lock buzzed.

They walked up three flights of thickly carpeted stairs to the second-floor landing. That this was a well-maintained building was clear from the gleaming woodwork and freshly painted walls. Probably cost an arm and a leg, but then Vivian Elmsley could no doubt afford an arm and a leg.

She was dressed in baggy black exercise trousers and a white sweatshirt. Still, Banks supposed, it didn't matter what you wore if all you had to do was sit around and write all day. She looked tired, bags under her eyes, broken blood vessels crisscrossing the whites. Banks could see what Elsie Patterson meant: there was no mistaking those slanted eyes. She also looked strained and edgy.

'Please, sit down.' She gestured Banks and Annie towards two matching chrome-and-black-leather chairs, then sat down herself. 'How can I help you?'

'First of all,' Banks asked, 'are you Gwynneth Shackleton?'

'I was, though most people called me Gwen. Vivian is my middle name. Elmsley is a pseudonym. Actually, it's my mother's maiden name. It's all perfectly legal.'

'I'm sure it is. You grew up in Hobb's End?'

'Yes.'

'Did you kill Gloria Shackleton?'

Her hand went to her chest. 'Kill Gloria? Me? What a suggestion. I most certainly did not.'

'Could Matthew, your brother, have killed her?'

'No. Matthew loved her. She looked after him.'

'May I ask why you haven't come forward in response to our requests for information?' Banks asked.

Vivian Elmsley paused before answering, as if composing her thoughts carefully. 'Chief Inspector,' she said, 'I admit that I have been following developments, but I honestly don't believe I can tell you anything of any value. I have also found it all very distressing.'

'Oh, come off it,' said Banks. 'Not only did you live in Hobb's End throughout the war and knew the victim well, you were also her sister-in-law. You can't expect me to believe you know nothing at all.'

'I can't honestly say I knew her very well. I wouldn't say we had much in common. I was always a bookish sort of girl, whereas Gloria was the more flamboyant type. As with many extroverts, she was also a secretive person, very difficult to get to know.'

'Did you see a lot of her?'

'Quite a bit. We were in and out of one another's houses. Bridge Cottage wasn't far from the shop.'

'Didn't you ever do things together?'

Vivian shrugged. 'I suppose we did. We went to the pictures, to dances.'

'Dances with American airmen?'

'Sometimes, yes.'

'Was there anyone in particular?'

'I suppose we were quite friendly with several of them.'

'Do you remember their names? What about Brad? Ring a bell?'

'Brad? Yes, I think he was one of them. Brad Szikorski.'

Banks checked the list of Rowan Woods personnel he had brought with him. *Bradford J. Szikorski, Jr.*

'And PX? Billy Joe?'

'Edgar Konig and Billy Joe Farrell.'

They were on the list, too.

'What about Charlie?'

Vivian Elmsley turned pale; a muscle by her jaw began to twitch. 'Charlie Markleson,' she whispered.

Banks checked the sheet. 'Charles Christopher Markleson.'

'How did you find out their names? I haven't heard them in so long.'

'It doesn't matter how we found out. Was Gloria having an affair with Brad Szikorski when Matthew came back?'

'I don't know what you're getting at. You've been misinformed, Chief Inspector. Gloria was married to Matthew, whether he was there or not. Yes, we went to the pictures and dances with those boys on occasion, but that's all there was to it.'

'How did Gloria behave when she thought her husband was dead. Surely an attractive woman like her must have had boyfriends?'

Vivian paused again. 'Gloria had a very gregarious side to her nature. She liked parties, group excursions, that sort of thing. She liked to keep things superficial. You must understand, Chief Inspector, we never gave up hope that Matthew would return.'

'You haven't answered my question. Did Gloria have a romantic affair with Brad Szikorski, or with anyone else?'

She looked away. 'Not that I knew about.'

'How did Brad take it when Matthew came back alive?'

'How should I know? Why would it matter to him?'

'It might have. If he fell in love with Gloria, and if she rejected him in favour of her husband.'

'Are you suggesting that *Brad* killed Gloria?' Vivian sniffed.

Banks leaned forward. 'Somebody did, Ms Elmsley, and the most immediate suspects that come to mind are Matthew, one of the Americans, Michael Stanhope, or you.'

'Ridiculous. It must have been a stranger.'

'You must see how the discovery casts suspicion on your brother, most of all. Gloria was buried in an outbuilding adjoining Bridge Cottage. Matthew was living with her there at the time.'

'But I had never known him be violent. Never.'

'War can change a man.'

'Even so.'

'Did he go out much after his return. Was Gloria often alone in the house?'

'He went to the pub of an evening. The Shoulder of Mutton. Yes, she was alone there sometimes.'

'Would it surprise you to hear that Gloria posed nude for a painting by Stanhope in 1944?'

'Yes, it would. Very much.'

'Was Gloria having an affair with Michael Stanhope?'

'I shouldn't think so. He was too old for her.'

'And homosexual?'

'I wouldn't know about that. I was very young.'

'Did she ever tell you about her son, Francis?'

'She did mention him to me once, yes. But she said she'd cut off all relations with him and his father.'

'There is one thing that really puzzles me,' Banks said, 'and that's what you *did* think had happened to Gloria? Surely you can't have thought she had simply disappeared from the face of the earth?'

'It wasn't a mystery at the time. Not really. She left because she couldn't stand it any more, taking care of Matthew, the way he was. After all, it wouldn't have been the first time she'd run away. She had clearly broken off all contact with whatever life she had had in London before coming to Hobb's End.'

'When did she disappear?' he asked.

'Shortly after V-E Day. A week or so. I had accompanied Matthew to his doctor in Leeds. When we got back that evening, she was gone.'

'Did Gloria ever say anything to you about leaving?'

'She hinted at it once or twice, but I didn't take her seriously. It was as if she was joking. You know, "Some day my prince will come. I'm going to leave all this behind and run off to untold wealth and riches." Gloria was a dreamer, Chief Inspector.'

'Did she take anything with her when she left?'

'A few clothes, personal items. She didn't have much.'

'That's interesting. What did she carry them in?'

'An old cardboard suitcase. The same one she arrived with.'

Banks paused. 'Ms Elmsley,' he asked, 'knowing what you know now, where do you think her clothes and suitcase got to?'

'I have no idea. I'm only telling you what I thought must have happened at the time. Perhaps someone stole them. To make it *look* as if she had gone away.'

'Ah. And who do you think would feel the need to risk taking time burying her body under the outbuilding floor?'

'Someone who wanted to avoid suspicion.'

'Exactly. Which brings us back very close to home, doesn't it? Why try to avoid suspicion? It had to be someone who felt suspicion was likely to fall on him or her: Matthew, Brad Szikorski or *you*.'

'Well, it wasn't me. And I told you, Matthew never raised a finger to her.'

'Which leaves Brad Szikorski.'

'Perhaps. Though I doubt it. Anyway Brad Szikorski was killed in a flying stunt in the desert outside Los Angeles in 1952.'

'What about Charles Markleson?'

'Charlie was killed in the war.'

'Edgar Konig? Billy Joe Farrell?'

'I don't know what happened to them, Chief Inspector.'

'Had either of them reason to kill Gloria?'

'Not that I know of. Though Billy Joe, I remember, did have a violent temper, and PX was rather smitten with Gloria.'

'Did she go out with him?'

'Not to my knowledge. He . . . He just seemed so *young* and shy.'

'Did you notice any blood in Bridge Cottage following Gloria's disappearance?'

'No. Obviously, if I had done, I would have been suspicious and called the police. Anyway, what makes you think she was killed in Bridge Cottage? She could have been killed outside, in the back yard, or even in the outbuilding.'

'Possibly,' Banks allowed. 'What happened next?'

'Nothing. We just carried on. Actually, we only stayed on in the village a few weeks longer, then we got a council house in Leeds.'

'What about Matthew? Did you kill him?'

'I did not. He committed suicide.'

'Why?'

'It wasn't related to Gloria's disappearance. He was ill, confused, depressed, in pain. I did my best for him, but it was no use.'

'He shot himself, didn't he?'

'Yes.'

'Where did he get the gun?'

'He always had it.'

'Always? Since when?'

'I don't know. Since he came back from the war, I suppose.'

'From the Japanese POW camp?'

'Yes.'

Banks got to his feet, shaking his head.

'What's wrong, Chief Inspector?' Vivian asked.

'Everything,' said Banks. 'Your brother Matthew shot himself with an American service revolver he just happened to bring back from a Japanese POW camp? *You* write detective novels. Ask yourself if your Inspector Niven would believe it. Ask yourself if your readers would believe it.' He reached in his pocket. 'Here's my card. I want you to think seriously about our little talk. We'll be back. Soon.'

Once they were out in the street again, Annie turned to Banks, whistled and said, 'She was lying.'

'Of course she was.' Banks looked at his watch. 'Want to grab a bite to eat?'

'Yes. I'm starving.'

They found a small café and Annie had a Greek salad, while Banks went for the prosciutto sandwich.

'But why was she lying?' Annie asked. 'I don't get it.'

'She's protecting herself. Or someone else.'

'So what do we do now?'

'Nothing,' said Banks. 'Leave her to stew overnight. I get the impression she has a lot on her conscience. If I'm right, she's near the end of her tether on this. We'll have another go at her tomorrow.'

'And in the meantime?'

'First, we'll go and see if we can find Francis Henderson. And then if it's OK with you, I'd like to head out to Bethnal Green and see my son. We've got a few things to talk over.'

'Of course. I understand. Maybe I'll go to the pictures. What about later?'

'Remember that naughty weekend you mentioned?'

Annie nodded.

'I don't know if you're still interested, but there's this discreet little hotel in Bloomsbury. And it *is* Friday. Even CID get to work regular hours sometimes.'

Annie blushed. 'But I didn't bring my toothbrush.'

Banks laughed. 'I'll buy you one.'

'Last of the big spenders.' The corner of her mouth twitched in a smile. 'And I didn't bring my nightie, either.'

'Don't worry,' said Banks. 'You won't need your nightie.'

OVER THE NEXT couple of weeks, as I continued to mourn Charlie, I noticed no improvement in Matthew's condition. He remained at Bridge Cottage with Gloria. I don't really think it mattered to him *where* he was, as long as his basic creature comforts were taken care of. There wasn't a day went by when I didn't spend time sitting with him, talking to him, though he never responded.

We soon got Matthew fixed up with Dr Jennings, a psychiatrist at Leeds University. Once a week, Gloria or I would take him to his appointment, spend an hour or so looking round the shops, then collect him and take him home. Dr Jennings admitted to me on the third visit that he was having little success and was considering narcosynthesis, despite the problems.

Matthew wasn't any trouble; he just wasn't there. He did, however, get into the habit of going to the Shoulder of Mutton every night and sitting alone in a corner drinking. At first, friends and neighbours who knew him would approach and ask how he was doing, but soon they left him alone. Once in a while he would have an angry outburst and smash a glass or kick a chair. But these were infrequent and soon passed over.

Gloria gave me a key, so I was able to pop in and out of Bridge Cottage whenever I could. She took as much time off from the farm as possible, of course, but she needed the income, and I don't think she could have borne the pain and heartbreak of being with him twenty-four hours a day.

You could smell victory in the air. The Americans had crossed the Rhine, and so had Monty's men. The Russians had Berlin surrounded. In April and May we started hearing the first rumours about concentration camps and atrocities on a scale that had only been hinted at. All the newspapers seemed at a loss as to how to describe what the liberating armies had found at places such as Belsen and Buchenwald. I also read about the appalling tortures inflicted on prisoners like Matthew.

BANKS WALKED into the cavernous East London Victorian pub, all smoked and etched glass, brass fittings and mirrors.

He and Annie had just been to Dulwich to see Francis Henderson, only to find that he was out. A neighbour told them she thought he had most likely gone on holiday, as he had cancelled his newspapers and milk. Banks slipped his card with a note through the letterbox and left it at that.

It was half past five, and the band was due to start at six to draw in the after-work crowd. Brian stood on the low wooden stage along with the others who were setting their equipment up.

He waved Banks over. Brian looked a little nervous, but that was only to be expected; his mates would no doubt tease him about his old man coming to a gig. He introduced Banks to Andy, the keyboard player, Jamisse, the bassist, who was from Mozambique, and the percussionist, Ali.

'I've just got to tune up,' said Brian, 'then I'll come over.'

'Fine. Pint?'

'Sure.'

Banks bought a couple of pints at the bar and found an empty table. Occasionally, feedback screeched from the amps, Ali hit a snare drum or Jamisse plucked at a bass string. It was a quarter to six when Brian detached himself from the others and came over. Tall and skinny, he wore threadbare jeans, trainers and a plain red T-shirt. His dark hair was long and straight, and he had three or four days' growth around his chin. He sat down, avoiding Banks's eyes.

Banks didn't want to launch right into the midst of things. 'I'm looking forward to this,' he said. 'I haven't heard you play since you used to practise at home.'

'I hope I've got better since then, Dad.'

'Me, too.' Banks smiled. 'Cheers.' They clinked glasses, then Banks lit a cigarette. 'What kind of music do you play?'

'You'll have to wait and hear it for yourself. I can't describe it.'

'Blues?'

'Not straight blues, no. I write most of the lyrics, Jamisse does most of the music. Andy can read music, so he arranges and stuff. We do some cover versions, too.'

'Anything an old fogey like me would recognise?'

Brian grinned. 'You might be surprised. Got to go now. Will you be around after?'

Banks looked at his watch. Six. Plenty of time. 'I don't have to leave until about eight,' he said.

'Great.'

The next thing Banks knew, the band had started. There was blues underlying the music, definitely. Andy's ghostly keyboards floated around it all, and Brian's guitar cut through the rhythms clear as a bell. When he soloed, which he did very well, the sound reminded Banks of early Jerry Garcia and Eric Clapton. There was an improvisational, jazzy element to the music, but it was accessible, *popular*.

Then the first set ended. The band acknowledged the applause, then Brian came over. Banks bought them both another pint.

'That was great,' Banks said.

Brian glanced away. 'Thanks.'

There was no point in putting it off any longer, Banks thought, taking a deep breath. 'Look,' he said, 'about what we said on the phone the other day. I'm disappointed, of course I am, but it's your life. If you think you can really make a go of this, I'm certainly not going to stand in your way.'

Brian met Banks's gaze, and Banks thought he could see relief in his son's eyes. So his approval *did* matter, after all.

'You mean it?'

Banks nodded.

'Architecture was just so boring, Dad. I'm sorry if I caused you any grief. But it was only partly because of the band. I didn't do enough work last year because I was bored by the whole subject.'

'Have you told your mother yet?'

'I left a message on her machine.'

'Look, when you get a bit of free time, why don't you come up to Gratly? You haven't even seen the cottage yet. We can go for long walks together, the way we used to? I'm not asking you to put a date to it. It's an open invitation. OK?'

Brian looked up from his beer and smiled. 'OK,' he said. 'I'd like that. It's a deal.'

ONE DAY GLORIA ASKED if I would mind closing the shop for an hour or so and walking with her. She looked pale.

It was the beginning of May, I remember. Hitler was dead, the Russians had Berlin, and all the German troops in Italy had surrendered. It could only be days from the end now.

We walked into Rowan Woods, wandering in the filtered green light of the new leaves. The woodland flowers were all in bloom, clusters of bluebells here and there, violets and primroses. The air was pungent with the smell of wild garlic.

'I don't know what to do with him, Gwen,' she said, close to tears. 'Nothing I do to try to reach him does any good.'

'I know,' I said. 'We just have to be patient.' Even as I spoke I felt the inadequacy of my words.

'It's all right for you. He's not your husband. It's not the same. I'm living with a stranger. I don't know what to do. Brad is still pestering me to run off back to America with him. Just imagine it, Gwen: Hollywood! A new life in the sunshine. A young, healthy, handsome, vigorous man who dotes on me . . .'

'But?'

She turned away, eyes downcast. 'A dream. That's all. I can't go. Silly, isn't it? A few years ago I did exactly that. Walked away from a life I didn't want and ended up here.'

'But you'd lost your whole family then. You had nothing to stay for. Anyone can understand your doing that.'

'But I'd walked away even before I lost them.'

'What do you mean?'

She paused. 'There are things you don't know about me, Gwen. I've been selfish. I've hurt people. But I want you to know that Matt is the only man I have ever truly loved. Not Brad, not . . . Never mind.'

'What were you going to say?'

Gloria paused and looked at me with those blue eyes of hers. 'I won't ask you to forgive me,' she said. 'You might not be able to do that. But at least hear me out.'

I nodded. She leaned back against a tree.

'When I was sixteen,' she began, 'I had a baby. I didn't love the father, not really. I was infatuated. George was good-looking, popular with all the girls. I was flattered by his attentions. We only did it once, but I didn't know about . . . you know . . . then, and I got pregnant. George would have married me like a shot—he said he loved me—but . . . I *knew* deep down that it would be the worst mistake of my life. He drank, like they all did down on the docks, and I really believed it was just a matter of time before he would start beating me.'

'But what about the baby?'

'After I had Francis I got very depressed and I didn't . . . I didn't feel what they said a normal mother should. I'm ashamed to say it, but I hated my own baby, Gwen. That's why I could never be a real mother to him or to anyone else.'

She sobbed and fell forward into my arms. I held her and comforted her as best I could. Sniffling, dabbing her handkerchief to her eyes, Gloria went on, 'George's sister Ivy couldn't have any children of her own. She and her husband are decent people. They'd got away and bettered themselves. They said they would take care of Francis. I knew he would be better off with them.'

'What did George say?'

'He couldn't understand it when I didn't object to giving up Francis to Ivy and John. He said that a boy needed a real mother to love. But, of course, he agreed. He could hardly bring up Francis on his own. He wasn't a bad man. It's me who's bad. I think he loved his son more than I did. He wanted to be a father as much as he could. But he got called up, of course. Anyway, he always thought I would change my mind. He's already been up to see me once with Francis. He said he still loves me, urged me to go back. I told him I was married and we had an argument.'

I didn't know what to say.

'Say you don't hate me, Gwen, please! I couldn't bear it if you hated me. You're my only real friend.'

'Of course I don't hate you. I just don't understand.'

'I don't know if I do, either, but don't you see that's exactly why I *can't l*eave Matt? Because of what I did before. This is my punishment, Gwen. Don't you see? Matt is my penance.'

'I think so,' I said. 'Are you and Brad still . . .?'

'Sometimes. Don't be angry. Brad brings me comfort from time to time and as long as Matt doesn't know . . . To be honest, though, he's more trouble than he's worth right now. I just can't keep him off the subject of running away together. It's all getting to be too much of a strain. I told him if he didn't stop pushing me I'd run off and leave the whole lot of you behind, him included.'

'Have you had any more trouble from Billy Joe?'

'No, not really. I got the impression he was secretly pleased that Matt had come back and spoilt things for me and Brad. I don't think he gives a damn about what it's all doing to *me*. Look, Gwen, I don't know if I should be telling you this, but I've been having a few problems with Michael.'

'Michael? Good Lord. You don't mean he's—'

'Don't be a fool, Gwen. The man's only interested in boys. No. But, last summer and autumn, you might have noticed I spent quite a bit of time at his studio. He was painting me.'

'But that's wonderful, Gloria. Can I see it? Is it finished?'

'Yes. And it's very good. It's a nude.'

I swallowed. 'You posed in the *nude* for Michael Stanhope?'

She laughed. 'Why not? There certainly wasn't much chance of him trying to put his hands on me, was there? Anyway, the point is, I begged him not to exhibit it, as long as Matthew is alive. I just don't know how it would affect him. Who knows if seeing a nude painting of his wife won't send him right over the edge?'

'That sounds reasonable,' I told her. 'What did Michael Stanhope have to say?'

'Oh, he's not happy about it. Thinks it's one of the best things he's done, blah blah. Says his career needs a boost and this could give it one. But he agreed in the end. He likes to play the miserable cynic, but he's pretty decent, deep down.'

There she finished and we walked back to Hobb's End.

I didn't see Gloria again until a couple of days later, and by then everyone knew Germany had surrendered. The war was over.

'ENJOY THE FILM?' Banks asked, when he met Annie outside the Leicester Square Odeon at nine o'clock. She had been to see the latest megamillion special-effects extravaganza.

'Not much,' said Annie. 'I suppose it had its good points.'

'What?'

'*The End*, for one.'

Banks laughed.

'How were things with your son?' Annie asked.

'We mended a bridge or two.'

He took Annie to a small bistro-style restaurant just off Shaftesbury Avenue. The place was busy, but they managed to get a table after a short wait.

They chose a claret and Banks went for roast lamb with rosemary, while Annie settled for a green salad and some bread and cheese.

Their food arrived more quickly than Banks expected, and they paused until the waiter had gone. Beyond the hum of conversation, clinking of cutlery and glassware, Banks could hear Tchaikovski's String Quartet No. 1 playing in the background.

After his talk with Brian, he felt as if a burden had been lifted from his mind. He and his son were talking again. And from what he had heard, the kid had talent; he might make it in the business yet.

The candlelight brought out the slight wine flush on Annie's cheeks and filled her dark eyes with mysterious reflections. Her hair tumbled over her shoulders in sexy waves.

'What are you thinking about?' she asked, looking up.

Perhaps this was the moment, Banks thought, emboldened by his buoyant mood. 'Annie, can I ask you a personal question?'

She arched her eyebrows and Banks sensed a part of her scurry back into the shadows. Too late now. 'Of course,' she said. 'But I can't promise to answer it.'

'Fair enough. What are you doing at Harkside? It's a nowhere posting. You're bright. You've got a future ahead of you if you want it, but you'll not get the job experience you need at Harkside.'

'I think that's rather insulting to Inspector Harmond and the others up there, don't you?'

'Oh, come on, Annie. You know as well as I do that's where they want to be. They chose the easy life.'

'Well, maybe it's what I've chosen, too.'

'Is it?'

'I didn't promise to answer your question.' Her mouth took on a sulky cast Banks hadn't seen before.

'No, you didn't,' Banks said, leaning towards her. 'But let me tell you something. Jimmy Riddle hates my guts. He isn't in the business of putting me in the way of anything I might find even remotely pleasant. The only reason I'm asking you now is because . . . because I'm afraid you're being used, too. Riddle had to have a reason for putting us together, something he thought would be unpleasant for me.'

She tilted her head. 'Perhaps this is it?' Annie suggested. 'What he expected. That we'd get together somehow, break the rules and get caught. That way he could be rid of both of us.'

'No, that's too easy. What we're doing isn't . . . I mean, it's only the same kind of thing he thought I was doing before. He has a far more sadistic mind than that.'

Annie shook her head slowly and then she seemed to come to some kind of decision. She looked at Banks. 'All right,' she said. 'I'll tell you, but only if you'll tell me something, too.'

ON MAY 8, 1945, it poured down all morning, despite the fact that this was V-E Day. By early afternoon, the rain was tapering off and we were left with as beautiful a warm May evening as you could ever ask for, the grass green and moist from the rain.

Gloria gave me a pair of stockings she had got from PX, and helped me with my make-up. First, we spent an hour or so at the Hobb's End street party. People had brought little tables and put them together in a row all along the High Street. It was a dull affair, though, as there were so few people left in the village.

Mother sat at one of the tables with her friend, Joyce Maddingley, and she told us to behave ourselves when we slipped away to the celebration dance at Harkside. Matthew refused to come out of the cottage at all. Mother said she would look in on him.

From the minute we got to Harkside village green, we were swept into a mad whirl. Most of the soldiers and airmen from the nearby bases had come. It didn't take Gloria long to meet up with Brad. Billy Joe was there with his new girlfriend, and PX was tagging along, too. I felt a sudden pang of missing Charlie, then I tried to enter into the spirit of victory.

First we went to the dance at the Mechanics Institute. There was a big band playing Glenn Miller, Duke Ellington and Benny Goodman tunes, and people kept throwing coloured streamers across the dance floor. At one point, I noticed Gloria and Brad slip outside. It was over an hour before I saw them again, and Gloria had retouched her make-up. I resolved to say nothing. I had thought a lot about Gloria and what she was sacrificing to care for Matthew, and I decided that she deserved her little pleasures.

The band was still playing when we piled out into the street. There was a huge bonfire on the village green and people were singing and setting off fireworks. The air was full of the acrid smell of smoke and the sky full of exploding colours. Everyone was drunk. I could see Gloria and Brad through the flames having an argument.

At one point we went to someone's house and drank some whisky. It was a wild party. People were packed in like sardines and the house was full of smoke. Gloria was dancing, but I couldn't see Brad. PX was drunk, and I saw him try to kiss a woman. She pushed him away and his face turned red. Then he stormed off. It was almost one o'clock when I told Gloria it was time for us to go.

The two of us were a little drunk. It was on emotion and excitement as much as alcohol. We danced and laughed our way home.

Bridge Cottage was dark. I went in with Gloria to make sure everything was all right and we heard Matthew snoring on the chesterfield. Gloria gestured me towards the kitchen. She poured us both another whisky, which was probably the last thing we needed. When she put her handbag on the countertop, it slipped off and fell on the floor. I bent over to pick it up and noticed how heavy it was. Curious, I opened the clasp and nearly fainted when I saw a gun.

Gloria turned.

'You weren't supposed to see that.'

'But, Gloria, where did you get it?'

'From one of the Americans at the party. He was so drunk he won't miss it.'

'What do you want a gun for?'

She shrugged. 'I just feel more comfortable knowing it's there, that's all.'

'But Matthew's harmless. He wouldn't hurt you.'

She looked at me as if I were the biggest fool she had ever met. 'Who said anything about Matthew?' she said, then took the gun and put it in one of the kitchen cupboards behind the tea and cocoa. 'Now will you have that drink?'

VIVIAN ELMSLEY was having a difficult time. Close to midnight she was sitting in her sparse living room, her third gin and tonic in her hand and some dreadful rubbish on television. Sleep refused to come. Chief Inspector Banks knew she was lying; nobody who had been as close to the people involved as she had been could know as little as she had professed.

Why *hadn't* she told them the truth? She didn't want to go to jail. But would they really prosecute her after so long? Were there not mitigating circumstances? She didn't know what they would do, and that was the problem. On the other hand, if she didn't tell them, then they would never find out the truth. Nobody else knew.

Only one thing was certain: the police would be back. Tonight she had to make her decision.

'YOU'RE RIGHT about one thing,' Annie began. 'I'm in Harkside because I was a naughty girl.'

'What happened?'

'Depends on your point of view. Look, I'm not going to tell you where it was or who was involved. OK?'

'OK. Go on.'

'This is hard.'

'You don't have to.'

She held up her hand. 'No. I've come this far.' She played with a spoon. 'It was when I made DS,' she said. 'Nearly two years ago now. There was a celebration at the local coppers' pub. The private room upstairs. I suppose I was dead chuffed with myself. I'd always wanted to be one of the boys. It got down to just four of us left. One of them suggested we go back to his place and drink some more.'

She was speaking very quietly so that no one would hear. Banks had to strain to hear her.

'We were already three sheets to the wind,' Annie went on, 'and I was the only female. I didn't know the others well. Things were getting pretty wild. I suppose I should have known what was coming by the way the conversation was going. But I'd been drinking, too, and I didn't really think much of it until one of them suggested we go in the bedroom, said he could tell I'd been wanting it all night. I laughed and brushed him off. I thought he was joking. He got angry. Things got out of hand. The other two grabbed me and held me down over the back of the settee while he raped me.'

Annie took a deep breath and went on. 'When he'd finished, they started rearranging positions, and I knew what was coming, so I slipped free, kicked the one who'd raped me as hard as I could in the balls and caught another on the jaw with my elbow. I managed to make it to the door. The third one caught me, and by then the one I'd hit with my elbow was up again. They were mad as hell. One of them punched me in the stomach and I went down. I thought they were going to do what they'd intended, but they'd lost their bottle. Suddenly they were individuals again, each looking out for number one, and they knew what they'd done. They told me to get out. I left.'

'Did you report it? For crying out loud, Annie, you'd been *raped*.'

She shook her head. 'You know what I did? I walked the city most of the night in a complete daze. I remember trying to feel some sort of emotion. There was nothing. Just a deep, cold numbness. When I finally found myself back at my flat, I had a long hot bath. Hours I must have lain there, just listening to the radio. That was soothing somehow. And do you know what? I understand every one of those rape victims who never comes forward to report the crime.'

Banks could see tears glistening at the corners of her eyes.

'What happened?' he asked.

'By morning I'd got a bit of nerve back. I went to see the chief super to tell him what they did. Two of the others had got there before me. Pre-emptive strike. They told the super there'd been a spot of bother at a party last night, just an initiation rite that got a bit out of hand, nothing serious, like, but that I'd probably be coming to complain, making up all sorts of wild allegations.'

'And he believed them?'

'Their word against mine. Besides, people around the station already thought I was a bit weird. You know, I did yoga and meditation and I didn't eat meat. I also had a reputation for not being very interested in men. As it happened, I did have a boyfriend at the time, but I kept my private life separate from the job.'

'Did you tell the chief super what really happened?'

'Yes. Every detail. He looked very embarrassed.'

'Didn't he initiate some sort of inquiry?'

'Like I said, their word against mine. And apart from a pair of torn knickers, I'd pretty much destroyed the evidence, hadn't I? The chief super also told me that that sort of internal investigation hurts everyone, especially the force. He said the officers involved would be disciplined for their excessive high spirits, but it would be best for all concerned if it went no further than his office.'

'He should have been kicked off the force.'

'I'm glad you agree.'

'So all that happened was they got a slap on the wrist.'

'Not quite.' Annie looked down into her coffee cup. 'There were complications.' She stared down for a few more seconds before looking up at Banks. 'Remember, I told you I kicked one of them? Something went wrong. They had to operate. He'd only been married a year. Planning a family.'

'Jesus. I can imagine you were popular after that.'

'Exactly. The chief superintendent suggested it might be better for all concerned if I transferred somewhere else, and they came up with Harkside. I think that our ACC used to work with Chief Constable Riddle, so Riddle knows all about what happened.'

'Which means that to him you're a troublemaker? A ball-busting lesbian bitch?'

Annie mustered a crooked smile.

'No wonder Riddle put us together. I'm sorry about what happened to you, Annie. Sorrier than I can say. I'm also amazed you would even consider getting involved with me. I would have thought that what happened would have been enough to put you off your fellow coppers for life.'

'Oh, Alan. You do yourself a disservice. I've never, for one moment, seen any similarity between you and the men who assaulted me. I wanted you. I was terrified, but I wanted to overcome my fear. The thing is, I thought I'd faced up to it and got on with my life.'

'Haven't you? You seem to be doing all right to me.'

'I thought I was over it but I've been in hiding at Harkside. I get by. I have my nice safe little life. I go to work, I do my job, and then I come home. No social life.' She paused. 'Let's face it, I know I'm good at the job but I haven't done any serious detective work in Harkside, until this case came along.'

'And now?'

She shrugged. 'I don't know. You're the first person I've told. Now it's your turn. You promised to tell me something, too.'

'Did I? What do you want to know?'

'Did you really punch Jimmy Riddle?'

Banks stubbed out his cigarette and slipped his credit card on the little tray the waiter had left. It was snatched up almost immediately.

'Yes,' he said. 'I did.'

She laughed. 'Bloody hell. I wish I'd been there.'

Banks signed the receipt, then they walked out into the busy West End evening. The streets were packed with people standing drinking outside the pubs.

As they turned onto Great Russell Street, Annie slipped her arm through Banks's. It was only the second time they had had any intimate physical contact in public, and it felt good. Annie rested her head on his shoulder; her hair tickled his cheek.

They passed the dark mass of the British Museum, set back behind its railings and courtyard, then crossed Russell Square.

'Here we are,' said Banks. 'Did you buy a toothbrush?'

'Yup.' Annie held up a bag. 'And a nightie.'

'I thought I said you wouldn't need one.'

She laughed and moved closer. 'Oh, don't worry. It's only a *little* nightie. I promise you'll like it.' And they walked up the stone steps.

I COULDN'T STOP thinking about the gun. Usually, the way the scene ran in my mind was that Gloria shot Matthew first and then herself. The images were so vivid I could even see the blood gush from their wounds. Finally, I determined I had to do something.

So the next time it was Gloria's turn to take Matthew to Leeds, I let myself in to Bridge Cottage.

I found the gun in the same place Gloria had left it in the kitchen cupboard. I put it in the shopping bag I had brought with me, put the cupboard back in order and left. The best I could hope for was that by the time she missed it she wouldn't feel the need for it any more and would realise what a favour I had done her.

Chapter Eight

It was about eleven o'clock on Saturday morning when Banks and Annie arrived back at Vivian Elmsley's building. Before Banks could even press the buzzer, the street door opened and Vivian almost bumped into them.

'You?' She put her hand to her heart. 'I didn't think . . . So soon . . . I was just . . . You'd better come in.'

They followed her upstairs to the flat. She was carrying a large buff envelope. Banks glanced at it and saw his name on it.

She turned to face them as they entered her living room. 'You've saved me the postage.'

'What were you sending me?' Banks asked. 'A confession?'

'Of sorts. Yes. I suppose you could call it that.'

'So you *were* lying yesterday?'

'Fiction's my trade. Sometimes I can't help it. Anyway,' she went on, handing Banks the envelope, 'I'd like you to take this away with you and read it. I'm not going to run anywhere, I promise you.'

'Why the change of heart?'

'Conscience, would you believe? I thought I could live with it, but I can't. The telephone calls didn't help, either. I've decided to tell the truth. I'd rather do things this way than answer a lot of questions, and I think it will help you understand. Of course, you'll have questions eventually. I have to be in Leeds next week, so you'll soon have the opportunity. Will you allow me this much, at least?'

If Banks were to go by the book, he wouldn't let a murder suspect hand him a written 'confession', then go away. But it was time for a judgment call. He believed that Vivian Elmsley wasn't going anywhere. She was in the public eye, and he didn't think she had anywhere to run, even if she wanted to. The other possibility was suicide. It was a risk, to be certain, but he decided to take it.

'You mentioned telephone calls,' he said. 'What do you mean?'

'Anonymous calls. Sometimes he says things, other times he just hangs up. He sounds vaguely threatening. And he calls me Gwen Shackleton.'

'Have you any idea who it might be?'

'No. The voice sounds muffled, as if he's speaking through a handkerchief or something.'

'I honestly wouldn't worry too much. In most cases people who make threatening phone calls don't confront their victims. But you should get in touch with your local police station. They'll be able to help.' Banks held up the envelope. 'We'll do as you ask,' he said, 'but how do we know this is the truth and not just more fiction?'

'It's a bit of both, but the parts you'll be interested in are true. You'll just have to take my word for it, won't you?'

THE DAY IT HAPPENED began like any ordinary day; I opened the shop, made lunch and tea for Mother and settled down to an evening's reading and the wireless. The Americans were having a farewell party up at the base that night, as they had heard they would be moving out in a matter of days. Neither Gloria nor I had felt like going. Somehow, that part of our lives seemed over. Charlie was dead and Gloria had made it clear to Brad, after their last fling on V-E Day, that it would be best if they didn't see each other any more.

I wouldn't normally have gone to Bridge Cottage so late in the evening except that Cynthia Garmen had dropped off some parachute silk. I thought Gloria might appreciate a small gift; she had been very depressed since V-E Day. I can't say that I heard any small voice telling me to go; nor can I recollect any feeling of apprehension. I thought the prospect of making a new dress might cheer Gloria up.

It was just after ten o'clock and Mother had gone to bed. I assumed Matthew would still be at the Shoulder of Mutton, so I thought I would call in there first and persuade him to walk home with me. As it turned out, he had been asked to leave a little earlier because he had had one of his outbursts and broken a glass.

I walked down the dark, deserted High Street to Bridge Cottage. There was light showing between the curtains. I knocked at the door but no one answered. I knocked again. Still nothing. I put my key in the lock, turned it and entered, calling out Gloria's name.

There was no one in the living room but I noticed a strong smell of whisky. I thought I heard a movement in the kitchen. Puzzled, I walked over and when I got to the doorway I saw her.

Gloria lay on the flagstone floor, legs and arms splayed at awkward angles. One of her little fists was curled tight, as if she were about to hit someone, except for the little finger, which stuck out.

I remember being surprised at how little blood there was. Her royal-blue dress was stained with it all over, yet very little had flowed to the floor. Not far from her body lay a broken whisky bottle. Bourbon. An unopened carton of Lucky Strikes sat on the countertop. Above it, the cupboard was open and tea and cocoa had spilt all over the counter and the floor nearby.

Kneeling beside her, holding a bloody kitchen knife, was Matthew. I went over to him, took the knife gently out of his hand and led him through to his armchair. He accompanied me meekly and flopped back in the chair.

'Matthew, what happened? What have you done? You've got to tell me. Why did you do it?'

I gave him pencil and paper, but he just drew in on himself and I could get nothing out of him.

In the end I gave up and went back to the kitchen. I wasn't thinking clearly. I suppose if I assumed anything at all it was that someone must have told him about what his wife got up to while he was out, and that one way or the other it had set off the explosion that had been building in him. Now Gloria was dead.

My heart wept for her; I had come to love her almost as much as I loved Matthew. But there was nothing I could do for her. It didn't matter now what happened to her. Or so I told myself. All I could think about was to protect Matthew. If anyone found out about this, he might be hanged, or, more likely, found insane and put in the lunatic asylum. I knew he wouldn't be able to bear that. I would have to care for him from now on.

The blackout cloth was still rolled up below the windows, where it had been left after I helped Gloria take it down a couple of months before. I gently rolled Gloria onto it, then wrapped it round her as tightly as a shroud. Before I had finished I kissed her on the forehead and said, 'Goodbye, sweet Gloria. Goodbye.' She was still warm.

Where could I hide her? The only place I could think of was the old outbuilding. In the light of a small oil lamp I started to dig the hole. I couldn't manage more than about three feet. I went back to the house, where Matthew hadn't moved, and managed to drag out the roll of blackout cloth and drop it in the hole. There was no one around. Only the black night sky with its uncaring stars.

With tears running down my cheeks, I shovelled back the earth. Some heavy stone slabs stood propped against the wall and I levered them down on top of the makeshift grave. It was the best I could do.

In the house, I swept up the broken glass, the spilt tea leaves and cocoa powder, and put the tins back in the cupboard. As I said, there was very little blood and I scrubbed it off the floor easily enough.

I had to explain where Gloria had gone, so after I had managed to lead Matthew upstairs and put him to bed, I packed his bloody shirt and trousers in a small suitcase and added Gloria's favourite clothes. Then I put her personal odds and ends in too. I wrote a note—Gloria's childlike handwriting and style were easy to imitate. After that, carrying the suitcase, I took the back way to the shop. Matthew didn't seem aware of what was happening and I had no idea whether he would remember what he had done.

Early the next day I went back to Bridge Cottage, found Matthew still in bed, 'found' the note and proceeded to tell everyone we knew that Gloria had run away during the night because she couldn't bear her life with Matthew any more. She said she loved him, but she couldn't be responsible for her actions if she stayed. Then I showed them the note, which said exactly that. She ended by saying that we shouldn't go looking for her because we would never be able to find her. Everyone believed the note without question.

I gave up Bridge Cottage, sold the contents and brought Matthew to live with us above the shop.

One evening when Mother was at Joyce Maddingley's, I took Matthew's bloodstained clothes and Gloria's dresses and burned them in the grate. I disposed of her trinkets in Leeds the next time I went there on shop business. I just stood on Leeds Bridge and dropped them one by one into the River Aire.

As I had expected, it was Brad who gave me the most trouble. He just couldn't believe that Gloria had simply left. If she wanted to go, he argued, then why didn't she go with him? He had asked her often enough. I told him I thought she wanted a completely new start. It hurt him deeply, which I hated to do, but he had to accept what I said in the end. The 448th Bomber Group moved out of Rowan Woods and I heard nothing more from Brad.

Michael Stanhope expressed sorrow that such a beautiful spirit had left. He said something about Hobb's End having glimmered briefly, before turning dark again. He was free to sell the nude now, not that I ever heard anything of it again. Perhaps it wasn't as good as he thought it was.

As for Matthew, he went on drinking and staring into space as before. I had to stop the visits to Dr Jennings, of course. Who knew what narcosynthesis might draw out of Matthew?

Soon, we were hearing rumours that the village was to be sold as a reservoir site, and when I looked around it didn't surprise me. I hadn't noticed it happening, but hardly anyone lived there any more. Those who had come back from the war had had a taste of more interesting locales or had been trained for jobs they could only get in the cities. The mill closed. Buildings fell into disrepair. Old people died. Finally, there was nobody left.

One day, before we left for Leeds, a man came into the shop with a little boy of about eight or nine and asked to see Gloria. I knew immediately who they were.

'Are you a relative?' I asked him.

'No,' he said. 'Just an old friend, that's all. I was passing this way, so I thought I'd look her up.' He sounded rather sad, and I noticed he had a cockney accent.

I asked him more questions, to show interest. Most of all, I wanted him to be satisfied by my explanation of Gloria's disappearance. I needn't have worried. When he left, he just said, 'If you do see her again, tell her George and little Frankie dropped by and send their love.'

I assured him I would. The little boy had said nothing at all, but I felt him staring at me the whole time. On impulse, I gave him a quarter of gumdrops. He thanked me solemnly and then they left.

The following week, Matthew, Mother and I moved to Leeds and Hobb's End ceased to exist.

ON SUNDAY MORNING, Annie was lying back in Banks's front room, barefoot, her feet dangling over the arm of the settee, reading about Gwen Shackleton's war.

'It's a confession of sorts, isn't it? she said. 'She does admit to interfering with the body. That makes her an accessory.'

'I very much doubt that any judge would admit the manuscript as evidence. All she has to do is say it's fiction. Any decent lawyer would make mincemeat of it. She makes her living writing detective fiction.' He ran his hand across his head. 'Believe me, the CPS can't even keep up with today's crimes, let alone put staff on prosecuting yesterday's on evidence so flimsy a puff of wind would blow it away.'

'So that's it? We go no further? To be honest, it looks to me as if the poor woman's suffered enough. What a blighted life. She still committed a crime, though.'

'Yes, but she's not the killer.'

'Unless she's lying in the story.'

'I don't think so. She did what she did to protect her brother, who had already suffered terribly in the war. If she'd called the police at the time, it's almost certain he would have been convicted of Gloria's murder. Unless . . .'

'Unless what?'

'Unless he didn't do it. There are a number of things in Gwen's version that bother me. Gwen notices that Gloria's fist is clenched apart from the little finger which appears to be broken. Right?'

'Right.'

'And Gloria's body is still warm. Which means that the clenched fist wasn't caused by rigor mortis; it was caused by a cadaveric spasm. What if the killer, the *real* killer, had been trying to take something out of Gloria's hand when he was disturbed by Matthew coming home? Something that might have incriminated him.'

'The button? It's certainly possible.'

Banks shook his head. 'But they'd still probably have arrested Matthew. The crazy husband would have looked the most obvious suspect, and the button, even if they had found it, could have been explained away.'

'So what do we do next?'

'We could hand the report to Jimmy Riddle and get on with our lives. Or look into those one or two little inconsistencies I mentioned. For a start, I'm not convinced that—'

The doorbell rang.

Banks went to answer the door. Annie heard a woman's voice, then in she walked. Blonde hair, black eyebrows, attractive, good figure, dressed in a pastel skirt and a white blouse. For a moment, she seemed speechless, a slight flush suffusing her pale complexion, then she moved forward and said, 'Hello, I don't think we've been introduced.'

Feeling foolish, Annie stood up. 'Annie Cabbot,' she said.

'Sandra Banks,' said the other. 'Pleased to meet you.'

Banks stood behind them looking uncomfortable. 'DS Cabbot and

I were just discussing the Thornfield Reservoir case,' he said. 'Maybe you've read about it?'

Sandra looked down at Annie's bare feet, then gave Banks a withering glance. 'Yes, of course,' she said. 'And on a Sunday morning, too. Such devotion to duty.'

Annie felt herself blush to her roots.

'Anyway,' Banks gibbered on, 'it's really nice to see you. Would you like some coffee or something?'

Sandra shook her head. 'No, I don't think so. I just came up to Eastvale to see to some things. I thought I'd drop by to talk to you about our son, but it'll do some other time. Don't let me interrupt.'

She opened the door and was gone.

Annie stood facing Banks in silence for a few moments, aware only of her fast and loud heartbeat and burning skin. 'I didn't know what to say,' she said. 'I felt foolish, embarrassed.'

'Why? Sandra and I have been separated for almost a year.'

'Yes, I know. It was just a shock, meeting her like that.'

Banks gave a nervous laugh. 'You can say that again. Look, let's sit outside, OK? Put Vivian Elmsley on the back burner for a while. It's a beautiful day, shame to waste it staying indoors.'

'OK.' Annie followed him outside, still feeling dazed. She sat on a striped deck chair. Banks read the *Sunday Times*, trying to pretend everything was just fine, but she knew he was rattled, too. Perhaps even more than she was. After all, he had been married to the woman for more than twenty years.

Annie stared into the distance at Witch Fell, whose massive shape took up most of the western skyline.

'Are you OK?' Banks asked, looking up from his paper.

'Fine,' she said, mustering a smile. 'Fine.'

But she wasn't. She should have known how fleeting happiness was; and what a mistake it is to allow oneself to get too close to anyone. Closeness like that stirs up all the old demons—the jealousy, the insecurity. A shadow had blotted out her sun, just the way Witch Fell obscured the sky.

RAIN HAD FINALLY come to the Dales, and the Golden Grill was almost empty. Doris, the proprietor, claimed Banks and Sergeant Hatchley, who had walked across for toasted tea cakes and coffee, were only the fourth and fifth customers to pass through her door that day.

'Does that put us in line for summat special, like?' Hatchley asked. 'Maybe a free cuppa?'

She slapped his arm and laughed. 'Get away with you.'

'Worth a try,' said Hatchley to Banks. 'Never ask, never get.'

Banks laughed, then he asked, 'Have you heard anything on that nationwide inquiry you put out yet?'

'Something came in this morning, as a matter of fact,' said Hatchley. 'Lass called Brenda Hamilton was found dead in a barn. Strangled and stabbed. In that order.'

'It certainly *sounds* promising.'

Hatchley shook his head. 'Don't get your hopes up. I only mentioned it because it was the same MO. There's a couple of problems. It happened near Hadleigh, Suffolk, in August 1952. That's seven years after Gloria Shackleton was killed. It's a long gap. It also happened in another part of the country.'

'There could be reasons for that.'

'And I doubt there'd be any American air force personnel around by then, would there? I mean the war was long over.'

'You're probably right, Jim, but get onto East Anglia and ask for more details. I'll ask DS Cabbot to contact the Americans again and see if she can find out anything.'

'Will do.'

Back in his office, Banks put off phoning Annie at Harkside, smoking a cigarette instead and staring out of the window. A warm, slow rain fell on the market square, darkening the cobbles. It wasn't bringing much relief; the air was still sticky and humid.

Sunday had gone badly after Sandra's visit, and it annoyed him that he felt that way. After all, *she* had a new boyfriend. Conversation had been awkward, and Annie had eventually left just after lunch, claiming she had things to see to back in Harkside.

At the time, Banks had not been sorry to see her go. He was more upset than he had let on by Sandra's visit. Why did she have to turn up just then, when everything was going so well? What gave her the right to act so shocked that *he* was seeing someone, knocking everyone's feelings out of kilter?

Finally, he plucked up the courage and picked up the phone. 'How's it going?' he asked.

'Fine.'

'You sound distracted.'

'No, I'm not. Just a bit busy. Really. It's fine.'

Banks took a deep breath. 'Look, if it's about Sunday, I'm sorry. I had no idea Sandra was going to turn up.'

'Well, as I said, I'm fine. Except I've got a lot on my plate.'

'OK, if that's how you want to play it. See if you can find out anything about an American air force presence in Suffolk in 1952. And, if there were any bases left, which was the nearest one to Hadleigh.'

'Right.'

'Annie?'

'What?'

'Can't we get together and talk about things?'

'There's nothing to talk about. Really. Look, you know I'm off home on holiday in a couple of days. I've got a lot to do before I go. Maybe when I get back. OK?'

Feeling more depressed than ever, Banks glanced at the pile of paper on his desk: SOCO search results, post-mortem, forensic odontology. None of it told him anything more.

'IT'S JENNY.'

'I know. I recognised your voice. How are you?' said Banks.

'Well, don't sound so excited to hear from me.'

'I'm sorry, Jenny, really. It's just that I'm expecting a call.'

'Well, I won't take up much of your time. I just want to apologise for dumping all over you on our last meeting.'

'What are friends for?'

'Anyway,' Jenny went on, 'by way of an apology, I'd like to invite you to dinner. If you think you can tolerate my cooking, that is?'

'It's bound to be better than mine.'

She laughed a little too nervously. 'How about tomorrow, sevenish?'

'Sounds fine.'

'Are you sure it won't cause any problems?'

'Why should it?'

'I don't know . . . I just . . .' Then her voice brightened. 'That's great. I'll see you tomorrow about seven, then?'

After he hung up, Banks sat back. Dinner with Jenny. At her place. That would be interesting. Then he thought about Annie, and her coldness yesterday, and it cast a shadow over him.

But whatever their personal problems, he *was* anxious to hear from Annie about East Anglia. Shortly before eleven, he did.

'I'm sorry for the delay,' she said. 'What with time differences and faulty fax machines, well, I'm sure you know . . .'

'That's all right. Just tell me what you've discovered.' Banks had already come to one or two conclusions of his own, and he felt the usual tremor of excitement as the pieces started to fall together.

'First off,' Annie said, 'there *was* an American air base near Hadleigh in 1952. The Americans came back in 1948, during the Berlin blockade and airlift. The first thing they did was deploy long-range B-29 bombers from four bases in East Anglia.'

'Any familiar names?'

'Just one. Guess who ran the PX?'

'Edgar Konig.'

'The very same. You don't sound so surprised.'

'Not really. What did you find out about him?'

'He left Rowan Woods in May 1945, and spent some time in Europe, then he returned to America. He was assigned to the base near Hadleigh in summer 1952. Tell me, why doesn't it surprise you? Why not one of the other Americans?'

'The whisky and the Luckies. In Vivian Elmsley's manuscript. She said there was a bottle of whisky smashed on the floor and an *unopened* carton of Lucky Strikes on the kitchen counter.'

'Brad could have brought them.'

'Possible. But it was PX who had access to the stores, PX who always supplied the goodies. The manuscript mentioned a farewell party at Rowan Woods that night. PX must have finally plucked up courage. He'd brought the presents. One last-ditch attempt to buy what he yearned for. Gloria resisted and . . . poor Matthew came in afterwards. Any idea where PX was between 1945 and 1952?'

'No. You're thinking there might be others.'

'Possibly.'

'I can check.'

'Good. See what you can do. I'll talk to you later.'

When Annie had hung up, Banks felt restless. Sometimes waiting was the most difficult part; that was when he smoked too much and paced up and down. There were a couple of things he could do in the meantime. First, he dialled Jenny Fuller's number.

'Alan,' she said. 'Don't tell me you want to cancel?'

'No, no. Actually, I need you to do a little favour for me.'

'Of course. If I can.'

'You said at lunch the other day that you trained with the FBI profilers? Do you have any contacts there? Anyone close enough to ask for a personal favour?'

Jenny paused a moment. 'Well, there is *one* fellow, yes.'

Banks filled her in on the new developments, then said, 'This Edgar Konig, I'd like you to ask your friend to check his record. DS Cabbot's working with the military authorities, but any information they can supply us with is limited.'

'I'm sure Bill will be happy to oblige, if he can,' said Jenny.

When Banks had finished giving Jenny the details, he asked DS Hatchley to call East Anglia and find out if a US airman called Edgar Konig had ever been questioned or suspected in connection with the Brenda Hamilton murder.

ON FRIDAY, it was after four o'clock when the publisher's rep dropped Vivian at her Leeds hotel, and the sky looked heavy and dark. In the distance, she could hear hesitant rumbles of thunder and see faint lightning flashes. Even the Metropole's façade, lovingly restored to its original orange terracotta, looked as black as it had when she had stayed there with Charlie all those years ago.

She would have liked nothing better than to rest in her room for an hour or so, perhaps take a long bath. Tomorrow would be taken up with signings in York and Harrogate. She supposed she could put off her trip . . . make the visit on Sunday morning. No. She would not procrastinate. She called the concierge and asked him to arrange for a taxi, then she put on her raincoat and waterproof boots.

Beyond Otley the roads were narrow, and for a while they got stuck behind a lorry doing only about thirty. It was after five o'clock when the driver pulled up in the car park near Thornfield Reservoir. The rain was coming down hard now. Vivian asked the driver to wait.

The path through the woods was treacherous, as if the parched earth had been yearning for the chance to suck up every drop of rain that fell, and Vivian had to be really careful not to slip as she made her way slowly down the embankment.

The ruined village lay spread out before her under the dark sky. Every few seconds a flash of lightning lit the scene.

Vivian paused at the fairy bridge, hardly able to believe that this was the same bridge where she had stood and chatted with Gloria, Matthew, Alice, Cynthia, Betty and the others all those years ago.

She moved towards Bridge Cottage. There was nothing left of the place except the foundations, but she remembered where every room and cupboard had been. The area around and inside the cottage had been dug up. They had been looking for more bodies, Vivian supposed. Well, they would, wouldn't they? Inspector Niven would have done exactly the same thing.

Now, standing there in the driving rain, she was beginning to wonder why she had come. At least when Hobb's End was under water she could imagine it as a place preserved. Now it was exposed as a heap of rubbish and memories, mostly painful. She had in mind only a simple sort of pilgrimage, an acknowledgment of some sort. Well, she had done that. Time to head back.

Lost in her thoughts, she hadn't noticed the gaunt, stringy-haired man who had followed her taxi from Leeds. When she passed Bridge Cottage on her way back, he stepped from behind the outbuilding and held out a gun, then he grabbed her round the throat, and she felt the hard metal pushing at the side of her neck.

Then a dogeared photograph appeared in front of her. It took her a few moments to realise that it was Gloria, perhaps a year or two before she had come to Hobb's End. Rain spattered the photograph and the hand that held it. Such a small hand. *Gloria's hand*, she thought. What was he doing with hands like Gloria's?

By SIX O'CLOCK on Friday evening, Banks was starting to get nervous about his dinner with Jenny. He had already showered and shaved; now he was trying to decide which version of casual he should put on tonight. It was a decision made a lot easier by the overflowing laundry basket: chinos and a blue denim shirt.

He thought of Annie. Did he owe her fidelity, or were all bets off after the way she had cut him? He didn't know. At the very least, he owed her an explanation of the case. Late that afternoon, Bill Gilchrist of the FBI had sent him, at Jenny's request, a six-page fax on Edgar 'PX' Konig, and Banks had been gobsmacked by its contents. DS Hatchley had also determined that Konig *had* been questioned in connection with the Brenda Hamilton murder.

Annie wasn't at the section station, or at home, when he phoned. He dialled her mobile number but still got no answer.

He was just heading into the bathroom to brush his teeth when the telephone rang.

'Don't you watch the news?' growled Chief Constable Riddle.

'No, sir. I've been getting ready to go out.'

'Then you'd better cancel. I'm calling from Thornfield Reservoir. Shortly over an hour ago, a woman was taken hostage. She had taken a taxi out there and told the driver to wait. When he thought he'd waited long enough, he went to look for her and saw her standing with a man who appeared to be holding a gun to her head. The taxi driver ran back to his car and phoned the police. The woman's name is Vivian Elmsley. Ring any bells?'

Banks's heart lurched. 'Vivian Elmsley? Yes, she's—'

'I know damn well who she is, Banks. What I don't know is why some maniac is holding a gun to her head and demanding to talk to the detective in charge of the Gloria Shackleton investigation.'

'What's his name?'

'He hasn't said. We, however, have gone into full bloody Hollywood production mode out here, with a big enough budget to bankrupt us. A hostage negotiator has spoken with him briefly from a distance. He won't say any more until we get you to the scene. There's an Armed Response Unit here already. Get yourself down here, man. Now!'

When Riddle hung up, Banks reached for his raincoat and shot out of the door.

ANNIE HAD MANAGED to get away from the station early, and by six o'clock she was approaching Blackburn on the M65. It was Friday rush hour; lightning forked and flickered over the humped Pennines, and thunder rumbled and crashed like a mad percussionist in the distance. Annie counted the gaps between the lightning and thunder, wondering if that really *did* tell you how far away the storm was.

What was the gap between her and Banks now? Could it be counted, like that between the thunder and the lightning?

It was all getting to be too much: first, there was the annoyance she had felt when he went out boozing with his mate; then the time he had gone to meet his son and made it clear she wasn't welcome; and then Sandra's appearance on Sunday morning. If every little thing like that was going to rub up against her raw nerve ends, then where would she find any peace?

If she stayed with him, she would have to meet his son and to pass the Dad's-new-girlfriend test. And there would be the divorce, something else they'd have to go through. She didn't think she could face all the emotional detritus of someone else's life impinging on her own.

Annie had the electronic gismo in the car stereo set so that no matter what programme she was listening to, the nearest local station would cut in with its weather and travel updates. Just as she was overtaking a convoy of lorries churning up so much water she could hardly see, the weather cut in, and she also caught a news bulletin about a hostage situation at Thornfield Reservoir. Unfortunately, the same gismo also cut the bulletin off halfway through the item. Annie jabbed at the search buttons. When she finally did get the right frequency, all she heard were the final words '. . . the hostage-taker has asked to talk to the detective in charge of the so-called Hobb's End skeleton case, Detective Chief Inspector Banks.'

Well, Annie thought, she would have to go back.

BANKS ARRIVED at Thornfield car park, put on his Wellington boots and hurried to the scene. Riddle hadn't been far wrong when he compared it to a Hollywood production. Though the patrol cars, Armed Response Vehicles and Technical Support Unit vans couldn't drive right to the rim of the reservoir because of the trees, some of them had forced their way through as far as they could, and long, thick wires and cables trailed the rest of the way. The local media people were there, too. The entire bowl of Hobb's End was floodlit. At the centre of it all, two small, pathetic figures were cruelly illuminated just beyond the fairy bridge.

Riddle stood by the phalanx of TV cameras clustered behind the police tape. Banks ignored him and went straight over to the hostage negotiator. He looked young. Banks guessed this was his first real-life situation. Officially, the local superintendent was in charge of the scene, but as a rule the negotiator called the shots.

'I'm DCI Banks,' he said.

'Sergeant Whitkirk,' said the negotiator.

'Let me go and talk to him.'

'You're not going down there,' Whitkirk said. 'Do your talking on this.' He held a loudhailer out. Banks didn't take it.

'No. You listen to me.' Banks pointed to the two figures. 'I don't know how many scenes like this you've handled successfully, but I know what this situation's all about and I think I've got a hell of a lot better chance than you or anyone else of making sure no one gets hurt. I know who he is and what he wants.'

'How can you know that? He hasn't communicated any demands.'

'Except to talk to me.'

'And our first rule is that we don't comply. He's a nutter and he's unpredictable. We can't give in to him, and you can't just walk into the situation. Maybe you're the one he really wants to kill.'

'I'll take my chances.'

Whitkirk thrust his chin out. 'No, you won't. I'm in charge of the scene here and you're not going in.'

'What do we do, then?'

'First we do all we can to turn an imprecise situation into a precise one.'

'Oh, stop quoting the textbook at me,' Banks said. 'Look, he's asked for me. He must have something to tell me, and there's only one way to find out. I think I can talk him out of doing any harm. Can't you give me a bit of leeway?'

Whitkirk chewed on his lip for a moment. 'Securing the scene's my responsibility,' he said.

'Let me go in.' Banks pointed over to the chief constable. 'Believe me, there's a bloke over there will give you a medal if I get shot.'

Whitkirk managed a thin smile. 'One condition,' he said. 'You wear a bulletproof vest.'

'All right.'

Whitkirk sent someone to pick up the vest from an Armed Response Vehicle, then he told the hostage-taker over his loudhailer what he was planning.

'Send him in,' the man shouted back.

Kitted out with his bulletproof vest, Banks set off down the side of the reservoir. About halfway down, he slipped and went the rest of the distance on his backside. It reminded him that he had put on his best trousers. He had forgotten to phone Jenny and cancel.

He heard a curse behind him and turned to see Annie Cabbot come sliding down after him. At the bottom, she flashed him a grin. 'Sorry. It was the only way I could give them the slip.'

'I take it you don't have a bulletproof vest?'

'No.'

'I could be gallant and give you mine, but we're a little too close to the scene now. Just stay back, behind me.'

They approached the fairy bridge and Banks told the man who he was. The man told them to stop at the far side. They faced one another over the bridge. Vivian Elmsley looked frightened but otherwise unhurt.

'This is DS Cabbot,' Banks said. 'She's been working on the case with me. Is it OK for her to be here?'

The man nodded. 'I know who she is,' he said. 'I saw her on television, then down here a week or so ago.'

'So it was you,' Annie said. 'What were you doing?'

'I've been here a lot at night. Thinking.'

'Why did you run?'

'I couldn't risk being caught, having to explain myself, before I'd finished what I had to do.'

Banks decided it was time to take charge. He held his hands up and gestured for Annie to do the same. Rain dripped down the back of his neck. 'We're not armed, Francis,' he said. 'We just want to talk. Let Ms Elmsley go.'

'So you know who I am?'

'Francis Henderson.'

'Clever. But my name's Stringer now. Frank Stringer.' So he had adopted his mother's maiden name. Strange. That told Banks something about the situation they were dealing with.

'Anyway,' Frank went on, 'I'm not ready to let anyone go yet. I want to hear her confess, then I'll decide whether to kill her or not.'

'OK, Frank. What do you want to hear?'

'She killed my mother. I want to hear her say so, and I want to know why.'

'She didn't kill anyone, Frank.'

'You're lying. You're trying to protect her.'

His grip tightened on Vivian. Banks caught her sudden intake of breath and saw the gun barrel pushed into the flesh under her ear.

'Listen to me, Frank,' he said. 'You want the truth, don't you? It didn't happen the way you think it did.'

'All those years,' Frank went on, as if he hadn't heard. 'Do you know he worshipped her, my father? He said she was a dreamer, a free spirit, a beautiful butterfly who just had to spread her wings and fly away. She always wanted to be one of those Hollywood actresses. But I hated her for leaving us. I hated her and I loved her. All my life dominated and blighted by a mother I never even knew. What do you think Mr Freud would make of that?'

'She *was* very young, Frank. When she got pregnant, she was frightened. She didn't know what to do. For some people to run away seems like the only solution. She obviously wanted the child, *you*, to live. She didn't have an abortion. Did she keep in touch?'

He sniffed. 'A postcard every now and then, telling him she was doing fine. My dad took me up to Hobb's End to see her. It was the only time I . . . the only time I really remember seeing her, hearing her voice. She told me I was a fine-looking boy. I loved her then. She was a magical creature to me. Dazzling. So beautiful and so tender.

But she told him she had a new life now and we should leave her alone if we wanted her to be happy.'

'What did your father do?'

'What she asked. He was devastated. We tried once more, when it was all over.' He turned so he was speaking into Vivian's ear. 'But this lying bitch here told us she had run away. All my life I believed that, believed my mother had run away and abandoned us for ever. Now I find out she was dead.'

'Let her go, Frank!' Banks shouted over a peal of thunder. 'She didn't know.'

'What do you mean, she didn't know? She must have known. Even if she didn't do the actual killing, she was involved.' Frank glared at Banks. His eyes were wild, his lank hair was plastered to his skull.

'You've got it all wrong, Frank. Vivian had nothing to do with your mother's death.' As he spoke, Banks noticed Vivian's eyes fill with curiosity, despite the gun at her neck. Annie stood beside him now. Banks's clothes stuck to his skin and rain stung his eyes.

'What do you mean?' Frank said.

'As far as she was concerned,' Banks said, 'your mother *had* gone away. She had spoken about running away often. Life was miserable for her. It was only natural for Gwen to assume that she'd go, just like she left you and your father in the first place.'

'No!'

Frank's grip tightened on Vivian's throat and she gasped.

'OK, Frank,' Banks went on. 'Calm down. Please.'

They waited a moment, all silent but for the pattering of the rain and the storm disappearing into the distance.

Then Banks felt things relax. Frank didn't say anything for at least a minute. Banks could see him processing information, trying to shore up his defences.

'If it wasn't her, who was it?' Frank said eventually.

Annie stepped forward. Frank turned to her and blinked the rain out of his eyes.

'His name was Edgar Konig,' Annie said. 'He ran the PX at Rowan Woods USAF Base, about a mile from here.'

'PX?' Vivian gasped.

'I don't believe you,' said Frank.

'It's true,' said Banks, picking up the thread. He realised that Annie didn't have the full story yet. 'Konig killed your mother. He also killed at least one other woman, down in East Anglia. There were others, too, in America. Edgar Konig was attracted to your mother, but he had serious problems with women. He was always tongue-tied around them. He brought her presents, but even then she didn't offer herself to him. She went out with other men. He watched and waited. All the time the pressure was building up in him.'

'How do you know it was him?'

'We found a collar button from an American airman's uniform. We think your mother must have torn it off as they struggled.'

Frank's grip round Vivian's throat had loosened a little.

'Edgar Konig went to Bridge Cottage to collect what he thought your mother owed him while her husband was at the pub. He'd been drinking and he thought he could overcome his inadequacies. She must have rejected him, maybe laughed at him, and the next thing he knew he'd killed her in a rage. Do you understand what I'm saying, Frank?'

'If that's how it happened, why did no one know about it?'

Slowly, Banks reached for his cigarettes and offered Frank one.

'Gave them up years back,' he said. 'Thanks, though.'

Banks lit up. Definite progress. Better not cock it up now.

'No one knew about it,' Banks went on, 'because Edgar Konig covered his tracks well.' He looked at Vivian Elmsley as he spoke. She averted her eyes. 'He buried the body in the outbuilding. Then he packed a few of her belongings in a suitcase to make it look as though she had run off. He even faked a note.'

Frank spoke in Vivian's ear. 'Is that right, what he's saying?'

Banks couldn't hear her, but he saw her mouth form the word 'Yes.'

'Frank,' Banks pressed on. 'The gun. I know you don't want to hurt anyone, but it's dangerous. It's easy to make a wrong move.'

Frank looked at the gun.

Banks stepped onto the fairy bridge and moved forward slowly. He knew there were probably two or three trained marksmen aiming in his direction, and the thought made his stomach churn. 'Give the gun to me, Frank.'

Frank released his grip on Vivian Elmsley's throat. She staggered aside and slipped down one of the muddy holes the SOCOs had dug in the Bridge Cottage floor. Annie ran to help her.

Frank handed the gun to Banks. 'What happened to him?' he asked. 'This Konig. Did he ever get caught?'

'I'll tell you all about that later, Frank,' said Banks, taking Frank by the elbow. 'Just for now, though, we're all a bit tired and wet. OK? I think we should go somewhere to dry off, don't you?'

Frank hung his head. Banks draped an arm across his shoulder. Several police officers had already come dashing and sliding down the embankment. Two of them grabbed Frank roughly and started handcuffing him.

'There's no need to be so rough with him,' said Banks.

'Leave this to us, sir,' said one of the officers.

Banks sighed and handed over the gun. They hustled Frank Stringer away. Banks turned to see Annie and the other policemen helping Vivian Elmsley to stumble over the fairy bridge.

'Thank you,' Vivian said. 'You saved my life.'

'I lied for you,' said Banks. 'I also sullied Gloria's loyalty to Matthew.'

She paled and whispered, 'I know. I appreciate what you did.'

'There was a chance, you know. If you'd come forward after you found Gloria dead, if you'd gone to the police . . .' Banks held his anger in check; this was neither the time nor the place for it. 'Ah, to hell with it. Too late now.'

Vivian bowed her head. 'Believe me, I know what I've done.'

Banks turned and slogged on alone through the mud to his car. All he wanted was a long hot bath and a large Laphroaig. And Annie.

She was already leaning against her car, arms folded.

'Are you all right?' Banks asked.

'I'm fine. Fine as anyone can be who's spent the last half-hour standing in the rain wondering if someone was going to get their head blown off. I respect what you did out there, by the way.'

'What do you mean?'

'You lied to get us all out of there alive.'

'It worked. What next?'

'Onward to St Ives. After I've stopped off for some dry clothes. I was already on my way when I heard. I couldn't just leave it.'

'Of course not. Thanks for being here.'

'You?'

'Home, I suppose.' Banks remembered dinner with Jenny. Too late now, but he could at least phone her and apologise.

Annie nodded. 'Look, I'll be gone for two weeks. Right now I'm still a bit mixed up about my feelings. Why don't you phone me when I get back? Maybe we can have that talk?'

'OK.'

She grinned at him crookedly. 'If there weren't so many policemen about I'd kiss you goodbye.' With that she opened the car door, got in and started the engine. Banks watched the red taillights disappear down the muddy track.

Epilogue

After a long, rainy winter and overdue repairs by Yorkshire Water, Thornfield Reservoir filled up again and Hobb's End once more disappeared. On July 27 of the year after the Gloria Shackleton murder had entered and left the public's imagination, Vivian Elmsley, in the midst of a national book tour, lay on a king-size bed in her Florida hotel room, alone with her memories, a bottle of gin, ice and tonic water, propped up with pillows, and watched the local news channel.

Tonight was the night, and after everything she had been through, Vivian desperately needed *some* sense of an ending.

Crowds gathered outside the gates of Starke Prison, about twenty-five miles away. One or two were quietly carrying placards that asked for an end to capital punishment, but by far the majority were chanting, 'Fry Konig! Fry Konig!' Vivian had been shocked when Banks told her that Gloria's murderer was not dead, but on death row in a Florida prison—a serial killer.

Vivian had visited Frank Stringer several times in jail and told him she would help him get back on his feet when he came out. It was the least she could do for Gloria's memory. In his turn, Frank had told Vivian how the re-emergence of Hobb's End had caused his obsession with the past to escalate. His father had been the first to recognise Gwen Shackleton as Vivian Elmsley on television, but Frank had confirmed it; he had memorised her eyes and her voice so many years ago. He couldn't explain why he had approached her at the bookshop. He meant no harm at first. Then the skeleton was discovered, and he knew she must have lied. He hated her after that; he telephoned to scare her, to make her suffer.

It was almost time. Edgar Konig, just turned seventy-six, was finally getting what he deserved.

Vivian felt a twinge of guilt when she realised that she *might* have helped put an end to his killing all those years ago. She had tried to rationalise it to herself so many times. Even if she had reported what happened, she told herself, they would have still probably arrested Matthew. What could she have told the police that would have pointed them towards Edgar Konig? It was all very well to say in retrospect that *she* could have stopped all those deaths, but it wasn't fair. Twenty-twenty hindsight. And who wouldn't, given the chance, go back and change *something*? Besides, Vivian told herself, she had acted only from the purest of motives: love for her brother.

And it was all over now. A cheer went up from the crowd outside the prison. Edgar Konig was dead.

Why was it that Vivian felt no relief, felt nothing but the stirrings of a bad headache? She closed her eyes. *All over.* She was so tired.

With her morbid imagination, Vivian saw Gloria run into the kitchen as she became frightened by PX's erratic behaviour, saw her pulling tins of tea and cocoa out of the cupboard, looking for the gun, shocked and scared to find that it wasn't there. Did she realise that Gwen must have taken it? *The gun.* Vivian was the one who had taken the gun, the one thing that *might* have saved Gloria's life.

Then, for all those terrible years, she had cared for Matthew, believing he was a murderer. Poor, gentle Matthew, who wouldn't harm a soul, who couldn't even kill himself. She had a vivid memory of the afternoon when she had come back from the shops and seen Matthew sitting with the gun in his mouth, trying to find the courage to pull the trigger. But he hadn't been able to do it. His eyes had pleaded with her, and she had walked over to him, tenderly wrapped her hand round his, kissed his forehead and pressed his finger on the trigger.

Outside Starke Prison the crowd was chanting. Vivian Elmsley let her tears flow freely for the first time in over fifty years.

PETER ROBINSON

Born and brought up in Yorkshire, author Peter Robinson already had a degree in English Literature from Leeds University under his belt when he chose to cross the Atlantic to continue his studies at the University of Windsor in Ontario.

Peter fell for Canada, and decided that he wanted to stay there, eventually making his home in Toronto, with his wife Sheila. His many successful detective novels, however, are set in the old country.

Part of the idea for *In a Dry Season* struck Peter Robinson in the late summer of 1995 when he was on holiday in England with his wife. They visited Thrushcross Reservoir, near Otley in Yorkshire. The reservoir had dried up, and the remains of the old village of West End were on view for the first time since it had been flooded in 1967. They could see the foundations of houses, the ruined flax mill and a tiny packhorse bridge that had survived under water for almost thirty years. As a crime writer, Peter Robinson's first thought was: What an interesting place to discover a body!

Needless to say, the drought in Yorkshire did not last, but the author's fascination with his plot idea did. He created a fictional reservoir, borrowing the name Thornfield from Charlotte Bronte's *Jane Eyre*, and wove ingredients from the Second World War into the story. It was a period that interested Peter. Although he was not born until five years after the war ended, it cast its long shadow over his childhood, in the form of sweet rationing and bomb sites. For his hero, he already had the redoubtable Detective Chief Inspector Alan Banks, who has featured regularly in his novels since the first one, *Gallows View*, was published in 1987.

24
HOURS

GREG ILES

Will Jennings is on his way to a conference in Biloxi, Mississippi, leaving his wife and daughter alone in the family's prestigious home. Joe Hickey, like any predator, waits for the right moment to seize his prey.

For the next twenty-four hours Will, Karen and five-year-old Abby will be part of a kidnapping plan that he has masterminded down to the very last second.

one

'The kid always makes it. I told you that.'

Margaret McDill had not seen the man until yesterday, but he had dominated every second of her existence since their meeting. He had told her to call him Joe, and claimed it was his real name, but she assumed it was an alias. He was a dark-haired, pale-skinned man of about fifty, with deep-set eyes and a coarse five-o'clock shadow. Margaret could not look into his eyes for long. They were dark, furious pools that sucked the life out of her, drained her will. And now they carried knowledge about her that she could not bear.

'I don't believe you,' she said quietly.

'Have I lied to you about anything else?'

'No. But you . . . you let me see your face all night. You won't let me go after that.'

'I told you, the kid always makes it.'

'You're going to kill me and let my son go.'

'You think I'm going to shoot you in broad daylight in front of McDonald's?'

Margaret looked down at her hands. She didn't want to look at Joe, and she didn't want to chance seeing herself in one of the mirrors. The one at home had been bad enough. An unhealthy glaze filmed her eyes, and make-up had failed to hide the bruise along her jaw. There was a long scratch on her forearm.

They were sitting in her BMW, in the parking lot of a shopping centre about fifty yards from a McDonald's restaurant. She had often shopped at the mall. Her husband, a cardiovascular surgeon, had recently bought a big-screen television at the Circuit City store, for patient education at his clinic. But all that seemed part of someone else's life now. As remote as the moon . . . And her son, Peter . . . God alone knew where he was. God and the man beside her.

'I don't care what you do with me,' she said. 'Just let Peter live. Kill me if you have to, just let my son go. He's only ten years old.'

'If you don't shut up, I might take you up on that,' Joe said wearily.

He started the BMW's engine and switched the air conditioner to high, then lit a Camel cigarette. The cold air blasted smoke all over the interior of the car. Margaret's eyes stung from hours of crying.

'Where's Peter now?' she asked, her voice barely a whisper.

Joe took a drag of the Camel and said nothing.

'He's dead, isn't he?' Margaret heard herself say. 'You're just playing games with me. He's dead and you're going to kill me, too—'

'*Christ*,' Joe said through clenched teeth. He glanced at his watch, then punched a number into the BMW's cellphone, he muttering, 'I do believe this has been the worst twenty-four hours of my life. And that includes our little party.'

She flinched.

'Hey,' he said into the phone. 'You in your spot? OK. Wait about a minute, then do it.'

Margaret jerked erect, her eyes wide, searching the nearby cars. 'Oh my God. Peter! Peter!'

Joe picked up the gun and jammed the barrel into her neck. 'You've come this far. Don't blow it now. You remember what we talked about?'

She closed her eyes and nodded. Tears rolled down her cheeks. 'I remember.'

A HUNDRED YARDS from Margaret McDill's BMW, Peter McDill sat in an old green pick-up truck, his eyes shut tight.

'You can open your eyes now.'

Peter opened his eyes. The first thing he saw was a McDonald's restaurant in the middle of a parking lot. It reassured him after his night of isolation. He recognised it. It was only a few miles from his house. Now that he knew where he was, Peter thought about jumping out. But the man behind the wheel of the truck was faster than he looked. Peter looked at his wrists, which were bound with duct tape.

'Can you take this off now?' he asked.

Peter had never seen or heard of Huey before yesterday, but for the last twenty-four hours he had seen no one else. Huey was six inches taller than his father, and weighed at least 300 pounds. He wore dirty mechanic's overalls and heavy plastic glasses with thick lenses that distorted his eyes.

He looked at Peter, his too-big eyes apologetic behind the thick lenses. 'I'm sorry I had to tape you up. But you shouldn't have run. I told you not to run.'

Peter's eyes welled with tears. 'Where's my mom? You said she was going to be here.'

'She's gonna be here. She's probably here already.'

Peter scanned the sea of parked cars, his eyes darting everywhere, searching for his mother's BMW. 'I don't see her car.'

Huey dug down into his front overalls pocket. 'Look, boy,' he said in his deep but childlike voice. 'I made you something.'

The giant hand opened to reveal a carved locomotive. Huey put it into Peter's bound hands. 'I finished it while you was sleeping,' he said. 'I like trains. I rode one once. When I was little. From St Louis, after Mamaw died. Joey rode up by hisself on the train and got me. We rode back together. I got to sit in the front with the rich people. We wasn't supposed to, but Joey figured a way. Joey's smart. He said it was only fair. He says I'm good as anybody. Ain't nobody no better than nobody else. That's a good thing to remember . . . Whittlin's a good thing, too,' Huey went on. 'Keeps me from being nervous.'

Peter closed his eyes. 'Where's my mom?'

'I liked talking to you. Before you ran, anyway. I thought you was my friend.'

Huey dug into his overalls again and brought out his pocketknife. He opened the big blade, grabbed Peter's bound wrists and with a quick jab thrust the knife between them and sawed through the duct tape. Then he reached over and unlocked the passenger door.

'Your mama's waiting for you. In the playground at the McDonald's. Go see her, boy.'

Peter pushed open the truck's door, jumped to the pavement, and started running.

JOE REACHED ACROSS Margaret McDill and opened the passenger door of the BMW. 'Your kid's waiting in the McDonald's Playland.'

Margaret's heart lurched. She looked at the open door, then back at Joe, who was caressing the BMW's leather-covered steering wheel.

'Sure wish I could keep this ride,' he said with genuine regret. 'Got used to this. Yes, sir.'

'Take it.'

'That's not part of the plan. And I always stick to the plan. That's why I'm still around.' As she stared, he opened the driver's door, got out, dropped the keys on the seat, and started walking away.

Margaret sat for a moment without breathing, mistrustful as an injured animal being released into the wild. Then she bolted from the car and ran towards the McDonald's.

WHEN JOE HICKEY climbed into the cab of the green pick-up, Huey looked at him with relief.

'Twenty-three hours, ten minutes,' Hickey said, tapping his watch. 'Cheryl's got the money, nobody got hurt, and no FBI in sight. I'm a goddamn genius, son. Master of the universe.'

'I'm just glad it's over,' said Huey. 'I was scared this time.'

Hickey laughed and tousled the hair on Huey's great unkempt head. 'Home free for another year, Buckethead.'

A smile slowly appeared on the giant's rubbery face. 'Yeah.' He put the truck into gear and joined the flow of traffic leaving the mall.

two
ONE YEAR LATER

Will Jennings swung his Ford Expedition onto the airport road. The field was less than a mile away, and he couldn't keep from watching the planes lifting over the trees as they took off. It had been nearly a month since he'd been up, and he was anxious to fly.

'Keep your eyes on the road,' said his wife from the seat beside him.

'Daddy's watching the airplanes!' Abby chimed from her safety seat in the back. Will looked at his rearview mirror and smiled at their five-and-a-half-year-old daughter. Facially, she was a miniature version of Karen, with strawberry-blonde curls, piercing green eyes, and a light dusting of freckles across her nose.

Will laid his right hand on Karen's knee. 'I sure wish my girls would come along with old Dad. Just jump in the plane and forget about everything for three days.'

'Can we, Mom?' cried Abby. 'Can we?'

'And what do we do for clothes?' Karen asked in a taut voice.

'I'll buy you both new wardrobes on the coast.'

'Yaaayy!' Abby cheered. 'Look, there's the airport!'

The white control tower had come into sight.

'We don't have any insulin,' Karen pointed out.

'Daddy can write me a subscription!'

'*Pre*scription, honey,' Will corrected.

'I want to go to the beach!'

'I can't believe you started this again,' Karen said under her breath. 'Daddy won't be spending any time at the beach, honey. He'll be nervous as a cat until he gives his lecture to all those other doctors. Then they'll spend hours talking about medical school. And then he'll tear his joints trying to play golf for three days straight.'

'If you come,' Will said, 'we can beat the bushes around Ocean Springs for some undiscovered Walter Anderson stuff.'

'*Noooo*,' Abby said plaintively. Their art-buying explorations entailed hours of searching small-town back streets. '*You* won't be playing golf, Mom. You can take me to the beach.'

'Yeah, Mom,' Will echoed.

Karen's eyes flashed like green warning beacons. 'I agreed to chair this flower show two years ago. It's the sixtieth anniversary of the Junior League, and I don't know whose brilliant idea it was to have a flower show, but it's officially my problem.'

'You got everything nailed down the day before yesterday,' Will told her. There wasn't much use in pressing the issue, but he felt he should try. Things had been tense for the past six months, and this would be the first trip he had made without Karen in a long time. 'You're just going to agonise until the whole circus starts on Monday. Four nights of hell. Why not forget it until then?'

'I can't do it,' she said with a note of finality. 'But if you want to take Abby by yourself, you can certainly do that.'

'You know I can't,' Will said with exasperation. 'This is once a year, Karen. I'm giving the keynote speech and the whole thing is very political. You know that. With the new drug venture, I'll have to spend hours with the Searle people—'

'You don't have to explain,' she said. 'Just don't try to make me blow off my obligations when you won't do the same.'

Will swung the Expedition into the general aviation area. Lines of single- and twin-engine planes waited on the concrete apron. Just seeing them lightened his heart.

'I'm not joining the Junior League when I grow up,' Abby said from the back seat. 'I'm going to be a pilot.'

'I thought you were going to be a doctor,' said Will.

'A flying doctor, silly!'

'Flying doctor sure beats housewife,' Karen said *sotto voce*.

Will took his wife's hand as he braked beside his Beechcraft Baron 58. 'One day she'll understand what you sacrificed, babe.'

'Sometimes I don't understand it myself.'

He squeezed Karen's hand. Then he got out, unstrapped Abby from her child seat, and set her on the apron.

The Baron was ten years old but as fine a piece of machinery as you could ask for, and Will owned her outright. She was white with blue stripes and her tail read N-2WJ. The 'WJ' was a touch of vanity, but Abby loved hearing the controllers call out November-Two-Whiskey-Juliet over the radio. When they were flying together, she sometimes made him call her Alpha Juliet.

Will took a suit bag and a leather sample case from the back of the Expedition and set them on the concrete. When he reached back into the car for his laptop computer, Karen picked up the sample case and suit bag and carried them to the plane. As they loaded the luggage, she said: 'You're having pain today, aren't you?'

'No,' he lied, closing the cabin door as though the fire in his hands did not exist. Under normal circumstances he would have cancelled his flight and taken a car, but it was far too late now to reach the Gulf Coast except by air.

Karen looked into his eyes, started to say something, then decided against it. She walked the length of the wing and helped Abby untether it while Will did his preflight walkaround.

'What's the flight time to the coast?' Karen asked. 'Fifty minutes?'

'Thirty-five minutes to the airport, if I push it.' Will was due at the Beau Rivage Casino Hotel in Biloxi at 7.00pm. His lecture would open the annual meeting of the Mississippi Medical Association. 'I'm cutting it a little close,' he conceded. 'That aneurysm ran way over. I'll call you after my presentation.' He pointed to the beeper on his belt. 'If you want me during the flight, use the SkyTel. It's new. Digital. Hardly any dead spots.'

'I just type in the message at home and send it like email?'

'Right. But if you don't want to fool with that, just call the answering service. They'll get the message to me.'

Abby tugged at his hand. 'Will you waggle the wings after takeoff?'

'Sure I will. Just for you.' Will took Karen by the waist. 'Thanks for giving me time last night to finish the video segment. I'd have been laughed out of the conference.'

'You've never been laughed at in your life.' Her face softened. 'How are your hands? I mean it, Will.'

'Stiff,' he admitted. 'But not too bad.'

'You taking anything?'

'Just painkillers and the methotrexate.' Methotrexate was a chemotherapeutic agent developed for use against cancer, but it was used in much smaller doses against Will's form of arthritis. He slipped an arm round Karen's shoulder. 'Don't forget to turn on the alarm system when you get home.'

She shook her head in a way that conveyed several emotions at once: concern, irritation and, somewhere in there, love. 'I never forget. Say goodbye, Abby. Daddy's late.'

Abby hugged his waist and he bent and picked her up. His joints protested, but he forced a smile and kissed her on the forehead. 'Take care of Mom. And don't give her any trouble about your shots.'

'But it doesn't hurt as much when you do it.'

'That's a fib. Mom's given a lot more shots than I have.'

He set her down with a muffled groan.

'Oh!' Karen said. 'I forgot to tell you. Microsoft is going to split again. It was up twelve points when I left the house.'

He smiled. 'Forget Microsoft. Tonight starts the ball rolling on Restorase.' Restorase, a new drug Will had helped develop, was the subject of his presentation. 'In thirty days, Abby will be set for Harvard, and you can start wearing *haute couture*.'

'I'm thinking Brown,' Karen said with a grudging laugh.

It was an old joke between them, started in the days when they had so little money that a trip to Wendy's Hamburgers was a treat. Now they could actually afford those universities, but the joke took them back to what, in some ways, had been a happier time.

'I'll see you both Sunday,' Will said. He climbed into the Baron and started the twin engines. After contacting ground control, he waved and taxied to the runway.

The Baron lifted into the sky. Instead of simply banking left to head south, Will executed a teardrop turn, which brought him right over the black Expedition on the ground. He could see Karen and Abby standing beside it. As he passed at 600 feet, he waggled his wings like a fighter pilot. On the concrete below, Abby whooped with glee.

FIFTEEN MILES NORTH of the airport, a battered green pick-up truck with a mower and two strimmers in the back rattled along a curving lane known as Crooked Mile Road. It stopped beside a wrought-iron mailbox at the foot of a wooded hill. An ornamental biplane was perched on the mailbox, and below it gold letters read: JENNINGS. The pick-up turned left and chugged slowly up the steep driveway.

At the top stood a breathtaking Victorian-style house. Wedgwood blue with white gingerbread trim, it seemed to watch over the expansive lawns around it with proprietary interest.

When the pick-up reached the crest of the drive, it continued fifty yards across the grass and stopped beside an ornate playhouse, an exact replica in miniature of the main house, standing in the shadow of pine and oak trees that bordered the lawn. When the engine died, but for birdcalls and the ticking of the motor there was silence.

The driver's door banged open, and Huey Cotton climbed out. Clad in his customary brown overalls and heavy black glasses, he stared at the playhouse with wonder in his eyes.

'See anybody?' called a voice from the truck.

'It's like Disneyland, Joey.'

Huey walked round the playhouse and looked across a glittering blue swimming pool to the rear of the main house. Peeking from two of the four garage bays were a silver Toyota Avalon and the white nose of a powerboat. He turned back to the playhouse, bent and examined it more closely.

Joe Hickey climbed out of the truck. He wore a Ralph Lauren polo shirt and Tommy Hilfiger khakis, but he didn't look natural or even comfortable in the costume. The lower half of a crude eagle tattoo showed on his biceps below the shirt's left sleeve.

'Look at the real house, Buckethead. See the third downstairs window from the end? That's it.'

'I see it,' Huey said straightening and glancing over.

Hickey reached into the truck bed and took out a rusted toolbox. 'Let's take care of the alarm system.'

Twenty minutes later they emerged from the back door of the house and stood on the fieldstone patio. 'Put the toolbox back in the truck,' Hickey said. 'Then wait behind the playhouse. As soon as they go inside, you run up to the window. Got it?'

'Just like last time.'

'There wasn't any freakin' playhouse last time. I don't want you fooling around back there. The second you hear the garage door close, get your big ass up to that window. If some nosy neighbour drives up and asks you a question, you're with the lawn service. Act like a retard. It shouldn't be much of a stretch for you.'

Huey stiffened. 'Don't say that, Joey.'

'If you're waiting at the window when you're supposed to be, I'll apologise.'

Huey shrugged and shambled across the patio towards the tree line. Hickey walked into the house through the back door.

KAREN AND ABBY sang tunes from *The Sound of Music*, Abby's favourite musical, at the top of their voices as they rolled north on Interstate 55. The Jenningses lived just west of Annandale in Madison County, Mississippi, twelve miles north of the capital city, Jackson.

'*That will bring us back to doe, oh, oh, oh . . .*'

Breathing hard from the singing, Karen reached down and punched a number into her cellphone.

'Anaesthesiology Associates,' said a woman's voice.

'Is this the answering service?' asked Karen.

'Yes, ma'am. A-1 Answer-all. The clinic's closed.'

'I'd like to leave a message for Dr Jennings. This is his wife.'

'Go ahead.'

'We already miss you. Break a leg tonight. Love, Karen and Abby.'

'With sugar and kisses on top!' Abby shouted from the back seat.

'Did you get that last part?' asked Karen.

'With sugar and kisses on top,' repeated the bored voice.

FIFTY MILES SOUTH of Jackson, Will settled the Baron in at 8,000 feet. Below him lay a puffy white carpet of cumulus clouds, before him a sky as blue as an Arctic lake. As he bent his wrist to check his primary GPS unit, a burning current of pain shot up his right arm. It was worse than he'd admitted to Karen, and she'd known it. A month ago, she'd threatened to tell the FAA that he was 'cheating' to pass his flight physicals. If she thought Will's arthritis put him—and the family—at risk while flying, she wouldn't hesitate to stop him.

If she did, Will wasn't sure he could handle it. Flying was more than recreation for him. It was a physical expression of how far he had come in life, a symbol of all he had attained, and of the lifestyle he had created for his family. His father, Tom, had never even ridden in an airplane. Will had paid $300,000 for one.

But for him the money was not the important thing. It was what the money could buy. Security. When growing up, Will had learned that lesson a thousand times: money was an insulator, like armour. It protected people who had it from the everyday problems that besieged and even destroyed others. And yet it did not make you invulnerable. His arthritis had taught him that.

In 1986, he graduated from medical school and began an obstetrics residency at University Hospital in Jackson. It was there that he met a nurse with stunning green eyes, strawberry-blonde hair, and a reputation for refusing dates. After three months of patience and charm, Will persuaded Karen to meet him for lunch. They dated for the next two years and, after a yearlong engagement, married. Will entered private practice the day after his honeymoon, and their adult life together began like a storybook.

But during the second year of his practice, he began experiencing pain in his hands, feet and back. Soon the pain was interfering with his work, and he went to see a friend in the rheumatology department. A week later he was diagnosed with psoriatic arthritis, a severe, often crippling disease. Continuing as an obstetrician was impossible, so he began to investigate less physically rigorous fields. His old college room-mate suggested anaesthesiology—his own speciality—and in 1993 Will began his anaesthesiology residency at University Hospital in Jackson.

The same month, Karen, who had always felt she had aimed too low with nursing, quit her job and enrolled at nearby Millsaps College for twenty-two hours of basic sciences in the premed programme. It meant they would have to put off having children for several more years. While Will trained for his new speciality and learned to deal with the pain of his disease, Karen racked up four semesters of perfect grades. She was luminous with happiness.

Then during her freshman year of medical school she got pregnant. Will was happy, Karen devastated. She believed that a baby would mean the death of her dream of being a doctor. For three agonising weeks, she considered an abortion. The fact that she was thirty-three finally convinced her to keep the baby. She managed to complete her freshman year, but after Abby was born there was no question of continuing. While Will joined the private anaesthesiology group led by his old room-mate, Karen went home to prepare for motherhood.

Will was phenomenally successful in his work, and Abby brightened their lives. But Karen's premature exit from medical school haunted her. Over the next couple of years, her resentment began to permeate their marriage, from dinner conversations to their sex life—or, more accurately, their lack of one. Will responded by focusing on his work and on Abby, and whatever energy he had left he used to fight his slowly progressing arthritis.

He treated himself, studying his condition until he knew more about it than most rheumatologists. He had done the same with Abby's juvenile diabetes. Being his own doctor allowed him to do things he otherwise might not have been allowed to, like flying. He only wished the problems in his marriage were as easy to solve.

A high-pitched beeping suddenly filled the Baron's cockpit. Will reached down, pulled the new SkyTel off his belt, and hit the RETRIEVE button. The pager displayed a message: WE ALREADY MISS YOU. BREAK A LEG TONIGHT. LOVE KAREN AND ABBY. WITH SUGAR AND KISSES ON TOP.

He smiled and waggled the Baron's wings.

KAREN STOPPED the Expedition beside her mailbox, reached into it and withdrew a thick handful of envelopes and magazines.

As she drove up the long drive and the house came into sight, she felt the ambivalence that always suffused her at the sight of it. Her first emotion was pride—she and Will had designed the house. But she could not escape the feeling that she'd constructed her own prison, a gilded cage like all the others on Crooked Mile Road.

Karen pulled into the garage. Abby unhooked her own safety straps but waited for her mother to open the door.

'Let's get some iced tea,' Karen said, setting Abby on the concrete. 'How do you feel?'

'Good.'

'Did you tee-tee a lot this afternoon?'

'No. I need to go now, though.'

'All right. We'll check your sugar after. Then we'll get the tea.'

Karen opened the door that led to the walk-through pantry and kitchen. Abby went inside and trudged up the hallway while Karen stopped at the digital alarm panel on the wall and punched in the security code. Then she took the tea pitcher from the refrigerator, set it on the counter, and began slicing a lemon.

Passing her bedroom, Abby glanced through the half-open door. Her dolls were arranged against the headboard of her bed, just as she'd left them. Five more steps carried her to the bathroom, where she stretched on tiptoe to reach the light switch. She used the toilet,

glad that she didn't tee-tee very much. That meant her sugar was
OK. After fixing her clothes, she climbed up on a stool before the
basin and washed her hands. Then she started for the kitchen.

As she passed her bedroom, she noticed a funny smell. She started
to walk in and check, but her mother's voice echoed up the hall,
saying the tea was ready.

When Abby turned away from the bedroom, something grey fluttered in front of her eyes. She swatted the air, but her hand hit something solid behind the grey. The grey thing was a towel, and there was
a hand inside it. The hand clamped the towel over her nose and
mouth, and the strange smell she'd noticed earlier swept into her lungs.

HUEY COTTON stood outside the Jenningses' house, nervously peering through Abby's bedroom window. He heard the scuff of a heel on
wood, saw his cousin walking through the bedroom with the little girl
in his arms, the kicking of her skinny legs getting weaker and weaker.

Joey walked to the open window and passed her through. Huey
accepted Abby as gingerly as he would a wounded bird.

'You're a genius,' Joey said, a crooked grin on his face. 'I apologise,
OK? She'll be out for two to four hours. Plenty of time.'

'You're going to call me, right?' Huey asked.

'Every thirty minutes. Don't say anything but "Hello" unless I ask
a question. Shut off the cellphone when you get there. Just put it on
for the check-in calls. And remember the back-up plan, right?'

'I remember.'

'Good. Now, get going.'

Huey started to walk away, then stopped and turned back.

'What's wrong now?' Joey asked.

'Can she have one of her dolls?'

Joey leaned back inside the window, snatched up a Barbie off the
bed, and handed it out. Huey took it.

'Don't start the engine till you hit the road,' Joey said.

'I know.'

Carrying Abby with maternal care, Huey turned and lumbered
towards the playhouse and his concealed pick-up truck.

KAREN STOOD at the kitchen counter, thumbing through the *New
England Journal of Medicine* and feeling the twinge of anger and
regret she always did when confronted by tangible reminders of the
profession she'd been forced to abandon. Two glasses of iced tea

stood on the counter beside her. Beside the glasses lay a plastic device for pricking Abby's finger. Without taking her eyes from the magazine, Karen called: 'Abby? You OK, sweetie?'

There was no answer.

She took a sip of tea and kept reading, thankful for a few moments of silence before the maddening last-minute details of the flower show would have to be dealt with.

BENEATH THE TALL PINES behind the playhouse, Huey opened the driver's door of his pick-up and slid Abby's unconscious body across the bench seat to the passenger side. She lay still as a sleeping angel. He reached into the truck, shifted it into neutral, and pushed it round the playhouse like a normal-sized man pushing a motorcycle. Then he steered it towards the steep driveway.

When the wheels hit concrete the truck gathered momentum, and Huey climbed inside as the old Chevy rolled down the hill.

He hit the brakes just before the truck reached the road, and the vehicle shuddered to a stop. Then he started the engine, and turned onto Crooked Mile Road, which led to Highway 463, and from there to Interstate 55. He had a long night ahead.

KAREN'S EARS pricked up at the rumble of a starting engine. It seemed out of place at this time of day. She glanced through the kitchen window but saw nothing. Maybe it was a delivery truck making a turn in the drive.

'Abby? Do you need help, honey?' she called.

Still no answer. A worm of fear turned in Karen's stomach. She was compulsive about controlling Abby's diabetes, and panic was always just beneath the surface. She started towards the hall. Relief surged through her as she heard footsteps on the hardwood. She was laughing at herself when a dark-haired man of about fifty walked through the hall door and held up both hands.

Her right hand flew to her heart, and in some sickening subdivision of a second, her mouth went dry, her throat closed and sweat broke out from her head to her toes.

'Stay calm, Mrs Jennings,' the man said in a reassuring voice. 'Abby's fine. I want you to listen to me. Everything is OK.'

At the word 'Abby', tears filled Karen's eyes. The panic that lived beneath her skin burned through to the surface, paralysing her. She tried to scream, but no sound came from her throat.

three

As Karen stood gaping, the stranger said, 'My name's Joe, Mrs Jennings. Joe Hickey. I'm going to help you through this thing. And the first thing to remember is that Abby is absolutely fine.'

Her temporary paralysis finally broke, and Karen jerked as though she had taken a physical blow. *'Abby!'* she screamed.

'Calm down,' the stranger said softly. 'Look at me. I'm Joe Hickey, OK? I'm telling you my real name because I'm not worried that it's going to matter later. You're never going to report this, because Abby's going to be fine. Abby, you, me, everybody's going to be fine. The kid always makes it through. That's my rule.'

Karen batted the man aside as she raced into the hallway. She yanked open the bathroom door and cried, 'Abby! Where are you?'

She tore through the ground floor, checking every room and closet. She raced up the back stairs and began searching the first floor. Every room was empty. She picked up the nearest phone, and dialled 911. Instead of an operator's voice, she heard: '. . . Preacher Bob's Fount of Life Church is a Full Gospel church—'

She clicked the disconnect button, but the voice droned on. Hickey must have dialled the prayer line from the kitchen phone and left it off the hook. She slammed down the phone, ran round the bed and picked up the private line. This time a female voice was speaking: '. . . the satellite farm forecast is made possible by Chemstar . . .'

Karen dropped the phone and stood staring at herself in the dressing-table mirror. She needed to calm down, to think rationally, but she couldn't. As she struggled to gain control, an image came into her mind with the power of a talisman.

She ran to the back stairs again, but this time she crept down the carpeted steps. When she reached the ground floor, she tiptoed up the hallway and darted into the master bedroom, locking the door behind her. Then, heart thumping, she walked into the closet and stood on the wooden box that gave her access to the top shelf.

Her hand barely reached over the edge, but she felt what she wanted: Will's .38 revolver. She pulled down the gun and opened the cylinder, as her father had taught her. Six rounds filled the chambers. She snapped the cylinder home. Clenching the pistol like a lifeline, she walked to the bedroom door and opened it quietly, then edged towards the kitchen. She stopped just outside and peered in.

Joe Hickey was sitting calmly at the kitchen table, drinking from one of the glasses of tea. Karen stepped into the kitchen, raised the gun, and aimed it at his face. 'Where's my daughter?'

Hickey swallowed some tea and slowly set down the glass. 'You don't want to shoot me, Karen. Can I call you Karen?'

She shook the .38 at him. 'Where's my little girl!'

'Abby is perfectly safe. However, if you shoot me, she'll be stone-dead in thirty minutes. And there won't be a thing I can do about it.'

Karen felt as though she'd been pushed from a great height, her stomach rolling as she went into free fall. 'Tell me what's happening!'

'Listen carefully, Karen. This is a kidnapping-for-ransom. OK? It's about money. M-O-N-E-Y. That's all. So, the last thing I want is for anything to happen to your precious little girl. Right now she's with my cousin Huey. After you got here, I passed her outside and he drove her off in his pick-up truck. He's got a cellphone with him. If I don't call him every thirty minutes, he'll kill her. He won't want to, but he will. That's rule number two. So don't get any crazy ideas about calling the police. It would take them an hour just to get me fingerprinted and into lockup, and by the time I saw a payphone Abby would be dead. But that's not going to happen,' Hickey said, smiling. 'You're a smart girl. And Huey's a good boy. Loves kids. He's practically a kid himself. He's a little slow. Since I'm the only person who was ever nice to him, he always does exactly what I tell him. So you want to be real careful with that gun.'

Karen looked at the weapon in her hand. Suddenly it seemed more of a threat to Abby than to the man in front of her.

'You pick things up real quick, I can tell,' Hickey said. 'So keep paying attention. This is a kidnapping-for-ransom, like I said. But it's not like you've seen on TV or in the movies. This is a work of art. A perfect crime. I know, because I've done it five times before and I haven't been caught yet. Not even a whiff of Johnny Law.'

The gun wavered in Karen's hand. She steadied it.

'I know what you're thinking,' Hickey said. 'What happened to the kids those other five times, right?'

She nodded slowly, forcing back tears, unwilling to give Hickey the satisfaction of seeing them.

'Right this second, every one of them is living a carefree life, watching *Barney* or *Rugrats* or swimming in their private swimming pool. You know why? Because their mamas didn't shoot me and their daddies were calm and methodical after the first few minutes. Just like you're going to be.'

Karen didn't want to put the gun down, but she saw no choice. She tossed it onto the table beside Hickey.

'Good girl,' he said, leaving the .38 where it had fallen. 'Yes, ma'am, that's exactly what a good mother does in a situation like this. I hope your husband's as smart as you are.'

Fear gripped Karen. 'Where's Will? What have you done with him?'

Hickey looked at his watch. 'Right about now, hubby's winged most of his way to Biloxi's beautiful Beau Rivage Casino Resort.'

The level of Hickey's knowledge crystallised the fear in Karen. He knew their lives, their plans, their exact schedules—

'We're going to let hubby give his little speech. Then he's going to get a visit from a partner of mine, and he'll find out the way things stand. Then we're all going to wait out the night together.'

'Wait out the night? What are you talking about?'

'This operation takes exactly twenty-four hours. I'm talking from the time Huey and me cranked up this afternoon. A day's work for a year's pay. We've got about twenty hours left to go.'

'But why do we have to wait? If you want money, I'll get it for you. All you want. Just bring my baby back!'

Hickey shook his head. 'I know you would, Karen. But that's not the way this operation works. Everything's set up according to a timetable. That way there's no surprises.'

'But we *can't* wait twenty hours!'

'You'd be surprised. This is a nice place. We'll get to know each other a little, have supper, pretend everything's fine. Before you know it, I'll have my money and you'll have Abby back.'

'Listen to me, you stupid son of a bitch!'

Hickey paled. 'You want to watch what you're saying there, Mom. It's not smart under the circumstances.'

Karen tried to keep her voice under control. 'Mr Hickey, if we wait until tomorrow, Abby is going to die. She's a juvenile diabetic. She'll die without her insulin.'

'Bullshit.'

'My God . . . didn't you *know* that?'

'Talk's cheap. Let's see some proof.'

Karen went to a kitchen drawer and pulled out a plastic bag full of syringes with needles. She threw the bag onto the table, then opened the refrigerator, where a dozen glass vials waited in rows. She took out a vial of insulin and tossed it at Hickey.

He caught it and stared at the label. It read: *Humulin N*. PATIENT: Abigail Jennings. PRESCRIBING PHYSICIAN: Will Jennings, MD.

'Damn,' Hickey said under his breath. 'I don't believe this.'

'Please,' Karen said. 'We must get this medicine to my daughter. She's due for her shot in an hour. How far away is she?'

'We can't go,' Hickey said in a flat voice.

Karen grabbed the .38 off the table and pointed it at his chest. 'Oh yes we can. We're going right now.'

'I told you about that gun.'

She cocked the revolver. 'If Abby doesn't get her insulin, she's going to die. Now you do what I say!'

Hickey held up his hands. 'Take it easy, Karen. I meant we can't go *yet*. Abby's being transported to a safe place. Maybe we can go later. How long before she's in trouble?'

Karen did the maths in her head. If Abby ate only low-sugar food she could make it through the night. But Karen had no intention of taking that risk. What if Hickey's cousin fed her candy?

'Juvenile diabetics are very unstable,' she said. 'If Abby eats too much sugar, she could go into a coma and die very fast.'

Hickey pursed his lips, obviously doing some mental maths of his own. Then he reached over the little built-in desk where Karen paid the household bills, picked up the cordless phone, and punched in a number. Karen stepped up to the desk and hit the SPEAKER button on the phone. Hickey looked down, trying to figure out how to switch it off, but before he could, a deep male voice said: 'Joey? Has it been thirty minutes?'

'No. What happened to "Hello"?'

'Oh, yeah. I'm sorry.' The man's voice had an incongruous sound, like the voice of a fifty-year-old child.

'How does the kid look?'

'OK. She's still sleeping.'

Karen's heart thudded. She jerked the gun. 'Let me talk to her!'

Hickey warned her back with a flip of his hand. 'Abby can't talk right now. She's sedated.'

Sedated? 'You son of a bitch! You—'

Hickey half rose and slugged Karen in the stomach. The breath left her in an explosive rush, and she dropped to the kitchen floor, the gun clattering uselessly in front of her.

'Look, Huey, don't give the kid any candy or anything like it. OK?'

'She needs fluids,' Karen gasped from the floor. 'Plenty of water!'

'Give her some water. Plenty of water.'

'Water,' Huey echoed.

'I may be coming out to see you tonight.'

Karen felt a surge of hope.

'That'd be good,' Huey said. 'I wouldn't be so nervous.'

'Yeah. Drive slow, OK?'

'Fifty-five,' Huey said dutifully.

'Good boy.' Hickey hung up and squatted before Karen. 'Here's the deal. Before we do anything, we have to let my partner make contact with your husband. We've got to make sure old Will's on the same page with us before we move. With this diabetic thing, he might just flip out. I hope not, because if he does, all the insulin in the world won't save Abby.'

Hickey walked past her to the opposite wall of the kitchen, where a four-foot-wide framed silk screen hung. It was a semi-abstract rendering of an alligator, brightly coloured like a child's painting, but with the unmistakable strength of genius in it. 'You've got paintings by this guy all over your house,' he said. 'Right?'

'Yes,' Karen replied, her thoughts on Abby. 'Walter Anderson.'

'Worth a lot of money?'

'That silk screen isn't. But the watercolours are. Do you want them?'

Hickey laughed. 'Want them? I don't give a shit about 'em. And by morning, you're going to hate every one. You're never going to want to see another one again.' He turned from the painting and smiled.

FORTY MILES SOUTH of Jackson, in a forest clearing, an old white AMC Rambler rested on blocks beside a small, tin-roofed cabin. Birdcalls echoed through the small clearing, punctuated by the *pock-pock-pock* of a woodpecker, and grey squirrels chased each other through the upper branches of the oaks.

A new sound entered the woods. A motor. The noise grew steadily until the green hood of a pick-up truck broke from beneath the trees into dappled sunlight. The truck trundled down the rutted lane and stopped before the cabin porch.

Huey Cotton got out and walked round the front of the truck, the Barbie sticking out of his pocket. He opened the passenger door and lifted Abby's limp body off the seat. Cradling her in his massive arms, he closed the truck's door and walked up the porch steps.

WILL LANDED THE BARON at Gulfport-Biloxi airport, taxied to the general aviation area and pulled into the empty spot indicated to him by a ground crewman.

As soon as the props stopped turning, he climbed out and unloaded his luggage from the cabin. Lugging it all to his rented car, a blue Ford Tempo, made his inflamed joints scream, even through the deadening layer of ibuprofen.

Will hoped the traffic was not too bad between the airport and the casino. He had less than an hour to reach the meeting room, and he needed to shower and shave before he took the podium.

It took him five minutes to reach US 90, the highway that ran along the Gulf of Mexico, then he pressed down the accelerator, figuring it was worth the risk of a ticket.

As he neared the casino, the traffic slowed to a crawl, but he was already in sight of the words BEAU RIVAGE glittering high in the fading sunlight. He turned off and pulled into the tasteful entrance of the casino resort, thankful for the bellboys waiting to take his bags. Keeping the computer and sample cases for himself, he gave his keys to a valet and walked through the massive doors and over to the check-in desk. When he gave his name, the hotel manager came out of an office and shook his hand. His name tag read: GEAUTREAU.

'Your colleagues have been getting a little nervous, Dr Jennings,' he said with a cool smile.

'I had a long surgery this afternoon.' Will tapped his computer case. 'But I've got my program ready to go. Just get me to a shower.'

Geautreau handed over a credit card key. 'You've got a suite on twenty-eight, Doctor. A Cypress suite. And our audio-video consultant is waiting for you in the Magnolia Ballroom. You'll find the VIP elevators past the jewellery store. Don't hesitate to call for anything, Doctor. Ask for me by name.'

'I will.'

As Will crossed the lobby, making for the elevators, a heavyset man in his forties shouted from an open-air bar to his left. It was Jackson Everett, an old medical school buddy. Everett was wearing a Hawaiian shirt and held an umbrella drink in his hand.

'Will Jennings!' he boomed. 'It's about time!' Everett shouldered his way across the lobby and slapped Will on the back, sending a sword of pain down his spine. 'Where's Karen?'

'She didn't make it this trip, Jack. Some Junior League thing.'

Everett laughed. 'You're giving the speech tonight, I hear.'

Will nodded.

'Hey, without Karen, you'll have to hit the casino with me. High rollers, stud!'

'I'd better pass. I had a long surgery, then the flight. I'm whipped.'

'Pussy-whipped, more like,' Everett complained. 'You gotta live a little, son.'

Will gave an obliging laugh. 'Let's get a beer tomorrow and catch up.'

'Hey, don't put us to sleep tonight, OK?'

'But that's my speciality, Jack.'

Everett groaned and walked off gulping his drink.

As Will waited for an elevator, he saw a few more faces he recognised across the lobby, but he didn't make an effort to speak.

On the twenty-eighth floor, he opened the door to his suite and found his bags and golf clubs waiting for him. He set his cases on the sitting-room sofa, then walked into the bathroom and turned on the hot water. As the bathroom filled with steam, he unzipped his suit bag and unpacked a shirt. Then he stripped to his shorts and lifted his sample case onto the bureau beside the television. From it he removed a bound folder and laid it on the desk. The paper summarised three years of work in the laboratory and in clinical trials. The culmination of it was a drug, Restorase, that represented potential profits on a vast scale, enough to make Will a truly wealthy man.

He checked the other contents of the sample case: a video-adapter unit that would allow his computer to interface with the convention room's projection TV; several drug vials, some of which contained Restorase; and some syringes. Will closed the case and hurried into the steamy bathroom.

HICKEY AND KAREN sat facing each other across the kitchen table. 'I don't understand why we have to wait until tomorrow,' she said. 'Why don't you just let me empty our accounts and give you the money?'

'For one thing, the banks have closed. You can't come close to the ransom with automated withdrawals.'

'What will be different tomorrow morning? How do you plan to get the ransom money?'

'Your husband is going to call his financial adviser here—Gray Davidson—and tell him a great little story. He's just discovered the missing centrepiece of Walter Anderson's largest sculpture. Many people believe it was stolen from Anderson's house. The value is—'

'Higher than any painting he ever did,' Karen finished. 'Because he didn't do much sculpture.'

Hickey grinned. 'Pretty good, huh? I do my homework. These damn doctors, I tell you. Every one of 'em collects something. Cars, boats, books, whatever. You can't believe the money these guys piss away. Anyway, tomorrow morning, Will's gonna call Davidson and tell him he needs two hundred grand wired to him in Biloxi. He's got a one-time opportunity to buy this sculpture, and the owner wants cash. And just in case Mr Davidson is suspicious, Will's lovely wife Karen is coming down to the office to authorise the wire. It isn't strictly required, but it's a nice touch. Then you and I are going to drive down to Davidson's office. I'll wait outside while you go in and sign off on the money, and the two hundred grand is off to Biloxi at the speed of light. My partner drives Will to the bank in Biloxi, Will goes in, comes out with the cash, and hands it to my partner.'

'You're doing all this for two hundred thousand dollars?'

Hickey laughed and shook his head. 'See? To you, two hundred grand is nothing. You can get it easy, and you don't feel any pain when it's gone. You're happy, I'm happy, and your kid's back safe at home. What more could you ask for?'

'Abby here now! Why can't she stay with us?'

Hickey's smile vanished. 'This whole little machine runs on fear, Karen. Your fear for Abby. Will's fear for you, and for Abby. Right?'

She said nothing.

'Most kidnappers are brain dead,' he said. 'They get busted the minute they go for the ransom. Or right after. No ransom pick-up method is safe from the FBI. The technology's just too good now. But I'm not picking up any ransom. Your husband's doing it for me. You're sending it, he's picking it up. I'm not even involved. Is that beautiful or what? The other way people screw up is taking the kid off with them and sending a ransom note asking for more ransom money than they could raise in a week. That leaves the parents at home, alone and scared shitless. What else are they going to do but call the FBI? My way, nobody calls anybody but me and my partners, every half-hour like clockwork. And as long as we do that, nobody gets hurt. Nobody goes to prison. Nobody dies.'

'You like listening to yourself talk, don't you?'

He shrugged. 'I like doing things right. This plan is as clean as they come. It's run perfectly five times in a row. Am I proud of that? Yeah. And who else can I talk about it to but someone like you?'

Hickey was talking about kidnap the way Will's partners bragged about inside stock trades. 'Don't you have any feelings for the children involved,' she said. 'How terrified they must be?'

'A kid can stand anything for twenty-four hours,' Hickey said softly. 'I stood a lot worse for *years*.'

'But sooner or later you'll make a mistake. You're bound to.'

'The parents might. Not me. The guy I got keeping these kids. He loves 'em. Weighs about three hundred pounds. Looks like goddamn Frankenstein, but he's a giant teddy bear.'

Karen shut her eyes.

'Don't worry,' Hickey said. 'Huey's not a child abuser or anything. He's too slow. Only he doesn't like kids running away from him. When he was little, kids at school treated him pretty bad. When he got bigger, they just yelled things and ran. Kids are pretty damn cruel. Now when he sees kids run, it makes him lose his head. Your kid the panicky type?'

'Not usually, but . . . can't we please spend the night where they are?'

'I'm getting hungry. Why don't you see about fixing some supper?'

'When can we take Abby the insulin?'

'Food,' Hickey said, rubbing his flat belly. 'F-O-O-D.'

four

Will looked out over an audience of close to a thousand people.

'Lights, please,' he said from the podium.

The lights dimmed. Will clicked a file icon with the trackball on his notebook computer and the 61-inch Hitachi television behind him flashed up a high-resolution image of an operating room. A patient lay unconscious on the table as the OR team prepared for surgery.

Will glanced at his script and said, 'This patient looks thoroughly prepped for surgery, doesn't he? Twenty minutes before this picture was taken, he assaulted a doctor and two nurses with a broken coffee carafe, causing serious injuries.'

The image on the television cut to a jiggling, handheld shot of a wild-eyed man jabbing a broken carafe at whoever was behind the camera. The camera jerked wildly towards the ceiling as its operator leaped back to avoid being slashed.

In the background, a nurse cried, 'Where is security?' The man with the carafe charged her and began weeping and howling at once. 'Where's my Rhelda Jean? Somebody call Rhelda, damn it!'

Suddenly the video cut back to the man lying prepped in the operating room.

'If I were to tell you that this man was subdued in the ER, not by police but by me, using a drug, you might guess this was accomplished with a paralysing relaxant like curare or succinylcholine. And you'd be right. Nowadays, emergency physicians routinely resort to the use of such drugs, because they sometimes offer the only means of compelling violent patients to accept lifesaving treatment.

'All of you know how dangerous the paralysing relaxants are, both medically and legally, because they leave patients unable to move or even breathe until they're intubated and bagged.'

The television showed a nurse standing over the patient in the ER, working a breathing bag. Will glanced into the crowd. At the first table, a stunning young woman was staring at him with laserlike concentration. She was twenty years younger than most of the women in the audience and wore a short black dress accented by a diamond necklace. She seemed to be alone, and Will had an unobstructed view from her tapered legs and well-turned ankles to her impressive *décolletage*. He had to remind himself to start talking again.

'Tonight,' he said, 'I'm going to tell you about a revolutionary new class of drug developed by myself and the Searle pharmaceutical company, and tested in clinical trials at University Hospital in Jackson. It can completely counteract the effects of succinylcholine, restoring full nerve conductivity in less than thirty seconds.'

Will heard murmurs of disbelief and then the television showed the screaming man again. This time, as he charged a nurse, a tall man in a white coat stepped up behind him with something that looked like a small white pistol. The white-coated doctor was Will. As the patient jabbed the glittering shard at the brave nurse, Will moved in and touched the side of his neck with the white pistol—a compressed-gas syringe. There was an audible hiss, and the man's free hand flew up to his neck. When he threw up both arms and collapsed, Will caught him and dragged him towards a treatment table, and two nurses hurried over to help and to restrain the patient with straps. Then Will stepped up and injected him with a conventional syringe.

'I am now injecting the patient with Restorase, the first of these new drugs to be approved by the FDA. Look at your watches, please.'

The camera operator focused on the patient's face. His eyes were half closed. Every doctor in the audience knew that the man's diaphragm was paralysed. He could not move or breathe, yet he was fully conscious of what was going on around him.

Will heard shuffles and whispers as the seconds ticked past. At twenty-five seconds, the patient's eyes blinked, then opened. He gasped twice, then began to breathe.

'What's your name, sir?' Will asked.

'Tommy Joe Smith,' he said, his eyes wide.

'Are you going to try to stab anyone else, Mr Smith?'

He shook his head violently.

'I know how shocking that footage can be,' Will said. 'But remember the scene that preceded it. In emergency rooms, psychiatric wards and prison infirmaries, healthcare workers are suffering grave injury at the hands of violent patients. Now their safety can be ensured without fear of fatal outcomes or costly lawsuits.'

A collective murmur of approval swept through the darkened ballroom, followed by a wave of applause.

'As you know,' Will said, 'the relaxants interrupt the normal flow of impulses from the brain to the skeletal muscles . . .'

He continued almost without thought. The woman in black was still staring from the front table. She wasn't smiling exactly, but there was a suggestive curve to her lips that signalled interest in more than drug therapy. He tried to make eye contact with other audience members, but every few seconds his gaze returned to the young woman, and she was always watching him. She had large eyes that never seemed to blink, and a mane of blonde hair. The strapless black dress revealed a fine collarbone, strong shoulders and a graceful neck. But what held him was her eyes. They never left his face.

He turned to the television to check the video feed, and when he turned back, she shifted in her seat, uncrossed her legs, then recrossed them. As Will dropped his gaze to look at his speech, he realised that he had fallen behind the video. He looked back up and skipped ahead to the proper cue line.

The ghost of a smile touched the woman's lips.

HICKEY SAT at Karen's kitchen table, eating a huge sandwich and drinking iced tea.

Karen was standing by the refrigerator, packing syringes and insulin into a small Igloo ice chest when the garage doorbell rang.

Hickey was instantly on his feet, Will's gun in his hand. 'Who's that?' he asked. 'You expecting somebody?'

Karen shook her head. She had no idea who it could be.

'Don't answer it. We'll just let them go on their merry way.' He took a step towards the pantry. 'Which door are they at?'

'The garage,' she whispered, shocked by the sense of conspiracy she felt with Hickey. But the last thing she wanted was someone disrupting his carefully organised plan while Abby was under his control.

The bell rang again. 'How come I didn't hear a car?' Hickey asked.

'Sometimes we don't.' As she spoke, she realised who the visitor might be. Stephanie Morgan, the co-chair of the Junior League flower show, who drove a Lexus that ran so quietly Karen never heard it pulling up the driveway. Of everyone she knew, Stephanie had the most reason to drop by over the next couple of days.

She and Hickey jumped when the kitchen window rattled. Karen turned and saw Stephanie Morgan's face pressed against the glass. She was shaking a reprimanding finger, and beside her was the little moon face of her eleven-month-old son, Josh.

'Open the door,' Hickey said in a flat voice.

'*Hide*,' Karen told him.

'I can't. She's looking at me right now.' He slid the gun behind his right leg. 'Go open it.'

Karen didn't want to invite Stephanie into her nightmare, but if she refused to open the door now, Steph would throw a fit and Hickey's plan would come apart. She motioned towards the garage. Stephanie nodded and disappeared from the window.

'Let me handle this,' Karen told him. 'Please.'

He looked sceptical. 'Let's see if you can.'

When Karen opened the door, Stephanie pushed past her with Josh in her arms, talking as she went. 'Karen, you've got to come down to the Coliseum. They were supposed to have those livestock people out of there by lunch today, but there are still cows on the floor. Cows, Karen.' Stephanie had reached the kitchen. 'Hello,' she said to Hickey. 'Are you Karen's secret lover? I always knew she had one.'

Karen stepped into the kitchen. 'Stephanie, this is Joe, my second cousin. He's from Washington State. Joe, Stephanie Morgan.'

Stephanie gave Hickey a little wave and turned back to Karen. 'I want to know why you didn't answer that doorbell.'

'I had some Mormons around before,' Karen said. 'I thought they'd come back for another try.'

Stephanie pulled a wry face. 'Likely story. I know what you're doing. Hiding from me. But I've got news for you, honey. You can't. You're the queen bee of this show, and I need you.'

'I'll be down in the morning,' Karen promised. She took Stephanie by the arm and walked her back towards the garage. 'But Joe's father passed away recently, and he's down here to work out some estate problems with me. We only have tonight to do it.'

'Nice meeting you, Joe!' Stephanie called.

'Yeah,' he said.

Karen pushed her into the garage. Sure enough, Stephanie's white Lexus was parked just behind the Expedition.

'Your cousin looks interesting,' Stephanie said. 'A little rough, maybe, but interesting. You sure I didn't just stumble onto a tryst?'

Karen forced a laugh. 'Positive. Joe can't stand me. He's just here to settle the estate. I'll see you in the morning, Steph.'

Stephanie had leaned down to strap Josh into his car seat. 'Don't you dare be late. I cannot handle cow shit, OK?'

Karen forced another laugh. Stephanie got into the Lexus, started it, and backed round to go down the hill.

Something brushed Karen's shoulder. Hickey was standing beside her and she hadn't even realised it. He waved at the Lexus. Stephanie honked her horn in reply, then disappeared over the lip of the drive.

'Not bad, Mom,' Hickey said. 'That skinny bitch owes you her life and she doesn't even know it.'

Karen realised she was shaking.

Hickey slapped her lightly on the behind, exactly the way Will would have. 'Let's get back inside.'

WILL'S LECTURE was nearly done. Behind him, the television showed a maternal-foetal medicine specialist injecting Restorase into a foetus. The foetus had been paralysed before undergoing a blood transfusion to save its life. Restorase would bring it out of paralysis in a tenth of the time it would normally take.

'I think this last shot is pretty self-explanatory,' Will said.

The pregnant belly was replaced by a sequence of Will teeing off at the Annandale golf course. With creative editing, he had made his drive appear to conclude with a hole-in-one. When the ball hit the pin and dropped into the cup a wild whoop went up from the dark (probably from the throat of Jackson Everett) and enthusiastic applause followed as the lights came up.

'I'll be at the Searle booth tomorrow afternoon with samples of Restorase. I look forward to speaking with all of you.'

This time the applause was more sedate, but also more sustained. Will began disconnecting his computer while the Mississippi Medical Association's president moved on to announcements. Will zipped up his computer case and stepped down from the podium.

He was immediately swallowed by a congratulatory mob that swept him out of the ballroom and into the atrium area. For fifteen minutes he shook hands and accepted compliments. Then, as he made for the main elevator, Jackson Everett reached out and pulled him into the waiting area.

Everett had another drink in his hand and the smell of rum came off him like a Caribbean perfume. He opened his mouth to say something to Will, but just then an elevator opened and disgorged an elderly woman holding a cigar box full of quarters.

'Take 'em to the cleaners, Grandma!' he yelled. 'Break the bank!'

The woman grinned and hurried towards the lobby.

Everett pushed Will into the elevator. Two more doctors wearing name tags stepped in after them, and the door began to close.

'Hold the door!' cried a female voice.

Will's right arm shot out to stop the sliding door, despite the pain the sudden move caused him. As the door retracted, the blonde woman in the black dress stepped into the elevator.

'Thanks,' she said, turning to face the closing doors. The elevator was lined with mirrors. Will looked to his right and studied her reflection in profile. She clutched her handbag and looked at the floor.

The elevator stopped on the eighth floor. The doctors brushed past her. Everett followed, then turned back and pointed at Will. 'Come on to the casino with us! You'll love it. And even if you don't, we're going to take in a little *dancing*, later. Know what I mean?'

'I've got to call Karen,' Will said, before Everett could get more explicit. 'You guys knock the walls out.'

'We always do.' Everett smirked and flicked his eyebrows up and down like Groucho Marx.

Will leaned forward and hit the CLOSE DOOR button.

'Thanks,' the woman said as the doors slid shut.

'He's OK really. Just a little drunk.'

She nodded, and as the elevator began to ascend, Will caught himself staring at her trim figure again. When he looked up, her reflected face was watching him. He blushed and looked at the floor.

'What's your floor?' she asked. 'There's no floor button lit.'

'Oh. I forgot to hit it. Still nervous, I guess. Twenty-eight, please.'

'You've got a Cypress suite? So do I.' She smiled. 'Your presentation was great, by the way. I can't believe you were nervous.'

'Are you a physician?' he asked. He didn't believe in stereotypes, but he'd never met a woman doctor who looked like this.

'No, I'm with the casino company.'

'Oh. I see. Hey, what's your floor?'

'I'm twenty-eight, too. Most of the Cypress suites are up there.'

He nodded and smiled, but when the woman turned away he gave her a hard look. A hooker? he wondered.

The elevator opened on twenty-eight.

'Bye,' the woman said. She got off and walked down the hallway to the left. Will got off and watched her seductive motion, then turned left himself and counted the numbers down to Suite 28021. He was inserting his credit card key when a female voice called, 'Dr Jennings?'

He looked up the long corridor. The blonde in the black dress was walking hesitantly towards him, fidgeting with her handbag. 'My key doesn't work. Could you try it for me?'

'I'll give it a shot.'

Will put his computer case inside his room and followed her. He inserted her card key but, no matter what he did, the lock refused to open. 'I think you're out of luck,' he told her.

'Would you mind if I used your phone to call the desk?'

He started to say he didn't mind, but something stopped him. A sense of something out of place, not quite logical. 'I think there's a house phone by the VIP elevators. I'll be glad to wait with you.'

She looked momentarily confused, but after a moment she smiled. 'That's right. I appreciate you waiting with me. You never know who's creeping around the casino. My name's Cheryl, by the way.'

He escorted her back towards the elevators, walking a little ahead.

He glanced into the waiting area and saw what he was looking for: a cream-coloured house telephone. 'Here it is,' he said, turning to her.

The words died in his throat. Cheryl was pointing an automatic pistol at his chest. She must have taken it from her handbag.

'What is this?' he asked. 'I've only got a few bucks on me, but you're welcome to it. Credit cards, whatever.'

'I don't want your money,' she said, looking anxiously at the elevators. 'I want you to go in your room.'

'What for?'

'You'll find out. Just hurry up.'

'I'm not going anywhere. Not until you tell me what's going on. In fact—' he stepped towards the telephone—'I'm going to call the front desk and have them call the police.'

'Don't touch that.'

'You're not going to shoot me, Cheryl.' He picked up the phone.

'If you call the police, Abby is going to die. And there's nothing I can do to stop it.'

His arm froze. 'What did you say?'

'Your daughter was kidnapped two hours ago, Doctor. If you want her to live, take me into your room right now.'

A paralysing numbness spread from deep within Will's chest. 'What are you talking about?'

Cheryl glanced at the elevator in panic. 'Doctor, if somebody gets out of that elevator and sees me with this gun, the whole thing's going to come apart. Abby's going to die, OK? And I don't want that to happen. I'll tell you everything you want to know, but you'd better get me into your goddamn room right now.'

Will hung up, stared at her for another few seconds then walked down to his door, unlocked it, and held it open for her.

Cheryl walked past him, across the sitting room and into the bedroom. He closed the door and followed her. She put the bed between herself and Will, still pointing the gun at him.

'Tell me about my little girl!'

'This is a kidnapping-for-ransom. My partner is with your wife, at your house in Madison County. Someone else is holding Abby at a third location. This is what's going to happen from this point on . . .'

Will listened, his brain working frantically. Whoever was behind this plan had created a situation in which any aggressive response was impossible. Cheryl's gun was only there to control Will's initial panic. The real coercion was Abby. He could pick up the telephone and call the police. But if they came and arrested Cheryl, and she didn't call her partner on their thirty-minute schedule, Abby would die.

'If I do what you want,' he said, 'what guarantee do I have that we'll get Abby back?'

'No guarantee. You have to trust us.'

'That's not good enough. How are we supposed to get her back? Tell me the details. Right this second!'

Cheryl nodded. 'Abby and your wife will be driven to a public place and set free within sight of each other.'

She sounded like she believed it. And she'd told him they'd carried out the same plan five times before.

'What's to keep me from going to the police after you let Abby go?'

'Because if the police start looking for us, we'll know and my partner will come back and kill Abby. Believe me, he'll do it. We've done this to five other doctors just like you, and none of them reported it. Not one. You won't, either.'

He turned away from her in frustration. Through the bedroom's picture window he saw the lights of a freighter out on the darkening gulf. He had never felt so impotent in his life. It made him crazy with rage. 'I'm supposed to just sit here all night while some stranger holds my little girl prisoner? Scared out of her mind? Lady, I will rip your head off before I let that happen.'

She jerked the gun back up. 'Stay back!'

'What kind of woman are you? Don't you have maternal feelings?'

'Don't you say anything about my feelings!' Cheryl's face reddened. 'You don't know anything about me!'

He was about to respond when a thought burst into his mind like a starshell. 'Oh Jesus. What about Abby's insulin?'

Cheryl's face was blank. 'What?'

'Abby's a juvenile diabetic. You didn't know that?'

'Calm down.'

'You've got to call your partner. I've got to talk to him right now!' The telephone beside the bed rang loudly. They stared at it. Then Cheryl walked to the phone and laid her free hand on the receiver.

'You want to talk?' she said. 'Here's your chance. But be cool, Doctor. Very cool.'

five

Will took the phone and held it to his ear. 'This is Will Jennings.'

'*Doctor* Will Jennings?' said a male voice.

'That's right.'

'You got some unexpected company down there, Doctor?'

Will looked over at Cheryl, who was watching intently. 'Yes.'

'She looks hot in that black dress, doesn't she?'

'Listen, I need to explain something to you.'

'Don't explain anything, college boy. *I'm* in charge tonight. You got that?'

'I've got it, but—'

'But nothing. I'm going to ask you a question, Doc. We're going to see if your answer matches your wife's. Kind of like the *Newlywed Game*, I guess. The question is . . . does your child have any serious medical condition?'

A trickle of hope flowed into Will's veins. 'She has juvenile diabetes.'

'That's a match! You just won the all-expense paid trip to beautiful Puerto Vallarta!'

'Abby needs that insulin, sir. Immediately.'

'Sir?' The man laughed darkly. 'I like that. This is probably the only time you'd call me "sir". Unless you had to tell me I was dying.'

'I'm an anaesthesiologist. I don't handle things like that.'

'No? You never told anybody they were dying?'

Will hesitated. 'When I was a gynaecologist, I did.'

'Ahh. So, no means yes. You ever kill anybody, Doc?'

'Of course not.'

'Nobody ever died on the table while you were passing the gas?'

'Well, of course. But not as a result of my actions.'

'No? I've got to wonder how honest you're being about that.'

'Would you mind telling me your name?'

'Joe Hickey, Doc. You can call me Joe.'

'Are you a former patient of mine, Joe? Or a relative of a patient?'

'Let's leave that for now. 'Cause I'm about to show you what a nice guy I am. I'm about to set it up so your little princess gets her insulin. Let me talk to my partner.'

'Could I speak with my wife for a moment?'

'Put Cheryl on, Doc.'

Will held out the phone to Cheryl.

She shook the gun at him. 'Get in the bathroom while I'm talking.'

Will backed into the spacious white marble cubicle. He kept the knob turned as he closed the door, and after he heard Cheryl's voice resume, opened it a couple of inches and put his ear to the crack.

'Why didn't we know about this medicine thing?' she asked. 'OK . . . I'm all right, I guess. But this guy isn't like the others, Joey . . . He's like a wolf, waiting for his chance . . . I know. OK. Thirty minutes.'

Will put his eye to the crack and saw Cheryl grimace as she hung up. 'All clear?' he asked, pushing open the door.

'Yeah.'

'What did he say?'

'He's taking the medicine to your little girl. I mean, he's taking your wife to give her the shot. See? If we didn't care what happened to her, would we take the risk to get her medicine to her?'

'Yes. Because you know if anything happened to Abby during the night, you wouldn't get your money.'

'You wouldn't know if anything had happened to her or not.'

'If I don't get confirmation that Abby's gotten her insulin within seven hours, I'll assume she's gone into ketoacidosis. And you'll talk then. You'll talk if I have to break every bone in your body.'

'Don't make threats, Doctor. Joey could do a lot of things to your little girl besides kill her. You're not holding any cards here.'

Will closed his eyes and fought a nauseating rush of terror. 'Who the hell is this Joey?'

Cheryl looked at him. 'He's my husband.'

ABBY LAY SLEEPING on an old sofa in the cabin. Huey sat on the floor beside her, whittling a piece of cedar. He was nervous. He knew the little girl was going to be scared when she woke up, and that scared him. He wished she was a boy instead of a girl. Boys were easier. Three out of the five times they had taken boys. Girls made him think too much, and thinking made him sad. He barely remembered his sister now, but he remembered some things. Long, terrible coughs with wheezing whistles between them. Huey had slid Jo Ellen's little bed over by the stove to keep her warm, but it hadn't done any good. By the time they got her to the doctor in a neighbour's pick-up, she was dead. Just four years old. Diphtheria, they said.

Abby groaned again, louder this time, and Huey picked up the Barbie doll Joey had passed him through the window.

'Mama?' Abby moaned, her eyes still closed. 'Mama?'

'Mama's not here right now, Abby. I'm Huey.'

Her eyes popped open, then went wide as she focused on the giant sitting before her. 'Where's my mama?' she asked in a tiny voice.

'She had to go somewhere with your daddy. They asked me to baby-sit for a while.'

Abby looked around the dilapidated cabin, her cheeks turning bright red. 'Where are we? Where is this place?'

'A cabin in the woods. Not very far from your house. Your mama will be back soon.'

Abby whimpered, on the edge of panic now. Huey took the Barbie and set it gently before her. 'Your mama left this for you,' he said.

She snatched up the doll and clutched it to her chest. 'I'm scared.'

Huey nodded in sympathy. 'I'm scared, too.'

Abby's mouth opened. 'You are?'

He nodded again, his eyes wet with tears. Abby reached out and squeezed his little finger as if to reassure him.

FORTY MILES NORTH of the cabin, in the heart of Jackson, a white-columned mansion stood gleaming in the beams of spotlights fixed to stately oak trees. Dr James McDill sat across the dinner table from his wife, Margaret, feeling a deep apprehension. After weeks of struggle, he was about to speak his mind on a very sensitive matter. He had no choice. The closer the convention got, the more convinced he had become that he was right.

He put down his fork. 'Margaret, I know you don't want me to bring this up again. But I've got to.'

His wife's spoon clattered against her bone china plate. 'Why?' she asked. 'Why do you have to?'

McDill sighed. A cardiovascular surgeon of wide experience, he had never approached any surgery with the trepidation with which he now faced his wife. 'Maybe because it happened exactly a year ago. Maybe because of the things they told us. I couldn't get it out of my mind in the OR this morning. How this thing has poisoned our lives.'

'Not mine. Yours! Your life.'

'For God's sake, Margaret. The convention started tonight on the coast. We're not there, and for one reason. Because what happened last year is still controlling us. We were wrong not to go to the police a year ago. And I have a very bad feeling now. That woman told me they'd done it before, and I believed her. She said they'd done it to other doctors. They took advantage of the convention . . . of our separation. Margaret, what if it's happening again? Right now?'

'Stop it! Don't you remember what they said? They'll kill Peter!'

'We've got to face this. We simply cannot let what happened to us happen to another family.'

'To us? What happened to you, James? You sat in a hotel room with some slut for a night. Don't you ever think for one minute of anyone but yourself? Peter was traumatised!'

'Of course I think about Peter! But I refuse to let another child go through what he did because of our cowardice.'

Margaret wrapped her arms tight around herself and began rocking back and forth in the chair. 'If only you hadn't left us here alone,' she murmured. 'All alone and unprotected . . .'

'Margaret, please—' He fell silent as their eleven-year-old son appeared in the dining-room door. Peter was a pale, thin boy, and his eyes never settled in one place long.

'What's the matter?' he asked timidly. 'Why are you guys yelling?'

'Just a misunderstanding, son. Nothing for you to worry about. What time are you going over to Jimmy's?'

'His dad is picking me up in a minute.'

Margaret took a gulp of wine and said, 'Are you sure you want to spend the night over there tonight, darling?'

'Yeah. Unless . . . unless you don't want me to.'

'I like having my baby under this roof,' Margaret cooed.

'Nonsense,' said McDill. 'Go have some fun, son.' A car horn sounded outside. 'You'd better run. We'll see you in the morning.'

Peter crossed the room and kissed his mother. Over his shoulder, Margaret glared at McDill.

'We'll be right here if you need us for anything,' she said. 'Just call. We'll be right here. All night.'

McDill stared dejectedly at his plate. He had lost his appetite.

THE EXPEDITION bounced along rutted ground beneath black trees, Hickey sitting stiff behind the wheel. Karen gripped the handle on the windshield frame, the ice chest cold between her legs. Hickey had let her remove the blindfold after the last turn, but she felt like she was still wearing it. With only the sidelights on, she was astonished that he could pick his way through the dense trees.

'We're going to meet Huey on this road,' he said. 'You will not get emotional, you hear? You can hug your kid long enough to calm her down. Then you take her blood sugar and give her the shot. After that, one last hug, then we go.'

'I understand.'

'Be sure you do. She's going to go crazy when you start to leave, but you'd better tough it out. Just like the first day of school. Huey's told her he's baby-sitting her for one night. You reinforce that. Tell her everything's OK, we're all friends, and you're going to pick her up in the morning. If you flip out . . .' Hickey turned to face her for an instant, his eyes hard as agates. 'I'll have to hurt you right in front of her. You don't want that.'

A pair of headlights flashed out of the dark. Hickey stopped the Expedition and blinked the headlights twice. Then he left them on, creating a long tunnel of light that merged with the headlights pointing at them.

'Come on,' he said, shutting off the engine. 'Bring your stuff.'

Karen picked up the ice chest and climbed out.

Night mist floated through the headlight beams as they walked along them, and the humidity was heavy on Karen's skin. She was straining for a sight or sound of Abby when a giant form blotted out the other pair of headlights. The silhouette was about thirty yards away, and it looked like the outline of a grizzly bear.

Suddenly a squeal cut through the night. 'Mama? Mama!'

Karen rushed forward, fell to her knees and embraced the tiny shadow that had emerged from behind the massive one.

'I'm here, honey!' she said, squeezing Abby as tight as she dared and choking back a wave of tears. 'Mama's here, baby!'

Abby keened and cried and screeched. She wanted to speak, but each time she tried, her little chest heaved and caught, and she kept repeating the same syllable over and over. 'Wh—wh—wha—'

Karen kissed her cheeks and nose and forehead and hair. 'It's OK, baby. Take your time. Mama's here. I can hear you, baby.'

'Wh—why did you leave me here, Mama? Why?'

Karen forced herself to appear calm. 'I had to, honey. Daddy and I have an important meeting. One we forgot about. It's only for grown-ups, but it won't last long. It's only for tonight.'

'Are you *leaving* again?' The confusion in Abby's eyes was the most wrenching sight Karen had ever seen.

'Not for a while yet. We need to check your sugar, baby.'

'*Nooooo*,' Abby wailed. 'I want to go home!'

Karen opened the ice chest and took out the spring-loaded device, which she had already loaded with a needle. Abby let her middle finger be immobilised. Karen pressed the tip of the pen to the pad of the finger and popped the trigger. Abby yelped, and Karen wiped off the first drop of blood and forced out another. She wiped that against a paper test strip, which she fed into a small machine containing a microchip. After fifteen seconds, the machine beeped.

'Two hundred and forty. You need your shot, sweetie.'

Karen drew three units of short-acting insulin from one vial then, using the same syringe, added five units from a long-acting vial. This was more than usual, but she suspected Abby would sleep little

321

during the night and would probably be given food of some kind.

'Has Mr Huey fed you anything, sweetie?'

'Just some crackers.'

'That's all?'

Abby looked at the ground. 'And a peppermint.'

'Abby!' Karen started to pull up Abby's dress to inject the insulin into her stomach, but with the men standing so near, she decided to inject it right through the material. She pinched up a fold of fat and shot the insulin into it. Abby whimpered softly and locked her arms around Karen's neck. Karen lifted Abby into her arms. There, on her knees in the dirt, she rocked her daughter back and forth, singing 'Itsy-bitsy Spider', Abby's favourite childhood rhyme.

'I love you, pumpkin,' she murmured. 'Everything's going to be all right.'

'Keep singing, Mama,' Abby said.

Karen started the song again, but as she sang, she tuned her ears to the male voices drifting back to her on the night air.

'You doing OK?' Hickey asked.

'Uh-huh,' said a deeper voice. 'She's nice.'

Karen put her mouth to Abby's ear. 'Do you remember what I taught you about calling the police? What numbers to call?'

'Nine?' Abby thought aloud. 'Nine-one-one?'

'Good, honey. Now, Mr Huey has a cellphone. If he goes to the bathroom, he might forget it. If he does, use it to call nine-one-one. Run and hide outside with it, tell them you're in trouble, then hide the phone. Don't hang up. If you can do all that, people will come and bring you home to Mommy and Daddy early. Do you understand?'

Abby's eyes were wide. 'Will the policeman hurt Huey?'

'No, baby. But don't even try it unless you can call without him knowing. OK? It's like a game.'

'Old home week's over,' Hickey called. 'Tell princess bye-bye.'

Abby screamed and grabbed Karen's neck. *'Nooo!'* she wailed.

Karen looked at Hickey, her eyes pleading. 'I'm begging you. Let me stay here with her until morning. What can it possibly matter?'

'I told you about this crap.' He held out his arms. 'Hand her over.'

Karen backed away, clutching Abby in her arms. Hickey lunged forward and grabbed Abby under the arms, then yanked at her as if pulling on a sack of feed. Abby shrieked.

'Stop!' Karen yelled at Hickey. 'Stop it! You're hurting her!'

'Then let go, damn it!'

With a cry of desolation, Karen let go.

A heart-wrenching scream burst from Abby's lips.

Karen snatched up the ice chest, then ran to Huey and hooked its handle round his huge fingers. There were more syringes inside, and five vials of insulin. 'Please keep this! If Abby gets sick or passes out, call me and I'll tell you what to do!'

The giant's face was a mask of bewildered fear. 'Yes, ma'am. I—'

'Shut up!' Hickey shouted. He thrust Abby into Huey's arms, then grabbed Karen and dragged her towards the Expedition.

'I'll be back in the morning, Abby!' Karen promised.

Abby continued to shriek so loudly that Karen put her hands over her ears to blunt the agony of hearing her child's terror. But it didn't work. Then she heard a door slam and the squeal of a loose fan belt as Huey's truck backed slowly down the road.

HIGH IN THE BEAU RIVAGE HOTEL in Biloxi, the phone rang in Suite 28021. Will grabbed it before Cheryl could. 'Joe? Is this Joe?'

'Will?' said an uncertain voice.

'Karen!'

The sound of weeping came down the line.

'Did you see Abby?' he asked through the lump in his throat. 'Did you get her the insulin?'

'Will, she's so scared! I gave her eight units and left some extra vials and syringes. It was awful—'

Karen screamed, then her voice was replaced by Hickey's. 'You can calm down now, college boy. Your kid got her medicine. It's *sayonara* for now.'

'Wait!' Will was shouting at a dead phone. He exhaled slowly, trying to control the wild anger swelling in his chest.

'Hey,' said Cheryl. 'Everything's gonna be OK.' She reached out to touch his shoulder.

Will slammed the phone into the side of her head. As she fell across the bed, he tried to wrench the gun from her hand, but she held it tight. They wrestled on the bed, clawing and fighting for the weapon. Will's joints shot fire through his limbs and torso, but he grabbed the gun blindly with both hands and yanked as hard as he could.

Something ripped, Cheryl screamed, and the gun came away in his hands. He jumped up and pointed it at her.

'What the hell?'

Cheryl's dress had torn, exposing her from the waist up. Will stared at the bruises that covered her abdomen and ribs.

'What happened to you?'

She backed against the ornate headboard. 'Nothing.'

'That's not nothing. That's a beating.'

She picked up a pillow and covered her chest. 'It's nothing. And you just screwed up big-time.'

After venting his rage in the attack, Will found himself puzzled about what to do next. 'I want to ask you something, Cheryl. Are you committed to this kidnapping?'

She said nothing.

'Because I have a feeling you're not. I have a feeling this kind of thing is what Joe gets off on, but not you. I think you tried to talk him out of it. That's why you got the beating, isn't it?'

Her face was blank. 'Don't need no reason for a beating,' she said, her earlier elocution gone. 'Ain't never no reason.'

Will flashed back to his days as a resident, working the Jackson ERs. He'd seen more physical abuse in six months than he'd thought existed in the world at the time. And many of the responses he got from women sounded exactly like Cheryl's. Sullen, angry, resigned.

'There's nothing you can do to me that hasn't been done before, Doctor. I mean, nothing.' Cheryl tossed the pillow aside, exposing the relief map of bruises. 'Face it, Joey's got you beat, right down the line.'

IN AN UPSTAIRS BATHROOM Margaret McDill sat at her dressing table, taking off her make-up. She looked into the mirror at her husband, who hovered in the door behind her like an accusing ghost. 'I refuse to discuss it,' she said. 'How many times do I have to tell you that?'

Dr McDill gave a long sigh. 'I'm just trying to understand.' He took a deep breath and pushed into forbidden territory yet again. 'Is there something I don't know about?' He'd asked this before and been rebuffed. Tonight he would press it. He had to. 'Did this man hurt you?'

'Hurt me?' Her lips tightened to white. 'Did he *hurt* me?'

'I'm your husband, Margaret. I only want to help you.'

She whirled from the mirror, her eyes wild. 'All right! All *right*! You want to know why I won't report it? Because he raped me.'

McDill flinched.

'He raped me, James. Do you feel better now? Is that what you want to tell the police? All the gory details? He told me to take off my clothes and I did. He told me I'd have to do things I'd never done before'—she covered her face with her hands—'and I did. All I could think of was Peter. They had my baby!' She exploded into unintelligible screams, thrashing her arms until McDill rushed forward and hugged her so tightly that she couldn't move.

'It's all right, Margaret . . . It's going to be all right. You didn't do anything wrong.' Tears stung his eyes. 'It's all right . . .'

Her screams subsided.

'Margaret? I'm afraid the same thing is happening again. Do you understand? To another family. Another mother. Another child.' He took her firmly by the shoulders and peered into her eyes. 'We can't let that happen. It wouldn't be Christian. Would it?'

Margaret slowly shook her head, her eyes glassy.

'I'm going to call the FBI,' McDill said. 'But we don't have to tell them anything about what happened to you. It's irrelevant.'

His wife's only response was fresh tears sliding down her cheeks.

'I love you, sweetheart,' he assured her. 'More than I ever have.'

s i x

'You can take off the blindfold now,' said Hickey.

Karen untied the scarf he'd taken from her room. The dashboard lights shone like a coastal city viewed from the sea. Glancing up, she saw they were on a two-lane road, and she knew by the speed and sound of the outgoing trip that they had driven on an interstate for at least half an hour after leaving Jackson. That left two options: I-55, which ran north and south, or I-20, which ran east and west. If he left the blindfold off, she might soon know for sure. She decided to make an effort to keep him in a good mood.

'Thank you for letting me give Abby the shot.'

Hickey rolled down his window a crack and blew cigarette smoke outside. 'That's what I like to hear. Gratitude. You don't see much of it these days. It's a forgotten courtesy. But you're an old-fashioned girl, I can tell.'

Karen looked at Hickey's profile. Heavy brows, the nose a bit flat, the chin like an unspoken challenge. It looked like a face that could take a lot of punishment, and probably had.

'We've got a whole night to kill,' he went on, glancing away from the road long enough to find her eyes in the dark. 'Why make it like breaking rocks, you know? Let's be friends.'

Her internal radar went to alert status.

'You're a beautiful woman. And I'm not a bad-looking guy, am I? You got some good tan lines, I bet. With that pool out back.'

Karen stared straight ahead, her cheeks burning.

'Get those jeans off.'

A ball of ice formed in Karen's chest.

'You think I'm kidding? We've done this gig five times, and every time the wives and me had a little party. A little bonus for the executive in the operation, and nobody the wiser.'

'No party tonight, Joe.'

'No?' He laughed and tapped a finger on the cellphone. 'Lose the jeans. Or I reach out and touch your precious princess.'

Karen held out for another few seconds. Then she unzipped her jeans, arched in the seat, and pulled them off. No sooner had she done this than he reached up and hit the passenger light switch, flooding her side of the interior with yellow light.

'Nice legs,' Hickey said. 'Far as they go.'

She felt his gaze on her lap like the heat from a lamp. 'Are you going to leave the light on all the way back? It seems dangerous.'

'I gotta admit, I'm tempted. But it wouldn't be too smart, would it? Like I said, we've got all night. What the hell.'

He flicked off the light, and the protective blanket of night closed around her again. But she was not safe. Nowhere close. Of course, safe didn't really matter, not in the usual sense. What mattered was survival. There was only one priority: Abby. Other mothers had walked through fire for their children; she could do the same. She could endure the worst that an animal like Hickey could dish out, and be there to hug Abby when it was over.

WILL STARED at the telephone in the bedroom of his suite. It had just rung, and though he was holding Cheryl's Walther in his hand, he knew it was useless. If she told Hickey he had assaulted her, anything could happen. If he didn't let her answer, Hickey would assume things were not as they should be and might retaliate against Abby.

The phone rang again. 'What are you going to do now, smart-ass?' Cheryl asked. She was leaning against the headboard of the bed, her torn dress around her waist.

He tossed the gun into her lap. She picked it up then answered the phone. After listening for a few moments, she said, 'It is now. The doc flipped out . . . He hit me and took my gun. OK.' She held out the receiver to Will. 'He wants to talk to you.'

Will took the phone.

'Doc, you screw up again, and the biggest piece you find of your little girl will fit in a thimble.'

'I hear you, Joe.'

'You hit my old lady?'

'It doesn't look like I was the first.'

Silence. Then, 'You remember what I said about your little girl.'

'I understand. I made a mistake. I just want my daughter back.'

The phone went dead.

'You're pathetic,' Cheryl said. 'Like some kid stopped by a highway patrolman. Totally submissive.'

'You know all about that, don't you? Submission.'

She shrugged. 'So he smacks me around sometimes.'

'Those bruises weren't caused by a couple of smacks. I see signs of systematic abuse.'

'You never smacked your wife?'

'No. We argue. We don't hit each other. What did you and Joe argue about last? Going through with his kidnapping?'

'Hell, no. We've done this lots of times.'

'Maybe you're tired of it. I can see how you would be. Realising how much pain you're putting people through. Especially the kids.'

She looked away. 'Talk all you want. You know what I was doing before Joe found me? I was a bar girl in a truck stop. A *full-service* bar girl.'

'Being a whore is a lot more respectable than what you're doing now.'

'Sitting somewhere all day, all night, available to any scummy, shit-breath, disease-ridden son of a bitch who walks in the door with the price of admission?'

'You didn't have any choice about clients?'

'Clients? I wasn't a lawyer, OK? It's *johns*. And, no, I didn't have any choice. 'Cause if I said no, I didn't get the coke.'

'Joe got you out of that life?'

'That's right. He got me clean. It was the hardest thing either of us ever did. So, if you think you're gonna talk me into betraying him, think again. You think I care if he smacks me around?'

'Yes, I do. Because you know that's not love. You don't owe Joe a life of servitude because he got you off cocaine. You deserve to be as happy as anybody else.'

A bitter laugh. 'You ever go to a hooker?'

'No.'

'What guy admits it? I believe you, though. You're one of those one-in-a-million guys who were meant to be husbands, aren't you?'

'I don't want to pry. But I would really like to know how you ended up in prostitution. I mean, you just don't look like one. You look too fresh. You're beautiful, for God's sake. How old are you?'

'Twenty-six.'

'How old is Joe?'

'Fifty.'

Twenty-four years' difference. 'Where are you from?'

Cheryl sighed. 'Do we have to play *Twenty Questions?*'

'What else is there to do?'

'I could use a drink.'

Will walked over to the phone.

'What are you doing?' she asked, laying a hand on the gun.

'Ordering you a drink. What do you like?'

She looked suspicious. 'I guess it won't hurt. Rum and Coke.'

He called room service and ordered a bottle of Bacardi, a two-litre bottle of Coca-Cola, and a pot of tea for himself.

'You English or something?' asked Cheryl.

'I just like tea.' What he wanted was caffeine, enough to get him through whatever was going to be required of him in the next twelve hours. He needed a painkiller, too, for his joints, but he wasn't going to take anything that might dull his mind.

'So, where are you from?' he asked again.

'My dad was in the army. We moved a lot when I was a little girl. My father screwed up some way. He took it out on my Mom for one too many years, and she finally left him. We went back to her home-town, little nothing of a place in Marion County. Then she hooked up with my stepfather.' Cheryl's eyes glazed. 'I was about ten, I guess. When I turned sixteen, I got the hell out of there.'

'Where'd you go?'

'I had a girlfriend who shared an apartment in Jackson with two other girls. One of them was dancing at this club, making three hundred bucks a night. Just lap dances and stuff, no tricks out back.'

'You started stripping?'

'Not right away. But my girlfriend went back home and suddenly my share of the rent went up. So, I gave it a try. And it worked. I was a natural, they said. Plenty of nights I made six hundred bucks. But you get these long shifts. I mean, have you ever danced for eight hours straight? Drinking beer and mixed drinks? You do that, you start needing something to keep you going, you know?'

'And once you got on coke, they had you.'

'Yep. Pretty soon you're only breaking even on the dancing, just to keep up your habit. Then you're into *them* for money. And that's when they hit you. There's ways to pay off the principal.' Her eyes looked ancient in her young face.

'And Joe got you out?'

A cynical smile. 'Sir Galahad to the rescue. That's Joe. One night he paid for a trick, packed me into his car, and hauled me all the way to New Orleans. He put mattresses on the walls and locked me in.' She shuddered at the memory. 'Cold turkey. Talk about a nightmare.'

'How the hell did you wind up kidnapping kids?'

'We needed money. Joe tried some straight things, but they never seemed to work out. He put me in a nice club in Metairie, just outside New Orleans, no drugs, no drinking. I was making so much money we couldn't believe it. Everybody said I was better than the featured dancers who came through, you know.' Cheryl's eyes lit up, the way Abby's did when she was telling someone about her doll collection. 'I had a dozen different outfits, props, the whole works. I had a Jeep Grand Cherokee and we'd drive around the country. Texas, Colorado, Montana . . . Man, it was something. But Joe got jealous. I was so good that people started talking to me about other things. Movie people. Not like Sandra Bullock, but still Hollywood. Soft porn stuff. And Joe got nervous. He didn't . . . He—'

'He wanted you all to himself.'

She nodded sadly. 'Yeah.'

'You couldn't break loose?'

'I owed him.'

A knock sounded at the door. Will walked through the sitting room of the suite and accepted the tray from a young Mexican girl, then hung out the DO NOT DISTURB sign and carried the tray in to Cheryl. He poured Bacardi and Coke and a steaming cup of tea.

Cheryl finished her drink in one long sip and held out the glass for a refill. 'You don't just walk away from the kind of work I was doing at the club in Jackson,' she said quietly. 'I owed them money, and when I started dancing in Metairie they heard about it. They wanted me back at the club. The guy who owned the place sent a guy. To bring me back. A really bad guy. Joe punched his ticket.'

'You mean he killed him?'

Cheryl looked Will right in the eye. 'That's what I mean. Messy, too. So that anybody else they sent would know what he was getting into. You know? And it worked. Nobody else came. I was free.'

'You weren't free. You'd just traded one master for another.'

'Hey, I ain't nobody's slave.'

'Cheryl, if you'll help me save Abby, I can give you enough money to get you away clean. Really free. For ever.'

Hope flickered in her eyes, then died. 'You're lying, sweetie.'

He started to argue, but there was no point. She would not be persuaded.

Cheryl held up her drink in a mock toast. 'Don't feel bad, Doc. It's just the nature of things.'

Will had stopped listening. He was thinking about Hickey choosing to spend the night with Karen rather than him. And what Karen would or would not do to save Abby.

HICKEY PULLED THE EXPEDITION into the garage and shut off the engine. In the ticking silence, Karen felt dread settle in her limbs.

'Party time,' Hickey said. He opened his door and climbed out, then waited in the glow of the porch light. 'You're not doing anybody any good sitting there. You or me.'

She folded her jeans and got out. At the door she waited for Hickey to open it, but he handed her the key ring.

'You do it,' he said. 'Your house.'

She tucked her jeans under her arm, then bent and took hold of the doorknob with her left hand. Before this house existed, she had worked with the architect on the blueprints. If any place on earth belonged to her, personified her, this house did. And now it was about to be violated.

'Come on,' he said. 'Meter's running.'

A desperate thought flashed through her mind. She could open the door just far enough to slip inside, then lock it behind her and call the police. But what would that accomplish? Nothing but death for Abby. Hickey had his cellphone, and he could be talking to his cousin in seconds. No. There was no choice but to obey.

She turned the key and walked inside, right through to the kitchen, then stood there, waiting for a command.

Hickey walked up slowly and smiled. 'Up to your bedroom.'

She turned and walked up the hallway, heavy-footed.

'Stop,' Hickey said.

Karen stopped. He opened Abby's door. Moonlight shone through the window, falling upon the toy inhabitants of the room.

'Take a good look, Mom. This is why we're not going to have any trouble being friends tonight.'

Karen looked. Here was the justification for whatever she would have to do to get through the night. To bring Abby back.

Hickey poked her between the shoulder blades, pushing her until she reached the master bedroom.

Not wanting to enter it in the dark, she rotated the dimmer switch on the wall. The sight of the bedroom startled her. Everything was in its proper place, but the antique sleigh bed, the overstuffed chair and ottoman, the cherrywood television cabinet and the Walter Anderson watercolours struck her as furnishings in some nameless hotel.

'Looks like a nice place to pass an evening,' Hickey said.

He walked past her and fell into the oversized chair. 'I could use a drink. Bourbon. Kentucky bourbon, if you got it.'

The bourbon was kept on a sideboard in Will's study. Karen laid her jeans on the foot of the bed and went up the hall, thankful for a chance to postpone what seemed inevitable. She picked up the Wild Turkey bottle and walked back towards her bedroom.

Hickey was smiling as she stepped through the door. 'Wild Turkey!' he cried. 'I'll be damned. Bring that here!'

She gave him the bottle. He unscrewed the cap and drank liberally from the wide glass mouth, then set the bottle between his legs. 'Put your jeans back on. You know what a lap dance is?'

Lurid images went through her mind of scantily clad women hunching over bar patrons, wiggling their silicone-enhanced breasts.

'No,' she replied.

'You're lying. You know what one is. What you don't know is, my wife had to do them for a living for a while. That bugged me, Karen. All those bastards feeling her up, slobbering all over her.'

'That's your wife with Will right now?'

He took another slug of Wild Turkey. 'We need some music. You got a stereo in that TV cabinet?'

Karen walked over and switched on the CD player.

'Something with a steady beat. You need a good beat for a lap dance. Not too fast, but not too slow either.'

With a growing sense of unreality, she scanned the CD rack. At a loss, she finally chose a *Best of the Eighties* compilation. The first song was 'Every Breath You Take' by the Police. The bass and drums began to pulse sinuously from speakers. When she turned, Hickey was nodding to the beat.

'That's it,' he said. 'Yeah. Come over here and dance.'

She would have laughed, were the situation not so desperate.

'I said *dance*,' Hickey repeated.

Karen began to sway to the music, but she felt awkward.

'Closer,' Hickey said.

Karen danced nearer the chair, but jerked back as Hickey's hand reached towards her.

'It's just money,' he said.

He was telling the truth. In his hand was a folded one-dollar bill. She danced closer, and he stuffed it into the front pocket of her jeans.

'That means you gotta take something off,' he said.

She hesitated, then slowly unbuttoned her blouse until it hung from her shoulders.

'Shake it off.'

She did. Goose bumps raced across her back and shoulders. She focused on the wall and kept swaying to the music, but her mind was spinning. How fast could the Wild Turkey dull his senses?

'Lean over,' he ordered.

She bent slightly at the waist, and he stuffed a bill into her bra.

'You know what that means, babe. The bra. The bra next.'

Part of her wanted to scream, *If you're going to rape me, just get it over with!* But a wiser part of her knew that anything could happen between now and the moment he actually forced himself on her. Miracles could happen. She reached up and undid the catch.

'That's better,' Hickey intoned. He held up another bill. A five this time. She danced closer, close enough for him to slide the five into her pocket. 'Now the jeans.'

She unzipped the jeans but left them on. As she spun slowly, he took another slug of bourbon and stared mesmerised at her chest. His eyes looked darker than before, like flat discs of slate. Shark's eyes. No knowledge in them, only hunger. A vast, insatiable appetite.

'Come on,' he rasped. 'Let's see the goods.'

She didn't want to take off her jeans. The vulnerability she had felt without them was dehumanising. But she couldn't afford to make him angry. She had to keep him drinking, convince him that she was going along with it. She let the jeans ride down her hips, then lifted her knees one at a time and kicked her feet out of them.

'That's enough foreplay,' Hickey ordered.

He thrust himself to his feet and carried the bottle of Wild Turkey to the bedside table. Then he walked back towards her, pulling off his polo shirt as he came, revealing a pale, wiry torso. When he reached for his belt, Karen looked at the carpet.

'Watch,' he said, his voice full of pride.

She took a deep breath and looked up as Hickey's khakis hit the floor. A tingling numbness began to creep outwards from some place deep within her. The act would be bad, she knew, but the anticipation was worse. The knowing that absolute suffering was inevitable. That no help would come. There was only Hickey. And Abby. Abby hanging over her head like a sword, enforcing every command he gave.

As Hickey stared at her with his stupid schoolboy grin, something stirred deep within her. Not quite a thought, but the seed of one. A tiny spark of awareness, smouldering and darkly feminine.

Her moment would come.

seven

Huey sat across from Abby on the linoleum floor of the cabin, whittling slowly. He had dragged an old saddle blanket in from the bedroom and set her on it, so she wouldn't have to sit on the bare floor.

'Do you feel better now?' he asked.

Abby nodded. 'A little bit.'

'Are you hungry? I'm hungry.'

'Kind of. My tummy hurts.'

A knot of worry formed in Huey's stomach. 'What do you like? I got baloney. You like Captain Crunch? I love Captain Crunch.'

'I have to eat Raisin Bran.'

'You can't eat Captain Crunch? How come?'

'Well, when you eat, the food puts sugar in your blood. And you've got stuff in *your* body to make the sugar go away. But I don't have any. So, the sugar gets more and more until it makes me sick. And if I get too sick, I'll go to sleep. Sleep and maybe never wake up.'

Fear passed into Huey's face like a shadow falling over a rock.

'That happened to my sister. Jo Ellen. I wish I could give you some of my blood to make your sugar go away.'

'That's what's in my shots. Stuff to make the sugar go away. I don't like needles, but I don't like being sick, either. It hurts.'

'I hate needles,' Huey said forcefully. 'Hate, hate, hate.'

'My tummy still hurts.'

Huey's mouth fell open. 'You just play here with your doll. I'm gonna make you the biggest bowl of Captain Crunch you ever saw!'

Before Abby could remind him that she couldn't eat Captain Crunch, the giant got to his feet and walked towards the kitchen. After three steps, he stopped and put his hand to his head as though he had forgotten something. 'Dumb, dumb, dumb,' he said.

He came back to Abby, bent down, and picked up the Nokia cellphone he'd left beside her. 'Joey said, take this with me everywhere. Don't leave it anywhere. He gave me a extra battery, too.'

Abby looked forlornly at the phone. She was thinking about what her mother had said about calling the police.

'I'll be right back,' Huey promised. 'You just wait.'

He walked into the kitchen. Abby could see his back as he opened a cabinet. She turned to the cabin window. It was pitch-black outside. She hated the dark, but her mother's voice was playing inside her head. *Take the phone and hide . . .*

She heard a clink, then Huey humming something. She liked Huey. But he was a stranger, and her daddy had told her over and over how strangers could be bad, even when they seemed nice. Abby closed her eyes and pictured her mother's face. What would she say if she could talk to me now?

Run.

Abby stood up with her Barbie and took a tentative step towards the door. Looking back towards the kitchen, she saw Huey's shadow moving on the floor. She walked very fast to the front door, picked up the small ice chest her mother had left, and slipped outside.

Huey came out of the kitchen carrying a bowl of Captain Crunch in his left hand and his cellphone in his right. He looked down at the blanket Abby had been sitting on and blinked in confusion. Then he peered around the room. After several seconds, a grin lighted his face. 'Are you playing hide-and-seek?'

The screen door banged softly in the wind.

Huey looked and saw it hanging open. His face went slack, he dropped the bowl and the phone and charged onto the porch.

HICKEY TOOK two steps towards Karen, a lopsided grin on his face.

She kept her eyes on his and tried to keep the fear out of her voice as she spoke. 'I need to use the bathroom.'

'What's in the bathroom? Another gun?'

'My diaphragm, OK? I don't want to get pregnant.'

'Fine. Go do whatever. But when you come out of there, it's Lady Godiva time.' He picked up the Wild Turkey bottle and stretched out on the bed, his face glowing with anticipation.

The second Karen closed the bathroom door, her survival instinct kicked into overdrive. She turned on the basin taps, then opened the cabinet behind the mirror. She saw nothing that could help her. As she closed the door, she caught her reflection in its mirrored surface. She looked like a ghost.

Splashing water on her face, she reached down for a hand towel and froze. Standing in a ceramic cup by the basin beside three toothbrushes was a disposable scalpel, six inches of plastic and surgical steel, flatter than a key and lighter than a pencil, its blade shielded by a plastic sheath. She reached down and lifted it out of the cup.

'*How long can it take?*' Hickey complained.

He sounded like he was right outside the door. Dropping a flannel over the scalpel, Karen yanked off her panties, sat on the toilet, and watched the doorknob. It didn't move.

She got up and took the scalpel from beneath the flannel, then removed the clear protective sheath from the blade. Its edge was honed to a sharpness that could lay open the human dermis like the skin of a peach. She straightened before the mirror and looked at herself. Was the scalpel concealable? After a moment's thought, she opened the dirty clothes cabinet and stood on tiptoe. In the top section were two shelves she used to store clothes she rarely wore. She reached up and dug through them with feverish intensity.

There. A claret-coloured teddy Will had bought at the mall last year, a garment she'd never even tried on. She wriggled into it and the top half lifted and pressed her breasts together so that the cleavage reminded her of the beach bunnies on *Baywatch*.

Perfect. Somewhere in this outfit she could hide the scalpel.

CROUCHING IN A THICKET, Abby watched Huey lumber past her in the moonlight.

'Abby?' he called. 'Why did you run away? You're scaring me.'

She was trying not to make a sound, but her shins had already been scratched bloody, and they stung like a thousand paper cuts. She hadn't wanted to go far from the lights, but she knew Huey would find her if she didn't get into the dark.

He paused twenty feet to her left, looking into the wall of trees. 'Abby? Where are you?'

She wondered how long she could wait here. The woods didn't usually scare her. Their house was in the middle of the woods. But she'd never spent the night in them. Already she'd heard scuttling sounds in the undergrowth that made her shiver.

'Come out!' Huey yelled, sounding really mad now.

Abby watched him pick up a big stick and poke some bushes with it. Then he moved off farther to her left, going along the line of trees.

She looked at the cabin, the lovely yellow light streaming from the windows, and wished she could wait inside, where there were no animals or bugs. Huey's voice floated back to her on the wind.

'There's bad things in the woods at night! Wolves and bears and things! You need Huey to look out for you!'

She hugged herself and tried not to listen. There might be bears in these woods, but she didn't think so. And certainly not wolves.

'There's snakes, too,' Huey called. 'Creepy crawly snakes looking for warm bodies in the dark.'

A chill shot up Abby's spine. There were snakes in Mississippi, all right. Bad ones. She shut her eyes and tried not to cry.

WHEN KAREN EMERGED from the bathroom wearing the teddy, she saw Hickey lying under the covers in the middle of the bed. He gave a long, low wolf whistle. 'Man *alive*. That's better than naked. Talk about getting with the programme.'

As Karen moved towards the bed, she saw Will's .38 lying on the floor. That was how confident Hickey was about the diabolical cage of circumstance he had constructed.

He patted the side of the bed.

As she moved towards him, she slid the gun under the bed with her foot, then slipped under the covers.

'Damn, you're cold,' he complained.

'Sorry.' He smelt like a stale ashtray. She stared up at the ceiling as though she had nothing in her mind but enduring what was to come with stoicism. 'What do you want me to do?'

'You're not gonna whine about it?'

'Not if it keeps you from hurting Abby.'

'Thank God for small favours.' He turned sideways, propped himself on an elbow, and she felt him press against her hip. A deep shudder rippled through her and every fibre of instinct told her to jerk away, but she forced herself to lie still and turn her face towards his.

'You probably want something special, something you fantasise about when you see women like me.'

'Like what?'

'Lie back and relax. You'll see.'

A smile spread over his lips as she pulled the covers over her shoulders, and slid down towards his midsection. She swallowed her revulsion, then straddled his legs and took hold of him with her left hand.

'Mmm,' he moaned and groped for the back of her head.

Panic shot through her. 'I know what to do. Lie back and relax. You don't want it to be over too fast.'

'Yeah.' After a moment, his head lolled back, and his eyes rolled up towards the ceiling.

Carefully closing her fingers around the handle, she drew the scalpel from its place of concealment and pressed the blade against his skin.

'Look down, Joe,' she said in a cold voice. 'And don't make any sudden moves.'

'What?' She felt his abdomen tighten as he raised his head to look and his eyes went from blank confusion to shock. He had seen and understood. His pelvis didn't move an inch.

'*What the—?*'

He raised his hand to strike her, but didn't have the courage. Karen looked straight into his eyes, where fear crackled like electricity. The power was intoxicating.

'This is a number ten scalpel,' she said. 'We keep them to take out splinters, stuff like that. But it'll take off your equipment just as easily. I bet you'd hardly even feel it. Just a quick sting.'

'I'm gonna kill you. You and your kid.'

She pushed the scalpel point deeper, drawing blood.

'Stop!' he shouted, his face white and contorted in terror.

'You're bleeding, Joe. So listen very closely. You're going to telephone your cousin and tell him to bring my daughter back here.'

Hickey's eyes flicked from the blade to her face. 'You won't do it. If you do, your kid dies.'

'Oh, I'll do it.' Karen's heart felt like it was beating drum rolls. 'I was a surgical nurse for six years, Joe. I'll do it, and if you live through it, you'll be peeing through a catheter for the rest of your life. *Pick up the phone!*'

'Take it easy!' Hickey grabbed the phone off the bedside table. 'I'm dialling!' He punched at the keypad. 'What do you want me to say?'

'Tell him you already have the ransom money. Tell him to put Abby in the truck and drive her back here.'

'He won't do it. He'll know something's wrong.'

'You told me he always does everything you say!'

Puzzlement came into Hickey's face. 'He's not answering.'

'You didn't dial it right! Dial it again!' She pressed the blade deeper.

'*Shit! Wait!*' He hung up and redialled the number, then waited for an answer. 'He's not picking up,' he said, looking worried enough for it to distract him from his immediate peril. 'What the hell?'

'He hasn't missed a call yet! Why this one?'

Hickey shrugged. 'How do I know? He's a damn retard. Now get that knife away from me, will you? We've got to figure out what's happening up there.'

'Shut up,' Karen snapped. 'Let me think.'

'You can't sit like that all night.'

'I said, Shut up!'

Karen blinked, momentarily off guard, and Hickey slammed the telephone into the side of her head.

White light exploded in her brain and, as her thoughts scattered into meaningless electrochemicals, her cerebellum executed the impulse her cerebral cortex had been holding in check for the past minute. Like a frog's leg touched by an electrode, the hand holding the scalpel jerked back.

Hickey shrieked like a hog having its throat cut.

Karen looked down. All she saw was blood.

HAVING CIRCLED back round the cabin, poking at bushes and trying to scare Abby, Huey was now working his way along the dirt road.

She crouched in the dark, her head filled with images of snakes curling and uncurling in the weeds around her. During the last few minutes, beetles had crawled over her feet and mosquitoes had feasted on her exposed arms and face.

As she squashed a mosquito bloody against her forearm, a faint ringing sounded in her ears. She tried to focus on it, but it disappeared. Then it came again. Her heart thumped. It was a telephone. The ringing was coming from the cabin. Huey must have left his phone inside when he went looking for her! She grabbed her doll and the ice chest and raced out of the trees towards the glowing windows.

But Abby couldn't find the phone. It wasn't on the table or the broken old couch. But it was still ringing.

She looked at the floor. There was a puddle of spilt milk and cereal by the bedroom door. The phone was lying in it. Abby darted to the puddle and reached for the wet cellphone but, even as she did, she knew something wasn't right. The phone's window was dark.

The ringing sounded again. It wasn't coming from the cellphone. It was coming from the bedroom. She ran in and looked around. An old-fashioned black phone sat on the floor on the far side of the bed. She grabbed the receiver. 'Hello? . . . Hello!'

A dial tone.

She stared at the phone in disbelief. How could her mother stop ringing, just when she was about to pick up?

'Abby?' Huey's voice floated into the bedroom. 'Don't run away from Huey! You're going to get me in trouble. Big trouble.'

She froze.

The voice sounded close, but she didn't hear footsteps. She grabbed the cellphone and ran flat-out for the back door.

Outside, she ran past a small shed and crouched beside a tree. There was just enough moonlight to see the POWER button. She switched on the phone, carefully punched in 911, pressed SEND, and put the phone to her ear.

'Welcome to CellStar,' said a computer voice. 'You are currently in a non-emergency-service zone. Please—'

'Is this the police?' Abby cried. 'I need a policeman!'

Tears formed in her eyes as the voice refused to acknowledge her.

HICKEY CLUTCHED a pillow to his groin, his face a mask of agony.

'You've got to get to a hospital!' she told him. 'You could bleed to death.'

He lifted the pillow and looked down, then laughed maniacally. 'You missed! You *missed*. Look at that!' He lifted the pillow higher, and his smile vanished. His right thigh had been laid open and blood was pulsing out at an alarming rate. 'Your kid is dead. *Dead!*'

Her heart turned to stone. She had gambled and failed. As Hickey tried to stanch the flow of blood with the pillow, she scrabbled under the bed for the gun. She had to keep him from bleeding to death, but she didn't want to be at his mercy while he was in a fit of rage.

'Go in the bathroom!' she said, getting to her feet with the pistol. 'Tie a towel above the laceration. You've got to slow the arterial flow.'

'Look what you did!' he screamed, his eyes wide with shock.

She was going to have to tend to the wound, but she didn't think she could bring herself to touch him yet. She didn't even want to get close to him. 'Get a towel!' she yelled. 'Hurry! Make a tourniquet!'

Hickey hobbled into the bathroom with the pillow pressed to his thigh, groaning and whining and cursing at once. Karen held the gun on him while he tied a towel round his thigh. He was doing a fair job, good enough to slow the bleeding anyway.

'Why didn't Huey answer?' she asked. 'Why aren't they at the cabin? Has he taken Abby somewhere?'

Hickey looked up, his face red with strain. 'You don't need to worry about that. Look at this damn leg! I'm bleeding to death!'

'You need a hospital.'

'Bullshit. I need stitches is all. You were a nurse, you said. You do it.'

'It would take fifty stitches to close that.' She was exaggerating.

'So get the stuff! Your husband's got a black bag or something, right? To take care of the neighbourhood brats?'

Will did keep a bag at home for Abby but Karen didn't want to get it. She didn't want to hold the gun or look at Hickey's nakedness or anything else any more. She just wanted Abby locked in her arms.

'Why are you doing this?' she screamed. 'Why? It's not fair! It's not right—'

Hickey slapped her. 'Lady, if you don't get your act together and sew me up, Huey will snap your little girl's spine like a twig. One phone call will do it. One fucking call.'

'You can't even get him on the phone!'

'I'll get him.'

Karen stood shaking, Will's gun quavering in her hand. She had to keep herself together. Or Abby wouldn't make it.

'Move your ass!' Hickey yelled. 'Get the bag!' She nodded and hurried out of the bathroom.

ABBY THOUGHT she'd heard Huey outside again, so she crept into the little shed behind the cabin. There was a tractor in it, like the one her daddy used to cut the grass at home, only bigger. She climbed up onto its seat and started pressing numbers on the cellphone's lighted keypad. She was dialling the only number she could think of: home.

She hit SEND again. The phone began to ring.

KAREN WAS RUMMAGING through Will's medical bag when the phone rang on Will's side of the bed. Hickey was still in the bathroom. Though the caller was almost surely Hickey's wife, Karen answered.

'Hello?'

'Tell her to give me a minute,' Hickey called from behind the half-closed bathroom door.

'Mama?'

Karen's hands began to shake. 'Abby?' She had to swallow before she could continue. 'Honey, are you all right? Where are you?'

Abby's voice disintegrated into sobs. Karen heard her hiccupping and swallowing, trying to control herself enough to answer.

'Take your time, baby. Tell me where you are.'

'I don't know! I'm in the woods. Mama, come get me! I'm scared.'

Karen glanced at the bathroom door. 'I'm going to come, honey, but— baby, Mama doesn't know how to get to where you are. Are you still at the place where I gave you the shot?'

'Uh-huh. I ran outside the cabin. Then I heard the phone inside.'

'Listen, honey. Do you remember how to call nine-one-one? If you do that, the police can come get—'

'I already did that. The lady wouldn't listen! Mama, help me.'

'What the hell are you doing? Give me that damn phone!' Hickey was coming through the bathroom door, trying to move quickly but not wanting to put too much weight on his injured leg.

Karen transferred the phone to her left hand, covering the mouthpiece, grabbed the .38 off the bed, pointed it at him and fired.

Hickey hit the floor like a soldier under incoming artillery and covered his head with both hands.

'Tell me where my baby is, you son of a bitch!'

Hickey didn't speak or move. *'Answer me, goddamn it!'* Karen fired into the floor, missing him by inches.

'Don't shoot me!' he screamed. 'If you kill me, your kid is dead!'

'Right along with you! Get it?' Karen tried to speak calmly into the receiver. 'Stay on the phone, baby. Mama's fine, but she's busy. Are you in the cabin now?'

'I'm in a little shed outside. I'm on a tractor.'

Abby's captor was certain to focus on any structures as he hunted for her, no matter how simple-minded he was.

'I want you to go back outside, Abby, into the woods. Make sure Huey isn't around, then sneak out of the shed, get down in some bushes, and stay down.'

'But it's night-time.'

'I know baby, but tonight the dark is your friend. Don't you worry, sweetie. Mama's going to come get you.'

'You promise?'

'I promise. Now, I want you to look outside and then run into the woods. Take the phone with you and stay on the line. Don't hang up, OK? *Don't hang up.*'

'OK.'

Karen covered the mouthpiece with her hand again and pointed the gun at Hickey's head. 'Get up, you bastard.'

Hickey flattened his hands on the floor and raised himself slowly, then leaned against the frame of the bathroom door for support.

'What the hell do you think you're doing?' he asked.

She gave him a cold smile. 'I'm changing the plan.'

eight

Dr James McDill and his wife sat across from Special Agent Bill Chalmers, a bland-faced, sandy-haired man in his early forties. It was 11.30pm. McDill had called the Jackson Field Office of the FBI a few minutes after Margaret's mini-breakdown, and that call had resulted in this meeting.

He had planned to come to the Federal Building alone, but Margaret had insisted on accompanying him. Chalmers had led them to the office of the SAC, or Special Agent-in-Charge. A name-plate on the desk read: FRANK ZWICK.

'We're talking about a kidnapping-for-ransom, correct?' Chalmers said from behind his boss's desk.

'Yes,' said McDill.

'And this happened one year ago?'

'Give or take a few days. It happened during the same annual medical convention that's going on right now in Biloxi.'

Chalmers pursed his lips. 'I've got to ask this, Doctor. Why did you folks wait a whole year to report this kidnapping?'

'They threatened to come back and kill our son.'

'You must have feared that they would do it to another family.'

McDill looked at the floor. 'That's true. The hard truth is, I'm more selfish than I'd like to think. If I had to do it again—'

'I was raped,' Margaret said quietly.

'I see,' Chalmers said.

McDill laid a hand on his wife's forearm. 'Margaret, you don't have to do this.'

She waved his arm off. 'I wouldn't let James report what happened. I was alone with the man who was running the kidnapping, and my son was being held at another location. Peter and my husband were at the mercy of these people. The man made very sure that I understood that. Then he used that fact to extort sex from me. I was terrified that would be made public. I know now that I was wrong to keep it quiet. But I haven't thought about anything else since it happened. I'm going to pieces, I think.'

McDill took her hand. This time she didn't pull away.

Agent Chalmers picked up his pen and tapped it on the table. 'And now you think it's happening again.'

'Yes,' said McDill.

'Tell me why.'

McDill took a deep breath. 'The woman holding me at the hotel said they'd done the same thing before, more than once. She also said no one had ever reported them. And knowing what I know now about the leader's tactics, I believe that, too. I mean, we didn't report it. The man who conceived this damned scheme—Joe, or whatever his real name is—has so far gotten away with it. What reason does he have to stop?'

'Mrs McDill, did you have a feeling about whether the name this man used was his real name?'

Margaret had begun weeping softly. 'I think Joe was his real name,' she said. 'I think it was some perverse point of pride with him. Like he could do all this to us without any fear that we would report him.'

'Did he say the other kidnappings had taken place in Mississippi?'

'No. But I assumed they had.'

'Could you recognise him from a photo?'

'Yes.'

'And the woman?' Chalmers asked McDill.

'I'd know her anywhere.'

'OK, we'll start by going through the Jackson police department mug books. And the National Crime Information Center computer. Are you two ready to look at a stack of pictures?'

'PICK UP THAT PHONE,' Karen ordered, pointing at the cordless beside Hickey. 'That's the private line.'

Hickey obeyed, but his eyes had a manic gleam that kept Karen's finger on the trigger.

'Call my husband's hotel room.'

'You're making a mistake, Karen.'

She raised the gun until it was pointed at his face, then spoke into the phone in her left hand. 'Abby, are you outside yet?'

'Yes.'

'Good. Get down out of sight.' She shifted the phone into the crook between her right shoulder and cheek. Now she could keep the pistol in her right hand while taking the private line from Hickey with her left. The phone on which Abby waited—Will's phone—handled both lines, but she didn't want to put Abby on hold unless she had to. 'Are you down in some bushes?'

'Uh-huh. They're itchy.'

'You sit tight right there. I'm calling Daddy, and we're going to straighten this out and come get you. Don't hang up, remember?'

'I'm not.'

'Have you got Will yet?' she asked Hickey.

He raised his hands. 'I'm bleeding to death here. Can't you stitch up my leg first?'

'The sooner you get Will on the phone, the sooner you stop bleeding.'

Hickey dialled a number and asked for suite 28021.

'Throw the receiver onto the bed.'

He did. She picked it up with her left hand and heard the phone ringing, then a female voice said, 'Hey.'

'Put Dr Jennings on the phone.'

'Who is this?'

'This is Mrs Jennings. And if you don't put him on the phone, I'm going to shoot your husband in the head.'

There was a stunned silence. Then the woman said, 'You can't do that. We've got your little girl.'

'Your husband's bleeding pretty badly right now, missy. You'd better get a move on.'

She heard a fumbling with the phone. Then Will said, 'Karen?'

'Will, thank God.'

'What's going on? Is Abby all right?'

'She got away from the man guarding her. She's hiding in the woods with a cellphone. I've got her on the other line right now.'

'My God! Where's Joe?'

'I'm holding a gun on him. If we call the police, can they trace the cellphone Abby's using? Can they find her?'

'I think they can triangulate cellphones pretty well. How far away from Jackson do you think she is?'

'An hour. Maybe more, maybe less.'

'It won't work,' Hickey said.

'Shut up!' Karen snapped.

'What's the matter?' asked Will.

'Hickey says tracing the phone won't work.'

'To hell with him. Look, I know the guy who runs CellStar. I did a gall bladder on his wife, and I played in a golf tournament with him.'

'Call him! He'll know what the police can do.'

'We need to know what cellular company Hickey's people are using. CellStar is the biggest, and he might have picked it for anonymity. Tell him to give you his cellphone.'

Karen gestured at Hickey with the pistol. 'Give me your cellphone.'

Hickey took a Nokia from his pocket and tossed it across the bed.

'I've got it,' she told Will.

'OK. Dial star-eight-one-one and see who answers.'

Karen bent down and without picking up the mobile, used her trigger finger to switch it on and punch the keys. Hickey watched her with a puzzled look in his eyes.

'Welcome to CellStar customer service,' said a computerised voice.

Karen hit END. 'It's CellStar.'

'Yes!' Will exulted. 'We finally caught a break. Stay on the line. I'll use Cheryl's cellphone to call my guy.'

She heard Will tell Hickey's wife to call directory assistance for the home number of a Harley Ferris in Ridgeland, Mississippi. Then he said, 'Karen, ask Hickey why he thinks we can't trace the phone.'

'Why can't we trace Huey's phone?' she repeated.

'Let me talk to that husband of yours.'

Karen tossed the cordless phone onto the bed. Hickey picked it up. 'Doc? You there?'

Karen said to Abby: 'I'm going to put you on hold for a few seconds, honey. I'm not hanging up, I'm just going to listen to Daddy for a minute. OK?'

Abby's voice rose to a frantic whisper. 'Don't hang up, Mama!'

'I'll be right back.' She hit the button that switched that phone to the private line.

'Let me explain something to you, Doc,' Hickey said to Will. 'In some ways tracing a cellphone is easy. 'Cause a cellphone ain't nothing but a radio and you can triangulate a radio. You look at the relative signal strengths between towers and figure a location down to yards. The problem, Doc—for you, I mean—is that not many towers are equipped to measure that stuff yet. Mississippi's five years behind the rest of the country. As usual. That's why I feel OK using cellphones in this operation. So, if you think the cops are gonna find your kid before Huey does, you're out of your mind. And if you're wondering why I'm telling you this, it's simple. I still want this thing to work. I still want my money. But if you bring in the cops or the FBI, I've got to cut my losses and run. That means when Huey finds the kid, he kills her.'

'But we know who you are,' Will pointed out. 'My wife has seen you and Huey. If you kill Abby, you're opening yourself to murder charges.'

'You're not thinking, Doc. Kidnapping alone is a death penalty offence. So I've got nothing to lose by killing her.' Hickey smiled at Karen. 'You starting to get the picture?'

Will said, 'Screw you, Joe. Put my wife back on.'

'I'm here,' said Karen. 'Abby's on hold. Let me get her back.' She switched her phone back to the main line. 'I'm back, baby. You OK?'

'No! I was scared. Don't get off any more.'

'I won't.' She motioned for Hickey to toss his phone back to her, then held it to her mouth. 'Go ahead, Will.'

'Cheryl's got Ferris's number from directory assistance. I'm using her phone to dial it now . . .' There was a pause, then Will came back on the line. 'I'm getting an answering machine. I'll keep calling till they wake up.' He fell silent for a moment. 'Look, you saw the guy who was holding Abby, right?'

'Yes.'

'Do you think he would kill her if Joe told him to?'

Karen covered the mouthpiece of the phone that connected her to Abby. 'I can't answer that. He's huge, and he's simple-minded. Hickey says he gets angry when children run from him, something about the way he was treated growing up. And Abby just ran from him.'

'Do you think Abby could hide from him until dawn? Or maybe walk to a road?'

'It's the middle of nowhere, Will.'

'But you left some insulin with her, right?'

'Yes. Hang on.' She swapped phones again. 'Abby? Do you have your ice chest with you? The one I left with Huey?'

'No. I picked it up when I first ran. But when I went back inside for the phone I forgot it.'

'That's all right. You're doing great. I'm talking to Daddy.'

'Are you coming to get me?'

'Yes. We're figuring it out right now. Don't make a sound, baby.' She put the phone down and picked up the one on which Will was still waiting. 'She doesn't have her insulin. She doesn't know how to inject herself even if she did.'

'I think she could do it if she had to.'

'She's only five years old, Will. Do we have any alternatives?'

'Abby gives herself up and we trust Joe to give her back after he gets the money?'

Karen looked across the bed at Hickey's glittering eyes, the bleeding leg. 'No. We've got to try to save her now.'

'Let me talk to him again,' Hickey said.

Karen threw the phone across the bed.

'Doc? Let me tell you a story. Me and Huey are cousins. Our mamas were sisters, and they both married sons of bitches, only Huey's daddy was the leaving kind of son of a bitch, and mine was the ass-whipping kind. After Huey's little sister died, he had to move down to Mississippi with us. Pop takes us deer hunting one day. We didn't let Huey carry a gun, of course, but you couldn't beat him for hauling dead deer out of the woods. Anyhow, I was climbing through this fence, and my gun went off. Pop was drunk, and he started yelling how he'd felt the bullet pass his cheek. He threw down his rifle and started whalin' on me right there in the woods. I was about thirteen. Huey was twelve. He was a big boy, though. He walks up behind Pop and grabs him around the arms, like he's hugging a tree. And he just holds him there. Pop's kicking and screaming and I know when he gets loose he's gonna tear me to pieces. I pick up my rifle and point it at him. But I can't shoot him too easy with Huey holding him, except point-blank in the head, which wouldn't look right.

'So Huey gets this scared look on his face and says, "I just wanted him to stop hitting you, Joey. I don't want to hurt him none." I say, "He ain't ever gonna stop. Not till he's dead. You kill him, Buckethead, and we'll be done with it." So Huey thinks for a minute. Then he picks Pop up and carries him over to this big rock and smashes his head against it till he stops wiggling. Huey didn't *want* to do that, Doc. But he did it. He won't want to hurt your little girl, either. But if I tell him to, he will. 'Cause he can't envision a world without cousin Joey in it. And if he thinks your little girl living means me going to prison, she'll die sure as old Pop did.'

Hickey listened to whatever Will said, then laid the phone near the middle of the bed, a confident smile on his face. Karen picked it up.

'What are we going to do?' she asked.

'While Hickey was telling his story, I called CellStar and tried to find out if Ferris is even in town. I told them it was a medical emergency. Their security department said he should be at home.'

'But you're still getting the machine?'

'Yes, but I'm going to keep ringing it. Somebody's bound to wake up eventually.'

HUEY COTTON PAUSED in the rutted road leading to the cabin and looked up at the sky. His heart was full of sadness, and his eyes felt fuzzy from staring into the dark trees. Huey experienced much of the world as colours. Like the woods. The woods had a green smell. Even at night, when you couldn't see the green, you could smell it.

Joey was two colours. Sometimes he was white like an angel, a guardian who floated at Huey's shoulder. But there was red in Joey, too, a hard little seed filled with dark ink, and sometimes it burst and bled out into the white, covering it completely. When Joey turned red, bad things happened and Huey had to do things he didn't like to do. But by doing them, he helped the red fade away.

Huey lowered his head and breathed deep. He could smell people sometimes, the way he smelt animals. Abby smelt like a towel fresh out of the dryer. Cleaner than anything he'd ever smelt. And she sparkled. He didn't understand why he couldn't find her in the dark, because she was silver and gold and should be reflecting the moonlight.

He looked into the dark mosaic of foliage, straining his eyes. The tree trunks looked silver-black. Moonlight dripped down the black leaves and hanging branches. He relaxed his eyes, which was a trick he had learned while hunting with Joey. Sometimes, if you let your eyes relax, they picked up things they never would if you were trying to see. As he looked into the shadows, something yellowy winked in the darkness.

He focused on the spot, but the yellowy light was gone.

He was close. The light was important, but something else had stirred the blood in his slow veins. The green smell had changed.

Twenty yards from the tractor shed, Abby crouched in the darkness, clenching the cellphone. The thick branches of the oak above blocked the moonlight. She couldn't see anything beyond the bushes that shielded her. She had no idea where Huey was. Only the reassuring glow of the phone's read-out panel kept her from bolting towards the lights of the cabin.

Hickey was sitting against the bedroom wall. 'You going to sew me up or what?' he asked.

'I haven't decided.'

'I'm getting exactly nowhere,' Will said in Karen's ear, his voice tight with frustration. 'Goddamn answering machine.'

'Mama?' Abby said in her other ear.

'What is it, baby?'

'I think I heard something.'

Karen's heart fluttered. 'Whisper, honey. What did you hear?'

'I don't know. How long till you get here?'

'Not long. Has the noise stopped?'

'I don't hear it right now. I'm scared it's a possum.'

Karen felt a hysterical relief. 'It's OK. A possum won't hurt you.'

'Mom, I heard it again.' Her whisper was barely audible now. 'Like somebody sneaking up.'

Karen fought a surge of panic. 'You have to be quiet. I want you to stop talking.'

'I feel better when we talk.'

'I know, sweetie, but—'

'Mama—'

In two nearly silent syllables, utter terror travelled from child to mother. Karen squeezed the phone tight enough to bruise her hand.

There was only silence. Then she heard a whimper, so soft that Abby had to be fighting a heroic battle to suppress it. Then a crash like breaking branches came down the line and Abby screamed.

'I found you, didn't I?' Huey said loudly.

Karen's heart turned to ice. 'ABBY!'

'What is it?' Will shouted in her ear.

'Joey?' said Huey, grabbing the cellphone from Abby.

'Put Abby back on!' Karen demanded. 'Please!'

'Where's Joey?'

'Well, well,' said Hickey, standing up. 'The worm has turned.'

Karen pointed the .38 at his chest. 'Make him put Abby back on!'

Hickey walked fearlessly around the bed. 'If you shoot me now, she's dead.' He brushed the gun aside and slapped her face, then stripped the phone from her hand. 'Huey? This is Joey. If you hear a shot, strangle that brat. Don't even wait to ask me a question, because I'll be dead. This bitch already stabbed me.'

Hickey grabbed Karen's wrist and squeezed until she dropped the .38. He picked it up. 'Tie the kid and gag her, Huey. I'll call you back.'

Without warning, Karen snapped. She flew at Hickey's face, meaning to claw out his eyes, but before she reached them, he slammed his fist into her sternum. The blow dropped her to the floor. As she lay there gasping, he picked up the phone that connected her to Will.

'Huey just found your kid, Doc. I hope you haven't talked to anybody yet, because if you have, Abby won't see second grade . . .'

Karen struggled to her knees. 'Please don't let him hurt her. She—'

'Shut your mouth.' Hickey hung up. 'And stitch up this leg.'

She stared up at him, panting like a winded runner.

'I own you,' he said in a quiet voice. 'You know that now.'

'I just want my little girl safe. Whatever that takes.'

Karen tried to put Abby out of her mind. If she didn't, she wouldn't be able to function. Bracing her hand on the bed, she got to her feet and opened Will's black bag.

nine

Huey stumbled through the dark with Abby in his arms and fear bubbling from his heart. Abby shrieked endlessly, so long and so loudly that he didn't know how she was breathing. He wished to God he could put his hands over his ears, but he needed them to carry her. The fear in her screams was the same fear he had known as a little boy. It set something vibrating in his chest. Joey had said to tie her up, but Huey didn't want to.

MIDNIGHT HAD PASSED, and the Jenningses' house stood dark and silent on its hill. Crickets cheeped in the pine trees, a truck droned out on the interstate, but the house itself was silent.

On the sleigh bed in the master bedroom, naked but for a towel across his midsection, Hickey held the bottle of Wild Turkey in his left hand and a halogen lamp from Will's study in his right. He aimed the light wherever she told him to, occasionally yelling when the needle pierced his unanaesthetised flesh.

As Karen sewed, she said softly, 'Why us?'

'Why *not* you? Huh? You think because you live out here in this suburban palace, you're immune to pain? My mother had throat cancer. That's the worst, man. "Why me?" she'd rasp all the time. "Dear Jesus, why me?" I'd ask the same thing. Why my mother? I'd look at the ceiling like God was up there listening and ask why. Then I finally figured it out. The joke was on me.'

Karen gazed intently at Hickey. Bitterness was etched in every line of his face, and his eyes were like black oil wells.

'It must be awful to be you,' she said.

'Sometimes,' he conceded. 'But tonight it's worse to be you.'

WILL STOOD at the picture window of the Cypress suite, staring out over the Gulf of Mexico. The first seconds after he realised that Huey had recaptured Abby had been hellish. Even armed with a pistol, Cheryl had felt compelled to lock herself in the marble bathroom for protection, so terrible had been his rage.

As it dissipated, his frustration grew. There was so much he didn't know. Hickey's overt motive was simple enough: money. But it seemed to Will that Hickey's plan was constructed to satisfy deeper urges than money. And Will needed to figure out what those were.

'What are you thinking about over there?' asked Cheryl.

She came out of the bathroom and climbed back into the bed, using the pillows to prop herself against the headboard.

'Not speaking to me?' she asked. 'Look, you ought to try to sleep. I've got to take the calls from Joey, so I have to stay awake. But you should crash. I'll wake you when it's time.'

'You think I can sleep with this going on?'

'You need to. You'll be a basket case in the morning if you don't.'

'I can't. Leave me alone, OK?'

'Look, you're standing there blaming yourself and trying to figure out a way to rescue your little girl. That's what they all do. But you can't. You're not Mel Gibson. You save your little girl by paying Joey the money. It's that simple.'

'I should trust Joe?'

'Joey's got a motto on this deal, Doc. The kid always makes it. That's how we've managed to keep on doing this.'

He turned back to the window. Cheryl's reassurances didn't mesh with the voice on the other end of the phone. There was hatred in Hickey's voice, a resentment so deep that Will could not see it stopping short of the maximum pain it could inflict.

'You want me to help you calm down?' Cheryl asked. 'I can chill you out. Whatever, you know. Back rub?'

'No, thanks.'

'Front rub?'

'Are you kidding?'

She smiled. 'Don't worry. Wifey won't ever know about it.'

'I said no, OK?'

Cheryl turned to the television, her lower lip pushed out like an angry child's.

SPECIAL AGENT BILL CHALMERS opened the door of the police squad room. Dr McDill and his wife had followed the FBI agent's car the few blocks from the Federal Building to police headquarters, and what they had come for now lay on the metal table in front of them. A stack of mug books two and a half feet high.

'There must be thousands of photos here,' McDill said.

'Easily. I'll be outside, accessing the NCIC computer. I'll check all past records of kidnappings in the Southeast, then hit the names "Joe", "Cheryl" and "Huey" for criminal records under actual names and aliases. "Joe" is common as dirt, but the others might ring a bell.'

After he went out, Margaret sat down at the table and opened one of the mug books.

'Are we doing the right thing?' she asked, looking up at her husband.

McDill gently squeezed her shoulder. 'Yes.'

'How do you know?'

'The right thing is always the hardest thing.'

ABBY SAT IN THE CORNER of the tatty sofa, crying inconsolably, her Barbie held tight against her. Huey sat on the floor six feet away, looking stricken.

'I didn't mean to scare you,' he said. 'I just did what Joey told me to. I have to do what Joey says.'

'He stole me from my mom and dad!' Abby wailed. 'You did, too!'

'How come you ran away? It's because I'm ugly, isn't it?'

Abby resumed crying, but she shook her head.

'You don't have to say it. I know. The kids in my school ran too.

Nobody liked me. But I thought we was friends. All I wanted to do was be nice. But you ran. How come?'

'I *told* you. You stole me away from my mom.'

'That's not it. You don't like me because I look like a monster.'

Abby fixed her swollen eyes on him. 'What you look like doesn't matter. Belle taught me that?'

Huey blinked. 'What?'

Abby rubbed her eyes and held out her gold-lamé-gowned Barbie. 'This is Belle. *Beauty and the Beast* Belle. Belle says it doesn't matter what you look like. It only matters what you feel inside. In your heart. And what you do.'

Huey's mouth hung slack.

'You never saw *Beauty and the Beast*?' Abby said incredulously.

He shook his head.

'Let's pretend I'm Belle, and you're Beast.'

'Beast?' He looked suddenly upset. 'I'm a beast?'

'Good Beast.' Abby wiped her runny nose. 'Beast after he turns nice. Not mean like at first.' She slid off the couch and held Belle out to him. 'Say something nice. And call me "Belle", remember?'

Tentatively, Huey said, 'I'm not going to let anything happen to you, Belle. I'm going to keep you safe till your mama comes.'

Abby smiled. 'Thank you, Beast. And if the villagers come and try to kill you, me and Mrs Potts and Chip will make them go away. They won't get you!'

Huey swallowed, his eyes bright.

'Now you say, "Thank you, Belle."'

'Thank you, Belle.'

Abby petted the doll's hair. 'Do you want to brush her hair? Just pretend like?'

Huey reached out and petted Belle's hair with his enormous hand.

'Good, Beast,' Abby murmured. 'Good Beast.'

KAREN WATCHED THE CLOCK beside her bed flash 2.30am. She was sitting in the chair in the corner, hugging her knees; Hickey lay on the bed, his injured leg propped high on some pillows, the Wild Turkey bottle beside him along with Will's .38. He was watching a Humphrey Bogart film on the television.

Karen had never known time to pass so slowly.

'You alive over there?' Hickey asked.

'Yes,' she replied.

'Then you ought to feel lucky.'

She sensed that Hickey was looking for a fight. She didn't intend to give him one.

''Cause a lot of people who ought to be alive aren't,' he said. 'You know?'

She wondered who he was thinking of. 'I know.'

'Bullshit you know.'

'I told you, I was a nurse.'

He glanced at her. 'You proud of it? People in agony waiting for pain medicine while nurses sit there painting their fingernails, watching the clock, waiting for their shift to end.'

She could not let that pass. 'I am proud I was a nurse. I know that happens. But nurses are stuck with doctors' orders. If they break them they get fired.'

Hickey scowled and drank from the Wild Turkey bottle. 'Don't get me started on doctors.'

Karen thought she remembered him saying that all the previous kidnappings had involved children of doctors. He'd said something about doctors collecting expensive toys. But that couldn't be the only reason he targeted them. Lots of people collected expensive things. Somehow, doctors were part of a vein of suffering that ran deep in Hickey's soul.

'When did your mother pass away?' she asked.

'What do you care?'

'I'm trying to understand what makes you so angry. Angry enough to do this to total strangers.'

'I'll let you in on a little secret, sunshine. You ain't strangers.'

'What?'

He smiled, and a wicked pleasure came into his face. 'The light dawning up there?'

A shadow seemed to pass behind Karen's eyes, a flickering fore-knowledge that made her shudder in the chair. 'What do you mean?'

'Your husband works at University Hospital, right?'

'That's right. That's where we met.'

'How romantic. But I have a little different feeling about the place. My mother died there.'

The transient fear that made her shudder before now took up residence in her heart.

'She was in for her throat cancer,' he said, almost to himself. 'They'd cut on her a bunch of times before. It was no big deal. But they were supposed to put some kind of special pantihose things on her during the operation. STDs or something.'

'SCDs,' Karen corrected him. 'Sequential compression devices. They keep the blood circulating in the legs while the patient is under anaesthesia.'

'Supposed to, anyway,' Hickey said. 'But they left them off, and she got some kind of clot. Sounds like Efrem Zimbalist.'

'An embolus.'

'That's it.'

'Will was the anaesthesiologist?'

'Fuckin'-A right he was. My mother died right there on the table. They told me nothing could be done. But I went back later and talked to the surgeon. He finally told me. It's the gas passer's job to make sure those SCD things are on the patient.'

'But that's not true!' Karen cried. 'That's the job of a nurse—if the surgeon has written the proper orders. The surgeon himself should check to be sure they're on.'

'The cutter told me the gas passer's supposed to check for it.'

'He was probably scared to death of you! He was shifting the blame wherever he could.'

A dark laugh from Hickey. 'He was scared, all right.' He leaned up on his elbow. 'Don't worry. That asshole paid, too. In full.'

'You sued him for malpractice?'

'Sued him?' Hickey laughed. 'I said he paid *in full*.'

'You mean you killed him?'

Hickey snapped his fingers. 'Just like that. No telling how many people I saved by wasting that butcher.'

Karen tried to remember Will mentioning a case like the one Hickey had described. But she couldn't. 'When exactly did this happen? I mean, when did your mother pass away? Will—'

'She didn't *pass away*, OK?' Hickey sat up in the bed. 'She was murdered. By doctors who didn't give a shit. Your old man wasn't even in the room when she started to go. He was there at the start and the end. Some assistant was in there the rest of the time.'

Nurse anaesthetist, Karen thought, her heart sinking. More and more, nurse anaesthetists were handling the bulk of routine operations. It lowered the cost to the patient and freed up time for the doctor to concentrate on difficult cases.

'Probably yapping on his cellphone to his stockbroker while my mother was croaking,' Hickey said, lying back. 'The bottom line is, your husband murdered my mother. And that's why we're here tonight, babe. Instant karma.'

Karen tried to think of a way to convince him of Will's innocence, but it was useless. His mind was made up. Until now, Abby's kidnapping had seemed a stroke of fate, terrible but random. But this was infinitely worse. Because from the moment it was born in Hickey's fevered mind, the crime was suffused with malice, driven by hatred and focused on revenge.

'How long have you been planning this?' she asked softly. 'I mean, you said you've done this to other doctors. Were they all involved in your mother's case?'

'Nah. I picked doctors for the reason I told you. They collect expensive toys, go off to meetings all the time. They're perfect marks. Your husband was already on my short list when he killed my mother. He just went to the top of the list.'

'You just want the money, right?' she said, watching his face.

'Sure.' He smiled, but his eyes were dead. 'What else?'

Karen kept her face motionless, but her soul was falling down a dark shaft. Abby wasn't meant to survive the kidnapping. She would live until Hickey's wife got the ransom money. Then she would wind up a corpse in a ditch somewhere. Hickey's other victims might have lived, but this time was different. This time it was not about money. He wanted to punish Will.

WILL LAY ON THE SOFA in the sitting room of the suite, a hot towel over his face. He had paced out a couple of miles on the sitting-room carpet, trying to burn off the desperate energy produced by his inability to help Abby. That exercise, combined with his earlier wrestling match with Cheryl, had aggravated his joints to the point that he had to take a powerful painkiller that he kept for emergency situations. The drug and the hot towel had tamped down the pain, but his brain was humming like an overloaded circuit. The QVC shopping network babbled incessantly from the bedroom, where Cheryl lay drinking her rum-and-Cokes.

What would it take to erode her loyalty to Hickey? A million dollars? Will could get a million in cash. It would take a few days, though. Which killed the idea. To be effective, bribe money would have to be in his hands before the ransom pick-up tomorrow.

In spite of Cheryl's assurances that waiting out the night was the way to get Abby back, he was certain she was wrong.

The towel on his face had gone cold. He threw it on the floor and sat up on the sofa. He needed more information. Cheryl claimed this kidnapping was exactly like all the others, but it wasn't. What made it different? Was it something Cheryl herself did not know? With a groan of pain, Will got up and walked into the bedroom.

IN JACKSON, Dr James McDill took a sip of coffee and rubbed his eyes. He scanned the rows of unfamiliar women, then wearily turned another page. His breath caught in his throat. Staring up from the mug book like a graduation portrait was Cheryl's innocent face.

'Agent Chalmers! This is her!'

The FBI agent looked over. 'Are you sure?'

'Positive.'

Chalmers walked over, took the photo out of its plastic sleeve and read from its back. 'Cheryl Lynn Tilly. I'll be damned. She *did* use her real name.'

He walked over to the computer he'd been using and began typing in the information from the photo. After several seconds, data from Washington began flashing up onto the screen.

'She's got some small-time collars,' Chalmers said. 'One prostitution arrest. Nothing violent. You're positive it's her?'

'Absolutely.'

'I'll make a copy of this photo and fax it down to the Beau Rivage. Maybe someone on the staff down there has seen her.'

'What will you do if they have?'

Chalmers raised his eyebrows and took a deep breath. 'Call in the troops. If she's down there, we have to assume you're right. There's a kidnapping in progress. And that is a major situation.'

KAREN ROCKED SLOWLY but ceaselessly in her chair, her arms round her shins, her chin buried between her knees. Hickey was still lying on the bed, his eyes glued to Bogart. Externally, Karen could maintain calm, but inside she was coming apart. The knowledge that Hickey meant to kill Abby was unendurable. She had to warn Will.

Food was her best excuse to get out of the bedroom, but there was no guarantee that Hickey wouldn't follow her into the kitchen. For a while she had entertained the hope that the whiskey might put him to sleep, but he seemed immune to it.

She stopped rocking. Hickey had said something to her and she'd missed it. 'Did you say something?' she asked.

'I said I'm starving. Go fix something.'

She forced herself to sound peeved. 'What would you like?'

'Damn it,' Hickey said. 'I don't know. Something hot.'

'There's some crawfish étouffée I could heat up.'

'Yeah.' He glanced over at her, his eyes bleary. 'Put it in an omelette.'

'Sure.' She got up and went out.

As soon as she cleared the door, she sped to a silent run. In the kitchen, she slid a skillet onto the hob, switched the gas to high, then opened the refrigerator and took out eggs, margarine and a dish of seasoned crawfish tails in a roux. The étouffée went into the microwave, and a glob of margarine into the skillet. Then she grabbed the phone off the wall and punched in the number of Will's office.

'Anaesthesiology Associates,' said the answering service operator.

'This is Karen Jennings. I need to—'

'Could you speak up, please?'

She raised the volume of her whisper. 'This is Karen Jennings. I need to get a message to my husband on his SkyTel pager.'

'Go ahead, ma'am.'

'You've got to do something, they're going to . . .'

'Just a second. Is that the message?'

'Yes—no, wait.' She couldn't simply state the situation to a stranger—the operator was liable to call the police herself. With shaking hands she broke the three eggs into the skillet. 'The message is, "You've got to do something before morning. Abby is going to die no matter what. Karen." Do you have that?'

'Yes, ma'am. This sounds like a real emergency.'

'It is. Wait. Add "Confirm receipt by email".'

'I don't take many messages like this, Mrs Jennings. Shouldn't you maybe call nine-one-one?'

'That's not appropriate. This is a little girl with liver cancer. Will's working with the transplant team, and things are very dicey.'

'Lord,' said the operator. 'I'll get this entered right away.'

'Thank you so much.' Karen hung up the phone, her hand shaking.

'That doesn't smell half bad.'

Karen froze.

Hickey was standing in the kitchen door in his bloody towel. He looked into her eyes for a moment, then past her. His eyes went cold. 'What are you doing by that phone?'

To avoid Hickey's gaze, she turned and looked at the phone. Tacked around it were cards, photographs and Post-it notes. She reached into the midst of them and pulled a small photo off the wall.

'I was looking at Abby's school picture. I still can't believe this is happening.'

The microwave beeped. She took out the étouffée and spooned it into the omelette. She sensed Hickey moving closer, but didn't look up. With shaking hands she folded the egg over the crawfish.

His fingers fell on her forearm, sending a shock up her spine. 'Look at me,' he said in a hard voice.

She did. His eyes were preternaturally alert, the eyes of a predator studying its prey. 'What?' she said.

Hickey just stared, registering each movement of her facial muscles, every pulse beat in her neck.

'It's going to burn,' she said, reaching for the spatula. As she slid it under the omelette, he slipped his arms around her waist, as though he were a loving husband watching his wife make breakfast. She forced herself to continue, lifting the omelette from the pan and dropping it onto a plate.

'I own you,' he said. 'Don't forget that.'

'How can I?'

'Bring the food back to the bed,' he said. Then he let his hands fall, turned and limped up the hallway.

She had no idea how long she'd been holding her breath. Her legs felt like water and she gripped the counter to hold herself up.

ten

Will sat in the chair by the bed, facing Cheryl. She was still propped against the headboard—gun beside her, QVC chattering in the background—but she had finally slipped on one of Will's white button-down shirts. For an hour he had probed her about Hickey, but to no avail. She had given him all the biography she felt safe giving.

He changed tack by asking about Huey instead of Joe, but suddenly something buzzed against his side. He jumped out of the chair and, looking down, he realised it was the new SkyTel pager.

'What's with you?' Cheryl asked.

'Something crawled over me.' He made a big show of looking under the chair cushion. 'A damn roach or something.'

She laughed. 'I wouldn't be surprised.'

Will was dying to check the pager. He wasn't on call, so the message had almost certainly come from Karen.

'Do you mind if I use the bathroom?' he asked.

Cheryl shrugged and returned her attention to QVC. 'Hey, if you got to go . . .'

Will walked into the bathroom and closed the door, then whipped the pager off his belt and punched the retrieve button. The green back-lit screen scrolled: YOU'VE GOT TO DO SOMETHING BEFORE MORNING. ABBY IS GOING TO DIE NO MATTER WHAT. KAREN. CONFIRM RECEIPT BY EMAIL.

He scrolled the message again, staring in shock at the words. Had Karen learned something new about Hickey's plan? Her meaning was clear: he would have to risk Abby's life to save her life.

As he stared at the message, the phone beside the toilet rang. He looked at his watch: 3.00am. Hickey's regular check-in call. He heard Cheryl's muffled voice through the bathroom door as she picked up the other extension. A few words, then silence again.

Wetting a flannel with hot water, he wrung it out and pressed it to his face. As the blood came to his cheeks, his mind pierced the fog that had blinded him for the past hours. And at the centre of his brain was awareness of a single fact: he had exactly thirty minutes to save Abby. The thirty minutes between check-in calls. Whether it was this half-hour or the next, that was the window of opportunity.

He threw the flannel into the basin. He had to know what Cheryl knew. There was a chance that she'd lied before, that she knew exactly where Abby was being held. But it wouldn't be enough for her to spill what she knew. She would have to cooperate until Abby was found. Play her role for Hickey during the check-in calls. What could possibly persuade her to do that? The bruises on her body proved she could take punishment, and God alone knew what horrors Hickey had visited upon her in the past . . . And yet . . .

Her eyes had shone when she told him about the contract she'd had with Hollywood producers, the contract Hickey had terminated. She hadn't tried to make it more than it was, but it had been a step up. It was also a step away from Joe Hickey, and on some level Cheryl must have known that, too. Known it, and believed she'd been born for more than prostitution and crime.

To betray Hickey, she would have to believe she could escape him. That would take money. Enough not merely to run but to vanish. To

become someone else. He flushed the toilet and opened the bathroom door.

'Was that Joe?' he asked.

'Yeah. Everything's cool, just like I said it would be.'

Will walked into the bedroom, his eyes on the gun beside Cheryl.
But as he neared the bed, something made him continue round it
into the sitting room. He looked at his notebook computer on the
desk. Eight hours ago he had been running video clips from that
machine, dreaming of the royalties he would realise on the drug he
had worked so hard to develop. What would that money be worth if
Abby lay in a coffin beneath the ground? How much time had he
spent away from home, away from her, working on the trials for
Restorase? How many hours wasted thinking up the name?

His rambling train of thought crashed to a halt like a locomotive
hitting a wall. His eyes went from the computer to his sample case.
Restorase. He had four vials of the prototype drug inside the case.
But more importantly, he had two vials of Anectine, which was the
trade name for succinylcholine, the relaxant that Restorase counter-
acted. There was also a package of syringes: two conventional, and
two of the special contact syringes.

A chill went through Will as he remembered the clinical trials of
the past year, images that would scare the hell out of a layman.

He closed his eyes. The woman in the next room had put Abby's
life at risk. Dropped her down a black hole of terror. Whatever dis-
advantages fate had handed Cheryl, she had chosen to help Hickey
of her own free will—not once, but six times, by her own admission.
Six children put through hell. Whatever she had to endure now was
only what she deserved.

He walked back into the bedroom, stopped at the edge of the bed
and looked down at Cheryl.

She glanced up, her eyes curious. 'What?'

'I want to kiss you.'

Her cheeks went pink. 'You what?'

'I want to kiss you.'

'I don't do that,' she said in a flustered voice. 'That's too personal.
No kiss.' But then she undid the top four buttons of the shirt 'You
can kiss here.'

He smiled and bent towards her breast.

'What changed your mind?' she asked in a softer voice.

As his cheek brushed her skin, he reached across her as though to prop himself on the bed, then closed his hand around the butt of her Walther. When he rose up and pointed the automatic at her face, she blinked with incomprehension.

'What are you doing?'

Will handed her his pager. 'Hit the RETRIEVE button!'

She fumbled with the device, then found the button. Her eyes narrowed as she read the words scrolling on the screen.

'I just got that message. Do you understand what it means?'

She shook her head.

'Joe is going to kill my little girl whether he gets the ransom or not.'

'He is not!'

'If my wife says he is, he is.'

'Joey would never let her send this message. This is a mistake.'

'No mistake, Cheryl. Karen is smarter than Joe, and she found a way. It's that simple. Now, you're about to tell me where Abby is.'

She blinked at him. 'I can't. I don't know where she is.'

'For your sake, I hope you do.'

Confidence suddenly returned to her face. 'Are you going to shoot me? Come on, Doc. We've been over this.'

'I'm not going to shoot you. Not with a bullet, anyway.'

A shadow of fear played over her face. 'What do you mean? Joey's going to call back in twenty-five minutes. If I don't answer, Abby's dead. It's that simple. And if I do, and I say one word, the same thing. And you don't know what that word is. So give me back my gun, and let's forget this happened.'

'Remember when you said there was nothing I could do to you that hadn't been done before?'

She gave him a blank look. 'Yeah?'

'You were wrong about that.' He transferred the Walther to his left hand and grabbed her arm with his right. 'Unhook my belt and pull it out of the loops,' he said.

She did.

'Bring that chair over here.' He pointed at a straight-backed chair against the wall.

'Why?'

He slapped her face.

A bitterness beyond anything he'd ever seen came into her eyes. But with the bitterness came something else. Familiarity. This was a language she understood. She climbed off the bed, picked up the chair, and brought it back.

'Sit in it.'

She did. He put the gun down and wrapped the belt round her torso and the chair back, then buckled it. From the bathroom he took a terry-cloth robe belt and used it to tie her lower legs to the legs of the chair.

'I'm going to scream,' she said.

'Go ahead. Scream your head off. Then you explain to Joe why he won't be getting his money in the morning.'

'You're killing your kid,' she said. 'Don't you get that?'

Will stood back and considered his handiwork. Screaming could become a problem, even if Cheryl didn't mean it to be. Fear was an unpredictable thing. He went into the other room and brought back a pair of socks and his sample case, then stuffed the socks into Cheryl's mouth. Her eyes went wide.

He dragged the chair closer to the bed, then bent and flipped Cheryl and the chair onto the mattress. She lay moulded in the shape of the chair, feet sticking up like a woman in stirrups.

'If you listened to my speech last night,' he said, 'you know a little about paralysing muscle relaxants.'

Cheryl looked confused. She probably hadn't listened to his presentation; she had been trying to seduce him with her eyes, all the time thinking about the moment when she'd have to con him into taking her into his room in the hope of sex.

Will removed a conventional syringe from his sample case. Cheryl's eyes locked onto it as he popped off its cap, poked the needle through the rubber seal of the vial of Anectine and drew sixty milligrams into the barrel.

'This is succinylcholine,' he said in a calm voice. 'Shortly after I inject it, your skeletal muscles will cease to function. The skeletal muscles are the ones that move your bones. But your diaphragm is also made of skeletal muscle. So, while you'll be able to see, hear and think normally, you won't be able to move. Or breathe.'

Her eyes widened.

'You don't have to go through this,' he said. 'All you have to do is tell me where Abby is, and I'll put this syringe back in the case.'

She nodded frantically.

He pulled the socks from her mouth. She gasped for air, then said, 'I swear to God, I don't know! Please don't stick me with that!'

As he shoved the socks back into Cheryl's mouth, she tried to bite his hand. He climbed onto the bed and sat on her rib cage.

'You can scream,' he said. 'But the sound won't last five seconds after I inject you. Listen to me, Cheryl. I've seen murderers turned into whimpering babies by this stuff. They lay paralysed, soiling themselves, turning blue. It must be like being buried alive.'

Cheryl fought the restraining belts like a madwoman, rocking Will and the chair in her attempt to get loose. He jabbed the point of the needle into her jugular vein, and she stopped instantly.

'You have a choice. You can help me save my little girl. Or you can find out what it's like to be dead.'

She closed her eyes, then opened them again. Tears ran down from their corners. '*I nono!*' she choked through the socks. '*I sweahta gaa!*'

'You know something.'

She shook her head violently.

Will depressed the plunger of the syringe.

Cheryl's scream died in her throat. Her eyelids began to flutter, and her facial muscles twitched rapidly. Her arms flew up and across her chest, then her body went rigid. Her eyes were frozen open, filled with limitless horror. She lay as still as a stone angel on a grave. An angel with screaming eyes.

He pulled the socks from her mouth, then climbed off her chest and sat beside her. 'I know it's bad. Maybe you feel as scared as my little girl feels right now. We're going to do this over and over until you tell me where Abby is, so you'd do well to tell me everything as soon as you can.'

Cheryl's face was going grey. Hypoxia was taking its toll, and consciousness would soon wink out. In the time it took him to reach down to the sample case for a vial of Restorase, Cheryl's skin took on a bluish cast. He drew fifty milligrams into a syringe and shot the drug into the vein at the crook of her elbow. Twenty seconds later, her eyelids fluttered. She blinked, and then her lachrymal glands began draining tears again.

'I didn't like doing that but you forced me to. Joe forced me to. I know you don't want to go through it again. So, talk to me.'

'You buh . . . bastard,' Cheryl whispered.

'Where's Abby, Cheryl?'

'I told you I don't know!'

'You know more than you're telling me. You couldn't have pulled this off five times before without knowing something. Where's the pick-up? Where are you going to meet Joe to give him the money?'

'The Truckers' Rest. A motel. Near Brookhaven.'

'You see?' he said. 'That's something I didn't know before. Keep talking.'

'That's all I know. Please don't do it again. I'm begging you.'

'Where is Abby?' he asked.

Deep sobs racked her chest. Cheryl had seen a glimpse of hell and the experience had shattered her. 'If I tell you anything,' she said, 'Joey will kill me.'

'Joe is two hundred miles away. I'm right here. If you tell me where Abby is, the needle goes back into the case, and you can have all the money you need to start over somewhere else. Any place you want.'

'You've forgotten something. When Joey calls back, I can kill your kid with one word. And I think I'm going to, for what you did.'

Will kept his face calm. 'You don't want Abby to die. And you don't want to die yourself. It's one thing to talk about death, or flirt with it when you're depressed, but you've got a taste of it now. And it's bad. Isn't it?'

She closed her eyes.

'You think that because nothing happened to the kids those other times, nothing will happen to Abby. But you're wrong. There's something different about this time. And Karen found out what it is.'

He pulled her chin over until she faced him. 'Open your eyes and tell me why this time is different. Don't make me inject you again.'

She opened her eyes. 'You killed Joey's mother.'

Will blinked. 'What are you talking about?'

'Last year, Joey's mother died during an operation. The doctor who did the surgery told Joey it was your fault. He said you weren't paying attention. You weren't even in the room.'

'What?' He thought back over the past year's cases. Some were clear, others a blur. He did about 850 a year, but he almost always remembered a death. 'Was her name Hickey?'

'No. She'd remarried. Simpkins was her name.'

'Simpkins . . . Simpkins?'

'Joey said you wouldn't remember it. That's how little it mattered to you. But it matters to him.'

'I do remember! The SCD case. The surgeon operated without SCDs, and Mrs Simpkins developed a pulmonary embolus.' It was all coming back now. The surgeon had been a visiting professor. 'Viola Simpkins . . . I had nothing to do with that death. It was a terrible mistake, but it wasn't my responsibility.'

'The surgeon told Joey it was.'

'Well, I'll tell him it wasn't. I'll make the damn surgeon tell him.'

'That might be tough. He's dead. Joey killed him.'

Will suddenly felt cold. Hickey had murdered a surgeon because his mother died on an operating table? 'Karen must have found this out. And that's why Joey is going to kill Abby. To punish me.'

'He never told me that,' Cheryl insisted.

'Because he knew you might not go along.' Will gripped her arms. 'Cheryl, you've got to tell me where Abby is. Joe's going to murder her. She's only five years old!'

She looked him dead in the eye. 'I told you—I—don't—know.'

Will drew seventy milligrams of Anectine into the syringe and climbed back onto her chest. She began to fight beneath him.

'Please, *please*,' she begged. 'Don't do it!'

Will pressed the needle against her flesh.

'She's somewhere west of Hazelhurst!' Cheryl cried.

He kept the needle in her vein. 'Where Highway 28 crosses I-55?'

'That's it! There's a shack ten or fifteen miles up that road. You go down two or three logging roads before you get to it.'

'That's useless. There are a hundred logging roads through those woods. Hunting camps, everything.'

'That's all I know! For Christ's sake, I'm trying to help you!'

'How is Joe calling Huey? Is he using a land line or a cellphone?'

'Cellular. There's no regular phone out there.'

'What else?'

She shook her head. 'That's all I know! I swear to God!'

Was she holding something back? Will considered injecting her again, but he didn't want to risk it. He needed her alive and cooperative for Hickey's next call. The important thing was to get a cellular trace started around Hazelhurst, if possible. He dialled Harley Ferris's number yet again.

'Joey's going to be calling in a couple of minutes,' Cheryl said.

Will's watch read 3.26am. Three rings. Four. Ferris's answering machine clicked and began speaking. Will's finger was on the disconnect button when he heard a click, then a clatter.

'Hello?' said a male voice. 'Hello! Harley Ferris here.'

'Thank God. Mr Ferris, this is Dr Will Jennings. Do you remember me? I was the anaesthesiologist on your wife's gall bladder surgery. She requested me.'

'I know you,' Ferris said. 'We've played golf together. But it's three thirty in the morning, Doctor. What the hell's going on?'

'This is an emergency. I want you to listen very carefully. My daughter's in desperate trouble. You can help her. But before I tell you anything, you've got to promise not to call the police.'

'The police? I don't understand?'

'Mr Ferris, my daughter was kidnapped yesterday. I can't go to the police because the kidnappers will kill her if I do.'

Ferris processed this information. 'I hear you,' he said finally.

'I'm in a hotel in Biloxi. My wife's at home in Annandale. One of the kidnappers is with her. My daughter is being held somewhere in the woods around Hazelhurst, Mississippi. Every thirty minutes, the leader of the kidnappers calls the location where my daughter's being held. I know they're using a CellStar telephone. Can you trace that call for me?'

'Are both parties using cellphones?'

'The man on the receiving end is using one. There's no land line where he is. He's ten or fifteen miles from Hazelhurst, down some logging road. That's all I know at this point.'

'I'd have to get a vehicle down there to trace it, and our vans could be anywhere in the state right now.'

'Mr Ferris, if we don't find that phone, my five-year-old daughter will be dead by morning. Even if I pay the ransom. It's not really the money they want. They want to hurt me. Can you help?'

'Doctor, it sounds to me like we should call the FBI.'

'No! They've thought of that. Planned for it.'

Silence. 'Damn it. OK. I'll see what I can do.'

'I need your word that you won't call the FBI.'

'I'll keep quiet until morning. But if I get a trace on that phone, we're calling the FBI. Agreed?'

'You find that phone, I'll be begging for a SWAT team.'

'Where are you now?'

'I'm at the Beau Rivage Casino, Suite 28021. Call as soon as you know anything, but not on the hour or half-hour. That's when the kidnappers make their check-in calls.'

'I'll call as soon as I know something. Hang tough, Doctor. We'll figure something out.'

'Thank you.'

Will hung up, his heart pounding.

'Joey's going to call any second.' He turned to Cheryl. 'What are you going to tell him?'

'Wait and see, you son of a bitch. You'd better untie me.'

Letting Cheryl answer Hickey's next call could be the biggest mistake he ever made. But he had no choice. He could hold the needle against Cheryl's neck as she answered, but instinct told him to show some faith. He undid the ties that bound her.

'I don't think you want my little girl to die. You're not that far gone. You were a little girl once, too. Not so long ago, either.'

The phone began to ring. The sound constricted Will's chest. 'My daughter's life is in your hands. Help her, and anything I have is yours. All the money you'll ever need.'

'You'd better answer that phone, Doctor.'

He took a deep breath, then picked up the phone, handed it to Cheryl, and leaned down to listen.

'Yeah?' she said.

'Everything OK?' Hickey asked.

She looked at Will, her eyes inches away.

'Yeah,' she said finally. 'Everything's cool.'

He felt light-headed. He was squeezing her arm with gratitude when Hickey said, 'What's the matter? You don't sound right.'

Cheryl looked at Will. 'I'm getting tired,' she said.

'Take one of the pills I gave you. I need you sharp.'

'I know. I'll talk to you in a half-hour.'

Will heard the click as Hickey hung up. With shaking hands he took the phone from Cheryl and set it in its cradle. 'Thank you,' he said.

She scowled and rolled off the bed. 'Now what?'

'Now we wait for the phone trace. And pray.'

eleven

While Cheryl lay on the sofa sipping a can of Coke, Will had set up his computer on the dining table in the front room of the suite. He was composing an email to Karen to tell her about Ferris and the phone tracing, but he needed a code, in case Hickey read the message. He and Karen had watched thousands of movies together. It took him less than a minute to come up with a phrase he was sure she would understand. The message he typed was: ABBY IS GOING TO MAKE IT. TRUST ME. DO YOU BELIEVE THE CONDOR IS AN ENDANGERED SPECIES? He was sure Karen would understand it. He plugged his computer into the data port of the hotel phone and sent the email. Seconds later the phone began to ring.

It was only 4.15—halfway between the scheduled check-in calls.

'That has to be Ferris,' Will said, grabbing the receiver. 'Will Jennings.'

'Harley Ferris, Doctor. Our computers show a call just after four o'clock, processed through the tower that serves the Hazelhurst area. It came from one of the land lines at your house.'

'Did you get any idea of the receiver's position?'

'No. Even if we'd had a tracing van there, it would have been tough. The call lasted less than fifteen seconds, and the phone was switched off afterwards. It's time to bring the FBI in on this.'

'Not yet, Harley. Where are your tracing vans?'

'They're up in Tunica County.'

Will gritted his teeth. Tunica County was practically Memphis. That meant a minimum of three hours before the vans could get to Hazelhurst. 'That's eight o'clock before they could even start tracing.'

'Exactly. I told one crew to hit the road and come on down, but you're right about the time. Listen . . . there's a guy who used to work for us, an engineer. He's retired, but he keeps his hand in. I'll give him a call. He's probably got enough equipment in his garage to do a trace from his truck.'

Will's heart surged. 'Do you think he would?'

'He's a good man. We're probably looking at an hour or more to get him and his equipment on site, but that beats the Tunica crew.'

Will gave Ferris the numbers of the direct SkyTel line and Cheryl's cellphone. 'I should be here,' he said, 'but there's no telling what could happen. Call me as soon as you know anything.'

'I will,' Ferris promised. 'I hope God's paying attention tonight.'

As Will hung up, he felt Cheryl's hand on his arm. Despite what he'd done to her earlier, she was watching him with empathy.

'After you and I pick up the ransom from the bank, what are you supposed to do?' Will asked.

'I call Joey,' Cheryl said. 'Then we meet at the motel in Brookhaven.'

'You're supposed to bring me along?'

'Yeah.'

'Have you always brought the husband?'

She hesitated.

'Cheryl—'

'No. This is the first time.'

'I told you this time is different. Joe wants to kill Karen and Abby in front of me.'

'That's not it.'

'Yes, it is. Only I can't believe Joe would put himself, Abby, and the money in one place. If he does, he's vulnerable. He has to assume that I could torture the name of the motel out of you, which means the FBI could come down on that place like the wrath of God.'

'It's the truth. The Trucker's Rest Motel, in Brookhaven.'

'That may be what he told you. But that's not how it's supposed to go down. You must know something more, Cheryl. *Think*.'

'I think you should just pay Joey the money. That's the way to get your kid back. That's the way the other guys did it.'

'I'm not the other guys. I'm down for special treatment.'

KAREN DOWNLOADED Will's email at 4.25am. Getting into the study to check for it wasn't difficult because Hickey had finally passed out on the bed. She stared at the message. The first part was clear enough. But the last sentence stumped her. Do you believe the condor is an endangered species? It had to be some kind of code.

'Condor,' she said softly. 'Condor . . . condor.' And then she had it.

'Condor' was Robert Redford's code name in the film *Three Days of the Condor*. She'd had a crush on the star for years and knew almost every line he spoke in the film. The words 'Do you believe the condor is an endangered species?' had been spoken over the phone by Redford to Max Von Sydow, who played the assassin. It marked the turning point, when Redford turned the tables on the men trying to kill him. *That* was Will's message. He had somehow turned the tables on Hickey.

FIFTEEN MILES SOUTH of the Jenningses' house, Dr James McDill and his wife sat on a couch in the office of the Special Agent-in-Charge of the Jackson field office of the FBI. His name was Frank Zwick. A short, fit man in his late forties, Zwick had been on the phone for the past half-hour, talking to bank presidents, helicopter pilots and officials, constantly smoothing his too-black hair as he talked.

McDill's identification of Cheryl Lynn Tilly at the Jackson police station had precipitated a storm of FBI activity. After Agent Chalmers phoned Zwick, the SAC had summoned the McDills to the Federal Building along with eight field agents. Now they all stood or sat around his office, as Zwick addressed them.

'Here's where we stand. One: the ransom. Every bank within thirty miles of Biloxi is set to report incoming wire transfers greater than twenty-five thousand dollars to this office. Two: tactical capability. We'll use our special weapons team. We'll also have twenty more out of New Orleans for surveillance duty in Biloxi. Three: air support. We'll have choppers both here and in Biloxi, ready for aerial surveillance and/or pursuit and assault.' Zwick made a steeple of his fingers and looked each of his agents in the eye. 'Questions?'

Agent Chalmers said, 'Sir? I wonder if we're not jumping the gun a little on this. Dr McDill identified Cheryl Lynn Tilly from the mug books. But that doesn't necessarily mean that the crime she took part in last year is actually being repeated this year. Does it?'

Zwick gave them a patronising smile. 'Gentlemen, ten minutes ago, our resident agent in Gulfport showed a faxed photo of Cheryl Lynn Tilly to a bellboy in the Beau Rivage Hotel. That bellboy is positive he saw Tilly in the hotel yesterday afternoon. Our resident agent and that bellboy are reviewing the casino's security tapes as we speak,' Zwick went on. 'If they spot her, they'll do a video capture and email it up here for Dr McDill to look at. Until then, we have to assume that he's right. There is a kidnapping-for-ransom taking place within this jurisdiction. To quote Sir Arthur Conan Doyle—through the immortal words of Sherlock Holmes—the game is afoot.'

In that moment McDill had a premonition of disaster. At the core of all this frantic activity was a kidnapped child who could die at any moment. And that took the situation about as far from a game as you could get.

By 5.56AM, WILL WAS CLOSE to cracking. His overtaxed mind was running in circles, and his efforts to locate Abby by tracing Huey's cellphone had come to nothing because, at the time of Hickey's 4.30 check-in call, Ferris's retired engineer had not been close enough to Hazelhurst to do any good. When 5.00 had ticked round, Will had his hopes up. But the five o'clock call never came.

He waited ten minutes. After that he could stand no more. For all he knew, Karen had somehow provoked Hickey into killing her. An acid lump clogged his throat as he dialled home. But when the phone was picked up, it was Karen's voice, not Hickey's, on the line.

The second Will spoke, she began to sob. He was certain something must have happened to Abby, but Karen explained that her tears were simply a reaction to the stress. Hickey had missed the last check-in call because he'd passed out drunk in their bed.

'I woke him for the four thirty call. He told Huey he wouldn't be calling back for another hour at least. He said he had to sleep.'

Hickey hadn't bothered to inform Cheryl of this change of plan.

'What are you doing to help Abby?' Karen asked.

'I got Ferris. We're trying to trace Huey's phone. But if Hickey isn't calling him, we can't trace it.'

'Maybe I should wake him up and tell him I have to talk to Abby.'

'Do you think he'd let you?'

'Probably not. But what choice do we have?'

'Cheryl is helping us now. To a certain extent, anyway. I'll explain why later. But tell me why you think Hickey is planning to kill Abby.'

'He thinks you killed his mother.'

'That's what I got from Cheryl. OK . . . let Hickey sleep until six. But if he hasn't made another call by then, you'll have to get him up and on the phone to Huey. Tell him you won't wire the money unless you have proof that Abby's OK.'

'I will.' Karen whispered goodbye and clicked off.

When five thirty rolled round, the phone didn't ring. Now it was six. The ringing telephone stopped Will's breath in his throat. He prodded Cheryl, who was snoring softly. She rubbed her eyes, picked up the phone, then nodded to indicate that it was Hickey on the phone. She said her usual 'Everything's cool,' then signed off. In a few seconds her eyes closed.

Two minutes later, the phone rang again. Like an automaton, Cheryl stirred and started to answer, but Will grabbed the receiver. 'Hello?'

'Harley Ferris, Will.'

'What have you got?'

'The subject in your house made a land line call that went through the Hazelhurst tower just after six. The call lasted sixteen seconds, and the trace target switched off his phone immediately after the call, but my man down there has narrowed the search area to about seven square miles.'

Will groaned. 'You haven't notified anyone official, have you?'

'No. But it's time we did. These are very short calls, Doctor. And our next chance for a more exact trace—when the CellStar van gets down there—is an hour from now.'

'We've still got some time. There's nothing the FBI could be doing right now that we can't. You have all my numbers. Thanks.'

He hung up and walked back to the window. Dawn was coming, a lighter blue hovering in the indigo sky, far to his left.

'Think with your head, Joe,' he said softly. 'Not your heart. Think about the money, not your mother. The money's what you want.'

KAREN FELT HANDS on her body and screamed.

'Shut up!' snapped a male voice. 'It's time to get up.'

She blinked and saw Hickey leaning over her. He was shaking her shoulders. 'What happened?' she asked.

'You fell asleep.'

Hickey was dressed and daylight was streaming through the bedroom curtains. 'God, no,' she breathed, unable to accept she'd fallen asleep while Abby's life was in jeopardy. 'What time is it?'

'Time to shower and doll yourself up for the Man. Fix your face.'

Her eyes went to the digital clock on her bedside table: 8.02am.

'Is it time to get Abby?'

'You mean, get the money. Play your part right, *then* you get Abby.'

'I know what's supposed to happen today,' she said. 'I know . . . what you want to do.'

He looked intrigued. 'What's that?'

'You want to hurt Will. Because of your mother.'

His eyes went cold.

'I understand that anger,' she said quickly. 'And I'm not going to try to convince you that you're wrong about Will, even though I believe you are. You think you're right, and that's all that matters.'

'You got that right.'

'All I'm asking you to do—no, *begging* you to do—is to take pity on a five-year-old girl. Use me instead.'

Hickey's eyes narrowed. 'Use you?'

'To punish Will. Kill me instead of Abby.'

'Nobody's going to die today,' he said. 'Let me tell you a little secret. This is the last job I'll ever pull. In a few days I'll be in Costa Rica. A rich expatriate, safe from extradition. Today is my grand exit. Take that shower and get some nice clothes on. You've got to put on a good show for your broker this morning.'

THE STINK OF OLD EGGS drifted from the room-service tray Cheryl had ordered. All Will had managed to get down was some tea and a biscuit, but she had eaten a massive breakfast. Hickey's last check-in call had come three minutes ago—at exactly eight o'clock—after which Cheryl had informed Will that they would be leaving for the Biloxi branch of the Magnolia Federal Bank within the hour.

Harley Ferris had not yet reported in, but Will still held out hope. After their hell-for-leather ride from Tunica County, CellStar's first-string tracing team had reached Hazelhurst at 7.15am. At least they'd been on station for the 8.00am call—if Hickey had made one to Huey.

The ring of the telephone floated through the spacious sitting room. Will said a silent prayer, then picked up the phone. 'Hello?'

'Will, it's Harley Ferris. We didn't get it.'

'Why not?' he asked. 'What happened?'

'The calls are just too short. We're very close in absolute terms, but we're talking about undeveloped land, thick Mississippi woods, waist-high underbrush. The logging road you mentioned: there are dozens cut through there. And there are hundreds of shacks.'

Will ground his teeth and looked out at the gulf. The cool air that had settled over the land during the night was taking on the yellow density of a Mississippi summer morning, as the sun baked it and sent it skywards again. Skywards . . .

'My God,' he breathed. 'Cheryl!'

'What?' Ferris asked.

Cheryl came to the wide door that divided the sitting room of the suite from the bedroom. 'What's the matter?' she asked.

'What kind of car does Huey drive?'

'An old pick-up truck. Last time I saw it, it was green. With lots of primer on it. It's one of those old Chevys. You know, with the rounded cab.'

'Listen, Harley. If you'll make me a promise, you can call the FBI. I've just learned what type of vehicle the guy in Hazelhurst is driving. If the FBI could get a chopper up over that area, they might be able to find it pretty quick.'

'You're damn right they could!' Ferris cried. 'Leave it to me.'

'The FBI is going to ask you a hundred questions about me. You can't answer them. That's my condition. You can't even give them my name. If you do, they'll have someone at my house in ten minutes, and that could get my daughter killed. The FBI's job is to find that vehicle and that cabin. That's it. In ninety minutes you can tell them all you know, but for now, nothing. Just the vehicle.'

'Jennings—'

'Don't give them my phone number, either. If they called at the wrong time, that could get Abby killed, too. Understood?'

'I don't like it. But I understand.'

'Good. And tell the FBI to put a paramedic in that chopper. With insulin. My daughter's a juvenile diabetic.'

'Jesus. Insulin, I've got it. Well . . . I'd better make that call. What kind of vehicle should they be looking for?'

'A green Chevy pick-up with lots of primer on it. The old kind, with rounded cab.'

'Got it. I'll talk to you soon.'

Will heard the click as Ferris disconnected.

Cheryl was still standing in the door.

'I feel like I woke up with the flu,' she said. 'My bones ache and all my muscles are twitching.'

'That'll pass.'

'Um . . . there's something I didn't tell you.'

'What?'

'This is the last job. Joey's last kidnapping. He's been talking about it all year. He's bought some land in Costa Rica. A ranch. For a while I thought it was, you know, bullshit. But I think maybe it's real.'

This new information only confirmed what Will had thought all along. This kidnapping was different from all the others. Hickey meant to kill Abby—and possibly Karen and himself—then vanish for good.

'You calling in the cops?' Cheryl asked.

'Not exactly.'

'Are we still going to pick up the money?'

'Absolutely. And it's all yours.'

She looked sceptical. 'Once we get it, are you going to let me go?'

'I need you to bluff Joe a bit longer. Over the phone, you know. Like we have been. Just long enough to get Abby.'

'I'm dead,' she said in a toneless voice.

'No, you're not. Hang with me, Cheryl.'

She covered her eyes with a shaking hand. Will could almost read her mind. In some corner of her brain she was thinking she should pick up the phone and warn Hickey. That if she told him what Will was up to, he might forgive her and call the whole thing off before everything came apart.

'Cheryl, you've got to think straight. I'm going to do everything I can to help you. If you somehow wind up in police custody, I'll testify on your behalf. I swear it. But you can't save Joe. It's gone past that. I know you still feel loyalty to him. But if you try to warn him,

I'll have no choice but to tell him everything you've told me. He'll know I could only have gotten it from you.'

Her face closed into a bitter mask. 'I'll tell him you tortured it out of me with those damn drugs.'

'If anything spooks Joe now, he'll tell Huey to kill Abby, and then he'll run. But you won't get out of this room. The only place you'll go will be death row.'

'Shut up, OK? Just shut up!' Tears welled in her red-rimmed eyes. 'I see I got no place to go. I never have.'

'But you do. If you can keep it together for another hour, you'll get enough money to become anybody you want to be. To get free and clear for the first time in your life.'

DR MCDILL ACCEPTED the magnifying glass that Special Agent-in-Charge Zwick offered him and leaned down over the photograph on the desk. It was a high-resolution digital still, captured from video tape shot by a security camera at the Beau Rivage Casino on the previous afternoon. The camera had been covering one of the blackjack tables and yielded a perfect shot of a blonde in a slinky black dress.

'Is it her?' Zwick asked.

'No doubt about it.' McDill put down the magnifying glass and looked back at his wife, who was sitting on Zwick's sofa. 'I was right,' he said. 'It's happening again. Right this minute, another family is going through the same hell we did.' He walked over to Margaret, sat beside her, and took her hand. 'We did the right thing.'

She looked shell-shocked. He needed to get her home.

As McDill stood up, a young woman burst into the room.

Zwick glared at her. 'I assume you have a good reason for this interruption, Agent Perry?'

The agent nodded, her eyes flashing with excitement. 'Harley Ferris, president of CellStar, is on the line asking for the SAC about a kidnapping-in-progress.'

The blood drained from Zwick's face.

HUEY COTTON WAS SITTING on the steps of the cabin, using the point of his knife to put the finishing touches to his carving. When his cellphone rang, he put down the cedar and picked up the phone. 'Joey?'

'How you feeling, boy?'

'OK. I guess.'

'What's wrong?'

'I heard something a minute ago. A motor. In the sky. I think it was a helicopter.'

'It was probably the Forest Service. You just heard it once?'

'No. Back and forth, like a buzzard circling.'

'Is that right? Well . . . remember the back-up plan we talked about?'

'I remember.'

'It's time to start thinking about that.'

Huey felt a twinge of fear. 'Right this red-hot minute?'

'Not quite. But you be ready. I'll call you.'

'OK.'

'How's the kid?'

'She's nice. Real nice.'

'That's not what I mean. Is she still asleep?'

Huey heard the sound of the lavatory. 'She just woke up.'

'OK. I'll call you soon. Keep listening for that helicopter.'

'OK.' Huey hit END. When he turned, he saw Abby standing in the cabin door. Her face was pale, her eyes crusted with sleep.

'I don't feel good,' she said.

Huey's face felt hot. 'What's the matter?'

'My head hurts. I think I need my shot.'

'Soon,' he promised. 'It won't be long now.'

 twelve

Karen stood in the kitchen with the cordless phone in her hand, dressed in a navy suit with a cream blouse. Her face was made up to cover the bruises she'd sustained during the night.

'Still on hold?' Hickey asked. He was sitting at the kitchen table, his sutured leg propped on its tile surface.

'Gray's getting something from his car.'

Gray Davidson was one of the founding partners of Klein Davidson, an independent brokerage firm that handled most of the money in the wealthy suburbs north of Jackson.

'You're not going to listen in?' Karen asked.

Hickey shook his head. 'Just stick to the script.'

'Karen?' said a male voice. 'It's Gray. Sorry you had to wait.'

'That's all right. Did you get a call from Will a few minutes ago?'

'Did I ever. Two hundred grand for a sculpture. That's kind of steep, even for Will.'

'It's a very important piece.'

'Do you feel all right with this, Karen?'

'What do you mean?'

'It seems odd, is all. That this guy selling the sculpture is in such a hurry for his money. Will says it's a competitive bidding situation and that the art dealer is flying back to New York today and wants cash.'

'That sounds like an art dealer.'

'I guess so.' Davidson paused. 'I guess I just hate seeing that much money leave my computer in a single morning.'

She forced herself to laugh. 'Now, that I believe. I'll be down to sign for it in half an hour.'

'Look forward to seeing you.'

'Bye.' Karen hung up, then opened the refrigerator.

'You don't have time for breakfast,' Hickey said.

She took two vials of insulin and some syringes from the top shelf and put them in her bag. 'I want this with me in case Abby's in trouble. You have a problem with that?'

A strange light flickered in Hickey's eyes. 'No problem. I told you nobody was going to die today.'

'I'm glad to hear it.'

'Let's go. We'll take the Expedition.'

Karen picked up her keys and led the way. Hickey limped after her.

She hit the UNLOCK button on her key ring, then the garage door-opener on the wall. She had the Expedition in gear by the time Hickey got into the passenger seat. As she started backing up Stephanie Morgan's white Lexus crested the top of the hill and blocked her access to the drive. She hit the brakes with a screech.

'Who is it?' Hickey was already reaching for Will's gun, which he was wearing in the small of his back.

Karen grabbed his wrist. 'It's Stephanie Morgan, the same woman as yesterday.'

'What does she want now?'

'Something about the flower show, I'm sure. I'll get rid of her.'

'You do that.' He rolled down his window.

Karen got out and started towards the Lexus. Stephanie was already walking towards her.

'I just came from the Coliseum,' she said in a tart voice. 'I didn't call because I knew you'd try to blow me off.'

'What is it, Stephanie?'

'The same as yesterday! Only worse. The cattle show people swore that the whole place would be cleaned up by noon.'

'And?' Karen looked past her, trying to see if either of her kids were in the car. The Lexus looked empty.

'There's hay and cow manure all over the place! Karen. You've got to come down and light a fire under those people. They just won't take me seriously.'

'My cousin's in the car, Stephanie, and he's got a plane to catch. I'll get there as soon as I can. You'll just have to handle it until then.'

'I *can't* handle it. I'm maxed out on Prozac, and even that's not doing any good.'

Karen wanted to scream. But the sound of the Expedition's door stopped her cold. She turned and saw Hickey walking towards them, a concerned look on his face.

'Everything OK?' he asked.

'Oh, hello again, Joe,' Stephanie said with a Teflon smile.

Karen interposed herself between them. 'I told her we have to get right to the airport.'

Hickey looked puzzled, then he smiled. 'We *are* late for my flight. They make you check in so early now.'

Stephanie's eyes went wide. 'I've got it! I can run you out to the airport. That way Karen can get right over to the Coliseum.'

'No,' Karen said quickly. 'Joe and I still have some talking to do. The estate things. I told you last night. It can't wait.'

Stephanie's face darkened and her voice lost its sorority-girl veneer. 'You're the chairman of this show, Karen. You volunteered for it. That means it's your job to—make sure . . .'

Karen followed her gaze. Stephanie was staring at the right leg of Hickey's khakis. A bright-red bloodstain ran from above the knee down to his ankle. Some of the stitches must have broken loose.

'What happened to you?' Stephanie asked. 'That looks serious.'

Hickey looked down at his leg.

'Joe hurt himself,' Karen said quickly. 'Doing some work for me.'

Hickey was watching Stephanie, his dark eyes glittering.

Karen took her by the arm and started walking her back towards the Lexus. 'I'll get down there as soon as I can, Steph. OK?'

Stephanie looked back over her shoulder. 'Is your cousin all right? He looks . . .' She looked into Karen's eyes. Something was stirring in her Prozac-padded brain. 'Are *you* all right?'

'I'm fine.' Karen tried to push her towards the car.

'You don't look fine. In fact, you look like hell.'

'Thanks a lot.'

Stephanie looked over Karen's shoulder. Whatever she saw convinced her that something was very wrong. She took hold of Karen's wrist and began pulling her towards the Lexus. 'Keep walking,' she whispered. 'When I start the car, jump in the back seat.'

'I can't. Get your butt out of here, Steph. *Now*.'

Karen risked a glance back at Hickey. His trouser leg was completely soaked with blood now, and his right hand was behind his back. She turned back to Stephanie: 'I'll see you in a few hours, OK?'

Stephanie's brow was knotted in puzzlement. Suddenly she whirled and yanked open the door of the Lexus, all pretence of normality gone.

Hickey shot her. A crimson flower blossomed on her upper chest. Karen screamed and leaped forward, but not in time to catch Stephanie as she slid down the rear door of the car, leaving a bright trail of blood on the white paint. Even before Karen could check Stephanie's airway, Hickey's rough hands jerked her to her feet.

'Get your ass in the truck.'

'You shot her,' Karen said, still not quite believing it.

Hickey aimed the .38 down at Stephanie's head. 'If you don't get into that Expedition, I'll shoot her again.'

His enraged eyes left no doubt that he would put a bullet in Stephanie Morgan's brain. Karen backed towards the Expedition.

'You said nobody was going to die!'

'She called that play. She should've handled those damn cattle people herself.'

'She has two kids!'

'You'd better start thinking about *your* kid, Mom.'

Karen's mouth went dry. She climbed up into the driver's seat and sat there, trying to hold herself together.

'Take hold of the gear shift and pull it over to D,' Hickey said.

'You lied to me,' Karen said. 'You've been planning to kill us all along. You're going to get your money and kill us.'

'Listen to me. By tomorrow night, I'll be sipping umbrella drinks in Costa Rica. I'm not worried about who saw me shoot some airhead in a Lexus. What I *am* worried about is getting my money. And that's what you need to focus on. Are we on the same page?'

Karen took a deep breath, then reached down and punched 911 on the Expedition's cellphone.

Hickey jammed the gun into her ribs, driving the breath from her lungs. 'Your friend is dead. So hang up and start driving.'

The 911 line rang once before Karen pressed END. She hated herself for being a coward, but she could not die over an acquaintance who was almost certainly dead already. She had a child to raise. Nothing else mattered. She and Abby had to get through the day alive.

She put the Expedition into gear and drove.

WHEN THE PHONE RANG in the suite at the Beau Rivage, Will pounced on it. Now that he'd given Ferris the go-ahead to call the FBI, he wanted to hear that a fleet of helicopters was heading for the forest around Hazelhurst. He jerked up the receiver, aware that his sleep-deprived brain was slowly but surely slipping off its tracks.

'Will Jennings.'

'What are you doing answering the phone?' Hickey asked. 'You expecting a call?'

'No,' he stammered. 'I'm just ready to move. Ready to get your money and get Abby back.'

'That's good, Doc. Because it's time to leave for the bank.'

'I'm ready.'

'You sound sleepy. Cheryl's got some pep pills if you need them. I don't want you messing up because you can't think straight.'

'I'm not going to mess up. But I need to talk to my daughter, Joe. I'm not going to the bank until I do.'

'Is that right? Huh. Maybe you should talk to your wife a minute. We just had a little social call at your house.'

Sweat beaded on Will's forehead. 'Karen?'

'I'm here,' she said.

'Are you all right?'

'Will, he just shot Stephanie Morgan.'

Will blinked, certain that he'd misheard. 'Did you say—?'

'You heard her right,' Hickey cut in. 'She's busy driving now. But if I hear any more bullshit about what you will and won't do, the Lexus queen won't be the only one who dies this morning. You follow?'

'Yes.'

'Now, what about this helicopter?'

Acid flooded Will's stomach. 'Helicopter?'

'You been talking to the FBI?'

Harley Ferris couldn't possibly have got an FBI helicopter into the air and over Hazelhurst so quickly. It had to be a coincidence. 'Joe, I'm doing exactly what you tell me. Nothing else.'

'Let me talk to Cheryl.'

Cheryl was sitting on the sofa. She had gone downstairs to a clothing store in the casino lobby and had bought a white Lycra sheath to replace the torn cocktail dress. She took the phone from Will and began a litany of one-word replies. 'Yeah. . . . No. . . . Right. . . . No, he's cool . . . We'll be there. No problem.' She handed the phone back to Will. 'It's showtime.'

He hung up the phone then looked at her. 'Thank you. I owe you more than I can ever repay.'

She stood up and slung her bag over her shoulder. 'You just remember you said that.'

KAREN PULLED the Expedition into the parking lot of the Klein Davidson Building and parked two spaces over from Gray Davidson's Mercedes.

'You only want to be thinking about one thing in there,' Hickey said. 'Your kid.'

'I'm not taking one step until you let me call nine-one-one and report a woman shot at my address.'

Hickey held the gun against her ribs again.

'If you shoot me, you won't get your money. All I'm asking is a chance to try to save a woman's life. It won't cost you anything. She has two small children, and I can't live with myself if I don't do all I can to help her.'

Hickey expelled air from his cheeks in exasperation.

She closed her eyes and leaned back against the headrest. She expected to feel the gun barrel pressed to her temple, but instead she heard four beeps, one ring, and a click.

'Nine-one-one, emergency,' said a female operator.

Hickey said, 'A woman was just shot in the chest at number one hundred, Crooked Mile Road. She's dying.'

Karen looked over at him, amazed.

'One hundred, Crooked Mile Road,' said the operator. 'Sir, I'm showing that we already received a call for this emergency.'

Hickey's jaw clenched. 'When was that?'

'About two minutes ago.'

'Who called it in?'

'I don't have that information, sir. But we've already dispatched—'

Hickey hit END. 'I think your husband has made a very big mistake. First we get a helicopter over the cabin. Now somebody's at your house reporting a shooting.'

'You were outside when you shot her. A neighbour could have heard.'

'Your neighbours aren't that close.' Hickey rubbed the dark stubble on his chin. 'Get in there and move the money. And remember . . . one mistake will put you in a mourning dress.'

Karen got out and walked towards the entrance, his last sentence hanging over her like a pall.

THE BILOXI BRANCH of the Magnolia Federal Bank was an unprepossessing two-storey brick building. Will pulled his rented Tempo into the lot and parked. 'What now?'

Cheryl shifted in the seat beside him. 'Now we wait,' she replied. 'Joey will call after the money's on its way.'

Will took her cellphone from her lap and dialled Ferris's number.

'Ferris,' said a clipped voice.

'It's Will. Anything?'

'The FBI already had a chopper in the air when I called them. It's been over the woods at Hazelhurst for a while now, but the foliage is so thick, they're probably missing buildings, much less a pick-up.'

'What about the phone trace?'

'We're almost there, Will. We just had a quick call to the subject's number. Our crew is working its way down an overgrown logging road right now.'

'What will they do if they find the truck?'

'There's an FBI SWAT team en route from Jackson. The SAC says they can seal off the cabin without the subject's knowledge.'

A chill of foreboding went through Will. 'They're not going to try an assault?'

'I think they're going to play it safe,' Ferris replied. 'But my guess is that with your little girl's life on the line, if they get a clean shot at the guy holding her, they'll take it.'

'Sweet Jesus.'

'They're pros, Will. Just like you. They know their jobs.'

'I've got to clear this line. Harley . . . for God's sake, tell them to be careful.'

'Have faith.'

He hung up. *Have faith?* It took a supreme effort simply to sit in the parking lot while Abby's future unfolded. But he had to play the hand Hickey had dealt him. Hickey had to believe until the last second that his plan was ticking along like a Swiss watch.

SENDING THE WIRE was just like everything Karen had ever done at Klein Davidson: a matter of paperwork, signing on various lines while Gray Davidson led her through the pages and made chitchat about kids and schools. She was functioning on autopilot, tormented by images of Stephanie Morgan's chest blossoming red. The only thing that really registered was the receptionist handing her a receipt and saying, 'The money's on its way.'

'That's it? That's all we have to do?'

Gray Davidson patted her on the shoulder. 'Scary how fast you can spend two hundred grand, isn't it?'

'Very scary,' Karen replied, wondering if Will was already in the bank in Biloxi, waiting to collect what she'd sent.

'You look like you're going to faint,' Davidson said with genuine concern. 'Why don't you come into my office and sit down?'

'No. I've got to run.' Somehow Karen conjured a smile. 'It's just a summer cold. I'll be fine.'

'Go straight home and get some rest,' Davidson called after her.

She held up a hand in acknowledgment, and went through the rosewood door and down the steps to the parking lot.

THE PARKING LOT of the Magnolia Federal Bank in Biloxi was filling up fast. Will could see why Hickey had picked this branch.

When the cellphone rang, he snatched it up, but Cheryl put her hand on his wrist and took the phone from his hand.

'It's me,' she said. 'Right . . . OK.' She hit END and looked at Will. 'The money's here. He said you should go in and get it.'

Will looked at the glass doors of the bank. 'Give me the phone.'

'You don't trust me?'

'I didn't say that. I just said I'm taking the phone.'

Cheryl snapped her head away from him, but did not resist when he took the phone from her hand. He slipped it into his pocket along with the Tempo's keys, then got out and walked towards the bank.

HICKEY DROVE SOUTH along the interstate at fifty-five miles per hour, his face wet with sweat, his right thigh soaked in blood.

'I think some more stitches broke,' he said. 'You aren't much of a doctor. I think you're going to have to do some repairs here.'

Karen had not given the suturing her best effort. 'I don't have Will's bag. I could probably tape it up, if you stop at a drugstore.'

Hickey looked in the rearview mirror, then changed lanes. 'Start looking for a one.'

Karen searched the strip malls that lined the interstate.

'There's a cop back there,' Hickey said, straightening in his seat.

She started to turn, but he grabbed her knee. 'Don't look.'

'Cops are always patrolling this interstate,' she told him.

'This one's hanging on me like a trailer.'

'Were you speeding?'

'You think I'm going to speed today? This is your husband, god-damn it. The son of a bitch called somebody. That's the only way they'd know what to look for.'

'What about the shooting at our house?'

'They wouldn't have issued an APB on this vehicle off that. Not yet, anyway.' He checked the rearview again. 'That bastard is still there.'

'You're paranoid! And you're driving suspiciously.'

Hickey craned his neck and looked up through the sunroof. 'Paranoid, huh? Take a look.'

The sunroof was tinted but, even so, Karen could see the large dot against the sky. It was a helicopter. 'That's probably the TV traffic chopper,' she said. But she wondered.

'Traffic chopper, my ass.' Hickey reached down and punched a number into the cellphone. After a few seconds, it began to ring.

'Joey?' said Huey.

'That's right, boy. It's time to go to the back-up plan.'

'OK.'

Karen's chest tightened. 'May I please speak to Abby? *Please*.'

Hickey sighed with frustration. 'Huey, is the kid right there?'

'She's in the bathroom.'

Karen's maternal radar went on alert as she heard Huey's voice fill the vehicle. 'Has she been to the bathroom a lot this morning, Huey?'

'She sure has.'

'Oh God. Her sugar's going up. She needs her shot.'

'And I'm bleeding to death,' Hickey said. 'Stay cool. You've got stuff with you, and we'll be there in plenty of time.'

'Joey?' said Huey.

'You know what to do? Everything just like I told you.'

'I remember.'

'We'll talk when we see each other.'

'OK. Bye-bye.'

Hickey pressed END. 'Bastards,' he said, looking up through the sunroof again. 'If your husband had done what he was supposed to, you'd be going straight to your little girl right now.'

Karen's heart stuttered. 'You said we were!'

'We're not going anywhere until I lose this tail.'

'You don't know it *is* a tail.'

A scornful grunt was his only comment. 'Your husband had better be getting us my goddamn money.'

'He is! You know he is.'

Hickey checked the rearview again. 'The squad car dropped out of sight. They're playing us loose. They want to follow us to the girl.'

Oh, Will, Karen thought, what did you do?

Without warning, Hickey veered across two lanes of traffic and onto an exit ramp. At the bottom, he swung onto a wide boulevard.

'Lakeland Drive?' said Karen. 'This is the road to the airport.'

'That it is.' Hickey laughed softly.

'THIS WAY, Dr Jennings.'

Will followed the secretary up a flight of stairs. Upon entering the bank, he had identified himself, and told her he was receiving a wire transfer of $200,000 and wouldn't deal with anyone but the top man.

The staircase ended at a hall lined with doors. She led him to the one at the end, knocked, then showed him into a typical bank office. Behind a desk sat a balding man in his early fifties. He stood. 'Hello, Dr Jennings. That'll be all, Cindy.'

The door closed behind Will, and the man held out a plump hand. 'I'm Jack Moore, vice president.'

Will shook the hand and looked around the office. There was a door on the wall to his right, partially open.

'How can I help you, Doctor? Your wire came in a few minutes ago. What would you like to do with the money?'

'I want to withdraw it in cash. I also need to withdraw some personal funds. I have a hundred and fifty thousand deposited with this bank in Jackson.'

Moore wiped his upper lip. 'You want to walk out of here with three hundred and fifty thousand dollars in a case?'

'That's right.' Cheryl had retrieved a cheap briefcase from her suite as they left the Beau Rivage.

'I see. Well . . .' Moore glanced at a door to his right. It opened, and a tall man with sandy hair and blue eyes stepped out.

'Dr Jennings,' said the stranger. 'I'm Special Agent Bill Chalmers. I'm aware of your situation and I'm here to help you.'

Will was so stunned he simply stood where he was. 'What the hell is this?' he muttered. 'How did you get here? How did you know where to go? Harley Ferris didn't know where I was going.'

Chalmers nodded. 'There's a sofa behind you, Doctor. Please sit down. We don't have much time, and we have a lot to do.'

Will backed up until his calves hit something padded. He sat.

'Do you know a cardiovascular surgeon named James McDill?'

'McDill? Sure. He's a member out at Annandale. He doesn't play much golf. Collects cars, I think.' Even as he spoke the word 'collects', something ticked in Will's brain.

'Exactly one year ago,' said Chalmers, 'James McDill's son, Peter, was kidnapped in exactly the same way your daughter was yesterday. He didn't report the crime until last night, and nobody knows why better than you. But this week he was overcome with anxiety that it might happen again. He called our Jackson field office around eleven last night. I was on duty, and we've been working ever since to piece together what's going on.'

'Have you talked to Harley Ferris? Do you know where my little girl is?'

'Mr Ferris is working with us now. We've augmented CellStar's tracing crew with a SWAT team, and we just had a very lucky break. The man holding Abby just took a call on his cellphone, and he forgot to switch it off. The SWAT team estimates they're two minutes from your daughter's position.'

'What do they plan to do when they get there?'

'We think we should go in and get her. We have special entry devices. Heat sensors and video to accurately place human bodies in the structure. They'll use special stun grenades to incapacitate the tango, then—'

'Tango?' Will interrupted.

'Sorry, that's radio slang for terrorists. These guys train in rescuing hostages from terrorists.'

'Can't you try to talk him out?'

'We could do that. But it's our understanding that the man holding Abby is mentally handicapped. The leader is still loose. He could call this guy Huey at any time and order him to kill your daughter.'

'Can't Ferris shut off Huey's phone?'

'Yes, but that might panic him. Or he might be under orders to kill your daughter if his communications are cut off. Right now—while Huey and Abby are isolated from the leader—we have a golden opportunity to go in. Before the situation deteriorates any further.'

'I still don't understand how you knew to come to this bank.'

'We didn't. We put an agent in every bank of any size in Gulfport and Biloxi. I requested this one because it was the largest. I flew down early this morning. The minute your wire came in, I contacted my Special Agent-in-Charge in Jackson. His name's Frank Zwick.'

'Is he in contact with the SWAT team?'

'Yes.'

'Please call him. Tell him there's a woman outside in my rental car. One of the kidnappers.'

Chalmers nodded. 'Cheryl Lynn Tilly. We'll leave her alone until the team hits the cabin. If she gets suspicious and comes inside, you can tell her there's some delay with paperwork. We have more agents converging on the bank right now, but they'll be discreet. Would you excuse us, Mr Moore?'

'Of course.' The banker, who looked as though he couldn't quite believe what was happening before his eyes, made a hasty exit.

Chalmers dialled a number on Moore's phone.

'The leader's name is Hickey. He has my wife with him,' Will said. 'Do you know where they are now?'

'Driving towards Jackson International Airport.'

'*What?*'

'Don't worry, they're not going anywhere. We're watching them from a helicopter. Hang on.' He spoke into the phone. 'Chalmers here. I've got Dr Jennings with me . . . He's on board with us . . . Yes, sir. Any word on the little girl?' Chalmers gave Will a thumbs-up.

'I want to talk to him,' Will said, standing.

'I'll tell him,' Chalmers said, and hung up. 'The SAC has a lot on his plate right now, Doctor.'

'What's happening?'

'SWAT found the cabin.'

Will closed his eyes and began to pray.

EIGHT FBI AGENTS in camouflage fatigues and black headgear crept silently through the trees, their submachine guns tight against their bodies. A ninth agent was already under the cabin, scanning the floor with a supersensitive microphone and headphones. Their leader was Special Agent Martin Cody, and Cody was in radio contact with the agent under the house.

'Got anything?' Cody said into the microphone mounted inside his ballistic glass face mask.

'Not yet.' Special Agent Sims Jackson was observing the cabin through a thermal-imaging camera. 'Nothing but a hot-water heater.'

Cody didn't like that. The pick-up truck was there, but the people weren't? Could the tango have detected their approach and fled into the woods?

'Cody to tracing van,' he said into his mike. The CellStar van was seventy yards back up the logging road. 'Has the cellphone moved?'

'Negative. Still in the same position.'

'We're going in,' Cody said into his mike. 'Prepare for explosive entry. Stun grenades through the windows, ram the front door.'

A staccato burst of mike clicks answered him.

'Shoot high,' Cody reminded them, though they knew the drill. 'This kid probably isn't much over three feet. OK . . . deploy.'

Moving forward without sound, in thirty seconds the team had deployed around the cabin, grenades and guns at the ready.

Agent Cody checked to make sure his ram team was in position. It was. 'On my five-count,' he said. 'Five—four —three—two—GO!'

The cabin windows shattered one second before the front door went down. Even in daylight, the blue-white flash of the stun grenades lit up the windows, followed by ear-shattering bangs. Cody saw his men vanish into the cabin. He followed.

The cabin floor shuddered under the impact of boots. The interior was filled with smoke, but it cleared quickly through the broken windows. There were no cries of 'federal agents', because no one could have heard them after the stun grenades.

'Bedroom! No joy!' cried the speaker in Cody's helmet.

'Kitchen, no joy!'

Cody checked the front room. He found nothing.

'Cellphone!' someone shouted. 'Cellphone in the kitchen!'

'Got another one!' cried someone else. 'Land line in the bedroom!'

Land line? Cody had been told there was no land line in the cabin, and he had seen no wires outside. Maybe there was a buried cable running to the building. He went into the kitchen and saw one of his men holding the cellphone. He took it and just then the phone began to ring. Cody yanked off his helmet, and hit SEND. 'Yeah?' he said.

'Do you have Prince Albert in the can?' asked a male voice.

Cody stood dumbfounded for a moment. 'Who is this?'

He heard wild laughter; then the caller clicked off.

Cody put his helmet back on and keyed his mike. 'Tracing van, did you hear that call?'

'Affirmative.'

'Where did it come from?'

'Unknown. We're checking.'

Cody pulled a digital cellphone from his pocket, and dialled the private number of SAC Zwick in Jackson.

WILL PACED BACK AND FORTH across the banker's small office. Agent Chalmers sat behind Moore's desk, speaking quietly to Zwick. Suddenly, he groaned and covered his eyes with his free hand.

'What happened?' Will asked. 'What happened, goddamn it?'

Chalmers looked up, his face pale. 'The cabin was empty when SWAT went in. Huey and your daughter weren't there.'

'*What?*' Will searched in his mind for an explanation. 'It must have been the wrong cabin.'

'It wasn't. They found the cellphone inside. And someone actually called them on it while they were there. Made a joke out of it.'

Will shook his head in disbelief.

'They also found a land line in the cabin, which means Hickey could have given Huey new instructions without anyone knowing. The phone company has no record of that line. It's probably an illegal tap.'

A land line. He should have known Hickey wouldn't let Huey operate without some sort of back-up. 'But the truck was still there?'

'Yes, but the battery had been removed. It looks like there might have been another vehicle.'

'Are you kidding me? Give me that damn phone!' Will snatched the phone from Chalmers's hand and shouted into it: 'Are you the guy in charge of this Chinese fire drill?'

'This is Frank Zwick, Doctor. Special Agent-in-Charge. Losing your temper isn't going to help your little girl.'

'You just tell me, what do you plan to do now?'

'I'm deciding that at this moment. You can help me. Did Cheryl Lynn Tilly mention any destination that would require air travel?'

'Costa Rica. She said Hickey has some land down there.'

'Costa Rica? You can't fly direct from Jackson to Costa Rica. And there's no reservation for a Joe or Joseph Hickey on any flight out of Jackson today. So, he must be flying out under an alias, with a connecting flight to South America.'

'Look, if Hickey called your men at the cabin, he knows you're involved. You may have just killed my little girl, Zwick.'

'I seriously doubt that, Doctor. Hickey wants two things: his money and his freedom. Killing your daughter won't help him get either. She's half his total leverage now.'

'You don't know what's going on! It's not about money. Hickey thinks I killed his mother on the operating table. This is about revenge. He *wants* to kill Abby. To punish me.'

Silence. Then, 'That's a disturbing new perspective, Doctor.'

'You're goddamn right it is.'

Will heard another phone ringing. It was the cellphone in his pocket. Cheryl's phone. 'Hang on, I think Hickey's calling me.' He dug the phone out of his pocket and hit SEND. 'Hello?'

'What's up, Doc?'

Will nodded at Chalmers. 'I'm in the bank, getting your money.'

'You're lying. You called the FBI. Where's Cheryl?'

'In the parking lot. I brought the phone in with me. So I could tell you what was happening if you called.'

'Well . . . the plan has changed. Your wife and me are about to take a little airplane ride. And if I see a cop or an FBI agent within a mile of me. I'm going to put one right in her ear. You follow?'

'Joe, I'm getting your money! Just tell me where you want it!'

'We'll work that out later. You just get it all ready to go. And tell your new friends to keep clear of that airport.'

'I don't know what you're talking about! Where's my daughter?'

Hickey laughed. '*Hasta luego, amigo*. Just remember, whatever happens, you called the play.' The phone went dead.

Will picked up the other phone. He told Zwick what had transpired.

The SAC said, 'I'm going to pull back my men and let them get into the airport.'

'Why? Won't Hickey be harder to stop with lots of people around?'

'Yes, but it's possible that this Huey character and your daughter are already inside the airport waiting for him. If we bust Hickey outside, they might just disappear.'

'But if they are inside, what can you do? How can you stop Hickey then? What's to keep him from putting a gun to Abby's head?

'I can promise you this, Doctor. If your little girl is in the airport, and Hickey makes a move towards her with a weapon, his brain will be removed from his cranium without benefit of anaesthetic. Sharpshooters will be in position before Hickey gets inside the building. Now, I have a lot to arrange, Doctor. Put Agent Chalmers back on.'

As Will handed over the phone, several thoughts came to him. Right now Zwick was almost certainly telling Chalmers to make sure Will stayed under FBI control. But Will's primary concern was Hickey. Even now, the man was controlling everyone involved. At the cabin he had proved he could stay two steps ahead of the SWAT team and laugh while doing it. Opposing his proven brilliance was Frank Zwick. Will had to assume that Zwick knew his job, but instinct told him that the events of the next few minutes would not be as easy to control as the SAC believed. As Chalmers listened to his boss on the phone, Will walked quietly out of the office.

'Where are you going?' Chalmers called. 'Doctor?'

Will paused in the hall. 'To get the ransom money.'

'It's no good to you now.'

'You don't know that. Hickey said to get it, so I'm getting it. I'll be back in a minute.' He took the stairs two at a time going down.

FIVE MILES EAST of downtown Jackson, Hickey turned Karen's Expedition onto the main airport access road.

'Where are we going?' she asked.

'You just watch.'

'We've got to get to Abby, Joe. Her sugar's going up.'

'Just shut your damn mouth. I got everything under control.'

Karen looked through the sunroof. The helicopter was still there. It had stayed practically on top of them all the way from the interstate. It had to be the police. She gripped the door handle as Hickey swerved into the lane for long-term parking.

He stopped at the barrier, took a ticket from the machine, then accelerated into the concrete-roofed garage. The brakes squealed as they neared the elevator on the terminal side of the building. He rounded the curve and almost ran over a young woman pulling a suitcase from the trunk of a silver Camry. He screeched to a stop, then pulled into the parking space beside the Camry.

He jumped out and smashed Will's .38 into the side of the woman's head. She dropped like a stone.

'Get out!' Hickey shouted at Karen. 'Help me!'

A wave of nausea nearly overcame her, but she forced herself to get out of the Expedition. Hickey was bent over the prostrate woman, rifling through her bag. He snatched his hand from it with a jangle of car keys and hit the UNLOCK button on the ring. 'Get in the back seat of the Camry! Move!'

Hickey grabbed the woman under the arms and heaved her upper body into the Camry's trunk. She moaned in pain and confusion, but Hickey took no notice. He slammed the lid shut. When he turned to Karen, his eyes were as cold as any she had ever seen.

'Get your ass in that car, or you'll never see Abby alive again.'

He didn't wait for her to obey. He jumped into the driver's seat, cranked the Camry, and backed out of the parking space.

Snapped from her trance by the realisation that he might leave without her, Karen jumped in the back and pulled the door shut.

'Get on the floor,' Hickey ordered.

She lay stomach-down across the carpeted hump behind the front seat. Hickey drove at normal speed through the lines of parked cars.

'Are we leaving the airport?' she asked.

'Yes, we are!' he cried. 'That nice lady left her parking receipt right here on the dashboard!'

Karen couldn't believe it. Hickey was going to drive right out from under the nose of the helicopter hovering overhead. The strange thing was that she wanted him to succeed. She had seen enough of him to know that if he were arrested, he would clam up and smile at the police while Abby died in a diabetic coma somewhere.

Hickey paid at the exit booth and joined the flow of traffic leaving the airport.

A sound like a muffled drum suddenly echoed through the car. The woman in the trunk was beating on the back seat. *'Help!'* screamed the muted voice. *'I can't breathe! Please let me out!'*

Karen shut her eyes and prayed for the woman to be quiet. If she kept screaming, Hickey was liable to pull over and shoot her.

The knocking behind Karen went on, but the cries decreased in intensity until they became a keening wail, like that of a small child.

'Traffic update!' Hickey cried. 'I thought you might like to know, that helicopter's still hovering over the airport, three miles back. Amateurs, baby. Amateurs.'

'Are we going to get Abby now?'

He laughed. 'We're going somewhere. That's one thing you can count on. We got an appointment with destiny!'

thirteen

Once he had the ransom (Moore had personally packed it into the briefcase at his feet), Will could not make a decision about what to do next until he knew the outcome of the FBI's attempt to arrest Hickey at the airport. So, he returned to the vice president's office on the first floor.

When the call from SAC Zwick finally came, Agent Chalmers lifted the phone, listened for a few moments, then turned paler than he had when the SWAT team had found nothing at the cabin.

'Tell me!' Will demanded. 'What happened?'

'I'm putting you on the speaker, Frank.' Chalmers hit a button on the phone. 'Go ahead.'

'Is my wife all right?' Will asked. 'Was my daughter there?'

Zwick's voice came from the bottom of an electronic well. 'Hickey and your wife pulled into the long-term parking garage, but they never came out. We found your Expedition. We're searching the airport, but it's just possible they got out of that garage in another car. We're getting the parking lot security-camera tapes.'

'Jesus!' Will stood up, holding the briefcase that held the ransom.

'What are you doing?' asked Chalmers.

'Going back to the car and waiting for Hickey's next call.'

'That's not an option, Doctor,' Zwick said from the speaker-phone. 'The only way you can participate in the resolution of this situation is our way. Otherwise, we'll have to arrest you.'

'For what? I haven't done anything.'

'I'll have the Gulfport police arrest you for reckless driving. You've got a hooker in your car. How about prostitution?'

'What do you want me to do?'

'By now Agent Chalmers has some special equipment at his disposal downstairs. A tracking device will allow us to follow you from a very discreet distance. We can wait for Hickey to arrange an exchange, then be ready to take him down at the safest moment. We also have an undetectable wire. With the wire, we'll know just when that moment is, and we'll have everything Hickey says on tape.'

'Undetectable, my ass. A wire helps you guys at trial, but it doesn't do squat for my wife and daughter. And they're my only priority.'

'This is non-negotiable, Doctor.'

'You think so?' Will reached into his pocket and brought out Cheryl's pistol. 'Ask Agent Chalmers if it's negotiable.'

'Bill?' said Zwick.

'He's holding a gun on me, Frank.'

'You just committed a felony, Doctor,' Zwick informed him. 'Don't make this worse for yourself.'

Will laughed. '*Worse?* Are you out of your mind?' He backed towards the door. 'You guys had your chance. Two chances. And you blew it both times. It's my turn now.'

Agent Chalmers held up both hands to show that he had no intention of going for Will's gun or his own. 'At least take the tracking device. Forget the wire.'

'Where is it?' Will asked.

'I'll call downstairs and have it waiting for you.'

Zwick said, 'Agent Chalmers, as soon as he leaves that room, you will call downstairs and order the agents down there to arrest him.'

Chalmers looked into Will's eyes. 'They'll have to shoot him to stop him, Frank. I say we let him go.'

'Damn it.' The speakerphone crackled for a moment. 'All right, just give him the tracker—Jennings, you're making the biggest mistake of your life.'

'I'm out of here,' Will said. 'Please don't try any cowboy stuff.' He turned, and bounded down the steps.

In the lobby, he made a beeline for the door. A secretary saw the gun and screamed, but a business-suited man by the doors held up his badge and yelled: 'FBI! Everyone stay calm! It's all right!'

As Will neared the door, the FBI man held out a small black box with a blinking red LED on it. 'GPS,' he said. 'Military grade. We can track you down to the square foot you're standing on.'

Will stuck the unit in his pocket, went through the automatic doors, and raced for the Tempo. When he hit the driver's seat, Cheryl said nervously, 'Where the hell have you been?'

He pulled out of the lot and onto Highway 90. Traffic was heavy, but he didn't see any obvious pursuit vehicles.

'Where are we going?' Cheryl asked.

'That's up to Joe. Right now, we're headed up to I-10. Wherever the meet is, it's going to be north.'

Will swung into the right-hand lane and overtook a dawdling pick-up truck. As he came alongside it, he rolled down his window, tossed the GPS device into the bed of the truck, and sped past.

'What was that?' Cheryl asked.

'A false trail for the FBI to follow.'

'The FBI? Was the FBI in the bank?'

'Yes. They raided the cabin, but Huey and Abby weren't there. All they found was the green truck and Huey's cellphone.' He turned and gave her a hard look. 'They also found a regular phone. A land line. You told me there was no regular phone service at the cabin.'

'I didn't know there was! I told you I never went there.'

He lifted the briefcase from the floor and set it in her lap. 'Open it.' When the lid rose high enough to reveal the neatly stacked 100-dollar bills, Cheryl's face lit up.

'That's three hundred and fifty thousand dollars,' he said. 'I told you I'd give you enough to start over. Now you've got it. That's freedom, Cheryl. Mexico, Bermuda, any place you want to be.'

She turned to him, eyes guarded. 'Can I leave right this minute?'

'No. Joe is going to call any second to set up a meeting. I need you to tell him everything's still all right.'

'No way. I've already done too much. Joey will—'

'He won't do anything! You'll never even have to see him again.'

'You're lying. To bluff Joey, you're going to need me up to the very last second. Then I'll be with him. And he'll *know*.'

'He's going to kill my little girl, Cheryl. You don't want to believe that, but deep down, you know.'

'Would you let me go if you knew where she was?'

Will nearly slammed on the brakes. 'Do you know where Huey's going?'

'Would you let me go if I did?'

'That depends on whether I believe you.'

She pursed her lips and looked down at the money on her lap. 'I was supposed to bring you to the motel, like I said. Then Joey was supposed to pick us up. I think he was going to take us back to the cabin where Huey was keeping Abby. But if the FBI raided the cabin, and Joey knows that . . .'

'He knows.'

'Then he's going to his back-up plan.'

'What's his back-up plan?'

'For Huey, I don't know. I'm still supposed to go to the motel in Brookhaven. Look, you've got the name of the motel. Just give that to the FBI and let me go. They'll find your little girl.'

'Not in time, they won't.'

'OK, listen. If Joey calls in a minute and tells me to go to the back-up plan. I'll say, "Fine, see ya soon." The motel's a hundred and fifty miles north of here. That gives you plenty of time to set something up. I don't know what you're doing anyway. If you want to save your kid, why are you running from the FBI?'

Will sighed. 'The FBI wants to bust Joe, OK? And you. And Huey. I don't care about that. I just want Abby back alive. And my wife. The FBI already spooked Joe twice. If he sees them anywhere close again, he might tell Huey to kill Abby. If he hasn't already.'

'But you can't do anything by yourself. And Joey's closer to the motel than we are. A lot closer.'

'Not necessarily.' Will pointed through the windshield. A Continental Airlines 727 was settling over Interstate 10 as it landed at the nearby airport.

Cheryl's mouth fell open. 'Jesus . . . your plane. But there's nowhere to land up there.'

'Let me worry about that.' Will had once lost an engine over the Mississippi Delta and set down on a deserted stretch of Highway 61. To save Abby, he would land the Baron on a driveway if he had to. 'One hour of acting, Cheryl. One hour, and you're free for ever—'

The ringing cellphone silenced him. He pulled onto the shoulder and shoved the Nokia towards her hand.

She refused to take it.

ABBY HAD SEEN amazing things in the last few minutes. When it was time to leave the cabin, Huey had picked up Belle and her ice chest and led her out to the green pick-up truck. But instead of getting in, he opened the hood over the motor and lifted out a big black thing he said was a battery. He carried it over to the white car sitting on the concrete blocks, opened the lid over the white car's motor and put the battery inside. While he was doing that, Abby had to run into the trees. Ever since she woke up, she'd had to go a lot, and that meant her sugar was going up fast.

After Huey got the battery into the white car, he worked under the hood for a minute, and the car started, rattling and puffing smoke. He then went back inside the cabin. Abby followed. In the kitchen, he took his cellphone from his pocket, turned it on, and set it on the counter. Then he lifted Abby and carried her out to the porch steps.

The white car was running, but it couldn't go anywhere because it was sitting a foot off the ground. Huey walked to the back, put his hands under the bumper, and started pulling on it. The back of the car tipped off the blocks and the tyres hit the ground. Huey helped Abby into the front seat and drove right off the blocks.

They rode under big trees hardly far enough apart for the car to fit between. Soon they hit a road, two mossy ruts through the dirt. Then the ruts hit a gravel road, which got Huey laughing until they had the puncture. He told Abby it wouldn't take long to change the tyre, but it took long enough that she had to run into the trees again.

That was when she realised she was in trouble. Her head hurt and she felt really tired. She started back towards the car, her eyes on Huey as he tossed the flat tyre into the trunk. He was grinning and waving. She tried to wave back, but fell face down in the dirt. The next thing she saw was Huey's eyes inches from hers, behind the heavy black plastic glasses.

'My sugar's too high,' she said. Huey must have carried her to the car, because she was sitting in the front seat. 'I need my shot.'

Huey got the small ice chest from the back seat and set it beside her. 'Do you know how to do it?'

'I've seen Mom and Dad do it lots of times. But I've never done it. You suck some medicine up into the syringe and then stick the needle in me and push the plunger. Will you give me the shot?'

Huey screwed up his face. 'I can't. I hate needles.'

'But I have to have it.'

'I can't do it, Belle.'

Abby bit her lip and tried not to be scared. 'Can you open the ice chest for me?'

Huey pressed the button on the side of the Igloo and opened it. Abby reached in and took out a bottle of insulin. She took a syringe from the ice chest and pulled off the cap, then drew a little clear fluid from the bottle. She pulled her dress over her right thigh and pinched up some skin and fat.

Huey's eyes were wet. 'You sure are brave.'

Abby wondered how a giant who could pick up a car could think she was brave, but he did. And that gave her the courage to stick the needle in. She pressed down the plunger, and by the time she felt the pain the needle was out again.

'You did it!' Huey cried.

'I did!' She laughed and leaned back in the seat, then reached up and hugged Huey. 'Let's go see my mom!'

He pulled back and looked at her, the awe in his face replaced by sadness. 'I'm never gonna see you again.' His bottom lip was shaking. 'Your mama's gonna take you away, and I'll never see you.'

'Sure you will.' She patted his arm.

'No.' He shook his head. 'It always happens. Any friend I ever make gets took away. Like my sister.'

Abby felt his sadness seeping into her. She picked up Belle and pushed the doll at his hand, but he wouldn't take it.

'We'd better get going,' she said. 'Mom's waiting for me.'

'Take it!' Will shouted, shoving the Nokia at Cheryl. 'Answer the damn phone!'

She crossed herself, then took the phone and hit SEND.

'Hello? . . . Yeah, I've got it . . . He's right here . . . No, not that I saw. No cop cars . . . We're on I-10. We turn on I-55 North, right? . . . Oh. OK.' She looked at Will. 'How come? . . . Oh God . . . OK. Just a second.' She handed the phone to Will.

'Joe?' Will said.

'You just had to play hero, didn't you?'

'Joe, I'm doing exactly what you told me to do. All I want is—'

'You called the FBI!'

'They were waiting for me in the damn bank! But I didn't call them. It's your fault.'

'What are you talking about?'

'A heart surgeon named James McDill called them. Does that name sound familiar?'

Hickey didn't reply.

'McDill was worried you were going to do to some other family what you'd done to his. He called the FBI last night. That's what started all this. The helicopters, the alerts for wire transfers, the whole thing.'

'Shit. McDill? His wife was a pill, too.'

'Joe, I've got the money. I'm ready to make the trade. The FBI agent in the bank tried to make me wear a wire, and I told him to stick it. I pulled Cheryl's gun on him and got the hell out of there. He gave me a GPS tracking device and I trashed it. Ask Cheryl. I *want* you to get to Costa Rica, OK? All I want is my daughter back.'

There was a long silence as Hickey considered his options. 'All right, listen up. Tell Cheryl to take you back to the Beau Rivage. Give her the money and the cellphone, then go back up to your suite.

You sit there till the phone rings. It'll be me. That phone's going to ring a lot during the next few hours. You just keep your ass in that room and answer it. Because if I call and you ain't there, your kid is dead. I get a busy signal? She's dead. Got it?'

'Look Joe . . . I know you don't just want the money, OK? You want to hurt me, and you want to do it through my family. I've got three hundred and fifty thousand dollars here. It's yours. But I've got to be there when we make the trade. When I see Karen and Abby drive away, I'll give you the money. You can do what you want then. You can kill me. Just let them live. That's all I ask.'

'Still trying to play hero, aren't you? The big martyr. Well, forget it. It's my way or the highway. You got no choice, son.'

The phone went dead in Will's hand. He hammered the steering wheel with his fists.

'What is it? What's wrong?' Cheryl screamed.

He explained Hickey's last demand.

'I told you,' she said. 'Joey's always three steps ahead.'

Will leaned back in the seat, his head and hands throbbing. 'I could get somebody to sit in the suite and answer my phone,' he said. 'Pretend they're me. One of my friends from the convention.'

'Joe wouldn't buy that for two seconds. He knows things about you that you don't even know. One trick question and it would be over.'

Another plane roared overhead—an F-18 Hornet. As the thunder of its jet engine shook the car, an idea flashed into Will's mind . . .

He took out his wallet, removed a card from it, and dialled a number on Cheryl's cellphone.

'Beau Rivage Casino Resort,' said the hotel operator.

'Give me Mr Geautreau, please. It's an emergency.'

'Who are you calling?' Cheryl asked.

'This is Mr Geautreau. May I help you?'

'This is Dr Will Jennings. We spoke yesterday when I checked in.'

'Of course, Doctor. How may I help you?'

'You've had the FBI in this morning, right?'

Geautreau hesitated. 'That's right.'

'Are there still FBI agents in the hotel?'

'The last one left a few minutes ago.'

'Listen, I don't know what the FBI told you, but they were there because my daughter was kidnapped last night. She's still missing. I'm not in the hotel now, but I need one of the kidnappers to think I am. He's going to call my suite several times over the next few hours and I need all those calls forwarded to the cellphone I'm using now. Can you do that?'

'Doctor, this sounds like a matter for the FBI.'

Will had considered calling Zwick. The SAC could have an agent at the Beau Rivage in ten minutes to handle this, if Will would share his plan with the Bureau. But that would put him back under the control of the FBI, which was the last place he wanted to be.

'Can you *technically* do it? he asked. 'Just tell me that.'

'Technically? Yes, we have that capability. But hotel policy—'

'Forget hotel policy. Let's talk about your personal policy. If you make sure those calls are forwarded to my cellphone—*personally* ensure it—I'll pay you ten thousand dollars.'

'Ten thousand . . . ?'

He had the man's attention. 'Let's make it fifteen thousand. Fifteen grand for three hours' work.'

'I'd need some security,' Geautreau said. 'Part of it up front.'

'Would a thousand dollars do?'

'I think that would be sufficient.'

'Connect me to Dr Jackson Everett's room. But stay on the phone.'

'As you say, Doctor.'

The phone rang five times. Will sweated. Then he heard a click. 'Son of a *bitch*,' said a ragged voice. 'Have a little mercy.'

'Jack? Wake up. It's Will Jennings.'

'Will? What's so important it can't wait till a decent hour? I've got the hangover from hell.'

'I'll tell you later. Right now I need you to go downstairs and write the hotel desk manager a cheque for a thousand dollars. I don't have time to explain. I just need a thousand dollars at the front desk in five minutes. His name's Geautreau. G-E-A-U-T-R-E-A-U. My life depends on it.'

'I'm on my way. But you owe me big-time.'

'Anything you want. Now hang up. He's waiting.'

'Hey, don't worry. I've got you covered on the money.'

The phone clicked.

'I heard,' said Geautreau.

'Fourteen thousand more where that came from. Write down the number of my cellphone. It's six-oh-one, three-three-two, four-two-one-seven. You can*not* screw this up.'

'Don't worry, Doctor. A pleasure doing business with you.'

Will hung up and headed for the airport.

fourteen

The sign beside the chain link gate read: WELCOME TO GULFPORT-BILOXI REGIONAL AIRPORT. PRESS INTERCOM BUTTON FOR APPROVAL.

Will pressed the button on the post beside his window and waited.

'Good morning,' said a male voice. 'Welcome to US Aviation Corp. How can we help you?'

'This is Dr Will Jennings. I flew in yesterday in Baron November-Two-Whiskey-Juliet. My daughter has been gravely injured in a traffic accident in Jackson, and I must get airborne as soon as possible.'

'Understood, Doctor. We are contacting the tower. Be advised that the Air National Guard has flight operations in progress, and that might cause some delay. Please wait at the gate. We'll get back to you ASAP.'

Air National Guard operations. Will didn't like the sound of that, but it explained all the activity in the sky.

The speaker on the post squawked. 'Dr Jennings, this is Gulfport Tower. We understand your situation and will do everything we can to expedite your takeoff. This is a timed operations exercise and it cannot be stopped. However, we should have a brief window eleven minutes from now during which you can depart.'

Eleven minutes. Hickey and Karen could be halfway to Hazelhurst in eleven minutes. But he had to be careful. If he sounded too upset, they wouldn't open the gate for him.

'I understand, Tower. What do you suggest?'

'When the gate opens, proceed to the white line and stop. An employee of US Aviation Corp will escort you to your plane and assist with your preflight walkaround.'

'Thank you, Tower. Much appreciated.'

The gate slid open. Will pulled up to the white line and put his foot on the brake. He could see his Baron seventy feet away.

Eleven minutes. Evidence of military operations was all around them. Sleek F-18 fighters were on their way to the primary runway. The Hornets lifted into the sky one after another, every thirty seconds. Will also saw two C-130 transports hanging in the sky to his right, preparing to land on the shorter, general aviation runway.

Ten minutes. Hickey would want to be moving towards the money.

And whether he was bound for somewhere near Hazelhurst or the motel in Brookhaven did not matter. Both towns lay on a straight line south from Jackson. Hickey was almost certainly driving south on Interstate 55. Keeping to the speed limit, he could reach Hazelhurst in thirty-five minutes, and he could have left the Jackson airport up to twenty minutes ago. By flying northwest at max cruise, Will could probably reach Hazelhurst before him, but it would be a matter of minutes, perhaps even seconds. How he would find Hickey and Karen—or Huey and Abby—once he got there was something he'd have to figure out on the way. What mattered now was getting airborne.

'Listen,' he said to Cheryl. 'When I give the word, I want you to get out of the car and follow me on foot. To my plane over there.' He pointed at the Baron. 'If I drive past this white line without permission, all hell will break loose. But if we just walk away, they may not notice a thing.'

'You go,' Cheryl said in a tight voice. 'I'm staying here.'

'What?'

'You don't need me.'

Will started to pull out the Walther, but a simpler idea struck him. He took the briefcase off Cheryl's lap, got out, and walked briskly towards the plane. Before he was halfway there, he heard the door of the Tempo slam and the sound of running feet behind him.

'Change your mind?' he said without turning.

'You bastard.'

He opened the Baron's door, tossed the briefcase between the cabin seats, then turned and helped Cheryl into the plane. She settled into the right-hand seat up front. Will sat down in the left seat, then switched on his avionics and started his engines.

A high-pitched sound cut through the engine noise. A siren. Will looked up and saw a boxy airport security vehicle bearing down on them, its red light flashing.

'Shit.' He throttled up and pulled forward, then turned right and started down the taxiway that paralleled the general aviation runway. The vehicle was following, but it couldn't keep up with the rapidly accelerating plane.

'Beechcraft Baron November-Two-Whiskey-Juliet,' crackled the radio. 'This is Gulfport Tower. Return to the ramp immediately.'

Will increased speed. He had thought he might take off from the taxiway, but he saw now that was impossible. A giant C-130 Hercules transport sat astride the taxiway ahead of him, its four props slowly turning. He would have to pass beneath the wing of the Hercules and turn onto the next taxiway.

'Baron Whiskey-Juliet,' said the tower, 'you are endangering the lives of military aircrew and ground personnel. Cut your engines immediately.'

Will swerved left, buzzed under the left wingtip of the C-130, then slowed for the turn that would carry him onto the next taxiway.

Eight hundred feet ahead of him, F-18s were taking off, flashing left to right across his line of sight.

He was going to have to time his takeoff so the Baron would pass between two of the departing Hornets, but he felt confident he could. This was the last takeoff he would ever be allowed to make from this airport, probably any airport. It might as well be his best.

He took his feet off the brakes, and the Baron rolled forward with nauseating slowness compared to the jets. As they approached the intersection with the main runway, an F-18 hurtled towards the same point with a roar. Cheryl screamed and covered her eyes, but Will knew the Hornet would be airborne before they reached the runway. He gave the twin Continentals everything he could.

Seconds before they reached the intersection, the F-18 blasted into the blue. Cheryl was still screaming, but Will let himself ride the rush of adrenaline flushing through his system. All the fatigue of the past twenty-four hours had disappeared. After hours of impotence, he was finally *doing* something.

'Baron Whiskey-Juliet!' barked the radio. 'You are not, repeat not, cleared for takeoff!'

They crossed the intersection at eighty-five knots and the Baron rocketed into the air.

WILL WAS BANKING north at 1,000 feet when he sighted the helicopter a mile behind him. He increased speed and kept climbing, his eye on a bank of cumulus clouds to the northwest.

He had turned down his radio to dampen the sound of the tower, but as they ploughed towards the clouds he detected a new voice competing with that of the furious controller.

'Baron Whiskey-Juliet, this is the helicopter on your starboard side. I am FBI Special Agent John Sims. You have committed multiple felonies. Return to the airport immediately. Please acknowledge.'

'Can he catch us?' Cheryl asked.

'Not a chance. We can do two hundred twenty knots, and we've got clouds ahead. He's history.'

'Baron Whiskey-Juliet,' crackled the radio. 'I'm patching my Special Agent-in-Charge through on this channel. Stand by.'

Will kept climbing towards the cloud bank, pushing the twin engines as hard as they would go. 'Can you see the chopper?'

'Getting smaller by the second,' Cheryl reported.

'Dr Jennings,' crackled the radio. 'This is Zwick. You're putting the lives of your wife and daughter at risk by cutting us out. You're going to need back-up. Without it, your family will end up dead.'

Will keyed his mike. 'That's a risk I'm prepared to take. The best thing you can do is get some agents into Brookhaven. I'll call you back.' He switched off the radio, then the transponder, which would normally broadcast his position to air traffic controllers.

'You've got a bigger problem than that helicopter,' Cheryl said.

'What?'

'You told that guy at the hotel to forward Joey's call through to my cellphone, right? That means that whether Joey tries to call you at the Beau Rivage, or me on my cellphone, he's going to get this phone. How do we decide who answers?'

Will suddenly felt cold. If Hickey called Cheryl and got 'the hotel' instead, his whole plan would be blown. 'We're all right for ten or fifteen minutes,' he said, thinking aloud. 'I'll answer. I'll say we're stuck in traffic on our way back to the Beau Rivage.'

'And after that?'

'By then we'll be halfway to Hazelhurst.'

'Is that where we're going?'

'North is where we're going right now. That's all we know until Joe calls and tells you something else.'

The Baron shot into the clouds and Will's heart lightened. The FBI chopper couldn't see him now unless it had radar.

'When the FBI raided the cabin, they found Huey's truck,' he said. 'Were there any other cars at the cabin?'

'I told you, I never went there.'

'But you must have heard them talking.'

Cheryl shook her head in exasperation.

In the switchboard centre at the Beau Rivage, a young operator sat reading a Stephen King novel. When the hotel's main line rang, he answered the way he always did: 'Beau Rivage Casino Resort'.

But when the caller asked for Suite 28021, he punched a key on his computer. A digital connection was made and a forwarding number dialled, as requested by Remy Geautreau, the front desk manager. The operator went back to his novel.

THE CELLPHONE RANG. Will jumped, dug it quickly from his pocket and checked his watch. 'I'm going to answer,' he said. 'Hold the phone up to my ear, and hit SEND when I tell you.'

Cheryl held up the phone, but Will said nothing. He had just realised something. Telling Hickey they were stuck in traffic wouldn't explain the roar of the Baron's engines.

The phone kept ringing. 'Are you going to answer?' Cheryl asked.

Will pulled back to idle, feathered his props and killed both engines. In the eerie silence, the plane began to fall.

'*Shit!*' Cheryl screamed. 'What happened? Are we going to crash?'

'We're fine! Hit SEND!'

He heard a beep, then the hiss of the open connection. 'Joe!'

'How's it hanging, Doc? You taking a nap up there?'

Up there? Will's heart thudded. Then he realised that Hickey meant the hotel suite. He'd assumed Hickey would call Cheryl before he called the Beau Rivage, to verify that she'd got the money. But Hickey had clearly expected Will to answer this call. And Geautreau had successfully patched it through.

'Where's Abby?' Will asked, trying to picture himself in the suite at the Beau Rivage rather than dropping towards the earth at a thousand feet per minute. 'I want to talk to her.'

'Everything in its season, Doc. I'll be talking to you soon.'

The phone went dead. Will dropped it in Cheryl's lap and began his midair engine-start sequence. He felt a rush of exhilaration as the Continentals fired up. He adjusted the pitch of his props and felt the plane leap forward as the blades bit into the air.

Cheryl's face was bone white.

Will began climbing to regain the lost altitude. 'Cheryl, I've got to know what kind of car Huey's driving.'

'If you'd keep the damn engines running, maybe I could think.'

'Think like you've never thought before in your life, goddamn it! We're at seven thousand feet. We can glide for seven minutes without engines before we crash.'

'I'm trying to help you!'

'Try harder.'

The cellphone rang in her lap. 'Who answers this time?' she asked. 'You. He just called me. And try to find out what Huey's driving.' 'OK.'

'Wait till I cut the engines.'

'Sweet Mary . . .'

Once again, Will starved the engines into silence.

Cheryl hit SEND as the plane began to glide earthward. 'Joey? . . . Yeah, I've got it.' She gave Will a thumbs up. 'Yeah. No problem. I think he's about wasted by the whole thing . . . I'm on 110 now, headed up toward the interstate. Am I still going to the motel? . . . Yeah, I remember . . . Uh huh . . . What about Huey and the little girl?' She jerked the phone away from her ear. 'I'm sorry . . . I'm on my way.' She clicked off.

Will restarted the engines, and once again the Baron began to climb. 'What did he say about Abby?'

'He told me not to talk about it on the phone.'

'What else did he say?'

'Go to Paco's place.'

'What's that?'

'A club. It's on the county line near Hattiesburg. I danced there for a while. They've got rooms out back for the girls.'

'He said the name of the club on the phone?'

'No. The name of the club is Paradise Alley. Paco works there.'

Will pulled out a map. Hattiesburg was southeast of Jackson, down Highway 49. It was closer to their present position, but there was no way he could cover both I-55 and Highway 49. And the fact that Cheryl had been told to go to Paco's place didn't mean Hickey was going straight there, or that Huey had been given the same instructions.

'Son of a bitch,' Cheryl said.

'What?'

'The Rambler! Joey's mom had an AMC Rambler. An old white thing. It was the club made me think of it. Paradise Alley. Joey's mom got to where she couldn't drive, and one night Joey showed up at Paradise Alley in her car. When we tried to leave, it broke down. It supposedly sat up on blocks for a couple of years, but I never saw it. Maybe the Rambler was at the cabin.'

Will couldn't suppress his excitement. At last, he had something. A white Rambler. And Abby might be in it. But where was it? 'The FBI found a cellphone at the cabin,' he reasoned aloud. 'So, unless Huey had two cellphones, Joe can't contact him while he's on the road.'

'I'm pretty sure Huey only had one,' Cheryl said.

'Does Huey know about Paradise Alley? Has he ever been there?'

She laughed. 'Are you kidding? You can't take Huey in there. One glimpse of a naked woman, he blows a gasket. Joey brought him to see me dance once, and he jumped up on stage trying to throw his coat over me.'

'Has Huey spent any time in or around Hattiesburg?'

'Not that I know of.'

'Then Huey isn't headed for Paco's place. He's probably going wherever he was supposed to go according to the original back-up plan. Joe changed your instructions, but I don't think he'd do that to Huey. So, what was Huey's original back-up destination? Where would Joe have told him to go if there was a problem?'

'Joey wouldn't want him driving too far. Not with your little girl along. Too much chance of the highway patrol stopping him.'

'I think Huey's going to the motel in Brookhaven, then. It's only twenty minutes from Hazelhurst, less than an hour from the cabin. Joe could get there from Jackson in fifty minutes, pick up Huey and Abby, then head east to Hattiesburg to meet you.'

'Makes sense to me.'

'If I'm right, Joe is driving south on I-55 right now. Huey is, too. They're probably twenty minutes apart in the southbound lanes. To hell with Highway 49.'

Will gripped the yoke with both hands and put the Baron into a steep turn.

KAREN LOOKED into the trunk of the Camry and put her hand to her mouth. The woman Hickey had carjacked had beaten her hands bloody in her attempts to get out of the trunk and the left side of her head was swollen from the pistol blow.

'Get out,' Karen said. 'Hurry! Before he changes his mind.'

Hickey was sitting in the Camry, talking on the cellphone, checking on Will. At Karen's urging, he had pulled off the interstate at a deserted exit to let the woman out of the trunk.

'Come on!' Karen hissed. She reached in and pulled the woman up by the arms. Somehow she got her on her feet, then pushed her towards the trees on the side of the road.

The woman looked around. The only sign of civilisation was a boarded up gas station. 'Are you going to leave me here?' she asked.

'You're safer here than you are with us. Run! Go on! Run!'

IN THE SWITCHBOARD centre at the Beau Rivage, the operator was heavily into his Stephen King novel. Trivialities like gainful employment simply could not compete. The young man answered the primary line on autopilot, and when the caller asked for Suite 28021 he said, 'Just one moment' as he usually did and made the connection.

Twenty-eight floors above him, the phones in Will's suite rang, faded, and rang again. The operator read another paragraph, then blinked and raised his head from the page. He was certain that something was wrong, he just couldn't place what it was. It took a few seconds to realise his mistake, but he thought he still had time to correct it. He was reaching for the computer keyboard to execute the call-forwarding command when the phones in 28021 stopped ringing.

'Shit,' he whispered. Geautreau had promised him a hundred bucks if he'd forward the suite's calls for the next three hours.

THE BARON ROARED northwards above Interstate 55 at 200 knots. Will didn't think they had covered enough distance to sight Huey's Rambler yet—if in fact he was driving the Rambler but he was flying parallel to the southbound lanes just in case.

The cellphone began ringing again. From habit Will reached for the throttles, then stopped himself. If he cut the engines at 300 feet, the state police would soon be hosing them off the interstate.

'Who answers it?' Cheryl asked.

'You.'

'Joey already told me where to go. He wouldn't call again.'

Will considered not answering at all, but he couldn't risk it. He pulled the throttles back as far as he dared, then picked up the Nokia and hit SEND. 'Hello?'

He heard only the open connection. Then someone said, 'Jennings?'

'Joe?'

'You wanna tell me how I dialled Cheryl and got you?'

Will gripped the phone tighter but kept his voice calm. 'You must have dialled the wrong number. You thought you were dialling her, but you dialled the hotel instead.'

Hickey didn't reply.

'Joe?'

'Put Cheryl on the phone.'

Will's breath caught in his throat. 'How do I do that?'

'You hand her the fucking phone, that's how.' The coldness of Hickey's voice was worse than any blast of temper.

'Joe, I'm telling you—'

'No, I'm telling *you*, Doc. I'm gonna let you in on a little secret. You're never going to talk to your kid again. It was always going to be that way. Had to be. From the day you murdered my mother. You took what was precious to me, so I gotta take what's precious to you.'

Hickey's words cut to the bone, but something more terrible struck Will like a hammer. There was no way Hickey could speak that way if Karen were in the car with him. She would be screaming at the least, possibly even trying to kill him.

'Where's Karen, Joe? I know she's not with you. What have you done to her?'

'You don't need to worry about that. No point at all.'

The phone went dead. A numbness began to spread through Will's body. It was like being cut adrift in space.

KAREN CLOSED the Camry's trunk and looked over her shoulder at the woman, who was making for the abandoned gas station. Karen walked to the passenger door and climbed in beside Hickey. He was off the phone, just staring through the windshield.

'Did you talk to Will?'

'I talked to him.'

'What did he say?'

'It's not what he said. It's where he said it. He wasn't in his suite.'

She felt a stab of alarm. 'What?'

'He answered Cheryl's cellphone. I told you he was pulling something. You just remember, he asked for every bit of this.' Hickey spun the Camry in a 180-degree turn, and sped back to the interstate.

WILL REDUCED HIS AIR SPEED to 100 knots. They were far enough north now that spotting Huey and Abby was a possibility. It was more than that, in fact. It was his only hope.

He prayed that Hickey had no way to contact Huey while he was out on the road. That Abby would remain alive for the next fifteen or twenty minutes while Will tried to locate her from the air.

He switched on his radio. He had just thought of a way in which the FBI might help him after all.

'Baron November-Two-Whiskey-Juliet,' crackled the speaker. 'This is an emergency call. Please respond.'

He keyed his mike. 'This is Baron Whiskey-Juliet, over.'

There was a brief silence. Then a voice said, 'Dr Jennings, this is

Frank Zwick. Where are you? Let us help you.'

Will shook his head. The FBI man didn't give up easily. There was no knowing how long they had been making that emergency radio call. Ever since he'd switched off the plane's radio, probably.

'Where I am doesn't matter.' He kept his eyes on the interstate. 'Tell me, did you figure out how Hickey escaped from the airport?'

'We're pretty sure he carjacked a Toyota Camry. A silver ninety-two model. We got it off the garage security tapes. Doctor, we need to know where you are. We can't—'

Will switched off the radio.

'Have you seen anything?' he asked Cheryl.

'I'm looking. I've seen every other kind of car, but no Rambler.'

'Scan, don't focus.' He saw Lexuses, 4WDs by the dozen, semi-trucks, Winnebagos and motorcycles. But no Rambler. 'Be right,' he said softly, holding the image of a Rambler in his mind. 'Be right.'

'Oh my God,' Cheryl said. 'I saw it.'

'The Rambler?'

She turned to him and nodded, her eyes wide. 'It was them. I saw Huey's face. I saw your little girl in the passenger window.'

Will craned his neck to look back, but the spot was far behind them now. Climbing skywards, he pulled the Baron round.

fifteen

As soon as Will completed his turn and settled the Baron back over the oncoming traffic, he saw the small white car. Box-shaped and splotched with primer, it was idling along compared to the other traffic, constantly being passed. Cheryl was right: it was a Rambler. Will reduced power, slowing the plane until it was practically drifting up the interstate towards the car.

Then he saw it. A small head in the passenger compartment, sitting close to a huge figure behind the wheel. As the Baron closed on the Rambler, Will made out the form and face he would have known by the dimmest candlelight. Relief unlike any he had ever known rolled through him. Abby was alive. And nothing on God's earth would keep him from her now.

'Hello, Alpha-Juliet,' he said softly. He waggled the plane's wings.

HUEY AND ABBY were singing 'Itsy-Bitsy Spider' when the plane first appeared, flying straight towards them at treetop level.

'Look!' Huey cried. 'A crop duster!'

'He's not supposed to fly that low,' Abby said in a concerned voice. 'I know, because my daddy flies an airplane.'

The plane shot past them. Abby whipped her head round and watched it climb, then vanish beyond her line of sight.

'I rode a airplane once,' Huey said. 'When Joey took me to Disneyland.'

Abby patted Belle in her lap. 'I met the real Belle there. And the real Snow White. And I got a dress just like she had.'

'If I made you something,' Huey said softly, 'would you like it?'

'Sure I would.'

'It probably wouldn't be as nice as the things you got at home.'

'Sure it would. Presents you make are better than ones you buy.'

He reached into the side pocket of his overalls and brought out what he had spent the previous night carving. The chunk of cedar had been transformed into a figure of a bear holding a little girl on its lap. The little girl's hair fell to her shoulders like Abby's and she wore a dress like Abby's. But what riveted Abby's attention was the bear itself. On its face sat a pair of heavy glasses, just like Huey's. The bear was clearly watching out for the little girl.

She opened her mouth in wonder. 'You really made that?'

Huey nodded shyly. 'Beauty and the Beast. I tried to make it as pretty as I could. I know you like pretty things.'

She took the carving from his hand. The wood was still warm from Huey's pocket. But more than that, it felt alive somehow.

'I love it,' she said. 'I *love* it.'

Huey's eyes lit up. 'You do?'

Abby nodded, her eyes still on the figures.

'Maybe you'll remember me sometimes, then.'

She looked up at him with curiosity in her eyes. 'Of course I will.'

Huey suddenly cried out and hit the brake pedal. Abby grabbed the dashboard, fearing they were about to smash into something.

The airplane was back, only this time it was right over the road and zooming straight at them. As Abby stared, its wings rocked up and down: first the right wing, then the left, then both again.

A thrill went through her. 'He waggled his wings! My daddy does that! Just the same . . .' Her face suddenly felt hot, and she had to squeeze her legs together to keep from wetting herself. Her daddy was in that plane. She knew it. And nothing in her life had ever felt quite the way that knowing that did. She reached out and touched Huey's arm. 'Everything's going to be OK now.'

AS THE BARON BLASTED past the Rambler, Will saw Abby's face pressed to the glass of the passenger window. Tears temporarily blinded him.

'I told you!' Cheryl cried. 'You saw them?'

'Yes,' he said, wiping his eyes with his sleeve.

'What are you going to do now?'

'I'm going to land.'

'On the *road*?'

'Absolutely.'

Cheryl's face went so white that Will thought she might pass out.

'Tighten that seat belt.'

As she scrabbled at her belt, Will climbed to 500 feet and took the Baron to 180 knots.

'Where are you going? You said you were going to land . . .'

'We've got something to do first. Watch for a silver Camry.'

Cheryl's hand flew to her mouth. She had heard Zwick on the radio, and she knew who was driving a silver Camry.

'Keep it together,' Will said. 'Everything's fine.' He hated to let the Rambler out of his sight for even one minute, but he could cover five miles of interstate in ninety seconds, and if Hickey was close enough to give him problems on the ground, he needed to know.

'I see a Camry!' Cheryl said. 'It's silver.'

Will climbed quickly to 1,000 feet. He would have liked nothing better than to descend and see whether Karen was in that car, but if he got close enough to see her, Hickey could spot him. The silver Camry below might not be the one Hickey had stolen—there were a lot of silver Camrys in the world—but it could be. He needed to get on the ground fast.

He executed a teardrop turn, pointed the Baron south at 200 knots, and began to consider the task he had set himself. There was really only one way to stop a car with an unarmed airplane. Land in front of it.

'There it is!' Cheryl said, pointing through the windshield.

She had good eyes. About a mile and a half ahead, a long line of cars had backed up behind a slow-moving vehicle in the right lane, while faster-moving traffic shot past them on the left.

Will cut his air speed and dropped to 400 feet. The vehicles below were moving between seventy and eighty miles per hour. At ninety knots, he was rapidly overtaking them, moving into position to land in front of the Rambler. As he approached the congested line of cars, he lowered his landing gear and went to full flaps. This further reduced his speed, bringing him more in line with the speed of the vehicles below, though he was still overtaking them.

He descended to 100 feet. Airspeed was eighty-five knots, still too fast. Cheryl leaned forward, watching the concrete rise towards them and endlessly repeating Hail Marys.

A brief crosswind tried to push the tail round, but Will corrected for it. He shut everything out of his mind but the scene ahead. In the right lane: the white Rambler, moving slowly. A Mercury Sable about sixty yards ahead of it, and a minivan some distance ahead of that.

It was now or never. He centred the Baron on the broken white line and dropped towards the roof of the Rambler at eighty-two knots. He couldn't see what was happening behind him, but he felt sure that the sight of a twin-engine plane dropping towards the road with its gear and flaps down had sent a lot of feet to a lot of brake pedals.

The Baron overtook the Rambler with a speed differential of thirty miles per hour. Will flew half the distance to the Mercury Sable, then eased the yoke forward and reduced power further. The Baron seemed to stutter in midair. Then it fell like a stone.

THREE MILES BEHIND the Baron, Hickey gaped and pointed through the windshield of the Camry.

'Look at that crazy son of a bitch! If he's got to crash, the least he could do is get off the highway to do it.'

Karen said nothing. The instant the Baron had dropped out of the sky and lined itself up over the interstate, her heart had jumped into her throat. It had to be Will. It *had* to be.

'What's he doing up there?' Hickey wondered aloud. 'He's a kamikaze, this guy. He must have lost an engine.'

He looked to Karen for a response, but she sat still and silent, staring at the dashboard. If Will was risking his life to land on the interstate, that could mean only one thing. Abby was somewhere up ahead. And she was alive.

'What's with you?' Hickey said. 'You gotta see this. This'll make CNN tonight.' He punched her on the shoulder. 'You sick or something? Why are you—'

He faced forward again and watched the plane drop to the level of the cars ahead, then disappear.

'Son of a bitch!' he said. He floored the accelerator and started to pass the Cadillac ahead of them.

Karen grabbed the wheel and wrenched it towards her, throwing the Camry into the right lane and forcing the Cadillac off the road.

'Let go!' Hickey yelled, hammering her head with his fist.

Karen clung to the wheel like a sea captain in a gale. The Camry veered onto the shoulder, which dropped precipitously to the woods below. She didn't care if they crashed into the trees, so long as it kept Hickey from reaching Abby.

'Let go, you crazy bitch!' He slammed an elbow into her ear and yanked the car back onto the road. Karen blacked out for a moment. She knew she had because, when she came to, her hands had slipped from the wheel, and the Camry's engine was whining as Hickey streaked past the cars ahead. She saw then that he was steering with only his left hand. His right held Will's .38, pointed at her stomach.

'Do it again and I'll kill you,' he said in a matter of fact voice.

She backed against the passenger door. As the speedometer needle went to ninety, then a hundred, Karen studied the gun in Hickey's hand. It was somehow more frightening than the idea of a wreck. A wreck at this speed would certainly kill them both, but the gun might kill only her. And Abby was so close—

Hickey cursed and applied the brake. A long chain of flashing red lights had appeared ahead. Brake lights. Something was happening up there. And that something had to be Will Jennings's plane. Hickey swerved onto the central reservation and raced past the braking cars, hatred burning in his face like a sulphurous fire.

Fixing an image of Abby in her mind, Karen began to pray. The image she saw was not Abby as she was now, but as an infant, the miracle of flesh and bone and smiling eyes that Karen had given up her career for, that she would give up everything for. A profound sadness seeped outwards from her heart, but with it came a peace that transcended her fear. She closed her eyes.

'I love you, Abby,' she said softly. 'I'm sorry, Will.'

'What?' Hickey said, fighting to keep the Camry moving past the bumper-to-bumper cars.

Karen curled her fingers into claws and launched herself across the console with murder in her heart.

Hickey fired.

THE BARON HIT THE CONCRETE hard, and Will's plan instantly began to disintegrate. The driver of the Sable must have slowed, because the Baron was racing towards it far too fast to stop. Will hit the throttles and hopped over the car, but when the wheels hit again he saw that the minivan that had been comfortably ahead of the Sable had also braked, probably to watch the crisis unfolding behind it.

He pulled up his flaps, cut power and applied the brakes, but he saw in an instant that he wouldn't be able to stop in time. He no longer had enough power or distance to skip over the minivan as he had the Sable, and his props were spinning with enough force to chop the van into scrap metal. Yet the driver wouldn't get off the damned road to avoid the crash. Then Will saw the group of heads in the back of the van.

Kids.

He swerved left and shut off his fuel and electrics. He felt a moment of euphoria as they passed the van, but it turned to horror as his right wingtip clipped the vehicle and they began to spin.

Cheryl was shrieking, and at some point in the whirling chaos Will saw a log truck barrelling up from behind them. Sitting in front of the log truck like a Matchbox toy was the white Rambler. As they spun round to face it again, Will saw the little car suddenly scoot forward out of the log truck's path, but his relief died as it went over the narrow shoulder and plummeted down the slope towards the trees.

'We've got to get out!' he shouted, gripping Cheryl's arm.

The plane had come to rest, and the thirty-ton juggernaut of steel and wood that was the log truck was speeding towards them with the sound of burning brakes. Will unbuckled both seat belts, then leaned over Cheryl and unlatched the door. 'Get out!' he shouted.

But she didn't. She was trying to look back into the cabin. Will scrambled over her and onto the wing, then pulled her from the cockpit. She was yelling something at him, but he shoved her onto the ground and jumped off after her.

'*The money!*' she screamed. '*We left the money!*'

'Forget it!' He grabbed her arm and tried to pull her clear, but she jerked free and jumped back onto the wing.

Will ran for the edge of the road.

AS THE RAMBLER hurtled down the grassy slope towards the trees, Huey pumped the brake, but it seemed to have no effect. Abby was screaming in his ear. His mind went blank for a second, but then a thought flashed like a Roman candle. He grabbed Abby with both hands and tossed her into the back seat like a sack of flour.

The Rambler crashed into a wall of saplings, hurling Huey forwards and smashing his head against the windshield. Abby smacked into the back of the front seat and bounced backwards.

She couldn't seem to get her breath, but other than that she felt OK. She got to her knees and looked over the front seat.

The windshield was smashed to pieces. Huey was bleeding from his forehead, and he wasn't moving. 'Huey?' she said. 'Beast?'

He moaned and held his ribs. Abby climbed over the seat and took hold of his right hand. 'Wake up, Beast.' She shook the hand again, then pinched it. 'Can you talk? Daddy didn't mean to hurt you!'

A loud boom sounded behind her, followed by a whoomph that made the air around the car glow for several seconds. Terror for her father went through her like a knife. 'Beast? Wake up!'

His right eye blinked, and he groaned in pain. 'Run,' he whispered. 'Run, Jo Ellen. I smell gas. And there's a bad man coming. Run to Daddy.'

Jo Ellen? And then she remembered. Huey's little sister was named Jo Ellen. Abby looked down at the floor. Belle and the carved bear and child lay in a mosaic of shattered glass. She picked up Belle and put her in Huey's lap, then grabbed the bear and climbed out of the passenger door. She wished she could pull Huey out, but trying to pull Huey would be like trying to pull a mountain. She turned away from the car and looked up the steep hill.

A tall man was looking down at her out of the sun. She couldn't see his face, only his silhouette. Then the shape of the man stirred something in her. 'Daddy?' she said hesitantly.

The shadow began running down the hill.

CHERYL CRAWLED onto the grass of the central reservation. Her knees were cut to pieces, her hair stank of gasoline, her eyelashes were gone, and her left forearm had a big red blister on it.

But she had the money.

Behind her lay what was left of the plane, a burning mass of twisted metal. A mile-long line of cars had stacked up behind the wrecked plane, and dozens of people were gawking

Cheryl coughed up black smoke, and the spasm hurt like a wire brush inside her rib cage. She thought she might have breathed fire during the explosion. What the hell. It was a small price to pay.

She got to her feet, then picked up the blackened briefcase and started for the trees on the ridge that divided the northbound and southbound lanes.

KAREN LAY against the passenger door of the Camry, staring at the small hole in her upper abdomen. Hickey was gone. He'd shot her and left her for dead.

Through the windshield she saw cars but no plane. She'd heard an explosion a few moments before, one she hoped was not Will's Baron. But it could have been. And if something had happened to Will, Abby might be alone up there with Hickey and the others.

Karen opened the Camry's glove box, found a wad of Kleenex, and stuffed it into the bullet hole. Then, steeling herself against the pain, she forced herself to turn and pop open the Camry's door.

Half falling onto the road, she decided to let her legs follow. After they did, she rolled onto her stomach, annoyed by the numbness of her midsection. Getting up seemed impossible. Then the smell of burning aviation fuel reached her, and she changed her mind.

WILL SNATCHED ABBY up and hugged her as tight as he dared.

'Where's Mom?' she asked. 'Is Mom with you?'

He had no answer. 'Come on, sweetie. Let's find her.'

'Wait. Huey's hurt. He's stuck in the car and he's bleeding!'

Will moved close enough to the Rambler to see that Abby's kidnapper was badly hurt. The tang of gasoline was in the air. If the car caught fire, he'd be burned alive.

Will set Abby down and ran to the driver's door. It had not been jammed shut in the crash, but the man was most definitely jammed behind the wheel. Will could scarcely budge him.

'Huey!' he yelled. 'Help me! *Move!*'

The man's left forearm was like a ham. Will grabbed it with both hands and pulled with all his strength. With a groan, Huey twisted in the seat and heaved himself out onto the ground. There was just enough slope for Will to roll him away from the car.

'Let's go find Mom!' Abby called.

He wasn't sure what to do. The smart thing would probably be to duck into the woods and wait for the police to show up. But what if Hickey *had* been in that silver Camry? And what if Karen was still with him? She might be bound and gagged in the back seat, or lying wounded in the trunk. He wished he had Cheryl's pistol, but there was no point in wishing. The gun had exploded with the plane.

He scooped Abby into his arms and looked up the shoulder. A dozen people stood along the crest, looking down at him. There were probably hundreds of cars backed up already. A world-class traffic snarl. If Hickey was up there with them, so be it. Somebody up there would have a gun. This was Mississippi, after all. They might *all* have guns. He hitched Abby up on his hip and climbed up the shoulder.

'*EVERYBODY BACK!*' screamed a male voice.

Will thought it was a cop until the men around him began to scatter, half of them sliding down the shoulder behind him, the others running back to their cars. His eyes picked out a man standing thirty feet away. He had dark hair and black eyes, and one of his trouser legs was soaked with blood. As Will watched, he raised his arm. A revolver gleamed blue-black in the sun.

Hickey.

There was nowhere to run. If he made a dash down the hill with Abby in his arms, Hickey could simply take a few steps and shoot them as they tried to reach the trees.

'Where's my money, Doc?' Hickey asked, his eyes smouldering.

Will pointed at the burning plane. 'In there.'

'You'd better be lying.'

'I'm too tired to lie.'

'Where's Cheryl?'

'I don't know.'

Keeping his gun trained on Will and Abby, Hickey backed to the edge of the shoulder and looked down. 'That's the way, Huey!' he shouted. 'Come on, boy! You can do it! You know what happens now?' Hickey asked, focusing on Will and Abby again.

'What?'

'This.'

He fired, and Will felt his right leg buckle. He almost collapsed, but he managed to keep on his feet long enough to set Abby down and move in front of her. She was screaming in terror. He considered telling her to run for it, but he doubted she would, and any such move might cause Hickey to shoot again. He felt her clutching his trousers from behind.

'Shot by your own gun,' Hickey said. 'How does it feel?'

Will looked down. The bullet had caught him in the thigh, but away on the lateral side, away from the femoral artery.

Hickey yelled back over his shoulder: 'Come on, Buckethead! Train's leaving!'

'Get out of here while you can, Joe,' Will said.

Hickey laughed. 'Oh, I'll be gettin' on soon. But you and me got an account to settle. And that little girl behind you is the legal tender.'

He took two steps closer. Will was about to snatch Abby up and try to run for it when a female voice stopped Hickey in his tracks.

'*I got the money, Joey!*'

Cheryl was standing on the far side of the road, by the central reservation. The smile on her face was forced, but she was making an effort. 'Let's get out of here, Joey. Come on!'

'Well, well,' Hickey said. 'The prodigal slut.' He shook his head. 'Gotta finish what you start, babe.'

Her smile vanished. 'There's no reason to hurt that little girl, Joey. Not any more.'

'You know there is.'

'Killing her won't bring your mama back.'

His eyes blazed. 'He'll feel some of what I've felt!' Hickey lowered his aim to Will's legs, which hardly shielded Abby at all.

'Joey, don't!' Cheryl opened the ransom briefcase, took out her Walther, and aimed it at Hickey's chest. 'It wasn't even his fault! Let's go to Costa Rica. Your ranch is waiting!'

Hickey looked at Will and laughed bitterly. 'Turned her against me, didn't you? Well . . . she always was a stupid cow.'

He turned casually towards Cheryl and fired, blowing her back onto the central reservation and spilling 100-dollar bills across the grass. Then his gun was on Will again, his aim dancing from head to chest to legs. As he played his little game, a strange beating sound echoed over the interstate. Will recognised it first: the *whup-whup-whup* of rotor blades. Hickey soon understood its meaning, but instead of bolting he took two steps closer to Will.

'What do I want with a ranch in Costa Rica? *This* is what I came for. What goes around comes around, Doc.'

Will felt a hard tug on his trousers. 'Daddy, *look*.'

As Hickey steadied his aim, Will threw himself on top of Abby. Then he turned and looked death full in the face.

He expected a muzzle flash, but what he saw was a forearm the size of a ham slip round Hickey's neck and lift him bodily into the air.

'You can't hurt Abby,' Huey said. 'You can hurt Huey, but you can't hurt Abby. She's my Belle.'

Hickey's eyes bulged with surprise. He tried to bring his pistol far enough back to shoot his cousin, but the first shot didn't come close. The forearm just lifted him higher, closing off his windpipe. Hickey's legs kicked like a badly hanged man's. He somehow managed to choke out three words, but they were poorly chosen.

'*You—goddamn—retard—*'

Will watched in fascination as Huey choked the life out of his cousin, his face as placid as that of a mountain gorilla at rest. Hickey's last bullet tore off part of Huey's ear, then the gun clicked empty.

Hickey's limbs went limp as rags, and his gun clattered onto the concrete. After a few seconds, Huey set him gently on the side of the road, sat beside him, and began to pet his head. Then he shook him gently, as if he might suddenly wake up.

'Joey? Joey?'

The beating of the helicopter was now much louder. Will rolled off Abby, unbuckled his belt, and tied it around his wounded thigh.

'Look,' Abby said in a small voice. 'Huey's crying.'

Huey had knelt over Hickey and put a hand over his mouth to feel for breath. When he felt none, he started mewling like a baby. 'Why'd you want to hurt Belle?' he sobbed. 'It's not right to hurt little girls. Mamaw told us that.'

'We've got to help him, Daddy.' Abby started towards Huey, but Will limped after her and brought her back.

'I need you here, baby. We've got to find Mom.'

'I'm right here,' someone said from behind them.

Will turned. Karen was standing on the other side of the road, an automatic pistol in her hand. It was Cheryl's Walther. She was pointing it at its owner, while Cheryl crawled over the grass stuffing 100-dollar bills back into the briefcase.

Abby started to run to Karen, but Will caught her arm and pulled her back. Karen was not herself. If she was, she would have run to Abby as soon as she sighted her.

'Bring me the gun, Karen,' he said.

She seemed not to have heard. Dazed, she continued to point the Walther at Cheryl's head, two feet away. For her part, Cheryl seemed not to notice. She just kept stuffing bills into the briefcase. Will saw blood on her shoulder, but apparently Hickey's bullet had not done major damage.

He limped across to his wife. 'Karen? May I please have the gun?'

'She's one of them!' Karen cried suddenly. 'Isn't she?'

'It's over,' he said, holding out his hand. 'Hickey's dead. And she's not going anywhere.'

Karen jerked the Walther out of his reach. As she did, Will saw a large bloodstain on her upper abdomen.

'What happened?'

'He shot me,' she said, still following Cheryl with the gun.

'Drop the weapon!' shouted a male voice. *'Police! Drop the gun and lie down on the ground!'*

Will turned and saw two uniformed state troopers pointing revolvers at Karen. 'Hold your fire!' he yelled. 'She's in shock!'

'Drop that weapon!' one trooper shouted again.

Karen turned towards them but did not drop the gun. Will knew they might fire at any moment. He stepped forward and put his body between their guns and Karen, but even as he did, a fierce wind sprang up, driving gravel across the road in a punishing spiral.

A Bell helicopter with 'FBI' stencilled in yellow on the fuel tank set down near the dwindling fire that had been Will's plane. Two men in suits leaped out of the cockpit and ran towards the state troopers, their badges held out in front of them. A hurried conversation resulted in one of the troopers lowering his gun, but the other did not seem impressed. One of the agents interposed himself between the stubborn trooper and Karen, and addressed himself to Will.

'Are you Dr Jennings?'

'Yes.'

'I'm Frank Zwick, Doctor. I'm glad to see you alive.'

'I'm glad to see you. Can you help us? My wife has been shot, and she's disorientated.'

'Can you get her to put down the gun?'

Will turned to Karen and held up his hands. 'Honey, you've got to give me the gun. These people are here to help us. You can't—'

Karen wobbled, then crumpled forward onto the ground.

Will ran forward and knelt beside her. Her pulse was weak. Carefully he rolled her over and unbuttoned the blood-soaked blouse. The bullet had struck her in the left upper abdomen.

'What's wrong with Mom?' Abby wailed. 'Daddy?'

'She's all right,' he assured her, though the wound could be fatal if not treated quickly in an operating room.

'We've got paramedics about five miles out,' Zwick said. 'They're coming up the shoulder in an ambulance. I'd estimate fifteen to twenty minutes.'

'I want her in your chopper,' Will told him. 'You can have her on the helipad at University Hospital in ten minutes.'

'That's not an air ambulance, Doctor. It's just a row of seats.'

'It beats waiting. Make it happen, Frank.'

The SAC nodded and ran over to talk to his pilot.

'Abby?' said Karen, her eyes fluttering. 'Where's Abby?' She struggled to rise. 'Where's my baby?'

'Right here, Mom.' Abby knelt beside her mother.

Karen seized her hand, then raised her head, looking right and left. 'Where's Hickey?'

'Dead,' Will told her again. 'We're all safe, babe.'

It took a few moments for this to register, but at last Karen sighed and closed her eyes again. Will checked her pulse. She was going into shock. They needed to get moving.

'Daddy's going to make you all better, Mom.'

Karen smiled a ghostly smile. 'I know, baby.'

'Does it hurt a lot?'

'With you holding my hand, nothing hurts.'

Abby laughed through tears.

'All set,' Zwick said, coming over. 'Ready to move her?'

'I'm a little under the weather,' Will told him.

'My daddy got shot in the leg,' Abby said proudly. 'He was trying to save me.'

'Whose money is this?' called a state trooper, holding up the ransom briefcase. Beside him, his partner was cuffing Cheryl's hands behind her back.

'Mine,' Will said. 'That woman was shot in the shoulder, and she was in a fire. Put her aboard the ambulance as soon as it gets here.'

'That's *my* money!' Cheryl yelled. She pointed at Will. 'Ask him!'

'Take it with you,' Will told the trooper. 'We'll sort it out later.'

'How much is in here?'

'Three hundred and fifty thousand.'

The trooper whistled long and low.

'You lying bastard!' Cheryl yelled at Will. 'I knew it!'

'I won't forget what I said,' he told her. 'I'll come to court and tell them what you did to help us.' He turned back to Zwick. 'Let's get Karen into the chopper.'

Zwick motioned for the troopers and the pilot to help.

'What about Huey?' Abby asked. 'Can he come, too?'

Will pointed at the spectacled giant, who was still trying to rouse

Joey from his permanent slumber. 'That one isn't for the county jail. He needs a psychological evaluation. If you'll take him to University, I'll get him onto the ward.'

The trooper holding the briefcase nodded.

Someone had made a pallet of blue FBI windbreakers on the floor of the chopper, and they laid Karen on it.

As the chopper beat its way into the sky, Will went forward and radioed the attending physician in the University Hospital emergency room, outlining Karen's case.

When he returned to the cabin, Karen's eyes were open. She said something he couldn't hear above the noise of the rotors, so he leaned down to her mouth.

'Family,' she whispered. 'Again.'

'We're a family again!' cried Abby, looking at Will with wide eyes. 'That's what she said!'

'That's what she said, all right,' he agreed. Suddenly something broke loose in him, and waves of grief and joy rolled through his heart.

'You're shaking, Daddy,' Abby said.

'I'm OK. It's been a long day.'

She smiled uncertainly, searching his eyes for the invincible father she had always known, for signs that everything would soon return to normal. Will took her free hand in his, just as she held Karen's. Together they formed a circle that he vowed would never again be broken. He had made such vows before, usually after seeing some tragic death in the hospital, but eventually the grind of daily existence dulled his awareness of the central truth of life. Chaos was working beneath everything, and death always waited in the wings, watchful as a crow. This time he would not forget how precious was the time he shared with those who loved him. This time he would keep that knowledge close in his heart.

This time . . .

GREG ILES

Before he became a writer, forty-year-old Greg Iles was a dedicated member of a band called Frankly Scarlet that toured all over the Southern USA. 'Music is so powerful,' he says. 'Once you're involved in it, either it won't let you go, or you won't let go of it.'

When he married his wife Carrie, however, it became clear that a life that entailed spending fifty-one out of fifty-two weeks on the road would be impossible to sustain. A turning point came on New Year's Eve 1990 when Iles was holed up in a motel alone, having rowed with the other band members. 'I called Carrie and I told her I was quitting music for ever. I said, "I'm gonna write a book. If I don't sell it in a year, I'll get a real job."'

She supported his decision, and he considers himself very lucky that his first two novels, *Black Cross* and *Spandau Phoenix*—both Second World War thrillers—did very well. *Mortal Fear* and *The Quiet Game*, which tackled the very different subjects of Internet crime and race relations in the Deep South, were even more successful, and Greg Iles's following grew.

With a Hollywood feature film of *24 Hours* now in the making, Iles has achieved an enviable degree of financial security for his family. It meant that when his son, Mark, was born prematurely in 1996 and had to have three blood transfusions while still in the womb, he could be at his wife's side. 'It's unbelievable when you see him now to think that he was born that small. He's doing great.' The couple, who also have a six-year-old daughter, Madeleine, live in Natchez, Mississippi, in a dream home that includes a huge sound studio where Greg, still passionate about music, does most of his writing while listening to favourite artists like Joni Mitchell and Sting.

Nora, Nora
Anne Rivers Siddons

In the 1960s Lytton, an insular small town in America's Deep South, offers few chances for a bright young twelve-year-old like Peyton McKenzie to spread her wings.

Not, that is, until Peyton's cousin Nora drives into town in a bright pink Thunderbird. The red-haired, fiercely independent Nora freely speaks her views on everything, shocking the narrow-minded townsfolk to their core.

To Peyton, she is a breath of fresh air.

PROLOGUE

The Losers Club met every weekday afternoon at four o'clock in the toolshed behind the Methodist parsonage on the corner of Peyton McKenzie's street. Peyton would be out of her seventh-grade classes at the Lytton Grammar School and sometimes through her homework by then; her father would be cloistered away in his study; and Clothilde would be moving ponderously about the kitchen preparing supper for them. Peyton would have shed her school clothes and skimmed gratefully into her jeans and a T-shirt, looking like a starved pullet, all air-light bones and translucent razor angles.

Ernie Longworth, the second member of the club after Peyton, would be dressed in the bursting coveralls he wore all day in the pursuit of his duties as sexton of the Methodist church. Ernie was thirty-four years old, very fat and pale and fish-eyed behind his thick glasses, and sullen and rude to almost everyone but the members of the Losers Club and his darting tarantula mother, the parsonage housekeeper, with whom he lived in a little house behind the minister's official residence. He read voraciously, and fiercely loved classical music.

Ernie had been Peyton's friend ever since she was old enough to toddle up the street alone and discover him pottering around his lair, a meticulously kept corner of the toolshed that held a bookcase, a gut-springing easy chair, a tape-mended ottoman and a black pot-bellied stove. Ernie kept a small white plastic Philco radio on a shelf there, and there were usually three Coca-Colas in an old red metal ice chest, waiting for the club members when they congregated. Though Ernie treated Peyton as an equal, talking to her as if she were his age, he was generally so waspishly ineffectual that no one, including Peyton, took him seriously. But she was still proud to have him in the Losers Club, because of his obviously superior mind and opinions on cultural matters, and she often parroted these to Clothilde, who only snorted.

'What good they do him if he can't get himself no further than that ol' toolshed and his mama's supper table,' she would say.

'He *wants* to do what he does,' Peyton would say. 'It leaves him more time for cultivating the mind than a real job in Atlanta would do. Ernie cares more for things of the spirit than of the flesh.'

'Look to me like he care plenty about his flesh,' Clothilde said, but she said it good-naturedly. The McKenzies' housekeeper did not see anything amiss with the time Peyton spent in the parsonage toolshed with Ernie Longworth. Everyone knew Ernie was harmless, if strange. Everyone knew that Peyton McKenzie was nothing but a thin, frail, 'nervous' child; the Peytons, her long-dead mother's family, had always been aristocratically nervous and frail. Lila Lee Peyton had, indeed, died of that frailty at Peyton's birth.

Clothilde—or Chloe—did not even mind that her own grandson, eight-year-old Boot, was the third member of the Losers Club. Almost dwarfishly small for his age, Boot had been born with a clubfoot. Chloe had been bringing him to work with her ever since he was two, when his own mother vanished into the haze of neon light that was Atlanta. She was grateful that he had a place to go in the afternoons for a couple of hours, so that she could prepare the McKenzie supper in peace.

Boot was always the last one to appear at Losers Club meetings, because his infirmity slowed him down, and the toolshed lay at the far end of the parsonage garden. This was an overgrown jungle of crazed rosebushes, rampaging wisteria, and kudzu-shrouded cement benches and plaster statuary. Boot had a hard time threading his way through this virulent green maze; they could hear his floundering in the undergrowth and the clump-scrape of his heavy leather boot on the gravel path long before his cheerful face appeared in the doorway. It gave them time to change the subject if they had been talking about him, or about some topic that might be offensive to him. In Lytton, Georgia, in 1961, there were many of those, and no one else in the town, black or white, thought to spare the tender sensibilities of a clubfooted little Negro boy. Wise, pragmatic Boot did not mind. He appreciated the gesture of the stopped conversations and always pretended that he had not the faintest idea what they had been talking about.

'Awright,' he would pipe, heaving himself down on the ottoman, 'Who done the dumbest thing today?'

1

Peyton McKenzie changed her name when she was six years old. All her life she had been called Prilla or sometimes Priscilla, her first name, but that stopped with rocklike finality when the first scabby classmate at elementary school began to chant, 'Prilla, Prilla, mother-killer.' By the time the entire first grade in the Lytton Grammar School had taken up the refrain, Peyton McKenzie had been born.

'It's a man's name, for heaven's sake,' her Aunt Augusta had said in exasperation. 'What's wrong with "Priscilla"? It's a lovely name.'

'Peyton is my middle name,' Peyton had muttered. 'It's as much mine as Priscilla.' Both she and Augusta McKenzie knew there would be no changing of Peyton's mind, but Augusta saw it as her duty, as the dominant woman in Peyton's life, to do battle with the granite streak of wilfulness in her niece. On the death of Peyton's mother, Frazier McKenzie had placed the day-to-day shaping of his daughter in his sister-in-law's hands. By the time of Peyton's first great rebellion, aunt and niece were old adversaries. Augusta McKenzie knew full well she wasn't going to win this one. But she would never know why, because Peyton never told anyone about the cold, whining little chant at school that morning, not until much later. Her beleaguered teacher soon forgot about the name change entirely.

Only Peyton remembered, each day of her life and deep in her smallest cell, that she had, indeed, killed her mother. If her father never so much as hinted to her that he held her responsible for the extinguishing of the radiant flame her mother had been, Peyton put it down to Frazier McKenzie's natural reticence. He had been, all her life, as politely remote as a benign godparent. He was so with everyone, except Peyton's older brother, Buddy. When Buddy died in an accident in his air-force trainer, when Peyton was five, Frazier McKenzie closed up shop on his laughter, anger, small foolishnesses, and large passions. Now, at twelve, Peyton could remember no other father than the cooled and static one she had. Her father seemed to remember her only intermittently.

She told the Losers Club about the name change on a February day when it seemed as if earth and sky were made of the same grey sodden cloth. It happens sometimes in the Deep South when winter can no longer muster an honest cold but will not admit the warm tides of spring lapping at the gates. It is a climatic sulk, and can last for weeks, exhausting spirits and fraying nerves. Ernie had been so petulant that Boot had told him to shut up if he didn't have anything to add to the day's litanies of abasement. Even Boot seemed more dutiful than enthusiastic over his contribution to the club's itinerary, a lustreless account of wiping out the Canaday children's hopscotch grid with his orthotic boot.

'Well, if I couldn't do better than that, I just wouldn't say anything,' Ernie sniffed.

'You *ain't* said anything,' Boot pointed out. 'And I jes' as soon you didn't. You as mean as an old settin' hen today. Peyton gon' have to come up with something really fine to make up for you.'

Two pairs of cool eyes turned towards Peyton.

'I killed my mother,' she said, her heart beating hard with the sheer daring of it, and the first opening of the pit of that old pain. The others were silent, looking at her.

'You ain't, neither,' Boot said finally.

'You flatter yourself,' Ernie said.

But they knew they were bested by a long shot.

'I did, too,' Peyton said. 'She died not a day after I was born. She bled to death. Everybody knows that. I've always known it.'

'Then why didn't you say?' Boot asked.

'You'd have only said I was showing off. Not only did I kill her, but when I was in first grade I changed my name to Peyton because the kids were singing a song about "Prilla, Prilla, mother-killer".'

She folded her arms over her thin chest complacently.

Ernie leaned back in his armchair and picked up his copy of *The Inferno*. 'Meeting adjourned,' he said coldly.

They watched him for a couple of minutes, but he did not look up, and finally Boot said, 'Come on, Peyton. He just mad because you outdone him. Let's go to your house.'

At the edge of the sidewalk in front of Peyton's house, he looked up at her. 'You really kill your ma?'

'I really did,' Peyton said.

THAT EVENING her father's sister-in-law, Augusta Tatum McKenzie, came for supper, bringing white rolls from the A&P grocery store. Peyton knew this made Chloe furious; she prided herself on her light, melting biscuits and rolls. But Augusta had pronounced that they were made from lard, which was very unhealthy, as well as being common.

'Where's Charles?' Frazier McKenzie asked, taking the box of rolls from her. 'Thanks, Augusta. These look very good.'

'Charles has gone fox-hunting with that lowlife Floyd Fletcher,' Augusta snapped. 'No matter that it's out of season. If Floyd weren't chief of police Charles would have been in jail long since. Sorry, that's all Floyd is. Sorry as a yard dog.'

'It's good for a man to get out in the woods sometimes,' Frazier said. 'I ought to do it more often.'

'You're too busy to hunt, Frazier,' Aunt Augusta said. She used a different voice with Peyton's father than with anyone else. 'It's been a long time since you've had time to fool around in the woods with Floyd Fletcher and that poolroom crowd. You've given up a lot for the law and your family. At least one of us knows it.'

Peyton stared at her aunt. She could not recall a single time when her father had gone off into the woods to slay foxes.

'I don't see how you can give up something you never did anyway,' she said. Her aunt brought out the mulish worst in Peyton. In her presence, Peyton turned into just what Augusta thought she was: a tall, shrinking, sulking, ungrateful preadolescent badly in need of a firm, womanly hand.

'There are a lot of things about your father you don't see,' Augusta said. 'You're old enough now to think about some of the sacrifices he's made for you, to say thank you once in a blue moon.'

Peyton got up and slammed rudely out of the breakfast room and into the kitchen, where Clothilde was whipping cream for strawberry shortcake. Chloe only looked up at her, but Peyton could feel the warm surge of her sympathy. Then she heard her father say, 'She says thank you often enough, Augusta. She's not an adult, after all. All that will come later.'

'You think?' Augusta replied relentlessly. 'Have you looked at her lately? She's taller than her mother already, taller than me. She's getting hair on her arms and legs. It's time she shaved her legs, but who is there to teach her how? And I'd get that hair cut and curled in a jiffy. You remember Lila Lee's hair, so lovely . . . I wish you'd let me take her in hand, Frazier. She'll never have any friends, boys or girls, unless we do something about that attitude. The only people she sees are that awful Ernie and that poor little Negro boy.'

Her father did not reply. Peyton stood silently, looking at Chloe, and could not get her breath.

I will not grow up, she thought. Not with her on my neck. I'll run away first. But she knew that she wouldn't. Peyton had never even taken a Greyhound bus into Atlanta alone.

She knew, too, that in a terrible way her aunt was right. She would never join the crowd of twittering, lipsticked girls and jostling, large-handed boys at the soda fountain after school. Yet each new inch of height brought her closer to a forced exit from the Losers Club. Augusta would see to that. Peyton would be isolated from the only confidants she had, the only living souls to whom she could say anything peevish and perverse that she pleased.

She stood on a frail bridge between childhood and womanhood and stared into an abyss.

'TELL ME ABOUT my mother,' she said to Chloe the next morning. It was Saturday, but Frazier McKenzie had already gone to his office above the garage and Peyton was heavy with the shapeless hours ahead of her. There was no Losers Club on Saturday.

'I done told you about your mama a million times,' Chloe said softly.

'Well, tell me again. Tell me what she looked like. Tell me what made her laugh.'

Chloe slipped eggs and bacon in front of her. 'Eat that,' she said. 'Eggs give you breasts.'

'I'd rather eat dog food,' Peyton said, near tears.

'Well, that's easy enough to get,' Chloe said. She did not push the eggs. She sensed, though she could not have articulated it, that Peyton was going to need her childhood for a long time yet.

'So, she looked like . . . what?'

'Well, she was real pretty,' Chloe said. 'She was little and slim, and light on her feet. She had hair that kind of spun around her head, real fine and blondelike, and curly. She never had to go to no beauty shop. She used to sing and dance around the house even when by herself, and she and your daddy and Buddy used to act silly all the time and play games. She was real popular; she went out all the time, to lunch at the country club, or to Atlanta to shop, or to play tennis at the club. She was gone 'most every afternoon.'

'I'm not like her at all, am I?' Peyton said in a small voice. She knew that she was not, but it was as if she had to hear it regularly lest she start to imagine a relationship that could not have been, and then feel the loss of it in her deepest heart.

Peyton had not known her grandparents George and Priscilla Peyton, but she knew about them. They were aristocrats, people who got for themselves a dazzling dryad of a daughter, people who gave her to Peyton's father, along with the gift of this great old house in Lytton, with thinly disguised apprehension.

Peyton could imagine why. Her father's family were Scots who had backed the wrong horse at the Battle of Culloden and then departed hastily for America, with nothing but their flinty reserve and the fireshot passions just beneath it that smouldered like burning peat, and their own private mythology, dark with stunted gods of water and mountain. Time, however, had mellowed the passions out of the McKenzies, so that they were now respectably Presbyterian. Peyton would not have known the dark Hebridean side of her family if it had not been for her paternal grandmother, Agnes MacLaren McKenzie.

Nana McKenzie was a throwback, a raven among the pale, fluttering female birds of Lytton. She lived alone now, since Peyton's grandfather had died ten years before, in a farmhouse at the edge of town. Nana walked into town when she wanted something, spurning her son's offers to drive her and his invitations to come and live with them in the big house.

'Surely you know that wouldn't do,' Augusta had said to Frazier when he proposed it. 'It would be a terrible influence on Peyton. Your mother's half crazy, and the whole town knows it. She makes a commotion every time she comes to town with her prophecies. We all know it's just hokum, but Ed Carruthers at the hardware store said his Negro boys have started carrying charms, to warn off the evil eye or some such nonsense. She stood in the middle of Monument Square the other day yelling "Go tell the Devil!" at a flock of crows.'

'She's not crazy, you know, Augusta,' Frazier had said tightly. 'The things she says and does have come down a thousand years in the Highlands. They make sense to her and to me, too, though I wish she wouldn't do them in the middle of town. When I was little I thought she had the Sight. She still says she does.'

He had looked levelly at Augusta, who fell silent, then turned to Peyton, who was doing her homework at the breakfast table nearby, and winked. Peyton's heart had soared. She loved her Nana McKenzie without boundary, believed with her whole heart that the old woman had the Sight, and was so warmed and energised by the wink that she said, 'Everybody knows that crows watch all week to see what sins we've committed, and on Friday they go down to hell and tell the Devil. Jaybirds do it, too. Haven't you heard of Jaybird Friday?'

'I have not, except among the Negroes,' Aunt Augusta had said. 'It's a Negro superstition, Peyton, not a Scottish one.'

'They've got crows in Scotland, too,' Peyton said rudely, and she knew at once that she had cranked it one ratchet too far.

'If I hear of Mama McKenzie creating one more scene in public I am going to speak to Floyd Fletcher,' her aunt said. 'This can't continue, Frazier.'

'I don't want to hear of your doing that, Augusta,' her father said, in a voice as austere as his profile. 'It is not your place. She is your mother-in-law, you know. She's Charlie's mother.'

'And he has not invited her into his home for more than a year now. Did you ever wonder why?'

Frazier McKenzie had turned his head slowly and looked at his sister-in-law. The sea-grey of his eyes turned to ice and his thin mouth thinned even further. 'That is enough, Augusta.'

Aunt Augusta had dropped her eyes. Soon after, she had gathered up her shopping bags and gone home. Peyton had felt exultation at her aunt's virtual banishment.

'Nana thinks I'm going to have the Sight when I'm older,' Peyton said now to Clothilde.

Chloe put down her iron and looked at her. 'I like your grandmother,' she said, 'and I believe it when she say she see stuff. But it ain't what you ought to be doing right now in your life. Look at you: you don't talk about much but your mama and your brother and you don't see many people but your grandmother and that Ernie and my own po' little Boot . . . Maybe you ought to spend some time with folks your age.'

Peyton shrugged, and went upstairs and put on her blue jeans. Then she climbed the dogwood tree at the side of the house to the tree house where she spent a great deal of time, and she opened her book. She had just discovered *The Catcher in the Rye*, and felt that somehow this book was going to change her life.

THAT NIGHT AFTER SUPPER, after her father went out to his office to polish up the Sunday-school lesson he would teach the next morning at the First Methodist Church, Peyton went into her room behind the cavernous downstairs bathroom and pulled the old projector out of her closet and hung a white sheet on the door.

She had volunteered to learn to use the old school projector when she was in the fourth grade. She proved to be deft with the wheezing old machine, and for the past three years had been the one excused from her classes to thread up and show films on the agriculture of the Urals and the Battle of Agincourt and, at Christmas, *A Christmas Carol.*

By now Peyton could have set up and operated the projector in her sleep, and in fact often did do so in the dark, when her father thought she was sleeping. She had found the projector and the cans of film one day when she was poking around in the spider room, a forbidden cubicle at the back of the garage where her father had once seen a black widow spider. She had asked him about them that night, and he had said that they were old home movies. 'You know. Things around town. This house. The church, and Nana's farm. Nana and Grandpa.'

'And us? Are we there?'

'Well . . . there are a few of your mother and your brother and me. Some birthdays and Christmases and things . . .'

'And me? Are there any of me?' Peyton asked.

'Well, you weren't born yet. About that time I moved my office out to the garage and the movie stuff got put away and I just forgot about it. What were you doing in the spider room, anyway?'

'Just looking,' Peyton mumbled, warm salt stinging her eyes. She knew that the reason her father had never made movies of her was that the pale little life that had taken his wife was nothing to be recorded. But after that the movies drew her like a magnet and it was the next week that she volunteered to be projectionist at school. After two or three weeks of practice, she went out to the garage while Frazier was in Atlanta, and moved the projector and the film into her room. She kept the projector behind her raincoat in the closet, and the round, flat cans of film under her bed. Twice a week she lay in the dark and watched a world without her whirr and flicker against her wall.

First she would put on the footage of Lytton and study the flickering images of her home town. The post office and the dry cleaner's, then the rest of the small businesses and services that made up Lytton's Main Street—a tiny grocery, a hardware store, a barber-shop, a butcher shop, a lunchroom with a poolroom at the back, and a drugstore with a black marble soda fountain. Then came a ten-cent store, the Lytton Banking Company, another attorney's office, the town municipal offices, and the solitary wooden movie theatre.

Because very little in Lytton had changed appreciably since the middle thirties, the Lytton of Peyton's time was the Lytton of her family's time, too, and that soothed her. When she thought about Lytton, Georgia, it was a town of erratic sepia images bathed in silence. Peyton's reel world was also her real one.

When she had reassured herself that the town in the films was still as it had been the last time she looked, she let herself follow the camera down the side streets, where people actually lived. In one of these sequences Peyton saw her own house, looking almost precisely as it did now except for the striped awnings over the front porch that had been there then. She saw her mother, Lila Lee Peyton McKenzie, waving from the front door and doing a pantomime of a movie star being photographed. As always, when she reached this spot in the film, Peyton felt a relief so profound it almost brought her to tears. Once again she had travelled the road home and come safely to this place where her mother smiled and held out her arms in welcome. It did not matter to Peyton that the welcome was not for her. In the films and in her mind, it was always a sweet sepia summer, and time stopped on the walkway to her house, and she was home.

Once she was safe, it was easy for Peyton to watch the other films. Most of them were, she knew, made by her father because they were of her mother, so young and light-struck and beautiful that she seemed to shimmer with colour even though there was none on the film. Her mother, small and slender, her blonde hair a nimbus around her little cat's face, dancing to unheard music on the porch; her mother vamping for the camera in the back yard, where a barbe-cue was going on; her mother standing at the net at the little Lytton Country Club holding a tennis racket and smiling up at a tall, trim young man in tennis whites who had raised both hands and clasped them over his head in victory. He was dark and, Peyton thought, brooding and romantic-looking, as she imagined Heathcliff must have looked, and the one time she had asked her father about the scene, when he had showed the movie for her brother when he was home on his first furlough, he had said the young man was the tennis pro at the club, and had been teaching her mother tennis, and she was such a natural that soon they had played together in tournaments. In the film they had just won the all-club tournament.

Soon her brother appeared, fat and blond and toddling stolidly around the big, flower-bordered back yard. Peyton knew that her mother had made these films, because in every one of them Buddy was attached in some way to his smiling father. Frazier McKenzie had been an attractive young man, Peyton thought, a little dour, maybe, with his long Scot's nose and sharp chin, and the peat-dark hair falling over his grey eyes, but when he laughed—and in the films he was almost always laughing—his face lit up with something powerfully magnetic, and he had a loose-limbed grace that made him seem a teenager. He almost was: Frazier McKenzie had married Lila Lee Peyton when he was twenty-two and she just eighteen. He had been only twenty-four when Buddy was born.

There followed an hour of Christmases and birthdays, in which Buddy stopped being the heavy-bottomed cherub and became the heavy-jawed, frowning young nimrod squinting into the distance with his first shotgun broken across his arm. And finally there she was, in a Christmas morning portrait posed before a big tree, along with her father and her brother. There she was, in the middle of the Christmas tinsel: a round melon, a knot of darkness in her mother's stomach, the cancer that would soon end the movies for good.

IN THE MORNING she got up and cut her hair. She did it swiftly and ruthlessly before the bathroom mirror, not meeting her own eyes, grasping each long braid and sawing it clumsily with the kitchen shears. She stood for a long moment, staring at the peat-brown ropes that had bound her to childhood, now lying on the worn linoleum, and then she lifted her head to the mirror. An apparition looked back. Her hair hung in tattered hanks around her pale face, stopping a few inches below her ears. Medusa, she thought. That's who I look like. Medusa. Well, then, OK. If they try to get all over me I'll turn them to stone. She grinned savagely, ran warm tap water over her hands, slicked it onto her hair and fluffed it out of its limp helmet. It has some curl in it. In her mind she saw soft, tumbling waves drifting around her head. They would make her eyes larger, soften her face, make her thin mouth bloom. She knew, as she looked into the mirror, that she hoped to see her mother there.

Medusa still looked back. How could the loss of two pigtails have made this malevolent difference? Peyton took a deep breath, said aloud, 'I don't give a damn,' and walked into the kitchen.

Clothilde was washing the breakfast dishes, her dark hands slipping in and out of the sinkful of steaming suds. She turned to look at Peyton and dropped the Fiestaware creamer into the water.

'Peyton, what in the name of God you done?' she breathed.

'Obviously, Clothilde, I have cut my hair. Maybe you've heard of haircuts?' Peyton said with a cold aluminium brightness.

'I heard of haircuts,' Chloe said. 'That ain't no haircut. That look like you took a lawnmower to it. Your daddy gon' have a fit. What was you thinkin' of?'

'I was tired of it,' Peyton said airily. 'Pigtails are for babies.'

'Well, your daddy gon' grow you up real quick,' Clothilde said fiercely, and then her dark face softened. 'Why don't you go try to do something with it, maybe wet it and push it back behind your ears, and let me tell him. Get him used to the notion. You can get Miss Freddie at the beauty shop to even it up some tomorrow afternoon.'

'Where is Daddy?' Peyton said in the new bright voice.

'He out in his office. You know, Peyton, you got that pretty straw hat Miss Augusta bought you for Easter. Why don't you wear it to Sunday School this morning? Maybe with your blue dress.'

'I'm not going to Sunday School or church,' Peyton said. 'I'm tired of that, too. I'm going to read all day. Sunday is a day of rest.'

She stalked out of the kitchen, and went into her room and closed the door. She waited all day for her father to come to her room. She had never done anything so overtly grotesque before, and she had no idea what he would do. She was afraid of his anger, but she was more afraid of simple, cold contempt. By supper time she could stand it no longer, so she smoothed the ragged spikes as best she could and went into the living room, where her father sat with the Sunday paper. He had lit only one lamp, which stood beside his cracked leather easy chair, and in its pale glow she could see only his profile.

'Peyton,' he said, not turning his head. His voice was weary.

'I guess you want to see it,' she said.

He turned his head and looked at her. He was silent for a long while. Peyton felt tears like acid rising in her throat.

'We haven't taken you very seriously, have we?' Frazier McKenzie said at last. His voice was still weary, but there was nothing in it of shock or anger. Perhaps it might still be all right . . .

'Daddy, it was a mistake, I don't know why I did it . . .'

'I don't care about your hair, Peyton,' he said. 'We can get that fixed; Augusta is going to take you into Atlanta and get you all prettied up. It's that you were so unhappy, and needed attention so much, and we didn't notice it—*I* didn't notice it. I wish you had come and talked to me about whatever is bothering you instead of chopping off your pretty hair, but I'm not exactly the kind of father a young girl comes running to, am I?'

The tears began to spill over Peyton's lower lashes. 'I'm not unhappy,' she quavered. 'I don't need attention. You're a good father, Daddy. I don't know why I did it. It just seemed all of a sudden something I needed to do . . . But it looks pretty awful, doesn't it?'

He gave a tired smile. 'You're a pretty girl, Peyton. I think you'll be a pretty woman one day. But we're going to have to make some changes. Augusta was right. You're at the point now where you need a woman in your life. You'll be thirteen in—June, isn't it? You can't be a child any more. You can't just run wild.'

'I don't run wild,' Peyton whispered, the unfairness of it loosening the tears again. 'I've never run wild in my life.'

'No, you haven't,' he said. 'It was a bad choice of words. But you've got to grow up some, and you've got to do it the right way. It's got to start now, and I can't do it, so on Tuesday your Aunt Augusta is taking you to Rich's for a hairdo and some clothes and maybe to lunch at the tearoom. You may find that you have a good time.'

'I won't,' Peyton cried, panic rising in her chest.

'You will,' he said, and he turned back to his newspaper.

Peyton went back to her room and threw herself across her narrow bed and cried in the winter twilight, knowing that change was upon her and it was going to be terrible, and that she and she alone had summoned it with a pair of kitchen shears.

2

Peyton went to school the next day with a scarf that had been her mother's tied under her chin. It was cream silk, splashed with huge red poppies and green vines, and must have looked festive and exotic on her mother. On Peyton, it looked almost shocking. But it was better than the hair. Peyton had it all planned: she would tell people she had an earache and had to keep the cold air off of it. 'We're going into Atlanta tomorrow to see a specialist,' she would say.

But no one asked and no one even mentioned the scarf.

After school she went straight to the Losers Club. When she came into the toolshed Ernie and Boot were waiting for her.

Peyton jerked the scarf off, heart surging up into her throat, and assumed the Betty Grable bathing-beauty pose. *'Taadaa!'* she cried.

'Holy cow!' Boot said reverently. 'You done won the stupidest prize for the next two years. You looks like a picked pullet, Peyton. What you go and do that for?'

'So I could win the stupidest prize for the next two years.'

'Well, it ain't no contest,' Boot said. 'What you daddy say?'

'He said it was very becoming.'

'Then he crazy as batshit,' Boot said mournfully.

Peyton looked at Ernie, who was sitting still and looking back at her. She knew he could flay her alive if he wished.

Ernie cocked his fuzzy head and studied her. 'You know, it's really not bad at all,' he said finally. 'You need to get it evened up a little, but I think you might look quite chic. Better than just pretty, really. Perhaps you're going to amount to something as a woman after all.'

Peyton felt a hopeful disbelief. Could he mean what he said? Of course not; anyone could see how she looked. But Ernie had never spared anyone's feelings before. She smiled, a silly, quivering smile.

Boot simply stared.

'Well, you little people run on now,' Ernie said. 'I've got to take Mama to the dentist. Maybe this time he'll drill her tongue out.'

Peyton laughed. The Losers Club had found its proper place in her firmament and her life was suddenly all right again.

It was early. No one would expect her home for a couple of hours yet, so she decided to go and see her grandmother. The walk took only about ten minutes. Her grandmother would understand, even if she didn't like the hair.

Peyton found Agnes McKenzie in her dim, cluttered kitchen, icing tea cakes. Nana always made them for Peyton, and they were sublime. A sweet vanilla smell told Peyton that there was another sheet of them in the old black woodstove. She stood still and breathed deeply. This was the very smell of childhood, rich and succouring.

Her grandmother did not turn round.

'Knew it was you,' she said. 'Saw it in the washtub this morning. Saw that you could do with a mess of tea cakes, too. Right now I need you to bring me some more wood in from the pantry.'

Peyton went into the pantry shed that opened off the kitchen. The wood basket stood there, along with a pristine electric stove and a new washer and dryer that Frazier had given to his mother two years before. Agnes McKenzie had never used them. She had simply thanked her son sweetly and gone on with heavy iron stove lids and dark soapy water. Only Peyton knew why.

'I see things in the fire and the water,' Agnes had told her once. 'The bad things in the fire and the good ones in the water. It's how I know things.'

Peyton picked up an armful of kindling and went back into the warm, dim kitchen.

'If you saw me in the water, that's good, isn't it?' Peyton said to her grandmother.

Agnes turned and looked at her, and then smiled. In the dimness she looked perhaps thirty, a smoky-haired, ocean-eyed thirty. Beautiful. Wild.

'Child,' she said. 'Look at you. I knew you'd lost something. I saw that in the fire. Come sit and we'll have coffee and tea cakes. There's not much that good strong coffee and tea cakes won't put right.'

Peyton took the cup gratefully and sipped the steaming coffee. She didn't like it very much—it was sludgy and bitter—but no one else let her have coffee. It made another bond with her grandmother.

'You look like you been whupped through hell with a buzzard gut, as our old washerwoman used to say,' Agnes said. 'But that doesn't matter. It won't last. You're going to be a handsome woman. You're going to look a lot like me, I think, when you get really old. And that's pretty good, if I do say so myself. What bothers me is why you did it.'

'I don't know,' Peyton said miserably, realising that she had been counting on her grandmother to say that she looked fine.

'Big change coming. Is that it?' Agnes said.

'I guess,' Peyton said. 'Everybody's going on about it. "You have to change, Peyton." "You won't have any boyfriends, Peyton."'

'You think making yourself ugly is going to change that? You'll grow up, my heart, ugly or not. Whacking off your hair isn't going to stop it.'

'Well, it just might put it off a while,' Peyton said, stung.

'Don't think so,' Agnes said. 'I see that it's right on top of you.'

'Do you see what's going to make me change? Daddy and Aunt Augusta are making me go to Rich's tomorrow and get styled and buy some new clothes. I think that's just the beginning . . .'

'I see a woman in your life, Peyton, for a long time to come. Yes. That much is clear.'

'Is it Aunt Augusta? Is it you?'

'I don't think it's Augusta. I wouldn't allow that, in any case. And it isn't me. I don't know who it is, only that she's coming.'

'Did you see her in the water or the fire?'

'I saw her in a bowl of Campbell's tomato soup.' Her grandmother smiled and reached out to touch the murdered hair gently. 'I don't know what that means. It doesn't feel like it's bad, though. Only . . . very different.'

WHEN PEYTON GOT HOME, the house was very quiet. She listened hard, heard the burring grumble of the old Electrolux upstairs somewhere, and followed the sound up.

She found Chloe vacuuming in the big upstairs back bedroom that they had always called the guest room, only Peyton could not remember any guests ever being in it. It would have been her room if she had not clung to her small one downstairs.

A thought rooted her in the doorway. They were making her move upstairs. It was a part of Aunt Augusta's adulthood campaign. Peyton darted into the room. 'What are you doing, Chloe?' she shouted. 'Because if anybody thinks they can make me move up here, they've got another think coming.'

Clothilde turned off the Electrolux. 'It ain't for you,' she said. 'We're going to have a guest in this room pretty soon.'

'A guest?' Peyton said stupidly. 'What guest?'

'Your Cousin Nora coming to see us. Your daddy called from his office this afternoon. He said to get the room ready and to tell you he had to go into Atlanta to the courthouse this evening and not to wait up for him. Oh, and your Aunt Augusta said she'd pick you up at nine Wednesday morning, and to wear your Easter dress and straw hat.'

Peyton's head spun. 'What cousin? I never heard of any Cousin Nora. Who is she?'

'She your mama's younger cousin's girl,' Clothilde said. 'I never met her. Her mama and your mama had some kind of falling-out right after Miss Lila Lee and your daddy got married, and your mama didn't talk about her. I reckon Nora is your second cousin, and she'd be about thirty now. Seem to me they lived in Florida. I know she's coming in from Key West.'

Peyton felt a great gust of terror. 'How long is she going to stay?' she asked.

'Not long, I don't think. Your daddy say she on her way up north for a job. She just need a place to stop on the way.'

'There are about a million motels up on the interstate,' Peyton muttered. 'I don't want any visitors.'

Clothilde rolled her eyes. 'Why should she stay in a motel when she got folks here? Git on now, Peyton, and let me finish. I ain't even started supper yet.'

Peyton started to slam out of the room and then stopped. 'Chloe—Nana knew she was coming! She told me this afternoon there was a woman coming! She saw it in . . . the water.'

Peyton was not about to reveal that her grandmother had seen this troublesome cousin in a bowl of tomato soup.

'Huh. Most likely she saw it in a telephone,' Clothilde grumbled. 'You know your daddy call her every afternoon.'

'So when is she getting here?'

'I don't know. Two or three days, your daddy says. By the time she gets here you'll be all prettied up and have some new clothes and all. She'll look at her cousin and say, "Woo-woo!"'

It was Clothilde's most favoured superlative. Peyton hated it. She turned and stumbled down the stairs to her room. The important thing, she decided, was to manage never to meet her cousin.

'YOU HAVE A LITTLE bitty head in proportion to your neck,' Mr Antoine said, squinting at Peyton in the mirror. 'And you're really long and thin through the waist and legs. I think we'll balance that with a cloud of curls. And maybe just a few highlights to bring out your nice eyes. How does that sound?'

Peyton, feeling pinheaded and as attenuated as an El Greco, did not answer. Indeed, since Aunt Augusta had picked her up that morning in her Lincoln, Peyton had said as little as was humanly possible without incurring her aunt's wrath.

Aunt Augusta was hovering behind the chair in Rich's Beauty Salon, where Peyton sat swathed in a pink drape, while Mr Antoine danced around her like a dervish, darting in to snip, fluff, stand back, snip again.

'So did you get bubble gum in your hair, or what?' he asked her as he snipped. 'I see that a lot. Not to worry. You left us plenty to work with. You're going to leave here looking like Sandra Dee.'

Peyton closed her eyes then. She did not open them as he worked in the permanent solution or when he pulled her hair onto rollers, or put her under the dryer. It seemed hours later when Mr Antoine shook her awake for what he called the comb-out. Peyton opened her eyes then, but she did not look into the mirror.

He combed and brushed and fluffed and sprayed, humming tunelessly as he worked. Finally Peyton heard him step back.

'*Voilà!*' he cried gaily. 'The new you. And just *look* at you!'

'Oh, Peyton, it looks just lovely,' Aunt Augusta trilled.

Peyton lifted her eyes, and her stomach lurched. All you saw was the hair. It was a tall, round helmet with a perfectly smooth exterior, inside which a surf of tiny curls and waves swirled.

And it was blonde. Butter yellow. Cadmium yellow.

'You're an entirely different person, Peyton,' her aunt said. 'There's absolutely nothing babyish about you now.'

Peyton could not speak. Were they both insane? Could neither of them see what they had done to her?

'Told you you'd love it,' Mr Antoine said, and he whirled away into another cubicle to answer a telephone.

'Truly, isn't it remarkable?' her aunt said happily, guiding Peyton out of the chair and towards the salon door.

'Yes,' Peyton whispered.

'I think we'll do a little something extra before lunch,' Augusta McKenzie said. 'Your hair is lovely, but it sort of overpowers your thin little face. I think we'll go down to Max Factor and get you made up. Nothing garish, of course, just a little blush and shadow and pink lipstick, to pop out those eyes and that mouth.'

Peyton found to her horror that she could do nothing but follow her aunt blindly out of the salon.

Augusta squeezed her hand. 'Well, this turned out to be fun, now, didn't it?' she said, smiling. 'You seem older already. We're like a couple of girls, skipping school and out for a shopping spree. I haven't had such fun in a long time.'

Peyton let her aunt lead her to the Max Factor counter as docilely as a lamb to the slaughterer's knife. There was nothing more they could do to her. Whatever they did would pale beside the hair. She sat down on a tall stool and closed her eyes again. She would endure. It would be over. They would go home. She would do something to the hair, something, anything.

Peyton felt a soft brush dancing over her face, and a thick smear of something that smelt like bubble gum being slicked onto her mouth. She went far away behind her closed eyes and waited.

At last her aunt caroled, 'Well, just look at our debutante!'

Peyton looked, blurring her eyes. She saw nothing but colour: the yellow aureole that she supposed was the hair, two pink blotches that must be blush, a slash of deeper pink that was undoubtedly lipstick.

'Wow,' she said, not really seeing.

'Wow, indeed,' her aunt said. 'Let's get you these things, and I can help you practise putting them on until you've got it down. It takes a little practice or it looks unnatural.'

'No kidding,' Peyton whispered. Another dreadful thing that could be fixed when she got home.

They ate frozen fruit salad and little chicken-salad sandwiches in the tearoom, then they stopped at the Tween Shop, a terrible place of posturing prepubescent mannequins with impossibly slim waists and gently swollen breasts, most wearing pencil strokes of pink or blue or yellow, a few in shirtwaisters with drifts of skirt and neat little collars and belts. A curly, flowered placard said that these offerings were suitable for young misses aged eleven to fourteen. Peyton knew that no matter what they put on her face or body, she wasn't ever going to look like the women of Rich's Department Store.

Aunt Augusta, accompanied by a clucking saleslady, dug among the racks of clothes like a terrier. She pulled out a horrifying cerise dress and jacket and a dark, plain sheath with a little coat to match. She selected two slim skirts and white blouses with little round collars, and a shirtwaister with tiny blue flowers and a little round collar.

'A Villager,' the saleslady said solemnly, as if she were offering a Fabergé egg. 'All the girls are buying them.'

Obediently, Peyton let Aunt Augusta and the saleslady lead her into a small cubicle walled with mirrors. She closed her eyes and let the legendary Villager slide over her rigid hair and down her body. She stood, desperately unfocused, as the saleslady buttoned up the front of the bodice and pulled the belt snug around her waist.

'If I might make a suggestion,' the saleslady said. 'There are some sweet preteen bras in Lingerie, with just a little light padding to give clothes some shape. Shall I just run over and pick a few out?'

'No,' Peyton all but wept. 'I won't wear one. I don't have anything to put in it. I wouldn't wear one if I did.'

Aunt Augusta raised her eyebrows at the saleslady and shook her head, smiling ruefully. The saleslady smirked back.

'Why don't you just pick out a couple that you think would be suitable and add them to my charge account?' Aunt Augusta said. 'I guess the smallest size they have. Do they make them small enough?'

'Oh yes. The sizes start at twenty-eight triple-A. Now, could I show you a little garter belt and some stockings?'

'I think I'm going to throw up,' Peyton said.

The trot to the rest room seemed endless. Swallowing hard against bile, Peyton plodded dumbly behind her aunt, who was leading her by the hand and saying, 'You can hold it, now. You know you don't want to throw up in the middle of Rich's . . .'

Peyton did hold it, but only just. She lurched into one of the stalls and vomited before she could even latch the door. When she finally stopped, she was weak and sweaty. She leaned against the cold steel of the cubicle and breathed in deep, desperate gasps.

Presently her aunt opened the cubicle and produced a handful of wet paper towels. She began to dab and scrub at Peyton's dress.

'Come on out here and let's wash your face,' she said. 'Oh, goodness. Just look at you. Your make-up is all smeared . . .'

Peyton stood mute, splashing her face in the sink when her aunt told her to, rinsing her mouth, letting Augusta pat her dry.

'Better now?' Augusta said. 'Your colour's coming back. Here, let's just touch you up a little. I wonder if it was that chicken salad—you're really not used to rich food. Come on, let's get you home. We'll get a Coca-Cola in the parking lot. That'll settle your tummy.'

Peyton followed Augusta out of the ladies' room and down the escalator to the basement parking lot. She sat there dumbly while their car was brought round, sipping the Coca-Cola her aunt bought her and knowing in her heart that there had been nothing asked of her, no test put to her, that she had not, on this day, failed.

IN THE LINCOLN Peyton put her head back against the seat and slept, waking only when the car stopped at last.

She opened her eyes slowly. Perhaps, if it was still early enough, she could get to her room and lock the door and begin the undoing of the horror before anyone saw her.

What she saw was her father and Clothilde, wrestling a mattress down the front steps and onto the lawn. Her father had on his white office shirt, but the sleeves were rolled and the collar was unbuttoned, and his hair fell over his face. Behind him, at the other end of the bouncing mattress, Chloe shone with sweat, like basalt.

Aunt Augusta tooted the horn gaily. 'Frazier McKenzie, come here and look at your grown-up daughter,' she trilled, and then she got out of the car the better to see the first viewing of her handiwork.

Peyton did not move. Her father shielded his face against the sun with his hand and walked slowly towards her side of the car. When he reached it he stopped and stared in. Peyton met his eyes and saw in them sheer shock and revulsion. They were gone in an instant, replaced by a smile, but they had been there.

'Well, my goodness,' he said. 'Get out and let's have a look at you.'

Peyton sat rooted in the Lincoln.

'She's had a little upset tummy,' Aunt Augusta offered across the roof of the Lincoln. 'She probably needs some iced tea and a nap. But first we're going to have a fashion show . . .'

Peyton jerked her door open and leapt out and ran past her father and the wide-eyed Clothilde and into the house, and into her room, and closed her door. She heard the murmur of voices out on the lawn, a hum like bees, with an occasional fragment of a sentence spiking up: '. . . at least she might have said thank you. Look, she's just left all these new things in the car. Frazier, I really think . . .'

Then her father's voice: '. . . maybe a little extreme for her age, Augusta. Let her get used to it. Let *us* get used to it. Good Lord, I didn't even recognise her.'

'Well, I guess ingratitude runs in the family,' she heard her aunt huff, and after that the solid thunk of the Lincoln's door closing.

She crawled onto her bed and pulled the faded afghan that her grandmother had made for her at her birth up over her ears. She did not move for a long, long time. By the time Chloe came to her door, her windows had darkened with the still-winter twilight.

'Peyton, you come on out to supper now,' Chloe called. 'Your daddy gone to a meeting up to the church, he say he want to see you before you go to bed. He say he think you looks pretty as a princess, and he wants to tell you himself. And I think we can fix that hair so it ain't so hard, and take some of that stuff off your face. It's gon' be all right. Come on out now, and after supper you can show me your new clothes. Your aunt left them for you.'

Peyton did not reply. Presently Clothilde went heavily away.

She was back in an hour. 'I got to go home,' she said. 'Ain't nobody with Boot. I'm settin' this tray right outside your door. You stop actin' like a baby now and come on out and eat it. Your Cousin Nora comin' tomorrow. You don't want her to think you a baby in a tantrum.'

Peyton still did not reply. She heard Clothilde mutter, and soon the closing of the front door, and then silence and darkness fell over the house. Peyton padded to her door and opened it and pulled the tray inside so that her father would not see it sitting there, set it on her desk and crawled back into her bed.

She heard her father at her door some time later, dimly. 'Peyton, you awake?' he called softly.

She did not answer. She lay motionless until at last, aeons later, she heard him click off the television and start up the stairs to bed. She waited another hour, and then she got up and tiptoed through the dark to the downstairs bathroom and ran a tub of water. She ran it very slowly so that her father would not hear it thundering into the porcelain tub.

When the bath was full Peyton got in and submerged herself. She felt the hair helmet soften stickily. She got the Ivory soap from the soap dish and scrubbed her head until it stung. The water around her yellowed. Some kind of rinse, then. Good.

She scrubbed herself all over, then got out of the tub, wrapped her hair in a towel, dressed in jeans and a T-shirt, and stole back to her room. She sat down in front of the maple dressing table and closed her eyes for a long time, and then she jerked the towel away. A towering mound of dun-coloured Brillo sat atop her head, lightless and dense. She could not get her comb through it.

Peyton got up, took the afghan and a pillow from her bed, and went out of her room. She got an apple, some cheese and a Coca-Cola from the refrigerator and went outside and climbed the dogwood tree where her father had constructed a shelter for her, more elaborate than a platform but less so than a roofed tree house. It had railings and one solid wall against the tree trunk. Two years before she had dragged an old air mattress up there, and now she propped her pillow on it, and lay down and covered herself with her afghan.

She prepared to cry, but instead she slept.

SHE AWOKE WITH A JOLT. Pearly morning light was streaming through the tree's bare branches, and her father was calling her from the ground. 'Come down from there right now, Peyton.'

Clothilde's voice joined his, shrill and angry. 'Well, I hope you happy,' she squalled. 'Your cousin here waitin' to meet you, and you stuck up in that tree like an ol' possum. She drove all night, she say. You git down from there this minute.'

Peyton did not look down at them, and she did not answer. She looked instead out towards the street. A blur of pure, shocking flamingo pink flamed there against the asphalt. She brought it into focus. It was a Thunderbird coupé, a fairly old one, from what she knew of those exotic cars, covered with road dust, but still fabulous in the morning light. Nobody in Lytton had a Thunderbird.

There was a creak of the steps to the tree house, and a woman's face appeared over its edge. It was freckled with copper and long and sharp-chinned, and a thick sheaf of dark red hair fell over one of its pale green eyes. It was an exaggerated face, almost a grotesque one, and Peyton simply stared. Then the mouth quirked up into a smile, and it was transformed into something near beauty.

'Dr Livingstone, I presume?' the woman said, and her voice was as slow and rich as cooling fudge, with a little hill of laughter in it. It was a wonderful voice, magical.

The woman swung herself up onto the platform and sat down, legs crossed, chin on hands. Her arms and legs were long, and in her blue jeans she was very thin. She looked solemnly at Peyton. Peyton stared back, as mesmerised as a cobra in a fakir's basket.

'I'm your Cousin Nora Findlay. I've driven all night to meet you, and I'm tired and I need my breakfast, and I want you to have yours with me. I don't have any other cousins. Then we'll do something about that hair. Sweet Jesus, what on earth were they thinking?'

Peyton put her head down and began to cry, and her Cousin Nora pulled her over and held her until Peyton had cried herself out, and then they climbed down the tree to breakfast.

3

The first thing you noticed about Nora Findlay, Peyton thought, was that she gave off heat, a kind of sheen, like a wild animal. There was a padding, hip-shot prowl to her walk, and she moved her body as if she were totally unconscious of it. She had a long Roman nose and a full mouth and with her slanted yellow-green eyes and thick, tumbled red hair, Peyton thought she looked like some sort of wild-cat: a leopard, a ruddy puma, a cheetah.

Clothilde had bacon and eggs waiting for them in the yellow

breakfast room. Peyton had a couple of hours yet before school. She would have liked to retreat to her room and think about the enormities of the past twelve hours, especially this strange, leonine cousin who had arrived in a pink chariot and laid siege to her tree. But she did not dare. Disapproval shone out of Chloe's face like steam off asphalt, and she could still hear the steel in her father's voice. She was in disgrace. There was nothing for it but to sit down at the blue lacquered table and wait for what would come. For a long time no one spoke, and she did not raise her eyes from her plate. There was only the chink of silver on china as Nora ate.

She smelt cigarette smoke then, an alien smell in this house, and she looked up at her cousin. Nora was smoking a cigarette from the fresh pack of Salems that sat on the table beside her.

'Have I broken a taboo?' she said in the rich, slow voice. 'Am I going to have to sneak behind the woodshed to smoke?'

She swept the heavy hair off her face with one long hand and turned to Peyton. 'Might as well join you in Coventry,' she said. 'Two's company, they say.'

'Coventry?' Peyton said in a small, tight voice.

'It means disgrace. For some reason, being sent to Coventry means the ultimate punishment; it means shunning. I don't know why. It means we're both of us in deep shit.'

Peyton gasped. She had never heard such a word used in this house. It hung in the warm air, and in the ensuing silence she heard a snorted 'Huh!' from Clothilde that meant her direst disapproval. She wondered if Chloe would tackle Nora directly.

'I'm sorry, Clothilde,' Nora called out. 'I hope I haven't blotted my copybook too badly.' She smiled into the kitchen at Chloe.

'It ain't like I never heard "shit" before,' Chloe said. 'It just that Mr Frazier ain't gon' want Peyton to hear it.'

'It's not like I haven't heard it before, either,' Peyton surprised herself by saying. And then she looked down at her plate and blushed. She would speak no more to this usurping stranger. Her cousin was not going to charm her with sweet cigarette smoke and soft 'shits'.

Nora finished her coffee. She stretched and yawned and said, 'I have never eaten a better breakfast. I mean that, Clothilde. It is all right if I call you that?'

'What else you gon' call me?' Chloe grumbled, but there was a smile at the corners of her black eyes.

'I'm bushed,' Nora said, getting up from the chair. Peyton saw that she wore tennis shoes over bare feet, and that her feet were small and neat, out of all proportion to her height.

'You upstairs in the back bedroom on the right,' Clothilde said. 'Mr Frazier said to let you sleep as long as you wanted to, that he'll see you for dinner. See all of us, I means.'

Peyton would not look up. She felt rather than saw her cousin come round to stand behind her chair. In a moment Nora's long hands were cupping her head, smoothing back the electric hair, pulling it sleekly behind her head and winding it.

'Got bobby pins, Chloe?' Nora said, and Chloe produced some from somewhere in her vast necessities drawer. There was a final tug and the feeling of the bobby pins slipping firmly home, and then Nora took Peyton's shoulders and stood her up and led her to the old mirror over the oak chest that held linens and silver.

'What do you think?'

Peyton looked. A small face under a smooth crown of hair looked back at her, sitting atop a long neck that seemed, now, slender instead of scrawny, and round the sharp chin and slanted cheekbones a few wisps of the horrendous curls lay softly. The image was not appalling. But it was not her. She merely stared.

'It's a French twist,' Nora said. 'It's not really right for you, but it gets that mess off your face and shows off those fabulous bones. If you like, we'll work on it some more tonight.'

Still Peyton stared.

Nora gave her shoulders a small shake, then went up the dim staircase towards her room.

Only then did Peyton look at Clothilde.

'That's right nice, Peyton,' Chloe said. 'Shows off them eyes.'

'I hate it,' Peyton said, but there was no heat in her voice. She went into her little room to get dressed for school, and for the first time in her life she felt almost confident, almost anticipatory, about going into the swarm of flips and bouffants that awaited her.

Nobody's got a French twist, she thought. This ought to shut up a few of them. Of course, I'm not going to keep it . . .

She realised as she walked to school that she could not wait to show her new hair to the Losers Club that afternoon.

But it was not her hair that the Losers Club wanted to talk about. They did not even mention it. Instead the subject was, first, her night in the tree, and, second, her Cousin Nora Findlay.

'Guess you gets the stupid prize, Peyton,' Boot said, eating

Planter's peanuts out of the big can from which Ernie doled a grudging inch or two for each of them once or twice a week.

For the first time, Peyton felt no hummingbird dart of triumph in her chest. She felt cross, waspish. The night before had been a source of stunning pain and revelation to her. She was not going to have it cut down to the status of stupidity of the week.

'It wasn't stupid. It was something I planned, a protest. I'm proud of it,' she said.

'I should think you might make your point better face to face,' Ernie drawled, but Peyton knew somehow that he envied her her flight into the dogwood tree. She realised then that Ernie would never dare leave his mother to go and sit in a tree all night.

'OK, so it ain't stupid. Tell about your cousin,' Boot said. 'I heard she redheaded as a woodpecker and ain't got no brassiere.'

'She has long red hair like a waterfall and green eyes, and real long legs, and she smokes Salems. As for the brassiere, I don't know about that.'

In Peyton's mind, her Cousin Nora was rapidly being transmuted into something fabulous, a unicorn, a young griffin.

'How did y'all know about that stuff last night?' she said.

'Huh. Half of Lytton probably know it by now,' Boot said.

When Peyton got home, Nora was nowhere in sight, but her Aunt Augusta was, sitting at the breakfast table with a cup of coffee and a slice of Clothilde's pineapple upside-down cake. She was stabbing the cake and waving it on her fork and haranguing Chloe at the same time.

Chloe ironed on, unconcerned and uncommunicative. Every now and then she would say, 'Uh-*uh*,' when Augusta made a point.

Peyton tried to slip past her back and into her own room, but Aunt Augusta rounded on her. 'Well, so here's our grown-up little lady,' she said with heavy sarcasm. 'The one who, by now, the whole town knows spent the night in a tree after her daddy and her aunt bent over backward to fix her up some. If your daddy doesn't listen to me now about boarding school, I'll be mighty surprised. Just look at that hair! Now what did you do to it?'

'It's a French twist,' Peyton said coldly. 'My cousin fixed it for me. She's going to fix it some more when she wakes up.'

Peyton had completely forgotten that she herself had planned to murder the French twist as soon as she could get to a mirror. In a heartbeat it became a powerful amulet against Aunt Augusta.

'Everybody at school loved it,' she lied. 'Grace Kelly wore one at her wedding. Some of the girls said I looked just like her.'

None of this was true, but Peyton did not care.

For a moment her aunt was speechless. Then she recovered.

'Oh, yes, your Cousin Nora,' she said venomously. 'Who drove in here at daybreak in a dirty pink convertible, with her shorts rolled up to her whatever, and got in bed and slept all day. Oh, yes, that's just wonderful. What a shining example. When I think what her mother did to your mother, when I think what little tramps those Vandiver women were, I shouldn't be surprised at anything this one does.'

'What do you mean, what her mother did to my mother?' Peyton said in a small voice.

'Well, it's time you knew,' her aunt huffed. 'Her mother stole your mother's fiancé away from her and ran off with him, and we all heard that she had your famous Cousin Nora way before she ever married that no-good Creighton Findlay. Not that that little affair lasted long; he walked out on her before Nora was two years old. After that she lived all over the place, with one relative or another, dragging that child with her. I guess it's no wonder . . . anyway, she and the child lived with almost every Peyton and Vandiver family except your mama and daddy. Your mama never spoke to her after that business with Creighton Findlay.'

'My mother's fiancé?' Peyton said. 'You mean . . . not Daddy?'

'Of course not! Your daddy is worth a million Findlays. He met and married your mother just after that. It was the saving of her. Creighton Findlay was as no-good as they come, but he was a handsome devil and she was crazy about him.'

'My mother's cousin—Nora's mother—where is she?'

'She died in a sanatorium for alcoholics in St Petersburg, Florida,' Aunt Augusta said with satisfaction.

'Not so,' a black-coffee voice said from the stairs. 'Everybody knows she married the Emperor of Bhutan and is living in splendour in the shadow of Everest. I see her often.'

Nora padded into the breakfast room, smiling amiably at Aunt Augusta, her green eyes slitted and her mane of hair tangled. She wore a long T-shirt that said 'Jesus Is Coming. Look Busy', and obviously nothing else. She smiled at Aunt Augusta.

'Well, Nora,' her aunt said, extravagantly avoiding looking at the Jesus T-shirt and the bobbling wealth of Nora underneath it.

'Well, Cousin Augusta,' Nora said, the smile widening as she sat down opposite Aunt Augusta at the breakfast table.

'How long do you plan to be with us?' Augusta McKenzie said.

Peyton could not imagine that anyone could miss the animosity in her aunt's voice, but Nora seemed to. She smiled sleepily. 'I hadn't thought, really,' she said. 'I just got here. I'd like to look around Lytton some. And then I'd like to see Atlanta.'

'Frazier said you were on your way to a job?' Aunt Augusta said. 'What sort of job might that be?'

'Clothilde, do you think I might possibly have a sliver of that cake?' Nora said, smiling into the kitchen. 'It smells like pure heaven. Well, I don't have any specific plans, Cousin Augusta. I'm just looking around to see what's what.'

Chloe brought the cake and poured a cup of strong, hot coffee for Nora. 'More where that came from,' she said.

Nora smiled her thanks around a mouthful of cake and rolled her eyes. 'Bliss,' she said. 'Nirvana. Maybe you could teach me to cook while I'm here. I really don't have any domestic skills.'

'What *are* your skills, Nora?' Aunt Augusta said. 'We never exactly knew.'

'Well, I'm good at English, and I write a little. I've been teaching for the past few years, in Miami and Key West. I've enjoyed that. I taught special English classes to Cuban and Haitian children.'

'Oh, really?' Augusta's nostrils flared as if she had smelt something dreadful. 'Coloured children, you mean?'

'Oh, yes. Black as the ace of spades, some of them. It was a real revelation for me to get acquainted with such different cultures.'

'Well, you won't find much opportunity for that kind of thing here,' Augusta said.

'Oh, really?' Nora said. 'I've already seen quite a few black people around here. Surely their children go to school?'

'Not our school,' Aunt Augusta said. 'They have their own school, and it's a good one. Frazier is on their school board, just as he is on ours.'

'Strange,' muttered Nora, looking ingenuously up at Aunt Augusta. 'I thought *Brown versus Board of Education* must be fairly familiar around the South. Hasn't the news gotten to Lytton yet?'

'There's no need to be sarcastic,' Augusta snapped. 'That desegregation rule is all about choice. None of our coloured people have chosen to come to Lytton Grammar and High Schools. And why should they? Their own school is just fine.'

'Maybe I'll apply there, then.' Nora smiled. 'You asked about my skills, Cousin Augusta? I am a truly superior lay. I am the best lay east of the Rockies. Lots of people say so. Although it doesn't look like there's much market for that in Lytton. Oh, well. We shall see.'

Peyton stared, her mouth open, and Chloe snorted.

Aunt Augusta got up from her chair, wheeled on her sensible heel, and sailed in palpitating silence out of the room. Peyton heard the front door slam. She could not speak and only continued to stare.

Nora reached over and ruffled her hair. 'I'm really not all that good,' she said. 'At least I don't think I am. I don't consider it a skill, more a pleasure. But when I saw your aunt I thought, "Now there's a lady with very little to occupy her time, and I think maybe this will do it for a good while to come." Now'—and she looked at Clothilde—'how long do we have before Cousin Frazier gets home? I need to bathe and change.'

'He be home in about an hour,' Chloe said, and Peyton saw with astonishment that she was trying to hide a smile.

'Good,' Nora said, and she went back up the stairs.

Peyton turned to Chloe. 'You like her, don't you?' she said.

'Don't know her yet,' Chloe said. 'But she kind of like a fresh little breeze in here.'

Peyton slumped out of the kitchen to her room and threw herself on the bed to think about everything that had happened since the morning. Instead she slid so deeply into sleep that when her father came to wake her for supper she did not, for a moment, know where she was.

THEY ATE THAT EVENING in the big dining room off the other side of the kitchen, and Nora had dressed for the occasion. Her hair was up in a burnished French twist, and she wore a pink oxford-cloth shirt with the sleeves rolled up and a pink plaid madras skirt. She looked, Peyton thought, like money, though she could not have said how. According to Aunt Augusta, Nora did not have a pot to piss in.

Candlelight. The table set with heavy old silver, crystal glasses and the good china that had been her mother's. Peyton hated all of it. Her father had bidden it for this unknown cousin, when he had never bidden it for her, not even on her birthdays.

When Clothilde came in with plates of pot roast and mashed potatoes, her father said, 'This was a good idea, Chloe. I'd forgotten how nice this room is. We ought to do this more often.'

So it had been Chloe's idea, then. It made no difference to Peyton.

She was not going to forgive her cousin. If it had not been for her, they would be eating pot roast comfortably in the breakfast room.

'I can't tell you what a perfect dinner this is,' Nora said. 'I've gotten so accustomed to getting my own meals that I'd forgotten what a pleasure good food and a beautiful table could be.'

'What do you usually eat?' Peyton said, forgetting to sulk.

'Pizza,' Nora said, smiling at her. 'Hamburgers. Kentucky Fried Chicken. Anything I can take with me in the car.'

'Oh,' Peyton said. 'Why don't you just stay home and eat?'

'Well, I'm not really sure where that is right now.'

'You must have a home. Everybody lives somewhere,' Peyton pushed it. Her father's eyebrows rose.

'I've lived a lot of places,' her cousin said, her face serene. She was, Peyton knew, going to refuse to be baited. 'I've lived all over Florida, and in Cuba for a while, and California. I realised I was getting sort of old for that kind of thing, and I thought I ought to look and see if I could find a nest somewhere. I'd like to settle for a while.'

'Nora taught coloured children,' Peyton said, looking sidewise to see how her father would take it. In the Deep South of her time, change had not even swept a wing over the small towns, and the federal government be damned.

'A good thing to do,' Frazier McKenzie said. 'There are never enough qualified teachers for the children who need them most. I've often wondered what's going to happen to us if we don't educate all our children.'

Peyton goggled, her mouth full of apple cobbler. She had no idea that her father thought about things like that.

'I thought I might find some kind of minority teaching job around Atlanta,' Nora said. 'What with Dr King and all, it's the real epicentre of the Movement. It's what I do best, what I love.'

Her father looked at her cousin thoughtfully. 'When was it that your mother died?' he said.

'About twelve years ago. I hadn't lived with her for a while. You know she was sick? She drank an awful lot, and it got so that she couldn't take care of me or herself. One of my father's sisters put her in an institution, and I lived with her family for a year or two. Then I got a scholarship and went to Rollins, and I've essentially been on my own ever since. Don't worry about me, Cousin Frazier. I'm absolutely accustomed to taking care of myself. I'll find a place in Atlanta. I'm looking forward to it.'

'It would be nice to have you that close to us,' her father said. 'I know Lila Lee would want Peyton to know her cousin.'

'I'm sure,' Nora said, looking down.

When Chloe had taken away the last of the dishes, her father said to Nora, 'I usually watch a little TV after dinner. You're welcome to join me. Peyton's going to be doing her homework.'

'I'd love to,' Nora said.

'I don't have any homework,' Peyton said.

'I think you probably do,' her father said, and he rose from his chair. He held Nora's chair as she stood up. Peyton got up from hers and went through the kitchen and the breakfast room to her room. She was suddenly tired, but she did not sleep. Her father would be in, she knew. There was no escaping it. There would be an accounting for her actions of the night before.

She heard the television set go on, and then, a little later, incredibly, she heard her father laughing. Nora's rich laughter followed.

I hate her, Peyton thought clearly and roundly.

When her father came in at last, she was awake. He sat down on the edge of her bed. His face looked cold, carved from granite in the low lamplight.

'Peyton, last night was not acceptable,' he said. 'I've gone to bat for you with your aunt more times than you know, but after this I've got to admit she's right. You've got to have some supervision.'

'No,' Peyton whispered.

'Yes. Nothing like it can happen again. So here are your options. One, you can go to boarding school. Two, I can put you entirely in your Aunt Augusta's hands. You'd live here, of course, but she would decide what was best for you and see that you did it.'

Peyton felt tears of enormity and betrayal well into her eyes.

'Three,' her father said, 'your Cousin Nora can stay with us for a while and oversee things. I've asked her if she would consider it, and she's said she'll think about it.'

'Nora would mean more work for Chloe,' Peyton whispered miserably. 'And it'll cost you a lot extra.'

'She'll be finding a job around here. She's adamant about that.'

'You'll have to talk to her. You don't like to do that.'

'Nora's pleasant to talk to. Besides, I work most nights.'

Peyton was silent. It was no contest. Boarding school was unimaginable, Aunt Augusta too terrible to contemplate.

Her father got up and walked to her door and then stopped and looked back. 'Incidentally, I like your hair that way,' he said. 'I can see more than a little of your mother in you.'

Peyton turned off her bedside lamp. She burrowed under her covers, feeling warmth that came from somewhere inside her as well as out. For the first time in a long time, she did not show herself her movies.

PEYTON GOT UP EARLY the next morning and shuffled into the kitchen, patting her hair. She had not combed it since Nora fixed it for her and was halfway hoping her cousin would offer to refresh it. Peyton had no idea how to make a French twist.

'Where is everybody?' she said grumpily to Chloe, who emerged from the kitchen bearing a gluey mass of oatmeal. 'I *hate* that stuff, Chloe; you know I do. You wouldn't dare serve it if Daddy was here.'

'It ain't your daddy needs fattening up,' Chloe said, banging down the dish in front of Peyton. 'Your daddy's gone to a breakfast meeting of the school board up at the café, and Nora took off early this morning. Say she want to get a look at the town before it has a chance to get a look at her.'

'Did she take the Thunderbird?'

'She sho' did. You could hear that little old car peeling off a mile away. She got the top down and the radio going full blast, and she singing along with it. Town gon' get a look at her, all right.'

'They'll kick her out of here,' Peyton said with obscure satisfaction, not realising that she hoped this would not happen until after Nora fixed her hair.

'I 'spect Nora could kick back right good,' Chloe said. 'I'd hate to be the one who tries to run her off.'

'Do you know when she's coming back?' Peyton asked.

'She say she be back late this afternoon. We gon' eat a little early. She going into Atlanta to see a movie later on.'

'What movie? Is Daddy going with her? Am I going?'

'I think she mean to go by herself.'

'All the way up there at *night*?'

'Nora almost thirty years old,' Chloe said. 'And she done drive that car from one end of this country to the other. I 'spect she be OK at a movie in Atlanta.'

'Huh,' Peyton grumped, but in her mind she could see it: the little pink car slicing through the dark towards the smear of light that was the city, Nora with the red hair flaming out behind her. Something in her heart squeezed.

It was a strange day in school. At recess one of the senior boys, an Adonis so exalted by position on the football team as to be near sacred, said, 'Hey, Peyton, I hear your cousin came to see you and that she's a good-looking broad. You tell her that any time she wants a real man's company she can call me. I bet we'd get along real good.'

Peyton, who would have passed by this icon a day earlier with her eyes averted, looked him in the face. 'Don't hold your breath,' she said. 'She's got about a million boyfriends.'

'She really got a pink T-bird?' said one of the Adonis's appendages.

'Yeah, she does,' Peyton said grandly. 'We're taking it into Atlanta tonight to a movie. She's going to teach me to drive it.'

There was no reply, and she walked away, floating on power.

NORA DID NOT EAT dinner with them, but she sat at the table smoking and chatting pleasantly. She wore an astonishing outfit of tight black ankle-length pants and a loose, heavily embroidered blouse of some rough, gauzy material, and her hair was down again. It shone like molten copper in the light from the brass overhead lamp.

'I'll get something after the movie,' she said when Frazier McKenzie raised an eyebrow at her empty plate. 'I ate lunch real late, and I hear there's a nice little Italian restaurant next door to the movie theatre. I haven't had clam linguine for a long time.'

'Neither have I,' Frazier said. 'Maybe we'll all go sometime. I don't think Peyton has ever tasted clam linguine.'

'I've had clams,' Peyton said. 'I've had them at Howard Johnson's. I think they're overrated. I find that most seafood is.'

Even she could hardly believe the affected sentences coming out of her mouth. She looked up at Nora, expecting laughter.

Nora only smiled. 'That's because you've never had it fresh out of a tropical sea and cooked over an outside grill. I agree with you, frozen seafood is ghastly. I'll make you my special *sopa caliente* one day. That ought to change your mind about seafood.'

'What's in it?'

'Oh, rice. Sweet potatoes. Fresh coconut milk. Crab and langouste—little warm-water lobsters. Chunks of fish. Broth. Spices. I learned to make it when I lived in Cuba.'

'It sounds hideous,' Peyton said.

Her father gave her a look. 'It sounds good to me,' he said. 'Might make a nice change from southern cooking, not that Chloe doesn't do that better than anybody. Sometimes I think we just don't get out into the world enough down here in Lytton.'

Nora stubbed out her Salem in the ashtray Chloe had put at her place—two days and already it was her place, Peyton thought resentfully—and lit another. Then she put that out, too.

'This can be pretty offensive if nobody else in the house smokes,' she said. 'I'll confine it to my room, or go out on the porch.'

'No, don't bother,' Frazier said and Peyton frankly goggled. 'I used to smoke. I still keep a pipe out in my office. Maybe I'll bring it in and we can smoke Peyton out of here.'

Peyton stared. Her head spun. Her father, smoking? Cigarettes, a pipe? This cool, abstemious man?

'So, did you have a tour of Lytton like you planned?' her father asked. 'It must have taken you all of twenty minutes.'

'It's a charming little town, Frazier. I looked into both churches and walked into all the neighbourhoods. The houses aren't grand, but they're so neat, so right somehow. Roses on trellises, and vegetable gardens . . . It feels like nothing bad could ever happen here.'

'You ought to try Lytton Grammar School, Peyton thought grimly.

'It's a pretty little town,' her father said mildly. 'But there are a lot of things that need changing here.'

'You mean like the "Coloured" and "White" entrances to the movie theatre? Maybe you could start with those.'

'It'll come,' he said. 'But it's going to have to come in its own time. If you tried to force that kind of change on Lytton all at once you'd hit a brick wall. Nothing would ever change.'

'But Frazier, it's the law of the land.'

Her father put down his coffee cup. 'Yes. It is,' he said. 'And we're lucky to have those laws in place at last. There's great change going on in the cities; you know that. But out here, in the backwaters, we're a hundred years behind the cities. It's going to be a matter of years. It's going to happen one mind at a time, one heart at a time. Meanwhile, we try, and we measure our victories in inches.'

Nora regarded him thoughtfully. 'Like what?'

'Well, like something I want to talk to you about. We talked about it at the school-board meeting this morning. The county education folks are about to get all over us for making no move towards compliance, and if they do that they'll never get any. So I thought—*we* thought—that a compromise might work for a while. Maybe one shared class, maybe an honours class so that everyone could see the idea working. You could hold it one week at Lytton High and the next at Carver High, and so on. I think maybe, once it got going, everybody might be able to live with that.'

'What kind of class?' Nora said.

'What do you think of English? An honours English class that maybe addressed the literature of blacks and whites alike. A small class, so there could be a lot of discussion . . .'

Nora raised her head. The bell of coppery hair swung forward over part of her face. 'I want that class, Frazier,' she said.

'I thought you might,' he said. 'I sold you and the class as a package. I said you might be willing to do some intensive tutoring, too. The black children are going to need it.'

'I would *love* it,' Nora breathed. 'It's just what I've hoped I'd find, but I never dreamed it could be here. When will you know?'

'The chairman's going to take it to the county meeting this next week, but I don't anticipate any problems. The county is going to be so relieved to see that we're making some sort of effort '

'Of course I'd get my own place,' Nora said excitedly.

'No, we'd want you here if you'll stay,' her father said. 'That is, if you're still willing to spend some time with Peyton.'

'I can't think of anything I'd like more,' Nora said. 'We will teach each other wondrous things. As long as we all understand that I'm not trying to be a mother or a disciplinarian. Just a friend.'

'It's all we ask, isn't it, Peyton?' Her father was smiling.

'Uh-huh,' she said.

'So I'll let you know as soon as I do,' her father said. 'But I should think you might plan on starting in a couple of weeks.'

They sat in silence for a time, and then Nora said, 'I met your grandmother today, Peyton. Your mother,' and she nodded at Frazier, who grimaced.

'I can't wait to hear about that,' he said.

'Well,' Nora said. 'I was sitting on a bench in the square reading a book and this old lady sat down beside me. She looked at me and said, "I know you. I saw you coming in a bowl of tomato soup."'

'Oh, Lord,' Frazier said. 'I hope she didn't bother you.'

'God, no.' Nora giggled. Unlike the rich laugh, it was silvery, flute-like. Peyton felt the corners of her own mouth tug upwards. 'I thought she was fabulous. How many of us have been foreseen in a bowl of tomato soup? We talked about some amazing things. Then she raised her fist at a limb full of crows over by the railroad tracks and yelled, "Go tell the Devil!" and they flew off and so did she. I like her better than anybody I've met except you all.'

'That's a folk tale. She's Scottish,' Peyton said.

'I know the tale. I loved hearing somebody actually say it. I'll bet the Devil is getting an earful right now.'

Peyton looked at her keenly to see if she was making fun of her grandmother, but there was no indication of that. Nora's face was soft with enjoyment.

'How did you know she was my grandmother?' Peyton said.

'Oh, she introduced herself. But I'd have known anyway. You look just like her, Frazier, and you're probably going to, Peyton. I thought she was beautiful.'

'I'm glad you got along,' Frazier said almost primly.

'I'm going down to see her sometime over the weekend. She wants to ride in my car. Peyton, you come, too, if you want to.'

'I have a lot of homework,' Peyton said. Was this amoeba-like cousin going to absorb her grandmother, too?

Presently Nora got up and gathered up a huge straw bag and went out into the twilight, jingling her car keys. Peyton and her father sat in silence while the engine growled into life and then faded away down the street.

'Are you glad she's going to stay awhile?' her father asked her.

'I don't know,' Peyton mumbled.

4

In the night Peyton was woken by the crash of thunder and pelting rain. Before she fell back asleep she heard the slam of a car door and the pounding of footsteps on the front porch, then the softer opening and closing of the front door. Nora, coming back from Atlanta. It was, Peyton knew, very late. Her father wasn't going to like this one little bit.

Peyton slept late and woke up cross and disorientated. She wrapped herself in her grandmother's afghan and stumbled into the breakfast room, trailing it, blinking into the overhead lamplight.

'Tell Mr De Mille I'm ready for my close-up now,' Nora said from her seat at the table. She was smoking and smiling at Peyton. Her face, too, was crumpled with sleep and her hair poured into her eyes like a sheepdog's. She wore a black silk kimono, belted tight and crawling with scarlet and gold dragons and tigers.

'Who's Mr De Mille?' said Peyton thickly, slumping down into her seat and looking at the cuckoo clock on the wall. It said ten fifteen.

'It's from a movie called *Sunset Boulevard*,' Nora said, inhaling deeply and letting the smoke drift from her nostrils. 'It's one of the great movies of all time. Next time it's at an art theatre, I'll take you.'

'Huh,' Peyton said, poking at the curling strips of bacon and the scrambled eggs on her plate. 'I was going to ride my bike down to Nana's today. But it looks like it's going to rain for the next hundred years.'

'I'll take you later,' Nora said. 'Right now we are going up to my room and I am going to fix that hair. Don't argue. It looks like a bird's nest caught in a windstorm.'

Peyton followed her cousin up the stairs to the big back bedroom without protesting, mainly because her hair did indeed look like a fright wig. Nora sat her down in front of the mirror at the old walnut dressing table that had been there ever since Peyton could remember. Formerly it had worn only yellowing antimacassars and a vase of dried flowers. Now it was littered with bottles and tubes and brushes, and smelt of spilt powder and cologne. Despite herself, Peyton studied the array of cosmetics. There had been none in this house but her father's aftershave since her birth.

'I'll show you what they're for after,' Nora said, moving her and the chair beside the window and bringing a towel to drape around her shoulders. She combed out her tangled hair gently and walked round and round her, studying her head from all angles. 'Peyton, do you like Audrey Hepburn?'

'Better than anybody,' Peyton said. '*Breakfast at Tiffany's* is my favourite movie. I sat though it three times.'

'I did twice. You know what I think we'll do? I think we'll cut this hair into a kind of Audrey Hepburn cap. Very short and pixieish, a little curly. It would look wonderful with your features and your long neck. You game?'

'Yes,' Peyton whispered, with the sense of leaping blindly into a bottomless abyss.

She kept her eyes closed while Nora snipped and patted and studied. Somehow it was not like the ministrations of Mr Antoine. As she worked, Nora talked about her night in Atlanta.

'Well, first,' she said, as if Peyton had asked, 'I went to the movie. *La Strada*. Have you seen it?'

'No,' Peyton said, trying to imagine herself walking alone into an Atlanta movie theatre after dark.

'You've got to see it, kiddo. I'll take you to a matinée. OK, so then afterward I walked up the street to Buon Giorno's and had my clam linguine and a bottle of awful, wonderful Chianti. That's a red Italian wine, very raw and gutsy.'

'I know what it is,' said Peyton, who didn't.

'Well,' Nora continued, 'so then I went down to this little place by the bus station that has the best Dixieland jazz I have *ever* heard outside New Orleans. And I danced and whooped and hollered till about one, and then I came home.'

'By *yourself*?' Peyton squawked. 'Down by the *bus* station? Aunt Augusta would *die*!'

'Which is why we aren't going to tell her, isn't it?' Peyton could hear the smile in Nora's voice. 'Besides, I wasn't by myself. I went with somebody I met at Buon Giorno's. He knew about the place.'

'*He?*' Peyton's head was literally spinning with the enormity of it.

'A soldier who was eating his dinner alone. So I joined him. It's more fun to eat Italian *with* somebody. He was on his way to Fort Benning and had to catch a bus at two in the morning. So we figured we might as well hear some jazz before he left, and dance a little.'

'You picked up a soldier and went to the bus station?'

Aside from sitting down on a bare toilet seat in a public rest room, going to the bus station was the number-one taboo in Aunt Augusta's pantheon of crimes and misdemeanours. Prowling soldiers were unthinkable.

'For God's sake, Peyton, he was all of eighteen, and homesick for Tennessee. He was a sweet boy. You get so you can tell who's OK and who isn't. We had a wonderful time, and I kissed him goodbye and put him on a Trailways bus.'

Nora produced a bulbous hand-held hair dryer and aimed it at Peyton's head. Until the hot air hit her, Peyton did not realise that her neck was completely naked. She looked down. A mat of wiry hair lay on the floor under the chair.

'You cut it all off,' she wailed.

'Yep. Now look.'

Nora stepped back and Peyton looked. A thin deer of a girl with a short tousle of hair looked back. It was its own colour again, with tendrils framing her face. Something Nora had done to it made it shine softly, and it was somehow fuller than usual. It had curve and lift and bounce to it. The girl in the mirror was . . . interesting. Pretty? No, assuredly not. But for the first time in her life Peyton could see what she might look like as a woman.

Nora smiled down at her. She lifted one eyebrow: 'Well?'

'I . . . gee. I don't know. It isn't me, is it?'

'Yes, it is. It's you like you ought to be. That stuff on your head was like a dead muskrat lying up there. This sets you free. Now I can really see your father and your grandmother in you.'

Peyton, who had spent her entire life searching for signs of her mother in her undistinguished visage, felt something inside her lighten and lift, as if she had tossed out a heavy burden. At least she looked like *someone* now—if not her mother, then just maybe her mad, beautiful grandmother, her blade-featured father.

Her smile widened. 'Nobody at school has hair like this.'

'Precisely,' Nora said. 'Peyton, take it from one who knows. You aren't ever going to look like Brigitte Bardot or Jackie Kennedy. Don't waste your time wishing. Go with what you've got. It may not ring many bells at school, but I assure you there *is* a world beyond Lytton Grammar, and it's a lot more interesting. You're going to shine in that world like a star. Come on, kiddo, let's go try it out on somebody. Is your daddy in his office?'

'No! Not yet.'

'Chloe, then?'

'She's gone home. She works only half a day on Saturdays.'

'OK, your grandmother. I promised, anyway. Dump that afghan and put on some clothes. Your chariot awaits.'

Peyton tiptoed down the stairs to her room and put on a pair of slim blue pants and a white sweater she had got for Christmas and never worn. The sweater was too big, but somehow the drooping amplitude of it was all right with the long neck and the small shining head. She put on her sneakers and went hesitantly out into the kitchen.

'Miss Hepburn, as I live and breathe,' Nora said, smiling. She had changed into tight, faded blue jeans and a sweat shirt.

They dashed through the rain to the Thunderbird. Peyton scrunched herself into the passenger seat, loving the sleek, feral feeling of the car as it leapt away from the kerb and skimmed into flight.

Her grandmother was in the kitchen, stirring something in a pot.

She heard them come in and turned from the stove. She looked first at Peyton, and a slow smile warmed her wild hawk's face. 'Well, here you are at last. I've waited a long time for you.'

Then she turned to Nora. 'It's nice to see you again,' she said, almost formally. 'Will you stay and have a cup of tea?'

They sat down before the blazing kitchen fireplace. Agnes McKenzie brought cups of the steaming brew and slices of seed cake almost shyly, as if offering them to royalty. She sat down then and sipped her own tea.

There was a silence. Finally Peyton could stand it no longer and said, 'How do you like my hair, Nana?'

Her grandmother studied her. 'You're not our little girl any more,' she said. 'But you're who you're going to be now, and that's a start. I can see the shape of you like a minnow in deep water. Or something in long grass. Something wild and shy, but the power's there. Oh, yes, it is. I always knew it would be.'

'Power?' Peyton said, appalled. She did not want power any more than she wanted wealth or celebrity. She would settle gratefully for the old anonymity, so long as no one laughed at her any more.

'Oh, yes. It'll be a long time until you grow into it, and it won't be any easy journey, but power.'

'Is it good power?' Nora said interestedly.

'It depends on who guides it,' Nana said. 'I plan to be on top of it like a duck on a june bug, but I'm not going to be able to go all the way with it.' Abruptly she got up from the table and said, 'Peyton, come on in the pantry with me. I need a load of firewood.'

Peyton rose to follow her grandmother.

Nora half rose, too. 'Won't you let me help?' she said. 'I don't want to feel like company.'

'But you are,' Agnes said, and smiled faintly at her, and went out of the kitchen with Peyton trailing behind her.

In the cold little pantry she fished in her apron, pulled something out and dropped it into Peyton's hand. It was a primitive and rather beautiful object: an intricately woven knot that formed a rough cross on a leather thong.

'It's a special amulet. It protects you. I want you to put it on now, and I don't want you to take it off again.'

'Protects me against what?'

Her grandmother was silent, and then she said, 'I saw her again, your Cousin Nora. I saw her this morning when I built the fire.'

'The fire—that's not so good, is it? She wouldn't hurt me, Nana. I know she wouldn't. I don't think I like her very much, but she's always taking my side and doing things for me, and she absolutely hates Aunt Augusta. That can't be all bad, can it?'

Her grandmother shook her head impatiently. 'I can't see bad or good this time,' she said. 'I just know that I saw her first in the soup, and this time in the fire—I don't see bad; I don't see anything. It's like fog. I don't know what it means.'

Suddenly Peyton was tired of all of it—the dark pantry, the visions of fire and water. She wanted light, air, normalcy, laughter, the sound of her record player.

'I think we need to go, Nana,' she said. 'Daddy's going to be in before long and Nora's making Cuban black bean soup for supper.'

Her grandmother looked at her and sighed. 'So it begins,' she said. 'All right, Peyton. You run on and have your soup.'

AT SUPPER HER FATHER frankly stared at her. He said nothing, only nodded as Nora talked lazily about her trip to Atlanta the night before, and ate the rich, dark soup appreciatively and had another bowl, saying it made him feel as if he were at a real fiesta, and all the while Peyton was aware of his eyes on her.

Finally he said, 'I really like your hair, Peyton. I like the new clothes, too. You remember to thank your aunt, now.'

'She's going to hate the hair,' Peyton said.

Her father smiled, a small smile, but a smile nevertheless. 'I expect you're right,' he said. 'Never mind. This is good. She'll come around. Did you thank Nora for the haircut?'

'She did,' Nora said before Peyton could remember that she had not. 'We went down to her grandmother's afterward, to show her. I think she liked it, too.'

Her father looked at Peyton.

'She really did,' Peyton said, bending over her soup bowl.

'Well, then, you've got a hard row to hoe ahead of you,' Frazier said, but he smiled again. 'Nora, tell me where you learned to make this soup. Cuba, you said? Were you there long? I've always wanted to see Cuba.'

'It's a wonderful country,' Nora said. 'I might still be there if the revolution hadn't heated things up. I believe in it, but I don't want to live with it. I don't take easily to sacrifice and nobility.'

She smiled through smoke, and Peyton thought how plain she was, and yet how utterly arresting. It was hard to look away from her. She had brought out fat wax candles from somewhere, and painted wooden candlesticks, and they ate by the flickering light. In it, Nora looked like some impossible firebird that had alighted in a small southern town and decided to stay awhile, unaware that her plumage roiled the air around her. She wore a heavy cabled white turtleneck sweater and the black pants, and her long, thin hands weaved in and out of the candlelight as she talked of Cuba.

'I went there in nineteen fifty-two with a friend,' she said. 'I was just out of school and didn't know what I wanted to do, and I had always wanted to see Cuba. He had a motorcycle. We put it on a ferry and took off. He came back two months later. I stayed five years.'

Peyton saw her father remark the 'he', though he said nothing. It emboldened her to say, 'Why didn't your friend stay, too?'

'Tootie was a priest,' Nora said. 'He had to get back to his parish.'

'Tootie?' Peyton said.

'Tootie LeClerc, fresh out of Loyola in New Orleans. I met him on the beach in Miami and we spent the afternoon drinking beer. Once I saw the motorcycle and heard he was going to Cuba, I knew what my next move was going to be.'

'So you stayed on,' Frazier said.

'I did. At first I just wanted to be a tourist—we poked around Havana and did all the touristy things—but soon we both got restless. So we got on the motorcycle and headed west, toward Mariel. It's beautiful country, or it was then—wild and empty, with blue, blue water. And poor. That's where we began to see little adobe shacks with chickens going in and out of the open windows, and the village men hanging around the lone flyspecked cantina because one or another of the cement factories had shut down and there was no work. And the children, some naked, some in rags, playing in the roads with not a sign of any supervision, or a school anywhere. Tootie thought he'd found paradise; he went straight to the Catholic church and asked if he could sign on sans pay, and the old priest almost kissed him. I went into the cantina and told the barkeeper that I would start a little school for the children, teach them English and some geography and what all, in exchange for room and board in the village. I had a little money. I was going to stay until it ran out. So they found me a room with a village family and I moved in and fell in love with them and it and everything else, and when Tootie went back to New Orleans, I stayed. They were some of the great years of my life. It was as if that's what I was meant to be doing—living there with those people, teaching those children.'

'But you left,' Frazier McKenzie said.

'Things change. One day it was time. I came back to Miami and got a job with a programme they had for the Haitian refugees pouring into Florida from Papa Doc and his benevolent Tontons Macoute. But you don't want to hear all this.'

'I do,' he said. 'It's fascinating. Peyton and I both would love to hear your stories. You've done something really valuable.'

'One day I'll tell them all to you.' She smiled and got up and said, 'Leave the dishes. Peyton, come with me. I have something for you.'

The something was a tiny tiger kitten with slanted green eyes and a little spike of a tail. Nora brought his box out of the bathroom and set it down, and the kitten scrambled out onto the floor, mewling furiously. He looked at Peyton and she looked back.

'I found him behind a trash can at the bus station last night,' Nora said. 'Somebody had obviously dumped him. His name is Trailways, and he needs a friend.'

The kitten mewed again. Peyton put out a hand and he sniffed her fingers and then climbed into her lap and curled up. Something in her heart softened into a spreading pool. 'Is he for me?' she asked.

'If you want him. He'll need a lot of taking care of. Shots and most certainly a flea bath. We need to get a vet to check him.'

'Can I take him to my room?' Peyton said. Her voice was tight with love for the angry little cat.

'In a little while,' Nora said. 'You stay with him right now. I want to go down and tell your father about him. I get the idea that there haven't been many pets in this house.'

'Buddy had a dog, I think, but I don't remember it . . .'

'You just sit tight.' Nora got up and went down the stairs towards the breakfast room. Peyton wrapped a small towel around the kitten and took it and sat with it on the second step, out of sight but not out of hearing.

' . . . not set up here for a cat,' she heard her father say. 'Chloe isn't going to have time to take care of it when she gets tired of it.'

'She's not going to get tired of it, Frazier,' Nora said, and her voice was cool and utterly level. 'I wish you had seen her face.'

'Did you ever think of asking me first?'

'I did, and vetoed that idea in a second. Would you have permitted it? And besides, it isn't your kitten. It's Peyton's.'

There was more talk but the voices dropped and Peyton could not hear. She sat on the step and rocked the kitten against her.

Presently Nora came into the hall and looked up and made a circle with her thumb and forefinger. Peyton felt tears sting her eyes.

She slept that night with the susurration of the wind and rain in the trees outside and, just at her ear, the rusty purr of the kitten.

WHEN PEYTON WOKE on Sunday morning the house was still and full of pearly grey light, and the rain was a blanket of sound that muffled wakefulness. She was just putting an unwilling foot out from under her covers when she heard Chloe shriek from the kitchen.

Peyton was halfway into the kitchen before she remembered the kitten and registered that it was not in her bedroom. 'Oh, shit,' she said softly.

Chloe was standing, arms akimbo, in the middle of the kitchen, glaring down at her skirt. Trailways hung from it, fastened by his needlelike claws, swinging gently and lashing his meagre tail.

Peyton ran and unhooked him from Clothilde's skirt and folded him protectively into her arms, where he struggled and yowled.

'What that sorry thing doing in this house?' Chloe demanded. 'I was just standing here fixin' breakfast and he come barrelling out of your room and grab on my skirt before I even seen him.'

'I'm sorry, Chloe,' Peyton said miserably. 'I thought he was still with me. Nora brought him to me. His name is Trailways.'

'His name mud for all I care. Does your daddy know about him?'

'Yes. It's all right with him.'

'Well, if it get under my feet one more time I'm gon' stomp on it.'

'He won't,' Peyton said fervently. 'I'll keep him in my room. I'll feed him and clean up after him. He won't be a bit of trouble.'

Trailways stuck his sharp little head out of Peyton's arm and looked up into Chloe's face. He put out a tiny paw and patted her arm, seven or eight rapid, whisper-soft pats. 'Rowr?' he said.

Chloe's face struggled with implacability but lost. An unwilling grin broke its surface. 'Well, he's a feisty little thing, ain't he?'

'He's a good boy. You're going to love him, Chloe.'

'I ain't gon' love no flea-bitten stray cat. But maybe I ain't gon' hate him, either,' Clothilde said.

When Nora finally straggled down to breakfast, Peyton and her father were playing with Trailways, tossing a ball of kitchen twine for him. Peyton was laughing, and her father was smiling.

Peyton looked up as Nora came down the stairs and into the breakfast room. Instead of the dragon robe, she was wearing a short black sheath, a strand of pearls, and high-heeled black shoes. She had her hair pulled back into a chignon and had tied a red and black paisley silk scarf around it. She looked absolutely wonderful.

'I thought we'd be going to church,' Nora said. 'Am I too late? Is this wrong for church?'

'You look just fine,' Frazier said. 'You just took us by surprise. Here you are all dressed and Peyton's still in her pyjamas. I wasn't sure you'd want to go to church, but we're glad to have you.'

'I'd really like to. So, I see you've met Trailways,' Nora said. 'He's a cutie, isn't he?'

'He's not so bad. Where on earth did you find him?'

'Behind a garbage can at the restaurant,' Nora said easily. She smiled at Peyton. *We will always have our secrets, you and I,* the smile said. Peyton smiled back at her cousin. *Yes, secrets of our own, which nobody else will ever know,* her smile said back to Nora.

She went to dress, and Nora came into her room with her.

'Now. What are you going to wear to church?'

Without stopping for Peyton's answer, Nora went to her closet and opened the door. She shook her head a little and then reached in and pulled out the dress and jacket that Aunt Augusta had selected from the Tween Shop. They were just as bad as Peyton remembered.

'This?' Nora said.

'I hate it. It looks like a missionary-society dress.'

'Just you wait. Put it on and I'll be right back.'

Peyton slipped on the dark, sleeveless dress, which gaped and billowed on her, the skirt flapping at her calves, and she would not look into the mirror on her dressing table. There was no way anyone was going to get her into the Lytton First Methodist Church in this.

Nora came back with a shopping bag and began to spread things out on Peyton's bed. First she brought out safety pins and pinned the waist and armholes of the dress snugly. Then she took a big roll of two-sided tape and doubled the hem up and secured it with the tape. Peyton felt it just skimming her knees.

Nora clasped a string of irregular freshwater pearls around Peyton's neck, then she produced stockings and black suede shoes with low, shaped heels.

'Cuban heels,' she said. 'Do you think you can squinch your feet into them just for an hour?'

Peyton nodded, wondering how on earth she was going to walk.

'Now the jacket,' Nora said, and she slipped it over Peyton's arms and buttoned it at the throat, pulling out the pearls so that they lay just along the neckline. She puffed Peyton's hair, whisked on a bit of blusher and a slicking of lip gloss and stepped back.

'Wow,' she said. 'This is even better than I thought.'

Peyton minced over to the mirror in the too-tight heels, and looked. Holly Golightly did indeed look back, standing poised and straight, her stalk of a neck rising from the collar of her dress, her long legs graceful.

'I can't,' Peyton whispered. 'I can't wear this.'

'Oh, yes, you can, and you will,' Nora said, putting an arm around her shoulder. 'You're going to walk into that church with your father and me and you're going to hear a great big swoosh of breath from everybody there.'

'I'd hate that.'

'No, you wouldn't. Once you've heard it, you'll want to hear it everywhere you go.'

THERE WAS NO WHOOSH of indrawn breath as Peyton walked into the Methodist church, the church she had attended all her life. There was, however, a small silence from each pew as she passed, and then a little hum of conversation.

'Let me die,' Peyton whispered to the God who never seemed to hear her, and she slipped into the McKenzie pew. When she turned to seat herself, she looked back. Everywhere she looked, there were smiles. Her Uncle Charles held up his thumb and forefinger in an OK sign. Only Aunt Augusta was not smiling. She looked as if she had swallowed something rancid.

The sermon seemed interminable. When it ended, Peyton trotted dumbly up the aisle behind her father. Nora walked ahead of them, head high. Peyton thought that there had been nothing like her in this church in its living memory, though Nora wore plain black, like half the women there, and pearls, and just the silk scarf. Still, eyes tracked her, heads went together, a soft babble rose wherever she passed. When the eyes turned to Peyton the babble swelled. Finally, the three of them gained the cold freedom of the porch, and then they were in the car.

'You ladies surely kicked up a fuss,' her father said. 'I never saw so much whispering and eye-rolling and what-all.'

Suddenly Peyton was wild to be home, to skin out of the pinned-up clothes, to curl up with Trailways under her afghan and read away the long afternoon.

'Augusta has asked us to lunch,' her father said. 'I thought we'd go and get it over with. If we don't, she's going to be at the house every morning until she finds out all she wants to know about Nora.'

'*Daddy,*' Peyton wailed.

'It's not for long, Peyton. And it's been a while since you've seen your Uncle Charlie. I want Nora to meet him.'

'I look forward to it,' Nora murmured.

Augusta McKenzie met them at the doorway of her home, a rambling brick ranch-style structure with black shutters and a path bordered with azalea bushes.

Augusta kissed Frazier lightly on the cheek and nodded to Nora.

'Your new clothes suit you very well, Peyton,' she said. 'I'm sorry you didn't think so much of your pretty permanent. Did your Cousin Nora cut it for you?'

The smile she bent on Nora was sharklike and brief.

'Yes, I did,' Nora said sweetly. 'We thought something a little simpler, maybe. I don't think Peyton quite knew how to take care of the permanent. I know she appreciated it, though.'

'I'm sure,' Augusta said.

She led them into her living room, done in turquoise and rose and beetling with bulbous brocade pieces. Charles McKenzie was perched uncomfortably on a wing chair, stiff in a blue suit and a red and blue tie. He clashed with the room.

Charles was a squashed and spread version of his older brother. You could see the resemblance in the grey eyes and dark hair, but the rest seemed blurred and sagging like a melting snowman. His nose was traced with red veins, he had two shiny-shaved chins poised over his starched collar, and his stomach pushed unhappily over his belt. Except on Sundays, Peyton could not remember ever seeing him in anything but hunting boots or desiccated old moccasins. She loved him. When she was very small, he used to toss her in the air and catch her, and she remembered her shrieks of joy.

He got up and hugged her briefly. He smelt as he always did, of whiskey and cigar smoke and his aftershave and, somehow, of the hunting dogs he kept over at Chief Fletcher's house.

'You look mighty pretty, honey,' he said. 'All grown up.'

'This is Peyton's cousin, Nora Findlay,' her father said, and Nora put out her hand, smiling. Uncle Charlie took it, reddening.

'I'm glad to meet you finally,' Nora said.

'Pleasedtomeecha,' Charles McKenzie mumbled.

'Please sit down,' Aunt Augusta said. 'Lunch will be only a minute. Now, Nora, tell us all about yourself. I knew your Lytton cousin, Lila Lee, for ever, of course, but I don't believe I ever met her Cousin Carolyn. Your mother. She's passed away, I understand?'

'Yes, she has,' Nora said. Peyton knew that Aunt Augusta knew that. She knew also that Nora knew she knew. Her stomach knotted, but Nora only said, 'As you know, she was sick for a long time before she died. I don't remember much about my father. So the only family I can come close to claiming is here in Lytton.'

'And you'll be moving on to a job in Atlanta, you said?'

'Well, actually . . .'

'I hope Nora will be staying awhile with us, Augusta,' Frazier McKenzie said. 'There are plans for a new joint English class with Lytton and Carver Highs, and I've suggested Nora for it. We'll know this week, but I'd say it was a done deal.'

'Well, Nora, you've landed well, haven't you?' Augusta said. And then, 'I think I heard Doreen say lunch was ready. Let's go on in.'

Aunt Augusta's table was spread with linen and china and crystal and silver, most of it in turquoise and rose. A prim tower of artificial fruit rose from a silver epergne in the middle of the table. Rose candles burned on either side of it.

'My goodness, it looks like a wedding with the candles and all,' Nora said. 'Beautiful, Aunt Augusta. Or should I say "Cousin"?'

' "Augusta" will do,' Peyton's aunt said. 'You're a bit too old to be my niece, and we're really not cousins. Thank you. I thought the candles because it's so dreary outside.'

A young black girl came into the dining room carrying a tureen. She wore a black dress and a starched white apron.

Peyton stared. 'Doreen! What are you doing in that thing?'

Doreen was the grandniece of Clothilde, a quiet girl only a few years older than Peyton. Her mother had died when she was small, and she did not know who her father was. Chloe looked after her and her younger brother, Tyrone. Peyton had played in the woods with both of them all through her childhood.

Doreen grinned but did not move her eyes from the tureen. She set it down in the middle of the table, where it slopped a bit of soup onto the tablecloth.

'Towel, please, Doreen,' Aunt Augusta said evenly, and when the girl had left the room she added, 'I'll never get her properly trained to serve. But she's helpful with the cleaning.'

'What's she doing in that apron thing?' Peyton asked curiously.

'For heaven's sake, Peyton, it's what people's maids wear,' her aunt said. 'Just because Chloe comes to work looking like a ragpicker does not mean it's proper. I bought the uniform for Doreen because I want her to learn how to be a good maid. She didn't go to school past the third grade because she had to look after Tyrone, and at least she can always find work if she's trained.'

No one spoke. Doreen came back into the room with a towel, looking as though she would burst into tears. Nora leaned towards her and took the towel. 'Let me,' she said. 'It's easier to reach from here. No, wait a minute, Doreen, don't go yet. I'm Nora Findlay, Peyton's cousin.'

Doreen looked at her wildly.

Nora smiled and said, 'You're a good maid, Doreen, but I wonder if you might not like to go back to school?'

'No'm,' the girl said, casting a look at Aunt Augusta. 'I've missed too much now. This is fine.'

'Well, look. I'm starting a special English class at Carver. You might enjoy sitting in sometime, when you're done with your work, of course. And I do tutoring, too. We could catch you up.'

'That will do, Doreen,' Aunt Augusta said, and the girl fled.

Augusta turned to Nora. 'It may not be the custom in some of the places you've lived,' she said tightly, 'but in Lytton people do not steal one another's maids.'

'I wasn't stealing her, I was emancipating her,' Nora said, and there were two round spots of colour high on her cheekbones. 'It was a notion Mr Lincoln had, a long time ago. I thought perhaps you'd heard of it.'

'You may bring in the plates, Doreen,' Augusta called. The girl did, and handed them round. The table was silent.

The meal was heavy and not particularly good, and it seemed to go on for years.

When at last it was over, they went back into the living room, and then Charles McKenzie said, 'Got a new shotgun the other day, Frazier. It's out in the garage. Want to go have a look?'

'Charles, let Frazier sit and digest his lunch,' Aunt Augusta snapped.

Nora stood up. 'I would love to see it, Charles,' she said. 'I learned skeet and trap shooting when I was in Cuba. I'm a pretty good shot, if I do say so. Will you show me?'

Charles McKenzie's ears reddened. He had no choice. He got up and shambled out of the room. Nora followed him.

After they left, the silence seemed to swell and shimmer. Even Peyton knew that what Nora had done had crossed some sort of boundary, though she did not know what it was. Aunt Augusta's eyes were almost popping out of her rosy face. Peyton knew, too, that whatever it was she was bursting to spill would not come forth while she was in the room.

'Aunt Augusta, may I go in the den and listen to the radio?' she said.

'Of course, Peyton.'

Peyton got up and wobbled on Nora's heels into the den, where the radio had been banished when the new Motorola TV was given pride of place in the living room. The den had started life as a small screened porch and was barely large enough to accommodate the radio and two battered Leatherette recliners. It smelt of cigars and, faintly, of sweet bourbon whiskey. Peyton turned on the radio and closed the glass French doors that separated the den from the living room. She then kicked off her shoes and curled up on the floor next to the big radio and laid her cheek against its fretwork as she had when she was a child, feeling the warmth and the living vibration from the station in Atlanta seep into her like sun. She must have slept. The next thing she knew someone had opened the glass doors and she could hear her father saying, 'Well, it's been a treat as usual, Augusta, but we've got to be on our way. I don't think Peyton has done her homework yet.'

Nora and Uncle Charles stood at the door, laughing.

'Thank you, Charles,' Nora said, her rich voice lilting with pleasure. 'What a lovely way to spend a rainy afternoon. Maybe you'll let me shoot it one day. I don't hunt, but I'm a terrific shot.'

Uncle Charles said heartily, 'It would be my pleasure.' Then he looked at Aunt Augusta's face and dropped his eyes to study his shoes.

'Thank you, Augusta,' Nora said, kissing Augusta on the cheek; Augusta flinched as if she had been bitten by a blue-tail fly. 'It was a wonderful lunch. Your house is just extraordinary.'

Peyton ran with Nora through the rain to the car. Behind them, they heard Augusta saying to Frazier, 'How can you possibly think she can stay in your house? I smelt whiskey on her breath, Frazier. Surely that should be enough for you.'

Nora laughed and shook out her wet copper hair. 'A little shot of Uncle Charles's stash wouldn't hurt her any,' she said.

Peyton was silent. In her world, no living white woman had ever been known to drink anything but eggnog at Christmas and a glass of champagne at weddings.

Her father was quiet on the drive home, and as they were putting away their wet things, he said, 'I've got a good bit of work to do. I'll be out in my office for a while.'

Peyton looked after him as he left the kitchen. Sunday afternoon was always their time to drive up to the Howard Johnson's on the interstate and have ice cream, and afterwards to watch television. Peyton had never known her father to work on Sunday afternoons.

Nora looked after him thoughtfully, then said, 'Get Trailways and I'll show you some of the things I brought with me from Cuba.'

'I think I'll read,' Peyton said. Tears were smarting in her eyes.

'This is better than any book,' Nora said, ruffling her hair.

Peyton brought Trailways to Nora's room and settled down in the middle of her unmade bed. The kitten burrowed under the bed-clothes and down to the bottom of the bed, scrabbling furiously, then curled into a ball, and started purring loudly.

Nora opened a big box that had been tied with twine and pulled out her treasures for Peyton's delectation. There were bolts of vivid, printed cloth—batik, Nora said. Big, bursting scrapbooks, too, came out of the trunk—'I'll show you some day'—and an ornate cigar box holding what Nora called her voodoo charms, which were small carved figures, bound clumps of feathers, mirrors, and a chicken's foot.

'Yuck,' Peyton said.

'Yeah, well, it's got power, no matter how it looks,' Nora said. 'Chickens are powerful carriers in voodoo. This chicken foot will protect you from were-tigers. That's probably why you never see them in the South—all those chickens.'

Peyton grinned unwillingly. The hurt of her father's defection eased slightly. 'What's that?' she asked, looking at a beautifully carved ebony box with a lock. It looked very old.

'That's my private stuff,' Nora said. 'The things that only I see. Photos, my journal, letters . . . Do you keep a journal, Peyton?'

'No,' Peyton said, suddenly on fire to open the box and let Nora's secrets fly out into the room like Pandora's furies.

'Well, that's one thing you simply have to do,' Nora said. 'How will you know what you think if you don't write it down? How will you remember who you were? I'm going to get you a good leather one next time I'm in Atlanta.'

Dusk was falling outside. The rain had stopped, and long, stabbing rays of brilliant red sun were piercing the clouds.

'Look at that. Red as sin,' Nora said. 'Does your father usually come in for dinner? If he doesn't, I'll fix us something.'

'He always does,' Peyton said, the pain welling back. 'Always. I don't know why he's acting like this.'

Nora was silent for a moment and then said, 'I do. He's mad at me. I think I shouldn't have gone out to the garage with your Uncle Charles, though God knows what your father and your aunt thought we were doing out there. You stay here and look through this stuff, if you want to. I'm going out there to talk to him.'

She pulled a sweatshirt over her thin T-shirt and padded out of the room, in her soft moccasins. Peyton sat still on the bed for a time after she left. Then she got up and went down the stairs and out of the back door to the foot of the stairs that led up to her father's office over the garage. She had no compunction about eavesdropping. This was about her, too.

'. . . if I've broken any of the house rules, I'm sorry, Frazier,' Nora was saying. 'But you'll have to tell me what they are. I can't read your mind, and I'd hate to have you running out here every time I cross some border I don't know is there.'

'I don't want to set rules for you, Nora,' her father said evenly. 'But I should think it would be apparent that young women don't go off with men and come back smelling like whiskey.'

'Maybe not in Lytton,' Nora said. 'But they do in the places I've lived, Frazier. In those places, it's an honour to be shown someone's treasures. Couldn't you see how proud Charles was of that shotgun? He wanted somebody to see it. And yes, I did have one drink with him. In the Latin countries, it's an insult to refuse someone's hospitality.'

'You're in a small southern town now, Nora. There's nothing Latin about it.'

'Nothing Latin in Lytton,' Nora said, and Peyton could hear laughter in her voice. 'No, there certainly isn't. But, Frazier, don't you see what she's made of him? He's like a ghost afraid to haunt his own house. How can a woman do that to a man? I wanted to give him back something . . .'

'Nora, I'm glad you're here. I thought it was a good idea and I still do. But there are some things that I just can't have Peyton learning.'

'What? Like racism? Like the fine art of inflicting humiliation?'

'Nora—'

'Frazier, your daughter is withering before she even blooms. She knows nothing, expects nothing. She doesn't even know how to laugh, as far as I can see. It breaks my heart. It may well be that I'm not the right person to teach her, but someone must do it besides Augusta. I've spent a long time finding out the way I want to live, and if I'm not free to live that way I just can't stay. I can accommodate some of your rules, of course, but, if I do, you'll have to accommodate some of my un-Lyttonly notions. But first we have to be able to talk. If you find you just can't do that, then I'll find another place to live. But I have to know what your . . . rules for living are.'

'I guess I just never thought about it,' her father said.

'Then how on earth do you know who you are?'

Abruptly the door leading to the landing opened, and Nora stepped out into the dusk. Peyton ducked behind the big camellia bush that sheltered the side of the garage. After Nora went into the house, she crept out and tiptoed through the kitchen and into her small room. She curled herself under her afghan.

Later—much later, it seemed—she heard her father come into the living room and click on the television set.

'Anybody want some supper?' he called. 'All of a sudden I feel like Howard Johnson's fried clams. Have I got any takers?'

She heard Nora's step coming down the stairs, and her voice answering. Peyton skinned out of bed and into her jeans and a sweater, light flooding back as if it had never been dark.

5

The next morning Nora said at breakfast that she planned to spend the day getting to know the inside of Lytton.

'What inside?' Peyton said, feeding the clamouring Trailways bits of her bacon under the table.

'You know, the insides of places and the people who run them. The library. The bank. The luncheonette. Who knows? Maybe the pool hall and the barbershop.'

'People are going to talk about you if you go in the pool hall and the barbershop,' Peyton said.

'People already are,' Nora said, smiling. 'Your aunt undoubtedly has the jungle drums going about my little fling with your uncle.'

'Don't you care?'

Nora blew smoke. 'No. I don't give a tinker's damn about what most people think about me; I stopped that a long time ago. Now I only care about a very few. You. Your daddy. Chloe. Your grandmother. And that about does it.'

Chloe came in with fresh biscuits and placed them on the table. Then she turned to Nora. 'Doreen told me you said you might teach her a little bit. I sho' would appreciate that. Maybe just enough to read better. She could go to high-school classes at night up to College Park if she could read better. She's a real bright girl. She don't need to be a maid the rest of her life.'

'I'd love to,' Nora said. 'Let me get a week or so of my new job under my belt—if I get it, of course—and then we'll set something up. But you better tell her not to tell Mrs McKenzie. She's already accused me of maid rustling.'

THAT MORNING at school Miss Carruthers said, in front of the entire class, 'Peyton, you look very nice with your new haircut. Very chic.'

After that no one said a word about her hair.

She took Trailways with her to the Losers Club that afternoon, and had to carry him in Chloe's lidded sewing basket because he writhed and howled so. When she got to the shed behind the parsonage, Boot and Ernie were waiting.

'What you got in that basket?' Boot said.

'A king cobra, at the very least,' Ernie said sourly.

'Never heard of no cobra spit like a cat.' Boot grinned. 'Come on, Peyton, let's see him. Mamaw told me about him.'

Peyton opened the basket and Trailways leapt out. He stood glaring at them, his little bowed legs planted apart, his spiky tail quivering. Then he found himself a spot on the frayed rug in front of the space heater and settled into a ball of sleep.

Ernie was heating water for instant cocoa. 'Cats make me sneeze,' he said. 'He can't stay very long, Peyton.'

'He's a special cat,' Peyton said. 'My Cousin Nora went up to Atlanta for dinner and met some soldier, and they were at the Trailways bus station and she saw him behind a garbage can. She brought him home to me. Trailways is his name.'

'What she doin' hanging around that bus station?' Boot said.

'It figures,' Ernie said prissily.

'She wasn't hanging around it,' Peyton retorted. 'She was only there to drop off the soldier. He was on his way to Fort Benning, and anyway, he was only about eighteen. Nora met him in the restaurant where she had dinner. An Italian restaurant.'

She cut her eyes at Ernie and Boot to see how her cousin's lone dinner in Atlanta was being received. They were silent.

'They went to a jazz place and danced after that,' she added. 'She's going to take me with her to Atlanta next time she goes.'

'Man, that is *something!*' Boot said. 'When y'all going?'

'Probably next weekend. We're going to spend the day.'

'Well, you and your new haircut have got a full social schedule,' Ernie drawled. It was the first time he had mentioned her haircut.

Peyton looked at him. 'Nora cut it,' she said.

'It's quite pretty, if you like that kind of thing,' Ernie said, stirring hot water into three paper cups.

'Everybody thinks it looks like Audrey Hepburn's,' Peyton said.

'More like Aldo Ray's. But never mind me. If your cousin did it, it must be holy.'

They were silent again for a while, sipping the cocoa, and then Ernie said, 'I'm going to suspend the club for a while. Nobody's heart seems to be in it, and I've got better things to do.'

'Naw,' Boot cried. 'My heart is in it good!'

'Peyton's isn't. She's all tied up with her sainted cousin.'

Fear flooded Peyton. Not to have the Losers Club . . .

'No, I'm not,' she said. 'I'm not going to do things with her much. She's dumb. She does crazy things. And everybody's going to be talking about us because of her. She's made Aunt Augusta mad as a wet hen. She went out to the garage with Uncle Charlie yesterday, and came back smelling like whiskey. Isn't that just the pits?'

'Everybody knows about that,' Ernie said.

'See why I don't like her?' Peyton said, close to tears.

'It doesn't sound to me like you don't like her,' Ernie said.

'What if I brought her one afternoon?' she said desperately. 'You'd see for yourself how awful she is.'

'You know we said we'd never let outsiders in here,' Ernie said.

'She wouldn't have to come more than once, Ernie, just so you could realise why I'm not going to get tied up with her. Besides, she might fit right in. She does the most awful, embarrassing things.'

'I'll have to think about it,' Ernie said, and the conversation gradually faded and died. Presently Peyton picked up Trailways and stuffed him back into the basket and went home with him.

Nora came in pink-cheeked and windblown from her day around the town and went upstairs. She did not put her head into Peyton's room, and Peyton did not climb the stairs to hers. From now on, she thought, she was going to exclude her cousin from her life. The club; oh, she could not let the club go, not yet . . .

That night, Nora wore a white cashmere sweater and grey flannel slacks to dinner. The candlelight gave her face a deeper glow and lit her hair to what Peyton fancied, having lately read Tennyson, was titian red. Chloe had made her famous vegetable beef soup and cornbread before she left, and there was an apple pie warm on the stove.

'Perfect for a cold night,' her father said, sliding into his seat. 'We're not done with winter yet, I don't think. You girls look mighty pretty, or is it the candlelight?'

They were back in the little breakfast room off the kitchen, but Nora had brought in the wooden candlesticks and lit the candles.

'I had a call from the chairman of the Fulton County Board today, Nora,' Frazier said. 'Everybody thinks the idea is a good one. We can't offer you much in the way of a salary, but I think that could be negotiated if we do the class more than one semester. I'd be pleased if you'd accept. I know Peyton would, too.'

Peyton dropped her eyes. 'Yes,' she mumbled.

'We wouldn't start for a week or so, but as it happens we need a substitute in sophomore English on Thursday and Friday. Mrs Camp is going to see her daughter's new baby.'

'I'd love to substitute,' Nora said. 'I'll get her lesson plans tomorrow, or if she'd rather, we could do a book-discussion group.'

'I think at this point she'd be grateful if you'd simply sit there and keep them quiet,' Frazier said. 'She's been trying to get away to see her grandchild for two months now. I think the book discussion sounds interesting. Why don't you try it? Give you an idea of how your class will work.'

'I will, then. In fact, I think I'll use *To Kill a Mockingbird* for my book discussion and first class.' She turned to Peyton. 'You've read *To Kill a Mockingbird*, haven't you?'

Peyton shook her head.

'Well, then, that's our first priority. It catches the small-town

South better than anything I've ever read, and it says some things about the South that need to be said.'

'Like what?'

'You'll see.'

NORA MET her substitute English class on Thursday morning, and by lunchtime it had passed into legend. Word leapt from Lytton High to Lytton Grammar like wildfire, and Peyton, eating her sandwich and reading *Little Women* alone in the lunchroom, looked up to find herself encircled by other students.

'Hear your cousin's over at the high school teaching nigger stuff,' Wesley Cato said. Wesley was fifteen and had repeated the seventh grade three times. Peyton merely looked at him.

'She's reading some kind of book about a nigger who raped a white girl and got shot by the police,' LeeAnne McGahee said. LeeAnne was twelve and looked eighteen, and was much admired for her immobile blonde bouffant and her projectile breasts.

'That's *To Kill a Mockingbird*,' Peyton said loftily. 'It's won all kinds of prizes. Nora gave it to me to read but I haven't yet.'

They stared at her, uncertain after this unexpected reaction.

'Well, it must be good if they shot the nigger,' Wesley said.

'It's about intolerance and prejudice in a little southern town,' Peyton said. 'You really ought to like it, Wesley.'

'I hear there's a retard in it, too,' LeeAnne said.

'Yep. So you'd like it, too.'

Shorn of their weapons, they sidled away. Peyton's heart was hammering, but she was also elated. She had stood down two of Lytton Grammar's most treasured icons and had come out the better for it. A flame of pure power leapt in her blood.

Maybe that's the power Nana was talking about, she thought. Maybe I have power in my words.

By the end of the day the rumours were a conflagration. Nora Findlay was reading tenth-graders a story about niggers raping people and about other people killing them. And it was the gospel truth that three of the boys—football players all, repeating the tenth grade for the second time—had offered in graphic terms to service Nora right there on her desk, and she had looked at them and laughed and said, 'Not on your best day, you horny little bastards,' whereupon the rest of the class had broken into cheers. And it was also gospel that when the class was over, she had waked out lighting a cigarette. The entire student body of Lytton Grammar School was buzzing with Nora.

'But when the principal stuck his head in to see how she was doing, she just smiled and said, "Fine, sir. You have nice students here," and he like to busted his face smiling back,' a student told Peyton on the school steps. 'My brother said that after he'd gone she just looked at the class and winked. He said everybody hoped nobody tells on her. They thought she was great.'

Peyton knew that nobody would tell parents or faculty about Nora Findlay. She was life, rebellion, even affirmation to them. No teacher had ever been anything but the oppressor. They would simply say, 'Oh, just fine, thanks. She's nice,' to their parents, and the faculty would say to each other what a sweet girl she seemed to be, so deferential to the older ones.

Peyton did not think it could last, of course; Nora was bound to be found out in this small, airless arena. But for now she was flying high, and Peyton soared with her. One of the cheerleaders actually asked her to sit with them at lunch the next day.

'I'm going home, thanks,' Peyton said. 'My cousin and I always have lunch together.'

That evening as they sat at dinner Frazier McKenzie said, 'Well, how did it go at the high school today?'

'Just fine,' Nora said. 'Peyton, please pass the butter.'

PEYTON WENT BACK to the Losers Club the next afternoon, expecting it would be a triumph to have a cousin who had embarrassed her in front of the entire town.

But Ernie and Boot said nothing about Nora.

'I'm reading *To Kill a Mockingbird*,' Peyton said, trying to sound offhand. 'Nora gave me a copy. She's teaching it to her class, too.'

'A nice little book,' Ernie said. 'Not, of course, the great American novel, but nice.'

'That idiot,' Nora said, grinning, when Peyton told her that night what Ernie had said. 'That's just what it is.'

On Saturday morning they went to Atlanta. The fresh cold had given way before the green surf of spring rolling north from Florida, and the earth smelt wet and new and rich. The sun was mild.

'If you'll put on your sweater we'll put the top down,' Nora said. 'I'll turn the heater on. I used to do that all the time in the winter in Miami, whenever it got a little chilly. There's nothing like spring wind in your face and warm air on your feet.'

And there wasn't. By the time they rolled into downtown Atlanta, Peyton was drunk on air and light and wind and warm feet.

'We'll park at Rich's because it's a good starting place. But I assume you don't want to go in,' Nora said.

'Never again.'

'Never say never.'

They walked up Peachtree Street from Rich's in the spring sun. The streets were full of people moving languidly.

'This is nice,' Nora said. 'This reminds me of a Saturday afternoon in Havana. Everybody came out into the streets.'

'To do what?' Peyton asked.

'Just to be there,' Nora said. 'You need to learn the fine art of just being, Peyton. I don't think your daddy or your Aunt Augusta is going to teach you that, so I guess the job falls to me. The first thing you do when you're being is to kind of float around seeing what you can see. Listen hard. Smell the smells—like that peanut shop over there. And the narcissus and daffodils from that lady on the corner.'

Peyton slowed down, consciously slackened her muscles, and sniffed the air. It's Atlanta in the spring, she thought in surprise. I'll never forget it. I'd know it anywhere. It's not like any other smell.

They stopped at a little stationery store in the Peachtree Arcade, a wondrous hall between two buildings, two storeys high, completely arched over with glass. The arcade was full of people, milling and chattering and examining wares spread out on tables. They did not look, to Peyton's eyes, very prosperous. This was just the sort of place Aunt Augusta was always warning her about. Not as bad as the bus station, but in the same arena.

'*Exactly* like Havana,' Nora said. 'Wonderful.'

In a far corner of the shop there was a dusty pile of old books. All were leather and some were stamped with faded gold. Nora riffled through them, smiling appreciatively. 'Lovely,' she said. 'Whole lives, right here in these books. What do you think of this one, Peyton?' She held up a green, soft-leather book, faded to a pale sage. Inside, in a faint copperplate hand, was written on the flyleaf, *Anna Marjorie Stephens. Her book.* There had been a date, but it was lost now. The thick ivory pages were edged with dull gold. Some of the first pages had been torn out, but the rest were blank and ruled with sepia ink.

'Do you like this? I think it's gorgeous,' Nora said. 'You'd always have Anna Marjorie looking over your shoulder, wouldn't you? She'd be the only one you'd have to share your secret thoughts with.'

'It's pretty,' Peyton said dutifully. She had thought they would go to the Cokesbury Book Shop and select a proper diary. A new one.

'I think you should have it,' Nora said. 'When you're grown and you look back over this, you'll see that there's a resonance to it that a mass-produced teenager's diary could never have.'

She paid for the book and they went out into the street. 'I guess it's about lunchtime,' Nora said. 'There's a delicatessen over there. Have you ever had a pastrami on rye?'

'I don't think so,' Peyton said faintly.

'Well, then, come on,' Nora said, starting towards the big delicatessen across from the arcade. 'Best in the world. But I expect they could rustle you up a hamburger if you'd like.'

When they approached the deli they saw a crowd on the sidewalk. People were milling about and there were policemen with nightsticks.

'They must hate the day's special,' Nora said, pushing through to look in the window. 'Look, Peyton, it's a sit-in. See those black kids at the counter? There's no food in front of them and not a living soul at the entire counter. Looks like we'd have our choice of seats.'

'Are we going in there?' Peyton squeaked. She knew that people went to jail for sitting in. Why, she could not quite remember.

'I thought we might.'

'Will we get arrested?'

'Oh, no. It's OK for us to eat in there. Just not them.'

'Is it against the law? Will they be arrested?'

'Probably not, unless they start a fuss. Sit-ins are a nonviolent protest. But the restaurant owner gets to decide if he'll serve Negroes or not. Obviously this one doesn't.'

'I can't go in there, Nora. There's a television camera over there. What if Daddy and Aunt Augusta saw me on TV?'

'I hope they'd be proud of you. Come on, Peyton. Sometimes it's necessary to do what scares you. I think this is one of those times.'

They went inside. There was a faint garlicky smell and stratas of cigarette smoke hung in the air. Behind the counter, two red-faced waitresses were sitting on stools and staring out of the window.

Nora sauntered to the counter and sat down beside one of the young Negroes. He looked at Nora, who smiled. Tentatively he smiled back. The other three men looked over, and nodded.

'What's good here?' Nora asked.

'I don't think we're likely to find out,' said the first young man.

Nora nodded thoughtfully. Then she raised her voice slightly and said, 'Miss? My cousin and I would like to order some lunch.'

'We don't serve Negroes,' the waitress said tightly.

'Well, we shouldn't have any trouble, then, should we? I think we'd both like a hamburger, and pickles and coleslaw on the side, and a coffee for me and Coca-Cola for the young lady.'

The woman stared 'You may not be Negroes, but you're sitting with them,' she said. 'I'm not going to serve you.'

'I thought this was a public restaurant,' Nora said mildly. 'If that's not the case, I think that guy out there with the television camera is just waiting to know about it.'

'The owner won't let the newspeople in,' the woman said.

'Now I don't believe that's legal. That guy out there would be real surprised to find that you all hadn't heard of the Constitution.'

A bald man put his head round a door at the end of the counter.

'She's threatening to bring the TV in here if we don't serve her,' the waitress squealed.

'Then serve the bitch,' he shouted, and shut the door.

'All right. What was it, hamburgers?' the waitress snapped.

'Yes. Six. With six sides of pickles and coleslaw and five coffees and a Coca-Cola.'

'Mr Stern!' the waitress shrieked.

'Do it,' he snarled from behind the door. 'Do it and get that trash out of my place.'

When the hamburgers came, they all ate silently and neatly. Peyton's face was burning. When they had finished and Nora picked up the bill, the first young man said, 'Thank you. We were getting pretty hungry. I hope we didn't scare the young lady.'

'I wasn't scared,' said Peyton, surprising herself.

They pushed through the crowd outside. 'What's going on in there?' asked a reporter. A cameraman started filming. Peyton sidled behind Nora, who merely smiled.

'Absolutely nothing,' she said. 'Just some people having lunch.'

They walked back to the parking garage in silence, the afternoon shading towards dusk. Peyton realised that she was trembling.

When the car came, Nora said, 'You still up for an early dinner? Or do you just want to go home? By the way, Peyton, I'm proud of you.'

'I'm still a little hungry,' Peyton lied. 'I'm really in the mood for some Italian food.'

'You got it,' Nora said, smiling, and she turned the car north up Peachtree Street.

'ARE YOU GOING to tell him?' Peyton asked later as Nora swung the car to the kerb in front of their house.

'Tell him what?'

'Any of it. You know. The sit-in and all that stuff. That I drank wine.'

'You didn't drink enough wine to make a chicken blink. It's a sin to eat ravioli without wine. No. I'm not going to tell him, unless you do first. I won't lie, but I won't tell him, either. That's for you to decide.'

'I don't think I will,' Peyton said. The day hung glittering like a Christmas ornament in her mind.

'Good. Everybody ought to have one or two private things.'

The house was dark. It was still early, but her father often went to bed early and read. Peyton's muscles relaxed slightly. It would not be required of her, then, to share this perfect day and night.

They tiptoed inside, and a light went on in the kitchen.

'Oh, shit,' Nora said softly.

Frazier McKenzie came into the room. He was still dressed, wearing his tan Perry Como cardigan, tweed pants and house slippers. His face was remote. Peyton knew he was displeased.

She heard her voice spilling out of her like a broken water main: 'Oh, Daddy, it was just wonderful! Nora bought me a journal in the Peachtree Arcade and then we rode through Buckhead—you should see the houses there, Daddy, they're mansions—and then we went to this Italian place and I had ravioli, it's like these little pouches with sausage in them and sauce on them—'

She stopped and looked up at him.

His face remained closed and still, and then he smiled. 'You had a big day, didn't you?' he said.

'Oh, yes,' Peyton breathed in relief and exultation.

'It *was* a good day,' Nora said. 'Maybe next time you'll come with us.'

'Maybe I will,' he said.

THAT NIGHT, Peyton wrote in her diary. She sat cross-legged on her bed, Trailways snugged into the curve of her thigh, and stared at the blank first page. I have no idea how to write in a diary, she thought.

'It's just for you,' Nora's voice repeated in her head. 'Nobody will ever see it unless you show it to them. Write anything you want to. Write who you hate and who you love. What you're reading. What Trailways looks like when he lies in that patch of sunlight on the dining-room table. The whole point is to have a record of how you really were at twelve going on thirteen. I can promise you you're not going to remember yourself that way. It'll be good to be able to look back and check in with the real Peyton McKenzie *circa* nineteen sixty-one.'

Tentatively, Peyton wrote the date and then: *Today I went into Atlanta with my Cousin Nora. We had lunch at a delicatessen and dinner at an Italian restaurant. I had ravioli and Chianti wine. It was good. We sang Nora's college songs on the way home. I thought Daddy would be mad, but he wasn't.*

She stopped, and then she wrote: *I was at a sit-in. There wasn't much to it but I think I'm glad I did it. It's very late and Trailways looks like a pile of feathers from a chicken. I can feel his purr all the way up my leg and into my chest. Goodbye. Peyton McKenzie.*

NORA'S FIRST EXPERIMENTAL English class was held the following Monday at Carver High, the black school literally across the railroad tracks from the main body of Lytton. It consisted of honours English students from both high schools, grades ten through twelve. It was held at Carver because the school board thought it only courteous for the white school to make the first visit.

The class was scheduled for ten in the morning. By noon the news of it was scattering through the grammar school like spilt mercury. Jerry Mooney, the massive, truculent captain of the wrestling team, had attacked a Negro boy, much smaller, in the cloakroom at recess. Miss Findlay threw him out of the class with both hands and a foot on his bottom. Miss Findlay made the white students sit by the Negroes and threatened to fail anyone who opened his mouth about it. When two white cheerleaders made whispered fun of a fat Negro girl, Miss Findlay put her arms around the sobbing child, and told the cheerleaders she was going to do everything she could to get them suspended for the rest of the year. Then she sent them back to Lytton High. They left smirking and switching their trim behinds, but there was unease in their blue eyes that had never been there before. Somehow nobody doubted that Miss Findlay could and would do what she said she would.

Students swarmed around Peyton when school was out. Was her cousin going to have Negro teachers over for dinner at Peyton's house? Was it true that she had made the white students use the Negro cloakrooms? Would the Negroes use the white ones when they came to Lytton High? Was she going to join St John's African Methodist Episcopal Church?

Nora laughed so hard when Peyton relayed these concerns that she choked on her cigarette and smoke exploded from her nostrils. 'Well, here's what you tell them,' she said. 'A: Maybe, if they ask me over to theirs first. B: If anybody wants to pee, they'll do it in the nearest bathroom, wherever that happens to be. C: I'll probably go to some services at St John's. I love the singing.'

'What did you do for your first class?'

'Well, after I got all the sniggering quieted down, I read to them from *To Kill a Mockingbird*. Then I picked out passages and asked them to read them aloud.'

'What parts?'

'The earliest parts, where Scout tells us about Maycomb, and about the people who lived there. I wanted them to see how close literature comes to the lives they know themselves, even though it happened in another time and place. And I think they got it, finally. Of course, none of them reads aloud very well, black or white, but towards the end nobody was embarrassed any more, and everyone was raising their hand to say how they thought Lytton was like Maycomb. They're very quick, if not articulate.'

'I wish I could take that class,' Peyton said. 'My English class is stupid. Mrs Manning just assigned us *Little Women*. I stopped reading that stuff when I was ten.'

'Well, I can't let you come to this one, but maybe we could sort of review what I've been doing in class every afternoon or so. You can read along with us. Or even better, you write down what you think about it and we'll go over it and compare it to what my high-schoolers said. I bet you'll be way ahead of them.'

'Maybe,' Peyton said. 'If you're still here next year, Nora, maybe I could take one of your classes. I'll almost be in high school then.'

'My Lord, so you will,' Nora said, looking at her and smiling. 'And you have a birthday this summer, too, don't you?'

'In June. Right after graduation.'

'Ah, graduation. Is there a commencement? When I started high school all you did was just show up.'

'Not really a commencement,' Peyton mumbled.

Peyton had been thinking with dread about that for some time. 'Just this thing in the school auditorium where the school choir sings and a preacher says something, and there are some speeches and stuff.'

Nora shot her a keen look. 'What sort of speeches?' she said. 'Who makes them?'

'Oh, you know. The ones who make good grades and stuff.'

'You'll be asked to make one.'

'No, I'm sure not. Besides, I'd hate it. I'd never in the world know what to say. I'd make such a fool of myself that I'd be the winner in the Losers Club for the rest of my life.'

Nora tapped her unlit cigarette thoughtfully on the table and studied her. 'The Losers Club. Is that the club you go to every afternoon? Why is it called that?'

'We tell each other what dumb things we've done that day, and the one who did the dumbest wins. It's usually Boot, because his foot makes him clumsy. He's always falling over things. It's really nothing. Just something we got in the habit of doing a long time ago. And it's not all stupid stuff. Ernie plays music for us and tells us about the theatre and literature and all.'

'Hmmm,' Nora said. 'Sounds like fun. Can I come sometime?'

'Well, it's in the bylaws that nobody but us can come. I asked Ernie and he got all cranky about it, but I'll ask him again. Boot would love it. He thinks your car is the greatest.'

'Never mind. I don't want to make Ernie uncomfortable. I'll meet Boot sometime here.'

Nora met Boot the next afternoon, when he came to the McKenzie house after the Losers Club. When she was much younger Peyton had played with him on those occasions, but at some point they had grown apart except for the Losers Club and, on those afternoons when he was visiting, Peyton was usually reading, and he pottered around the kitchen with his grandmother. It bothered neither Boot nor Peyton. At the Losers Club they were fully equal, and that was what counted.

Boot came in shortly after Peyton had got home, slamming the back door and shouting for his grandmother. Peyton heard, from the snug harbour of her bed, Chloe saying, 'Now, you just stay in this kitchen and be quiet. Peyton studying and Miss Nora coming in from the library any time now.'

'She comin' in that car?'

'Of course she is. You think she flying?'

'Maybe if I held the door for her she'd take me for a ride,' Boot said ingenuously. 'I could probably wash it sometime, too.'

Peyton heard the front door open and close, and heard Nora's voice: 'Is that the incomparable Meatloaf à la Chloe I smell?'

Peyton got up and went into the kitchen, drawn out of her room like a moth to a leaping flame. Light and air and noise came in with Nora. The old house had not felt their like in Peyton's lifetime.

It must be what it was like when my mother was alive, she thought.

Nora dumped her armful of books onto the breakfast table and plopped down in her seat. 'Coffee before I die?' she said. 'And maybe some of that pecan pie from last night? Peyton, are you game for some? I swear I . . ." Her voice trailed off. Boot's grinning face had appeared round the door into the kitchen, 'Well, who have we here?'

'This is my grandbaby Boot,' Clothilde said. 'He promised not to bother anybody. Boot, this is Miss Nora. You know, I told you. She's staying with us for a while.'

'Hello, Boot,' Nora said. 'I've been hearing about you.'

He hung his head and dug at the linoleum with his toe, and then looked up at her and gave her the full wattage of his smile. 'That your car out there?' he said.

'It is,' Nora said, sipping her coffee.

'I heard you drove it all the way up here from Cuba.'

'Well, from Key West, Florida. That's about as far as you can go before you come to Cuba.'

'With the top down?'

'A lot of the time.'

'You get bugs squashed on you?'

Nora smiled then. 'Pounds and pounds of them.'

Boot's joyous, froggy laugh rang out. 'Ain't that somethin? Boy, I'd like to seen all them bugs . . .'

It was obviously time for Nora to say, 'I'll take you for a ride sometime,' but she did not. 'A few bugs go a long way,' she said.

There was a small silence, and then Boot said, 'You could drive that car to our club meeting sometime. It right up the street. And if it got bugs on it I could wash and wax it for you.'

'Well, I'll think about that,' Nora said, and she gathered up her books as if to leave. Peyton watched as Boot's heart leapt into his black eyes, and she knew she had just witnessed love at first sight. Because Boot was staring at her cousin with such naked adoration, she said, 'Nora says she doesn't think she'll come to club meetings.'

'I bet you ain't never done nothin' stupid,' Boot said to Nora.

'Dumber than you can possibly imagine,' Nora said.

'Tell one!' Boot crowed with joy. This was too much for him, a copper-crowned madonna who drove around in a pink chariot and did dumb things.

'Maybe one day,' Nora said, and she went out of the room and up the stairs. Peyton stared after her. So did Boot and Chloe.

After Boot and Chloe had gone home, Nora came down to Peyton's room and settled onto the end of the narrow white bed as she sometimes did. 'What's happening, kiddo?' she said.

Peyton closed her book. 'Did Boot make you mad or something?' she said. 'He makes a lot of noise, I know, with that boot thing, but he's nice, and he can be real funny sometimes.'

Nora looked at her and then out the window into the back yard, where the first forsythia was beginning to spill like a fountain.

'I'm just not wild about children,' she said. 'There's no use pretending I am. I'll try to be nicer to Boot, though. I just hope he isn't underfoot all the time.'

Peyton saw a curtain fall behind Nora's green eyes. Something in her was closing like a door. There were secrets inside Nora, places she would allow no one to go. She realised that what she had been given of Nora was carefully edited, that an entire continent lay underneath.

As if possessed of some perverse incubus, Boot was indeed underfoot after that. His infatuation knew no bounds. Whenever Nora got out of her car in the afternoon, Boot would rush to hold the door for her, to carry her books and her parcels. Whenever, at a weekend, she set out on one of her slow cruises around town, she would see Boot in the rearview mirror, thumping after her like one of the Seven Dwarfs. Nora said nothing, but began to disappear into her room the minute she came home from school, and stopped coming down to breakfast, where, often, Boot would be lurking like a happy frog.

'Doesn't that child have anybody else to look after him?' she said once to Peyton, after Boot had offered once more to clean the Thunderbird.

'Well, we all sort of look after him,' Peyton said. 'And he's with me and Ernie almost every afternoon. He's never any trouble.'

'Maybe not to you,' Nora said under her breath, taking the stairs to her room two at a time.

Clothilde had, Peyton knew, recently forbidden Boot the house except in a real emergency. But Nora never mentioned him to

Chloe, and Chloe did not speak of him, either.

Not until the day in March when Nora came home early from her tutoring session at the black high school and found Boot in her car, top down, engine running, radio booming out country music. Boot's eyes were squeezed shut, and his face was rapt with bliss. He did not see Nora until she jerked the car door open and clutched him by his collar and dragged him out of the car. Her face was blanched with fury, and her eyes were slitted. Peyton, watching through the screen door, gasped and went still. This was going to be bad.

Nora bent and looked into Boot's face, only inches from it. Her hands gripped his shoulders, and she shook him slightly. 'Don't you ever, *ever* touch my car again, you hear me? Don't come near it. Don't come near me. *Nobody* touches that car but me! Where did you get those keys?'

'They was laying on the kitchen table,' Boot whispered. He was trying to pull away from Nora's hands. She let him go abruptly, and he staggered a little, then took off round the house.

Nora stood with her head bent, her eyes closed. Then she turned towards the house. Peyton scuttled into her room. She did not want to talk about this. She did not want to see Nora's face like that. She did not want to see Boot's humiliation.

No one mentioned the incident at supper. Nora ate with relish and chatted of insignificant things, and Frazier took out the pipe he had resumed smoking and smiled at them both through sweet smoke. That night Peyton showed herself her movies. She wrote in her diary, *Even the air hurts*.

Nora finally went to Boot's house and apologised to him, largely, Peyton knew, because Chloe's face was so miserable. She didn't know what had come over her, she said, except that she was terribly tired and had not been sleeping well.

'Of course I'll take you for a ride in the car,' she said, and Chloe and Boot nodded in unison. But Boot did not come back to the house. Peyton saw him at the Losers Club, where he dutifully recited his litanies of abasement; she said nothing about Nora and the car because he did not know she knew about the incident. But he was somehow diminished, and though he could still make her and Ernie laugh, he did not often laugh with them. He was, somehow, a wise and wizened little man, not a child any more.

It seemed a long time before Chloe began to sing again in the kitchen.

6

On St Patrick's Day Nora took Peyton and Frazier into Atlanta for dinner.

'I think there's some sort of parade down Peachtree Street, too,' she said. 'We really ought to see it.'

'You want to take a Scotsman to a St Patrick's Day parade?' Frazier said. He was smiling, though.

'Why not? Loosen you up a little. We'll have you drinking green beer before you know it.'

'Faith and begorra,' he said. Peyton laughed happily. She could not remember her father ever making a real joke before.

It was a sweet, soft day, and they went in the Thunderbird, all three of them squeezed into the front seat. Nora laughed at the sight of Frazier folding his long body into the little pink car, sitting with his knees under his chin. Peyton, crammed between them, felt a swoop of joy that seemed to have its provenance in nothing at all but the rush of clean wind past her face.

They parked the Thunderbird in Davison's parking lot and walked up to Peachtree Street. Both sides of the street were crowded with people wearing all shades of green. Vendors were selling four-leaf clover pennants. Although Peyton could see no bars on the length of the street, there must have been ready sources for green beer because nearly everyone around them was carrying paper cups of it.

The parade itself was modest. The handsome, white-haired mayor came first, in a green Lincoln convertible, followed by sundry other dignitaries in convertibles. On a throne draped in green sat the queen of the parade, in a cloud of virulent green tulle and a headdress of woven shamrocks.

Behind the queen and her court came a band, and then a surging straggle of green-clad, beer-carrying people, waving banners and shillelaghs and singing. It was not a big parade, but it was a loud one, and when they got back into the Thunderbird to drive out along Peachtree Street to Buckhead, Peyton's ears still rang with it.

They had dinner in the same Italian restaurant where Peyton and Nora had eaten before. Nora and her father split a bottle of Chianti, and Peyton had a splash of it in a small glass. Her father ordered clam linguine for two, and Nora studied the menu and then said, 'Peyton, I think the scungili for you. It's light, and it has a nice lemony taste to it.'

'What is it?' Peyton said doubtfully.

'Fish cooked with some wine. Really special.'

'OK,' Peyton said. 'I'll try it.'

They talked in the flickering light of a candle, and the waiter hovered over Nora and brought another bottle of Chianti, 'on the house', he said. Nora smiled.

Their dinner came then. Peyton's plate was steaming, and a wonderful smell curled up from the browned medallions on it.

'Mmmm,' she said, taking a bite. The swirls of lemon butter and wine the fish was bathed in were exotic and rich. She finished most of it and mopped up the sauce with a piece of bread.

'That was good,' she said. 'What kind of fish did you say it was?'

Nora leaned back and lit a cigarette and smiled at her. 'Squid,' she said. 'Some people call it octopus.'

Peyton's stomach muscles contracted. And then they subsided. 'Not bad at all,' she said, thinking that the squid was going to earn her a place of honour in the pantheon of awfulness at the Losers Club. Let's see Ernie top that, she thought.

On the way home Nora put the top up on the Thunderbird. The inside of the car was small and dark and warm, and the radio played softly. Nora sang along with Dean Martin: 'Return to Me'. Her voice was soft and gritty. Wedged between them, Peyton closed her eyes and let the roaring of the road beneath them swell in her ears until she slipped off on its tide. Once she lifted her head and saw black, star-pricked sky and knew they were sailing through the fields near home. She heard laughter, and put her head back on her father's shoulder and slept again.

WHEN PEYTON CAME in from the Losers Club the next Monday, Nora told her the awful news. Her grandmother had suffered a stroke. It was severe, and Agnes McKenzie stayed in the hospital in Atlanta for weeks. She could not speak, and all efforts to make her accept therapy failed. When she was able to leave the hospital, Frazier found a nearby nursing home for her. It was clean, cheerful, and well staffed, and it cost the very earth. Agnes seemed, if not happy, then at least content there.

Peyton visited often at first, but she could not be sure that her grandmother even knew her. Nora visited once, with Frazier, and her grandmother became violent, trying to rip out her tubes—trying, it seemed, to get at Nora. That night she had another small stroke, and after that she was gone from them, only her slight body remaining.

Peyton did not visit any more after that. Only Frazier went, night after night, to hold his mother's hands. When he came home from these visits he usually spent an hour or so in his office before he came in to watch television with them.

After her last visit to her grandmother, Peyton wrote in her diary, *Why do people have to be wrecked like that? Who will there be in my life like her now?*

In her heart she knew the answer to that, but she could not bear the weight of it, and buried it deep.

ALL THROUGH the early days of that spring, Nora incised herself deeply and vividly into the small life of Lytton. It was as if, content that she had safe harbour in the house on Green Street, she felt emboldened to flash out into the town and the school like a comet, trailing delight and outrage in equal parts in her wake.

Late afternoons became Nora and Peyton's special time together. Much of it was spent up in Nora's room, Nora with her long length curled on her bed, smoking, Peyton in the red canvas butterfly chair her cousin had brought with her, a hectic anomaly in that dim room of polished mahogany and white chenille. Trailways would desert Peyton temporarily to curl into the curve of Nora's waist or legs and purr his rusty, room-shaking purr.

They talked endlessly, but almost never about themselves. It was too soon for that. They talked about books, about music, about movies. Or rather, Nora talked. Peyton had no sense of being instructed, but she knew in some way that Nora was tutoring her. She began, once in a while, to venture an opinion about whatever it was they were talking about.

'Why do you listen to me?' she asked Nora once. 'I don't know anything about anything yet.'

'You will.' Nora smiled.

Sometimes, in the warming nights, they did things: they went, the three of them, to a movie in Atlanta occasionally, or a symphony at the Municipal Auditorium, and once to *Our Town*, a play put on by an Atlanta company. Nora said it was oversentimental claptrap and overdone, but she wept along with Peyton when the dead of Grover's

Corners reached out, in vain, to the living. They went to a couple of baseball games, and once to a square dance at the Lytton Veterans hut. Frazier laughingly refused to dance, and Peyton would not have if someone had held a gun to her head, but Nora danced every set with every man who asked her.

Once, in the middle of a tender night heavy with the smell of wisteria, Nora woke Peyton and they took the Thunderbird, top down, out into the country to a small lake that fed into the Lytton reservoir, where they slipped naked into the blood-warm water and swam under the moon.

But mostly Nora seemed to want simply to be in the house on Green Street. Sometimes, after dinner, instead of watching television, she would read to them out of whatever esoteric book she was reading, and once in a while she made martinis before dinner and she and Frazier had one. Peyton ate the olives.

Peyton knew via the grammar school jungle drums that almost none of the female teachers at Lytton High liked Nora, and that most of the male ones did, and that almost every unmarried male teacher had asked her out. But she never talked about it, and she never went out on a date.

'You should get out some,' Frazier said. 'It's just not right for you to sit in this old house all the time when you should be out meeting people your own age.'

'Maybe later,' Nora said. 'Right now I'd rather just be here with you all. You have no idea how tired of flitting around I am.'

'Didn't you date in Florida and Cuba?' Peyton asked her in one of their late-night talk sessions on Nora's bed, where Nora sometimes let her have a drag of a Salem. In her head, Peyton had invented a lavish, exotic life for Nora back in those fabled cities she had left. Men were a large part of it—handsome, mysterious men unlike any she knew in Lytton. There must have been men.

'She's had hundreds of affairs,' Peyton told the Losers Club. 'She had lovers in every city, but eventually she got bored with them and left. I think she still gets letters from some of them.'

'Tell about that,' Boot said, enchanted.

Ernie sniffed. 'If she had all those lovers it seems to me one of them might have finally married her,' he said.

'She doesn't want to be tied down,' Peyton said. 'She told me that.'

Nora had done no such thing, but Peyton thought it was true.

Nora would not talk about Cuba or Miami or Key West, at least not about the men she had known there, except to say that of course she had had dates, but for now no one was as interesting as the people in this funny old house. Peyton could not imagine why anyone would think her or her father interesting, but she was warmed as she could not remember having been in her life. She mattered, at last, to someone who did not have to love her.

'You know, Chloe,' Nora said one morning, 'I promised you and Doreen that I'd tutor her in the afternoons so she can get her high school equivalency certificate. Would you tell her that now would be a good time for us to start?'

'Doreen ain't around afternoons no more,' Chloe said. 'She got a job up in Hapeville at the McDonald's. They likes her a lot. Look like she be able to be an assistant manager in a year or two.'

'Chloe, she doesn't need to sling hamburgers all her life!' Nora said. 'No telling where she might go if she gets that certificate. Why on earth did she leave Mrs McKenzie's? I know she's awful, but at least Doreen had enough free time to study.'

Chloe was silent, and then she said, 'She ain't leave. Miss Augusta fired her. Didn't even give her no notice.'

'Why?' Nora cried. 'Who on earth wouldn't want Doreen working for them?'

'She come home from church early and found Doreen sittin' in the bathtub,' Chloe said without looking at Peyton or Nora. 'She like to bust a gut. She tell Doreen to put on her clothes and get out and not come back.'

'Oh, *Chloe*,' Nora said, stricken.

'Thing is, Doreen ain't never had no bathtub,' Chloe said. 'We always wash in washtubs. I guess she just wanted to see how it felt to sit down in that hot water. It ain't like Miss Augusta was going to catch anything from her. Doreen is a clean girl.'

Peyton watched Nora's face in silence. It was blanched white and there was a spot of red high on each cheekbone. She went out of the room silently and did not open her bedroom door that afternoon to Peyton and Trailways.

That evening Peyton heard her father's car door slam out front, and at almost the same instant heard Nora's running steps on the stairs. She went to her own bedroom door and opened it an inch or so, but she did not go out into the living room.

'Do you know what that woman has done?' she heard Nora shout.

'What woman?' her father said. His voice was alarmed.

'Your sister-in-law! The famous Augusta McKenzie of Lytton, Georgia, social and moral arbiter to a generation, font of compassion for the frail and lowly—'

'Sit down,' Frazier McKenzie said. 'Tell me.'

'I hate her, Frazier,' Peyton heard her cousin say. Her voice was trembling. 'She is the worst, most evil woman I have ever known.'

'Nora, what has she *done*?'

'She fired Doreen because she found her in her bathtub,' Nora said. 'She thought Doreen had contaminated it.'

And she burst into tears.

There was a brief silence, and then Nora continued, her voice strangled with sobs. 'You know, we said I was going to tutor Doreen so she could get her reading up to par and take the high school equivalency test. You were there that day at lunch. So this morning I told Chloe I'd like to start and she told me that Doreen had been fired and was working at the McDonald's up in Hapeville. Frazier, what future can she possibly have now? Oh, I *hate* Augusta . . .'

There was a silence in which only Nora's muffled sobs resounded. Peyton opened her door a few more inches and peered out. Nora sat on the sofa with her face in her hands. Her father, looking drawn and weary, sat beside her, patting her awkwardly on the back.

'Nora,' he said presently. 'You need to understand about Augusta. I don't mean to excuse her; what she did was an ugly thing. A lot of what she does is downright unacceptable. But we do accept it, our family, because we know what she came out of, we know how hard she's worked building a life for herself.'

'What life?' Nora cried. 'It's certainly no life for Charlie! It's certainly no life for Peyton. What life are you talking about?'

'She was born in a mill-village shack,' Peyton's father said slowly. 'It was worse, in a way, than most of our Negro neighbourhoods because the folks who live there have strong family ties and often white families who care for them. But they didn't have that in Augusta's little settlement. Everybody was too intent on digging his own way out to put out a hand to a neighbour. A lot of them just gave up. Augusta's parents were like that. When Charlie met her, her father was dying of white lung and still smoking like a chimney, lying on an old sofa they had dragged out onto the front porch. Her mother was drunk most of the time. There was an older brother who had long since left and was in jail in the North somewhere. And there was a younger sister, about eleven, who stayed out of school and did whatever she pleased. Augusta was the pretty one, and the smart one, and she really is both of those things. She worked at the perfume counter at Rich's in Atlanta, and she taught herself how to act like a lady and dress like one on the measly little salary she made. It can't have been much, and she had to pay a lot of the family's rent and grocery bills every month, and keep her little sister in clothes, because both the parents were on disability.

'So one day Charlie went into Rich's to buy Mother some perfume for Christmas, and he took one look at her, and that was that. She sold herself right along with the perfume. They were married not three months later. I guess she thought she was marrying way up with Charlie, but I think if she'd known him a little longer she'd have realised that what she saw in Charlie was what she was going to get. I love Charlie; he's my brother and he's a sweet man. But he's no Prince Charming, no rescuer of maidens. Augusta never got over that. She'd seen herself as totally safe and secure, the most socially sought-after woman in this part of the county, the absolute oracle of manners and propriety and elegance. But I guess she's known for a long time now that she's only as safe as Charlie's last pay cheque, and the only people she can lord it over are her servants and sometimes my daughter. She's forgotten that Charlie gave her two things she'd never have had without him: a ticket out of the mill village and his love. He really loves her. Always has. Don't think he doesn't know how disappointed in him she is. It's made her mean. We all know that. Most of us have learned just to overlook the silliest of her pranks and dodge the really hurtful ones. I sometimes think she really does care about Peyton and me, but I can't think why . . .'

'Oh, Frazier!' Nora said. 'If you can't think why, then you're more oblivious than I thought. It's obvious. She's got an awful crush on you, and she's trying to get at you through Peyton.'

'Oh, I don't think so,' Frazier said doubtfully. 'But you're right about this thing with Doreen. We can't let that go. I'll talk to her about it. Maybe she'll take Doreen back. If she won't, maybe I can find her something closer to home that will give her time to study, and maybe we can help her out a little financially . . .'

'Frazier McKenzie,' Nora said, tears in her voice again. 'You are maybe the best man I've ever known.'

'Then God help you,' Frazier said. Peyton could hear the smile in his voice. 'Will you at least try to think a little better of Augusta now?'

'No,' Nora said. 'She's a bitch and I hate her. But I'll lay off her unless she does something else this bad, which she'll probably manage to do tomorrow.'

Peyton went into the bathroom and washed her face for dinner. She felt lighter than air. She knew that whatever bonds kept her tethered to earth, they were never again going to be of Aunt Augusta's making.

WHEN SHE NEXT WENT to the Losers Club, Peyton realised she had not been going so often and felt guilty and somehow resentful. She was tired of having to make excuses to Ernie. She was aware, as she knew he was, that she was lying regularly to the club when she said that Nora was tutoring her after school. It seemed that he reported on Nora's public antics with far more venom than usual, and it occurred to her that he was punishing her with the stories.

'Have you met Mr Lloyd Huey, who lives next door to your Aunt Augusta and Uncle Charles?' he asked, and when Peyton said that of course she knew him, Ernie continued.

'Well, then, you know he owns the sawmill and has a bunch of Negroes working for him. He also has an enormous fallout shelter in his backyard. Well, somehow Nora got the notion that he was mistreating his help, and she told him in the drugstore that if he didn't shape up she was going to tell everybody in town that he had asked her down to see the famous shelter and then tried to seduce her. It's the kind of talk that could ruin a man in a little town like this.'

'How could it ruin Mr Huey?' Peyton said. 'He's got five children and only one leg and he's in a wheelchair all the time.'

'Well, I guess Nora thinks that any man with breath in his body would try to seduce her. God knows, enough of them have.'

'I'm going home,' Peyton said, sudden anger shaking her. 'You've turned the club into a witch-hunt against Nora. That's not fair, and it's not fun any longer.'

'The truth is often not much fun,' Ernie said unctuously.

Peyton slammed out of the shed and stamped home, a feeling of heaviness and loss hanging over her.

Her father and her Uncle Charlie were coming out of the living room. Charles McKenzie looked miserable. Behind him, her father's face was set. Peyton murmured hello to both of them and slid into her room like a salamander going to earth. Nothing good was going to come of this visit. She knew it.

She peered through the almost-closed door of her room at her father, thinking that she was getting quite good at spying on people and not caring. He sat down in his accustomed chair and stared straight ahead. He did not open his newspaper or turn on the television set. This was as strange to Peyton as the fact of his being in the living room at all before dinner.

She was about to close her door when she heard Nora's light step on the porch, and the screened door creaking open and shut again.

'Well, what on earth are you doing in here in the daylight?' Peyton heard her say. There was a silence, and then Frazier said, 'Come in and sit down, Nora. We need to talk a little.'

Peyton froze at her spying post. Whatever great trouble this meeting portended, she needed to know about it. At the last minute she moved back from her door so that she could hear but not see. Somehow she could handle an assault on one sense but not on two.

'Charles was here,' her father said. 'He was pretty upset. I've never known him to tell tales on anyone, but he felt like he had to tell me about this. Lloyd Huey came over to see him this afternoon and told him what you said to him in the drugstore. Lloyd was mad and he was hurt. He thought Charlie would be the right one to tell me about it, and then he wanted me to speak to you.'

There was a silence. Peyton could imagine them sitting there, her father leaning forward with his hands clasped and resting on his knees, Nora slumping in the other chair and lighting a cigarette.

'This is pretty serious, Nora,' her father said. 'I don't think we can let it go as one more . . . escapade. The others have been on the side of the angels, even if they stirred up hornets' nests all over town. A certain amount of that is good for Lytton. But this has really hurt Lloyd. Charlie said he had tears in his eyes when he came over.'

There was another silence. Then her father went on: 'Nora, Lloyd is insensitive, to say the least. And I think he probably is tough on his help over at the mill. But I seriously doubt he mistreats Negroes. He may yell at them, but he yells at everybody. We let it go because it's a tough life he's living and because his mill has provided jobs for a whole lot of people, Negroes mostly. That kind of talk can hurt him in the town. Whether or not people believe it in the beginning, they'll talk.'

'Oh, Frazier,' Nora whispered. 'I really did hear that he abused his Negro workers physically, and withheld their pay when they displeased him. You know we can't let that go by—'

'What is this "we", Nora?' Frazier McKenzie said, and Peyton heard the ice in his voice.

'I can't imagine you would sanction that sort of thing,' Nora said. Her voice seemed to be losing force with every word.

'I wouldn't sanction that sort of thing if it were true, but it can't possibly be,' her father said. 'I've known Lloyd since we were kids. If he was seriously abusing his Negro help it would have got out way before now. The fact is you've jumped to a bad conclusion, and you've taken way too much on yourself. You cannot just come into this town and set yourself up as an avenging angel. It hurts people, and it will hurt you.'

'So what do you want me to do?' Nora whispered.

'I want you to go over and apologise to Lloyd,' her father said, 'and I want you just to stop with the . . . eccentricities. Just give it all a rest for a while. Even if I agree with you, and sometimes I do, I just don't have the energy to go on cleaning up after you.'

Nora gave a gasp of hurt and leapt out of her chair and ran up the stairs. Peyton heard the door to her room close. But before that, she heard the ragged catch of a sob. Peyton crawled under her afghan with Trailways and lay there until supper time. Nora did not come down, and her father did not speak. They ate in silence, and he went out to his office over the garage, and Peyton went back to bed and cried. She could not bear the trouble humming in the air.

For a couple of days Nora avoided all of them, eating her meals standing up at the refrigerator at odd times of the day and night, leaving for school early in the morning, and staying away somewhere until very late. The Thunderbird was not often at the kerb. Peyton's father ate his meals silently, the newspaper unfolded before him, and went early to his office and stayed late. Chloe did not sing, or linger to talk, or make special desserts. Peyton went back to showing herself her movies at night.

On the fourth day she heard her cousin's steps clicking rapidly up the path and into and through the house to the back door. She pulled aside her curtain and looked. Nora, windblown and scarlet-cheeked, ran up the steps to her father's office and rapped smartly on the door. When she saw the door open, Peyton dropped the curtain and burrowed under her afghan again. This was nothing to spy on.

Nora and her father did not come down for a long time. Peyton was foraging hungrily in the kitchen when they did, lifting the lids of the pots Clothilde had left on the stove. Nora was red-nosed and pouchy about the eyes, but the vivid life was back. Coming into the kitchen, she crackled with it. Peyton looked sideways at her father.

The ice had gone from his eyes, and the crinkles at their corners looked freshly incised, as if he had been smiling. Peyton's heart, for days bound and shut down in her chest, now soared. It was going to be all right . . .

'What are you doing in here munching like a goat?' Nora said teasingly. The rich music was back in her voice. 'The least you could have done was heat up supper and set the table.'

'I don't know where all that stuff is,' Peyton said, pretending it was ordinary talk on an ordinary day. 'I don't know how to work the stove.'

'That's absurd,' Nora said. 'I could cook when I was ten years old. Knowing how to cook well is a very sexy thing. This coming Saturday you're going to start learning.'

She set the green beans and new potatoes to warm and wrapped the chicken in foil and put it in the oven. Then she made martinis. Peyton heard them laughing desultorily at something when she went in to change for dinner. She snatched up Trailways and danced him around her room and squeezed him until he growled. Then she went into the living room to warm herself and eat olives. She would never know what had passed between Nora and her father in his office that evening, nor whether Nora finally apologised to Mr Lloyd Huey. Whatever it was, it sufficed.

Two nights later her father came home early and she heard Nora's steps come down to meet him, and something low being said between them. Her father laughed, and then Nora called, 'Peyton! Get out here! Your days of innocence are over!'

Peyton went cautiously into the living room. Nora had been almost manic since the trouble had passed; a shimmering like heat lightning was on her. It made Peyton want to hug her and pull away from her at the same time. Nora could burn you as easily as she could warm you, she thought.

Nora had brought her portable gramophone downstairs. She stood in the middle of the room, grinning. She wore blue jeans and a T-shirt, and her freshly washed hair almost gave off sparks. Peyton's father sat in his chair, smiling faintly at her.

'We are about to learn the twist,' Nora said. 'There is no hanging back and no salvation from it. By supper time I want to see those hips wiggling like there's no tomorrow.'

She put a record on the machine and started it.

'Come on, baby,' Chubby Checker growled. 'Let's do the twist . . .'

In the middle of the room, Nora planted her feet and threw back her head and held her hands out as if in a gesture of submission or supplication. Her hips began to gyrate in a circle and she seemed to swell with the music.

Peyton felt her face burn but something in her own hips and pelvis responded to the tug of the music. She smiled.

'Come on,' Nora said. 'Both of you, get out here. Keep your feet still, Frazier—that's right—and just move your hips in a kind of circle, in time to the music. Come on, Peyton.'

The music and motion took Peyton and flung her far away, and she was doing the twist as if she had known how all her life. She laughed aloud and looked over at her father. He danced fluidly opposite Nora. His dark hair hung over his eyes, and he was laughing.

The record ended and Nora put it on again. By the time it had played itself out two or three times they were flushed and sweating and moving as loosely as if their joints had been oiled. They had just sagged, laughing, into chairs and the sofa when Chloe came into the room. She stood in the doorway, not speaking. Her face was ashen under its deep ochre. There were tears in her eyes.

'I don't reckon y'all heard the phone,' she said. 'Miss Agnes done passed.'

Late that night Peyton heard her father come into the living room. He had been to the nursing home and then to the funeral home, making arrangements. His step was slow and heavy. Peyton did not get out of bed. The cold nothingness of her grandmother's death had tired her beyond rising. She turned into her pillow and hugged Trailways and closed her eyes once more. Even when she heard Nora come rapidly down the stairs from her room, she did not get up. Let them deal with it, this heavy blankness that was death.

Then she heard the sound of sobbing, dry and rough, as though the weeper did not know how to do it, and she got up and went to her door.

Her father sat slumped on the sofa. Nora knelt beside him, her arms around him, his face pressed into her shoulder. She was rocking him slightly, back and forth, and her face was pressed into his dark hair.

Peyton averted her eyes and, trembling all over, got the long-unworn amulet her grandmother had given her from her jewellery box, dropped it over her head and looked down. I'm getting breasts, she thought, and my grandmother is dead and my father is crying.

She slept heavily and long and got up aching as if she had been beaten. Neither her father nor Nora was about, and Chloe was silent in the kitchen as she put toast and eggs on the table.

'They gone to pick out a casket,' she said. 'You go on to school, now. There ain't nothing you can do till later.'

After school Peyton went as straight and swiftly as an arrow to the Losers Club. She longed with every atom of her being to be in a place where no strangeness was. When she got there, the door was padlocked. She went round to the window and stood on a cement block that lay under it. The chairs were gone, and the space heater, and the shelf that had held Ernie's library. Only the potbellied stove remained, black and empty.

Peyton walked home sobbing aloud.

Why is it, she wrote in her diary that night, *that if you have one thing you can't have another?*

7

After that, Peyton became obsessed with her Cousin Nora. She dogged her steps in the daytime, leaned close to her when they watched television at night. Everything Nora did and said and thought seemed, in these days, to be touched with mystery and glamour, and Peyton could not get enough of them.

One Saturday in May Nora went in the afternoon to tutor a Negro child in English.

'*Huckleberry Finn*,' she said, getting into the Thunderbird. 'He's having a hard time with Jim. I think it's the first time he's ever really thought about what slavery meant.'

She drove away and Peyton went back into the house. Her father was in his office, and Chloe had gone home. Peyton went in search of Trailways. She knew he would be on Nora's bed, lying on his back with his big paws folded on his mottled belly.

Peyton went up the stairs into Nora's room, knowing precisely what she was going to do and on fire with it. She closed the door behind her and opened the door to Nora's closet and looked on the top shelf. The ebony box was there, behind a warped tennis racket. It seemed to shine like a beacon in the gloom of the closet. Trembling, she lifted the box from the shelf and carried it over to Nora's bed. Part of the tremor was the fear of being caught and horror at what she was doing. Part of it was an anticipation so keen that it took her breath.

Peyton set the chest down on the bed. She took a deep breath and felt for the latch on the box. It was unlocked and opened easily.

She closed her eyes and breathed, 'I'm sorry for doing this, God,' and looked into the box for the core of her Cousin Nora.

Papers. Nothing but papers and envelopes. The papers seemed to be ordinary documents: birth certificate, passport, copy of a driver's licence, the sale papers and title to the Thunderbird. Some of the envelopes held letters, but they were disappointing: chatty notes from unknown women friends, a couple that might have been from tepid boyfriends. Nothing else. No photographs, no treasured bits of jewellery. Peyton leaned back, disappointment flooding her. Where was Nora in all this? Where was the source of the mystery that was so close it was almost palpable?

She started to close the box, and then she saw that the old velvet lining was slit at its top, some of the fabric rotting away. Her fingers felt the bulk of papers. Without hesitating she reached in and pulled out a thick manila envelope.

Photographs. Here she was, then. Here was Nora. Peyton's heart thudded high in her throat. She shuffled them slowly. The first few were landscapes. A shot of an ocean, clouds massing over its horizon, scabby palm trees in the foreground. Then a square in a town, with children darting about in the dirt street, laughing. Flowers hanging low from trees and bursting from pots and window boxes. Even in its obvious poverty and banality, the square had a holiday air.

The next photograph was the same view, but in its midst, beside a dry fountain in the middle of the square, stood the virulently pink Thunderbird. Peyton's breath caught. She lifted the photograph and took out the others. They were of people, people and Nora. Nora, her red hair molten in the sun, black sunglasses on her nose, laughing with her arms round a man and an old woman. A small group of people stood behind them. Nora wore short shorts and a peasant blouse. The men wore pants and bright flowered shirts, the women cotton skirts and tops like Nora's. The old woman held a small child in her arms, and there were other children at the feet of the adults. All the people except Nora were black. Against them, Nora burned like a pale flame.

Peyton thought that this must be the family Nora had lived with in Cuba. They were handsome people, but their blackness was so absolute that it was startling. Peyton had always thought Cubans were white with black hair and moustaches.

She picked up another photograph and saw the Thunderbird again, this time silhouetted against a beach. Here were the white sand and blue skies and turquoise water she had imagined; here was the paradisiacal backdrop she had built in her mind for Nora. There was no one in the Thunderbird. A faded inscription on the back of the photograph read *The famous Thunderbird, 1955.*

Beneath it was another photograph of the Thunderbird, only this time Nora was sitting in it, smiling at the camera, holding a small child in her arms, her cheek pressed into his hair. The child was reaching out to touch the glittering mirror on the driver's side. The sun was high; Nora's hair shone a pure, burnished red.

So did the child's.

Peyton's breath stopped in her throat. Slowly she turned the photo over. *Madonna and child* was written in Nora's slashing backhand. *Me and the baby, summer 1957.*

Whose child it was had not been written there. There was no need. Peyton knew. She closed the box and sat down on the edge of Nora's bed, trembling all over, her mind working feverishly to assimilate the photograph.

Nora had a child, a midnight-dark Cuban child with impossible red hair. He was perhaps a year old in the photograph. Nora obviously loved him. He was just as obviously gone from her life now.

Peyton sat there for a long time. She looked at the photo, but she heard and saw nothing. Then she did: the door opening, and Nora's footsteps coming into the room. Peyton did not lift her head. She wished that she could simply die, sitting there.

She felt rather than saw Nora sit down on the edge of the bed beside her. Nora did not speak, but she reached out and took the photograph from Peyton's fingers.

'I'm sorry,' Peyton whispered. Her voice was strangled.

Nora said, 'Don't be. I would have told you sometime. I wasn't quite ready to do it now, but now's as good a time as any. The baby is my son. His name is Roberto. He adored that car. I could always stop him from crying just by putting him in it.'

'Is that why it made you so mad when Boot got in your car?'

'I wasn't mad. But yes, that's what . . . got to me. For a minute it was like seeing Roberto when he would be eight or nine.'

'Like Boot?'

'Yes. Roberto is very black, as I'm sure you've noticed.'

'Where is he?' Peyton said, and then wished she had bitten out her tongue. It was obvious something had happened with the baby or else he would be with Nora.

'He's in Cuba, with his grandmother,' Nora said. 'If you've seen the other photographs, she's the old woman. She loves him very much. When I was about to bring him back to Miami with me, she hid him away somewhere. I get letters from her sometimes, telling me about him. I know that he's safe and happy. I probably never will know where he is, unless he finds me when he's older.'

'Weren't you scared for him?' Peyton said. 'Couldn't you have called the police or something?'

Nora laughed. There was little of amusement in it. 'The police probably helped hide him. No, I wasn't scared for him, and I'm still not. Cubans adore children; they're all that most of them have. The whole village will be Roberto's family. They'd never have let me take him away. Oh, they wouldn't have harmed me; the family I lived with loved me. But I was essentially an outsider, and Roberto wasn't. He's the jewel of the family. He'll have a better life in Cuba, even in that poor little village, than I could have given him here in the South. His colour would have made him a pariah, no matter how hard I tried to protect him. I couldn't have borne that.'

'Don't you miss him?'

'Like my arms and legs,' Nora said. 'Like my heart.'

Peyton felt a pang that was different from the shock of surprise and the surge of pity for Nora. It was jealousy.

'Will you go back there?' she said finally.

'No,' Nora said.

The silence spun out. Hesitantly, Peyton said, 'Does your husband help take care of him?'

Nora turned her head and smiled down at her.

'He's not my husband,' she said. 'He's a beautiful man, a sweet man. He adored me, and the baby is simply his heart. But when I . . . knew I had to come back, he wouldn't come with me. He was very angry. He had assumed I would stay in Cuba with them always. He helped his mother hide Roberto, and then he went into the mountains with Castro. He doesn't write. I presume he comes down to see Roberto occasionally, but I don't know where he is.'

'Maybe he'll bring Roberto here one day,' Peyton said.

'He'll never leave Cuba,' Nora said.

They were quiet again. 'It's awful,' Peyton said at last.

'Yes, it is,' Nora said. 'It wasn't smart of me. But I don't regret it. Raoul was the lover of a lifetime, and Roberto is in the world now. I'll always have those two things.'

Another silence, and then Nora said, 'You mustn't tell anyone, Peyton. Not anyone, not even your father. I'll have to decide when I'll do that, or even *if* I will. If anyone else knew I'd have to leave.'

'Daddy wouldn't care!'

'Maybe not, but there's no way it wouldn't get out eventually. Augusta would ruin both of you in a minute, just to get at me. I couldn't stay here. The rural South simply will not have it.'

Peyton's heart hurt. 'I promise,' she said. 'I'll never, ever tell anybody. It'll always be just our secret.'

After a time Nora stretched out on the bed and gathered Trailways to her and smiled up at Peyton. Her eyes were wet. Peyton was so giddy with shock and pride that Nora had confided in her that she could not speak.

'It seems to me that you know my secret now,' Nora said. 'But I don't know any of yours.'

'I don't have any secrets. I've never done anything,' Peyton said, feeling inadequate. Never, not even at the Losers Club, had she felt so utterly bereft.

'The best secrets can be the ones that you make with your mind,' Nora said. 'Didn't you ever have a secret dream? Didn't you want to be a ballet dancer or a spy or something when you got older? Didn't you ever have a great love affair in your mind?'

'No,' said Peyton, wincing.

'Oh, Peyton. The day that you will isn't far away at all. Don't be afraid of it. It won't happen until you're ready. And it's just the greatest thing, to be crazy in love with somebody. You wouldn't want to miss that.'

'I'll never get married,' Peyton said.

'I'm not talking about marriage,' Nora said, smiling.

Peyton blushed. 'I do have a secret,' she said suddenly. 'I have a huge one. I don't know how I could have forgotten.'

'And it is?' Nora said.

'I killed my mother.'

And this time, unlike the time at the Losers Club, Peyton did not feel dizzy with the enormity of it, only as if she had handed off something heavy to Nora.

Nora stared at her. 'What are you talking about?'

'Well . . . she bled to death after she had me.'

'Who told you that?' Nora's face was whitening as she spoke.

'Aunt Augusta. I must have been seven or eight.'

'And she told you you killed your mother?'

'Oh, no. Nobody had to tell me that. I mean, if I came and then she bled to death, what else could it be?'

'Peyton, did you ever talk to your father about this?'

Peyton looked down. 'No. Daddy and I never talked about her.'

'Why not?' Nora cried, hot anger in her voice.

'I thought he was grieving for her too much,' Peyton said. 'And then Buddy . . . I thought it would be just too awful to remind him. I thought it was enough that he thought about it every time he looked at me.' She felt the old salt in her throat.

Nora sat up and reached over and took Peyton's face in her hands. 'Now listen,' she said. 'I have something to tell you. It's about your mother, and you have to know it now. It's way past time. Peyton, you did not kill your mother. Your mother was just fine when you were born. She was bleeding a little, but a lot of women do. The doctor propped her legs up on a pillow and told her not to get up until the next morning, and he gave her a shot of something. She was asleep when he left. Your father and your aunt were taking care of you. Your father was ecstatic.'

Peyton's heart filled. He had held her, then, had looked down at her, had rejoiced that she was in the world.

'What happened, then, if she was all right?'

'What happened was that she got out of bed that afternoon and slipped out and drove to the country club and shacked up with the tennis pro,' Nora said calmly. 'She'd been doing it for months. She must have been out of her mind. She came home and bled to death in the bathroom. The tennis pro was gone the next morning.'

A great whispering whiteness, like snow, filled Peyton's heart and mind. She looked into it as if she were looking at a blizzard through a windowpane. 'How do you know?'

'My mother told me. Someone in the family obviously got wind of it, and told her. She told me not long before she died. I think now she told me out of spite. She and Lila Lee were always enemies.'

'Did . . . does my father know?' Peyton whispered.

'Yes,' Nora said.

'But he couldn't have told me,' Peyton said. 'He loved her so much. And he must have thought it would have hurt me awfully if he told me. . . . It was a kind thing, really.'

'I don't happen to think it's too terribly kind to let your child think that she killed her mother,' Nora said in a constricted voice.

'He didn't know I thought that. I've never told anybody that, except the Losers Club and now you.'

'Well, anybody with eyes could have seen that something's been bothering you all these years. He *should* have found out what it was, and the hell with his tender sensibilities.'

'Please don't be mad at him,' Peyton said, beginning to cry. She felt nothing about her mother, only the terrible possibility of the loss of Nora.

Nora got up. 'I'm going out to have a talk with your father,' she said, cheeks flaming. 'I want you to stay here until I come back and call you. I do not want you listening at the door this time. Oh, yeah, I know you do. I don't usually care, but I care about this. Hear what I'm saying, Peyton: if you eavesdrop on us I will know it and I will leave here this afternoon. Do you understand me?'

'Yes,' Peyton said through thick, stinging tears.

Nora had reached the door when Peyton cried, 'Wait! Could he be my . . . could I be . . . ?'

'God, no,' Nora said. 'You're every inch a McKenzie. He was a Neanderthal. His eyebrows met over his nose.'

She flung herself out of the room and slammed the door. Peyton pulled Trailways to her and curled into a ball around him. She stayed there until the cat fell asleep and the light outside the window went from yellow to blue, until she finally dozed.

She did not wake until Nora opened the door and put her head into the room. 'Your father and I are going to get a hamburger,' she said. Her voice was level, even light. There were silver tracks on her cheeks, though. She had been crying. 'There's cold roast beef in the fridge. Or we'll bring you a hamburger. But this time you can't come with us.'

'A hamburger would be nice,' Peyton said meekly.

But she had fallen asleep again long before they returned.

Peyton slept until morning, and when she woke she felt so much lighter that she thought she might float. Her mother was not, after all, a saint, and she herself was not a killer.

Presently Nora tapped on her door and then came in. She was dressed in her church 'lady' outfit, a soft yellow linen suit with a short jacket. The yellow linen cast a glow upon her neck and washed her tawny face faintly, as if she had held a bouquet of buttercups under her chin. Peyton thought she looked wonderful.

'You OK, kiddo?' Nora said, sitting down on the edge of Peyton's bed. 'You had a big day yesterday.'

'I feel funny,' Peyton said dreamily. 'Kind of floaty. Nothing seems very real. It almost feels like I'm in a place I don't know.'

'Well, in a way you are,' Nora said. 'Everything that shaped the world for you all your life changed yesterday. You want to talk about any of it?'

Peyton considered. 'I guess there's a lot I want to know about my mother,' she said. 'Will I ever know what she really was?'

'If you want to—as much as anyone knows anyone else. I'll tell you everything I know whenever you ask. Your father will talk to you about her, too. He hasn't before now because he thought it would be too hard for you. But he's promised that he will.'

'Did you all have a fight about this?'

'Mmm-hmm. A monstrous one. We were furious with each other. We yelled and screamed. Finally it occurred to both of us that this was not about us, it was about you, and then everything seemed just to fall into place. He knows he should have been closer to you all these years. He wanted to spare you any pain, and so he just didn't talk to you about anything. That's going to change, though.'

Peyton felt uneasy. Did she really want a father who bared his soul to her? 'Maybe Daddy and I can talk later,' she said. 'I just don't feel like I know what to say yet. I was the other way for so long that I don't know what way I need to be now.'

Nora laughed and hugged her. 'I'll relay the message. Do you want to come to church with us, or would you rather just mooch around here and collect yourself?'

'Mooch,' Peyton said gratefully.

Nora went to the door and looked back. 'She did love you, you know,' she said. 'And she loved your father a great deal. What she did had nothing to do with that.'

'How could it not?' Peyton's voice shook.

'They're not at all the same thing,' Nora said. 'Not at all. One is like scratching an itch. When the itch stops, the scratching ends. But the other is better in every way. It lasts. And the other is what she felt for you and your brother and your father. Your father knows that. You will, too, when you're older.'

Peyton heard her father's voice then, calling from the living room. 'You gals ready to go?'

'Let's let this gal sleep in,' Nora called back. 'She had a big day yesterday. She'll have lunch with us. Maybe Howard Johnson's fried clams again. Are you buying?'

'I'll flip you,' he said, and he came into the room.

He sat down on the edge of her bed as Nora had done and lifted her chin with his hand. 'I let you think a terrible thing, and I didn't even know it,' he said. 'We'll have to talk about that. But right now I just want you to know that you are my dearly loved daughter, and my best thing, and that I am very, very proud of you.'

Peyton nodded. She thought hopelessly that if she cried again her throat and nose would finally burst with it.

He leaned forward and hugged her hard and then got up and stood beside Nora. The scent of his pipe and shaving soap lingered.

'Your mother would have loved you totally,' he said. 'It would have been impossible for her not to. I'm telling you the truth about that. Can you be dressed and ready for clams in an hour or so?'

'Yes,' Peyton whispered. 'I can.'

The crystal shell burst, and the world came flooding back in, rude and loud and charged with joy.

8

Peyton went through the next week with the careful deliberation of the newly sighted, not quite believing that the old blindness would not strike her again. It was not the profound dissociation of the past Sunday, but it was strange enough to keep her preternaturally aware of everything around her, of her own body.

When she looked down she could see her chest, like a shelf. When had that happened? Jeremy Tucker from the tenth grade had run up and kissed her on the cheek at recess. What was she supposed to do about that? Her cheek burned all afternoon.

When Nora came in from her last tutorial that Friday afternoon she found Peyton and Trailways curled up on her bed, record player braying out Brahms.. Peyton was in a tight ball with her eyes closed.

Nora sighed. 'Who stole your bubble gum, toots?' she said, coming across the room to sit beside Peyton.

Peyton opened her eyes. 'I have to make a speech,' she said. 'I have to write it. I have to get up onstage at graduation. It's supposed to be some kind of honour, but I told Mrs Manning I'm not doing it.'

'You could do it wonderfully,' Nora said. 'We could practise it until you weren't frightened any more.'

'I'd die. I'd forget what I was supposed to say. I'd throw up. Everybody would laugh at me. They already think I'm drippy. You know I look like a stork.'

'No,' Nora said. 'I don't know you look like a stork. Haven't you looked at yourself lately? You have a waist and hips and breasts. Your hair is great. You're a pretty girl, Peyton; you have your father's wonderful profile, and his eyes. Lots of girls would kill to look like you.'

'Can you see me leading cheers?' Peyton said bitterly.

'No. But is that really what you want to do? Come on, Peyton. Let's do this thing. Let's work on your speech together. We can practise it. I'll stand in the wings grinning on speech night. We'll get you a knockout new dress.'

'I can't write. What would I write about?'

'I have an idea,' Nora said. 'You know how much you liked the play *Our Town*. What if you did an *Our Town* about Lytton? You could be the Stage Manager and read all the other parts.'

'You mean write about dead people? Nobody wants to hear about dead people at a graduation.'

Nora grinned. 'Dead people don't have to be tragic. You'd make them up to fit what you wanted to say. A young girl like you talking about how sweet it was to be young in Lytton, Georgia. An honoured old man telling about the past here and all the things he witnessed and what he learned over a lifetime. A person who thought Lytton was small potatoes and left, and wandered the wide world, and then came home because there was no place better. You'd talk about the things they remembered—that *you* remember: the long summer twilights, roller-skating in the fall, the town Christmas decorations. Your father would simply burst with pride.'

After a long silence, Peyton said, 'Would you absolutely and positively be there in the wings? Would you help me all the way, and fix the things that are wrong with it?'

'I'll most certainly be there,' Nora said. 'But you're going to have to fix the wrong things yourself. I'm not writing it for you. I'll read it all, though, and I'll rehearse you. You might just surprise yourself by having a good time.'

The next morning Peyton went to the library and checked out *Our Town*. She brought the book home, and she had not read more than two pages before she picked up her pencil and notebook and began to write. She wrote for a long time, and when she looked up it had grown dark and she could hear the voices of Nora and her father out on the front porch, where they sometimes sat after dinner in the soft, fragrant night. She could smell the cool bite of Nora's cigarette, and a sweeter, thicker scent that meant her father was smoking his pipe. The old porch glider creaked, and all at once Peyton was powerfully, giddily happy, and very hungry.

She went out onto the porch. 'Hey,' she said to them.

'Hey, yourself,' her father said. 'Did you just wake up? We saved you some supper.'

'I wasn't asleep,' Peyton said.

Nora looked at her keenly and then reached over and picked up her hand and squeezed it. 'We're off,' she said, grinning.

'Off where?' Frazier said.

'Off to see the Wizard,' Nora said, and she laughed joyously. 'Off our rockers. You just wait and see where we land.'

'I gather I'm not supposed to ask.'

'No. But you'll hear about it soon. Literally. Chicken salad in there, Peyton.'

And Peyton went off to eat her late supper and find a way to think about herself that was not, perhaps, so drippy after all.

IT WAS AS IF she had two sets of eyes in those first days of working on the speech. The first set was the one she had had since birth—more educated now, perhaps, focused on her rapidly expanding world, but still her own vision. The other set was somewhere inside her, and it filtered everything through the screen of her writing.

Coming back from Atlanta in the Thunderbird in the late afternoon she would see the Lytton water tank before she saw anything else of the town, and the setting sun would strike the metal into a million facets of glittering colour, and she would think, This is what the person who went away and came back would see first.

She spoke of it to Nora, shyly. 'It's like everything I hear and see and do wants to go into the speech,' she said.

'That's what makes a writer,' Nora said. 'That you see the story in everything. That you go through your life with all your senses open, that you think "what if" a thousand times a day. I knew you'd be good with words, but I didn't know about the seeing. It's not given to many people. It's a gift, Peyton. You can't ever again think of yourself as a loser, as you say. Or even ordinary.'

Peyton's head swam. Pride and fear in equal measure flooded her. And so she went back to her notebook and wrote furiously through the warming afternoons of May. Five weeks. She had only five weeks before graduation.

At night when she came out for supper, she felt as if she were breathing air and seeing lights for the first time. They sat long at the table, talking about their days, and when they finally got up it was to move onto the screened porch and sit in the dark, hearing the ghostly nighttime dissonance of the katydids. Nora and her father almost always lingered when Peyton got up to go to bed. Where once she would have spied on them, now Peyton wrote more in her notebook. But once she went into the living room to ask Nora how to spell something and saw her sitting on the couch watching the soundless television. Her father was stretched out on the sofa with his head in Nora's lap, fast asleep. Nora heard Peyton and looked up and put a finger to her lips.

'Don't wake him. He's had an awful day,' she whispered.

Peyton felt as though she were walking on tiptoe in those days, afraid she might crush something fragile.

She saw Boot one afternoon in the parking lot of the A&P store, where he had taken a job two days a week bagging groceries. He was pushing a full cart, limping along behind a large woman headed for a dirty Pontiac. When Peyton came out of the store with the eggs she had been sent for, he was waiting at the kerb.

'Hey, Peyton,' he said cheerfully.

'Hey, Boot,' she said, sweetness and familiarity flooding over her. She had, she realised, missed Boot enormously.

'Have you seen Ernie?' she asked.

'Don't you know nothin'?' Boot said. 'Ernie gone. His mean ol' mama broke her hip and he had to put her in a home up to Hapeville. He sold that little old house and moved in a 'partment to be near her. I think he workin' at McDonald's, like Doreen, only not the same one. He a manager; you know he real smart.'

Ernie in a little paper cap, taking orders from empty-headed teens and fat, blue-rinsed old women who would never in their lifetime know as much as one hundredth of what Ernie's brain held.

Peyton felt tears start. 'Oh, Boot, when?'

'Week and a half ago. It was real sudden. He came by to see me before they left. He working double shifts. That home cost an arm an' a leg, he say.'

'Did he say anything about me?' Peyton whispered.

'Naw. He ain't said nothin' about you since the last time you was at the Losers Club. We shut it down right after that. I miss it, though. It was a lot of fun.'

'I miss it, too,' Peyton said, and she turned away. The tears were streaking down her cheeks now. If Boot saw them he would broadcast it that Peyton McKenzie was crying in the A&P parking lot.

'I'll see you soon, Boot,' she called over her shoulder.

'Yeah,' he called back. 'Tell Mamaw I say hey.'

Peyton did not write in her notebook that afternoon. She lay on her bed and cried and cried, and when the tears finally stopped and she washed her swollen face, she saw for a moment the watery reflection of the pale, pigtailed girl in the too-large blue jeans who used to cut through the undergrowth every afternoon to reach the sanctuary of the Losers Club, and she began to cry again.

'WOW,' NORA SAID, shuffling pages. 'I don't know whether we need an editor or a surgeon.'

They were sitting cross-legged on Nora's bed on a Sunday afternoon, surrounded by drifts of paper. It was thickly hot and airless and Peyton was wearing one of her old sleeveless blouses—too tight across the chest now—and a pair of cutoffs. Nora wore underpants and an enormous, frayed blue oxford-cloth shirt. She was smoking and turning pages intently.

'Now,' Nora said. 'The thing to do first is decide what you want this speech to say.'

'Well . . . just how good it was to live in Lytton years ago, and how everybody sees it differently, but it's still Lytton.'

'Good. Now how would you go about telling that?'

'Through the people who are remembering.'

'OK,' Nora said. 'Let's start with the beginning. Since you're the Stage Manager, what do you want to say?'

'I want to say what the Stage Manager in *Our Town* says.'

'Well, you can't use his exact words, or you'd get sued, but you could say that the play inspired you to think about Lytton and how it must have been long ago, and that you wanted to show people that, because that Lytton won't come again.'

'I want to say exactly that,' Peyton said.

'OK. But it's the only part of it I'm going to write for you. Now let's get into the body of it. I think you could handle maybe three soliloquies. The old woman and the girl are perfect. Whom do you want for your third?'

'The horses,' Peyton said, seeing suddenly the shape of it. 'Their field is on the edge of town, and it would be a way to show Lytton as you came into it back then, and to talk about how it was when people were mainly farmers. And then the young girl, who lived in the middle of town. And then the old woman, because she lived on the other edge of it. It sort of takes you through the town, see?'

'I do indeed.' Nora smiled. 'You ready to start pruning?'

They worked all that afternoon and into the night. When at last they stopped, Peyton was amazed to see that it was nearly midnight. They had culled out the three segments, though.

The next afternoon Nora wrote out the brief introduction, and Peyton read it aloud for the first time: 'More than twenty years ago Thornton Wilder wrote a play called *Our Town*. I went to see it this year in Atlanta, and it made me cry and laugh and wonder. It takes place mainly in the cemetery of a little town, where the dead talk to the Stage Manager, but to me they are as vivid and real as if they were alive. In a sense, they are, through their memories, and I'd like to show you what I think Lytton might have been like through the eyes of some of us who aren't here any more.'

Peyton looked up at Nora, her eyes brimming. 'It's just right,' she said. 'I could never have thought of it.'

Over the next few days the speech took shape and Peyton grew, if not easy, then at least familiar with it. Nora listened and applauded. 'Fabulous,' she said. 'You'll be a sensation.'

And Peyton, flushed with success, began hesitantly to believe her.

Two weeks into their practice sessions, Nora came home and dumped her books loudly on the secretary and stood rubbing her forehead as if it ached.

'What's the matter?' Peyton said in alarm, coming in from the kitchen.

'Oh, nothing. Just a foul-up at school. I threw a kid out of class and I didn't want to do it, but I didn't have any choice.'

'Was it one of the Negro kids?' Peyton said.

'No. It was one of the cheerleaders,' Nora said.

'You didn't! How wonderful!' Peyton said. 'Which one?'

'Mary Jim Turnipseed. She called one of the black kids a dimwit, and the child cried in front of the whole class and ran out. Mary Jim started to laugh. I'm afraid I yelled at her.'

'Mary Jim! Lord, Nora, she's the cheerleader captain and homecoming queen. She'll tell her father. He's a judge.'

'I don't care if her father is the lord high executioner. I will not have that kind of thing in my classroom.'

Mary Jim not only told her father about the incident, but also informed her parents that Nora had been teaching them pornography for the last few months, and took home her heavily underlined copy of *The Tropic of Cancer* by way of proof. When her outraged parents asked why she hadn't told them earlier, she said that Miss Findlay had said she'd flunk anybody who told his or her folks. Margaret Turnipseed was on the phone before the words died on Mary Jim's trembling little lips.

They had finished supper and were sitting on the porch talking of the coming summer when the people came. Frazier heard them first, and looked up. There must have been ten or twelve of them, people he had known all his life, neighbours, clients. He did not speak. It was easy to see that they had not come in friendship.

Horace Turnipseed stepped out of the small knot of people and said, 'Frazier, we don't like doing this, but we can't let it go on. Your . . . cousin, or whatever she is, expelled my daughter from her class today. That might not be such a bad thing if Mary Jim deserved it, but she's always been a good girl. I can't imagine what she could have done to warrant that kind of behaviour. But the main thing we can't let pass is what Miss Findlay is teaching our children. I never read anything so dirty. The idea that my child—anybody's child—is reading this stuff is absolutely unacceptable. I'm afraid that we're going to have to ask that you to relieve Miss Findlay of her position.'

'What book are you referring to, Horace?' Frazier asked.

'This.' Horace Turnipseed held up the book. 'This *Tropic of Cancer* thing. There's filth on every page. Every single one.'

'It must have been a trial for you to have to finish it, Horace,' Peyton's father said. 'Every page, think of it. And it's a big book, too.'

Horace Turnipseed's face reddened. 'Have you ever heard of this book, Frazier?' he said.

'I've read that book,' her father answered. 'I didn't find it in the least offensive. Pretty basic and earthy, but not offensive.'

Peyton goggled. She knew her father had not read the book. She doubted he had even heard of it.

'I will not ask her to resign, Horace,' he said.

There was a shuffling, murmuring silence, and then Aunt Augusta stepped forward into the lamplight.

'You are a good man, Frazier,' Augusta McKenzie said. 'But we think perhaps you're . . . too close to this situation. This young woman is a troublemaker. She is a terrible influence on our young people. How can you subject Peyton to all that? It makes us all wonder in exactly what capacity you keep Miss Findlay in your house.'

Frazier McKenzie stepped forward. He crossed his arms over his chest and looked at his sister-in-law, and then he let his gaze slide over all their faces. Many looked away.

'Miss Findlay is in my house in any capacity she wishes to be,' he said. 'And it is my fondest hope that she will remain so—in any capacity she chooses. It is you who are the troublemaker, Augusta.'

Augusta McKenzie gasped and turned on her heel and clicked rapidly down the path.

Horace Turnipseed cleared his throat. 'Then we have no choice but to go to the whole school board, Frazier,' he said.

'Go,' her father said. Peyton could see that he was trembling.

The small crowd sensed that there was nothing more to say and melted away as silently as it had come. In a moment there was only lamplight and the smell of grass and the sound of crickets.

Her father turned to Nora and took her by the shoulders. 'I meant what I said,' he said. 'I want you with us. We need you. Don't let these idiots run you away. Any capacity, Nora. Any at all.'

Nora's face was as white as a lily in the dimness. 'Don't do this to me, Frazier,' she whispered. 'Don't need me. Don't. I can't carry the weight of it. I can't stay.'

And she wheeled and ran up the stairs to her room.

'Daddy . . .' Peyton said, near tears. 'Daddy, go get her. Don't let her go.'

'I don't think she'll go,' her father said. 'All this business upset her. I don't blame her. She's like a bird. You have to hold her in your open hand. I landed on her too hard tonight.'

'Did you want her to stay . . . you know, like my mother or something?' Peyton could not say, 'Like as your wife.'

'Go to bed, Peyton. We'll straighten it out in the morning.'

But they did not. Nora eluded them like a wild thing. She got up early and stayed late at school. She went often to Atlanta alone and did not ask Peyton and Frazier to go with her. When they did see her, she was noncommittal and pleasant. Her face was pinched and the fire seemed to have gone out of her. She still rehearsed Peyton in her speech, but with the mechanical capability of a paid coach.

Peyton couldn't speak to her of the night on the porch, mostly for fear of what she might hear. But she fretted about her speech. 'You *will* be there, won't you, Nora?' she asked.

'Peyton, you've gotten so good at it that you could do it by yourself,' Nora said. 'But yes, I'll be there. I promised, didn't I?'

The silence in the house spun out. Frazier was once more in his office until all hours. Clothilde trudged heavily about the kitchen. Peyton ached for the Losers Club, at the same time knowing that even if it were still meeting, she had somehow travelled beyond it and could not go back. It was a cold, dull time.

9

Sonny Burkholter was Lytton's claim to fame, its shining star. He had been born to the town's seamstress, a nervous little woman known in Lytton simply as Miss Carrie. They lived for many years in a tiny, neat cottage beside the railroad tracks. There had been a Mr Burkholter, but he had disappeared, leaving Miss Carrie to bring up Sonny. She idolised him. There was no doubt in her mind that he would touch the world in a very special way.

And he did. After an undistinguished academic career at Lytton High, Sonny cut and ran. For months his frantic mother did not know where he was. Eventually, Sonny surfaced. In a letter to his mother, in which he did not enquire after her well-being, he told her that he was in Los Angeles and had just been cast in a new Western drama as the second lead.

I'm going to come back and build you a house, he wrote. *Watch for me Tuesday night. It's called* Pecos.

Miss Carrie and the whole town watched, and there was no doubt in the collective consciousness that Sonny was going to be a very big television star. Besides his rather ordinary good looks—sharp, diamond-blue eyes, shock of yellow hair, square jaw, chiselled nose—Sonny had something ineffable and immediate on the little screen. The camera loved him. Sonny had only to grin and the set lit up along with the hearts of half of America; when he spoke in his slow drawl sighs were heard from L.A. to Bangor, Maine. He was nineteen years old at the time. The role in the Western was small. But it propelled Sonny into the small-screen stratosphere, and there he had stayed, ending up the season before in a turgid drama called *The Southerners*, in which he played a 'modern Rhett Butler born to raise hell and break hearts'. From the first episode the ratings were off the charts. Raising hell and breaking hearts became, to his adoring public, the very quintessence of southernness. Sonny played it so well that he became a southerner the likes of whom had never trod the red earth of the South.

Speculation about his love affairs was rife and lurid. But Sonny did not settle down. When he came back to Lytton for the first time since he'd left, to install his mother in the mammoth new house he had had built for her just outside town and to speak at the high school, he was unmarried, thirty years old, and richer than Croesus.

Lytton went berserk with pride and joy. There were WELCOME HOME, SONNY signs all over town, and plans were under way for a parade. But Sonny's publicist sent word that he wanted no special treatment. Sonny was, she said, coming back to find his roots and see his mother into the home they had dreamed about during the years in the cramped little railroad cottage. He would appreciate it if the town would treat him just like anybody else.

It was an inspired public-relations ploy. It let the town worship him for his down-to-earth humility and his devotion to his old mother and laid the groundwork for Sonny to get out of town afterwards as fast as his limousine would take him.

He and Nora collided like meteors. After they met, in the high school cafeteria on Career Day, Sonny decided to stay awhile.

Peyton heard about it from Chloe. Chloe had heard it from her cousin's daughter, who worked in the cafeteria and witnessed the whole thing. As local legend had it, Sonny was escorted to the cafeteria by the tongue-tied president of the student body and the grinning principal. He went through the line 'just like anybody else', and pronounced the lunch the best he had had since he left home.

'There's nothing in the world beats good old-fashioned southern cooking,' he said. This was a stretch, since the school had opted for flaccid grey steaks and uniformly yellow frozen French fries in his honour, but it was widely quoted all the same. He was just getting an Eskimo pie out of the freezer when Nora came into the room.

'She had on that yellow thing that makes her look like a birthday candle,' Chloe reported, 'and somebody had brought her a yellow lily, and she'd stuck it in her hair. That boy walked straight over to her and said, "Will you have lunch with me?" And she said, "Sure." And they sat down together and he ate lunch all over again. They left together, too, in that little pink car.'

Before the day was out, Nora was back with them. Not the coltish Nora who had climbed Peyton's tree in the beginning, not the gleeful Nora who had outraged and overjoyed Lytton in equal parts. And not the languid Nora who had coiled herself on the porch with them in the spring nights. But nevertheless, Nora. The dulled, dimmed stranger of the past few days was gone.

This Nora was not often at home for meals and spent virtually no evenings with Peyton and Frazier. She dashed in and out, hair a brazen banner behind her, green eyes sparkling. She sang in the bathroom and gave Peyton whirlwind hugs on her way out to meet Sonny and paused to kiss Frazier on the cheek and straighten his tie. She seemed to give off sparks. Looking at her, Peyton had the notion that if Nora stuck her finger into a light socket, all the fuses in the house would blow. Despite the hugs and kisses and laughter, there was something about her that was out of control, almost dangerous.

Chloe disliked Sonny Burkholter and was not polite about it.

'He look like an ol' yellow pug dog, with that squished-up nose,' she said after Nora made her watch Sonny's TV programme. 'And he don't act like no southerner I ever seen. Who you seen lately kissin' hands, or tippin' that hat what looks like a lady's?'

'That's a plantation hat.' Nora smiled, refusing to be baited. 'People used to wear them on the big plantations.'

'Ain't no plantation around here I ever seen.'

'Well, you just wait till you see the house Sonny built his mother. It's got everything: columns, oak avenues, horses, everything.'

'She gon' keep slaves?'

'Don't be a butt,' Nora said, and hugged her, and dashed out in a flurry of skirts and petticoats.

The skirts were new. They were not the blazing tropical prints that most of Nora's others were, nor were they willowy, like the rest. They were wide and sprigged with flowers, or made of candy-striped seersucker. And Nora no longer slouched about barefoot.

Peyton had not spent an afternoon or evening in Nora's room since Sonny came home. Pride and pique kept her from begging Nora to rehearse her on the speech, but anxiety about it mounted.

Finally she said, 'Could you possibly listen to my speech tonight? It sounds funny to me and it's only a week away.'

'I can't tonight, kiddo,' Nora said, climbing into a new white dress that drifted around her like a snowbank. 'We're taking Sonny's mother into Atlanta to Emile's. She's never had dinner in Atlanta. Besides, it's time for you to rehearse alone now. You'll be alone when you give it, and you really need to get used to it.'

'But you'll be there . . .'

'Sure, but I can't give the speech for you. Now's as good a time as any to start standing alone. You can do it.'

No, I can't, Peyton thought. She was suddenly very angry at her cousin. This was to have been her special time with Nora, but Nora had given it all to Sonny without a backward glance.

'You're going to look pretty silly, all of you jammed into that little car,' Peyton said.

'We're taking Sonny's limo. He hates to use it, but with his mother he has to, and besides, his driver is dying of boredom.'

Peyton could not leave it alone. 'I'd have thought a big TV star could drive his own car,' she said. 'Can't he drive?'

'Of course he can, but he doesn't like to drive the limo around here. He thinks it looks ostentatious. Knock it off about Sonny, Peyton. He's a nice guy. You'll see when you meet him.'

'I don't want to meet him.'

'Well, then, you can sit in your room all night, because I've invited him to dinner.'

'Daddy's just going to love that. Did you ask him?'

'Yes. He said he'd be honoured, and by all means to ask him.'

Peyton thought of the night on the porch when her father had taken hold of Nora's shoulders and said, 'I meant what I said. I want you to stay. I want you with us. We need you . . . Any capacity, Nora. Any at all.' She remembered his face as he said it. He had looked younger by far than she had ever seen him. He had looked happy. He did not look young now, or happy.

'I bet he didn't mean it,' she said to Nora.

'Well, if he didn't he'll never let me know about it, because he's a gentleman, and the kindest man I've ever met.'

Then why isn't that enough? Peyton said in her head. Her heart hurt as if someone had hit her in the chest.

She ploughed on with her rehearsing. At first the space where Nora was not swallowed her voice and her will, but after a few days she saw that, given no mishaps, she could probably read the speech competently. The magic and music had gone from it, though. But with Nora there in the wings, perhaps the magic would come back.

The judge and his coterie were as good as their word. Nora was dismissed only days after the confrontation on the front steps. She never spoke of it, did not seem to remember that she had had a job. She lived entirely in the wake of Sonny Burkholter.

Her father did not, this time, shut Peyton out or pull away from her. He spent his nights with her on the porch or in front of the TV, and he never missed breakfast or dinner with her, and she could tell he was trying to enter her world. He asked about her days and hugged her frequently, and made a small game of her graduation speech.

'Still not going to tell me?'

'No.'

'I know. You're giving it in Japanese.'

'You're silly.'

'Then you're going to tap dance while you're speaking.'

'Daddy . . .'

But she laughed. They both laughed. If they laughed enough, Peyton could not hear the emptiness where Nora's rich laugh should be. Once it would have been enough just to be this close to Daddy, she thought bleakly. Almost, it was.

She was still angry with Nora, and not the least of her anger was for her father. Nora had to know that Frazier wanted her to stay, she thought. If she wasn't going to be with us like she'd always been, she should have moved out so we wouldn't have to watch her carry on with that jerk.

Sonny came to dinner the week of graduation. Nora had asked for a completely southern meal and had presented Chloe with the menu: fried chicken, turnip greens with cornmeal dumplings, fresh corn, sliced tomatoes, biscuits, and chicken gravy. And peach cobbler for dessert. These were all the things Sonny pined for out in California, she said.

'They ain't got chicken in California?' Clothilde had grumped.

'Nobody in California fries anything, Chloe, and they've never heard of turnip greens.'

Promptly at six o'clock the long black limousine slid up the kerb in front of the house and Sonny got out of the back seat—or one of the back seats, Peyton thought. She was watching from the screened porch, behind a big fern.

Sonny came up the steps and Nora stood in the doorway to greet him. She wore yellow pique and he wore a bursting blue T-shirt, white pants, and black sunglasses. She took him by the hand and led him onto the porch.

'Frazier, this is Sonny,' she announced. 'He's heard all about you. He said he was almost afraid to meet you. Sonny, this is my Cousin Frazier McKenzie.'

'We're pleased to have you,' Frazier said, standing up and putting out his hand to Sonny. 'We've seen a lot of you on TV.'

'The pleasure is mine, sir,' Sonny said. He took Frazier's hand in both his own and pressed it, and looked into his eyes.

'Needless to say, you're all Nora talks about,' he told Frazier. 'You and Miss Peyton here.' He smiled over at Peyton behind her fern. His teeth were blinding white and his voice was small and high, as if he had a bee trapped in his jaws. They must do something on TV to make it sound lower, Peyton thought. She was so delighted with his voice that she came out from behind the fern and let him take her hand and bow over it and kiss it. She looked up at Nora to see if she was successfully concealing her laughter, but Nora was not laughing. She was smiling tenderly upon Sonny.

'Didn't I tell you they were special?' she said.

It was an awful dinner; Peyton felt as if it went on for aeons. Sonny did most of the talking. He began the moment they sat down.

The table was set with pink linen and flowers, and her mother's silver candlesticks held pale pink candles. When Chloe came in with their plates, Sonny mimicked a swoon. When she had left again, he turned to Frazier and said, 'It's what I've missed most, this good old-fashioned southern cooking. And nobody does it like these good old Negro mammies, do they? She's worth her weight in gold.'

At first Peyton thought she had not heard correctly. Then she looked at her father. He was looking down at his plate with interest. She looked at Nora. Surely she would demolish him with the cold knife of her tongue. 'Mammies' indeed!

But Nora merely said, 'She's the best cook I've ever known.'

From then on Sonny talked of Hollywood and the show; he tossed out words and phrases like 'production schedule' and 'ratings' and 'syndication'. Her father looked gravely interested. Nora looked as if she were hearing an Ave Maria.

What is *wrong* with her? Peyton thought. He's a jerk.

That night before she fell asleep, Peyton prayed: 'Please, God, don't let her go off with him. Please don't let her leave.'

The day after the dinner Sonny flew to New York for a few days and Nora was back in spirit as well as in flesh. It was as if she had never been away. No one remarked about it; they simply slid into their old life as if they were sliding into warm water.

On one of the days they went into Atlanta, and Frazier did some business at the courthouse while Nora and Peyton shopped. Nora had trimmed Peyton's hair and it was back in its lustrous tousle, and they found, at Rich's, an ivory polished-cotton sheath with a stand-away collar that made Peyton look, as Nora said, like a lighted candle. Even Peyton could see that it was an extraordinary dress. In it, a person could do anything, even make a speech on the stage of Lytton Grammar School. Nora bought it for her.

They drove home in the late afternoon, singing at the top of their lungs. Oh, yes, Nora was back.

'Do you think she's trying to say she's sorry about taking up with that jerk?' Peyton asked her father that night when he came in to tuck her in. He'd been doing that every night, and after the first embarrassed stiffness, both of them had enjoyed the ritual.

He was silent for a moment, and then he sat down on the edge of her bed. 'No, I don't,' he said, looking at her. 'I think she's saying goodbye.'

'No,' Peyton cried. It came out as involuntarily as breath.

'You know she never said she'd stay,' he said, smoothing the hair off her face.

'But she wanted to, I know she did . . . she always talked about how safe she felt here, and how she just wanted to be with us.'

'She needs to be able to do what's right for her,' Frazier said. 'We can't hold her if she wants to go.'

'Do . . . you want her to stay?'

He smiled. 'Let it be, Peyton. Be happy that she's happy.'

'I bet she's not. I bet it's just his stupid money. She'd hate living in Hollywood. Can you see her out there?'

'Yes,' he said. 'I can.'

On Thursday of that week Nora listened to a last run-through of the speech Peyton would give the next night. Peyton dressed for it in the ivory dress Nora had bought her, and her mother's pearls.

'That was perfect,' Nora said. 'And look at you. I'm going to have to hog-tie Sonny; he'll try to make a play for you for sure.'

'Is he coming?'

'Yes. He wouldn't miss it for the world. He's coming back tomorrow afternoon. I'm going to meet him at the airport and we're coming straight to the auditorium. It's practically his last night before he has to go back to California, so you should be honoured.'

'Are you going with him?' Peyton said, elaborately examining her hemline in the mirror.

'He hasn't asked me,' Nora said. 'But if he does, you'll be the first to know. Of course, it certainly wouldn't mean I'd go . . .'

'He's rich. You'd never have to worry about money again.'

'I don't worry about it now. That's not worthy of you, Peyton. Let's drop this right now.' Her tone was chilly. As she left the room, Peyton took a last look at her reflection in the mirror. The candle's flame had gone out.

Nora was not there the next morning.

'She gone to Atlanta to do a little shopping,' Chloe said.

Peyton pushed away her plate. Why had Nora left her on this morning? She didn't have to leave for the airport until late in the day.

Nora was not back in the afternoon, either. Peyton stayed in her room and looked at her watch a hundred times. Finally she knew that Nora would be on her way to the airport to retrieve Sonny and that she would not see her now until that night in the wings. When she had dressed and sat down to put on her make-up the way Nora had taught her, her hands shook so that she could manage only clownish red spots on her cheeks and a crazy slash of lipstick. She washed it all off.

'You look beautiful,' her father said as they got into the car to go to the school.

Those honoured sat in tiered rows on the stage, on bleachers borrowed from the gymnasium. The school choir sat in chairs just below them. It was very hot. Peyton felt lightheaded and removed, stricken with terror.

Nora . . . Peyton slid a look at the wings. She saw the drama coach, but no Nora. But she had thirty minutes yet . . .

They had the prayer. The principal stood up and welcomed everyone. The audience rustled and fanned.

Peyton heard the principal telling the audience that the valedictory address would be given by Miss Peyton McKenzie, and that he was sure they were all eager to hear what she had to say.

Nora did not come.

Peyton stood up and walked to the lectern. Her hands were so wet that they left prints on the pages of her speech. She looked out into the audience and could see nothing but the haze of lights.

Nora did not come.

'More than twenty years ago Thornton Wilder wrote a play called *Our Town,*' she whispered. Her voice shook.

'Louder,' the drama coach hissed from the wings.

Peyton ploughed ahead. She started into the segment about the horses.

'We are horses,' she faltered. 'Let us tell you how it was then, on the farms of Lytton, Georgia . . . .'

From the audience there was a muffled whinny, and a patter of smothered laughter. Peyton's hands and lips numbed. She read on. Nora was not there. Peyton would have felt her if she had been.

'We were happy here,' she finished up. 'We were fed and groomed with love, and nobody ever beat us in our lives.'

'You can't beat a dead horse,' a voice in the audience said. This time the laughter was not muffled.

Nora did not come.

Sickened and dizzy, Peyton started into the segment about the young girl. 'My name is Elizabeth,' she quavered. 'I was sixteen years old when I died, and I loved my life. There were no streetlights in my Lytton, but there were gas lamps, and I used to walk in their soft light in the spring nights, smelling the honeysuckle and mimosa, laughing with my friend, all dressed up. We did not always know where we were going, but it did not matter. Sometimes we just went to the little meadow behind the bandstand and lay in the cool grass.'

'Must have been a real good friend,' someone called.

'Yeah,' another boy yelled. 'I've had a lay behind that bandstand, too. I never knew you could die of it, though.'

There was a hush, and then the auditorium exploded into laughter. Peyton saw her father stand up and turn and glare at the audience, saw him hold up his hands for quiet. The laughter spiralled up.

Peyton turned and walked off the stage. She did not turn her head right or left as she went through the wings.

The drama coach put out her hand. 'Peyton, honey,' she said. 'It wasn't you. It was those idiot boys.'

In the schoolyard Peyton broke into a trot. By the time she was a block from home she had taken off her shoes and tossed them into the grass beside the sidewalk and was running flat out. Her stockings were shredded, and the cement of the sidewalk abraded her feet. She did not feel it. She felt nothing but a simple need to be in the tree house. In the dark.

Where Nora was not.

Without hesitation she went up her tree and huddled on the floor of the tree house. It felt cramped, too small, a toy. She knew she would not come here again.

She laid her head on her crossed arms and sank down into the leafy darkness of the tree branches. She waited.

In what seemed like an eyeblink she heard her father's voice under her tree. 'Come on down, honey,' he said. 'Come on down and let's go in and have some hot chocolate. It's not the end of the world, and it's not your fault. Those boys will be punished.'

Peyton burrowed her head deeper into her arms.

'Peyton, come down from there,' Aunt Augusta's voice shrilled.

She did not reply.

'Peyton, I can't just leave you up there,' her father said pleadingly. 'Please don't make me come up and get you.'

'Let me get her,' Nora's voice said. 'I did it once before. She'll come down for me, and we can talk this business out.'

Peyton lifted her head and looked down. Nora stood at the foot of the tree, hands on hips, looking up. She had on the yellow dress, and she shone in the darkness like foxfire. She was smiling. Beyond her, at the kerb, stood the little pink car; she and Sonny must have come home and Peyton had not heard. Sonny stood beside Nora, looking serious and concerned.

'I apologise, kiddo,' Nora said. 'We got hung up and couldn't get back. Listen, you don't care about those cretins. They think the backs of cigarette packs are literature. I'm just going to come up now. That's how we met, remember?'

She put her hands on the lower limbs of the tree to swing herself up. The yellow skirt belled out around her.

Peyton was on her feet before she even knew she was rising. She leaned far out over the railing of the tree house. 'Don't you come up here!' she screamed. 'Don't you dare come up here! What makes you think you can just come up here and take care of me, like nothing even happened? *You told me you'd be there and you weren't!* You can't take care of anybody! You can't even take care of your own baby!'

The silence was absolute. In it Peyton could hear the katydids start up, and her own blood thundering in her ears.

'Did you all know that Nora has a little boy?' she called down, in a voice of such ugly gaiety that it hurt even her ears. 'He's five years old and his name is Roberto and he lives in Cuba with his grandmother because Nora went off and left him. He's black, and his father is black, and he was never Nora's husband . . .'

A blindness was roaring down on her, but through it she thought she saw her father's face go still and blank, and saw Sonny Burkholter's slight recoiling, and heard Aunt Augusta's gasp. Nora said nothing; her face did not change. Then she turned and walked towards the house. She did not look back. The others did not move.

'Go tell the Devil!' Peyton screamed after her, leaning further out still. 'Go tell the Devil!'

The sodden railing gave, and Peyton followed her rage and anguish down into darkness.

IT WAS AS IF SHE lived and moved and slept in deep green water. It seemed like an eternity after she broke free of it, but her father said that it had been only three days.

'You have a doozy of a thing called a cranial haematoma,' he said. 'It knocked you out for three days. But you're fine now, and there won't be any aftereffects as long as you stay quiet. You've got a broken collarbone, too. And a couple of cracked ribs.'

Peyton remembered, dimly, about the night of the graduation and the tree, but she did not let her memory take her any further.

When she came home from the hospital she asked to be in the upstairs bedroom. Nora's room.

'You sure?' her father said.

'Yes. The other one's too small. And Trailways won't stay in any room but this one.'

So it became Peyton's room, with nothing left in it of her Cousin Nora. Peyton floated on pain medication, and slept and woke and watched the little television her father had brought her, and ate the meals Chloe brought, and stroked Trailways, and never thought of the room's last occupant except once or twice when she thought, in that place between sleep and waking, that she smelt Nora's perfume.

June seeped away, and July came, hot and still. Peyton did not ask about Nora. She did not ask about Sonny. She did not care.

On a still, hot day in the third week of July, Peyton finally looked into the mirror. A bleached, yellowed skull looked back, with shapeless, lank hair on one side of its head and stubble over white scalp on the other. There was a long, welted red scar in the stubble.

'I need a haircut,' she said, and then she realised that there would be no haircut because Nora was gone. She began to cry, and she cried, on and off, through the afternoon and most of the night. Her father lay on her bed beside her, holding her face to his shoulder. Grey light was just showing under her venetian blinds when she stopped.

'You better now?' her father said.

'I don't know,' she said. 'Daddy, do you pray?'

'Yes, I do.'

'Does it always feel to you like God is listening?'

'I don't always feel Him, but I think He does listen. Most of the time, anyway.'

'What good does it do if He's not listening all the time?'

'I think He wants us to handle what we can on our own. Why do you want to know?'

'Because I prayed for Nora to stay, and she might have, but then I ran her away myself. I thought maybe I'd done it wrong.' And she began to cry again. 'I hate Nora,' she sobbed. 'She ruined my life!'

'Well, you didn't do such a bad job of ruining hers,' he said.

'What do you mean?'

'I mean old Sonny was gone before you hit the ground.'

'When did Nora go?'

'I'm not sure. She was gone when I came home from the hospital the next morning.'

'She didn't even care whether I was badly hurt or not.'

'She did. She called from Alabama late that day to see about you. We knew then that you'd be all right. Chloe told her.'

'Have you talked to her?'

'No.'

'When you said . . . that Sonny was gone, you mean gone back to Hollywood, without her?'

'How would it look if the new Rhett Butler was keeping company with a lady who had a black baby out of wedlock?' her father said. Incredibly, there was laughter in his voice.

Peyton smiled tentatively, and then she began to laugh, too.

'Rat Butler,' she said, and collapsed against him in laughter.

Presently she stopped. 'So you know where she is?'

'Texas,' he said. 'I had a letter the day before yesterday. She's working in a library there. She says it's a funny little town but it doesn't hold a candle to Lytton.'

Peyton felt fresh pain flooding her. She closed her eyes against it. Nora, in a dusty little town in Texas, working in a library . . .

'What about the car?'

'She sold the car. She said she didn't like it any more. She has a Plymouth now.'

Peyton shook her head back and forth, grinding her face into her father's shoulder. 'I loved that car,' she said.

'There was a message for you in the letter,' he said. 'I've been carrying it around for days, waiting for you to want to hear it.'

He pulled a much-folded sheet of stationery from his shirt pocket. Peyton closed her eyes and waited.

' "Tell Peyton it wasn't her fault. If I know her, she'll carry around a wagonload of guilt for the rest of her life if somebody doesn't take it away from her. But it was all me. Tell her it's what I do best, run. I've been doing it all my life. I preach freedom and spontaneity; I know how to draw people out and get them to trust me. And when I have them hanging on to me, I run. I leave them twisting in the wind. The truth is that I'm dying for safety, and a place to be, but I can't stand it when somebody offers it to me. I punish the people who open themselves to me. Tell her that she was born with the gift of a constant heart, and that's worth a hundred of me. Tell her to stop feeling guilty and start writing, and that she did me a favour. Ol' Sonny is nothing but a redneck with money, and he'll be a real hog when he's forty. I knew that even when I was following him around like a puppy dog. He was my ticket away from the love and trust you both offered me. I deserved him, but I'm mighty glad to be rid of him. Tell Peyton I love her, just as I do you." '

It was signed, simply, 'Nora.'

'What does that mean?' Peyton said.

'I think it means that you grew up and Nora didn't.'

Peyton's heart cracked. Nora stood before her vivid, laughing. Peyton could count every copper freckle. Loss drowned her.

'I hate her,' she said, weeping, but she said it doubtfully. Surely hate did not hurt like this.

'Well,' her father said, 'you'd just as soon hate a butterfly. We didn't give one single thought to what *she* might need. We just

.mbed up on her wings. We loved it there; it was a wonderful ride. And she tried to hold us up, but we were too heavy. Finally she had to drop us and go. All the time she wanted an anchor, a place to light, and we were too busy riding her wings to see that.'

'She said I'd always be safe with her. She *said* that!'

Her father put his chin down on her head and began to rock her like a child. 'Nobody's safe, Peyton, and nobody's free,' he said. 'There's only somewhere between safe and free, and what people are. We all try so hard to be strong, or free, or safe, or whatever it is we think we need most . . . and in the end all we can ever be is just us. And it's enough because it has to be.'

'I don't know how to do that. I'm not even sure who me is.'

'Well, this is what we do,' he said. 'We try to give what little we have to somebody who hasn't got it, and maybe they try to give us back some of what they have that we haven't got. That's what love is. That's all it is. You can do that. You already do it.'

They were silent awhile. Then he said, 'We both still need Nora, I guess.'

'No. We don't.'

'Yes. For one thing, you need a haircut.' He smoothed her hair back from her forehead. 'Let's go get her,' he said.

'Are you *crazy?* Go get her? After what she did to you?'

'Yep. You and me and even Trailways if he'll behave himself. Drive to New Orleans and then on over to Texas.'

Peyton saw it in her mind, the empty, heat-shimmering roads. Small diners and gas stations and neon cactuses. Hamburgers and milkshakes in the car at McDonald's and Burger King.

'When would we go?'

'Now. This afternoon.'

'She wouldn't come,' Peyton whispered. 'Not after what I did . . .'

'Bet she would. She needs us, too. She really does. I should have seen that sooner.'

'What if she doesn't think so?'

He grinned suddenly. 'Then we'll pester her until she changes her mind,' he said. 'We'll plonk our guitars under her window and yowl like a couple of tomcats until she gives up. She'll come.'

Peyton began to laugh. She ran to the window and jerked the clattering blinds up. Red-gold light smote her. Joy took her then, and hurled her, still laughing, out into the brightening day.